MW01484812

Forever Fleeting

Forever Fleeting

Bret Kissinger

This is a work of fiction. With the exception of historical figures, all names, characters, places, and incidents are either the products of the author's imagination or have been used fictitiously. Any resemblance to actual persons, living or dead, events or locales is entirely coincidental.

Copyright © 2018 by Bret Kissinger

All rights reserved, including the right to reproduce this book or portions thereof in any form whatsoever.

ISBN-13: 9781728792033

Book Cover Design by 8 Little Pages.

Edited by PaperTrue

This book is dedicated to the millions of casualties of the most destructive event in human history—a true number that will never be known. They were soldiers and civilians, men and women, young and old, gay and straight, black and white—they were human beings. Lives were lost, souls were torn, cities destroyed, and the world, forever changed.

Special Thanks

To my family, for everything.

To Brandi, for allowing me to steal enough of your confidence to publish this book.

To Dayna, for allowing me to bounce around wording in sentences an annoying number of times.

Chapter List

First Glance

Even at a young age, Wilhelm knew there were a handful of moments that shaped—that defined—a person's life. But at that point in his life, he had only one. Things had finally turned around. Wilhelm could feel the resurgence in Germany. Unemployment dropped, food was plenty, and nationalism soared. It had begun five years earlier in 1933 when the Führer ascended to power and raised Germany from the ashes of the Great War. But there was no telling that to Wilhelm's father, Petyr—they still rationed their rations. He would never forget the hardships the end of the Great War had brought or how quickly things could descend back to that level.

Wilhelm had just turned eighteen and, though he hadn't told his father, he was planning to leave their small hometown of Schönfeld behind and move to Berlin with his best friend, Erich Brinkerhoff. Wilhelm was a confident young man with an inviting smile. He knew life had much to offer him and none of it could be found in the "Rote Blumen"—"Red Flowers," the flower shop his father had started with Wilhelm's mother. It seemed to be the only thing that brought his father any peace or comfort.

Petyr was a stern man and only spoke when he had a tirade of swear words to deliver. At six feet four, he was a few inches taller than Wilhelm and had giant hands that were somehow gentle enough to arrange bouquets.

He was a veteran of the Great War. He was also a victim. His hands shook, only staying still when he was working with "weeds," as Wilhelm called them. Wilhelm had absolutely no interest in flowers and could not believe the amount of money people were willing to pay for them. It was also hard to enjoy something that was so minutely scrutinized. His father was obsessed with creating the perfect bouquets and was prone to yelling when one of them was deemed unsatisfactory.

Unfortunately, Wilhelm had a tell-tale sign for when he was bored—running his hand through his wavy black hair. His father hated that. Sometimes, he did it unintentionally, but at other times, he knew exactly what he was doing. And if a verbal warning went unheeded, his father would slam his fist on the table. Wilhelm knew to stop. Otherwise, his face ran the risk of becoming the next "table" that bore his anger. He would then escape into his imagination and the places he'd rather be. That angered his father even more, but it kept his mind from curling its legs up and dying.

Schönfeld, south of Berlin, was a hushed city, and inside the "Rote Blumen," it was dead silent. It was a city with a large collection of homes and businesses, surrounded by fields, forests, and farmlands. Wilhelm had always imagined the city to be surrounded by living fences—there was nowhere to go. His father did not allow him to play the radio, and each afternoon after-school working at the shop felt like an eternity. He loathed it. But even if he lacked passion, he still deemed his work satisfactory. But he and his father had different definitions of the word. Wilhelm did everything he could to prevent his father from critiquing (criticizing) his work.

But his father had shown him how to arrange bouquets and dry flowers. His father had been somewhat of a mad scientist of flowers, often using dyes and pigments to create artificial colors.

He never understood how his father could be so patient with flowers yet so short with him. For most parents, children are the flower, not the weed.

"Have you completed your chores?" Petyr would ask.

"Yes, Father," Wilhelm would reply.

"Lock up when you are done," Petyr would instruct.

Petyr would then close the door behind him before Wilhelm could even say goodbye. And sometimes, these were the only words the two would share all night.

Even in the mild spring weather, the house was cold in a way that had nothing to do with temperature. Wilhelm had lost his mother to fever when he was nine years old, and his once hypothermic father had frozen into ice. Wilhelm was an only child, but he had vague memories of his mother crying over the loss of a baby. He had found out that she had had three miscarriages from the letters and sympathy cards he discovered in her dresser and, judging by the looks his father gave him, Wilhelm assumed that his father wished there had been four.

It was April, and the weather would soon turn pleasant. Pleasant weather meant a busy season at the "Rote Blumen." But Wilhelm would only give his father until the end of August before he would leave for Berlin. He would have to sacrifice both Saturdays and Sundays and after-school hours during the week to help his father out.

On one such Saturday, Wilhelm finished ringing up an elderly lady who had bought yet another dozen daffodils. She had made it a weekly habit, and Wilhelm felt inclined to remind her to water her flowers. But it was also good business, and his father would surely smack his knuckles with a ruler for doing such a thing. But Wilhelm knew there was no right answer. If he told her to start watering her flowers more, his father would chew his ear off for losing a weekly customer. However, if he said nothing at all, his father would be ashamed at how ungentlemanly he was.

The elderly woman smiled and walked toward the door at a tortoise pace. Nearly a minute later, the entrance bell rang, telling Wilhelm she had found the exit. He began wiping down the counter while reading his favorite comic book underneath the glass when the bell atop the entrance door rang once again.

"Good afternoon," Wilhelm said, nodding politely.

But he choked on his spit when he saw the young woman who had just entered the shop. He had never seen anything or anyone so beautiful as her in the shop, in the city or in the world. He may not have seen much of the world, but he still felt this declaration would hold true even if he had explored every last inch of it. She had the most striking blue eyes he had ever seen. The color was far more vibrant than any flower in the shop.

Even with the space between them, the attraction was magnetic, and he could not look away. Her nearly white blonde hair fell just short of her shoulders and radiated a feeling of summer. She wore a blue ribbon in it and was dressed in a gray flannel suit like the woman beside her. Wilhelm had not noticed her at first. She had the same eyes as the younger woman, only her hair was almost black. He could only guess it was the young woman's mother.

Wilhelm did not break his stare, even though he knew he should. But he could not. The young girl looked at him nervously. He was unaware that his innocent stare was making her uncomfortable. But to him, time had frozen. Those blue eyes had cast a spell on him. The older woman looked around the shop, keeping her white glove-covered hands away from anything that could stain them.

Wilhelm finally looked away, but only for a moment. The comic book that had captivated him before had transformed into a bouquet manual. The young girl twirled a dyed blue rose in her hand. His stare was powerful and obvious. She turned, her electric blue eyes meeting his warm brown ones. Her stare was like out of the pages of his superhero comic book. It made his knees weak. His stomach turned into a sea, churning nervous energy, and his smile drooped. Yet, the stare gave him strength and blind arrogance. He felt if he were to jump off the roof now, he would fly. He wanted to say something—anything. But he could only smile. She smiled back nervously.

"Come along, Hannah," the older woman called out.

Hannah. He now had a name for the beautiful young woman. Hannah set the blue rose back and took one final glance at Wilhelm before leaving the store. There were a handful of moments that shaped—that defined—a person's life, and such a moment had just walked into his father's shop—a moment named Hannah. Wilhelm knew nothing about her, but he wanted to know everything. But a temporary state of paralysis had taken hold of him. After staring at the door for nearly a minute, he snapped out of his comatose state, hopped over the cash register, and sprinted out of the shop. His heart raced and threatened to burst out of his chest. The nervous energy in his stomach rose to his throat. Dozens of cars zipped past him on the street, and even more pedestrians crowded the sidewalks. Even the sun was cruel in masking the enchanting young woman's location. Wilhelm had to cover his eyes from its blinding glow. He thought of dashing across the street, taking his chances of being hit, in the hope of finding her. But Hannah was gone.

He stepped back inside the "Rote Blumen" and grabbed the blue rose Hannah had held in her hand. At that moment, an idea struck him. He took the rose and began the long process of drying it. Drying flowers meant doing just what the title implied. It gave the flower a longer life, and if stored properly, it could last for eternity. He would carry the rose on his person, and if he ever saw Hannah again, he would give her the exact rose she had twirled in her fingers.

The next three months, he thought of her less and less, but her face would flash in his mind every night before bed. He made up conversations in his head of what he would say to her if he ever did see her again. Each conversation ranged from the bold declaration of his love for her to a simple question of how her day had been. He put many hours into the shop during the summer, and only on occasions was he able to meet with Erich.

The August heat dwindled, and September soon approached. Wilhelm had to tell his father he was leaving. He had planned on telling him in July, but the thought of his father's reaction had made him put it off till then. But he could wait no longer.

On the last Friday in August, while eating yet another silent meal, Wilhelm decided to tell his father. While his father read the newspaper—"Völksicher Beobachter" (National Observer)—Wilhelm played with the peas and carrots on his plate with his fork—the universal sign of having something on your mind. But Wilhelm could have changed skin colors and his father wouldn't have noticed. It was up to him to start the conversation.

"I am moving to Berlin," he blurted out.

His father looked up from his newspaper and removed his glasses.

"And what will you do there?" he asked.

"I don't know. But there is much work," Wilhelm said.

Wilhelm waited for the outburst. The last eighteen years of swearing and disappointment had led to this one moment. He had often wondered if his father's head would burst into flames if he unleashed his full anger. But Petyr did not yell. He simply slid his hand over Wilhelm's and squeezed it.

When the time had finally come to leave, Wilhelm did not expect to feel as sad as he did while packing his suitcase. It seemed silly, but even though his mother was dead, her spirit was in that house. And the moment he would leave, her spirit would too. Some fathers and sons only grew close when the son turned into a man. Wilhelm vowed to return when he was older in the hope his relationship with his father would take the same course. He had taken all that his suitcase could fit and had the dried blue rose neatly folded in a white handkerchief in his pocket. Wilhelm was on his way to Berlin.

Ich Bin Ein Berliner

The Brandenburg Gate with its six rectangular columns and four horse-drawn carriage, called the quadriga, atop the gate was one of the most recognizable sights in Berlin. In between each of the columns were six flags with a red background and a white disk enveloping a black swastika—the flag of the Nazi empire. Wilhelm smiled as the gates welcomed him to his new life—a life of endless possibilities and void of trimming flowers.

He carried a faded gray duffel bag and a pale blue suitcase and gingerly held a letter from Erich with his fingertips. His arm was tired after repeatedly lifting the suitcase and letter to read the address. Erich had moved to the city three weeks earlier and had found a place at a reasonable rent. Although the sun faded behind the gate, many hours would pass before Wilhelm went to bed, as a beer or two needed to be shared with Erich upon his arrival.

Wilhelm regretted not staying on the bus for a few more blocks. He traded the suitcase from hand to hand while the duffel bag, draped around his neck, nearly choked him. When he finally approached the tan-colored apartment building he was to live in, it certainly didn't sparkle with opulence, but somewhere up on the fourth floor was his new home. Wilhelm shouted Erich's name, stepped back, nearly onto the road, and gazed up toward the fourth floor. Seconds later, Erich's head popped out of the window and flashed a smile.

"Wilhelm!" he yelled, hitting his head on the window.

Erich disappeared back into the room, and Wilhelm waited for Erich to descend the four flights of steps. The door opened, and Erich rushed out, spreading his arms and drawing Wilhelm into a hug.

"Welcome to your new home!" Erich said.

His dark oak-colored hair was slightly longer than when Wilhelm had last seen him.

Wilhelm lugged his suitcase up the stairs, and it bounced with each step. Though the apartment was modest, Wilhelm could not help but smile. It had a sofa in the living room, a small kitchen in the left-hand corner, one bathroom, and two bedrooms. It appeared that Erich had taken the liberty of taking the larger bedroom.

"It's perfect," Wilhelm said with a beaming smile.

"We'll unpack later. Time for a beer," Erich said, slapping Wilhelm on the back.

Wilhelm tossed the suitcase and duffel bag into the empty room, and they hurried out of the apartment. They descended the steps three at a time and stepped out into the crisp Berlin nighttime air.

"I will introduce you to Heinrich," Erich said.

Erich had met Heinrich after only his third day in the city, and he had quickly become one of his best friends. As Wilhelm and Erich walked down the road, Erich pointed out various buildings—a deli with the best pastrami in Berlin, Max's grocery store, a pharmacy, and over half a dozen drinking establishments—that he thought Wilhelm should know. The one they approached had a wooden sign with a goat's head dangling over the front door by two gold chains. It was called "Die Verdorbene Ziege"—"The Spoiled Goat." Three-quarter of the bar was full, and the lightly stained wooden bar was covered with glasses filled with amber and dark brown beers.

A man of their age with short yellow-platinum blonde hair greeted them with a smile. He was the perfect German in the eyes of the Führer. His drooping smile and the glint in his soft blues eyes told Wilhelm it wasn't the man's first beer of the night.

"Erich!" the man yelled. He raised his glass of dark wheat beer, and the sudden movement caused the beer to slosh out of the glass and onto the floor.

"Heinrich, this is Wilhelm," Erich introduced.

Heinrich slid over two beers to Erich and Wilhelm. Erich took a sip of his and waited for Wilhelm and Heinrich to shake hands before handing the beer to Wilhelm.

"Nice to meet you," Wilhelm said.

"First night in Berlin belongs to Berlin," Heinrich said.

It was a peculiar comment, and Wilhelm wasn't sure how to take it. But after having finished his fourth pint of beer in less than twenty minutes, euphoria set in, and he was laughing at every comment, he understood—Berlin and its beer was going to beat him to a pulp.

Wilhelm had always been easy-going, and he got along with just about everyone. He could strike up conversations with strangers that could last an hour. But with alcohol, Wilhelm would almost profess his love for the entire human race. He developed an immediate liking for Heinrich—they shared the same kindred spirit and sense of life's unlimited potential. Of course, Wilhelm had to mention Hannah—the unicorn spirit of a woman that had appeared in his life and vanished. Erich was well-versed in all things Hannah. He had heard all about her during their phone calls. Heinrich shared a smile with Erich—it was not the first time he was hearing about it either.

"Berlin will make you forget about her," Heinrich said.

Wilhelm cast a doubtful look at Heinrich.

"Made me forget twice," Erich said, and the three laughed. Erich explained he had slept with two different women since his arrival in the city.

After another beer, the room began to spin. Wilhelm was on an invisible, motorized merry-go-round with no way of stepping off.

They stumbled outside, and the fresh air pushed Wilhelm off the merry-go-round—temporarily at least. The Nazi flag waved from every building as they crossed street after street. It was hardly the end of the night though, as they must have gone to a dozen more bars, and Wilhelm made the awful decision of switching from beer to liquor. He did not even remember making it back to their apartment. He woke up to the smell of vomit wafting out of the garbage can that had been placed beside his bed. He felt surprisingly well but, as soon as he shifted his head, he realized the grave error in his calculation. The only explanation to his pounding headache was that his brain was trying to break free from his skull. He thought he would never be able to leave his bed again. And, for most of that day, he did not. The first night in Berlin belongs to Berlin. But, based on how he felt even the next day, Berlin was in his debt.

Heinrich had gotten them jobs helping construct the new Reich Chancellery, the headquarters of the Nazi Party and the Third Reich. Heinrich's uncle was a member of the Schutzstaffel (SS) and had called in a favor. No other job instilled more pride in Berlin than building the headquarters of the Reich. The weather was still pleasant, and the work was good and honest. Each day ended with sore feet, a tight lower back, and dirt-stained hands, followed by drinks at the "Betrunkene Ente"—"The Drunken Duck."

Wilhelm adjusted to life in the epicenter of Germany well, and he found his thoughts about Hannah lessen and lessen with each passing day. It was only when he would take the dried blue rose out of his pocket and place it on his dresser each night that his thoughts would drift back to her. He would spend the next thirty minutes tossing and turning in his bed. After Hannah would finally leave his thoughts, he would think of his father and mother. Even if his childhood had been anything but great since his mother had died, there were areas in the house where she still seemed to be. It was a comfort greatly missing from his new home. He could only hope that the comfort his mother's ghost had given him gave his father the same. Wilhelm was constantly haunted by guilt for leaving him alone, but he knew that he needed to live his life.

Every night, he would drift off to sleep and awaken with excitement. Heinrich and Erich had become like brothers to him, and if either Wilhelm or Erich ever missed a good home-cooked meal, Heinrich's mother was more than willing to have them over. Berlin was everything Wilhelm had wanted it to be.

Dance of Lights

October came with a new cool breeze that signaled autumn was well on its way. October also meant the Oktoberfest. There was no argument to be made. Wilhelm, Erich, and Heinrich had all wanted to go. The bus they took was old, smelly, and jam-packed, but it was well worth the nearly eight-hour drive to Munich. They dressed in the traditional lederhosen—white, long-sleeve shirts, suspenders, and dark brown shorts, and they even wore festive Tyrolean hats. It seemed all of Munich, if not all of Germany, had gathered on the grounds. Every tent was filled beyond capacity. The day was filled with beer, pretzels, bratwursts, and schnitzels and the night, with only beer. With each sip, Erich and Heinrich's courage and lust increased tenfold.

"Time to meet a questionable Munich woman," Heinrich announced.

"Last one to speak to a girl buys the next four rounds," Erich added.

Wilhelm, although certainly feeling the effects of what seemed like a bathtub full of beer, was not at that stage to strike up a conversation with a group of women who gave the impression they were a pack of wolves.

The tents were strung with golden lights, and the sun had set outside. A rush of cold air filled the tents—the type of breeze that alerted people about how drunk they truly were.

With the number of people packed elbow-to-elbow, it was stifling. Wilhelm took big gulps of the crisp air before it turned into the same stagnant air he had been breathing all day. But in his moment of enjoying the cool breeze, Heinrich and Erich had begun talking to a group of no-less-than fifteen women.

Both held out their empty glass pints for Wilhelm to refill. Wilhelm yanked them from their hands and ignored the smirks that had spread across their faces. He shimmied past the dancers and chatty drinkers toward a long wooden table. It stretched the length of the tent, leaving no open spot to stand. The bartenders were outnumbered and overwhelmed. The masses held out their money and empty glasses for them to take and to fill. The male bartenders instinctively went to the best-looking women—something Wilhelm couldn't blame them for. Being caught up in the beauty of the lights and the laughter coming from every corner of the tent, he was perfectly content with having to wait. It was the sort of atmosphere in which every person was having the time of their life.

"Excuse me," a voice said from beside him.

"Sorry," Wilhelm said, snapping out of his daze and creating room for one more.

He caught a whiff of perfume that put his senses on alert. It filled him with a sense of hunger. But this hunger had nothing to do with food, but everything to do with how intoxicating the woman smelt. He caught a glimpse of her hair first, as her back was facing him. It was nearly white blonde in color. When she felt his gaze, she turned her head to look at him. Her eyes were strikingly blue. When she smiled nervously, Wilhelm smiled too. He had found her. It was the woman who had tormented his dreams and filled his thoughts since late April.

"Hannah," Wilhelm muttered, flashing a smile that would cause permanent wrinkles.

"Hello," she said, blushing as he stared at her, but she did not look away.

"It is you," Wilhelm said in disbelief.

"I am sorry. Do I know you?" Hannah asked.

She was even more beautiful than he had remembered her to be. Her face was tattooed in his thoughts, but it was only a photograph. It could not replicate the way her hair blew with the slight breeze or how she smiled tentatively at first before nearly laughing, nor did her eyes sparkle like they did inside the tent with the golden lights reflecting off them. And it definitely did not smell like her perfume—a scent of citrus and lavender.

"You were in Schönfeld in late April. At the 'Rote Blumen,' the flower shop," Wilhelm clarified.

He had rehearsed so many lines—he had thought about this moment ever since he had first laid eyes on her. But his mind had now been wiped clean. He was only aware of how beautiful and intoxicating she was. He could do nothing but smile.

"Yes, I was. You were working," Hannah said, smiling once again.

In a span of seconds, the line for the drinks had diminished by nearly half. Somebody would soon grab the glasses he had been dangling over the table for over ten minutes. He had waited two eternities and three lifetimes, but now that Hannah was here—the woman he had longed to see again—the line moved faster than cars on the autobahn.

An uncomfortable silence fell between Hannah and Wilhelm. She looked away. Wilhelm had always found having something in his hand to be comforting, but he had set the three empty pint glasses on the wooden table, and to pick them up while they were still empty would be awkward. Instead, his left hand disappeared into his pocket, and his fingers found the dried petals of the blue rose.

"You were looking at a blue rose," Wilhelm said, breaking the silence.

She turned back to him. "Yes. They are my absolute favorite," she said.

Wilhelm removed the rose from his pocket and held it out for her to take.

"This is the rose," Wilhelm said.

Her eyes went from the rose to his face. She took the rose and twirled it in her hand.

"You kept this?" she asked, her face blushing ever so slightly.

"Yes. It's been with me since the day you left. My name is Wilhelm Schreiber."

He offered his hand and hoped it was not too sweaty.

She shook it. "Hannah Goldschmidt."

Her hand was smooth and her grip, gentle. His was strong and confident. He held onto her hand longer than deemed appropriate. He could not help but think about how their hands fit perfectly into one another—like pieces of a puzzle. Hannah broke their gaze and looked at their hands.

"Sorry," Wilhelm said, realizing what he was doing.

Hannah laughed. The server came and took their order—Hannah another Spatenbrau and Wilhelm, three of the Oktoberfest special.

"Where are you from, Hannah?" Wilhelm asked.

"Berlin," Hannah answered.

Wilhelm's heart skipped a beat—two beats. But it made up for it and could be seen beating through his white shirt.

"I live there too now," Wilhelm said.

Their four pints were set down, sending a fresh coating of beer on the table. Wilhelm paid the server before Hannah got the chance to.

"Thank you," Hannah said.

"No need. Are you here with friends?" Wilhelm asked, hoping the dreaded word "boyfriend" would not follow.

"Yes. My aunt is here with me as well. They are probably wondering where I am," Hannah answered.

She cast a nervous glance at the hundreds, if not thousands, of people. But she did not appear eager to leave Wilhelm, only anxious about the idea of not being able to find her group.

"Let me take one for you," Hannah offered, seeing Wilhelm struggling to try and carry three large, filled-to-the-brim pints.

Wilhelm let Hannah walk in front so they wouldn't get separated. Hannah was much shorter and petite than him—where she was able to gracefully slide and shimmy past, Wilhelm bumped into nearly every person. Heinrich was well over six-feet tall, making it easy for Wilhelm to spot him. Wilhelm nodded in his direction, and Hannah followed the invisible line to the tall, blonde young man.

"Here you go," Wilhelm said, extending the pints to Heinrich and Erich.

Both of them were still talking to the group of women, but Heinrich paused mid-sentence when he noticed Hannah.

"Hannah, these are my friends, Heinrich and Erich," Wilhelm introduced, smiling arrogantly for every painfully long daily description of the mythical Hannah was now proven true.

"Nice to meet you," Hannah said.

"We cannot stay. I must help her find her friends," Wilhelm said.

It was probably unwise for him to leave Heinrich and Erich, as the likelihood of finding them again was marginal at best, but he did not care. He would rather be lost with Hannah than found with Erich and Heinrich.

He and Hannah made their way through the sea of dancing and conversing people.

"Tell me about yourself, Hannah," Wilhelm said, loud enough to be heard over the chatter and music.

The atmosphere was filled with a blend of beer and sweat.

"What do you want to know?" Hannah asked.

"Everything," Wilhelm said.

"I cannot believe you held onto this rose. You never even spoke to me," Hannah said.

"I have not stopped thinking about you since that day," Wilhelm said.

He had a nervous energy and a great smile that made his words seem innocent.

They made their way out of the tent and into the mass of people. Lights, both artificial and natural, shined and sparkled everywhere while music poured out of accordions, fiddles, and flutes.

"So, why did you leave Schönfeld?" Hannah asked.

"To see the world," Wilhelm answered.

"Don't you miss your family?" she asked.

"My mother died when I was young, and my father and I never really got along. It was my mother's shop, but I think my father is only truly at peace when he is there. But not me," Wilhelm explained.

"To your mother," Hannah said, raising her glass. Wilhelm smiled and clunked her glass with his. "I feel so sorry for you that you lost her at such a young age. I cannot imagine," Hannah said.

Her parents were her best friends. It was just the three of them, and she could not dare to imagine losing one and not being close to the other.

"I cannot believe I am standing here, next to you. I never thought I would see you again," Wilhelm said, still staring at her in disbelief.

Hannah smiled nervously. Wilhelm had a deep unabashed stare. He simply loved her eyes. They exuded a hidden strength that not even she was aware of, but there was vulnerability in them too.

As they watched the band and dancers, both kept stealing glances at one another. When they both caught each other, they laughed nervously before burying their faces in their beer.

"Will you dance with me?" Hannah asked.

"Always," Wilhelm said.

He took her empty pint and set it down on a close-by table. The music was fast, and the more advanced dancers slapped their hands against their thighs and feet in the tradition of the Schuhplattler. Wilhelm and Hannah laughed, for Wilhelm was not an innately gifted freestyle dancer. The music ended, and they both hunched over from fits of laughter and sore jaws from smiling too much.

"I need to get you another beer so that you do not remember this in the morning," Wilhelm joked.

"I am afraid this memory is going nowhere," Hannah said.

The music took an unexpected slower pace, and husbands pulled their wives in close while bachelors looked for eligible women. The single men stared at Wilhelm and Hannah, trying to figure out if they were a couple. Wilhelm had but seconds before a bold drunk grabbed Hannah's hand.

Wilhelm offered Hannah his hand. She smiled and took it. Wilhelm pulled her close with a sure, strong hand—one entwined with hers and the other wrapped around her waist. She was drawn to his confidence and the way he stood tall as they danced. Wilhelm may have struggled with the faster-paced dancing, but he knew how to waltz. Hannah was taken away by his ability and was no stranger to traditional dancing either. As a child, when her father and mother would dance in the silence, she would join them.

"You are very good," Hannah said.

Wilhelm led her into a spin.

"It is my strongest memory of my mother. We used to dance together in the kitchen," Wilhelm said.

Hannah could tell the reverence he held his mother in. The deep respect he had for her was the same way he treated Hannah—the constant gentleman.

At first, Wilhelm's stare was intimidating. Hannah had never liked people with such strong stares. It made her feel she was being judged—being watched. But his stare lacked judgment, and she was quick to admire it. When she spoke, he did not look around and half listen—he hung on every word. To him, it was as if all the other thousands of people had vanished—there was only Hannah.

The music died out, but the momentary silence was soon filled with applause. They both smiled nervously as they pulled away. The music came back with fervor and life. Hannah's hand was grabbed by a woman, and she was pulled into a long train of people.

She grabbed Wilhelm as hundreds, linked together by clinging hands, skipped along. But the train split and Hannah's grip broke, and before Wilhelm could grab her hand, ten people separated them. The number doubled when the train broke off again, and by the time the song ended, Hannah was gone.

Building the Reich

The next couple of days started and ended much the same way—Wilhelm awoke with a new sense of hope only to have it crushed. He had not seen Hannah for the rest of his time in Munich. Though there were nearly a thousand women for him to talk with, he had no desire to. He had nothing but odds on his mind—the odds of Hannah living in Berlin, the odds of her finding herself in the "Rote Blumen," the odds of her going to the Oktoberfest in Munich, and the odds of him running into her amidst thousands. But, to Wilhelm, there was only one easy explanation—fate.

He, Erich, and Heinrich slept most of the bus ride home and arrived back in Berlin at nearly nine o'clock at night. Despite sleeping for almost the entire eight-hour ride to Berlin, they had nothing but sleep on their schedule when they returned.

The next morning, Wilhelm woke to a large yawn and got ready for another day of building the Reich. He had enjoyed the job much more in September than he had in October. Cold gusts ripped through his clothes and caused the scaffolding to shake. But still, he could hardly complain. Less than ten years ago, there were hardly any jobs to go around and even less food. Plus, he was able to work outside with his best friends. Fresh air beat inside air any day of the week. While some refused to climb the scaffold for a fear of heights, Wilhelm loved it. He, Erich, and Heinrich could talk about anything and the boss, on street level, could not scold them if they happened to take a quick break.

On Thursday, a black car pulled alongside the curb and halted to a stop. As he was nearly four stories off the ground, Wilhelm was the first to see the car approach.

"It's the Führer!" a man yelled from ground level.

"Get down here!" another hollered.

Rushing down a scaffold was not safe or smart, as any quick change of weight placement could turn it into a teeter-totter. But they did not want to be the only ones not standing with respect for the Führer.

The Führer was the most famous man in Germany. Apart from his driver, who stood by the car, the Führer was accompanied by only two other men. One was nearly as famous as Hitler and the other, unheralded by a large majority.

The known was Joseph Goebbels—the Minister of Propaganda. He was a thin, short man and extremely loyal to Adolf Hitler. The unheralded was Albert Speer. Wilhelm had seen him before—often, actually. He was the designer of the Reich Chancellery.

"Hail, Hitler!" the workers shouted while raising their right arms in the Nazi salute. It was mandatory for civilians and punishable if not done. It was the reason Wilhelm, Erich, and Heinrich were willing to risk falling off the scaffold.

Hitler nodded and smiled.

"Back to work," the boss commanded.

After the three were back up on the scaffolding and above earshot, they criticized the laziest of the workers who had finally found the motivation to actually work. Men who had done nothing but scratch their heads and rearrange their underwear now moved with annoying frenzy.

Wilhelm had never taken notice of the traffic before, but after the Führer's visit, he kept looking at the streets below. When a black and white Ford Eifel drove past, his mouth dropped open. He immediately fell in love with that car—the way the paint glistened in the sun and the sound of the engine as it drove by.

"That's what I want to do," Wilhelm said.

When neither Erich nor Heinrich answered, he tapped the latter on the shoulder. Heinrich turned to look at the car and did not give it a second look.

"Drive cars?" Heinrich asked.

"No, sell them," Wilhelm corrected.

Heinrich gave a half-nod and returned to his conversation with Erich. Though Wilhelm enjoyed the work, he could not help but think of what winter would be like. Working outside in the freezing cold and snow did not seem like fun, nor did standing four stories up on a sheet of plywood held in place by aluminum cross beams when winter winds blasted through. Being able to escape the cold inside and being surrounded by cars was a much better alternative.

Wilhelm finished his shift and, while Heinrich and Erich went home, he went to the nearest car dealer. It was called "Der Berliner Autohändler." Though the cars were used, they were washed and cleaned, and everything possible to make them appear more enticing was done. Wilhelm opened the door and walked in. The person behind the front desk had his face covered by the day's newspaper.

"Can I help you?" the man asked.

"I want to work here," Wilhelm said.

"Know anything about cars?" the man asked, still reading the newspaper.

"No. Not really. But these cars will sell themselves. I will just stay out of the way," Wilhelm said.

The man lowered the paper and gave it a shake so he could fold it back up. He was balding and overweight.

"How much do you want to get paid?" the man asked.

"How much do you want to pay me?" Wilhelm asked.

"I do not know. If you sell nothing, I wish to pay you nothing," the man said.

He rose from his chair, tucked his shirt that was two sizes too small back into his pants, and hobbled toward Wilhelm.

"Then pay me nothing. But I will take five-percent commission," Wilhelm said.

"Five percent? Pull your pants up, son. I do not have to see them to know that you have them," the man said, "So, you know nothing about cars, but you want to make five-percent commission?" He shook his head while laughing.

"Pay me what you feel I have earned," Wilhelm said.

The man stared long and hard. He had exactly twenty-five cars on his lot, and he washed each one every other day. He hated it. And with winter coming, he would have to scrape the snow off the cars and shovel the lot. He loathed that.

"Do you have a suit?" the man asked.

The man himself wore a dress shirt and tie that hardly looked presentable. The shirt was already untucked, as there was only a mere inch of extra shirt to tuck into his pants. Maybe some number of years and pounds ago, it had fit.

"No," Wilhelm answered.

He had not realized how underdressed he was in a pair of dirt-covered slacks and a white shirt that now looked closer to gray or brown. He most certainly had grime on his face, dirt under his fingernails, and was stained with an invisible layer of offending body odor. One of the drawbacks of working on a scaffold was that the sun hung only a foot over his shoulders.

"Get a suit," the man said.

"Yes, Sir," Wilhelm said, beaming with a smile.

"Come back here tomorrow at eight. My name is Hans. Hans Rabe," the man said, extending his hand.

Wilhelm shook it and remembered what his father had said about handshakes ... "A handshake reveals the man. Be firm and look the man in the eye." He waved goodbye and left the dealership in prime spirits.

Though he had lived in Berlin for almost two months now, his knowledge of places was limited to his work and the places Erich had shown him on his first night. So, Wilhelm wandered aimlessly on the street. He had taken too many lefts and rights to know where he was. But as fate would have it, he came across a strip of stores—a bakery, a jeweler, and a shop with a modest sign that read "Tailor, Tux, and Touch Up."

The full-length glass windows of the two-story building were spaced with red bricks. Wilhelm opened the door of the shop and looked around. There were mannequins dressed in sharp, elegant suits and tuxedos and women's jackets of leather, cloth, and wool in varying shades of brown, black, gray, silver, and red. Each showcased a fine eye for fashion and a sure hand that measured, stitched, and sewed. But for how immaculate they looked in the early evening, the mannequins must have looked equally creepy at night.

"Just a minute," a man's voice yelled from somewhere in the back.

Wilhelm tried looking beyond the register and the black curtain that hung behind it. The voice had come from somewhere behind it. As he waited, he ran the suits between his fingers to get a feel of the different fabrics.

A bald man with a thin onyx-colored beard, speckled with white hair, bound through the black curtain, around the register, and to Wilhelm.

"A good day to you, young Sir, and welcome. My name is Josef. How may I help you?" the man asked and offered his hand.

"I need a suit, Sir," Wilhelm said, shaking his hand.

Josef wore glasses that sat on the tip of his nose, and Wilhelm thought if he leaned too far forward, they would slide off his face.

"You have come to the right place," Josef said.

He held his arm out, gesturing Wilhelm to follow him. Wilhelm did, and they walked to the back end of the shop. The wooden shelves against the wall were filled with different fabrics. When they reached the back, Josef pulled a cloth ruler, appearing to be nearly seven-feet long, from his breast pocket. "Step up here if you would please," Josef said.

Wilhelm stepped up onto a circular platform and observed himself in the mirror in front of him as Josef pulled shut the sliding door behind him. There was a mirror on the door as well so customers knew exactly how things fit and looked.

"Cough please," Josef said.

Wilhelm's face contorted.

"Bad tailor humor. Just relax, son," Josef reassured.

He used the cloth ruler to measure Wilhelm's neck, chest, waist, seat, shirt length, shoulder width, arm length, wrist, hips, and inseam. He jotted the measurements onto a sheet of paper attached to a brown clipboard. He was so thorough that Wilhelm thought he could tell him down to the exact millimeter. Josef had a soft voice with great diction and uttered phrases like, "Very good, Sir," "There it is," and "Fantastic." The man was warm and gentle in a way entirely different from Wilhelm's father.

"Excellent. Do you have a preference in color?" Josef asked as he rolled the cloth ruler back up.

"I love black. But something stylish. And I am not embarrassed to say that my funds are not as deep as my pockets."

Josef smiled. "It is always a pleasure to help a man buy his first suit—a suit you make a living in, a suit you live in. Perhaps, a suit you fall in love in," Josef said, arching his eyebrows for effect.

Wilhelm smiled. It was a strange thought, but Wilhelm would have loved to hear the man read some of his favorite books because he delivered his words like poetry.

"Now, about your thin pockets. To create a tux from new, I fear will be out of your price range. But we can use an existing suit, and my wife can tweak it to your measurements," Josef added.

"That would be appreciated," Wilhelm said.

"I shall return," Josef said, disappearing behind the black curtain once again. He sifted through the suit coats on the rack before finding one similar to Wilhelm's measurements. It was indigo and would need some adjusting, but Wilhelm smiled approvingly when Josef brought it to him.

"It is not black. But I think it will look sharp on you," Josef said.

"It is excellent. But how much?" Wilhelm asked.

"It is your first tux. We can work something out," Josef reassured him once again.

"Thank you."

"Pay for half the tux now. My wife will adjust it. Come back tomorrow and pay the remaining half."

Wilhelm put the coat on and examined himself in the mirror.

"You, my fine good Sir, are my last customer for the day," Josef said.

As Wilhelm stepped toward the register, Josef hurried toward the door to flip the sign and turn the lock to stop anyone trying to sneak in before the sign was flipped from "OPEN" to "CLOSED."

"You'd be surprised how many don't read the sign," Josef added.

He walked to the register and took the sheet of paper from the clipboard and attached it to the indigo suit.

"I did not get your name, son."

"Wilhelm Schreiber."

Josef wrote the name on the sheet of paper. His handwriting was as Wilhelm had expected it to be—almost calligraphic.

"Well, young Wilhelm, I smell my wife's brisket. My daughter will finish up. I shall see you tomorrow, my good young Sir," Josef said, nodding politely.

"Good night, Sir," Wilhelm said.

Josef disappeared in the back. The floorboards creaked as he ascended the stairs. Wilhelm waited patiently by the glass counter. One thing was for certain—you could not beat Josef's commute to work. It consisted all of twelve steps. The black curtain was brushed open once more, and Wilhelm's mouth fell agape before awkwardly forming a smile.

"Hannah," he mumbled.

"Wilhelm," Hannah said with a paralyzing smile.

"You are the tailor's daughter?" Wilhelm asked, struggling to speak.

"Yes," Hannah said, laughing at his choice of words.

Erich had warned Wilhelm that if he continued to think of Hannah, he would go crazy and start seeing her in the clouds and in his beer. Wilhelm stood dumbfounded as he considered this possibility.

"What is the suit for?" Hannah asked.

Her question snapped him out of his temporary paralysis. He took out the required amount of money from his pocket and put it down on the counter.

"I am going to be selling cars," Wilhelm said.

Josef's phrase, "a suit you make a living in," came to mind but was quickly replaced by "a suit you fall in love in."

Hannah took the Reichsmarks from the counter, opened the register, and placed them inside.

"I looked all over for you in Munich," Wilhelm said.

"That was my last night there," Hannah said.

"You live upstairs?"

Hannah nodded and held out his change for him. Wilhelm took it, their fingertips caressing one another as he did.

"I have to take you out, Hannah," Wilhelm blurted out.

"I have to ask my father," Hannah said.

"I will ask him."

Hannah nodded and disappeared behind the black curtain and came back moments later with her father by her side.

"Is there a problem, Mr. Schreiber?" Josef asked.

"With your tux? No, Sir. I would like to take Hannah out for dinner if you would permit it," Wilhelm said, taking a deep breath to summon his courage. He could sense the change in Josef's demeanor. He was no longer a tailor. He was now a protective father.

"You do," Josef said grimly.

It was obvious he did not approve of Wilhelm's desire to take his daughter on a date after having only seen her for thirty seconds.

"I have met Wilhelm before. Mother and I had gone to his father's flower shop when we were in Schönfeld last spring and when I visited Aunt Clara in Munich just a few weeks ago," Hannah mentioned.

Wilhelm's spirits soared higher than any Luftwaffe pilot ever had. Hannah was attempting to talk her father into allowing her to go on a date with him.

"And would you like to go out with him?" Josef asked.

"Very much," Hannah gushed.

The feeling of being able to fly swept over Wilhelm once again. It would take getting hit by a dump truck to wipe the smile off his face, and even that was not a certainty.

"You may take her out tomorrow when you pick up your suit. Hannah, you will be home by ten. Not a minute later. And, Mr. Schreiber, you have lost your discount," Josef said, pointing his finger at Wilhelm.

His face was stern, and whether he himself decided to crack the smallest remnant of a smile or Hannah non-verbally pleaded with him to do so, Wilhelm could not tell. Josef disappeared behind the black curtain and clambered up the steps with plodding feet. Something told Wilhelm that Josef would not enjoy his brisket nearly as much.

"Will you be here tomorrow? Or will you vanish like before?" Wilhelm teased.

"I will be here tomorrow. Come at five," Hannah said.

Wilhelm smiled and left the shop, taking one final glance at Hannah before he did. One thing was for certain—tomorrow would take forever.

Italy in Berlin

ime became lethargic—it barely crept by. It was his first day at his dream job, and Wilhelm could have sworn he had been at work for at least three hours, but every time he looked up at the clock, he was forced to face the reality that only minutes had passed. He was tempted to ask Hans if his clock was broken.

Hans went through every car on his lot in great detail. His sales philosophy, which he said was similar to that of a snake, was to play dumb and indifferent, and when the customers were close to buying, unhinge your jaws and bury your fangs in them. He showed Wilhelm how to fill out the paperwork and instructed him on the three tiers of pricing—above market for the desperate and dumb, market for the interested and educated, and below market for parking lot mold (the cars that weren't selling). Wilhelm did his best to seem interested, for he truly was, but his mind kept his upcoming date with Hannah at the forefront. Though he retained much of what Hans said, the minutia of it went in and out. Hans was displeased when Wilhelm showed up without a suit, but Wilhelm assured him a suit was being tailored for him.

"I do not expect you to remember everything," Hans said as they ate their lunch.

Hans had brought in sauerkraut and bierwurst for the both of them. Hans did not look like a man who knew how to cook, but Wilhelm gave an approving nod as he chewed.

"Are you having second thoughts about the job?" Hans asked, bits of food shooting from his mouth.

"No. Not at all. My mind is on a date I have tonight. I am sorry," Wilhelm said.

Honesty was his best play.

Hans smiled, and bits of his bierwurst squeezed out of his mouth and onto his plate. "Where are you taking her?" Hans asked with a mouthful. He grabbed a napkin and wiped his face.

"An Italian restaurant and then to a park by the river for music and dancing," Wilhelm said.

He had gone over every detail nearly fifty times. He was excited about it all but most excited to learn more about her.

"To be that smitten…" Hans said, reminiscing in his head about when he had looked at his wife in the same way. He said he still loved her, but a house full of five children was as noisy as the train station, and for that reason, he did not mind working six days a week. He would spend the first hour upon returning home arguing with his wife about it and spend the next two hours begging for forgiveness. By the time she was done cleansing him of his sins, they would be in bed, drifting off to sleep, and the cycle would start over the next day.

It had been quiet without a single customer before lunch. A middle-aged man had stopped by but left as soon as he saw Wilhelm approaching. Another customer had to "think about it," but the third had stayed and inspected the Adler Trumpf parked in the second row. He assured Wilhelm he would not be influenced into buying, but Wilhelm did not mention the car a single time during their conversation. He told the man his boss was watching and he only wanted it to look like he was pitching the car. They talked about the nice autumn day, the headaches of traffic, but Wilhelm snuck in hints about the car's design and specs every now and then. Once the man sat behind the wheel, Wilhelm bore his fangs and poisoned the man's thoughts with the sleek silver Adler Trumpf, and he bought the car at market price.

"Way to bear those fangs," Hans said, using his pointer and middle fingers to form fangs.

Hans took note of Wilhelm's enthusiasm for nearly everything—even the fly that kept landing on his head didn't perturb him.

"Are you picking her up?" Hans asked as they closed up for the day.

"No, I do not have a car," Wilhelm said.

Hans nodded to himself before tossing a key at Wilhelm.

"Bring it back in good shape or you will be buying it and at above market price," Hans stated.

Wilhelm smiled at the gesture, but his mouth dropped open when he read the label telling him which car the key belonged to—a 1935 Mercedes-Benz 500K convertible. It had a sleek, long front end and a small back-end design. It was not the best car in the lot, but it definitely was in the conversation.

"Are you sure?" Wilhelm asked, giving Hans the chance to reconsider.

"You did well today," Hans said, patting Wilhelm on the back.

It was less than an hour from when he had to pick up Hannah. As he drove off the lot and the wind blew his hair back, he felt like one of the heroes of American cinema. He returned to his apartment and showered and brushed his teeth. Then he combed his hair and dabbed some of his father's aftershave he had taken. Heinrich had stopped by to wish him luck, and he and Erich advised him on when to try and kiss her. The talk made Wilhelm nervous, and he brushed them off with a wave.

He was downstairs and in the car in less than twenty seconds and at Hannah's in just over ten minutes. He parked the car along the curb and opened the door to Josef's shop. He hoped Hannah would be there waiting for him. But it was Hannah's mother working behind the register. She was an elegant woman with a kind smile.

"Mr. Schreiber?" she asked.

"Yes, Ma'am," Wilhelm responded, walking to her and then shaking her hand.

"I am Hannah's mother, Emma. It's nice to meet you, Wilhelm. Let's see how this fits."

He had forgotten about the suit. Emma removed it from the hanger and helped Wilhelm put it on. She fixed his crooked tie and buttoned the suit and made sure it was wrinkle free with a pull here and a tug there.

"Handsome," Emma said.

"Will Hannah be coming down?" Wilhelm asked.

Emma bit the corner of her bottom lip—something was wrong. Her lips contorted somewhere between a frown and a reassuring smile—something Wilhelm translated as she had something she wanted to say. Her lips parted, but a rustle in the back caused her to close them again, and she elected to defer. Josef came through the black dividing curtain and smiled.

"Is the suit to your satisfaction, Mr. Schreiber?" he asked.

"Yes," Wilhelm said.

It could have been down to his knees and he would not have cared. It was not the reason he was there. But it did fit perfectly and the material, a blend of wool and cashmere, was the most comfortable thing he had ever worn. But an uncomfortable silence descended with only the buzzing of the lights above making noise. Josef looked adamant in his resolve toward an unknown issue while Emma looked sick over it.

"Josef," Emma whispered.

"Mr. Schreiber, I do not think it appropriate that Hannah go out with you," Josef said delicately.

He had said it in such a kind way that Wilhelm did not understand his words at first. But Josef had hit him with a rock, and even if he called it a pillow, it still hurt.

He should have taken Hannah out the night before. Fate had been cruel in Schönfeld and Munich, and he could sense it laughing at his expense now.

"As for your tux, I will give you the discount and an extra five percent off," Josef said.

"Thank you, Sir," Wilhelm mumbled.

Truthfully, he didn't even know what Josef had just said. He removed some Reichsmarks from his pocket and set it on the counter. It was well more than needed, but he neither knew how much change he should receive nor did he care. He glanced at the black dividing curtain, hoping it would brush open and Hannah would step through. But the curtain was as unmoving as a brick wall. He tried to smile in appreciation for the well-made suit and left.

"Oh, Josef," Emma sighed.

"We talked about this. You know why, Emma," Josef interrupted her before she could say anything further.

His decision had not wavered, but there were only five things that made Josef truly happy—a hot cup of lemon tea, the first snowfall every year, his business, his wife, and his daughter. But now, he was looking at a silent dinner with smoldering glances from his wife and tear-soaked ones from Hannah, a sight no father wanted to see, and it was a combination that created a painful steam directed Josef's way.

"Hannah," Josef called. It was loud enough for Hannah to hear from upstairs. The footsteps that followed threatened to break the floorboards, and Hannah came skidding to a stop with a hopeful smile. "Please be careful," Josef said.

Hannah hugged her father, and he embraced it with a soothing sigh. It comforted him in a way nothing else could. Hannah pulled away, grinned, and then dashed out of the shop. Her mother looked on with a smile. Emma had listened to Hannah's pleas for over an hour the night before.

"Wilhelm!" Hannah shouted.

Wilhelm had been too dejected to even start the car and, instead, he just stared at the steering wheel as if it contained his past, present, and future. But like the wheel, it was nothing but black.

"Hannah!" Wilhelm exclaimed.

She was stunning in a blue dress, emblazoned with white dots, that fell short of her knees. In her hair, she wore the blue rose Wilhelm had given her.

"Is this your car?" Hannah asked.

She was certainly impressed, even if she had been taught not to focus on such superficial things.

Wilhelm returned to his senses and dashed around the car to open the passenger door for her and nearly got hit by a passing car. A horn honked to voice the driver's displeasure. Wilhelm opened the door and held out his hand to help Hannah into the car.

"No. Hans, my boss, let me borrow it," Wilhelm explained.

"That was very nice of him," Hannah said.

Wilhelm stared long enough at Hannah that she self-consciously examined herself in the side mirror.

"Something wrong?" she asked.

Wilhelm slowly shook his head. "I hope if I look long enough, this image will photograph itself onto my mind and never leave me," Wilhelm said.

Hannah smiled as Wilhelm closed the door for her. He dashed around to the other side, again not looking for oncoming cars, and hopped into the driver's seat. The car roared to life, and Wilhelm tugged on the steering wheel to get the car to veer onto the street. It was a cognizant effort to keep his eyes on the road and not on Hannah. She had her right arm out of the open window, her fingers dancing with the wind.

Wilhelm parked a few blocks away from the restaurant—"Veni, Vidi, Edi" or "I came, I saw, I ate"—for two reasons. First, parking was a nightmare, and he did not feel comfortable squeezing into any tight space with a car that was not his and one he could not afford. Second, and more important, he wanted to walk with Hannah.

The weather was exceptionally fair for mid-October apart from sporadic gusts of wind. But the gusts were cold enough for goosebumps to spread on Hannah's arms. Seeing that Hannah was cold, Wilhelm removed his coat and draped it over her shoulders.

"Now you will be cold too," Hannah said.

"My heart is beating too fast to be cold," Wilhelm said.

"Where are we going?"

"Do you like Italian food?"

"I do."

The restaurant was nestled in the corner of an intersection and had the option of both indoor and outdoor seating. He had originally planned to sit outdoors, but after giving up his suit coat, he realized how thin his white, long-sleeved dress shirt was, and the wind's nips had turned into bites.

"Reservation for Schreiber," Wilhelm said to the attendant.

Hannah had found a man who planned to be romantic. It showed that the woman was on his mind and he had taken the effort to ensure the date goes smoothly. Her father was that way. He would "surprise" her mother and her with flowers every Friday.

Fortunately, Wilhelm had made reservations. Otherwise, they would most likely not have been seated before Hannah's curfew. Those who had been waiting a while for a table groaned when Hannah and Wilhelm moved past them. The seating area had dimmed lighting, and the walls were dark walnut in color. They followed the greeter to a booth, where he laid two menus next to two glasses of white wine. The booth cushions were black and the backing, a wash of silver and gold and extremely comfortable.

"I hope you like Riesling wine," Wilhelm said.

"I do, but I can't. I will just have water," Hannah replied.

But Wilhelm's gesture was not lost and was appreciated nonetheless.

Wilhelm took a sip of his wine to stifle his nerves. It was one of his favorite wines. It gave off an almost-perfumed aroma and a taste of apples.

They both reached for the menus and scanned through them. Wilhelm loved anything with pasta, and because of that, he found the menu to be a series of impossible choices. Hannah, on the other hand, loved cheese and picked out the cheese ravioli in a matter of seconds. But Wilhelm still had not decided when the waiter returned to take their order. Wilhelm was quick to decide on just about everything, but choosing food was something he toiled over. He studied the dishes on the other tables to see what looked best. As Hannah finished ordering, a surge of anxiety bull rushed him. Fettuccine Alfredo were the first and only words that came to his mind. It was only after the waiter had taken their menus and left did he realize he had forgotten to ask for chicken to be added.

"I am most certainly going to spill. I have to avoid tomato sauce," Wilhelm said.

Hannah smiled and took a sip of her water.

"Can I ask you a series of questions?" Wilhelm asked.

"Am I being interrogated?" she asked playfully, leaning forward with her eyes bulging in a suspenseful way.

"Where were you the night of August second?" Wilhelm asked, taking another sip of his wine. He had not planned on asking her a "series of questions." He had wanted a naturally forming conversation.

A nervous energy hovered over the table and between them, not uncomfortable, but both were aware of it.

"What is your favorite color?"

"You are getting a bit personal, aren't you?" Hannah asked, laughing. It was the last question she had been expected to be asked, but she found the randomness of it to be adorable.

"Blue," she answered.

It had been his guess based on the blue rose and her dress.

"Reason?" Wilhelm asked.

"There was a landscape painting I had seen when my parents and I were vacationing in Austria. It was of a mountain lake with trees alongside it, and the lake stretched and branched off past what we could see. Gray mountains with white tips rose in the background, and the sky was filled with clouds that looked like cotton balls. A single canoe on the water, not moving enough to even cause a ripple. I imagined I was in it. It seemed to be the most perfect place on earth. It was peaceful and tranquil in the most wonderful way. Things hadn't changed there for hundreds of years. I'll never forget the color of the water," Hannah described.

She smiled nervously before taking a sip of her water. Wilhelm's gaze had not broken the entire time she spoke. The blue of her eyes was that lake and the white around the blue, the clouds she spoke of.

"Thank you for sharing that with me, Hannah."

He had always been open, but for some, it took a lot of trust and faith to reveal such a thing.

"What is yours?" Hannah asked.

"Black," Wilhelm answered. There were no close seconds, yet Hannah's eye color ascended the charts.

"Any painting you've seen to make it so?" Hannah asked, making light of her story.

Wilhelm shook his head but then hesitated.

"My mother had black hair. When I was sad, she used to lie in bed with me, and I would run my fingers through it. It gave me the same comfort that painting gave you. When she died, my father made me wear black. He said it was the color of strength—that I should take all my sadness and tears and let the black soak them up. Black absorbs everything," Wilhelm said.

"You have her hair," Hannah remarked.

But she was more focused on the cold remarks Wilhelm's father had given him.

Wilhelm nodded. Not a day went by when he did not think of his mother. It was a loss he never accepted, never understood, and never let go of. He took a deep breath to steady his emotions. He was one more poignant memory away from crying.

"You said you are not close to your father?" Hannah asked.

She hoped she was not getting too personal, as it was quite the leap from discussing his favorite color.

"On different continents. I remember my mother telling me to be patient with him. When I was young, I was digging through his drawers one day, and I found the Honour Cross. I didn't know what it was at the time. But there was another medal—silver with a skeleton hunched over. The coin terrified me as a child," Wilhelm said.

"What was the medal for?" Hannah asked.

"The Battle of Verdun. But my father caught me looking at it, and he hit me. He was shocked and scared at what I had seen. I cried in my mother's arms."

"Did you ask your father about it later?"

"Once, but I was told to never bring it up again. My mother kept saying, 'be patient,' 'be patient,' like it was some kind of mantra."

Wilhelm acted as though he was beyond caring, but the reality was he did. The man was his father, and he longed to have a great relationship with him. But the older he got, the more he accepted the truth that the two would never become close. The problem with being somebody who conveyed every emotion they were feeling was that it also revealed their more personal emotions. Memories of his mother brought tears and those of his father too, but those were caused by anger.

Hannah reached over and squeezed his hand. "I am sorry for asking."

"No. I am happy you did."

It was far too early for Hannah to make assumptions or judge Wilhelm in any way, but she thought that his mother's early and sudden death and the distant relationship with a father who had no use for life had given rise to a fire and thirst for life in Wilhelm.

The waiter finally arrived with the two dishes, leaving a trail of smoke that wafted off the ravioli and alfredo. He also took the liberty of refilling Wilhelm's Riesling and Hannah's water. They both thanked him, and the waiter nodded and left.

"I will trade you one ravioli for one fork swirl of your alfredo," Hannah said.

"You strike a reasonable bargain, Ms. Goldschmidt. I agree to your terms," Wilhelm said.

He offered his hand. Hannah shook it. Her face turned slightly red, and her touch sent shivers across his arm and into his heart.

Wilhelm slid his plate over, and she did the same, and they sampled each other's order. They ate in silence. Wilhelm was afraid of speaking with a mouthful of food or, worse, sending bits of food flying like noodle shrapnel at Hannah's face. He also made a conscious effort to not eat past the point of full. He was used to eating with Erich and Heinrich, where eating usually turned into a competition, and the winner received burps and flatulence as a prize.

The waiter returned and asked if either were interested in dessert, to which both refused. Wilhelm had always loved chewing gum, and as a child, he only received it on his birthdays or holidays. But he always saved a pack for special occasions. It was clove flavored, and apart from using it to freshen his breath, he simply loved to chew it. He offered a piece to Hannah, and they rose from the table. Wilhelm placed enough money for both of the meals and a tip into the black check holder, and the two left the restaurant.

It was dark, and the city was lit by streetlights and headlights. But Wilhelm led her away from the artificial light and toward the Spree River and its reflection of the stars.

"We are not going to the car?" Hannah asked.

"Not unless you want to go home," Wilhelm answered.

"No. I am just curious," Hannah said.

The air had a deep chill, and Wilhelm did his best not to shiver.

"Do you want your jacket back?" Hannah asked.

"No. I am fine," Wilhelm lied. What he wanted was to hold her hand, but the cold wind had numbed his courage. He counted to five in his head and reached for her hand. Her hand met his, and he entwined his fingers with hers. The cold shivers were met with a rush of warmth from her touch.

"Do you paint?" Wilhelm asked.

"What's that?" she asked.

"You mentioned the painting. I was wondering if it made you want to paint," Wilhelm explained.

"I do. I am not any good, but I do like to paint," Hannah said.

"I will not agree to that until you let me see one of your paintings," Wilhelm argued.

"And then you would say I am no good?" Hannah asked.

He thought she was serious until she smirked.

"Well, I would not want to lie to you," Wilhelm said.

Hannah playfully punched his shoulder before wrapping her hand around his arm. It sent an army of warm shivers up his arm that warmed him in a way no jacket could.

They had to cross one more intersection to reach the banks of the Spree River. The Berlin Cathedral, with its three green domes, was cast in the moonlight in the distance. A string of golden lights connected to the lampposts strung along the paved pathway.

Bicyclists and pedestrians peddled and strolled along the river's edge. Musicians played violins and harps. Some people stopped to listen, others to dance.

"Do you want to sell cars for the rest of your life?" Hannah asked.

"I do not know. I just want to enjoy life right now. I want to see the world," Wilhelm answered.

"You are a wanderlust," Hannah said.

She loved her home and could not imagine permanently leaving it or moving far away. Yet, she was always slightly envious of people who could leave on a whim.

"I have never even been to Paris," Wilhelm said.

"Nor have I. It is a beautiful city. I love the lights," Hannah said.

"I love the stars. They are the same for everybody. No matter where you are, you can be anywhere when you look up at them," Wilhelm said.

The musicians, bicyclists, walkers, and dancers, along with the string of lights, were behind them. Here, it was only the two of them and the hundreds of stars overhead. They seemed to have transcended to a different time, and only the faint glimmering of the city lights across the river brought them back.

Wilhelm pulled Hannah close.

"Close your eyes," he whispered, his voice tickling her ear. She closed her eyes. "Where do you want to go?" he asked.

"New York City."

Wilhelm guided her four steps to the left.

"Open your eyes," he whispered.

He had her head arched gently backward, and when she opened her eyes, she found herself gazing up at the night sky. It was littered with stars of white and blue and some, a melted swirl of both. There was nothing but the stars—no buildings of steel or concrete, no bushes or trees, no shrieking trains or honking cars. It was completely silent. She allowed herself to only look at them. The world around her was gone. She truly was somewhere else. Hannah was among the stars.

"Africa," Hannah whispered.

She closed her eyes again, and Wilhelm spun her and moved her forward and backward and left and right. Hannah screamed with excitement.

"Open your eyes," Wilhelm said.

She smiled when she did.

"Beware of the lions," Wilhelm said, standing behind her, his arms wrapped around her waist. She rested her head against his chest, their fingertips flirting with one another. "Next stop—Austria. Close your eyes," Wilhelm whispered.

He swept her off her feet and dashed forward with her in his arms, she laughing as he did. He set her feet back on the ground and leaned in.

"Keep your eyes closed. You are on that lake. On that canoe. You are surrounded by trees on the edge of the lake. The mountains are ahead of you. Can you see it?"

She opened her eyes. Each star warranted her stare, but there were too many to fixate on just one. It was an inside view of heaven itself. A deep relaxation spread over her. Though her nerves caused her heart to pound fast with excitement, the stars relaxed her exactly how that lake had in western Austria. Hannah turned to face Wilhelm.

"Where is it you want to go?" she asked.

"There is no place I would rather be than right here with you," Wilhelm said.

He inched his face toward her. Their noses almost touched—each subjected to a radical spectrum of emotions that blended to form a euphoric feeling and lightheadedness. Without either fully realizing, they had started to dance—their fingers doing what their lips desperately wanted to. They had danced under the lights in Munich too, but before Wilhelm had been able to kiss her, they had been pulled apart. He would not let that happen again. A strong invisible hand pushed him closer to her. His lips gravitated toward hers. Her eyes closed, her heart raced. She bit her lower lip, and her final exhale tickled his lips before he gently pressed his against hers.

He cupped her face with both his hands. She balled the front of his shirt into her fist and squeezed it. When they pulled away, they stared into each other's eyes—both smiled. The wind blew Hannah's hair over her eyes. Wilhelm gently brushed it behind her ear.

"I need to go," Hannah said.

Wilhelm had spent all his teenage years waiting for the future yet, at that moment, he would have been perfectly content if time stood still forever and he was forced to relive that singular moment for all eternity.

They walked hand in hand back to the car. A feeling of invincibility took hold. Hannah had turned Wilhelm into one of the superheroes he read about it in his comics. He was indestructible. The cold wind that had caused shivers to erupt in his body was now powerless. He had the power of flight and the power to fly to the stars themselves.

Lena Hauser

Even after returning home, the high hadn't gone away. Wilhelm laid in bed, going over every detail in his head for nearly two hours. When he finally drifted off to sleep, it was nearly one in the morning. He awoke at five after five. Even after only receiving four hours of sleep, he awoke with the same smile he had fallen asleep with.

He usually slept in until 6:30 a.m., but he knew no more sleep would come to him. His night with Hannah had rejuvenated him in a way no amount of sleep could. He showered, shaved, brushed his teeth, and dressed. With time to kill, he went for a walk around the surrounding blocks. The city slowly rose to life, and when the streets were bustling with cars, it was time to return home and get ready for work.

He was at the dealership and had finished washing the Mercedes-Benz before Hans had even arrived. When Hans pulled into the parking lot in a rusty, faded car, Wilhelm was tempted to pitch him one of the cars in the lot.

As Hans stepped out of his car, he used his thumb to gesture up and down, silently questioning how the date went. Wilhelm gave a thumbs up, and Hans smiled and victoriously shook his fist. Wilhelm handed Hans the keys to the Mercedes-Benz, and Hans nodded his approval of the wash job.

Wilhelm sold two cars that day, including the Mercedes. He was sad to see it go, as it had been something of a wingman on his date with Hannah. But what sold it to the young man was the way Wilhelm had described the car and his date with Hannah. Hans had said people were willing to pay for an experience, and Wilhelm had sold the experience of taking a good-looking girl out on a date—the experience of the wind pushing your hair back as you sped down the street and the engine roaring like a horse begging to go faster. Hans gave Wilhelm another thumbs up from inside the dealership. If the kid kept it up, he would be able to leave for home much earlier. The thought made his smile vanish.

"I am going to have to get some more cars in here," Hans said.

Wilhelm's routine over the next few days did not vary. He would wake up at 5:30 a.m. and go for a walk around the city, and by the time he would return, Erich would have left for work. Wilhelm would work until six and would expect Erich to be home by then, as he worked until five. But he wouldn't be, and Wilhelm would be asleep before he returned. If it had not been for the unwashed dishes in the sink and the dirty clothes strewn about in the hallway, Wilhelm would have thought Erich had moved back to Schönfeld. He had gotten so used to returning to an empty apartment that he was startled when he found Erich sitting on the couch later that week. But he was not alone. Wilhelm had not seen her at first because her hair color—long, thick, sable brown that bounced with volume—was an almost identical shade as the couch. Both stood when they heard the front door close.

"Wilhelm, I would like you to meet Lena Hauser. Lena, this is my other best friend, Wilhelm Schreiber," Erich introduced.

Lena was fair skinned with chameleon-like eyes that looked blue when the sun hit them and faded gray during cloudy days.

"It is nice to finally meet you," Lena said, shaking Wilhelm's hand before entwining it back in Erich's. She had a great smile, and Wilhelm could tell by her clothing that she was high society.

"Nice to meet you. I guess this explains why I have not been seeing Erich much of late," Wilhelm said.

"We met at the Reich Chancellery. Her father is Sturmscharführer Hauser. He was there for a tour, and she had tagged along," Erich said.

"He nearly fell off the scaffold from staring so hard," Lena teased.

"Please, I stared an appropriate amount of time," Erich clarified.

Lena rolled her eyes, and Wilhelm recognized the look in Erich's. He had found his own Hannah. Perhaps now, Erich understood the incessant ramblings about Hannah.

"We stopped here tonight to see if you would like to join us at my parents' house for dinner," Lena said.

"Certainly," Wilhelm answered.

He and Erich had no food in the fridge, save for a few eggs that had a questionable expiration date.

"You are welcome to bring Hannah," Lena added.

Wilhelm was desperate to see Hannah again and wanted Erich to properly meet her.

"Heinrich is meeting us there as well. He was trying to hunt down a date. But the women of Berlin have proven to be an evasive prey," Erich joked.

"That seems doubtful. Anyway, I need to change," Wilhelm said.

"That's fine. Erich needs to shower. He smells like a sewer," Lena teased.

"That smell is hard work," Erich said in his defense.

"That smell is repulsive," Lena jabbed back.

Wilhelm could have used a shower, but his days of sweating at work were over. He was either inside or outside in the cool autumn air, and his work was anything but back-breaking. He changed, washed his face, and gave his wavy hair a quick run-through with his fingers. While Erich showered, Wilhelm walked to Hannah's. Josef had yet to flip the sign on the glass door, and it saved Wilhelm from having to knock.

"Need another suit coat, Mr. Schreiber?" Josef asked when Wilhelm walked in, but he knew the reason Wilhelm was there had nothing to do with suits.

"May I take Hannah to dinner, Sir?" Wilhelm asked.

"You may," Emma answered, stepping out from the black dividing curtain.

Josef took a deep breath before he moved into the back and went upstairs.

"I have heard good things about you, Wilhelm," Emma said, beaming at Wilhelm.

"Hannah is very close to you and Mr. Goldschmidt. I can tell by the way she talks about you," Wilhelm said.

"That is sweet of you to say. Thank you," Emma said.

"Your suit coat fit perfectly. Thank you."

"I'm good with a needle."

"Hello, Wilhelm," Hannah said, emerging through the black curtain. She was breathtaking in a gray pea coat and gloves of the same color—so much so that even the mannequins turned their heads to stare at her.

"Will you join me for dinner, Hannah?" Wilhelm asked.

"Of course. This time I won't have to borrow your jacket," Hannah joked.

"Hannah, grab your father's gloves for Wilhelm. His hands will freeze otherwise," Emma said.

"Oh, that's not necessary," Wilhelm said, holding up his hand to stop any generosity on his behalf. But, truthfully, his hands had gotten cold on the walk over.

"Please, Wilhelm, it's no trouble," Emma insisted.

"First, my daughter, now, my gloves," Josef blurted out from behind the black curtain. He stepped through, reading from his clipboard, his glasses hanging precariously on the tip of his nose. "Ten. Sharp," he said.

"Yes, Father," Hannah said.

"And, Mr. Schreiber, we need to discuss back payments on your purchase. I think I may have missed some taxes and fees," Josef added.

Emma gave him a playful, back-handed slap across his chest.

"Ignore him, Wilhelm," Emma said, apologizing with a smile.

"Love you both," Hannah said.

"Love you," her parents replied.

Hannah left, closing the door behind them.

"No car?" she asked Wilhelm.

"Cinderella's curfew was at seven this morning," Wilhelm said.

The walk back to his apartment started with a nervous silence. But it dissipated quickly. They talked about how delicious their food was on their date and what a typical day consisted of for both. But the nervous energy crept back, as it always did around a crush. It was unspoken but shared.

Lena and Erich were already outside, leaning against the apartment building. Erich wore a new jacket, and Wilhelm suspected it was a gift from Lena. Hannah was surprised to find out that they would be going to dinner with the two. Wilhelm introduced her to Erich and Lena as they walked to Lena's house, some two and a half kilometers away.

Lena had an air of confidence about her that hovered on the line of arrogance. It was likely she did not know what colors the sidewalks were, for her head was always high and her chin, raised. But she was not lacking in manners. She asked both Wilhelm and Hannah questions to get to know them better and was genuinely interested in their answers. Lena loved Berlin and was quick to point out some of her favorite places.

Neither Hannah nor Wilhelm had expected such a long walk and waited for either Lena or Erich to say they had arrived. The air was frigid, and it felt more like late December than early November. When the winds swept off the Spree, it traveled right through their clothing like ghosts through a wall, and their exhales looked like smoke.

"It was Erich's idea to walk. I could have arranged for a car to pick us up," Lena said, casting Erich a dirty look.

Lena waited for a car to speed by and then dashed across the street before the next one came zipping past. She led them to a massive apartment complex. The iron gate swung open in advance. Wilhelm wished there was someone to open the front door to their apartment complex, especially after grocery shopping. He had to pin his bag of groceries against the door with his hip and catch it as he opened the door. Three oranges had been casualties of one such unsuccessful attempt. Only, Lena's home was not a single apartment. The entire building was her home—a three-story house with nearly twenty windows. The lawn was the greenest Wilhelm had ever seen and large enough to be a football pitch. The well-kept lawn had a stone walking path that led from the family garden to the front door and a flagpole that was taller than the house. The Nazi flag waved high and true in the strong wind.

"My father is having a gathering. It will be over soon," Lena said in response to the eight vehicles parked in the driveway that had gone unnoticed at first. She opened the thick oak door, painted in a pristine white. The knocker was a chrome eagle with a rat in its talons. Hannah's hand grew colder, and Wilhelm squeezed it to keep it warm. Hopefully, the two would be warmer in a few moments.

The entrance to the house had a small bench to sit on while putting on and taking off shoes and a closet for shoes and coats. To the left was the living room and to the right, a kitchen that any chef or food fanatic would envy. But it was not what they could see that had captured their attention. Their first deep breath was of hot, freshly baked pies and smoked meats that caused their stomachs to sit up like a dog that had just heard a strange sound. Erich's stomach gurgled louder than the laughter and chatter coming from one of the rooms.

A woman came toward the front door, wiping her hands on a towel. Her skin was fair like Lena's, but her hair was dark red. She wore an apron stained with flour and blood, and the makeup on her face was a tad much.

"Lena, you are back so soon. Supper is not quite ready," the woman said.

"Mother, this is Wilhelm and Hannah. Wilhelm and Hannah, this is my mother, Ida," Lena introduced.

Ida made sure her hand was dry before shaking theirs.

"Your father is in the study room. Best to wait in the living room until they are done," Ida said.

"Do you need help, Mother?" Lena asked.

"No. Be a host to your friends," Ida answered.

Lena led them left to the living room. The ceiling was nearly ten meters high with a staircase that spiraled up to what Wilhelm could not even guess how many rooms. The floor was a dark wood and neatly polished. The furniture was new and made from crisp black leather. Mounts of animals that Lena's father had shot hung on the wall. They varied from deer and elk to the more exotic, like lion and zebra. The fireplace alongside the eastern wall crackled. Sturmscharführer Hauser's pistol from his time of fighting in the Great War was placed over the mantle.

"Sit anywhere you'd like. Make yourselves comfortable," Lena said warmly.

As soon as Wilhelm sat, he felt like he would never be comfortable again if he ever got up. The leather of the chair sunk in and cushioned him everywhere. The heat from the fire wafted toward them like a spell of an enchantress, and Wilhelm was being sung to sleep. Moments later, the eagle knocker pounded against the thick white door. Lena left the room and returned moments later with Heinrich and his date, a woman neither Wilhelm nor Erich knew.

"Marry her," Heinrich told Erich as soon as he saw the house.

"I feel sorry for your date," Erich said.

The young woman had jet-black hair and almost equally dark eyes. Heinrich was too busy gawking at the house to notice his date's awkward stares. Her face reddened as she waited to be introduced.

"Right, sorry," Heinrich said after noticing every person staring at him, "This is Helga Stark. We met outside a brewery."

"Your home is lovely," Helga said.

"Thank you," Lena said.

Heinrich slouched onto the couch beside Wilhelm, and Helga sat on the edge of it, still too uncomfortable to fully relax.

"What does everyone want to drink?" Lena asked.

"Beer," both Erich and Heinrich nearly shouted in unison.

"Erich, will you help?" Lena asked.

But Erich was too preoccupied making faces at Heinrich and Wilhelm to notice.

"I'll help you," Hannah said.

She rose from the couch and Helga did too, but neither Hannah nor Lena had noticed so, instead of following them, she moved closer to the fireplace. Her cheeks were rosy and her nose, runny. It was obvious she had not expected such a long walk either. Men forgot details like mentioning when, where, and with whom when asking a woman to dinner.

Hannah was shy by nature and was not under the spell that Wilhelm was. But she was taught to be helpful when in a guest's home. So was Wilhelm, but he did not have the will to rise from the piece of heaven he was sitting on.

"You best be careful, Erich, or you may end up on these walls," Heinrich teased, standing between the elk and wild boar mounts and acting like he had been stuffed by a taxidermist.

Hannah made sure to stay close to Lena. It was a realistic possibility she could get lost in the house. They stepped into the kitchen. Two other women were helping Ida with preparing supper and the desserts. Hannah watched and took note of how it was being prepared.

"Do you need something, Lena?" Ida asked.

The black kitchen island's granite top was covered with cut vegetables and a dusting of sugar and flour. The stove top was covered with sizzling pans and boiling pots.

"Beer for the men. Wine for us women," Lena said.

"There is a bottle of '29 in the cellar. Be sure not to take your father's beer. His guests have a select taste," Ida said.

"Come on, Hannah," Lena beckoned.

She led Hannah toward the door that led downstairs. She flipped a switch and the light powered on. As they descended the steps, there was not a single creek. The basement was expansive, but it was the three horizontal racks of wine that housed over a hundred bottles that drew Hannah's attention. Each row was divided first by type and then by year.

"My parents are a bit of wine fanatics," Lena added unnecessarily.

Lena searched through the wine and every now and then, pulled one from the rack, and stated its year and importance. There was a bottle of Merlot from 1918, which Jakob had brought home to Ida after his time fighting in the Great War had ended. There was a bottle of Chardonnay from 1919 from Ida and Jakob's wedding, a bottle of 1896 that Jakob's parents had bought on the day he was born, and a bottle of Pinot Noir from Paris that was bottled in 1876, which Jakob's father had received on his sixteenth birthday.

Hannah enjoyed a glass of wine but was by no means a wine connoisseur. But she loved the stories behind each bottle, and even though Hannah lived above her family's shop and Lena lived in a castle, they were both family oriented.

Lena pulled a bottle of 1929 Cabernet Sauvignon from the rack.

"I have a bottle of Riesling from 1912 that I steal sips from when I'm having a rough day. Do you want to try it?" Lena asked.

"I would never ask," Hannah said.

"You are not asking. I am asking you," Lena reminded.

Lena crouched down and carefully slid the bottle from the rack. Hannah grabbed the bottle of '29 Cabernet Sauvignon to free Lena's hands so she could uncork the '12 Riesling.

"I like to think of where the wine has been. And think of the year in which it was bottled," Lena said.

"The English ship, the Titanic, which sank in 1912," Hannah suggested.

"Perhaps this bottle was on the ship, and it was picked up by one of the lifeboats. Or it floated all the way to Europe," Lena continued, pulling the cork out of the bottleneck. "Let it breathe for a moment"—no doubt she had heard the phrase a thousand times from her oenophile parents. She offered Hannah the first drink. Hannah took a sip and handed it back to Lena. It was remarkably smooth and strong and easily the best wine she had ever had. Lena took a swig before pressing the cork back into it.

"Now we have to find the beer for our big, strong men," Lena said, rolling her eyes.

Hannah smiled. She had expected to be shier than she was. She had a small circle of people she trusted, and almost all were blood. But Lena had been generous, friendly, and interesting. Hannah never got the feeling that Lena was judging, and for that, she liked her immediately.

"My father drinks this. He buys it from the brewery directly, and he serves it during his meetings," Lena said, lifting a pack of six bottles of dark beer. She set the beer back in the crate before moving to the hard liquors. "But, secretly, my father has a week spot for American Whiskey," Lena said. Her mouth formed an O that said, "Oh, the scandal."

The room was dim, and it seemed Lena had the entire inventory memorized and did not need to read a single label.

"Those are what we serve to obnoxious men," Lena said, pointing to a crate of bottled beer.

Hannah lifted the crate, and they climbed up the steps and hurried through the busy kitchen and back into the living room.

"I thought you had left," Erich teased.

"It is my house, you idiot," Lena said, tossing a pillow from the couch at his face.

Seeing Hannah struggle with the crate, Wilhelm snapped free from the spell the couch had cast and hurried to take it from her.

"We were hoping you men had taken the hint and left," Lena joked.

She sat on Erich's lap, and he wrapped his arms around her. The men finished two beers and the women, two glasses of wine before the door upstairs on the mezzanine finally opened. A veil of smoke wafted out. The chatter grew louder as the shadows inside crept out and down the steps. Each man was dressed in uniform adorned with medals and patches with the red armband of the swastika.

"Hail, Hitler!" the officers chanted as they struck the Nazi salute.

Lena nearly jumped off the chair, and the others too rose and repeated the words and saluted.

The Nazi officers smoked cigarettes or cigars that were complimented with Scotch or beer, the very same Lena had pointed out earlier.

"My daughter, Lena, is having some friends over for dinner tonight," a handsome, cleanly-shaven man said.

His hair was the same color as Lena's, thick, kept short, and parted to one side. The man was Lena's father, Jakob. The other officers nodded and smiled. Some outranked Jakob, some did not, but he was ascending more rapidly than any of them. Though Jakob liked to think of himself a lion, to Hannah, he resembled a coiled snake that could strike without warning.

"Lena, introduce us to your friends," Jakob said, taking a puff from his cigarette and leaning closer to the fireplace. It did not help the image of a snake Hannah had of him. The cold-blooded was trying to warm itself.

Lena obliged, and Jakob nodded at each when Lena recited their names, the fire dancing in the reflection of his eyes.

"I am Sturmscharführer Jakob Hauser. Welcome to my home," he said as he threw his cigarette into the fireplace.

Hannah had liked Lena almost immediately but had gotten a different vibe from her father. He seemed cold and calculating, and as he looked over each, it was as if he was trying to read their minds.

"Please don't hesitate to make yourselves comfortable. I see Lena has started you men out with beer. I'm afraid I must insist that you drink wine at dinner. A proper meal requires a fine wine," Jakob advised.

"Sturmscharführer Hauser, thank you for having us," one of the higher-ranking members said.

"It was my pleasure, Obersturmführer Lammers," Jakob responded.

The officers inclined their heads ever so slightly. One of the women who had been in the kitchen helping Lena's mother now stood at the entrance.

"Ellie, please help these men find their coats," Jakob instructed.

"Yes, Sturmscharführer," Ellie said.

The officers followed the attractive house help, stealing glances at her backside. Ellie handed them their coats and bid them a good night. She closed the door and went back into the kitchen.

"I will go help your mother in the kitchen," Jakob said.

"And by help, he means sample bits of dinner while my mother isn't looking," Lena teased.

"Such slander," Erich said.

"I'm afraid she is right, Erich," Jakob said.

"Then let me know if I can help," Erich joked.

"Remember to finish your beers. We drink wine at our table," Jakob said before leaving for the kitchen.

Erich, Wilhelm, and Heinrich debated over whether or not Mr. Hauser meant to finish the opened bottles in their hands or also the three unopened ones. Wilhelm would have been fine finishing his opened beer, but Heinrich and Erich had opened one more, and he did not want Lena to run back downstairs for a single bottle.

Helga's third glass of wine stifled her runny nose and warmed her still-chilled body, and she finally had the courage to include herself in the conversation. As none of the three girls were largely built, the bottle of '29 hit them like the Stock Market Crash of the year in which the wine was bottled. When Ida, now dressed in a red evening gown, came to tell them dinner was ready, all six were at various stages of inebriation.

A case of the giggles had taken over as they sat at the table. Ida and Jakob smiled at one another. The '29 and the strong German beer had done its job. None, apart from Lena, had expected the spread of food that stretched from end to end that included beef, pork, chicken, potatoes, yams, green beans, peas, carrots, and corn. The counter was decorated with cherry pie, apple pie, and white cake.

"You have overdone yourself, Mrs. Hauser," Erich said while the others chimed in their approval. The table, a thick oak, was nearly bowed and buckled at the center from the spread.

"I wanted to make sure everyone had something they liked," Ida said.

Nobody wanted to ruin the food. It looked like edible art. But as soon as Ida dug the spoons into the food, it was fair game. The table seemed to be divided between carnivores and herbivores. Erich had nothing but meat on his plate, and Helga had nothing but potatoes and vegetables. Hannah had elected for a small amount of beef and a large spoonful of potatoes. The loaf of bread disappeared quickly in an attempt to soak up stomachs full of alcohol. But Wilhelm, Heinrich, and Erich kept diverting their attention to the counter and the pies and cake atop it. Even if no one else had heard it, the desserts called their names and pleaded them to take a slice.

Jakob had insisted on choosing the wine for each person. The selection depended upon what was on each of their plates. Hannah was given a glass of Zinfandel, Helga, a glass of

Viognier, and Wilhelm, a glass of Pinot Noir. Erich and Heinrich had taken such a wide array of food that they had sampled every kind of wine. Jakob's selections did not disappoint.

"Lena tells me you are from Schönfeld too, Wilhelm," Jakob said, twirling his glass of Mourvèdre before taking a sip.

"Yes, Sir," Wilhelm answered.

"Did your father serve during the Great War?" Jakob asked.

"He did," Wilhelm answered.

"Good man. Victory would have been ours if we had the right leaders. We have that man now," Jakob said confidently.

"Now if we could only chase the rats out of Berlin," Ida added.

"Rats?" Helga asked.

"Jews," Jakob clarified.

The word made him nauseous as if his wine had suddenly gone bad.

"Rats are preferred," Lena said.

"The rats will be scurrying," Jakob promised.

Hannah finished her glass of wine, and Jakob took the liberty of refilling it. Wilhelm took note of how much of it she drank and thought of surprising her with a bottle, but when Jakob moved his hand, the year 1932 printed on the bottle was now visible and might have been the price too.

"We are the hawks. The rats can scurry. But they cannot hide," Jakob said.

He was the last to set his fork down. The Hausers were accustomed to fine dining and knew to savor the flavor, and because of that, their dinners were three times as long as any Wilhelm had had with his father. Added to that was the fact the Hausers actually spoke with one another.

Ida rose to clear the table, and the others unanimously stood to help, but Ida waved them away.

"I am fine. Please help yourself to dessert," Ida said, beaming with a polite smile.

Though the dinner satisfied every taste bud they had, they had made the right decision in saving enough room for two pieces of pie or cake. The only thing desired after dessert was a nap. But as Ida, Ellie, and the second helper cleared the table and started the commendable task of washing a mountain of dishes, Lena led the others up the spiraling staircase to the billiards room. Apart from the obvious billiard table, a dartboard hung on the wall, and there was a poker table in the middle of the room surrounded by black leather wheeled chairs with padded armrests. Cigarette smoke and booze had become permanent residents of the room, and the walls blew puffs of smoke and belched beer habitually. It was the room where Jakob lured the Reich's most influential people, coaxing them with fine wines and strong cigars to increase the favorable light cast upon him and his family.

The next two hours involved over fifty card games. The playing cards, which had been new during the first shuffle and deal, showed signs of wear and tear by the end of the second hour. The wine continued to be poured, but Wilhelm and Hannah had to refuse. They would have to leave soon to meet Hannah's ten-o'-clock curfew.

Helga had sat out the last hand of Schafkopf—Sheepshead. Erich and Wilhelm had played hundreds of hands with Erich's grandmother the summer of their thirteenth year. Hannah and Wilhelm, who had the Jack of Diamonds, therefore, making him partner, had won easily with Erich, Lena, and Heinrich not even getting *schneider* (30 points). They refused a rematch and rose from their seats.

"You are leaving?" Heinrich asked.

"Yes, I am getting tired," Wilhelm answered.

He would rather face the retaliation for leaving than have it placed on Hannah's curfew.

"Thank you so much, Lena," Hannah said, preparing to leave.

"Yes, thank you," Wilhelm repeated.

"My pleasure. It was great to meet you. Please tell me we can do this again sometime," Lena said enthusiastically.

Helga was slouched in her seat and fast asleep. Wilhelm knew Heinrich to be a man with a wandering eye and as someone who liked to roam. It was likely Wilhelm would never see her again. When the billiards room door opened, the silhouettes of Mr. and Mrs. Hauser cuddling together on the Chesterfield chair were cast by the fire, the cigarette in his hand flashing red when he puffed it. Hannah and Wilhelm descended the spiraling staircase.

"Leaving?" Ida asked as she sat up.

"We really should be going. We cannot thank you enough," Hannah said.

"Our pleasure. We want Lena to surround herself with good German stock," Ida said.

"Shall we see you again?" Jakob asked.

"I hope so," Wilhelm answered.

"Are you planning on walking?" Ida asked.

"Yes, we are not far," Hannah said.

If one kilometer was bending the truth, two and a half was breaking it.

"Are you sure?" Ida asked.

"Yes, thank you," Hannah said.

Wilhelm agreed with Hannah. They had eaten pounds of their food and drank hundreds of dollars' worth of their fine wine. To ask or even accept an offered ride would have been overstepping.

"Be careful tonight," Jakob cautioned.

Ida still disagreed with their choice to walk, but Jakob had grabbed her hand and pulled her back toward him.

Wilhelm instantly regretted not taking the ride the moment the chill November air hit his face. But, at least, he was more prepared than he was on their first date, and he would get nearly half an hour more with Hannah than the five minutes of silence in the back seat of one of Mr. Hauser's cars.

"I did not know we were going out with your friends," Hannah said.

She was not mad, only surprised.

"I am sorry. I just met Lena tonight, and she asked me to bring you," Wilhelm said.

Hannah only nodded.

"Did I do something wrong?" he asked.

"No. I had fun. I just want to know beforehand. I'm being silly."

"No, I should have told you."

Surprises were one thing, but meeting a group of strangers was something that was obviously out of Hannah's comfort zone.

"It is freezing," Hannah said.

Wilhelm had thought the night had gone well but, clearly, Hannah thought differently. It made it strange she refused a ride home.

"I do not like being in people's debt," Hannah explained.

"What do you mean?" Wilhelm asked.

"Lena's father—he is a member of the Schutzstaffel," Hannah began but paused.

The Schutzstaffel or SS was Hitler's die-hard loyal soldiers. Those two letters instilled fear in many.

Wilhelm was at a loss for words.

"My father trusts me to be smart. I want to be able to tell him where we are going. I'm sorry," Hannah continued, "I'm also sorry for making you walk."

"I do not mind walking," Wilhelm reassured her.

He reached for her hand and was elated when she did not pull it away. The further they walked, the more relaxed she became, and their conversation flowed. They discussed each wine they had had, the best part of the meal, the close losses in cards, and Lena and Helga. But the city buzzed more than usual that night. Three police cars sped past, their red and blue lights spinning and dancing off the side of the buildings. After a fourth sped by, it was hard to think of it as a coincidence. Something was happening.

The Night of Broken Glass

Hannah squeezed Wilhelm's hand. The streets, which had been eerily empty, were now filled with people quiet as ghosts. An ominous aura clouded the streets close to her home. Windows had been smashed, and the streets were littered with shards of glass. Some of the businesses were on fire, the smoke wafting toward the full moon. It cast an unearthly glow. Owners and spectators looked on helpless, terrified, and confused.

"I have to get home," Hannah gasped.

Jakob Hauser's words "be careful" had at first sounded like the plea of a worried parent but, now, they were the words of warning from someone with dangerous information.

Wilhelm secured his grip on Hannah. He wasn't going anywhere. They dashed across the crowded streets. Women and children screamed out as their husbands and fathers were forced onto trucks. Those who resisted were beaten. Sirens echoed, but the police did nothing but watch as the Gestapo—the Nazis' secret, ruthless police—rounded up their desired suspects. Hannah ran so quickly that even Wilhelm, nearly a foot taller, struggled to keep up, but his grip did not falter.

The ominous shadows grew with each step. Hannah's home was around the corner. They covered their eyes as an invisible blazing heat swept over them. Broken glass crunched under their shoes. The heat grew, and its origin was soon discovered. As Wilhelm and Hannah turned the corner, the windows of the shop shot out gusts of flame. Hannah tried to speak, but no sound came out. Her legs collapsed. Wilhelm fell to his knees to stop her from hitting the pavement. She was paralyzed, only able to gawk at the horror.

"Stay back," Wilhelm cautioned.

He brought his shirt over his mouth and nose and dashed inside. He yelled out for Hannah's parents, but the crackling fire roared each time and swallowed up his yells. The walls were as black as the smoke, but the east wall had stayed relatively unaffected by the fire. Painted on it in blood red was the Star of David, stretching from floor to ceiling. The words "Tod für Ratten und Juden"—Death to rats and Jews—were to the right of it. The letters looked like they were traced with the tip of a finger.

Hannah stood behind him silently, her greatest secret had been revealed.

"Hannah!" a voice cried out to her from behind.

Wilhelm turned. His eyes met Hannah's only for a moment through the thick fog of the black smoke.

"Mother!" Hannah cried.

She dashed toward her while Wilhelm stumbled out of the shop. Emma and Hannah pulled each other into a hug that temporarily blocked their airways. Wilhelm coughed violently as his lungs tried to reject the smoke they had been forced to inhale. He took quick breaths, and the cold November air flooded into his lungs.

Josef emerged from a small crowd and dashed to his wife and daughter.

"Thank God," Josef sighed. His lip was split open, and blood trickled from a gash on his forehead. Bruising had already commenced, growing in varying shades of purple and blue.

"Father?" Hannah gasped when her eyes fell upon his forehead. She flung her arms around him, pulling him into a hug.

"I am okay. I am just happy you are safe," Josef said, rubbing her back. "Thank you, Wilhelm," he said, looking up from the hug.

Firetruck sirens rang out, and the spinning red lights skipped off the streets. The Goldschmidts made room for the firetruck and firemen, but it drove past them. They would only extinguish non-Jewish homes and businesses.

Hannah and her parents hugged one another as they looked on, and even though memories inside their home flooded their thoughts, the fires still roared.

Wilhelm thought of his mother. He had always felt her presence in his childhood home. It was a great comfort to know he could always return to it and to her. But that same comfort would not be available for Hannah. Every memory would be tarnished because of this night. He took a deep breath and sprinted back inside.

"Wilhelm!" Josef called. He pulled free from Hannah and Emma and followed in after Wilhelm.

Wilhelm had accidentally started a fire at the "Rote Blumen" in his youth, and the ensuing beating he had received from his father had temporarily changed the way he walked. But it had taught him a valuable lesson on how to put out a fire. Wilhelm grabbed the black dividing curtain and pounded the fire before draping the curtain over it. The flames suffocated before it could spread. Josef and Emma had kept a few empty buckets near the customer bathroom, as it would often leak. Wilhelm and Josef filled them and poured the water over the small batches of fire that remained.

Hannah would not stand idly by. She dashed in, her mother close behind her. Emma ran by Josef and helped fill up the empty buckets. Hannah stared at the red Star of David. The symbol that had once been the shield that guarded her faith in God was now a blood-soaked macabre sword that inflicted grievous injury and spilled her secrets. Wilhelm looked from the wall to Hannah.

"Wilhelm, I wanted to but…" she started to say but fell silent.

It all made sense now. Her strange attitude had nothing to do with him but everything to do with being in the company of a man who despised and imprisoned Jews. He had unknowingly put her in a dangerous situation.

"I understand. It was not safe to trust me," Wilhelm said with a sorrowful look.

Her secret was hers to share, and he often forgot they did not know each other as well as he thought. He had been fully confident about his feelings for her, but perhaps she was not about her feelings toward him. Wilhelm stepped outside for fresh air and to give Hannah and her parents a moment alone.

Emma softly grabbed Hannah's hand. "Go," she said, signaling Hannah to follow him. Emma had a wonderful ability to sense sadness in others, and she could see the change in Wilhelm's eyes.

Hannah stepped outside. Wilhelm was sitting on the curb, taking puffs of fresh air like a cigarette. He had earned the right to hear Hannah reveal her secret her way.

"Wilhelm," she said, just loud enough to be heard.

He rose from the curb and turned toward her. His tux and face were stained black—his face temporarily, his tux permanently.

"You do not have to say anything," he said.

"I want to. Wilhelm, I'm Jewish. I wanted to tell you out loud. I trust you. I would have told you regardless of what happened tonight. I am sorry I lied to you," she said.

"You didn't lie. I never asked."

"You do not mind?"

"It is a part of who you are. One of thousands. And I like them all," Wilhelm said.

Hannah rested her head against his chest. He ran his fingers through her hair.

Inside, Josef and Emma tip-toed about the shop to assess the damage. Inconsequential cloths and fabrics, the hours labored into the hand-sewed suits, tuxes, and jackets to the irreplaceable photographs had all burned to ash. Hannah and Wilhelm stepped back into the shop. No one appreciated the possessions of loved ones more than Wilhelm. He knew there would be a time when Hannah's parents would be gone and that the mere sight of a cloth ruler and sewing machine would devastate her and bring her to tears. When Wilhelm's mother had passed away, his father refused to remove any of her clothing or toiletry items from the house. Her brush with her black hair woven between the bristles brought him to tears for a year, and as Wilhelm thought about the brush and the final remnants of smoke dissipated through the broken windows, his eyes filled with tears.

"You should be getting home, Wilhelm. It's not safe," Josef said.

Wilhelm's eyes went to Hannah.

"I'll be okay," Hannah said, squeezing his hand.

Wilhelm wanted to offer his apartment for them to stay in, but if they did, Erich was sure to ask questions, and just because he knew Hannah's secret, it did not mean it was his to share. He gave her hand a final squeeze and left.

The fires had been extinguished, and the silence outside made it appear the looting and vandalism were over. But Josef would not have his family sleep upstairs in case his shop fell victim to arson once more. They slept in the back room at the side of the steps. Blankets were laid out for comfort, and some were wrapped around them as the cold November winds whistled in. Even with a jacket, gloves, and knitted hat in addition to seven blankets, the wind and cold found ways to attack.

Blocks away, Wilhelm was in a warm bed. The wind and cold were powerless in its attempt to penetrate through the insulated walls of his apartment. But still, no sleep would come to him. He was scheduled to work in the morning but called Hans at home to tell him he was ill. Instead of a greeting, Hans had answered the phone with a curse word. There was little Hans cared about at 2:30 in the morning.

Wilhelm wanted to avoid seeing Erich, for there was no way he could keep the previous night from showing on his face. So, at ten after four, he dressed and returned to Hannah's home but first stopped at the car dealership for the mop, bucket, and soap he used to wash cars and carried it the nineteen blocks. The sun had yet to rise, and the wind was cruel.

As soon as he reached the Goldschmidts' shop, he began sweeping the debris and soot and decided to remove the disgusting racial epitaph from the wall next. It took nearly thirty minutes of scrubbing before it started to come off, but it still left a nasty reminder in the form of a red smear. The walls that had once been a clean white would never return to that color. Wilhelm went to the nearest hardware store and bought two cans of gold paint. He had always liked gold and thought it would look elegant amongst the fine tuxes Mr. and Mrs. Goldschmidt made. He applied the first coat of paint and, while that dried, he mopped up the water they had thrown onto the floor to extinguish the flames. He salvaged what he thought might be of importance, but he would let Hannah and her parents decide if they wanted to keep it. It was too much of a personal decision for an outsider to make.

"Mr. Schreiber," Josef said, stepping through where the black curtain had once hung.

He neither knew the time or why Wilhelm was in his shop. He had locked the door both out of habit and precaution, but Wilhelm had most certainly entered through one of the gaping holes where the glass windows had once stood. Josef's head looked swollen but, at least, it had stopped bleeding.

"Good morning, Sir," Wilhelm greeted without breaking the back-and-forth motion of the mop.

"What is it that you are doing?" Josef asked.

"I thought I would get started," Wilhelm said.

"Wilhelm, you seem like a nice young man. But this cannot work with Hannah. We are Jews. You are German. There are laws," Josef explained.

"You are German too," Wilhelm said. He turned away from him as he mopped the floor. Josef nodded, both annoyed and appreciative, and grabbed the broom.

"Gold?" Josef asked.

The color was hard to miss.

"Elegant, yes?" Wilhelm asked.

"It's tacky," Josef said, but his deadpan expression slowly curled into a smile.

Wilhelm chuckled and continued to mop. No matter how many times Josef or Wilhelm swept, a fresh layer of dirt and ash always remained.

"Why doesn't it bother you?" Josef asked.

"That you are Jewish?"

"Yes."

"I don't know. I was sheltered as a child. I did not see much but my school, my home, and the flower shop. My father never talked, and my mother died when I was young. I did not receive much input about anything."

"Thank you. For that and this," Josef said, nodding to the shop.

"Thank you for changing your mind and letting me take Hannah out. I still owe you," Wilhelm said.

"Consider those extra fees for your tux paid for," Josef said.

"Not quite. I will require a new suit coat."

"It would be my pleasure, my good young Sir."

It was strange to talk as much as they did. Josef was not one for silence and filled it with whatever thoughts crossed his mind—random in their transition. In the next hour, they talked about anything from what Schönfeld was like to family vacations Josef had been on. He even talked about life during the Great War and the extreme sanctions and limited rations that followed. He talked about how he had become a tailor and when he met Hannah's mother. After his university schooling, he and his friends had vacationed in Munich. He had drunk too much, and the train back to the city was crowded. He and his friends were forced onto different cars. While his friends got off at the right exit, he passed out and only awoke at the last stop in a city called Germering. The train station was almost entirely empty, but that's where he had met her—Emma had also gotten off at that station.

"I asked her where in God's earth I was! She was so polite, and they were both attractive in their nurse's uniform," Josef said.

"They?" Wilhelm asked.

"Yes. I was seeing two of her."

Wilhelm smiled. "Mrs. Goldschmidt said she was good with a needle," Wilhelm added.

At the time, he did not know what it fully meant, but now that he knew she was a nurse, it made sense. He didn't need to ask to know that it had become an illegal profession for Jewish people.

"When she spoke, I keeled over and vomited at her feet," Josef continued.

"She didn't run away?" Wilhelm asked.

"On the contrary, she nearly carried me to a nearby park and laid me on a bench and sat with me. When I awoke, we watched the sunrise. I took her to breakfast and then I got back on the train."

"You left?" Wilhelm asked.

"I missed my stop again—this time on purpose—showed up and never spent another day without her."

He went on to elaborate that Emma was not Jewish so, at first, his family did not accept her but grew to love her as much as he did. Wilhelm had no idea how his parents had met, and he would never know. His father absolutely cherished Wilhelm's mother, but the mention of her caused him great pain, and his pain transformed into tremendous anger.

By the time Hannah and Emma had woken, the floor was free of debris and the wall had a second coat of paint. Hannah and Emma stepped through where the black dividing curtain had once hung. Their eyes were red with bags drooping under them. Wilhelm had looked the same during the weeks after his mother's death. It was from crying oneself to sleep.

"Oh, my," Emma gasped, her eyes swiveling around the room. There was still significant damage to the western wall, but the fact that any of it looked as good or better than it had lifted her spirits.

"Do you like the color? If yes, it was my decision. If no, it was Wilhelm's," Josef joked.

"I love it. Wilhelm, you are too kind," Emma said. She put her hands on his shoulders, smiled, and hugged him.

"I know somebody who can help with windows," Wilhelm mentioned.

Refurnishing the inside would do little if they did not fix the gaping holes. The winds of November would blow in anything from leaves to old newspapers and, soon, winter would be upon them, sending in drifts of blowing snow.

"We can't ask that of you," Emma said.

"You didn't," Wilhelm assured her.

"I will go with you," Hannah said.

"Be careful," Josef said.

Things had quieted, but that did not mean it was safe.

"No harm will come to her. You have my word," Wilhelm said.

He held out his hand, and Hannah grabbed it.

Wilhelm's "somebody" was Hans, and although he had called in sick, he hoped he would understand. Hans had said the windshields came from the same place that produced windows for homes and businesses. The owner's name was Frederick, and the two had known each other from since they were young and, therefore, Hans felt he could have and should have received a better deal.

"You're not sick," Hans said when Wilhelm walked in.

"No. I am sorry," Wilhelm said.

"Is that Hannah?" Hans asked, lifting himself off his chair to gain a better vantage point.

"Yes," Wilhelm answered.

Hans nodded his approval. Hannah smiled politely yet uncomfortably.

"Were you out last night? The city was taken over by the devil," Hans said.

"Hannah's father's shop was looted by mistake," Wilhelm said.

Though he knew Hans to be a decent man, the prejudice of Jews ran rampant. It was something taught from parent to child as a scapegoat to problems.

"Windows broken?" Hans asked.

Wilhelm nodded.

"Broken glass everywhere. I had to take a different route to work today," Hans said, his explaining sounding an awful lot like complaining.

Wilhelm knew he did not mean to sound self-loathing, but he did. If only Hans knew how November 9th had affected some people. He and Hannah had seen first-hand men being forced onto the convoy trucks and taken away. The synagogue Hannah and her parents worshipped at had been burnt to the ground. Shops and homes had been destroyed.

"Well, since somebody called in sick today," Hans said, staring at Wilhelm for at least ten seconds of silence, "I can't exactly run to Frederick's. But I can give you his address." He scribbled on a piece of paper. "He is impatient, so make sure you talk quickly and get to the point."

Wilhelm took the paper, thanked him and then he and Hannah walked toward the door.

"Wait," Hans shouted. He rolled his eyes and reached in his pocket for his keys. "You're going to want to drive."

He tossed the keys, but Wilhelm dropped them, making Hans close his eyes in frustration at his compassion.

"I get done at four. I have a houseful of crying kids to return to. Please be late," Hans said.

Wilhelm smirked. Hans often talked about all the crying in his house, yet his desk was littered with his children's pictures, and every day, he snuck in a story of something new one of his children had learned.

Wilhelm thanked him, but Hans was already face-deep in his newspaper.

"Do you want to drive?" Wilhelm asked, looking at Hannah.

"I do not know how to," Hannah replied.

There had never been a need to own a car. Hannah's world consisted only of fourteen blocks.

"I will teach you," Wilhelm said.

As Wilhelm drove, he explained every knob, button, and stick. He answered every question Hannah had, even the questions she asked twice. The ride to Frederick's was only twenty minutes, but they stayed for only ten.

Frederick was a man of fewer words than Wilhelm's father, and Wilhelm wondered what grand conversations the two could have. Josef and Wilhelm had measured the windows and jotted down the measurements. Wilhelm only had to hand over the paper and Hans' note, and a couple of Frederick's workers loaded up the car. Wilhelm paid him, and Frederick waved goodbye with the hand that was not clawing at his head.

"Do you want to drive back?" Wilhelm asked Hannah.

"No, I do not think I am ready."

"Then practice here."

There were twenty men walking about, and the idea of practicing with so many eyes on her made her anxious. Hannah hated being the center of attention. She was perfectly fine with her back against the wall in silence. Often, her silence was misconstrued as her not having a good time, but she believed a person should only speak when they had something to say.

"Now you are being silly. You will do fine," Wilhelm insisted.

"Maybe at a later time," Hannah said.

It was her definitive answer, and Wilhelm did not push her further. Instead, he changed the topic, but Hannah's thoughts drifted back to the previous night. He left her in silence, knowing processing what had happened was something she needed to do. And sadly, it was something she had to do alone.

Though Hannah's parents were safe, there was no replacing the photographs and memories that had been burned to ash. But more than that, the innocence of youth was gone. Her father had always told her he could and would protect her, but for no fault of his own, he could not. For the first time in her life, she fully knew the world could and would harm her.

Wilhelm parked the car in front of Hannah's home, and Josef jogged out to help with the windows.

"You continue to surprise, Mr. Schreiber," Josef said.

Wilhelm had learned much during his time working at the Reich Chancellery, and the five windows were up in less than three hours, including a twenty-minute snack and water break.

"I have to return Hans' car," Wilhelm said after the work was completed.

It was later than Wilhelm had expected or wanted it to be, and it was unlikely he would get the car back on time. Hans would probably be waiting outside.

"May I join you?" Josef asked.

It was not the Goldschmidt Wilhelm had wanted to ask, but he nodded politely. Awkward situations rarely affected Wilhelm. But there was something strangely intimate and intimidating about being in such a confined place with Hannah's father. And even though he could see outside and his window was rolled down, sending bits of the outside world into the car, it was a feeling that could only be compared to claustrophobia. The silence killed him. He had an awful feeling Josef was watching him, but when Wilhelm looked over to check the mirror, Josef's attention was outside on the hundreds of shops that had been vandalized and destroyed—many he knew, many he didn't—but whether it was the sun reflecting off Josef's eyes or he had a tear that would not fall, Wilhelm could not tell.

The increase in traffic meant it was past four. As he drove into the lot, his presumption was proven true. The lights of the building were off, and Hans was waiting outside with a scowl on his face.

"Shit … sorry," Wilhelm mumbled.

Josef only smiled.

Wilhelm pulled the car up close and put it into park and exited the car so fast that he nearly tripped.

"You are late," Hans growled.

"I am sorry," Wilhelm said.

"Will you be at work tomorrow?" Hans asked, ignoring Josef completely. It was too late in the day to meet new people.

"Yes, Sir," Wilhelm said.

"Good. Sell something," Hans said, getting into his car.

Wilhelm could tell Josef wanted to say something, but Wilhelm pleaded with his eyes for him to stay quiet. Hans waved out of the window as he drove away.

"Does he look unkindly upon my kind?" Josef asked as they began walking back home.

"I do not know, but it's safer to keep it a secret," Wilhelm said.

The long walk back to Josef's was filled with an uncomfortable silence. Josef had something to say, but every time it looked as though he was going to speak, his mouth closed and he returned to his contemplation. He even started to speak on several occasions, but only the first portion of a word was audible, and each time, Wilhelm came up with his own conclusions.

"Is there something you wish to say, Mr. Goldschmidt?" Wilhelm asked.

The imagination was worse than the truth on most occasions.

"Wilhelm, I like you, son. You are a mensch. My daughter likes you. But I think we must accept certain facts, no matter how warped the facts are, how unethical they are. We are Jews. It isn't safe for you, and it isn't safe for Hannah," Josef said.

Forget about Wilhelm, both were worried about Hannah.

"I understand," Wilhelm said.

A sharp pain stabbed his heart for his own betrayal.

"Can I say goodbye?" Wilhelm asked.

"Certainly," Josef said.

Whether Josef continued to talk or was silent the rest of the walk, Wilhelm could not say, for his mind tortured him by replaying every memory he had with Hannah. Though they were depressingly scarce, each was treasured. He scrambled to think of what he would say, but he did not have a single word prepared when they returned to the shop. The sun had set, and the road basked in the streetlights.

"Thank you for your help today. It will not be forgotten," Josef said.

Hannah smiled when she saw Wilhelm, but for the first time, Wilhelm was unable to return it.

Josef silently motioned Emma to go upstairs, and after twenty years of marriage, she understood without a single quizzical look.

"Wilhelm, what is wrong?" Hannah asked.

"We cannot see each other again," Wilhelm said.

"Why?"

"It isn't safe, Hannah. I brought you to an SS officer's home. I could have gotten you into serious trouble."

"You didn't know," Hannah muttered, grabbing his hands.

Normally, hers were cold and his warm, yet the long walk had made the tips of his fingers ice and hers, cups of hot coffee.

"Goodbye, Hannah," Wilhelm said. He kissed her forehead—he hated the pain he was causing her. He turned to leave. He wanted to say so much more but knew further words would only cause them both more pain.

Hannah watched him leave. She was stuck in a trance and did not know how long she had stood there before she finally dawdled upstairs. The modest kitchen was clean but dark. Emma and Josef sat on two brown armchairs in the living room with looks of melancholy.

"You made him?" Hannah asked, looking at her father.

"Hannah, it is for the best. It isn't safe," Josef said.

"Mother?"

Josef had told Emma about his discussion, and her eyes, swiveling from Josef to Hannah, told Hannah that she was torn on what she thought was right and what was fair.

"We have to be careful, Hannah," Emma tried reasoning.

"He didn't run away. He stayed. I should have told him," Hannah argued.

"No. You did the right thing—keeping it hidden," Josef said.

"I am not ashamed of who I am, Father."

"Nor am I," Josef said. He rose and moved toward her. But Hannah dodged his hug and dashed into her bedroom. Josef followed after her.

"Let her be," Emma advised.

Josef paused half-way between Hannah's bedroom and the living room.

"Josef," Emma sighed.

"Emma, we need to keep her safe," he said adamantly.

"I know, but what if my father had stopped me?" she asked.

"He didn't and look what I've made you—a Jew."

"I chose that, and what you have made me is a wife and a mother. You have given me a great life."

Hannah wanted nothing more than to drift off into a dreamless sleep but, instead, she stared at her off-white ceiling. It did not seem fair to be told what to do. She was nineteen. Her mother was married at her age and a year later, pregnant. Hannah had never missed her curfew once and had never snuck out of the house. But both streaks would end that night.

When she thought it was safe, she slowly opened her door and hoped it would not betray her cause with a creak. All the lights in the living room and kitchen were off. Her parents' bedroom door was closed. She dressed as quickly as she could in the darkness and crept out of her bedroom. She grabbed her jacket draped over the back of the couch. She had gone from her bedroom to the kitchen for a glass of water nearly a thousand times and was therefore apt at moving around in the dark. The stairs were in her favor. They usually moaned and groaned when stepped on, but this time, they absorbed every sound. She had her reservations about breaking her parents' trust, but she had given Wilhelm hers, and he had done nothing to lose it. And her trust was not something she gave away like a flier at a parade. The entire shop was testament to Wilhelm's character.

She unlocked the door and slid out without fully opening it. She closed it, locked it, and stepped out into the cool, crisp air and walked as quickly as she could without drawing any attention. She had felt so safe with Wilhelm by her side on their walks, yet now, alone, Berlin was a city of unseen and unknown monsters. The city she loved had betrayed her, and it would never feel as safe again. She had to cross hordes of deserted streets and empty alleys until she finally reached Wilhelm's apartment building.

She opened the door and dashed up the steps toward apartment number four-fourteen. She brought her hand to the door to knock but paused with tentativeness. She could still turn back. She had broken her parents' curfew, not their trust. She knocked softly and paused. She took a deep breath and rapped on the door confidently. The door opened.

"Hannah?" Erich asked, his pale blue eyes too glazed to see properly. He yawned and rubbed his head. His hair stuck straight up, and he wore only a white t-shirt and boxer shorts.

"Is Wilhelm here?" Hannah asked.

"I think so. The door was shut when I got home from Lena's," Erich answered.

He looked still half-asleep and unable to remember such details.

"May I come in?" Hannah asked.

"Sure," Erich said.

He opened the door fully and pivoted to allow Hannah to step in.

Hannah thanked him and walked in. Erich closed the door behind her and stumbled back into his bedroom and collapsed face first onto his bed. Hannah staggered toward the closed bedroom door and slowly turned the knob. A figure sat up when the door opened.

"Hannah?" Wilhelm asked, startled.

Hannah closed the door behind her and removed her coat and shoes, kicking them off and draping her coat over his dresser. Without a word, she crawled into Wilhelm's bed and lifted his arm to cover her. The cold radiated from her body.

"Did you walk here?" he asked.

She only put a finger to his mouth. There would be time for words, but at that moment, she only wanted to sleep with Wilhelm by her side. Wilhelm reset his alarm clock to 3:30 so he could walk Hannah home before her parents awoke. Her shivering diminished as the heat trapped between their bodies increased. Their feet rubbed up against one another, and she entwined her hand with his. They only got three hours of sleep, but they were the best he had ever had. He awoke to taking in a deep breath of Hannah's hair and the annoying buzzing sound of his alarm. How time could be so cruel.

"I have to take you home," Wilhelm whispered into her ear.

The bed had never been warmer or more comfortable, and it called both of them back to it. Their eyes struggled to stay open, but as they stepped out of his apartment, the fresh, frigid air hit them like a cold shower.

"My father made you leave, Wilhelm," Hannah said.

"I want you to be safe," Wilhelm said.

"I want to live," Hannah said, mimicking Wilhelm's own words. She reached for his hand. "Dance with me?"

"Always," he answered.

He pulled her close, and they danced under the streetlights.

"Where do you want to go?" Wilhelm asked.

"Los Angeles," Hannah said with a smile.

"Close your eyes," Wilhelm whispered.

Hannah looked into his dark eyes one last time before she closed hers. A soft hand arched her backward.

"Open your eyes," Wilhelm whispered.

She opened her eyes. The moon and stars filled her view. She stared at them for only a moment before Wilhelm leaned in, blocking out a part of the moon, and kissed her.

Falling

It had been six weeks since Hannah had been forbidden to see Wilhelm, but each night since, she had snuck out. Her stomach would turn into a knot of guilt each time she crept through her own home like a burglar. But when she opened the shop door to find Wilhelm there, it was worth it. He had insisted he escort her, as he did not like the idea of Hannah walking alone. Their walks consisted of both deep conversation and reflective silence. When the snow fell, they would walk to the Spree River and watch it dance to the ground. By the time they would get to Wilhelm's apartment, they would only get four hours of sleep before they needed to walk back to Hannah's.

With each successful trip, Hannah secretly longed to get caught. She hated to hide such a thing from her parents. Wilhelm was one of the best things in her life, and it was alien to keep such a thing from them. The lack of sleep was well worth it, but she missed their dates. There were too many variables for it to continue unknown. Some nights, her father would fall asleep on the chair, and Hannah had to whisper from her window she could not go. Other nights, her parents stayed up later than usual, and Hannah would oversleep.

"I am going to tell my parents," Hannah said, the guilt too heavy to fall asleep one night. She turned onto her back to look at Wilhelm as they lay in his bed. Wilhelm had been on the verge of drifting off to sleep.

"They may stop you from seeing me entirely," Wilhelm said.

"I won't let them," Hannah reassured him.

"I want to be there when you do."

Hannah smiled with appreciation. It was going to be the hardest thing she ever had to do. She had never lied to her parents, never kept secrets from them. They would be hurt but, at least, it would be out in the open and known, and Hannah liked to believe telling them rather than being caught showed greater respect and courage.

It was a Saturday morning, and they had gained an extra hour before her parents would wake, but she wanted to be certain she and Wilhelm were there when they did.

"Are you sure?" Wilhelm asked.

On the walk to Hannah's, Berlin was theirs apart from a few workers opening their shops. There were almost no cars on the streets and next to no one on the sidewalks.

"I am sure," Hannah said, but the terrible feeling in her stomach told her otherwise. Her feet refused to lift and walk up the stairs, and she felt light-headed and weak with each step.

Wilhelm had never seen her home, and though it was small, it gave a feeling of comfort. The paintings on the walls and the photographs on the dressers and cabinets made the home and the love inside something palpable. Wilhelm stopped to examine one of the paintings.

"Is this yours?" Wilhelm asked.

The painting was a scenic landscape of snow-covered evergreen trees.

"Yes," Hannah said, her face blushing. She avoided looking at her painting or Wilhelm.

"You are impressive, Ms. Goldschmidt," Wilhelm complimented before looking at a photograph of her parents.

"I love photography. The magic of it is something I cannot wrap my head around—to capture a moment forever with a single flash."

Wilhelm recognized the passion for it in her voice. She struggled to remain quiet as she showed him her favorites. If it were Hannah's choice, her home would be wallpapered with photographs.

The silent, dark, closed bedroom came to life. The floorboards creaked, and light cast out of the crack of the door. The color in Hannah's face vanished. Wilhelm took her hand in his. The door opened and Josef stepped out. A startled look hung on his face when he saw Wilhelm.

"Hannah, what is this?" Josef asked.

Emma stood in the doorway of her bedroom, not concerned, but not condoning the secrecy either.

"I have been seeing Wilhelm. I never stopped. I don't want to fight with you, and I don't want to lie to you," Hannah said, letting out a sigh of relief after she finished.

"Hannah, we discussed this," Josef said.

"You can't keep me safe, Father. Wilhelm can't keep me safe. But he makes me happy. You make me happy, and I don't want to lose either of you," Hannah said.

"He is a very nice young man, but you are Jewish, Hannah. Come to reason," Josef tried explaining.

"The Nazis punish me for being a Jew. Will you punish me too?" she asked.

Emma put her hand on Josef's—a subtle sign the power had been usurped.

"Your curfew is eleven. No more sneaking out. You will tell us where you are going and who you will be with," Emma said.

Hannah flashed a smile that had enchanted Wilhelm from the start.

"Yes, Mother."

"I do trust you, Hannah. My verdict is still out on him," Josef said.

Hannah's smile had enchanted Josef for far longer.

"He is teasing you, Wilhelm. He complimented you to the point of annoyance," Emma said.

"Looks like you've missed your stop," Josef said, shaking Wilhelm's hand.

"How about breakfast?" Emma asked.

Even if Hannah didn't consider seeing Wilhelm against her parents' wishes wrong, neither she nor Wilhelm was the type who thought doing something wrong felt good. But now that her parents knew, the varying degrees of guilt knotting in her stomach had disappeared. She and Wilhelm spent the entire day together and every evening the week after.

Wilhelm genuinely liked his job, but the normal nine-hour shift had somehow morphed into a full cycle around the sun. Hans had grown tired of hearing "Hannah stories" so much that he put a limit of five references per day. Wilhelm saved his fifth to ask if he could teach Hannah how to drive after closing up. Hans bartered by taking a half-day on Friday.

Wilhelm had taken Hannah almost everywhere in Berlin within walking distance, but she did not expect to go to Wilhelm's workplace. Wilhelm had shoveled off every car in the lot when he arrived that morning but now, almost twelve hours later, they were coated in a fresh, fluffy blanket of snow.

"Please tell me we are not going to be shoveling the cars off," Hannah said with deep sarcasm.

"We? No, I'll be inside. Knock on the door when you are done," Wilhelm said, matching her own sarcasm and raising it.

Wilhelm used his keys to unlock the door. He was given his own set after he sold his sixth car. He had presented an idea to Hans about buying the same model cars the Nazi hierarchy drove. He had spent hours outside the Reich Chancellery building and could name every car Hitler, Goebbels, Göring, Bormann, and Dönitz drove or rode in. Though Hans was leery of the idea, he agreed to buy one, and after the car sold the same day he had driven it into the lot, he was more open to the idea.

"It's cold," Hannah said.

Wilhelm turned the lights on. Heat was too expensive for after hours. One of the newer model cars was on display in the building. It was the most lavish car in the entire lot, and Hans hoped one of Berlin's most affluent citizens would make an offer on it.

"You are going to learn how to drive," Wilhelm said.

He had recognized her shyness in front of others but, now, it was only them—no prying or judging eyes. He opened the car door for her and, like a chauffeur, helped her inside. Hannah sat behind the wheel and put herself at ease. There was no worry of forgetting to break or running through a stop sign. After an hour of Wilhelm calling out scenarios, Hannah was ready for the real thing. He removed the key to one of the older models and smiled.

"No," Hannah said.

"It isn't driving unless you move," Wilhelm said, reaching for her hand and pulling her outside.

"Wilhelm, no," she insisted.

But she didn't even convince herself, for the truth was she was dying to learn. Her father had always kept her sheltered in fear of what the world could do to her. It was not without its merit, as proven true by Kristallnacht (The Night of Broken Glass), but there was so much Hannah wanted to learn but was afraid to. Wilhelm had a fearlessness when it came to doing everything he wanted. His comfort zone was ever expanding and, by association, Hannah's was forced to grow.

Wilhelm entered the passenger seat and left Hannah out in the cold. He had no plans of leaving the car, and Hannah loved him for it. She trotted through the snow and around the car and took the driver's seat. The door slammed shut, making the snow from the roof fall off.

"I'm only sitting here because it's cold out," she said.

"Fair enough," Wilhelm said.

He started the car.

"I'm not moving," Hannah said, crossing her arms.

Wilhelm put the car in drive, and the car strolled forward.

"Wilhelm!" Hannah yelled, wrapping her hands around the wheel.

"See, you are doing fine," Wilhelm said.

But she was only going five kilometers per hour. She cranked the wheel to turn down the ramp and onto the road, screaming in ecstasy as she did. Adrenaline stormed through her as she pressed down on the gas. They drove all around the city, and by the time Hannah put the car in park at the dealership, she had another love. She could not wait to drive when spring hit. There were so many places they could go. Her dormant wanderlust spirit flickered like an ember.

Afterward, they walked to Wilhelm's apartment to help prepare dinner. Erich had had the great idea of doing weekly dinners with Lena, Hannah, Heinrich, and whatever woman Heinrich was dating at the time. The only problem was that neither he nor Wilhelm could cook.

Wilhelm opened the door and a puff of smoke wafted out. The kitchen sizzled and coughed.

"Thank God," Erich said, trying to dodge the smoke and turn the stove down.

"It looks lovely," Hannah said, kissing his cheek.

"Thank you, Hannah. Someone who appreciates effort," Erich said.

"Your effort smells like shit," Wilhelm teased.

"Well, give me a hand so our effort can taste like shit too," Erich retorted.

Though there were no books available that would teach such things, Wilhelm had picked Hannah's brain on the rules of kosher, and he ensured each meal met the requirements. But Hannah assured him there were worse sins to commit. To guarantee the meat was from an animal slaughtered by a rabbi, Hannah and Wilhelm often "picked it up on their way."

"Lena should be here shortly. No doubt her mother is sending her with a dozen pies," Erich said.

"And hopefully a bottle of wine," Wilhelm added.

He slid his hand into an oven mitt and loaded a pan of Kartoffelpuffer—potatoes mixed with eggs, spices, and served with either meat or applesauce—into the oven. They were one of Wilhelm's favorites and something he was actually good at making. They were also another thing that reminded him of his mother. He would sit on the kitchen counter and watch her make it at least once a week, but after she passed away, it was made only once or twice a year.

Erich flipped the flank steaks and dodged clouds of smoke like a boxer avoiding jabs and hooks.

"Thank God you two are not in charge of rebuilding the Reich," Lena said.

Neither had heard her knock or enter. She held a cherry pie in one hand and two bottles of wine in the other. Hannah took the pie from her and placed it on the counter, and Lena set the two bottles of wine on the table.

"It is fun to watch them struggle, Hannah," Lena joked.

Hannah shimmied past Erich and Wilhelm to the cupboard and removed two wine glasses for her and Lena.

"Mother says to…" Lena started.

"Let it breathe," Hannah finished.

They hurried out of the smoky kitchen to the couch.

"It is excellent," Hannah said after getting the okay from Lena to drink.

"I wonder how many Jews are celebrating Hanukkah," Lena said, rolling her eyes.

It was only when Lena went off on one of her Jewish tirades did Hannah remember she could not fully trust her. But besides that, there wasn't a single occasion Hannah did not enjoy her time with Lena and, apart from Lena's anti-Semitism, their interests were extremely similar. The Nazi propaganda had portrayed Jews as having hooked noses and greasy black hair and olive skin. It was a stereotype Hannah defied with her porcelain skin, blue eyes, and light blonde hair. Luckily, the topic changed quickly when Heinrich entered without a knock.

"We are not going to want to eat, are we?" he asked, tossing his coat on to the edge of the couch.

Heinrich was with another woman, and though it seemed mean, none of the others took much effort in getting to know her, as they were usually gone after a few days. But they certainly weren't rude. Lena poured a glass of wine for her and finally, after getting dirty looks from Lena and Hannah, Heinrich introduced her. Her name was Eva, and she had moved to Berlin from Frankfurt.

"Ladies and gentlemen, please take your seats at the table. Dinner will be served shortly," Erich announced, taking a bow.

Lena and Hannah exchanged looks and laughed.

"Tonight's dinner is brought to you by Erich Brinkerhoff and Wilhelm Schreiber. If you feel the desire to tip, please do so," Erich said.

"I have a tip. Don't burn the food," Heinrich teased.

Eva punched him on the shoulder, garnering respect points from Hannah and Lena. They both liked Heinrich, and he definitely had his charm, but he also had no problem breaking hearts.

"We are going to need more wine," Lena said as the plates of food were set before them.

"A toast," Wilhelm said, standing over the table and raising his glass, "To friends who are like family and to these nights."

The others raised their glasses and nodded at each other.

"Let's get this over with," Heinrich said.

But there were no complaints to be made. Erich and Wilhelm nodded at each other victoriously. The wine went down smoothly and, once again, Ida Hauser had perfectly paired the wine with the food. Her pie was even more delicious, and it was a struggle to fight off the feeling of an on-setting food coma. Hannah had volunteered to wash the dishes. Lena dried them while Heinrich told one of his famous stories. Even if they were hardly appropriate, especially in front of a date, they were usually funny at his expense.

"I think Erich may propose soon," Lena said with a hopeful smile on her face.

"Really?" Hannah asked, handing over a washed plate needing to be dried.

"He has been talking with my father a lot lately. My father likes him," Lena continued.

"That is so exciting, Lena. I'm happy for you," Hannah said.

"You will be there, won't you?" Lena asked.

The wedding was sure to be populated with Nazi elites and Jew haters. There seemed no possible way she would ever be able to.

"Of course," Hannah said as it was easier to lie—something to worry about down the road. Hannah often wanted to know if their relationship would change if Lena found out she was Jewish—would it end? Or would Lena's outlook on Jews change?

"Say what you want about the French, but damn do they make great wine!" Erich said after finishing his glass.

Wilhelm reached into the kitchen drawer and removed five spoons. The gesture did not go unnoticed, and the others, apart from Eva, hurried to the table.

"What is it?" Eva asked.

It was one of the minor annoyances of Heinrich bringing new dates. They had to go over the rules of most games they played, including the agreed alterations to standard rules.

"It is a card game. Get four of a kind, reach for the spoons. See somebody else grab one, you grab one. There are only five spoons and six of us," Heinrich explained.

Though Wilhelm considered himself a gentleman, there was no gallantry in spoons. The game began in silence and then turned into hushed whispers, which was followed by false alarms being shouted when the players intentionally motioned for the spoons. Erich had tried to vote for the action to be punishable with the banishment of a hand. He had even written up the rules and regulations. But it was almost always Erich who fell for the bluffs and grabbed a spoon prematurely. Nobody had a great poker face and, often, their blank faces cracked with smirks and laughter. The game had the distinction of not rewarding the winner but punishing the loser. Erich lost game one, and as punishment, he had to down his glass of wine.

"Do we have another bottle?" Erich asked.

"Yes. It's in the fridge above the lettuce," Lena answered.

"We have lettuce?" Erich asked, bewildered.

She knew more about what Erich had than Erich did, and it wasn't hard to imagine them as an old couple shouting at each other from other rooms. Erich opened the next bottle of wine and made everyone else finish their glass before topping them off. Heinrich lost the second round and Wilhelm, the third. The girls did not miss an opportunity to brag about being undefeated. But through silent communication, the three men decided to work together to end the streak. They played thirty games, and each acquired enough losses to make the room spin.

"Do you care if I stay here?" Heinrich asked, already making the couch his bed.

"No. You are all welcome to stay," Erich said.

Erich raised his glass to his mouth, but Lena stopped it from touching his lips.

"You have had enough, handsome," she said.

She did not feel like taking care of him again. Her father had gotten Erich drunk on whiskey once, and Erich had vomited all over the bed. He vowed it would never happen again, but he had also sworn off drinking.

Hannah had gotten permission to stay the night. She told her parents drinking would be involved, so it would be safer if she stayed at Wilhelm's. Again, it was her mother who had won the argument for her.

"Let me know if you need anything, Eva," Lena said as she helped Erich to the bedroom.

Heinrich had passed out face first on the couch, so Eva would get no help from him. Erich and Wilhelm used the closet to store extra pillows and blankets, as it was common for Heinrich to sleep on their couch on Friday and Saturday nights. Hannah gave Eva a pillow and a blanket, and Eva moved to the chair.

"Good night, Hannah," Lena said from behind the door.

"Let me know if you need help," Hannah said.

"If he starts puking, I will need your help dragging him into the bathtub. He can puke as many times as he wants then," Lena said, cracking a smile and closing the door.

Erich and Heinrich were not the only ones feeling the agony of defeat. Wilhelm blinked slowly and sat on the edge of his bed, the room spinning violently. Hannah gave him a glass of water, and he drank it in three gulps.

"Poor loser," Hannah teased, wiping his chin.

As they lay in bed, Hannah gently scratched his back. Wilhelm and Hannah assumed they were the first to wake in the morning, and both experienced varying degrees of a hangover. But when they opened the bedroom door, they discovered they were not the first to wake. Heinrich was in the kitchen, frying eggs and buttering toast.

"Lena and Erich still sleeping?" Hannah asked.

"Still sleeping? They were up for at least an hour last night," Heinrich said.

"Good or bad?" Wilhelm asked.

"Two minutes of good. Fifty-eight minutes of bad," Heinrich answered.

Wilhelm laughed, and the uneasy queasiness sped vomit up into his throat like an erupting volcano. Heinrich smiled both at his joke and the sudden disappearance of color from Wilhelm's face. Heinrich was the type of guy that instilled envy. He was good-looking, charming, and the man did not fall privy to such a mortal thing as a hangover. And, apparently, he made a good breakfast.

He, Wilhelm, and Hannah had finished eating by the time Eva, Erich, and Lena stumbled awake. They ate their breakfast, lukewarm by that point, then Eva and Heinrich left.

"Have a good Christmas, Hannah," Lena said, holding out a bottle of wine she had removed from her purse.

"Lena, thank you. That is so thoughtful," Hannah said graciously.

"Just remember…" Lena started.

"To let it breathe…" Hannah continued—it was a commandment in the Hauser house.

"It is a Malbec. A good Christmas wine," Lena added.

Hannah wrapped Lena in a hug, and the small gift of wine and holiday wishes only reiterated her belief Lena was a good person, not deep down, but on the surface even with her anti-Semitic comments—Hannah knew it was the product of years of government propaganda. They were only twelve or thirteen when Hitler and his anti-Semite agenda rose to power—still children.

Wilhelm walked Hannah home and then returned to his bed for a much-needed nap. He had been invited to Hannah's house for dinner to celebrate the eighth day of Hanukkah and Christmas Eve. He had started saving for Hannah's gift weeks earlier and could not wait to see the look on her face when she opened it. He had arranged his own bouquet for Emma and had a box of chocolates for Josef.

Hannah waited by the locked shop door for him. She wore a deep garnet, velvet dress with white shoes, and to Wilhelm, Christmas had never looked better. Emma's talents knew no limits. She had made the dress based solely on a passing glance while she and Hannah were window shopping. The shop looked as it had before the fire, except for the color. But apart from fellow Jews and the occasional oblivious person who came in as customers, business was drastically down.

The smell of Christmas wafted off an evergreen-scented candle as they walked up the steps. Josef and Emma were dressed in their best and greeted Wilhelm with a handshake and a hug.

"Thank you for having me," Wilhelm said.

He handed the chocolates to Josef and the flowers to Emma.

"They are beautiful," Emma said.

"The chocolates more so," Josef quipped.

The Menorah, a candelabrum of nine candles, four on each edge and one lone candle in the middle, burned brightly and cast dancing shadows on the wall. Hannah eyed the present in Wilhelm's hand but made no mention of it, as it would have been rude. But as she took it from him and set it down next to the lamp and they moved to the table, her eyes moved back to it. Her mind scrambled to find out what it was.

Emma had made braised brisket with root vegetables and spiced apple-pear sauce. Wilhelm found the meat to be perfectly tender and spiced but absolutely loved the apple-pear sauce. While Josef and Emma ate theirs warm, Emma had placed Hannah's bowl in the freezer.

"What are you doing?" Wilhelm asked.

"Hannah is a bit of a strange duck. She prefers hers cold. Blame Emma's family," Josef joked.

"Finally, the kink in the armor I have been searching for," Wilhelm teased.

Hannah waited ten minutes before removing the bowl and bringing a spoonful to her mouth. It was chilled to her liking, but the skeptical look on Wilhelm's face lessened her enjoyment. She slid her bowl over.

"Try it," she offered.

Wilhelm had found his bowl of hot apple-pear sauce to be mouth-watering and had no problem accepting another spoonful. Yet, he could not deny the apple-pear sauce tasted even better chilled—somehow refreshing like a tall glass of ice water.

"It is okay," Wilhelm lied.

"Liar," Hannah sneered.

His eyes had lit up too much for her to believe his lie.

As Hannah and Emma washed and dried the dishes, Josef and Wilhelm sat in the living room as the record player played Christmas music. Josef grabbed a gift box from beside the couch and held it out for Wilhelm. Emma and Hannah paused to watch. Wilhelm lifted open the box and unfolded a black suit coat and black pants that were perfectly hemmed and tailored.

"This is more than I could ask for," Wilhelm said.

The jet black looked sleek and elegant, and he would feel like a better man in it. It was the type of suit that made a man stand tall and proud. The inside of the coat was inscribed with a ruby-red thread, like the first coat they had made him, with the letter J & E and a G overlapping the two.

"I remember you saying you liked black, and Hannah told me it was your favorite color," Josef said.

"Let me pay for at least half of this," Wilhelm insisted.

Josef put up his hands. "Wilhelm, it is a gift."

"But I only got you chocolates and flowers."

The gifts were fine to bring to a holiday dinner, but after Wilhelm had gotten a gift that took both money and hours to make, his gifts seemed tacky and cheap.

"Wilhelm, your gifts were thoughtful and appreciated. And I know you arranged the bouquet yourself. You did a wonderful job," Emma reassured.

The red roses were surrounded by noble fir and variegated holly to make heavy use of the traditional colors of Christmas. But they celebrated Hanukkah, not Christmas. Wilhelm had given her nothing more than weeds.

"I, for one, appreciate the chocolates and, in fact, will appreciate one right now," Josef added.

He opened the box and hovered his finger over it.

"There is a key as to what is in each space," Wilhelm said, trying to make the gift sound better than it was.

"I prefer a little excitement. Embrace the unknown, my good young Sir," Josef said.

But their kind words did little to stifle the embarrassment he felt.

"Is it okay if Hannah and I go for a walk?" Wilhelm asked.

Josef nodded as Emma sat beside him.

"Dress warm," Emma said.

Hannah reached for her coat and put on a knit hat her mother had made and her gloves. Wilhelm pulled his hat and gloves from the pockets of his jacket and grabbed the gift from beside the lamp. As they stepped outside, they were greeted by snowfall. The roads were blanketed with it, but there were no cars on them. It seemed all of Berlin was nestled beside fires and at dinner tables. The entire city was theirs.

"I love the snow," Hannah declared, spinning around with her head tilted back.

They walked without purpose, Hannah's eyes darting to the present in his hand every few minutes.

"Do you have a destination in mind? Or are we walking to Frankfurt?" Hannah joked.

"Maybe," Wilhelm said.

But, of course, he did. Nothing was spontaneous when it came to their dates. Even when he let Hannah choose, she knew he had every possible option planned.

Hannah and Wilhelm continued to cross block after block until the Brandenburg Gates opened before them. The Nazi flag hung between each column, and the gate was cast in a golden light.

"They are beautiful," Hannah said.

"I love the chariot above. Do you know what it is?" Wilhelm asked.

Hannah shook her head.

"It is the quadriga—the chariot used by the Greek Gods. It is a symbol of triumph, victory, and fame."

"I see why the Nazis hang their flag here."

"I passed through this on my first day in the city. It seemed to welcome me—made me feel like I belonged here. I know you feel like this city hates you, Hannah. But it isn't the city. Someday, you will look upon these gates and feel the city calling you to come home."

He held out the wrapped present. Hannah took it and unwrapped it as delicately as her excitement allowed her. She opened it and pulled a camera from the box.

"Wilhelm … how did you get this?" Hannah asked. Her eyes opened wide, and the smile she flashed was brighter than any camera.

"I sold a lot of cars."

"This must have cost you a fortune. I can't accept this," Hannah said and held it out for Wilhelm to take.

"No. It is yours. It comes with one stipulation. The first photograph you take must be of us."

Hannah examined the camera in her hand. It was black with two silver nobs on top and an adjustable silver lens in the front. She had held it before in different shops only to have to put it back. But she had asked enough questions to know how the camera worked and how to develop film. She leaned in close to Wilhelm and extended her arm as far as she could.

"Smile," Hannah said.

Wilhelm kissed her cheek, and the camera flashed. She took six more photos, and though she wanted them only of Wilhelm, he refused. He had said every photo was better with her in it.

"I love it," Hannah said, looking the camera over.

"I thought you could take photographs and then draw and paint them later," Wilhelm said.

Hannah pressed her lips against his. He pulled her close.

"We should get back," Hannah said.

"We should," he agreed, but he pulled her back for another kiss.

The walk back took twice as long because every street they crossed, they paused to kiss. When they arrived, their fingertips were icicles, and their noses were dripping. The heat inside the shop was minimal but increased with each step up the stairs. Josef and Emma were asleep on the couch, her head resting on his shoulder.

"After twenty years, they are still madly in love," Hannah said.

The coffee table in front of Josef and Emma was covered with playing cards. Josef's had fallen onto his lap, revealing a hand that would have been pathetic no matter the game.

The holidays had always been harder than any other time. Wilhelm's mother had loved Christmas, and she would make it a truly magical time. Christmas was not a day, but a month-long celebration that included building snowmen, baking cookies, and drinking hot chocolate. Every branch of their Christmas tree would be covered in ornaments and tinsel. If the Ghost of Christmas Past ever visited, Wilhelm would have been able to see the man his father used to be—the man his mother had loved. But he quickly scrapped that desire. If the white-robed ghost with its blazing head of candlelight did visit him, he would want to go back to Christmas in his kitchen with the smells of ginger and molasses and a Christmas ham in the oven and his mother humming Christmas music.

Hannah stared fondly at her parents before she raised her camera and snapped a photograph.

"How was your first Hanukkah?" she asked.

"Perfect," Wilhelm said.

Emma had made two glasses of hot buttered rum, garnished with a sprinkle of nutmeg. It was still warm, yet cool enough to drink. It was remarkably creamy from the melted butter with the perfect amount of spice and sugar.

"Stay with me," Hannah whispered.

She grabbed his hand and pulled him toward her bedroom, both setting their cups on the table. She slowly closed the door. A soft click came when the latch locked. She waited with her ear pressed to the door for any sound.

"Are you certain?" Wilhelm asked.

Hannah only nodded and bit her lip to stop herself from smiling. The darkness outside the bedroom ended, as a bright light from underneath the crack of the door flooded the room. The kitchen faucet turned on. Hannah and Wilhelm froze, each expecting the bedroom door to open. But the faucet shut off and, seconds later, the darkness returned.

Hannah stepped toward Wilhelm and unbuttoned his shirt. Electricity surged through his veins, and his breathing escalated. Her fingertips were ice, sending shivers when she ran them across his chest and took his shirt off.

"Unzip my dress?" Hannah asked, turning her back to him.

Wilhelm's thumb and pointer finger shook, but he steadied them enough to pull the zipper down. The dress fell to the floor. Goosebumps spread across her back and arms. She turned to face him, somehow self-conscious. They stared at each other, both vulnerable yet strong. They kissed softly and innocently at first, but their passion increased with each kiss.

Their hands traveled the length of their bodies and explored each other in the dark. They clumsily moved to the bed, their lips never separating. She squeezed his hand during moments of heightened pleasure, and Wilhelm only continued when she nodded. She traced her hands across his back as he kissed her neck. When it was over, they lay in bed, breathing heavily. It was only natural to feel awkward, but both smiled. The room was hot like an August day and contradicted the snow falling past the bedroom window.

Wilhelm had intended to wake up early and leave before Emma and Josef woke, but when he opened the door, Emma was in the kitchen while Josef futzed with the record player.

"Merry Christmas, Wilhelm," Emma greeted.

"Merry Christmas," Wilhelm greeted back.

"Do I get chocolates or was that box a two bird, one named Hanukkah and the other named Christmas, one stone kind of a thing?" Josef asked.

Hannah stepped out of her bedroom, a worried look on her face, but it was not needed, for there was no mention of Wilhelm staying the night. Hannah helped her mother in the kitchen, and Josef and Wilhelm played a game of chess that had to be paused so they could eat. The game lasted nearly an hour and a half but never truly ended. Josef was in check and in denial of a checkmate.

Each week became routine. Wilhelm and Hannah would spend the evenings together from Monday to Thursday, and Fridays were the weekly dinner at Wilhelm and Erich's with Lena, Heinrich, and one of his mystery dates. Hannah had secretly photographed a tender moment between Lena and Erich and had it framed. She gave it to Lena as a late Christmas gift.

On one particular Saturday, Wilhelm borrowed a car from the dealership, and he and Hannah simply drove north with no heading. They pulled over to walk the snow-covered trails or to eat before getting back in the car and driving off. They took turns driving until the once-peaceful snow turned into a white-out blizzard. They parked the car off the road, the winds whipping violent clouds of snow all around. It looked like the entire world had been wiped clean of all color but white.

"It's like God elected for a new canvas," Hannah remarked.

The wind's howl was only slightly muffled inside the car and, at times, seemed like it was strong enough to blow the car away.

Their fingers caressed one another before they moved closer together. Wilhelm stroked her hair and stared into her eyes. He loved those eyes. The world made sense when he looked into them.

"I love you," Wilhelm whispered. His strong gaze remained unbroken.

"I love you," she whispered back.

They brought their hands together before entwining them and succumbing to lust. They tried to remove their clothes without breaking their kiss. They laughed when Wilhelm struggled with his jacket. They climbed into the back seat and used their clothes for added warmth to the flannel blanket sprawled over them. They rubbed against one another. Their hands were explorers charting new territories. He kissed her neck, and she grabbed a handful of his wavy, dark hair.

The windows fogged, and steam rose off their bodies. They let out sighs as they pressed against one another, moving their hips to increase the quivering-inducing pleasure. Their bodies glistened with sweat. He rested his head on her heaving chest, and she ran her fingers through his damp hair.

He reached for the handle and rolled the window down. The cold air was opportunistic and rushed into the car with a piercing whistle. Their breathing returned to normal, and their trembling stopped.

"Play me a song, Wilhelm," Hannah said.

His guitar was on the floor, hidden under Hannah's bra and his shirt. He lifted it up and positioned it on his knee. He had learned guitar on the behest of his mother but had not played in months. But after letting it slip in a conversation, Hannah was insistent on hearing him play. He wrote his father, at Hannah's request, for him to send him his guitar. Much to Wilhelm's surprise, he sent it, and Wilhelm played for Hannah every Sunday morning while she painted.

Hannah sat up against the car with the blanket clutched in front of her to keep her warm. The crack in the window had done its job, and the car quickly became too cold. Hannah's shivers lessened when Wilhelm rolled the window back up. He took a deep breath and strummed the guitar. He had forgotten every song and some of the chords, but he did remember the major ones—G, E minor, E, A minor, C, and D. He played without direction, allowing the music to tell him which chord to play next. Music, like photography, was a magic that mesmerized Hannah. It was amazing how it could alter a mood, make someone dance, and even make someone cry.

The snowfall was relentless, and they were stranded in the car for hours. They filled it with conversation, music, cards, snacks and, when the desire for one another consumed them, they embraced each other. At nearly four the following morning, the snow subsided, and after shoveling the car free, they drove back to Berlin albeit slowly.

Trips like that were many and often. Sometimes, the two were joined by Erich, Lena, Heinrich, and Eva. Eva had temporarily stifled Heinrich's desire to wander. Lena had called Heinrich a "nomad" and said he simply scavenged an area and, after having consumed all it had to offer, moved on. Their trips took them north to a cabin Lena's family owned. It was hardly a shock to find it stocked with suitable dessert wines, dinner wines, and all other varieties of wines. The cabin made from cedar still cast its marvelous scent. It had been built nearly a hundred years earlier and had a historic aura both Wilhelm and Hannah loved.

Hitler had an affinity for stone. He thought of it as a symbol of strength. But Hannah had always found wood to tell a story stone could never tell. Trees lived for hundreds of years, and nobody could ever know the history that occurred around them.

The fireplace roared and heated the room to what Lena considered perfection and to what Wilhelm considered hell. The wine was imbibed, and appetizers were made. Hannah and Lena found it safe to get to know Eva a bit more and included her in on more "secret" talk. They played cards, went for walks in the snow, and had snowball fights, one of which prompted Lena to lock the men outside for nearly an hour. At night, in the privacy of their own rooms, they made love. The couple that lost the most card games the night before was forced to make breakfast for the others the following morning. After Wilhelm and Hannah had not won a single game during the thirty odd hands, a time when Wilhelm had the unfortunate misgiving of having crap hands that transcended a singular game and was crap in all the seven different games they played, it was decided they had to make breakfast the following week too.

Every Sunday afternoon was met with melancholy as they drove back to Berlin to face another week of work. But the mood would switch half-way home as they discussed their next adventure. Hannah surprised Lena with more framed pictures of Erich and her and

Heinrich with group photos. Lena often teased him and said Hannah should photograph his dates and write their names on the pictures so Heinrich could remember them.

Winter faded into spring and spring, summer. Erich had found out about a new club in Berlin called "Verdrehende Nächte" (Twisting Nights) that played American dance music. Wilhelm and Hannah both loved to dance, but Heinrich and Lena had to be coerced into going the first time. It took much convincing on Erich, Wilhelm, and Hannah's parts but, eventually, Heinrich and Lena conceded and agreed to go for "only an hour or so."

As they waited outside, they were teased with glimpses of the inside when patrons of the club left with smiles and bellowing laughter. The bouncer finally nodded for them to enter. Heinrich and Lena's complaining stopped the moment a rolling drum solo caused the walls to shake. The club was full of sweaty couples dancing, bars lined with people in conversation, and spectators watching the dancing. The lines for the bathroom were long and winding. Sporadic outbursts of laughter were frequent in response to a well-told joke or a mishap on the dance floor. The room was relatively dim, but the blue veil of cigarette smoke wafting toward the ceiling was cast in the chandelier lighting. The band pounded drums and symbols, blared trumpets and saxophones, and swayed with the music. The fun was contagious enough to be classified as a plague.

Hannah and Wilhelm moved right to the dance floor. Heinrich's date, Lieselotte, took his hand and, with surprising strength, nearly dragged him onto it. Erich knew better than to drag Lena, so he simply offered her his hand. She took it, and they hurried to the dance floor to claim a spot next to the others.

"I do not know this dance," Lena said.

"Neither do we," Hannah assured her.

Hannah gave Lena an encouraging smile. It was not about knowing the dance, but enjoying it, and enjoy it they did after they realized no one was there to ridicule them. Everyone else was there for the same reason they were—to have fun. After an hour of dancing, they took their first break. The men's room and ladies' room were on separate sides of the band stage. It was nearly a fifteen-minute wait, after which they ordered a few pitchers of beer. Any inhibitions they had had were gone after the beer buzz set in. Even when they weren't dancing, the room spun. Their clothes were drenched from sweat and spilled beer, and the lights above them made the sweat on their skin glisten like morning dew on grass. When they stepped outside, the fresh air was welcomed, even if it was stagnant and muggy.

"We have to go back. We just have to," Lena insisted.

Hannah, Wilhelm, and Erich shared smiles, as getting her to come had been like dragging a child to the dentist. Indeed, they did go back. But it was the only time they had seen Lieselotte. Heinrich had found the club to be filled with limber, long-legged women. They made a habit of going every Thursday night. At first, Heinrich and Lena needed to consume copious amounts of alcohol to make it onto the dance floor, but with each passing week, the amount needed diminished and, soon, they went right to the dance floor before their first drink. Their dancing improved, but it didn't matter. It was simply to have a great time with great friends.

Thursdays were spent at "Verdrehende Nächte" and Fridays and Saturdays at Lena's cabin. Heinrich was often joined by a woman he met the night before at "Verdrehende Nächte" and sometimes, he was without a date, but he eventually began dating Eva again. They would leave Berlin at 6:30 p.m. and arrive at Lena's cabin shortly before nine if no bathroom stops were required—a feat accomplished only once.

16 June was a particularly important Friday. Erich had given the others the heads-up he would be proposing to Lena. Heinrich and Eva had lasted all of two weeks, so Erich relied solely on Hannah to keep Lena preoccupied. Heinrich had rekindled things with Helga Stark, and though she knew Lena and Hannah, it was different. Both had grown to like Eva but knew it was ultimately destined to end. Lena still invited Eva along if she wanted to come, but Eva had decided against it. Neither could blame her.

The sun hung low, the weather was scolding, and the air almost too thick to swallow. The cabin was less than half a kilometer from a small lake. It had stayed hidden during the winter under ice and a blanket of snow but now sparkled like a gem, and apart from the cabin and family across the lake, it was all theirs.

"Do you think Erich is acting weird?" Lena asked.

"Isn't he always?" Hannah said.

"More so," Lena maintained.

Hannah, Lena, and Helga were cutting watermelon, cantaloupe, and pineapple in the kitchen as the three men were avoiding being caught on fire while cooking bratwursts and frikadelle (hamburgers) over a charcoal grill outside.

"Who gets hurt first?" Helga asked, laughing.

It would be Helga that got hurt first. Hannah and Lena both knew from each other's smirk they had had the same thought and suppressed the urge to break out in laughter.

They made a spread worthy of the Hauser house—bratwurst, hamburgers, potato salad, coleslaw, and cut-fruit salad with an artistic touch by using the watermelon rind as a fruit bowl. With so much food, the plates barely fit on the table. The wine was perfect for such a summer day with a subtle taste of citrus, and Jakob and Ida Hauser's streak of great selections continued.

After lunch and after clearing the table, they played a few hands of cards to let their food settle before swimming for most of that afternoon. At around six, Erich asked Lena to join him on the paddle boat. Heinrich, Wilhelm, and Hannah tried to be inconspicuous with the glances they exchanged. They played four-handed cribbage, but only Helga was vested in winning. After the dozenth glance at the lake, Helga asked what was wrong. Heinrich explained. Helga understood but felt out of place. Her face reddened, and the redness did not go away for the rest of the game.

The sunset sparkled off the calm water, and the four had finished playing their third game of cribbage when Lena and Erich paddled to shore. Hannah raised her camera and snapped a photo of Lena gleaming with a smile on her face and a diamond on her finger. Cheers and whistles came from the shore, and after Lena and Erich docked, both were bombarded with hugs. Lena had stocked enough wine for several weeks, but most of it was used up that night as they sat beside a peaceful campfire.

Erich and Lena went inside first, no doubt to celebrate their engagement. Heinrich and Helga were next, arguing the entire way to the house. Helga could not shake off the awkward feeling of being invited to something so personal. Wilhelm and Hannah had been alone countless times yet, now, they were joined by awkwardness. Wilhelm poked at the fire with a stick, his mind wandering. He was happy for Erich, truly, but he could not deny his jealousy. But what Erich had done was within the law. Both he and Lena were of strong German stock. But Hannah was Jewish, and in the eyes of the Reich, she was a half-breed.

After the Nuremberg Laws of 1935 were put into effect, "mixed" marriage was declared an offense punishable by imprisonment and even death. The Mischling (mixed-blood) Test determined whether or not a person had to identify themselves as a Jew. A person with three or four Jewish grandparents was considered a Jew. A person with exactly two Jewish grandparents is to be either a Jew or a Mischling of the first degree. A person with only one Jewish grandparent was considered to be a Mischling of the second degree.

Hannah's mother was not born Jewish but was a convert. But because Hannah had two Jewish grandparents, she had to face another series of tests, which she failed. She had taken part in the religious community after the laws had been put into effect, classifying her a Jew. A Mischling of the first degree was just a smaller step down from being classified as a full Jew anyway. But if Wilhelm married Hannah, he too would be classified as a Jew.

"Hannah, you know I want to," Wilhelm began.

He wanted to say more, but Hannah stopped him.

"I understand," she said.

Wilhelm wanted nothing more than to be her husband.

"Wilhelm, I know you love me. You know I love you. We just can't," Hannah said.

She walked around the fire and sat beside him and took his hands in hers. But the answer did not satisfy his discontent. "Walk with me," she said.

Together, they strolled to the lake. Hannah had told Wilhelm much of what she had sacrificed for being a Jew. But she never complained though Wilhelm would have preferred it. To listen to her accept as a truth the way things were was more gut-wrenching than her venting.

She could not go to university and pursue a career as a nurse. She had wanted to be one at a young age, but the dream had been taken away while she was still a child. No doubt she wanted to follow in her mother's footsteps before the law prohibited Emma's right to practice. She was able to only treat other Jews until that too was taken away. She traded her stitching of flesh with cloth but still helped those at the synagogue with cuts, scrapes, and minor injuries, as there was a strong likelihood they would not be treated by the city's clinics and hospitals.

"Will you be distant the whole night?" Hannah asked.

"I want that so badly," Wilhelm said.

"Tonight is Lena and Erich's night. Let's not make it about us," Hannah said.

She took his hand and wrapped it around her waist. They took a waltzing position.

"Dance with me?" she asked.

"Always," he answered.

The moon was barely visible but for the faintest curve, and it reflected off the tranquil water with only a slight ripple that came when something under the water moved. Crickets sang their loneliness for all to hear.

"Let me take you somewhere safe," Wilhelm said.

"Plan on taking me to the moon?" Hannah asked.

The whole of Europe held its breath. The exhale was coming. Though it was hard to get the truth from the Nazi-controlled newspapers, Lena often let little things slip. Germany had done much to garner the attention of France and the United Kingdom. In March, they had annexed Czechoslovakia. The British and French had drawn a line, and Hitler had stepped over it and continued to creep forward to see how far they would let him.

"France. England. The United States," Wilhelm said, rambling off names of nearly two dozen countries.

Hannah shook her head. "Wilhelm, they will not let me leave the country. My passport is marked Sara. Jews only leave when told," she reasoned.

Anyone who had to classify themselves as Jewish had their passport marked with the name Israel, if male, and Sara, if female. Remarkably, it was safer being in Berlin—better to be under the hawk's nose than in front of its eyes.

Hannah pushed the paddle boat into the water, and the two hopped on before it drifted off.

"Now we are somewhere else," Hannah said.

They laid down, using the life jackets as pillows, and gazed at the stars. But the feeling of disappointment and let down did not fade easily for Wilhelm. Over the next several days, he found it hard to be around Erich and Lena and all their wedding excitement and bliss. But guilt swept in. Lena and Erich had been nothing short of great friends. Hannah took it better than Wilhelm, in public at least, but he knew the laws had beaten her morale to a pulp.

After returning home from a long day at the dealership, Josef and Emma invited Wilhelm over for dinner. Wilhelm wanted nothing but a shower and a relaxing night on his couch with Hannah. But he did not want to refuse, and he knew he would enjoy both the food and the company.

The stairs leading up to Hannah's home usually alerted her parents of her arrival with a groan or a creak but the shouting coming from upstairs drowned them out. If someone would have entered the Schreiber home, the shouting was to be expected. If there was no shouting, something was terribly wrong. But Hannah had only heard her parents argue on less than a handful of occasions. Something was terribly wrong.

"What is going on?" she asked, reaching the top of the steps.

Josef and Emma fell silent and hoped they could get away with it.

"I heard you arguing," Hannah said.

"Tell her, Josef," Emma said.

Josef paused with a sigh and then said, "The Portnoes were taken."

"Who are the Portnoes?" Wilhelm asked.

"A family from our synagogue," Emma answered.

"What do you mean 'taken'?" Hannah asked.

"They were taken from their home and forced to board a train," Josef explained.

"A train? To where?" Hannah asked, her voice shrill.

Flashes of her and her parents ripped from their beds and forced onto a train filled her head.

"I do not know," Josef said.

"It's not just here, Hannah," Emma added. She said she had telephoned Josef's cousin, Abel, in Poland and he too said the Jews were being rounded up. The hawk the Goldschmidts and the other Jews of Germany had been hiding under had looked down to see them in its nest.

"We should have left when we had the chance," Hannah said.

The words broke Josef's heart. Aaron and Shoshana Kowalski were his and Emma's best friends for years. The four would meet for dinner every Friday night and play cards at either their own home or the Kowalski's. After Hitler was named chancellor in January of 1933, they had emigrated from Germany to England. They had told Josef and Emma they should consider the same. Though Josef knew Hitler to be an anti-Semite, he could not imagine the series of events that would unfold to allow Hitler to act on it. But now, it was too late.

"I am so sorry," Josef said.

Hannah rushed forward to hug her parents. Her pulse raced, and the strength in her body abandoned her. She desperately hoped she was in a nightmare—one she would wake up from immediately. It would only be a matter of time before they came for them—only a matter of time before they forced them to board a train to an unknown destination.

The useless feeling in Wilhelm had mutated exponentially.

"I fear by being your father, I have sentenced you to an awful fate," Josef said.

Though he fully believed in Judaism with all his soul and heart, he found himself wishing he had never practiced it. Had Emma divorced him prior to the Nuremberg Laws of 1935, the Mischling Test would have classified both her and Hannah as Mischling of the first degree.

To Wilhelm, it was watching the fever take over his mother, flushing the color from her skin and the warmth from it. But unlike then, there was something he could do.

"Let me be her husband," Wilhelm said.

The sobbing from Emma and Hannah along with Josef's pleads for forgiveness had drowned out Wilhelm's words. None turned to look at him.

"Let me be her husband," Wilhelm said louder.

They did not pull away from their embrace, and their three heads looking at him appeared to come from one body.

"I am German. I have no Jewish grandparents. Let me marry her and give her my name. She will no longer be Hannah Goldschmidt. She will be Hannah Schreiber," Wilhelm said.

"You will be classified a Jew," Emma warned.

"Hannah does not look Jewish. I mean, what they think Jews look like," Wilhelm said.

There was no apology needed, for they had all seen the propaganda that had been placed on every street corner for the last five years. Hannah appeared to be a beautiful Aryan, the caliber of which Hitler wanted to populate the world.

"You would do this for her?" Josef asked.

"I love her. I want to marry her. This gives me an excuse that you cannot refuse," Wilhelm replied, smiling both with excitement and nervousness—something he did not know whether it was appropriate or not.

"There are laws though, Wilhelm. No one will marry you," Josef said.

"I do know of a Roman Catholic priest who is marrying couples in secret," Emma said. She had several friends who had wed their Jewish daughters to non-Jewish men.

"I need to ask Hannah," Wilhelm said.

There were so many places he had thought of proposing and in so many different ways. He was the one who had given Erich the idea of proposing on the lake. Though he had considered it for himself, the cabin belonged to Lena, and the moment belonged to her. But of all the ideas as to how and where, none involved her parents standing by her or Hannah in tears. It appeared to be an almost forced marriage. He certainly wanted Josef and Emma's blessing, but he did not want them to command her to say yes.

"I need to get a ring," Wilhelm said.

And of all the scenarios he had mapped out in his mind's eye, each one involved placing a ring on Hannah's finger.

"May I have a word with you, Wilhelm?" Josef asked.

Wilhelm nodded and followed Josef into his bedroom. He had never been allowed to enter his father's bedroom and standing in Hannah's father's room once again brought to light the drastically different childhoods he and Hannah had had. Josef dug deep into the top drawer of the dresser in front of the bed. The inside of it was cluttered with letters, photos, and old tickets, ranging from bus and train to theatre and opera.

"I keep almost everything," Josef said as he sorted through the drawer. "I think Emma secretly discards old things, but I am sentimental about keeping things that bring back memories—the train ticket I took to Paris to meet Emma while she was studying there, photographs of my mother and father, my brothers, Asher and Azriel, twins, my sisters, Eliana, Maya, and Liora. A ticket to a truly awful musical. Come to think of it, this is something I should toss."

Wilhelm had never been envious of a dresser drawer until that moment. It was not junk in the drawer—it was proof of life. A person must be so fortunate to have so many memories. Fifty years from then, Wilhelm hoped his drawer to be as full.

"Here we go," Josef said, sighing with satisfaction as he pulled a ring box from its depths.

He opened the old, silver, felt box and a blue sapphire amongst a band of white diamonds sparkled with the same vibrancy as the day it had been crafted. Its tenure in the cramped drawer amongst ageless treasures had only increased its antique appeal.

"This ring has been in my family's possession dating back to my great-great-grandfather. He crafted it himself. It was given to his wife and passed to their eldest son and down the line. Though Emma and I have tried, a son never came to us that way. But God has given us you. I give you the ring, Wilhelm," Josef said and held out the box for Wilhelm to take.

It was far more expensive than anything Wilhelm could have afforded. Yet, it was not the monetary amount attached to the ring that made it special. It was a ring with history—much like what Hannah had said about all that trees had witnessed. The ring had been on the finger of her family for generations.

Wilhelm thanked him. His voice was scratchy and gave out. Unlike with his father, he had expected to be overcome with emotion. The generosity of the Goldschmidts knew no limits, nor would they ever know how much it meant to him.

Wilhelm was transfixed by the ring and who had worn it. It was a ring that had traveled hundreds of miles, seen thousands of people and entire lifetimes. He wondered why Josef had kept it hidden amongst what looked like junk to the untrained eye. But the junk was equally as important to Josef as the ring—much like the medals Wilhelm's own father had kept hidden away. They were memories his father wanted to forget, yet he never could. But it also was not safe for such a ring not to be hidden. The shop had been vandalized and broken into once. The city was on full alert, and the Gestapo was far more formidable than farmers with pitchforks.

"Mr. Goldschmidt, may I ask Hannah's hand in marriage?" Wilhelm asked.

He would do it in the traditional and proper way.

Josef put his hands on Wilhelm's shoulders. "You are a good man, Wilhelm, and I must say you wear fine suit coats."

Wilhelm could have asked Josef about every trinket, photograph, and ticket in the drawer, and he would have answered patiently and honestly. But the questions were for Hannah to ask. He could only hope she recognized what a gift she had waiting to be unwrapped. Josef patted his back as they stepped out of the room.

"Will you walk with me?" Wilhelm asked, approaching Hannah.

Hannah nodded, and her parents smiled as she and Wilhelm walked down the stairs. Something had changed in Wilhelm though. He did not feel excited about asking her hand in marriage. It seemed like a chore she was being forced to do. There was no excitement. The anticipation and surprise had vanished.

Hannah and Wilhelm walked longer than either had expected to. Wilhelm subconsciously led them to the Tiergarten. The trees were full of leaves and life. They paused on the bridge, where four lion statues, two on each end, rested on each side, carrying the decorative bridge cables in their mouths. The water looked to be the same color as the sky—a perfect watercolor blend of orange and purple sunset.

Wilhelm paused and looked down at the water. The lion statues glared at him, and even if they were fake, they looked capable of pouncing. Realizing if he delayed it any longer would make it look like he did not want to marry her at all, he turned to Hannah and drew the ring box.

"This ring has been in your family for generations, Hannah," Wilhelm said.

Hannah reached out and took the ring box from his hand.

"I do not want you to think I am only accepting because of what my parents want, Wilhelm," she said, falling to one knee. "Wilhelm Schreiber, will you marry me?"

Wilhelm got down on his knees and took her left hand in his right. He pulled the ring from the box and slid it onto her left ring finger.

"Will you let me be your man?" he asked.

"Yes," Hannah answered, rubbing the side of his face.

He pressed his lips against hers with enough force to nearly knock them over.

"I only have one condition. We wait until my father can come."

Secret Wedding

Wilhelm stared at his black telephone for ten minutes, contemplating what he would tell his father. A verbal bashing over the phone was preferred, but he elected to simply ask his father to come to Berlin. It was a gamble, as anything short of Wilhelm's life being on the line was bound to fail.

On 30 June, Wilhelm and Hannah waited at the bus station for Wilhelm's father to arrive. Each bus that came toward them made Wilhelm's stomach summersault. But Petyr Schreiber was not to be found among the scurrying passengers as each bus emptied. Wilhelm assured Hannah they were wasting their time, but Hannah's only response was "one more." But the final tally of "one more" was six when Petyr Schreiber finally stepped off a bus. He carried only a small suitcase and wore a suit and hat. He had aged since Wilhelm saw him last—almost a year and a half ago.

"Father," Wilhelm said. He foolishly motioned to give his father a hug, but his father simply put out his large hand for a shake instead.

"Are you going to tell me what I am doing here, Wilhelm?" Petyr asked.

His father had never been one for small talk. Though Wilhelm had zero hesitations in marrying Hannah, telling his father was a different story. But if he wanted his father to treat him as a man, he could not act like a boy.

"Father, I am getting married. This is my fiancée, Hannah Goldschmidt," Wilhelm said boldly.

Petyr looked from Wilhelm to Hannah, who smiled and extended her hand. His hand trembled as he shook hers, and his face contorted into a pained smile. It may have been his first in ten years.

"It is great to finally meet you," Hannah said.

Petyr only gave another quarter-hearted, pained smile and nodded.

"Will you require a place to stay?" Wilhelm asked.

"I have made arrangements," Petyr said sharply.

They walked one city block before Petyr put a hand on Wilhelm's chest to stop him from walking.

"May I have a word with my son in private, please, Ms. Goldschmidt?" Petyr asked.

"Certainly," Hannah said, moving out of eavesdropping distance.

"Is she pregnant?" Petyr asked.

"No," Wilhelm said.

"In trouble?"

"No. Does there have to be a nefarious reason for me to be able to marry her?"

The nervousness he had initially felt had quickly morphed into annoyance and anger. He didn't care about sounding rude for it was obvious his father didn't. Wilhelm was no longer living under his roof. He could do nothing to Wilhelm but leave.

"You said nothing on the telephone about it," Petyr said.

"I wanted to surprise you."

But his father hated to be surprised, and it was a failed tactic from the start. In a matter of words, his father had turned himself into the victim. Wilhelm could have given him a bit of information on the phone.

Petyr began walking again, and Wilhelm took silent note that it was arguably both one of the longest and best conversations the two had ever had. Petyr was not a dawdler and was a firm believer in walking like you had somewhere to be. If they ever presented legislation for sidewalk speed limit minimums, he would advocate it whole-heartedly. While Petyr sped past the human sloths, Hannah and Wilhelm moped behind.

Petyr had to be enlightened about Hannah's "condition," as the propaganda put it. Wilhelm hated to admit it, but his father had sensed something the moment he had set foot off the bus. But that was his nature by default. He was always negative and assumed the worst. He was bound to be correct once in a while. Of all the times his father had accused him of incorrectly drying a flower or having poor taste in designing bouquets, Wilhelm felt his father was wrong. It was all preference. But Wilhelm hated that his father had to be right about Hannah.

"Hannah, I will meet you at your house later," Wilhelm said.

Hannah did her best to not show her surprise. After all, it had been part of the plan to tell Petyr together. They believed it would lead to less likelihood of an incident, an incident being Petyr shouting at Wilhelm in front of passing pedestrians. Wilhelm gave her another nod, and Hannah crossed the street while Wilhelm and Petyr continued on.

The streets were too busy with people trying to reach their destinations on time, and there were far too many conversations for anyone to care about what Wilhelm and his father talked about. It was a bright-blue-sky kind of day, and the weather was thick and hot. But if there was one man who had the ability to produce clouds of gray gloom, it was Wilhelm's father.

"You have something to tell me?" Petyr asked, sensing trouble like a bird before a storm.

"I do. Hannah is Jewish, Father," Wilhelm said.

Petyr rolled his eyes and groaned. "How can you be so stupid, Wilhelm?"

He had nearly yelled it, and those close by stopped and looked. Perhaps Wilhelm had been wrong because, for a split second, all of Berlin had turned to look at him.

"I am not stupid. I love her. I do not care where she worships or what she believes in."

"If they find out, you will be shipped off and sent out of the country," Petyr said, his voice rising.

"I know," Wilhelm said.

Petyr was ready to either implode or explode. For the sake of the innocent people beside them waiting for the light to turn red so they could cross, Wilhelm hoped his father would choose to implode to lessen the number of casualties.

"I called you here because I want you to be there. For my mother's sake. If it is something you cannot do, please board a bus and return home. I am marrying Hannah with or without you there. And I did not invite you here to ask your permission," Wilhelm said firmly.

The light turned red. But Petyr and Wilhelm stayed on the curb as dozens moved past. There were a hundred things Petyr wanted to say, which he had expressed silently through a dozen facial expressions.

"You should have told me in advance. I could have prepared a floral arrangement," Petyr said.

Petyr was hardly an anti-Semite. He did not care enough about people to classify them, but he was not willing to meet Josef and Emma at their shop or their home above. Instead, they met at the Tiergarten where they could distance themselves from the bustling city and the hawk's eyes. Wilhelm had warned Hannah's parents that his father was a man of few words and it was best to not push the conversation if it was not natural.

"Expect a lot of one-word answers," Wilhelm had said.

After the awkward conversation of less than fifty words had run its course, Petyr went to his motel room, and Hannah and Wilhelm went to meet Father Declan, the Roman Catholic priest Emma had mentioned.

The Holy Cross Church was an ancient building that had seen some recent restoration to it. The inside was covered in a bright white paint that mimicked the light people professed to seeing during near-death experiences. A golden trim danced around it with sculptures of saints behind the altar. The giant cross with the figure of Jesus nailed to it hung in a way that made it look like he was looking into the eyes of every parishioner.

Both Hannah and Wilhelm thought it would have been discourteous to not join the mass. Hannah had to whisper answers to Wilhelm's questions throughout. She explained the differences between Judaism and Catholicism with the major difference in their belief—the Messiah was not Jesus Christ but was yet to come. When the mass ended, the priest, cloaked in white robes that drowned his thin frame, shook hands with many. After the entire clergy had cleared from the church, Hannah and Wilhelm approached Father Declan. His hair was as white as his robes. He appeared to be in his seventies, but his charming smile matched that of a man a quarter his age.

"I have not seen you here before," Father Declan said, extending his hand. Wilhelm shook it first and then Hannah.

"No, Father. I am Wilhelm Schreiber, and this is my fiancée, Hannah Goldschmidt," Wilhelm introduced.

"Pleasure," Father Declan said politely. He flashed his charismatic smile a second time as he surveyed the young couple. "You would like to be married here?"

"We understand that you help those with no other choice," Hannah said.

"I am an extension of the Lord our God, Miss," Father Declan said.

"You marry those the Reich would not allow," Hannah clarified.

The Nazis not only had problems with Judaism but with Catholicism as well. They did not like any organization able to bend thousands to its knees apart from their own. They were removing priests from churches, and they had many spies.

"I do not know what you are talking about," Father Declan said.

"Please, Father. We need your help," Wilhelm pleaded.

Declan was silent as he switched glances from Hannah to Wilhelm in an attempt to decipher if their plea was a well-practiced act or a genuine call for help. Hannah wanted to retract her eyes from his gaze but knew to do so would look as though she had something to hide.

"Who will be present?" Father Declan asked.

"My parents and Wilhelm's father," Hannah answered.

"Which of you is Jewish?" Father Declan asked.

"I am," Hannah said.

"Your passport?" Father Declan asked.

Hannah removed it from her pocket and handed it to him.

"You have been marked," Father Declan said, looking the passport over.

The front cover had the Nazi Eagle near the top with the words "German Reich" above it. Declan flipped open to the second page. A photo of Hannah was on the left-hand side and on the right page, her date of birth, address, hair color, eye color, and other pertinent information. But Jews had a large red J stamped over the information.

"We were told you can help with that," Wilhelm said.

Emma had also said that Father Declan had studied calligraphy as a part of his vocation, translating old texts into different languages. He had been born in Sheffield, England, and when the Great War broke out, he served as a priest and wandered the battlefields, giving last rights to not only the Allied powers but the Central Powers as well.

"I can. We must do this tonight. Thirty minutes past eleven. Enter through my rectory. There is a passage under the church. I will leave the door unlocked. Do not come all at once," Father Declan instructed.

"Thank you," Hannah said.

"I shall get to work on this," Father Declan said, waving her passport.

He had blank copies of the information page of the passport and would have to copy the handwriting perfectly from Hannah's passport to the new page and then glue it down perfectly so that, to the human eye, there was nothing to alert there was a hidden page underneath. It would not hold up under extreme scrutiny, but it would suffice for a quick glance. The Nazis had programmed their Stormtroopers to look for a certain type and failed to realize Jewish was not a race.

Hannah and Wilhelm stepped outside the church. The sun was high in the sky, and the temperature had not dropped in the hour they were at mass.

"I wish I could tell Lena," Hannah sighed.

"So do I," Wilhelm said.

It was weird to get married and not have Lena, Erich, and Heinrich present or any of their relatives apart from their parents. They would not be able to even mention it to them, for there could be no believable story to make them understand why they would have gotten married without them there. Lena's wedding was to have over two hundred people present. If the laws changed or a new power took order, perhaps the laws would be different, and Hannah and Wilhelm could have the wedding they both wanted.

The suits displayed in the windows of the Goldschmidts' shop had not changed in months. The only people who shopped there were fellow Jews, and as more time passed, the tighter their funds became, and necessity trumped wants.

"Wilhelm, may I have a word with you?" Josef asked.

Wilhelm followed Josef to the back of the store and the area where he took his measurements.

Hannah stepped through the black dividing curtain and walked up the steps.

"You are getting married. You will require something worthy of marrying my daughter," Josef said. He pushed his drooping glasses back on and glanced toward the black curtain to ensure Hannah would not step back through. He opened a cabinet and carefully pulled a white penguin tuxedo with a black bowtie from it. "Barring any sudden gain in weight, these measurements should be to your liking. Emma suggested the color though she knows you are partial to black," Josef said.

"It's perfect. But you shouldn't have," Wilhelm said.

"Please, Wilhelm, we had the fabric. It only cost us time."

"You have been so kind to me since the first day I walked into your shop."

"If I knew you were going to be stealing my daughter from me, I would have locked my doors," Josef quipped.

Wilhelm's father had rejected his hug hours earlier, but a handshake didn't display his gratitude. He hugged Josef, and Josef hugged him.

"Don't spill anything on it," Josef said, glaring at Wilhelm over his glasses. He gave Wilhelm a final pat on the shoulder, and the two went upstairs.

Hannah had been fasting all day as part of a Jewish custom, and Wilhelm could not fathom how hungry she must have been. There were numerous times when going seven hours without food while he slept seemed too long and he had gone into the kitchen for a midnight snack.

When the clock chimed nine times, Wilhelm bid goodbye and took his new tuxedo, covered in a black bag, and walked to his father's motel. He could not get dressed at his apartment for it was bound to raise questions from Erich and, possibly, Lena. Wilhelm knocked on the motel door and wondered whether or not his father had left town. But the door opened, and Petyr ushered him inside.

"Can I get dressed here?" Wilhelm asked.

Petyr nodded and turned away. Wilhelm disappeared into the bathroom, showered, and dressed while his father sat on the edge of the bed and stared at the same painting on the wall across from him the entire time. It was the sort of generic painting of flowers that most likely hung in every room of the motel. Wilhelm had always been a person who could walk through an art museum in ten minutes and his father the type who could stare at a single painting for an hour.

"Something wrong?" Wilhelm asked. He had stared at his father for nearly thirty seconds, but Petyr's gaze was fixed on the painting.

"Can you sit down?" Petyr asked.

Wilhelm almost didn't recognize it as a question and not his usual ordering. He sat on the bed, his bow tie still untied and half of the buttons of his shirt left undone. Petyr rubbed his thumb against something in his hand—only bits of silver visible. He stopped and held it out for Wilhelm to take. But Wilhelm knew what it was before he even grabbed it. It was the same medal he had been beaten for looking at. His fingers remembered every indent of it. The hunched-over skeleton that had traumatized him as a child was as harrowing over a decade later. "Die Weltblutpumpe" the inscription read.

"The World Blood Pump. And the world bled," Petyr said.

He took a deep breath to prepare himself for the pain his words were about to cause him.

"I've only told your mother this once, and I don't know if I am strong enough to tell you it now," Petyr started but paused to stifle his emotions already thickening in his throat, "but I will try. Verdun was called a meat grinder. That's what it was. Both us and the French would push forward, and Verdun would spit us back into piles of flesh and bone. The thunder from the artillery did not stop. You couldn't hear anything else, and that was fortunate. For everywhere you looked, there were people dying. The fields were littered with so many dead. I couldn't believe the world had that many people, and I didn't think there would be any left when the fighting stopped. We hid in trenches created from artillery, but when it rained, we had to crawl out or risk drowning in the mud. They picked us off and we picked them off. The men who were supposed to supply us with food and water were gunned down. We had no choice but to drink from the crater—drink the water laced with poisonous gas, blood, oil, and corpses. I had friends who were so sick of fighting that when the poisonous gas came, they took off their masks. It would take us six weeks to push forward a hundred meters only to be pushed back the same distance. When the artillery did break, I could only hear screaming as men looked for their legs and arms. Horses and cows neighed and mooed as they were shot. The grass was covered in blood and poison. It was hell and nothing short of it. Then, one day, the battle was over and another day, the war was over. They gave me this medal. It took me years to figure out what it meant to me and only after your mother died that I accepted what I had realized."

"What did you realize?" Wilhelm asked.

"I am the skeleton on the coin, Wilhelm. Everything that made me who I was was burned, shot, blasted apart, and washed away. Each time I press down on the pump, I'm forced to relive it. Flashes come to me when I close my eyes—moments where I can hear the artillery, the screaming of men and beast. I can smell the decay and death. I am just bones now, Wilhelm. Whatever fragment of my soul that remained was taken by your mother, and I'm truly sorry to say there is nothing salvageable to give you."

He squeezed Wilhelm's hand, rose from the bed, and left the motel room. Wilhelm traced his thumb across the medal as he looked at it. The medal held the fate of his father and, once again, Wilhelm was in tears from the pain it caused. It was not that his father didn't love him, it was simply he had nothing left to give.

Wilhelm wiped his eyes and stood. He finished buttoning his shirt and tying his bow tie and left the motel room. As he and his father walked to the church, Wilhelm made no further reference to his father's cathartic moment. They passed the Gestapo as they crossed the streets. To instill more terror, they had German Shepherds leashed up who disliked anyone or anything but their masters. They barked and growled at anyone who got too close. Wilhelm snickered—as if dogs could sniff the Jew out of someone.

Wilhelm and Petyr turned down the street of the Holy Cross Church and headed toward the rectory. It was the same color brick as the church, gray, and separated by less than ten feet. Wilhelm knocked on the door. Father Declan opened it.

"Is Hannah here?" Wilhelm asked.

"They are in the church," Father Declan answered.

Wilhelm and Petyr stepped inside, and Father Declan closed the door behind them, checking the streets for followers before doing so. Wilhelm introduced his father and Father Declan, and the latter led them into the basement of the rectory. He opened the wooden door, revealing a locked iron gate. Father Declan used his key, and the gate sprung forward with a scratching squeal. A fresh snowfall of dust fell from the ceiling. The mold inside the tunnel had gone untreated for decades. Father Declan held a rectangular flashlight with a single circular bulb as he led them through it. He was able to walk with his back straight, but Wilhelm had to bend his head and Petyr, nearly six feet four, had to almost crouch through the narrow tunnel. The ten feet between the church and the rectory seemed to be ten miles in such a cramped space. But they came to another gate, and Father Declan unlocked it.

Wilhelm had a terrible feeling that his once pure white tux was now peppered gray with dust. The father, son, and holy priest walked up the steps and into the church. His father's hand acted like a broom, but not as gentle, as he swept the dust off Wilhelm's shoulders and back. Josef and Emma were standing in the first row with their backs to them. When they heard the approaching footsteps, they turned. Wilhelm's heart froze, and his eyes refused to blink.

Hannah was a vision in a white strapless dress, designs intricately sewn throughout, accenting the dress. The blue rose Wilhelm had given her was in her curled hair. She flashed her mesmerizing smile—a combination of nerves and excitement. Wilhelm could only stare for moments until he returned her smile with one of his own. Hannah had always looked beautiful but, in a building of immaculate symbology and statues, none was more so than Hannah.

Father Declan moved to the back to put on his white chasuble and stole. He emerged from the back and ushered Wilhelm forward with a smile and a wave. Petyr took his place next to Josef and Emma. Wilhelm's legs shook the whole walk to Hannah. He stared long and hard when he was at her side. There was not a single thing about the way she looked he wanted to forget.

"I was thinking of secrets and how they pertain in the Bible. If you are married in secret with just a few witnesses, does it count? Does it count in man's eyes? In God's eyes? Matthew chapter ten verses twenty-six through twenty-eight came to my head. 'So, have no fear of them, for nothing is covered that will not be revealed or hidden that will not be known. What I tell you in the dark, say in the light, and what you hear whispered, proclaim on the housetops.' What we say in this dark church is heard by God, the father. These are dark days we live in, Wilhelm Schreiber and Hannah Goldschmidt. You are to be the light for each other," Father Declan began the ceremony.

Wilhelm was lost in memories and in Hannah's eyes. The day Wilhelm had envisioned almost two years earlier in the "Rote Blumen" had arrived. He slid her wedding ring onto her right index finger, as was Jewish custom. After the ceremony, the ring would be moved to her left hand to follow tradition. It was also a way to keep others in the dark about their marriage, as most Germans wore it on their right ring fingers.

Both repeated the vows spoken by Father Declan. They were not only vows but also Wilhelm's ketubah, the outlining of the three things—clothing, food, and conjugal relations—he would provide for Hannah. While Josef's hand was fully entwined with Emma's, Petyr's was conversely alone. His hand, which nearly always trembled, did so at a much greater frequency, his thoughts dwelling on his late wife, Saundra, and how she would have loved to see their son get married.

At the words, Wilhelm and Hannah leaned in and kissed. They were married under Jewish law, Catholic law, man's law and, most importantly, God's law. Josef and Emma stepped toward them, arms open wide. Josef set a glass bottle wrapped in cloth at Wilhelm and Hannah's feet, and Wilhelm smashed it with a stomp of his foot.

"Mosel Tov!" Emma and Josef screamed. They wrapped their arms around Wilhelm and Hannah while Petyr stood in the pew, trying to stifle his trembling hand by squeezing the top of the pew.

Father Declan led Wilhelm and Hannah into the backroom. A small plate of food, mostly bread, was on the table. In Jewish culture, it was called the yichud. Father Declan left them alone. Hannah ate almost all the loaf, and it helped suppress her gurgling stomach. Hannah and Wilhelm stayed for twenty minutes, sharing a glass of wine before walking back out into the church.

"Time for a first dance I should think," Father Declan said.

It was hard to care about the danger he put himself in by marrying couples against the law when the joy on the couple's faces was as prominent as any mole or freckle or when seeing the relief wash away a parent's worry.

The church was quiet without music, but it had never stopped Hannah and Wilhelm before. But the keys of the piano filled the quiet church with beautiful music. Wilhelm had expected either Emma or Josef, Father Declan or even a hobo from the street to be seated at it—anyone but his father. But he was there, his trembling hands steady and true as they hit the keys. It was a beautiful bit of musical melody, both loving and sad.

"I did not know your father could play," Hannah whispered.

"Nor did I," Wilhelm said.

What an angel Wilhelm's mother had been. She had hoped Wilhelm learning music would bridge the divide between the two men she loved. It was a gift she had given them both but had been unwrapped only now.

Hannah had shown Father Declan how to work her camera, and he photographed them as they danced. Hannah's parents held her veil over Hannah and Wilhelm's heads. When the music ended, they pulled away from each other.

"And a gift for you, Mrs. Schreiber," Father Declan said, holding out Hannah's passport. She took it and opened it. Her name, address, hair, and eye color, and other information were written perfectly in the same handwriting, only Goldschmidt had been replaced with Schreiber, and the large red J was absent. Hannah gleamed at the possibility of living a life unhindered.

"Thank you so much," Hannah said.

"We are all children of God. Not everyone has forgotten that," Father Declan said, putting a hand on her shoulder and flashing a charismatic smile.

"We will see you later," Josef said. He kissed Hannah's cheek, and Emma hugged both her and Wilhelm. It was another simple gesture that once again affirmed Wilhelm had gained not only a wife but also a family.

"Petyr, you are more than welcome to stay at our home," Emma reminded.

She was unwaveringly kind, much like his own mother had been. Petyr nodded in thanks and tentatively stepped toward Hannah and Wilhelm.

"I," Petyr said, but paused, "I wish your mother was here."

"Me too," Wilhelm said.

Petyr only nodded and shook Wilhelm's hand and squeezed his shoulder. To say anything further would cause him to surrender to his loss.

"You look beautiful, Hannah," Petyr said.

He followed Josef and Emma out of the church. After allowing five minutes for the others to leave, Hannah and Wilhelm walked to the staircase and through the secret passage to the basement of the rectory. They gave their thanks to Father Declan once more and left. It was nearly one in the morning, and the city was covered in a thick eerie feeling. They strolled hand in hand to Wilhelm's apartment. Erich was staying at Lena's.

Wilhelm unlocked and opened the door to his apartment and flicked the light switch on. Both knew what they needed to do to consummate the marriage, but it now had greater meaning than the countless other times.

"Are you still hungry?" Wilhelm asked.

A loaf of bread would have done nothing to stifle his hunger from a day of fasting.

"No," Hannah said.

Her mind seemed to be elsewhere.

"Do you regret it?" Wilhelm asked.

"No, the thoughts in my head about you are not what is troubling me."

His morale, which had nosedived, now skidded and bounced on the ground.

"Then please share what is?"

"I am happy but selfish. I am free to live a life. But my parents cannot. I am sad that I have to leave them," Hannah said.

"We can visit them any time you want, Hannah. I would not stop that," Wilhelm assured her.

"I know you would not, but they are watching the Jews more and more. They are taking many. Forcing them to board a train to relocate. What if my parents are taken and I never find out where they are?"

Wilhelm gently grabbed her hands and ushered her to the couch. He stared into her brilliant blue eyes. He wanted her to know the solemn vow he made would always hold true.

"I don't know what the future will bring, but I do know I will be there with you when it comes," Wilhelm said.

Hannah let her appreciation known with a slight curve of her lips. She rose from the couch and walked into the kitchen and poured herself a glass of water. Wilhelm unbuttoned his shirt on the way to his bedroom. He sat on the edge of the bed and yanked off his shoes. Hannah drank the glass of water in a daze. Wilhelm was obviously dejected, but Hannah knew it was not because she had not been in the mood for sex but because she was melancholy, and there was nothing he could do.

But he had done something. He truly cared, and there was not a more attractive quality than that. She set the glass down on the counter and took long strides to him. He stood in his pants and a tank top. Hannah helped him with the tight tank—a nervous sweat before and during the ceremony had caused it to stick to his body like glue. Wilhelm had taken it only as a helping hand until Hannah's fingers traced from his stomach to his chest. The shivers that spread were the likes of which no cold January night could ever bring. He looked into her eyes. She would have to advance it further. She did with a soft nod.

Wilhelm ran his fingers through her hair and kissed her. He lifted her off the ground, holding her with one hand and running the other through her light blonde hair. She locked her legs around his waist, and they fell onto the bed. They were two people unsure about everything in their lives but each other. But in that moment, they rejected all inhibitions and succumbed to desire, lust, and love.

The next couple of weeks greeted Hannah with a wide array of emotions. One moment, she was excited about starting her life with Wilhelm and creating a home for the two of them, but the smallest smell, sight or sound could change her mood drastically, as it brought on memories of her parents. She had seen them nearly every day, but to not live in the same house, to share meals, and share conversation was hard adjusting to. Wilhelm had found moving out easy, but he did not have the strong rapport with his father as Hannah had with her parents.

Erich had almost exclusively been living at Lena's, and Hannah and Wilhelm assumed he and Lena would be looking for a place of their own after their wedding, a date set for Saturday, 22 July. Hannah and Wilhelm had agreed to go but would be making an "unexpected" trip to visit Wilhelm's father who had fallen ill days before. The feeling was nothing short of despicable. Lena and Erich talked about nothing but their big day. Hannah, on occasions, tried talking both herself and Wilhelm into going or, at the very least, Wilhelm going. But it was far too dangerous for Hannah to go, and Wilhelm knew how much she wanted to, and he wouldn't let her face that truly awful feeling alone.

It was a week before the wedding, and Hannah and Wilhelm had just returned to their apartment from a long walk. Hannah nearly screamed when she opened the door and saw two SS officers, dressed in black, standing with their backs to them. When they turned, she recognized both as Erich and Sturmscharführer Hauser.

"Greetings, Hannah. Wilhelm," Sturmscharführer Hauser said, inclining his head.

It was hardly trespassing, as Erich lived there, but Hannah saw Jakob Hauser as nothing more than a burglar. No doubt his hawk eyes had examined every last inch of the place. Wilhelm had tried to defend Jakob, and she could not find fault in him or his logic, for Jakob and Ida Hauser had been kind, hospitable, and respectable every time she had seen them. When she thought long on it, she realized she condemned him for the patches on his uniform but was offended for being classified by the yellow Star of David she was supposed to wear.

Erich was dressed in black with two black diamond gorget patches with one having the double horizontal lighting S on it and a single black strap on his shoulder. He held out his hands to showcase his uniform. "What do you think?" he asked. He radiated self-pride through his smile that exposed every tooth.

"You are a soldier?" Wilhelm asked.

"Not just a soldier, Wilhelm. A member of the SS-Schütze," Sturmscharführer Hauser said, wearing a similar smile.

It seemed the sort of thing two best friends would tell one another. Yet, Wilhelm could hardly hold contempt over it. He kept hidden that he and Hannah were married, and they were going to lie to miss Erich's wedding.

"Lena never mentioned you were joining," Hannah said.

"Sturmscharführer Hauser has been telling me to enlist. He says conscription is coming and to enlist ensures a better post and more room for advancement," Erich explained.

"In a few months, he will be an SS-Sturmmann and maybe, in less than a year, an SS-Rottenführer," Sturmscharführer Hauser added. But he had secretly pulled strings to lessen the time of promotion. The higher the rank Erich procured, the more elite and popular his daughter's wedding became.

"You should consider it, Wilhelm. Germany will require you," Sturmscharführer Hauser said.

"I will have to think about it. I can't have Erich looking better than me," Wilhelm teased.

Jakob flashed a handsome smile—the kind that no doubt had first entranced Ida.

"Erich was showing me his place and what will need to be moved after their house is built," Sturmscharführer Hauser mentioned.

More news for Wilhelm.

"Sturmscharführer Hauser…" Erich started, but Jakob put a firm hand on his chest.

"Please, Erich, when in private, you may call me Jakob," Sturmscharführer Hauser said.

"Jakob got a great deal, and it is right down the road from their house," Erich continued.

"Congratulations, Erich!" Hannah said, rushing forward to hug him.

"Make sure my guest room is of adequate size," Wilhelm joked, then hugged Erich.

"I think Lena was planning on telling you, so when she does, act surprised," Erich said.

"Not going to start your wedding off on a good foot, Erich. The holes we dig with women are like quicksand and not easily escapable. Remember that," Sturmscharführer

Hauser advised. He smiled and marched toward the door and paused as he opened it. "By the way, in case you were thinking of kidnapping my daughter, remember it is my job to find those who try to hide," Sturmscharführer Hauser said.

It was common in Germany for friends of the bride and groom to kidnap the bride and leave a series of clues for the groom to find her. But Hannah found the warning to be extremely unnerving as if he had said it only to her. But indeed, Hannah, Wilhelm, and Heinrich did have plans to kidnap the bride.

That Friday, Hans, yet again, let Wilhelm borrow a car. Hannah and Wilhelm stopped at the Hauser house to pick up Lena and Heinrich and another of Heinrich's mystery dates. The plan was to stay at Lena's for less than five minutes, but they all knew and hoped Ida would have a quick supper for them. Ida did not disappoint. Heinrich had suggested a quick nap before hitting the road, but it was refuted. His new date, Susan, had been given the title "Susan the Silent" on the account that she had not said a single word the entire car ride to the cabin.

There were at least six credible drinking establishments only ten minutes away from the cabin, and they stopped at each and promised their friend Erich would be there soon to pay the tab. Erich had been forced to take the smelly, uncomfortable bus, and each bar he stopped at, he was greeted with a tab for five drinks. Susan was too polite for the act and found it hard to be mean to Erich without ever having met him and, therefore, only ordered water. Her sacrifice was in vain, for Heinrich ordered two beers. By the time Erich arrived at the cabin, Hannah, Wilhelm, Heinrich, Lena, and Susan were drunk, and Erich was broke.

"You bastards!" Erich shouted before the door was even fully open.

"What is it?" Heinrich asked innocently.

"You unhand my fiancé. I am to marry her!" Erich said with a dramatic and drunk effect.

"I do not know what you are talking about, Erich," Hannah said.

"Et tu, Hannah?" Erich asked, quoting Julius Caesar. He grabbed his chest from the invisible knife wound before turning his attention to the silent stranger.

"Sorry, don't know you, but I am disappointed in you all the same," Erich said, offering his hand.

"Susan," she said, shaking his hand and laughing.

"Pleasure. Have you seen my fiancé? Brown hair, shoulder-length. Soft gray eyes," Erich asked.

"Check one of the bedrooms," Susan said.

"Come on!" Heinrich shouted.

"You quiet down and pour me a drink!" Erich commanded.

Jakob had bought a keg of the finest beer. Rumor stated that simply breathing it in could intoxicate a person. Heinrich poured a pint to the brim and scraped off the foam and handed it to Erich. He downed it in six gulps, suppressed the urge to gag and scavenged the rooms. He turned the knob of the master bedroom, but it was locked.

"Erich," Hannah called.

He turned his drunken attention to Hannah and the bronze key in her hand. He staggered toward her and held his hand out for the key. Heinrich held a glass of beer, over a pint's worth, and Hannah dropped the key in. Like a great luxury liner, it sank to the depths of the amber beer.

"Sorry!" Hannah whispered.

Erich nearly whiffed on his first attempt to grab the glass. But he secured it with two hands and raised the bottom to the ceiling and chugged the delicious poison. A decent amount ran down his chin and onto the floor. He caught the key with his teeth.

"Please don't vomit on Lena," Wilhelm said.

"I make no promises," Erich replied.

He took a step backward for every three steps forward. He inserted the key into the lock and opened the door. Lena was on the bed with only the sheets covering her from her upper thighs to her chest.

"You found me. Now come and claim me," Lena said, lifting the sheet.

Erich closed the door behind him and moved straight and true to her.

"We will be by the lake," Hannah shouted through the door.

Wilhelm and Heinrich muscled the keg, and even though they had walked to the lake countless times, it now seemed like they had accomplished one of the great feats of human history. They downed another pint of beer. The sun had long set, but only then did the temperature drop.

"I am sorry, Hannah," Wilhelm said.

"For what?" she asked.

"This," Wilhelm answered, picking her up and sprinting into the water.

She screamed when the cold water hit her flesh.

Susan gave Heinrich a warning look as he approached her with the same intention.

"You did reveal Lena's location," Heinrich said, justifying what he was about to do.

A crime deserved punishment, so he scooped her up and dove into the water. Lena and Erich joined in less than an hour later, and after swimming and splashing around, they sat around a fire. Their drunkenness surrendered to exhaustion and consumed them. Hannah drove back with Lena and Susan early in the morning. Erich was no longer allowed to see her until the wedding day. Erich rode back with Wilhelm and Heinrich. But Erich barely opened his eyes the whole car ride home. They had to pull over more than a dozen times for Erich to vomit. Wilhelm was thankful Hannah had taken Hans' car. Otherwise, he would have some major cleaning to do.

Later that night, Wilhelm broke the news to Erich that his father had fallen ill, and that he and Hannah had to go to Schönfeld to take care of him. The disappointment in Erich's voice was evident, and a surge of guilt flooded Wilhelm, and it seemed like it would never go away. Hannah's phone call to Lena did not fare any better, but she was grateful Lena did not ask her to stay and let Wilhelm go alone. But in an effort to better their conscience, they did travel to Schönfeld. The bus ride was long and uncomfortable. The city had not changed. It was a comfort and, to Wilhelm, a dependable friend. The "Rote Blumen" seemed to carry the same flowers as it had when Wilhelm had left.

"It feels like ages ago," Hannah said.

Wilhelm stood in exactly the same spot he had when he first saw her. But now, he did not have to worry about running after her or losing her in the blinding sun and a bustling city. She was his. And he was hers.

Wilhelm should have known it would not be a straightforward visit. His father put him to work, and as Wilhelm mopped and swept, Petyr showed Hannah how to dry flowers, arrange bouquets, and create wreaths and centerpieces.

"You have such an eye," Hannah commented.

"From Wilhelm's mother. I was awful when we first opened. But she loved to do it," Petyr said.

"Do you have a photograph of her? I would very much like to see it," Hannah asked.

Petyr removed his ripped leather wallet from his pocket and took out a torn, battered photo from it. Saundra, with the same dark hair as Wilhelm, smiled with baby Wilhelm on her lap. She squeezed his pudgy fingers and pointed ahead, no doubt toward the camera to draw Wilhelm's attention to it.

"She was beautiful. Thank you for showing me," Hannah said.

Wilhelm's mood changed, and even though he loved to think about his mother, seeing her picture smashed his heart with a sledgehammer. The change was not just in Wilhelm. Petyr too remained quiet for the next forty minutes. He and Hannah arranged bouquets, and Wilhelm continued to do the same mind-numbing chores that had driven him insane throughout his childhood. Yet, somehow, he found it impossible to complain, as it brought a relaxing nostalgia over him. Hannah was able to get Petyr to open up in a way Wilhelm never could, and after years of failure, he had simply stopped trying. But Petyr told stories of Wilhelm's mother that made Wilhelm smile and tear up. He tried hiding his tears from his father and stayed outside for a few minutes after emptying the trash into the dumpster.

Hannah and Wilhelm stayed a week, working the shop, while Petyr stayed home to better sell the lie, as the Brinkerhoffs had many family and friends in the city. At night, they would make dinner and play cards. After a week, Hannah and Wilhelm drove back to Berlin. That night, they cooked dinner for Erich and Lena and apologized again for missing their wedding, but both were overly kind and only asked how Wilhelm's father was doing.

August came and more weekend trips to Lena's cabin followed. Sunday mornings were spent with Hannah painting or drawing and Wilhelm playing the guitar. But as the dog days of August winded down, Germany prepared for war.

Conscripted

The first of September 1939 was a Friday, and the tradition of dinners continued at Wilhelm and Hannah's apartment. Erich had moved in with Lena and her parents while their house was being built. But unlike the countless previous Fridays where after the dinner's dishes were washed, dried, put away, and cards played, the Führer had a special speech for all of Germany.

Erich fine-tuned the signal on the radio.

"For months, we have been suffering under the torture of a problem, which the Versailles Diktat created—a problem which has deteriorated until it becomes intolerable for us," Hitler's voice said.

The Führer was an exceptional orator, and his charisma was not diminished by the radio. When eyes were closed, it was like Hitler was in the very room, and for that reason, Hannah didn't blink. Murmurs had said fighting had broken out on the Polish border, and all of Berlin, all of Germany, and the entire world waited for the Führer's address.

"This night, for the first time, Polish regular soldiers fired on our territory. Since 5:45 a.m., we have been returning the fire, and from now on, bombs will be met by bombs. Whoever fight with poison gas will be fought with poison gas. Whoever departs from the rules of humane warfare can only expect that we shall do the same. I will continue this struggle, no matter against whom, until the safety of the Reich and its rights are secured," Hitler continued.

Wilhelm, Erich, and Heinrich exchanged looks. Fighting had started. War had started. And war needed young men to fight it. The address changed thousands of lives in seconds.

"And I would like to close with the declaration that I once made when I began the struggle for power in the Reich. I then said, 'If our will is so strong that no hardship and suffering can subdue it, then our will and our German might shall prevail!'" Hitler ended.

"We were left with no choice," Erich said as he switched the radio off.

The Führer had stated in his speech that he sought peace repeatedly only to be met with oppression and mobilization. But Hannah was not so quick to believe the Führer's words.

"We are taking back what is ours," Lena said.

Her pride in Germany and the Reich was fully evident. Her father had been promoted to SS-Untersturmführer and Erich to SS-Oberschütze. The Hauser name continued to ascend the Nazi ladder.

"We invaded Poland," Wilhelm said, disagreeing.

How could Lena say Germany was defending itself when Germany bulldozed into Poland?

"Our country starved for years after the Great War ended," Lena said, her face reddening and her voice rising, "We were not given humility in our defeat. I remember my father burning money during the winter because it provided nothing but kindling. Thousands of Germany's sons fought to better our lives, and their sacrifice went in vain until now. I commend the Führer for not bending to please France or England. Germany is not a domesticated dog. It is a wild wolf, and we will not take orders from sheep and sheepdogs."

No one argued with her. They had all been told of uncles or cousins who had been killed during the fighting. But the Great War was a war of attrition. Even the Hausers had suffered during the decade after the war. Bread cost .63 marks in 1918. In November of 1923, bread cost 201,000,000,000 marks. The exchange rate between the US dollar and the Deutsche mark was one trillion marks to the US dollar.

On 3 September, France, Britain, Australia, and New Zealand declared war on Germany, and Canada declared war a week later. On 17 September, the Soviet Union, under the leadership of Joseph Stalin, invaded Poland. The argument that the fight for mere feet of land would take months was poorly founded, as less than a month after the fighting had started, on 27 September, Warsaw surrendered. In less than thirty days, Germany had conquered a country. Wilhelm and Heinrich both expected to be notified of their obligation to serve, but September came without it, and they started to let the ember of hope breathe life into a roaring fire. Perhaps they would not have to go to war after all.

October brought windy gusts and falling leaves and November, frigid mornings and late-month snowfall. Wilhelm and Hannah carried on like normal. Wilhelm worked for Hans during the day while, on Thursday nights, they danced at "Verdrehende Nächte," and on Fridays were dinner with Erich, Lena, Heinrich, and a rotation of women. The snowfall and cold temperatures only increased Hannah's holiday spirit.

The Friday before Christmas, 22 December, Wilhelm was late in returning home from work. Lena, Erich, Heinrich, and his date would arrive in ten minutes, and his tardiness had put a handicap on Hannah having dinner ready in time. But Hannah was not at the stove or by the fridge. She was seated at the kitchen table, staring at the pile of mail as if expecting it to take flight.

"What's wrong?" Wilhelm asked, closing the door behind him.

Hannah pointed to the thick brown card, no larger than an index card, amongst the pile. Wilhelm stared at it from the safe distance of the entryway and then lumbered to the table, took the brown card, and read it.

"I have been drafted. I have to report on Christmas day," Wilhelm said. His strength traveled out of his body like an evacuation. It was a cruel nightmare. It had to be. He looked about the room for any signs of it being a dream. But every sight, every smell, and every sound were as they should be. Hanukkah had ended on the 14th, but the two celebrated Christmas as well. It was hardly the gift either had wanted.

"Don't go, Wilhelm," Hannah pleaded.

"I have to," Wilhelm said. If he didn't go, they would be forced to leave the country, and even if Hannah's passport worked, her parents would be left behind.

Fists beat against the other side of the door, and Heinrich entered. "Did you get it too?" he asked. Heinrich had always been full of color and confidence. But his face was ghost white, and he had a nervousness Hannah had never seen from him.

Wilhelm held up the draft notice.

"Maybe we'll get assigned together," Heinrich said, his voice filled with a dusting of hope.

"Maybe," Wilhelm said, his voice caked in doubt.

"I do not want to fight," Heinrich said.

There was another knock on the door. Lena and Erich came in and tossed their jackets on the back of the couch.

"You have gotten your notices?" Lena asked after seeing the brown card.

Wilhelm could only nod.

"Perhaps you will be serving under me," Erich said, somehow smiling.

Erich had been a brother but seeing him smile about leaving for war had made him a stranger.

"Can we talk about something else? Anything else," Hannah insisted.

Lena moved over to Hannah and squeezed her hand. "We took Poland in less than a month, Hannah. This war will be over in a year."

Each tried to do their best to enjoy the night, but only Lena and Erich were in high spirits. It was the least fun their Friday dinners had been. Hannah and Wilhelm kept reminding each other they still had Saturday and Sunday. Wilhelm stopped by Hans' house early Saturday to tell him he had been drafted and would no longer be around to work.

"You be careful. I've been there. It isn't pretty," Hans said.

It was obvious advice, but Wilhelm still appreciated it. Hans squeezed Wilhelm in an unexpected hug and promised him there would be a job waiting for him when he got back. He also let Wilhelm borrow one of his cars one last time, and he and Hannah drove to Schönfeld to tell his father of his draft notice. They had not mentioned it to Petyr for hours until they sat down for an early four-o'-clock dinner. But, like the dinner when Wilhelm had told his father he was moving to Berlin, his father ignored all the telltale signs, including glances between Hannah and Wilhelm, awkward silence, forced conversation, and the shifting of vegetables on Wilhelm's plate.

"Father, I have been drafted," Wilhelm finally said. Petyr did his best to keep his face void of emotion, but his mouth dropped a bit. The words had brought Petyr back to the fields of Verdun. "Many expect the war to be over quickly," Wilhelm added.

Petyr shook his head, almost laughing at the idea. "They said the same thing when I fought—just a few more weeks. Hundreds were dying every damn day. Look at me,

Wilhelm. This is the face of a survivor. Shadows and silhouettes of what we once were. War only takes. It doesn't give. You don't win."

Wilhelm's thoughts went to the medal. The blood pump of the world would run once again.

"Don't repeat my mistakes," Petyr said.

Wilhelm had never once heard his father plead, but his words sounded an awful lot like it.

"What can I do?" Wilhelm asked.

"I mean, during the fighting, don't ask the names of the men next to you. They may not make a day or a week. You stay detached," Petyr said sternly.

It was impossible to tell who was more alarmed—Wilhelm or Hannah. The mood had shifted so much that the plates of food could not be touched. When Wilhelm said goodbye, it was another handshake that met him. But it was the longest handshake his father had ever given him.

Hannah and Wilhelm left his father and his hometown behind. They had planned to spend the night alone, but when they arrived at their apartment, Erich was on the steps. He rose to his feet when Hannah and Wilhelm approached.

"About time," Erich said.

"What's wrong?" Wilhelm asked.

"Lena and I would like to invite you over to Untersturmführer Hauser's and Mrs. Hauser's home."

Lena and Erich's house was scheduled to be completed in only four months. To celebrate, they were going to have a weekend-long celebration. But now, in four months, Wilhelm, Erich, and Heinrich would be somewhere in Europe fighting a war.

"I do not feel like it," Wilhelm said.

"Please. It is the last chance we have before we leave," Erich insisted.

The next day was Christmas Eve and would be spent with their families. But Hannah and Wilhelm hardly felt like being with company, especially the war-happy Hausers. But they had missed Erich and Lena's wedding, and it would be the last time they would all be together for months.

"Fine," Hannah said, forcing a smile.

Erich returned it with considerably less effort. He gave Hannah and Wilhelm a ride in one of the cars the Hausers owned. Lena had said her family had taken over several businesses from Jewish people as a part of a law that had started in October 1938. To Hannah, it was riding in a coffin or grave robbing. She was sick thinking of how many families starved so the Hausers could have another automobile. The disgusted stomach she had had in the car amplified at the sight of the Hauser homestead. It was enough to make her vomit. The lawn and trees were covered in a blanket of snow, but the driveway was neatly shoveled, no doubt every hour by hired help. The front door of the house opened for them and Jakob, casually dressed, stood with a glass of whiskey in his hand and a cigarette between his fingers.

"Wilhelm! Hannah! Nice of you to join us. I hope your father is doing well," Jakob said.

"He is. Thank you," Wilhelm replied.

Hannah held out a bottle of wine for Jakob. Though it was cheap and did not have enough class to be mentioned with the wines the Hausers had in their cellars, it was the gesture she hoped they took.

"We don't drink wine," Jakob said with a deadpan expression, then smiled.

"Certainly not such quality as this," Hannah said.

"Nonsense. Thank you. We shall drink this bottle when the war is over and our fighting men return home," Jakob said.

Wilhelm, Hannah, and Erich sat on the entryway bench and removed their shoes while Ida rushed forward with a welcoming smile. "I can take your coats," she said and helped Hannah remove hers. Hannah thanked her, and Ida hung the three coats in the closet.

The heat from the fireplace was strong, and the feeling in their fingers and toes returned almost immediately.

"I'm glad you decided to come. I sent Erich an hour ago," Lena said.

"I'm only frostbitten from the waist down," Erich said, standing by the crackling fire to warm himself.

Heinrich sat on the couch with a familiar face beside him.

"Eva!" Hannah said, shocked to see her.

"It's about time Heinrich tightened the screws in his head," Lena teased.

"Hello, Hannah," Eva greeted.

Of all of Heinrich's dates, Eva had been Lena and Hannah's favorite. It was only too bad Heinrich had finally seen it two days before he had to leave. Heinrich was still not his charismatic, confident self. He had the appearance of someone battling the stomach flu.

Lena gave Wilhelm and Hannah a glass of red wine, and the two sat beside Heinrich and Eva on the couch. With each opening of the oven, the smell of seasoned goose and a wide array of pies crept out of the kitchen like an invisible fog and rose to their nostrils. After roughly half an hour, Ida announced dinner was ready. It was the type of spread Wilhelm and Hannah had grown accustomed to seeing when they visited the Hausers, and they only hoped their appetite would cooperate.

"Father met with the Führer today," Lena said, her pride and excitement on full display.

"Lena, it's not good to brag. I met with several other officers as well," Jakob said.

"Tell them what he said, Father," Lena said.

Ida and Jakob smiled at one another—both filled with pride over their daughter's nationalism.

"He understands the sacrifice and burden Germany's sons must undertake. He assures us our struggle is his struggle. He will do what is necessary to achieve absolute victory," Jakob said.

No one but Lena and Ida gave any sign Jakob had spoken.

"That should be enough talk of war at the table," Ida said.

"Lena tells me you enjoy photography, Hannah," Jakob said as he precisely cut through his goose.

"Yes. Very much so. Wilhelm bought me a camera last Christmas," Hannah replied.

"For Christmas?" Jakob asked. Hannah nodded. "Lena showed me the photos you had given her. You have quite the eye," Jakob added.

"They really are beautiful. Such a thoughtful gift, Hannah," Ida said.

When the last scraps of food were eaten off the plates, Ida served the pies and insisted the men eat a second slice even if they were full. "I want everyone to have fun tonight and to be safe. You are all more than welcome to stay here," she said. Everyone at the table offered to help clean the kitchen, but Ida waved them away. No doubt Ellie would soon appear in the kitchen to do the heavy lifting.

Lena and the others ascended the circular staircase and went into the card room. They played every card game they knew. Lena made sure the wine kept flowing, and it raised the mood. With each hand and game they played, they forgot about what the next few days, weeks, months and, possibly, years would bring. Eva was the first to pass out in the same chair she played cards in, and Heinrich and Wilhelm were close behind and fell asleep on the couch and Chesterfield chair in the living room. Erich and Lena stumbled out of the card room to the bedroom, kissing as they did.

Hannah collected the cards and arranged them back into a neat pile and into the case. She tried waking Eva to get her into a more comfortable piece of furniture, but she only groaned. Eva had a glass of water at the table, just inches from where her head rested, and a wastebasket beside her. Hannah shut the light off and walked through the hallway. A lone light shone in the private study. Jakob sat with one foot resting over the other leg, an open book obscuring his face. His back was to her, a cloud of smoke dissipating off the end of his cigarette. He turned to look at her, lowering the open book in his hand. He took another puff from his cigarette and blew a cloud of smoke to the ceiling.

"Hannah. The last survivor. Please come in," Jakob said.

Hannah wanted only two things—to go to the bathroom and find a couch or chair to sleep in. But she would have settled for a hundred different things than to sit alone in a room with Jakob Hauser. Her tiredness had little to do with drinking. She was certainly buzzed, but each night after finding the draft card, she had slept only an accumulation of minutes, not hours. But to refuse Jakob's request, a polite one at that, would have been terribly rude. There was a second black leather chair directly in front of the one Jakob was sitting in with only a circular wooden table between them. Beside both chairs was a lone bookshelf that stretched from the floor to the ceiling and contained what looked to be over a hundred books.

"Please sit," Jakob said.

Hannah took the offered chair and, whether it was sheer exhaustion or something else, the chair was the most comfortable one Hannah had sat on in the Hauser home. Each chair demanded high praise, for they were well cushioned and hugged and massaged every muscle. The chair hoaxed her into comfort, and she struggled to stay awake.

"I was just looking through some of my favorite books," Jakob said.

"You have quite the collection," Hannah complimented.

It would have been a blatant lie to say his collection wasn't impressive, as it no doubt contained first-edition hardbacks. But she knew whatever books were deemed approved by the Nazis were hardly the books she desired to read.

"Did you like the wine tonight?" Jakob asked.

"Yes. Mrs. Hauser knows how to pair the perfect wine with the perfect meal," Hannah said.

"Yes, she has great taste," Jakob agreed, taking another long drag from his cigarette and putting it out on the ashtray on the table between them.

"She has it down to a science," Hannah said, watching as the red ember of the cigarette died out and the last trail of smoke rose to the ceiling.

"Was it to your specifications?" Jakob asked, giving the glass of whiskey in his hand a quick swirl before taking a sip.

"I don't know what you mean," Hannah said.

Jakob set the glass of whiskey on the table, closed the book, and slid it back onto the shelf. "I believe the term is kosher."

Hannah's heart jumped into her throat and then plummeted into the pit of her stomach, trying to hide.

"I don't know what you're talking about," she said.

"Please, Hannah, don't disrespect my intelligence in my own home," Jakob said. Hannah froze. "You said you like photography. I am a fan of it as well. Photographs are honest. People can lie, deceive, cheat, steal. Words too. But a photograph you can take at face value," Jakob continued. He slid a black folder with the Nazi swastika embossed on it from the shelf. He opened it and tossed the photographs inside it toward Hannah—photos of Hannah and Wilhelm leaving Holy Cross Church, of her parents' shop, and her home upstairs.

"I have been taking note of what you eat at our table, what you drink. We've been watching the priest for months. You see, I differ in my approach to catching rats. Most want to stomp on the first one they see. But not me. I feed the rat. I let it come closer and closer. You lull the rat into a sense of safety and then rats you didn't know existed crawl out of the gutters and alleyways. And that's when you get them."

A lone tear cascaded down her cheek, one she did not know if from sadness or absolute terror.

"Hannah Goldschmidt. Hannah Schreiber. Sara Hannah Goldschmidt. Daughter of Emma and Josef Goldschmidt. It does not matter what name you go by. You are Jewish," Jakob stated.

"What will you do?" Hannah asked.

"Your time will come soon enough, Hannah," Jakob warned.

"What of Wilhelm?"

"Wilhelm will serve the Reich."

"And Father Declan?"

"Boarded a train."

Hannah did not dare mention her parents.

"Does Lena know?"

Had she been nothing more than a dedicated actress serving the Reich?

"No. She does not."

"Can I be the one to tell her?"

Lena was her best friend. The two shared things about Erich and Wilhelm. Hannah owed her the truth, no matter what it cost her. She owed Lena that much.

"You may," Jakob said.

The chair that had been a soothing comfort now held her down like a vice. She struggled to her feet.

"You know, I strongly support Minster Goebbels' agenda, but the problem with profiling Jews in one light is that it allows the ones like you to stay in the shadows and unseen. Blonde hair. Blue eyes. The perfect German. A sheep in wolf's clothing," Jakob said.

He rose to his feet, stepped toward the door, and gestured Hannah to leave.

"I would not try to leave the country, Hannah," Jakob warned.

Hannah lumbered through the opening. She checked behind her before descending the spiraling staircase. She had to keep a secure grip on the railing to counter her trembling legs. Wilhelm and Heinrich were both asleep. She walked toward the lone light shining from the kitchen. Lena was at the black kitchen island, taking sobering sips from the glass of water in her hands.

"I think Erich will miss Christmas," Lena said, grabbing a glass from the cupboard and filling it with water. She set it down on the island counter next to Hannah.

"I need to talk to you, Lena," Hannah said.

"Is something wrong?" Lena asked.

It was something Hannah had wanted Lena to know but under different circumstances and under the rule of a different leader.

"I have wanted to tell you. I didn't miss your wedding because Wilhelm's father was ill. I missed it because I couldn't be in a room with so many Nazis. Lena, I am Jewish," Hannah said.

Lena stared hard into Hannah's eyes, and even though none of her telltale signs betrayed Hannah as joking, Lena laughed.

"I am too tired and drunk for such a joke, Hannah," Lena said, then brought her glass of water to her lips and gulped it. But no smile came to Hannah's face nor any of the dozens of signs, both subtle and blatant. "What?" Lena asked.

"I'm Jewish," Hannah repeated.

Lena's confused smile changed. Contempt, even hate, sobered her up like a pot of coffee.

"You are a fucking Jew? You, my friend? A girl who slept in my family's home, drank from our glasses, ate from our plates?"

Hannah's first instinct was to apologize, yet being a Jew was nothing she had to be sorry for. What she was sorry for was keeping it from her best friend. But Lena's reaction completely warranted her secrecy.

"Lena…" Hannah began, but Lena cut her off.

"Get out of my house, you fucking rat," she ordered.

Hannah wanted to say more, even if it was best she didn't.

"Get the fuck out of my house!" Lena repeated, this time yelling. She pointed to the door, her face maroon with rage, and spit on Hannah.

Hannah wiped the spit from her face, pleaded silently one last time and hurried to wake Wilhelm. He awoke to the quick tapping, like the peck of a woodpecker, of Hannah's hand.

"We have to go," Hannah said.

"Okay," Wilhelm said.

He rose from the couch and struggled to keep up with Hannah. She had both of their coats in her hand before Wilhelm even made it to the bench. She opened the door before Wilhelm had a chance to put his coat on and defend himself against the brutal cold. It was nearly midnight, and it was so cold and dark that it was hard to believe the sun had risen in years. A permanent frost was in the air, and after mere seconds, the lining of their nostrils froze.

"Why did we leave?" Wilhelm asked.

"I felt like sleeping in our bed," Hannah lied.

Wilhelm did not need to worry about one more thing. She did her best to discretely wipe the tears from her eyes.

"You're shivering," Wilhelm said.

"It is freezing," Hannah replied.

But her shivering had nothing to do with the howling, biting wind or the frozen air. It had everything to do with Jakob and the horrible way Lena had reacted. When they arrived back at their apartment, neither could feel their feet, hands or ears. Even with the apartment well heated, neither wanted to remove their jacket and change into their pajamas. But they both did change, in near record time, and crawled into bed. They wrapped the blankets around them and covered every possible crevice where the cold could sneak in. They laid on their sides, not a space between them, rubbing their feet together to warm themselves.

When his shivering subsided, Wilhelm drifted off to sleep, but while Hannah's shivering stopped, her goosebumps stayed. Her thoughts shifted from Wilhelm's deployment to her parents, her own fate, and to Father Declan, a kind and good man whose life had drastically changed because of the generosity he had shown to her and Wilhelm.

The next morning took an eternity to arrive and Hannah, once again, had only been able to get two or three hours of intermittent sleep. They had a quick breakfast of toast and eggs, bathed, and walked to Hannah's parents. It was a Herculean effort to finish her toast, for her stomach was turning with too many knots to desire food. Her face was pale, something she blamed on the cold weather when Wilhelm took notice. Had Jakob Hauser had her parents taken?

When her hand trembled too much for her to put the key into the lock of her parents' shop, she again blamed it on the cold. She gave the key to Wilhelm, and he unlocked the door. The shop showed no sign of forced entry, and the fact the door was locked was of vital importance. It was highly unlikely the Gestapo or Nazis would lock the door on their way out. On her second step up the stairs, she could smell her mother's cooking wafting down.

Emma was at the sink, finishing washing the dishes of that morning's breakfast. Josef was playing a hand of solitaire, switching from a three-card draw to a one-card draw when a desired card came about. Hannah rushed forward and wrapped her mother in a hug. Emma tried to dry off her hands and hug Hannah at the same time.

"Merry Christmas, Wilhelm," Josef said.

"We will pray for you every day, Wilhelm," Emma added.

"I suppose my uniform will not be as well made as your tuxes," Wilhelm said.

"Sadly, it will not have our initials," Emma said.

Emma had sewn an E and J with a G overlapping the two into every suit, coat, and jacket they had made and sold. Gold was reserved for clothing for either herself, Hannah or Josef. The rest were in a deep ruby red. But after further review of his wedding tux, Wilhelm had seen his too was stitched in gold fabric.

Emma crocheted a black and white blanket while Hannah did her best to paint the Brandenburg Gate by memory. The hanging Nazi flags were left out. Josef challenged Wilhelm to finish their last hand of chess from a previous visit, a checkmate Josef would not accept, and only after twenty minutes of moving his King every legal move, they started a new game. When Wilhelm was two moves away from losing, Josef put a soft hand on Wilhelm's before Wilhelm moved his rook.

"We will finish it next time," Josef said.

Hannah and Emma joined them in playing cards, and it was a nice change of pace to play without the penalty of getting drunk. Josef had kept his record player on, but their laughter and talking nearly drowned out the festive music. The lunch Emma made was hardly enough to satisfy an appetite, but they had not sold anything for months. Josef had been pawning things off before the Nazis could take them. It was better to get something out of their valuable and invaluable items than nothing at all. It was obvious both had lost weight, but Josef shrugged it off when Hannah mentioned it.

"I'm simply losing my winter weight early," he had said.

After lunch, they played more cards and exchanged gifts. Emma's present to Hannah and Wilhelm was the blanket she had finished crocheting earlier that morning. Josef's gift, sewn by Emma, was a warm woolen sweater, off-white in color, and a thick pair of wool socks. Wilhelm had given Josef another box of chocolates and a new chessboard made of glass with black marble and white crystal pieces, and he made sure it included an instructional manual on how to play as a way to tease Josef.

"Oh, good, kindling!" Josef joked.

Wilhelm and Hannah had gotten Emma a new casserole dish, pine-scented candles, and three framed photos, one of Hannah and Wilhelm, one of Emma and Josef, and one of only the Goldschmidts. Hannah's gifts included a new knitted hat, gray winter coat, and a new blood-red dress she couldn't wait to go dancing in. As the sun set and darkness descended, Josef gathered them close and prayed.

"Dear God, please keep us strong and resolute. Do not let us turn from you or each other. Let us stay true. We ask you to look upon us kindly," he recited.

Hannah had awoken from her nightmare. She loved each of her gifts, but celebrating the holiday with her parents and Wilhelm was the greatest gift she could receive or ask for.

"Wilhelm, there's something I need to tell you," Josef said, placing both hands on Wilhelm's shoulders. "You are an awful chess player," he teased. Emma gasped and slapped his chest. "I'm only kidding," Josef said. His joking demeanor shifted. "Wilhelm, my good young Sir, how I thank God you needed a tux."

He didn't have to say more. He hugged Wilhelm, and Wilhelm hugged him back. Josef had been the opposite of his own father—Petyr was unable to speak the language of affection while Josef was fluent. Emma squeezed Wilhelm tight in her hug and kissed his forehead. "Come back to us," she whispered.

Hannah and Wilhelm smiled and left. The walk back to their apartment was filled with silence. Wilhelm had not given Hannah her gift yet, but Hannah's thoughts were elsewhere. How lonely the next few months would be. Wilhelm had saved up a nice bit of money, but Hannah would be living alone for the first time in her life. Her parents had told her to limit her visits, but it did not matter. Jakob Hauser and the Nazis knew she was Jewish. It did not matter what name she went by. But Untersturmführer Hauser would soon be leaving for war. Perhaps his secret would travel with him to Poland or Belgium or wherever the war brought him.

"Hannah," Wilhelm said.

Snowflakes danced to the ground and took forever to fall from the black canvas sky.

"So many people gone," Hannah said in response to the empty homes and businesses. She stopped as she finally noticed he was not beside her. "What's wrong?" she asked, turning back to face him.

Wilhelm removed a sterling silver round charm necklace from his coat.

"Merry Christmas," he said.

Hannah held it in her mitten-covered hand and read the inscription: "I am yours. Now and always."

"It's beautiful," Hannah said.

"I wanted you to know. In case…"

"I am yours. Now and always," Hannah said before he could speak the awful words the end of his sentence would surely bring.

She removed a gift of her own. It too was a necklace, a rectangular bar of white gold. Inscribed on it were coordinates: 52.5214 N, 13.454 E.

"It's our address. So you can find your way home," Hannah said, "even if I don't know where you are."

Worrying was never enjoyable, but when narrowed down to a smaller scale, it was easier to remove unlikely possibilities. But she had a scale the size of Europe to worry about.

Wilhelm pulled her close to him. "Look up," he said. Hannah did, snowflakes falling slowly onto her face. The blue and white-speckled black sky was as frozen as the air. "Whenever you look up at them, know that I will be too. And, at that moment, we will be right next to each other," Wilhelm said.

Hannah smiled. Wilhelm dipped her so low that her back almost touched the sidewalk. He pulled her back up and gently kissed her. Their lips were cold but radiated heat.

"Dance with me?" Hannah asked.

"Always," Wilhelm replied.

When they entered their apartment, they tossed their hats, mittens, and coats to the floor, leaving a trail of clothing from the door to the bathroom. They bumped against the wall, their lips never separating as their passion consumed them. The rest of their clothes formed a mound in front of the bathroom door. Their skin erupted in shivers, both from the cold and each other's touch. Wilhelm swung his arm backward and shut the door. They stepped into the tub. The blood in their feet froze the moment it touched the cold porcelain surface.

Hannah turned the water on. The shower head spat out freezing water, paused and then pelted them with liquid heat. Their fingers explored each other as the hot water ran down their bodies. Hannah used her foot to put the plug in place. The water filled as they laid down, Hannah atop of him, the water running down her front like tributaries of a river. His fingers followed the tracks from her stomach to her breasts.

The water splashed out of the tub as they rose to their feet. Hannah pressed herself against the shower wall while Wilhelm thrusted his hips slowly before going faster in obedience to her silent commands. Their moans were deafened by the running water. The room filled up with steam evaporating out of the tub and off their bodies. Both breathed heavily, staring into each other's eyes after they climaxed—their bodies hyper-sensitive to the trickling water. Wilhelm shut the water off, and they laid back down in the tub. She rested her head against his chest, the water falling short of her face. They stayed there, fighting off the urge to sleep, until the water turned lukewarm.

After having dried off and dressed, Wilhelm and Hannah were anything but tired. It was their final night together for only God knew how long. Side by side, lying in bed, they stared into each other's eyes, willing time to stop and for the other to become a mental tattoo that would never fade.

"I love you, Wilhelm. Don't ever forget that," Hannah said.

"From the moment I saw you, Hannah, I knew I needed you in my life," Wilhelm said.

"I'm scared."

"Me too."

It was the truth, plain and simple. Even with their minds racing through what had happened and what would happen, they eventually drifted off to sleep. Wilhelm was never more relaxed than he was when Hannah was beside him.

Barely a word was spoken as they sat around the table for breakfast the next day. Heinrich would meet Wilhelm at his and Hannah's apartment, and the two would leave together. The clock on the wall had betrayed Wilhelm and Hannah. The hour was at hand. The faded gray duffel bag he had jammed full of clothing for his new life in Berlin was now once again full as he left the city.

"I have something for you," Hannah said, walking over to the coffee table in the living room and grabbing a two-by-four-inch photo. It was Wilhelm's favorite photo of them and one of the hundreds of moments with the woman he loved. "I wanted to frame it. But this way, you can keep it on your person," Hannah said.

"I will look at this every single day until I come back to you," Wilhelm said.

"Come back to me," Hannah ordered and pleaded, twirling the blue rose in her hand. "Dance with me when you get home?"

"Always," Wilhelm replied.

A knock on the door served as the final alarm. Time was up. Wilhelm opened the door, and Heinrich stepped in.

"Sorry, my mother was having a tough time of it," Heinrich said. The color in his face still had not returned, and his handsome looks needed a long night of sleep. "Ready?" he asked.

Wilhelm only nodded. He could not respond with "yes" to a question that implied he was ready to shoot, to be shot at, to kill, and to be killed.

"Take care of yourself, Heinrich. The women of Berlin will miss you," Hannah said. She hugged him and kissed his cheek.

"And I will miss them. Stay safe, Hannah," Heinrich said.

Whether Heinrich knew she was a Jew or not, she did not know, nor did she really care to know. It was such an insignificant thing in comparison to the two of them marching off to war.

"I love you," Wilhelm said, wrapping his arms around Hannah and taking in the smell of her hair.

She kissed him, tears filling her eyes as she did. She had wanted to show strength and stifle her tears until after Wilhelm had left. He wiped them with his hand and tried to smile. As the door closed behind him, no more air filled her lungs. Her heart stopped and then pounded and pounded, her heart rate skyrocketing. She struggled to breathe, struggled to move, and struggled to accept.

The modest even small apartment had been home only seconds ago. But now, the person who had made it home was gone. It was now nothing more than four walls and

a ceiling. It seemed impossible that Wilhelm would not walk through the door later that evening—impossible he was not off selling cars with Hans. It was now not a question of when he would come back but if he would come back.

The thirty seconds since she had seen him, felt his touch, and kissed his lips felt like an anguishing lifetime. Air flooded her lungs, powering her body out of its temporary paralysis. She whipped the door open and dashed down the steps, yelling his name. Wilhelm and Heinrich were already a block away. She sprinted across the street, ignoring the passing cars, still yelling his name. He turned and ran to meet her. Her lips smashed against his as he lifted her off her feet. It was a high they were addicted to and a withdrawal that came not days or even hours after but minutes. She kissed him long and hard and he, her. But all of Europe was tearing them apart, and their hold on one another broke. Their fingertips clung to one another for as long as they could before they broke apart.

"Look up at the stars and you are anywhere," Wilhelm said.

Hannah watched him as he crossed street after street until he was nothing but a small figure in the distance before he faded entirely from sight.

Round-Up

Christmas, a time of giving, had taken the best thing in Hannah and Wilhelm's lives. The year 1940 came without much fanfare for Hannah, and the spring months crept by. Hannah visited her parents more often than they had wanted her to due to the danger of it, but they were the only people Hannah saw apart from the grocery clerks. The days moved like weeks and the weeks like months.

On one of her visits, Hannah's parents showed her a magazine they had been given by a family friend. The magazine's cover featured a Jewish family, and the articles inside were dedicated to the relocation of the Jewish people. The images inside were of luscious lawns, spacious two-story houses, and smiling families. Josef's remaining Jewish friends had told him that relocation seemed like a fair offer.

Hannah had not been contacted by any Nazi officials since Jakob Hauser had discovered her secret. She had not told her parents for the only thing that could come from it was an unrelenting worrying. She had been warned not to try and leave the country. She had not seen or spoken to Lena since that day but, no doubt, Jakob was among the forces that had invaded Denmark or Norway in April.

Her thoughts drifted to Wilhelm and where in Europe he was. When spring arrived, it brought sunnier, longer days that helped raise Hannah's spirits. Winter, with its short, dark, gloomy days had been lonely. She missed her winter walks with Wilhelm. Her parents insisted she limit her visits to once a week. For the other six days of the week, she was trapped in her apartment. She spent her days painting, drawing, and playing Wilhelm's guitar. The summer of 1939 had been filled with friends, dancing, and sun, but the summer of 1940 had been one of isolation.

On an early morning, Hannah left her apartment for her weekly visit to her parents. She had debated with them that arriving before most of the city woke and leaving after most of it had gone to bed was safe. But her true intention was to spend as much time with them as she could. But she had woken late that day, and the blocks between her apartment and her parents' home were full of people. Possessions were thrown out of windows. SS officers were on every street corner. People, all ages, races, and genders, were being searched. Hannah had stopped short of the search radius and planned on turning around and walking the block back to her apartment, but three SS officers swept the spectators forward like a broom. Lines formed, and people held out their passports. It was common practice to keep them on oneself, as random searches were prominent.

"Passports out!" an SS officer shouted.

Hannah weighed her options—sweat dripped down her brow as she did. Her fingers trembled. She discretely searched the lines for her parents. Their home, over five blocks away, could be safe, but if her parents had gone for a walk or an errand, they would have been led into the search. Hannah could not simply leave, as it would certainly draw attention to her. The search was cerebral and fast. Those dragged from the lines appeared to be random in their selection. But each, no doubt, had the giant red J stamped onto their passport, which was accompanied by the name "Israel" or "Sara."

The man ripping the passports from their hands and checking them was tall and thin with nearly black hair and a face that was terrifyingly familiar, but she could not put either a location to where she had seen him or a name. But Hannah recognized the patches on his collar and shoulder. He was an SS-Rottenführer. Lena had spoken incessantly about the rank, as she had hoped Erich would reach it within six months. But that itself was nearly six months ago, and for a second, she wondered if Erich had. But the wonder ceased and fear took over. Hannah was now at the front of the line.

"Your passport," the Rottenführer demanded.

Hannah had kept it next to her side and tried to kill her trembling hand. The passport would be useless if she showed such a level of fear. She took a deep breath through her nose and raised the passport. The Rottenführer's hand snatched it like the clamping jaws of an alligator. He opened it, his eyes going from the passport to Hannah. His thin lips curled into a smile.

"Father Declan," he said, waving two soldiers over to him.

The two soldiers grabbed clumps of Hannah's jacket and dragged her out of the line. Another officer took the Rottenführer's spot as he followed Hannah.

"You were seen at the priest's house, Mrs. Schreiber," the Rottenführer said. He stared long and hard at Hannah, but his near growl showed signs of confusion. Did he recognize her too?

"I go to church there," Hannah said.

"You are a terrible liar," the Rottenführer said.

"I'm not lying," Hannah said. Her face was on fire and, most likely, a beet-red in color.

"You are Hannah Goldschmidt," the Rottenführer said.

"I am now Hannah Schreiber. I married my husband before he went off to fight."

"You will board a train to relocate."

A thousand thoughts flashed through her head. She wanted to run, but her legs no longer seemed connected to her body. She wanted to ask about her parents, but to do so would be a gamble. If they had not been caught, the Nazis would definitely be aware now. But if they had already been relocated, she wanted to be sent to the same city.

"What city am I to be sent to?" Hannah asked.

"The one over the mountains," the Rottenführer answered, laughing at his inside joke, one he found amusing.

"Mountains?" Hannah asked.

"The gate of heaven," the Rottenführer said. He and the two guards shared a smile. The realization hit Hannah. There were no resettlements, no relocations, no "Jew cities" out of Germany. Those who had left never returned. Those who had left were most certainly dead. "Time to board the train," the Rottenführer said.

The two soldiers grabbed Hannah by the elbows and practically lifted her off her feet as they dragged her away.

"Rottenführer Weaver, what do you think you are doing?" a voice yelled out.

The voice was familiar and, unlike the Rottenführer, she knew why and to whom it belonged to—a voice she had not heard since late December of 1939. It was Lena.

"Mrs. Brinkerhoff, I am taking this Jew to a train," Weaver said.

"Jew? Do you not recognize her? She was a guest of mine on several occasions. My father introduced you to her," Lena said.

Hannah's mind took her to the memory and every detail of it—the crackling fire, the mouth-watering smells wafting out of the kitchen, the comfortable couch, the Nazi officers cloaked in leather, and the stench of cigarette. Judging by the Rottenführer's face, he had replayed an identical memory.

The two men ignored Lena and continued dragging Hannah away. "Stop!" Weaver yelled. The two men obliged. Weaver walked toward them. Lena followed behind him and, somehow, cast an even larger more powerful shadow than the much taller man.

"She is a Jew," he said, poking his finger into Hannah's forehead.

"You have been misinformed," Lena said.

"By your father?" he asked.

"My father told me of his suspicions. But she only has one Jewish grandparent. The Mischling Test is clearly defined as requiring at least two grandparents," Lena said.

"A Jew is a fucking Jew," Weaver snapped.

"I agree. But the order has not been given yet," Lena said.

"Her passport has been faked. She is Hannah Goldschmidt. It says Hannah Schreiber."

"And I am Lena Hauser. My passport says Lena Brinkerhoff. It is called marriage, Rottenführer Weaver."

"Her time will come. I do not think your father, a self-proclaimed hawk, would take kindly to having a daughter with a pet rat."

"You can ask him when he returns. He is fighting with the other hawks while the birds that cannot fly stay here and look for worms."

Lena had called a Nazi officer a chicken and hadn't flinched a muscle. If Lena had been born a man, she would have risen to the top of the Nazi hierarchy due to sheer determination and fierceness.

Weaver pinned Hannah's passport against her chest with his long, skeletal finger. He stood silent and statuesque. The two soldiers would not disobey his command, but both knew who Jakob Hauser was and his rank and, more importantly, how important his family was to him. "Let her go," Weaver commanded. The two soldiers released Hannah and gave Lena an apologetic frown. "Scurry along, rat," Weaver sniggered, and then he and the two soldiers returned to the search lines.

Hannah and Lena stared at each other. There had been a time when Hannah could read Lena's thoughts by just glancing at her face. But now, it was foreign and shrouded in mystery.

"Thank you," Hannah said.

"Don't," Lena said, cutting her off.

Hannah fell silent. If a conversation were to occur, Lena would have to start it.

"My father had told me the date they would be searching these blocks," Lena said.

"Why did you stop him?" Hannah asked.

"I don't know. But I won't do it again. They are forcing the last Jews out of Berlin. Leave Germany. Don't ever come back."

Hannah wanted to say so much more. She wanted to ask how Erich was, how Lena was. She wanted her to know she missed her. The months since Wilhelm had left had been the hardest of her life, and they could have been lessened had Lena still been a part of it.

"I wish you well, Lena."

The emotion in Lena's eyes was unmistakable. She had disobeyed her father and, possibly, tarnished his reputation. Rottenführer Weaver was a pawn of Jakob's, but if Lena's actions came to light, Jakob's allegiance to the Nazi cause could be called into question.

Hannah staggered away, keeping her eyes on her best friend, hoping Lena could still read her silent expressions—expressions that simply translated into "thank you." Hannah had no idea how long the searches would last. The SS officers knew her passport had been forged. There were two types of Jew hunters—those who did it out of necessity, the duties of a job, and those who were thrilled by the hunt. Hannah was a prey who had escaped, and Rottenführer Weaver would take it as a personal challenge to hunt her down. If she were to be caught by a different officer or soldier without Lena's help, which she may not get again, she would be boarded onto a train.

The city swarmed with SS, and even if it was foolish, it felt like every one of them had one goal—to capture her. Hannah had taken to hiding in alleyways until darkness descended. She had to leave the city and let time stifle Rottenführer Weaver's hunger for her capture. She returned to her apartment and grabbed her mother's old book bag from her medical-school days and gathered what would fit—a spare change of clothes, her camera, a manila envelope that she filled with some of her favorite photos, her paint brushes, and drawing pencils. She would have to leave so many of her possessions behind, but she told herself it was only temporary.

She slid the dried blue rose into the manila envelope and stood in the doorway, taking in her home before closing the door. She bolted to the bus station. She would have to leave town until the searches quieted down. Her parents' home was blocks outside the search radius, and Hannah would return when it was quieter. She had narrowly escaped once and to think it would happen twice was foolish even for a person of faith. There was only one place she knew to go—Schönfeld.

The bus ride was under two hours, and with each mile covered, safety dulled her fears. The sight of the "Rote Blumen" calmed her. She took a deep breath as she stepped in front of the window. Petyr with his tall frame was visible inside. He had never been overly warm to her, but he had an effortless ability to make someone feel safe and safe was something she had not felt since Wilhelm had left and Jakob Hauser had confronted her. Hannah stepped inside.

"Hannah?" Petyr said, setting down the bouquet he was working on. She took long strides to him and hugged him. "Is something wrong?" he asked.

"I need a place to stay for a few days. The Nazis are looking for me," Hannah explained.

"You can stay here as long as you need to," Petyr said.

Though the Jews in their community had been taken, it was such a small city that it was not subject to as many searches as the nation's capital.

"Thank you," Hannah said.

"Have you heard from Wilhelm?" Petyr asked.

"No," Hannah answered.

Petyr nodded. He understood how difficult it was to send letters.

"Are you hungry? Thirsty?" Petyr asked.

Out of politeness, Hannah wanted to say no, but she didn't think her stomach would accept such betrayal. She had not eaten since supper the night before, over twenty-four hours ago.

"If it is not too much trouble," Hannah said. Her stomach growled at her subtlety.

"No trouble. I was just going to finish this one up and close up shop," Petyr said.

"Please. Finish."

Her stomach now threatened to cannibalize itself for the treachery.

Petyr was a man of details and a perfectionist. Apart from walking, Petyr did not rush a single thing. Wilhelm had told her as much, and from the times she had been with him, it had been that way—not necessarily a bad quality, yet annoying when having to wait on that person. But Petyr was doing Hannah a favor and taking the risk, and because of that, she waited patiently. Even in her hunger and slight annoyance, she appreciated the amount of time, thought, and care that went into everything Petyr did. Wilhelm had taken that quality, and it extended far beyond bouquets and wreaths.

The supper Petyr prepared told Hannah he had gotten used to eating alone. There were no casseroles or meat pies. Each meal consisted of a piece of meat, potato, and a vegetable. It was the sort of monotony most would have hated, but Petyr found reliably comforting.

"Sorry," Petyr said, shrugging at how unappetizing the dinner looked. Petyr had a cupboard full of spices his late wife had used but had no idea how to use them. The spices and herbs he used were strictly limited to salt and pepper.

"You are a better cook than Wilhelm," Hannah said, smiling, even if it was untrue.

"Nearly burnt the house down the first time he cooked," Petyr said.

Hannah felt guilty at how naturally their conversations continued, knowing Wilhelm had never been able to hold such conversations with his father. Yet, she also knew it was hard to not argue with someone who was so similar. It was hard to tell what type of man Petyr would have been had the war not happened and had his wife still been alive. But Hannah recognized the kindness in his eyes, visible through the obvious pain.

Hannah stayed with Petyr for three weeks, helping out at the shop and spicing up dinners, both figuratively and literally, and on 1 November, she told him she was going to return to Berlin to join her parents. Petyr had tried to dissuade her from it but knew her intentions were pure even if dangerous and, honestly, Petyr wouldn't have thought much of Hannah if she had not wanted to.

"I'll come back," Hannah promised.

Petyr hugged her and watched her board the bus. The grey bus jerked forward with a discharge of black smoke. It was only as the bus sputtered out of the city did Hannah realize she had forgotten the manila folder and the photographs and blue rose inside. She had decorated Wilhelm's old room with the pictures. They were her most prized possessions, and she had purposefully put them all in the folder so she would not forget them. The dried blue rose was kept on the nightstand next to the bed. She had held it in her hands every night. It had served as something of a dreamcatcher, and without it, she was vulnerable.

Hannah had deliberately taken the last bus, the 10:30, so she would arrive in Berlin well after midnight while most were asleep in their beds. Only three other people were on the bus, and when each stepped off and branched off into different directions, Hannah exited.

The city she loved had turned on her. The street lights were no longer casting security in illuminating her surroundings. Instead, they were like giant searchlights that betrayed her location. She hurried across the streets to her family's home. She removed her key, but to her dismay, the door was unlocked. It was never unlocked. Her father had always locked it, and after Kristallnacht, he had become doubly paranoid and triple checked if it was locked. The shop was dark, and the mannequins made her jump more than once. In the darkness, the suits they wore looked like the black leather of the SS.

She crept silently through the black dividing curtain and up the steps. As soon as the black curtain parted open, the lights upstairs cast a glow on the base of the steps. It was certainly well past her parents' bedtime, but either her mother or father must have gone to the kitchen for a glass of water. Hannah smiled. She had been sick with worry the entire three weeks in Schönfeld. But neither her mother nor father was at the kitchen sink. The bathroom door was open and the light, off. Hannah's first thought was someone had left the kitchen light on but, like with the lock, her father could not clear his mind enough to sleep unless he had personally verified every light was off, candle was blown out, and window, shut.

"Hello?" she called out.

The walls of the living room had been stripped bare of the art, paintings, and photos that had hung. The dishes, silverware, and fine china were stacked on the kitchen table. Four figures, cloaked in black and wearing black field caps with the Totenkopf (skull and crossbones) stepped out of her parents' bedroom. They were SS, but to many, they were the Grim Reaper.

"What a late hour to be calling," the highest-ranking officer said.

The man had more medals and insignia patches than Rottenführer Weaver and Untersturmführer Hauser and was much older than both, appearing to be in his late fifties with bits of gray hair on the sides of his head, unconcealed by his field cap.

"I would greet you with a good evening, but we are well past evening and even night. Good morning, Miss, I am Obersturmführer Weitel. May I see your passport please?" he asked, removing the black leather glove from his right hand and extending it.

The other three stalked behind her. Hannah removed her own mitten and reached into her pocket. One of the three took two steps forward and watched her hand closely, no doubt to see if she was reaching for a weapon. Hannah pulled her passport from her coat and handed it to Obersturmführer Weitel. He nodded appreciatively. Weitel looked over the passport and, much to Hannah's shock, he handed it back over.

"Thank you, Mrs. Schreiber. Now, can I ask what you are doing here?" Weitel asked.

A lie needed to come to Hannah and fast.

"I came to check on the building. Will it be made available for Germans?" Hannah asked.

"It will," Weitel said.

"And the previous owners? They are Jewish, I was told," Hannah asked.

"They were," Weitel answered again.

Were—past tense. Even if Weitel could feel Hannah's beating heart, her shaking hands or see the cold sweat covering her body and forehead, he showed no signs of it. But like so many of the SS, it was not the kill that gave the greatest thrill but the hunt, and some loved to prolong it. But Hannah needed to know where her parents had been taken.

"Where are they now?" Hannah asked.

"No longer here," Weitel said.

Hannah was asking too many questions, and she knew it. She had to make herself seem more interested in the building than the previous occupants—a task easier said than done. She walked through the living room—her legs were gelatin, the bones in them, gone and glanced into the open rooms. Many of the possessions were gone or piled up to be removed from the home. Hannah's childhood home was being disemboweled. She had a memory in every square inch. She paused by her parents' bedroom. Her father's "junk" drawer had been pulled from the dresser, and the pictures, letters, tickets, and trinkets were scattered about on the wooden floor.

"Leave your contact information with Oberschütze Reinhart, and you will be contacted when the building is ready to have a tenant," Weitel said.

Hannah was no longer welcomed, and to stay any longer would be unwise. Yet, she would not leave until she received information about her parents' whereabouts.

"The previous owner made tuxes. I saw them downstairs. They appear to be well made. I wish to have their contact information so they can make dresses and suits for me and my friends," Hannah said.

"I do not have it. Now, if you would, Mrs. Schreiber, it is time for you to leave," Weitel insisted.

The man who Hannah presumed to be Reinhart went into her parents' bedroom, but the other two still remained standing in front of the stairwell. Reinhart sorted through the mess on the bedroom floor and discarded the pile with utter disregard for how valuable they may have been to the owner. He paused and lifted a photo from the heap. He marched to Weitel and gave him the picture. In the flash of a moment, the photograph went from Weitel's hand to his face, and not only did her parents' faces smile from the photograph but Hannah's too.

Hannah's survival instinct jerked her body into action. She turned and her legs, which had barely supported her weight when the SS stepped out of her parents' bedroom, now were steel beams, and she went from the living room to the top of the stairs in four strides.

"Stop her!" Weitel commanded. The two men at the top of the stairs grabbed her by the shoulders. "Bring her here," Weitel said. Hannah's feet dragged as the two men carried her to Weitel. "Your passport," Weitel demanded.

"I have shown you my passport," Hannah said.

"Now!" Weitel yelled. His voice had not struck Hannah as menacing before, but the way he had spoken caused Hannah's eyes to open wide and her breath to shorten. The men held her firmly from the back. Hannah removed her passport and gave it to him. Weitel drew a knife, black handled with the silver Nazi eagle on it, and pointed the blade at Hannah. He brought it to the passport and used the blade point to poke at the corners. A small curl betrayed the hidden layer. He ripped it off and revealed the true passport—"Sara Hannah Goldschmidt" with the giant red J stamped on it. "You are stupid," Weitel said, holding up the photograph, one of the hundreds Hannah had taken of the three of them.

"Where are my parents?" Hannah asked.

"They have been relocated east—to a Jewish community," Weitel said.

He removed a folded piece of paper from the inside pocket of his leather coat and carefully unfolded it. A picture of a home with a large spacious green lawn and a Jewish family smiling stretched the cover of it. Hannah, however, would not believe her parents would willingly leave without telling her. But if they had been told Hannah had already gone, maybe they would have.

"Where?" Hannah asked.

"Time to board a train."

Fall of France

Wilhelm hoped he and Heinrich would be stationed together but, shortly after their month-long boot camp was over, Heinrich was sent to another unit to invade Denmark. Wilhelm hated boot camp, but it was made bearable entirely because of Heinrich. He could be counted on to listen to and crack a well-needed joke. While most men simply gave handshakes to those who were reassigned, Wilhelm and Heinrich's relationship ran much deeper. Neither was too proud to hug the other on their last day together.

"If you see Erich before I do, give him a good backhand to the nuts," Heinrich joked.

"I'll be hung for treason. He's an officer," Wilhelm replied.

"God help Germany," Heinrich said.

They fell silent, both too terrified to acknowledge out loud they may never see each other again.

"Take care of yourself. We will have some stories to tell when we get back," Heinrich said.

"You too," Wilhelm said.

The early spring months of 1940 brought Wilhelm nothing but inactivity. But Wilhelm hardly complained for, in war, inactivity was heaven. May came and added to the months since he had last seen Hannah, and even boot camp with Heinrich was now months removed. But it was a comfort to know Hannah had her parents and Lena to keep her company.

With each new day, Wilhelm and the German army moved west. Hitler would make his biggest statement of the war thus far. The German Wehrmacht, the people's army, which was much different than the SS, pushed into France, Belgium, Luxembourg, and the Netherlands. Wilhelm was behind the 7th Panzer division as it bypassed the famed Maginot Line, a line of concrete fortifications, obstacles, and weapon instillations built by the French a decade earlier to stop an invasion by Germany. Instead, they blitzed through the Ardennes Forest led by one of Germany's greatest generals—Erwin Rommel.

While the tanks and forces went around the Maginot Line, the Luftwaffe (air force) simply flew over it. The artillery fire blasts exploding on the ground and the whizzing airplanes overhead put Wilhelm in a temporary state of paralysis. Bits of grass and dirt blasted into the air from shell explosions. The German army followed their tanks and kept cover behind them, but the seemingly unending heavy machine gun firing from the French struck many down. It was hard to believe a man who had been alive less than a second ago no longer was—dead from a random errant bullet. Some missed so narrowly that men paused to check themselves only to be hit by a different bullet.

When the Luftwaffe planes powered forward with a loud buzz like a swarm of angry hornets, Wilhelm and the German infantrymen cheered, and the cheering did not stop when the bombs were dropped. It was odd to cheer for death. Each and every German knew what the silence and break in shooting meant—the men on the other side were dead. To the outsider, it was barbaric. The cheering rose to higher volumes in response to the silence, but the uninitiated to war had never been shot at.

There had been the same response to "what is the weather supposed to be like?" The answer was always, "cloudy with a high chance of metal rain." Wilhelm needed to march on a battlefield once to accept it as an incontrovertible absolute truth. The weather in France in May 1940 was pleasant, warm, and basked in sunlight. But the battlefields were always covered in smoky clouds from artillery fire, and the skies drenched the fields in metal rain in the form of bullets. The forecast never changed.

There were more close calls than Wilhelm could count. It all fell on a pause, a duck, a crouch, a charge, and a dive. Some called it God's protection, others, sheer dumb luck, and others, fate. But one thing was for certain—each man gained an appreciation for life. The nights brought euphoria to the survivors as well as great pride. They had pushed further into France in five days than what had been accomplished over a year during the Great War.

But each mile they advanced, the faces of the dead stared up from the cratered, blood-soaked, grassy fields with open, unseeing eyes—French soldiers with names, families, and lives Wilhelm would never know. The fallen were scavenged for food, water, and supplies. Their possessions were taken—a right granted long ago as the spoils of war. The tanks bulldozed through, the debris on the ground floated momentarily, photographs stripped from the pockets of the dead slowly twirled in the wind, held up by ghost-like hands of the fallen.

Lost & Found

Hannah's feet dragged along the ground, skipping when the front of her shoes dipped too far forward. Two hands held her from under her shoulders. Even with her jacket, their grip pinched her skin. She tried to squirm free, but the two men dragging her were strong as oxen. She was powerless to resist and saved her strength as the men hauled her to the train.

The train, with its long line of cattle cars, seemed to stretch for a mile. The cars were made of wood and coated with a red paint that had severely faded from years under a strong sun. Hannah's first thought was Noah and his ark—only it wasn't animals shepherded onto a ship, it was people, and the ark was a train, though the wood looked no different. And the most glaring difference was that it was not salvation the train brought, but damnation. The two men gave Hannah a hard-enough push for her to fall to the ground. She covered her face to lessen the impact. Her book bag was thrown at her. She picked up the bag and hurried to her feet. The crowd behind her swarmed, and she barely made it onto the train before she was trampled.

The inside of the cars had nothing but open space, space enough for fifty to stand, but space slowly disappeared as more and more piled in. Soon, the space was gone.

"There isn't enough room," Hannah yelled.

She was forced further and deeper into the corner. The car was stifling. It baked like an oven under the sunlight, and as more people piled on, it became a furnace. The light from the open door did not reach Hannah nor did the fresh air. Her breathing escalated. She tried peering around those stacked in front of her, but the man in front of her was a skyscraper. She had to use her elbows to keep him from continuing to back into her.

"Where are we going?" Hannah asked.

She got a response in five different languages—two she recognized and three she did not.

The train shrieked and jerked forward, causing people to bump into those in front of them, as the train powered ahead with a menacing thud. The man in front of Hannah inadvertently pinned her against the back corner. His coat covered her mouth and nose, pressing against them. No air filled her lungs. Her hands were pinned helplessly to her sides. She was suffocating, and there was nothing she could do. Her eyes bulged open so grotesquely that the elderly woman beside her noticed. She hit the man's arm and yelled at him in Polish. He turned to look at Hannah and then pushed the man ahead of him for more room. Hannah thanked her, panting as she gulped in the stagnant air. The older woman only smiled at her, no doubt, not understanding Hannah's German.

The train car had only one barred window that provided ventilation, but none of it made it to Hannah. The train continued to power forward as the sun fell. They traveled hours packed elbow-to-elbow. Hannah kept her eyes closed, taking calming breaths and trying to force herself to someplace else.

Strong stale urine wafted through the dead dormant air. A wooden bucket was passed around. The elderly woman beside Hannah took it and lifted her maroon, dirt-covered dress and placed the bucket underneath. Urine hit the pail. After she finished, she offered the pail to Hannah. She gagged as she took it. Feces floated inside and urine dripped off the sides. It was nearly full, and one bump would spill the contents all over her. But Hannah hadn't gone to the bathroom since leaving Petyr's—a time that felt like not hours ago, but days. Her thoughts gravitated to her father and mother like the pull of a giant magnet. She had called out their first and last names early on, but there was no reply. A part of Hannah hoped they were on the train and in a different car, and another part of her pleaded with God they were not. Urinating into a pail in front of what appeared to be over a hundred people was embarrassing and degrading, and it caused the tears in her eyes to thicken. She passed the bucket up, and the person beside the barred window had the unfortunate duty of pouring it out.

How many people had bought into the magazine's promise of relocation? The train was oddly quiet, and some showed no signs of panic. There were no four-bedroom homes with spacious lawns waiting for them. They couldn't even give them a seat on the train or a proper bathroom.

The man in front of her took small but sure steps forward, and Hannah did not miss the opportunity to get out of the corner. As the people ahead of her swayed forward with small steps, the barred window became visible. People, one at a time, pressed their faces against the bars, breathing in the fresh air. They took puffs of it like the final breath before plunging underwater and moved on.

The cold wind hit Hannah's face before it was even her turn. The man ahead of her threatened to take it all with giant gulps and nearly cried from the relief it brought. He finally moved, and Hannah rested her face against the cold bars. The train was loud and rhythmic. With her eyes closed, the air was the same it had been on cold winter days. It filled her lungs with a rejuvenating vapor. But she was only able to take five deep breaths before a push on her back sent her forward. By the time the line finished, Hannah was back in the corner, but she stood sideways to ensure she would not be pinned and nearly suffocate again. She rested her head against the wall, her eyes growing heavy. Sleep seemed impossible standing, but when her eyes opened next, sunlight was pouring in through the window. Her mouth was so dry that swallowing became a manual effort that almost required her to massage her throat. Her stomach gurgled. An invisible fist punched from the inside out.

The elderly woman beside Hannah rested her head against the wall of the car, and when a change of direction caused everyone inside to let out sighs of fright, the elderly woman did not stir. Hannah tried to wake her, softly at first and then more forcefully. But the woman did not wake. Hannah placed her hand on her forehead. The old woman was ice cold in the boiling hot car. Hannah whipped her hand away and gasped. "She's dead," Hannah said. But nobody appeared to pay any attention to her, and in a multi-lingual car, it seemed no one spoke German. Hannah couldn't take her eyes off the woman. If she hadn't intervened, it would have been Hannah ice cold with open, unseeing eyes. It was a sobering, awful thought—there was a dead person in the car, and no one cared.

But as the tall man in front of her swung his shoulder out of her eyeline, there were at least three more people face down on the ground. The elderly woman stared blankly at Hannah—their faces mere inches away. Hannah ran her hand softly across the woman's eyelids to shut them. Those around the elderly woman created as much room as they could, and they helped lower the body down to the urine-and-feces-filled car floor.

The heat inside sweltered and only worsened the smell of human waste and decay. People vomited onto the floor or unintentionally onto other people. From what Hannah could tell, she was one of the few, if not the only one, to have any possessions in the car. She had inquired for information from as many people around her as she could, but only one understood her.

"We were given a number tag to put on our luggage and one to keep so we can claim it when the train stops," the woman said.

The woman spoke German but had a strong accent, English by the sound of it. She brushed her light blonde hair away from her face, revealing eyes blue ice in color.

"What is your name?" Hannah asked.

"Eleanor. And you?"

"Hannah."

"Are you Jewish?" Eleanor asked.

To Hannah, it was both safe and obvious to answer truthfully. There was no point in hiding it anymore. Hannah nodded. Eleanor shimmied past the three people between her and Hannah. Knowing her words would not be understood, she smiled apologetically as she bumped past instead of speaking.

"Aren't you?" Hannah asked.

Eleanor shook her head. There were other undesirables to the Nazis than just Jews— Gypsies, homosexuals, and the disabled were among them. Perhaps Eleanor was one of them. But inside the boiling car, no one cared who was gay or straight, Slavic or Polish, man or woman.

"I guess you could say an honorary member," Eleanor said. She smiled, finding her words to be delightfully cheery. It took all of ten seconds to see Eleanor had an unbreakable spirit. A quiet strength and an aura of positive energy emitted from her like a small sun.

"What do you mean honorary member?" Hannah asked.

Eleanor struggled to remove her passport from her pocket. She wore a nice coat that was more English in style than Central European. Hannah did not expect to see the red J stamped on the passport, but when Eleanor showed her, the red J was ever present.

"Look closer," Eleanor said. The J was not as calligraphic as the J on Hannah's or that of any other Jew. And unlike the other Jews, Eleanor's hadn't been stamped but written. "Terrible representation of the J. His handwriting is poor. Even for me," Eleanor said. She recognized Hannah had no idea what it meant. "I am a primary school teacher."

"Why are you here?" Hannah asked.

"There were Jewish children in my class. The principal told us the Nazis would be coming to collect them and that we should have them ready for when they arrived," Eleanor said. It was obvious Eleanor had not done exactly that or she would not have been on the train with her. "I went back to my classroom, gathered the Jewish children, and left the school with them. I told their families to leave the city," Eleanor continued.

"You don't believe the magazines?" Hannah asked.

"Not at all. Any hopes that it was true vanquished when I stepped foot on this train," Eleanor said.

Hannah was an adult, but the child in her longed for an answer of comfort and hope, no matter how naïve it was, instead of the cold, hard truth. But Hannah had come to the same conclusion. Lena would not have intervened if there was truly a two-story house with a spacious green lawn awaiting her.

"Do you have family on board?" Eleanor asked.

"I do not know. I was taken at my parents' house. They were gone," Hannah answered.

Eleanor gave her a silent apology.

"Your accent. Where are you from?" Hannah asked.

"York," Eleanor said.

"England?" Hannah asked.

Eleanor nodded. Hannah had been right in her assumption.

"Do you know where they are taking us?" Hannah asked.

"I do not know. Maybe they keep us on the train until we all die."

It was a truly horrifying thought. Hannah couldn't fathom being the last living person on board surrounded by a hundred decaying corpses. Bullets would have been much more humane and easier for the Nazis. But Germany was fighting a war and bullets were not reusable.

"Starve us to death. I'm well over half-way there," Eleanor said.

Hannah had one chocolate bar left in her bag. Petyr had offered her several, as he was a chocolate connoisseur, but she had only taken the one. Oh, how she wished she had taken every last one! Hannah turned to face the corner of the train and dug her arm elbow deep into her mother's book bag, keeping the security latch intact, and pulled out the chocolate bar. It was not enough to share with everyone, but she could not in good conscious not share it with at least one other person. She peeled the aluminum wrapper and broke the bar in half and placed one half in Eleanor's hand. The bar was half-melted and coated their hands.

"Eat it before anyone sees," Hannah said.

The milk chocolate was creamy and satisfied her taste buds. The sugar surged into her blood, and the shaking of her hands subsided. Eleanor thanked Hannah before and after eating it. Hannah had appeased her hunger but had traded one evil for another. Her mouth was coated in a thick melt of chocolate, and she had not a drop of saliva to help wash it down.

The bucket made its way around again, as it did every hour or so unless a series of taps on the shoulders was passed along the car to signal the bucket was needed. Both Hannah and Eleanor had to use it though it hardly mattered, as the floor was covered with human waste. They made the rounds to the window, taking in the life-saving gulps of fresh air. But equally life-saving was the companionship Eleanor provided. Her words killed time and diverted Hannah's attention away from their dire situation.

Hannah discovered Eleanor was married to a man named Liam Cole who was still in the United Kingdom. He had urged Eleanor to leave when war was declared. But Eleanor wanted to finish the school year. She had actually been born in Germany, but her family had moved to York when she was twelve. Even though she was fluent in English and German, she had retained a German accent on her English and an English accent on her German. Hannah told her about her parents and Wilhelm, her secret marriage, and about Lena, the friend she had lost and the friend who had saved her life.

"At least the sun has set," Eleanor said.

The number of people piled in kept the car constantly hot, but it did cool with the crisp, chilly nighttime air. But something even better happened than a drop in temperature—tapping hit the roof. Hannah's first reaction to the tapping was gunfire. The taps came fast and furiously. But it wasn't bullets. It was rain.

The cattle car was anything but in pristine condition, and shady repairs had left the roof with more than a fair share of cracks and holes. In some places, the rain was only a teasing drop, but in others, it was salvation. People scrambled over each other to reach the ceiling. The drops hit their faces and trickled into their mouths. The waste bucket was emptied and raised to collect the water. The corner that had been a desert, that had almost killed Hannah, turned into an oasis. Water poured through a silver dollar-sized hole and into Hannah and Eleanor's mouths. The repairs of the ceiling caused the water to flow toward the back, and during the peak of the rainfall, it looked as though a faucet had been turned on.

After the rainfall ended, Hannah repositioned her book bag so it could be used as a headrest for both her and Eleanor. Again, seeming impossible, Hannah was able to sleep, albeit intermittently, usually no longer than ten minutes without waking up. Her feet were ungodly sore, and her shoulders were tight with knots. The rain had quenched her thirst but had also dampened her clothes. They stuck to her skin, causing a hellacious itching. Her legs were ready to cave. Hannah and Eleanor leaned against one another and had found the perfect position that prevented them from collapsing but one jerk or twitch and they would surely fall.

A giant shriek woke the entire cabin. The train was finally stopping.

When Your Number Is Up

The stain of battle washed away. Wilhelm cupped his hands over the water basin and splashed his face. The white towel he had was now blotched with blood and dirt—blood that belonged to comrades and strangers and, although washed away, would stain him permanently.

A pause in battle came about. The planes flying overhead did little to even entice his wonder or attention any more. They had used the tactic of tanks with air support to keep the French in a continual state of retreat. It was only during times of rest did Wilhelm realize how far Germany had gone and how far he had gone. It was the furthest away from home he had ever been.

"Can't say we don't get to see the world," a soldier said as he sat beside Wilhelm.

But Wilhelm's world was in a small apartment in Berlin.

"I'd like to see to it without being shot at," Wilhelm replied.

"Price of admission, pal," the soldier said, lighting a cigarette.

Wilhelm kept a journal where, every night, he recapped what had happened. There was not a single entry that did not contain Hannah's name. His optimism about the war ending early rose to the heights of the Luftwaffe. In only the first half of May, Germany was deep into France, and the word throughout the camps was, by the time June came, France would be out of the fight.

"How are we fairing in Belgium?" Wilhelm asked.

"Better than us," the soldier said. He smiled a shit-eating grin, the cigarette dangling precariously from the edge of his lips.

Germany advanced at a rate Wilhelm's father would be astounded at. Though Wilhelm did not care for battle, he could not deny the pride it brought him with each piece of French land they conquered. It was Verdun where the German army had been stifled. Had things gone differently and had the German leadership not "betrayed" Germany, as so many people saw it, perhaps this war would not have been necessary. The Great War, the war to end all wars, was doomed the moment Germany signed the armistice.

Every soldier in the German army had been raised in the ashes. The Americans had aided in the "Golden Years" of 1924–1929 by lending Germany huge sums of money, but the Stock Market Crash in 1929 sent America into a depression and destroyed Germany. Unemployment and poverty had reached unparalleled heights. Perhaps if there would have been better hospitals with more adequate medicines, his mother would not have died. The thought sent a rush of heat and color to his face but lasted only seconds. His mother's smiling face came to his mind and a steam of anger rose, collected, and formed tears. He kept his eyes closed for a few seconds until the tears disappeared.

"Name's Höring," the soldier said, extending his hand, after tossing his cigarette.

"Wilhelm," Wilhelm said and shook Höring's hand.

"My father would shit his pants if I told him we made it this far into France," Höring said.

"Mine too," Wilhelm said.

"I guess this makes us men or, at least, it should," Höring remarked.

"What city are you from?" Wilhelm asked, setting his pencil into the spine of his journal.

He had only been half-committed to the conversation but could tell Höring was in the mood to talk. Some men handled battle differently. Wilhelm found writing to be extremely cathartic and did not feel the need to discuss it. He was able to address what had happened in his journal in a way he was uncomfortable doing with other men. Each night was a great relief of conscience. Other men replayed the day in their heads as they puffed on a cigarette. Others, like Höring, had to carry a conversation so they would not be alone with their thoughts. But Wilhelm was hell-bent on not allowing the horrors of war to eat and pick away at his soul like it had his father and so many others.

"Frankfurt. You?" Höring asked. He was overly excited, surely proud of his home city, but more grateful for the question and the continued conversation.

"Schönfeld. But I was living in Berlin with my wife," Wilhelm said.

"You're lucky. You got to wrestle in the bedroom a few times before leaving for this shit hole. I'm hoping a fine French woman invites me in for a match," Höring said.

Höring sounded like Heinrich although Heinrich would not have to hope. The thought of his good friend put a smile on Wilhelm's face and a worried knot in his stomach. He tried to trick his mind into saying Heinrich was young, tall, and strong, which meant he would be safe. Yet, these things did not mean anything in battle like they once had hundreds of years earlier. There was no way of accurately predicting the chances of Heinrich being alive or dead. The men had a phrase—"When your number is up, your number is up." Simply put, it meant there was nothing you could do if it was your time.

"Tell you one thing, I'm volunteering first chance I get to go up in the air," Höring said. He ran his hand through his cinnamon brown hair and lit another cigarette—they could always be counted on to stifle a case of the shakes.

Every soldier had had that thought while on the battlefield because, as chunks of Earth exploded and steel rain fell, the planes soared high above. It seemed so safe so far up in the sky—unreachable by even artillery. But the humming sound they brought struck a paralyzing fear in those on the ground. Wilhelm referred to planes, both German and otherwise, as hawks and the ground troops as worms. When the hawks came shrieking with their talons stretched out, there was nothing the worms could do but wiggle.

"We keep this up, you may be able to see her before '41," Höring said, giving Wilhelm an encouraging nudge on the shoulder.

The tents and impromptu barracks just didn't seem enticing in comparison to the open French fields, mild temperature, and star-covered sky. Two other men sat beside Wilhelm and Höring. Their faces were obscured with dirt. They each took a gulp from their canteen and poured some of the water onto their faces.

"Ever been to France before?" one asked.

"No. But it seems to be a family tradition to fight here," the other one answered.

The chubbier of the two was Jonas. He had what Wilhelm would guess was dirty-blonde hair that currently was literally dirty. The other was Rudolph. He was rail thin and looked as though he could not afford to ration anything. It was remarkable he was even able to raise a gun to fire. At forty years old, he was older than most of the troops.

"Your father fought?" Höring asked.

"My father. His four brothers. Father was the only one to return to Germany. Left his legs in France," Rudolph answered.

"Let's hope we fare better," Jonas added.

"We Webers sacrifice for Germany. Between my uncles and my father's cousins, we sent twenty-four during the Great War. We have thirteen fighting right now, with the fourteenth soon to come of age," Rudolph said.

"You have a son?" Wilhelm asked.

"Seven. Each prepared to fight and die for Germany when their time comes," Rudolph replied.

"I'm fighting so that when I have children, they don't have to do the shit we're doing," Höring said.

Wilhelm could not agree more. If he had a son, there would never be a circumstance where he would wish war upon him. His father, for all his shortcomings, had felt that way too.

"You have seven children?" Jonas asked. His jaw dropped open, and he wore a look of incredulousness.

"No. I have seven sons. I have twelve children. Wife wants two more girls to make the house an even match," Rudolph said. He smiled. It wasn't a good look for him. His teeth were shark-like and uncommitted to aligning in any way.

Wilhelm went over the numbers. If Rudolph's wife was roughly the same age as Rudolph, she must have spent most of her adult life pregnant.

The camp was subject to non-stop noise, whether it was the nearly hundred conversations, the humming of generators, tanks rolling by or planes flying overhead. It was doubtful Wilhelm would be able to sleep.

"How could you afford twelve children?" Jonas asked.

It was a personal question but Jonas, although younger, was not worried if Rudolph took offense. It was hard to be intimidated by a man so thin.

"It was tough. You three must have been too young to really know what it was like. People were burning useless money. Living in alleyways. France, Great Britain, the Americans—they all blamed the war on us. We didn't shoot that Duke. One man did. They took our country and split it among the winners like hyenas tearing bits of flesh from a wounded prey. We're taking it back now," Rudolph said. He hit the butt of his Gewehr 41 rifle into the dirt to signify where they now sat. "This isn't France anymore. It's Germany. This is German soil now."

French or German, it was still only soil. Soil thousands had already died for.

"I personally do not feel like dying for dirt," Höring stated.

Wilhelm and Jonas smiled. Rudolph took slight offense. He was a member of the SS and a devout believer in all that they were doing.

"Glory is not free. It requires blood," Rudolph said.

"And dirt apparently," Höring joked.

Wilhelm tried to meet Höring's gaze and give him a warning look. Rudolph outranked them both, and Höring was playing on the line of disrespect. Even though Rudolph was little more than skin and bones, it was the insignia on his uniform that was to be feared. Rudolph's mouth opened.

"Incoming!" a voice yelled.

Wilhelm and the others arched their heads to the sky. Bombs showered the earth like meteors. The planes overhead were not German. They were French. The ground exploded with hellfire and sent bodies catapulting through the air. As Wilhelm and the others sprinted for cover, one exploded within twenty feet of them. The blast knocked them over. A high-pitch whistle shrieked in Wilhelm's head. Sounds were warped and distorted. The blasted-up earth fell back down like hail, and a large portion landed on Wilhelm's chest. He grabbed the clump of earth by the grass on it. He lifted it, but to his horror, it was not grass he held nor a clump of dirt—it was hair and a human head. Rudolph's dead eyes stared into Wilhelm's. He had been blasted in half. His torso was feet away and his legs, even further. His entrails were wrapped around Höring like a squid.

The sky lit up with what looked like fireworks as the Luftwaffe fired at the French air fleet. It was almost beautiful the way the gunfire lit up the sky, but the reality was much more terrifying. Planes that were shot down plummeted and crashed into the ground. Wilhelm's hearing slowly returned, and the lip-syncing of an officer formed audible words.

But Wilhelm could only stare at Rudolph. Moments earlier, he had been speaking about his family. Seconds later, he was dead—nothing but a pile of blasted-apart bits of flesh and bone. When the shock wore off, he threw Rudolph's head aside. He was disgusted at how carelessly and with such disregard he had treated Rudolph's body. Höring grabbed Wilhelm's arm and forced him to cover behind one of the trucks.

"The bombers have run their course! We are safe now!" an Oberscharführer shouted, but his words were drowned out by the buzzing and firing from the sky.

Wilhelm's eyes scanned the battlefield. It was not just Rudolph who had been killed. At least twenty-five had fallen, and as medics rushed past with the injured, it was obvious the final fatality total would be much higher. But Wilhelm could only think of the twelve children who were now fatherless and Rudolph's widowed wife.

"When your number's up, your number is up," Höring said.

Arbeit Macht Freit

The relief the screeching train brought quickly turned into worry. Exactly where had the train brought them? The unknown was terrifying. The door roared like a lion as it slid open. Blinding sunlight barged in through the door and struck the back corner of the train, and even with dozens of people ahead of her, it still caused Hannah to close her eyes.

"Out! Quickly!" a voice yelled, repeating the command like a mantra.

The train emptied, and Hannah and Eleanor were able to move toward the exit. People were pulled and dragged off the train. It was impossible not to notice the twenty who had died. Hannah and Eleanor were both cautious of where they stepped. The fresh air from outside was welcomed. The inside of the train had been nothing short of purely putrid. As Hannah stepped off, it was obvious her train car had not been an anomaly. It had been the status quo. Hundreds of people stepped off the cars.

"Form lines! Your places will be determined shortly. Men, one line! Women, another! Form lines!" an SS officer commanded in German.

Nearly eighty percent had no idea what was being said. The passengers searched for their family members or for someone who spoke their language and could explain what the

Germans were shouting. The Nazi guards, with German Shepherds, formed a line to bottleneck the passengers in one direction. Soldiers pushed the elderly and young children into lines. Infants were ripped from their mother's arms. Mothers were put into separate lines from fathers. Nazi workers marched through the lines, taking away the possessions of those who still had any.

Hannah clutched her book bag tightly and tried to hide it between her and Eleanor, but a woman guard snatched it from her and threw it toward a cascading pile by the train. Her camera, no doubt, had broken. The suitcases, knapsacks, and bags were tossed from the train cars. The numbered tags had indeed been a ploy. German Shepherds barked, daring people to run. The two lines were massive, and Hannah tried to determine what they meant. It appeared random in their selection but, like those taken during the searches, they were certainly not random. The Nazis did nothing randomly. There was a method and a formula with an answer yet to be seen.

"What is happening?" Hannah asked.

"I don't know," Eleanor answered.

Shouting from a dozen languages broke out. Family members tried to rejoin each other in different lines but were pushed back. Children either cried or were too young to know what was going on and played with one another. The two lines branched apart. One went left, and the other went right. Several officers were taking down what appeared to be registration numbers. The line again forked.

"Women to the right. Men to the left," another guard shouted.

Huge crates were overflowing with eyeglasses and another with rings, earrings, and jewelry. Women unwilling to part from their wedding rings had them yanked off. Hannah concealed her ring, but a hand seized her charm necklace and snapped the chain. When Hannah reached to reclaim it, her ring flashed, and the woman guard grabbed her wrist and wrenched the ring from her finger. Eleanor took one last look at her own ring. The two rings were tossed into the crate of thousands. The ring that had been in Hannah's family for generations was gone. Even if the guards told her she could reclaim it, it would take days to sort through the crate.

"Just a ring, Hannah. It can be replaced," Eleanor said.

Hannah was terrified and confused, but she knew Eleanor was the type of person she should surround herself with. She had a flame of encouragement, strength, and resolve, and Hannah clung to it like a moth to a flame.

An SS woman handed out rectangular pieces of paper with registration numbers on it. She wrote the next number and gave it to Hannah. The number "19653" was written in black ink. Hannah followed those ahead of her, everything happening too quickly to fully understand. A man with stone-cold hands grabbed her left arm and twisted it so hard that Hannah grimaced. He stabbed a single-needle device into her flesh and carved into her arm. Each poke was like a wasp sting as he tattooed in black ink the number "19653." Her blood turned black and the area around the skin, red. He finished the tattoo with a small black triangle underneath the number—it was to permanently mark Hannah as a Jew. She would never be able to hide it again. Her forearm throbbed and continued to redden and bleed.

The guards kept yelling for them to hurry and move. Hannah and Eleanor were pushed into another room. The women undressed and laid their clothes on tables. Both men and women, in striped pajamas, pulled the clothing over the women's heads to speed up the process. They were called Kapos (prison workers).

Hannah had found it extremely uncomfortable to go to the bathroom in a bucket in front of people, and this was even worse. But she realized every woman in the room was equally terrified and worried as she was. After stripping nude, the women sat on benches, and the Nazis or Kapos cut their hair to almost a shaved length. Women cried as their hair was cut and fell at their feet. A Kapos pushed Hannah on her shoulders, forcing her onto a wooden bench. The Kapos grabbed a handful of her hair and nearly yanked it out. The scissors were dull, and they sawed her hair more than they cut. It was superficial, but she loved her hair. It was a part of who she was and how others viewed her. Tears trickled down her face as her blonde hair fell. She lost a part of what made her a woman. She trembled from both fear and cold. She was yanked off the bench and pushed forward toward a large shower room. Hannah ran her fingers across her head to feel it. The length of hair that fell short of her shoulders and she had habitually run her fingers through was now gone. The showers were clouded in steam, and the water struck her body like shards of glass but switched to scalding and back to freezing without warning or middle ground. Eleanor was at the shower beside Hannah, and though she tried to exude strength, there was no way she too did not crumble inside.

All the women looked the same. No hairstyles to differentiate them or allow them to express themselves. More Kapos handed out striped pajamas, wooden clogs, and a headscarf. The Kapos did not care what size was needed, and women tried to trade with one another. Hannah's pajamas were a size too large and her clogs, a size too small.

Eleanor and Hannah found each other and embraced in a hug. They had known each other for mere hours, but the immense worry, fear, and radical change in their life had to be shared with someone. They followed those ahead of them outside. They were still wet, their clothes sticking to their bodies, and the hot sun had set. To Hannah and the other thousands, it seemed as though the sun had set forever and abandoned them to the darkness of the camp. The masses were escorted toward a series of long buildings that looked like barns.

"Welcome to Auschwitz," the guard said, opening the door and stepping aside.

As they were brought inside, it did little to change Hannah's opinion it was a barn. Rows of beds, three-rows high, stretched the length of the barn. The mattresses were stiff and torn and the pillows, flat. Hannah kept a look out for her mother amongst all the women, but her mother's long, dark hair had surely been cut. It was impossible to decipher who a woman was without seeing her face. Like the train car, there were far too many people for the allotted beds, and the building smelt much like the train had.

Hannah and Eleanor climbed onto the third bunk. People laid down head to feet. Also, like the train, going to the bathroom at night required going into a bucket. Sobs from almost everyone filled the barracks, and even though there were a hundred people inside them, Hannah had never been more alone in her entire life. She closed her eyes and pleaded with God that she was only stuck in a nightmare—a nightmare she would wake up from and find Wilhelm beside her and her parents at home. But every cough, every sneeze, and every whimper was amplified, and every person who rose from the bunks to use the bucket caused enough noise to break a light sleep. A woman grabbed the full bucket and moved outside to empty it. A loud bang caused the invisible hair on Hannah's body to rise. The door to the barracks opened, and a tall handsome man with black eyes, like eyes of a great white shark, walked in holding up a dead woman with one arm.

"I would like to remind you that no one is allowed outside the barracks after hours. Caught and you will be killed. No exceptions," he announced. His hand was covered in a black leather glove and wrapped around the back of the woman's neck. He released her, and her body dropped to the wooden floor.

The barracks was closed, and the room went black once again. The name Standartenführer Usinger was whispered about. It appeared it was an unwritten rule about the barracks—the last one to fill the bucket must empty it, but at the risk of being shot. The barracks had no windows or lights but, instead, had a row of skylights at the top of the roof. Hannah stared at the few stars she could see. "I am anywhere," she whispered to herself. She fixated her thoughts and her gaze on the few stars. Her gaze became so strong that she could no longer see the feet on either side of her face. Her breathing calmed down, and she powered her imagination to take her back to her apartment in Berlin. Her eyes closed, and she fell asleep not out of comfort, but sheer exhaustion.

After what seemed like only seconds, a whistle blew, and she woke. Those who had been in the camp rose from the bed quickly. Hannah and Eleanor followed them, making sure not to be the last to leave. They followed the masses to another stable-type facility, only this one was the latrine. Circular holes—two across, spaced diagonally—ran the width of the building, and each was occupied. There was no toilet paper or sink or even water basin to wash hands. The longer-tenured prisoners did not give a second thought to using the open toilets, and even those who had arrived the previous night had been desensitized to it. The room was thick with a pungent foul smell with little ventilation to help clear it out. Hannah squatted over the hole and suppressed the urge to gag and cry. But the oddest thing was people mimicking showering motions.

"What are they doing?" Hannah asked.

The question was to no one in particular.

"Try to clean … best … can," a woman answered.

It seemed ridiculous, even mad, but the human psyche was an odd thing. If literally dusting oneself off helped keep morale from dropping further, Hannah was in no position to criticize—only to learn.

"First day?" the woman asked.

"Yes," Hannah answered.

"Stay close … me. Speak … German. Have chance … to live," the woman said.

Hannah and Eleanor followed in her wake. The woman had a strong odor to her, and she was nothing but bones. Her eyes protruded out in an alien way, and she was one of the oldest in the camp at what Hannah assumed was in her fifties. The woman was fortunate her scarf and shaved head concealed her gray hair.

"I have been … for one year," the woman said.

Her German was rough, and her sentences were more like puzzle pieces than a full image but, still, Hannah and Eleanor were able to decipher what she was saying. Eleanor told the woman her and Hannah's names and then asked for hers. It was Kitty, and she led Hannah and Eleanor, amongst the hundreds, for morning breakfast.

"No lose bowl. Lose. No eat," Kitty said, waving her finger in warning.

The bowl was nothing but a silver cup with a handle. The workers ladled out of wooden barrels either imitation coffee or herbal tea into the bowls. Breakfast was a word that encapsulated many different foods from pastries, eggs, hash browns, pancakes, and waffles, but it did mean food. But no food was present.

"I thought you said breakfast," Eleanor said, peering into her bowl and at her coffee. The water was barely colored.

"This breakfast," Kitty said.

Hannah had never cared for coffee. But what was in her cup was far from it. It tasted as if just two drops of coffee were dropped from a pipet into her bowl and the rest, filled with water.

"You come to like," Kitty said.

Hannah's gag reflex pressed to its limits when she swallowed her first gulp. It certainly did not rival a French café drink, but it was wet. Her dry throat regained much-needed moisture.

A second gong rang out, and a frenzy swept over the prisoners. They scrambled into lines.

"Appell," Kitty said.

Appell meant roll call Hannah discovered, and she and Eleanor hurried behind Kitty as the lines formed into rows of ten. Hannah, Eleanor, Kitty, and the hundreds of others waited for an SS officer to march forward. But nobody came. It was impossible to know exactly how much time had passed, but Hannah had no doubt that it was over thirty minutes.

"What is happening?" Hannah asked.

Kitty silenced her with a long hush. Hannah peaked from the corners of her eyes. Everyone was as still as a statue. An hour passed without any sign of a Kapos or a guard. Hannah's neck and back stiffened, and her feet were two slabs of meat that had been beaten with a meat tenderizer. Her wooden clogs, at least a size too small, caused her toes to curl downward, and her toenails to break off. A second hour passed, and Hannah's shoulders had meat hooks stabbed into them, and her lower back was as stiff as a two-by-four. Was this what they had to do all day—stand in silence and in a statuelike stature?

With what felt like a forever later, the Kapos of the barracks finally emerged. He held a clipboard in his hand and read off numbers from it. Again, they appeared to be random and, again, Hannah did not fall prey to it. The numbers weren't random. They were the registration numbers that had been tattooed onto the prisoners' flesh.

"There is one missing," the Kapos said.

"Yes, Sir. She was killed last night," a woman near the front said.

"Why has she not been presented before me?" the Kapos asked.

Was a dead person truly expected to stand for appell? But two women hurried to the barracks and dragged the dead woman toward the lines. The two women hoisted her up, and the Kapos again disappeared. The dead woman was frail and the two who held her equally so, and they struggled to support the dead weight. Another half hour passed before Standartenführer Usinger stepped forward. The two women collapsed under the weight of the dead woman.

"May I remind you that silence is required. You are to stand in your place without movement. If this simple task cannot be completed, you shall be punished. Step forward," Standartenführer Usinger said.

The junior officer next to him opened a leather-bound book and handed it and a black fountain pen to Standartenführer Usinger. The pen, with its blade-like edge, nearly carved into the paper. The junior officer took the pen, and Usinger tore out two perforated punishment cards. "SS-Schütze Kranger, please escort these two women to the site of justice," Standartenführer Usinger instructed.

It was the title Erich had had the last Hannah saw him. Was he also at such a place?

The two women followed Kranger, and though Hannah wanted to see exactly where the "site of justice" was, she knew turning her head to follow them would bring her a punishment card of her own. Once the appell concluded, the prisoners were once again separated. They were sent to work in either factories, construction projects, coal mines or farms. Hannah and Eleanor held each other's hand in an effort to not get separated, but a guard pulled them apart and pushed Eleanor one way and Hannah, another. Hannah's group was predominantly men.

They marched past the electric fences and guard towers. Hannah once again found herself behind a tall man and was unable to tell if it was the same man who had nearly suffocated her. Three Nazis rode in an open top car alongside the workers. Two were riflemen with Maschinenpistole 38 guns in their hands, and the other wore the familiar insignia of Rottenführer. The march, although fast-paced, was peaceful. Hannah loved walks, and even though she had no feeling in her toes, when she closed her eyes, she could pretend she was someplace else. But the destination wasn't her parents' home or the Hausers or the Tiergarten, but a farmer's field with a wagon in the middle and what looked like a million stones in a desolate field.

The Rottenführer stepped down from the vehicle and surveyed the twenty-five workers who had been assigned to him. He took long strides past them, his arms resting against one another behind his back.

"You will notice we have no walls in this field. But they are there—invisible to the naked eye. The field is your space. One step over without my permission, and you will be punished. This field is riddled with stones. You will remove the stones and place them in that wagon. When the wagon is full, you will push it to the edge of the field and empty it. A secondary truck will come, and you will reload the stones onto the truck. There will be no breaks. You work until I tell you," the Rottenführer instructed.

The prisoners immediately started lifting stones and tossing them into the wagon. The work got repetitive shortly after the first two hours. Hannah's lower back ached from all the bending and standing. The sun beat down on her neck and arms, and she was in a no-win situation with her sleeves. If she left them down, her arms roasted in an oven of fabric. If she rolled them up, they seared and sizzled like meat on a charcoal grill. Her mouth and throat had been packed with sand, and her rumbling stomach was a seven on the Richter scale from the lack of water and food. She had been used to day fasts, but now that she had gone three days with nothing but half a chocolate bar and a bowl of imitation coffee, she was beyond starved. Her malnourished muscles made her weak and even the modest of stones to be thirty pounds heavier.

167

"How long do we work for?" Hannah asked the large man. She had kept close to him, as his tall frame blocked the relentless ball of fire that was the sun.

He shook his head in annoyance. He most likely had not understood a single word. He was tall, thick, and strong, and he looked like he could take the three guards on himself. But if his body felt anything like Hannah's, his strength was at twenty percent capacity. She had never been a big eater and often could eat once or twice a day and be satisfied. This man looked like he ate every one or two hours and, therefore, had missed not a handful of meals but nearly two dozen.

As the guards kept watch, she could not help but think they were lions and she and the workers, a field full of gazelles. They salivated, studying the herd, searching for weakness. Hannah came across a rock, roughly half the size she was, and the Rottenführer watched her with unblinking eyes with only one thought—had he found the weakling? If she moved from the rock, it would only solidify his answer. She crouched down beside the rock and tried to hoist it free. She failed. The lion licked its lips. The sun blinded her, and then it went black. The large man had created a micro-eclipse. He looked down at Hannah and crouched beside her. He dug his fingers around the base and heaved it free. They lifted it together and hurried toward the truck and dropped it onto the bed. Hannah thanked him, but the man only nodded and went back to work.

Hannah's neck was on fire. She no longer worried about sunburns, but legitimate burns. She had thrown what must have been the five hundredth rock into the wagon when the whistle finally blew.

"Prepare to march back to camp for lunch," the Rottenführer said.

The idea of lunch was alluring, but the long, three-kilometer trek back was not. Hannah's arms were beet-red, her hands, black from dirt, and her face, remarkably ghost white. She was light-headed and dripping with sweat. She tried to find Eleanor in the lines, but without walking up and down them, she would not be able to decipher one scarf-covered head from the next.

The worker slopped ladles full of soup into bowls. Hannah glanced down at her silver bowl. There appeared to be nothing in it but water, save for a small potato peel. Hannah had been one of the lucky ones. Many bowls did not contain any potato peels. But the soup, although hot on a hot summer day, did moisten her mouth that had turned into a desert.

She sat next to the tall man. The disappointment on his face formed a frown as he drank his soup.

"What is your name? I am Hannah," Hannah said.

It was tough to tell if he was more annoyed at his liquid lunch or the question.

"Rafel Trugnowski," he answered.

"Where are you from?" she asked slowly as if it would help.

He only stared at her. She tried using her hands, and the more she did, the more annoyed he looked. "I am from Poland," he said in German. Hannah's face contorted at his flawless German. "My mother was German. Father, Russian," he added as he smacked the bottom of his bowl to get every last drop into his mouth.

"If anyone has to use the toilet, now is the time," the Rottenführer announced. Bits of food shot out of his mouth as he yelled. His plate was nearly spilling over with cut potatoes, sausage, and fruit. He used his fork to scrape, puncture, and bring food to his already-full mouth. When he ate as much as he wanted, he set his plate on the ground and let a German Shepherd slop it up with its long tongue. At that moment, every Jew, Gypsy, homosexual, and other non-desirable wanted to be that dog.

Hannah followed the rush to the latrines, used it, and joined Trugnowski and the twenty-three others on the two-mile march back to the field.

"You don't speak much," Hannah said.

"Not when I have nothing to say," Trugnowski mumbled.

"Do you have a family?" Hannah asked.

He nodded. "I have not seen them since the day we arrived. My wife, Natalie, and my daughters, Aloysha and Naenia." For a second, the constant annoyance changed into hope. He gave her enough details for her to sketch a face in her mind, but it was a face Hannah did not know. She told him the truth that she had not seen them but promised to ask about the camp. He was silent for the rest of the march and the day in the field.

With the sun relentlessly attacking her neck, Hannah removed her scarf at the cost of the embarrassment her shaved head brought her and covered her neck. It took twenty people to push the wagon forward and empty it. The moment the rocks fell to the ground, a second truck drove up. It seemed too cruel a coincidence to be accidental. The Nazis wanted to break their spirit, and with every stone, it cracked and tore.

"Day is over. Begin the march back," the Rottenführer announced after blowing his whistle.

Hannah was sore nearly everywhere, but her shoulders, lower back, and her feet were in a three-way fight with no winners. She could barely lift her feet to walk the long, arduous march back to the camp. When they reached the camp, there was another whistle, signaling another appell. Hannah wanted to look for Eleanor but knew she must keep her eyes straight ahead or risk receiving a punishment card. She wanted nothing more than a shower, a full plate of food, and a comfortable bed, but all three were dreams of fallacy. It was 6:30 when they returned to camp and after 8 when the Kapos stepped out for appell. They waited another forty minutes for Standartenführer Usinger.

Afterward, Hannah joined the long line for the evening meal of a piece of bread and a slice of cheese. The sight was enough to nearly make Hannah cry with joy and relief. She stayed close to Trugnowski, feeling like an annoying fly. Trugnowski did not share the same jubilation for his ration. Though each and every one in the fields had worked beyond exhaustion, it had been Trugnowski who had lifted the heaviest of the stones.

"Hannah," a voice beckoned.

Hannah turned. Eleanor and Kitty approached. It was easy to tell by appearance alone they had been given a better job than her and Trugnowski.

"Where did you get assigned?" Hannah asked.

"Toilets," Eleanor said, unable to contain her smile. It was customary for Eleanor to find the best in situations, but she was overly accepting of a job that required her scraping out human waste from toilets. "There are no guards in there," Eleanor added.

"Just you?" Hannah asked.

"No, one other woman," Eleanor answered.

All four sat on the ground. Their throbbing feet could not support their weight a moment longer. Even the hard ground was welcomed. "Sister?" Trugnowski asked Hannah, nodding his head at Eleanor. Hannah shook her head.

One of the oddest things had been the camp orchestra playing music while the other prisoners worked. The musicians themselves were prisoners, and Hannah could not think of a better duty than to play music all day, but she could not deny it lifted her spirit to hear it.

Trugnowski gently checked the man beside him. He had not moved since he and the three women had sat down. His skin had gone hard and cold. "He is dead," he said. He searched the man's clothes and removed the slice of bread. "He will not need it," he said in defense of his scavenge. It was alarming and sad at how little reaction death received. The man was nothing but bones cloaked in what could have passed as bed sheets. He surely had died of malnutrition. But to Hannah and most of the prisoners, and to the Nazis, he was simply a man with a number tattooed on his arm—a cog in the German labor machine.

Eleanor was generally a gregarious person and had asked Trugnowski how long he had been in the camp and where he had come from. She was relentless, and Trugnowski found it to be less annoying to answer her and accept he now had two flies circling him. Trugnowski had actually fought for the Germans during the Great War, fighting alongside his maternal uncles. His paternal uncles had fought for the Russians. He had been fifteen at the time of his fighting and was no stranger to hellish conditions.

They continued to talk until a gong rang out to signal for the prisoners to return to their quarters. Hannah promised to ask about the barracks for his wife, Natalie, and his two daughters, Aloysha and Naenia. Trugnowski nodded his appreciation and joined the other men. Hannah, Kitty, and Eleanor followed the long line of people waiting to use the bathroom.

After using the latrine, they returned to the barracks moments before a second final gong rang out. Nighttime silence was in effect. Any noise would be treated with punishment. Hannah and Eleanor clambered onto the top-level bunks. Somehow, the mattress seemed comfortable.

It had been the hardest day of Hannah's life, not only physically but also emotionally. She had been stripped of her dignity—stripped of her humanity. She was covered in dirt and human waste and shrouded in a foul odor. Eleanor slid her hand into Hannah's and squeezed it. It was her inaudible way of saying the same feelings were going through her mind. Eleanor, once again, kept the ember of Hannah's spirit flickering.

Paris

May of 1940 could not have gone better for the Germans. Belgium had surrendered on 28 May. Over three hundred thousand French and English Allied troops had escaped the city of Dunkirk, but the Germans took Paris on 14 June.

For the first time, Wilhelm could enjoy the pause in battle not in some farmer's field or village but in one of the greatest cities in the world. He had read about and seen pictures showcasing the opulence and romanticism of Paris. The city had been under bombing earlier in the month, but Wilhelm was delighted to see that the Eiffel Tower, along with most of Paris, remained undamaged. After the city had been fully secured by the Germans, the French signed an armistice on 22 June.

The next day, the Führer visited and was photographed in front of the Eiffel Tower. It was the second time Wilhelm had seen the Führer in person. He and Höring waited patiently until the Führer had his photograph taken in front of the famed landmark. Wilhelm and Höring gave him the Nazi salute, and Hitler shook their hands. He had a strong gaze that fell on Wilhelm and pierced through him to an unknown distance.

"I remember you from the Reich Chancellery," a voice said.

Wilhelm had recognized the man but did not think Albert Speer, the Reich Chancellery's architect, would remember one of a hundred workers, especially one who had spent most of the workday eight meters up on a scaffold.

"Hello, Mr. Speer," Wilhelm greeted.

"You have done Germany proud," Speer said.

He then followed Hitler and sculptor Arno Breker, whom Hitler had named the "official state sculptor" in 1937.

Wilhelm and Höring waited for Hitler to leave, not daring to rush the Führer. After the Führer, the architect, and the sculptor left to tour the Parisian art museums and galas, Wilhelm and Höring stepped in front of the tower, and the army photographer took their picture. Wilhelm could not wait to show Hannah and his father. He had advanced further than his father and the German army had during the Great War. The Mighty France had fallen to its knees in a first-round knock-out. Massive celebrations raged for the next two nights. German soldiers visited every French café and bar, stuffing their faces full with every French delicacy they could find. Wilhelm had refused countless pleas by Höring to visit a French brothel, but Höring and Jonas both went. The smile Höring and Jonas returned with were the same Erich and Heinrich had had on Wilhelm's first night in Berlin—how were his two best friends?

The next week was like a vacation. They seemed to visit every café Paris had to offer, from the "Prendre le Gâteau," "Le Plat Blanc," "Givre Strudel," to "Le Bon Depart." He attended the nightclubs, both risqué and conservative. Though he enjoyed himself, there was something missing—Hannah. Wilhelm stayed in Paris for the next three weeks until he was sent north to the city of Cherbourg.

In an operation known as Sea Lion, Germany was to invade England. But the Royal Air Force met the Luftwaffe over the White Cliffs of Dover and England. The skies were ablaze with Armageddon in the form of spectacular dogfights. Germany bombed London nearly every night, and the Battle of Britain raged on and was fought entirely in the air. The air battles continued as raiders bombed the English cities of London, Southampton, Bristol, Cardiff, Liverpool, and Manchester. The British did their own bombing of Berlin.

Wilhelm and the Sixth Army in Cherbourg were joined by the Ninth and Sixteenth Armies. Operation Sea Lion had been hindered by tumultuous waves and storms that made a sea invasion impossible, and it was thwarted by the unexpected defense of England by so few, and Hitler abandoned his quest to invade England—temporarily, at least. In August of 1939, Germany and the Soviet Union had signed the Non-Aggression Pact. Belgium, Norway, and France had all been defeated. The United States had stayed out of the war, and its people were adamant they remain free of the pit of war and a European conflict.

Perhaps, the war was over. Germany had nearly doubled its territorial size and maybe the Führer would be satisfied with it. Germany had reclaimed the Sudetenland, the areas of Czechoslovakia that had been taken from them as a result of the Treaty of Versailles. The reclaiming had been a major goal of Hitler's. More importantly, they had mended their pride. They were no longer the wounded sheep. They were the alpha wolf who had chased the British and French across the English Channel, and the two nations who posed the greatest threat, the United States of America and the Soviet Union, were no longer threats. If the Americans had any plan to join the war, they most likely would have when France was invaded and the Battle of Britain waged over the Channel. The idea of returning home to Germany had taken hold of Wilhelm, Höring, and Jonas, and they could do little more than discuss what they would do when they returned.

"Maybe the war is over," Jonas said. His expression was one of hope, and even if Höring and Wilhelm had knowledge to offer on the contrary, neither would have had the heart to burst his bubble.

"The operation has only been postponed," a soldier said in passing.

Postponed—not canceled. The soldier was unknown, but in the three seconds he came into Wilhelm's life, he dashed his spirits in a measly six words.

"Shit," Höring muttered.

"So where are they sending us now?" Jonas called after the soldier.

The soldier simply shrugged. The bubble of hope that had encompassed Jonas' chubby cheeks, that Wilhelm and Höring did not have the heart to pop, had been shot down, bombed, and set on fire by the unknown soldier.

In mid-September, Italy invaded Egypt, and on 27 September, Germany signed the Tripartite Pact with Italy and Japan.

"They're going to send us to fucking Africa," Höring said.

"It will be winter soon. No better place to spend it than the Southern Mediterranean," Jonas said.

Even if he looked at Wilhelm and Höring as he spoke, the words were more of a self-soothing pep talk.

The idea of having an ally had seemed like a necessity at the war's outset. But nobody could have predicted the sheer dominance Germany had exuded so far, and they had done it almost single-handedly. The Soviet Union had aided in the conquering of Poland, but it had only sped up the process of a certain fate.

Wilhelm, Höring, and Jonas spent a week detailing the positives of a North-African tour. Wilhelm would have a chance to see the Great Pyramids, which Höring countered with seeing a great desert. But he made up for it by stating they most likely would travel through Italy and its historic, intrinsic cities of Rome, Florence, and Venice and the small country of Vatican City. Wilhelm had spent the first eighteen years of his life in the city of Schönfeld while in the last year, he had seen Paris, Cherbourg, and Brussels. But after all their planning and talks, the three stayed in Northern France, repairing damaged tanks, vehicles, and even aircraft. Wilhelm had been fascinated by automobiles, but as he worked on the Arado Ar 96, the Luftwaffe standard airplane, weighing over three thousand pounds, he could not believe it could defy gravity and soar through the air. He became annoying to the returning pilots because he would ask them everything from top speed, max altitude, to what the sensation of flying felt like. It was hardly the talk a returning pilot wanted to engage in and, often, they ignored him.

But there was one pilot, Aaron Rind, who was always willing to answer a question. He was in his mid-thirties, and his face would be stained with sweat and grease upon his landings. He was always polite, and if he was ever pressed for time, he would ask for a raincheck, but he always cashed it in. He had gone to university to study physics, and airplanes were little more than building blocks to him. Aaron would let Wilhelm take the pilot seat and point to the many controls and dials and explain what they did. Wilhelm found working on the airplanes to be therapeutic, much like his writing was. There were so many things with war that could not be answered—things that could not be fixed. But each time a plane landed, there was a series of checklists that needed to be completed and a solution to any problem found. There was always an answer.

"That is why I love math. There is no gray line. Nothing open to debate. There is only one right answer," Aaron said.

Wilhelm despised math but could not find any fault in his logic.

He still saw Höring and Jonas during the mornings and nights, but they had been assigned to fixing tanks, and while the two wanted to fill their free nights with booze and French women, Aaron wanted to disappear into a good book. Wilhelm found copies of the books Aaron read from the local library, which had a surprising number of German-translated books, and as they would check over Aaron's plane, they would discuss what they had read.

"Want to go for a ride?" Aaron asked.

It had been nearly a month of daily checks and conversations.

"Is that allowed?" Wilhelm asked.

"I will tell them I was running a diagnostics check," Aaron said.

He climbed up the ladder resting against the plane and took his seat. Wilhelm smiled, checked to make sure no officers were around, climbed up the ladder, and took the seat behind Aaron.

"Run through the checklist," Aaron said.

"Control surfaces, fuel tanks and oil, fuel contaminants, weights and balances, plane's exterior was full of nicks and dings," Wilhelm recited.

Aaron laughed. It was a part of their running gag. Each inspection called for an eye examination of the plane and to catalog any damages. It was war. No plane was unscathed.

"Now what?" Aaron asked.

"Push the fuel-mixture knob," Wilhelm answered.

"Partially?"

"No, fully."

"Right. To increase the revolutions per minute and generate thrust."

"The plane will want to move left," Wilhelm said.

"Very good. Adjust with the rudders," Aaron stated.

The rudders were the foot pedals. The rubbers of your boots go on the rudder or, as Wilhelm remembered it, "rubbers to rudders."

Aaron slowly advanced the throttle, and the plane jerked forward and sped faster than any one of Hans' automobiles. The airspeed indicator light flashed.

"Meaning?" Aaron asked.

"We have achieved the necessary speed for liftoff," Wilhelm said.

"Excellent. Do I push in on the yoke?" Aaron asked.

"Only if you want to eat dirt," Wilhelm answered.

"Beats our rations," Aaron joked.

He pulled back on the yoke and the plane rose, nose-first into the air. The force caused every one of Wilhelm's organs to press against his back. It was equally terrifying and exhilarating. The ground was far below, and the stars seemed to be within reach. Aaron steadied the plane. The turn and bank indicator leveled, and the vertical speed indicator returned to zero. He would no longer quiz Wilhelm to allow him to enjoy an awe-inspiring view. At that moment, Wilhelm was an eagle with a view that the likes of Napoleon, Julius Caesar, Da Vinci, and not even Jesus Christ had ever seen. It was hard to believe the world was at war. There were no troubles, no worries at 6100 meters above sea level.

Aaron talked about the valor of the British RAF (Royal Airforce) pilots and the level of respect he had for them and stated Germany had not accounted for such resolute resolve. Aaron stayed close to the French coast, not wanting to go too far across the Channel and provoke the aforementioned RAF pilots.

"This is unbelievable!" Wilhelm exclaimed.

"It is. I rarely get to enjoy it like this," Aaron said.

"I suppose it is a lot different when you are being shot at," Wilhelm said.

"It is. I have been lucky so far, but if my fortunes should change, there are worse ways to go."

The black sky was speckled with stars—clearer, more vibrant, and larger than Wilhelm had ever seen. Wilhelm decided that when he would return to Germany and to Hannah, he would get his pilot's license. Hannah was as much of a star aficionado as he was, but to experience the stars from this altitude was to glimpse into the universe.

The Arado Ar 96 had a max altitude of 7100 meters, but Aaron found it unnecessary to test the accuracy of that statistic and cruised at 6400 meters. Aaron brought the plane into a descent, and the sheer wonder of the flight warped into worry. Aaron explained everything he did and had told Wilhelm the landing was the scariest part. And it truly was.

"We are still okay," Aaron said, his voice calm.

The ground grew and sped by. There was a jerk and a bounce as the wheels touched down. Wilhelm had floored the gas pedals of many of Hans' cars, but the plane traveled over double the speed of any. The breaks pressed down, the wheels grabbed the runway, and the plane decelerated.

"You alright?" Aaron asked.

"More than alright," Wilhelm answered. The droopy smile on his face was half-formed from the force at which they had traveled.

As they rechecked the entire plane and refueled it, Aaron explained things in greater detail. Somethings could only be explained through experience. His excitement caused him to rattle off in such great detail that Wilhelm could not keep up. But Aaron would always find a way to simplify it. It was no surprise to Wilhelm that Aaron flirted with the idea of becoming a teacher after the war. Aaron had taken Wilhelm up three more times, but on the landing of the third flight, his superior screamed so loud that the plane practically shook from turbulence.

The war had taken a temporary hiatus for Wilhelm during those weeks. The French Resistance was more active in Paris and the larger cities. The blitz in Britain continued every night, and each night, there were a handful of pilots and planes that never returned. Some nights were worse than others, and Aaron would only wave and leave Wilhelm to refuel and check the oil and fluid levels. But Wilhelm wondered if Aaron had gotten severely reprimanded for his unauthorized flights.

"I am sorry for making you take me up," Wilhelm said after four days of near silence.

Aaron shook his head. "If they banned us from flying, every last one of us would break the rules. We're flying over London. What other mad men will they find?" he asked.

Some would have used the word courage. It was hard to decide which was the worst fate—being shot down over England or being shot down over the Channel.

"How many men have you killed?" Aaron asked.

He had been holding the same wrench in his hand for twenty minutes, inspecting it more than his own plane. The monster in his chest finally left and breathed in the Channel air.

"I don't know," Wilhelm said.

It was the truth. He had fired at soldiers in the distance, and a part of him wished he had missed every time. But deep down, he knew he had not. He did not need Aaron to calculate the probability for him.

"Me either. But you shoot bullets. I drop bombs," Aaron said.

It was all he said the rest of the inspection, but his words stuck with Wilhelm all that night. Perhaps it was a hidden blessing Wilhelm was not in the Luftwaffe. In the

Wehrmacht, he shot at men, still horrible, but Aaron dropped bombs that exploded, burned, and buried in rubble women and children. From the God-like view, Aaron could see the sheer destruction he created.

Wilhelm, Jonas, and Höring had secured a pass to go to Paris for Christmas Eve. Aaron had been invited but refused. He was not one for large crowds. The city on the surface seemed to accept German rule, but there were pockets of French Resistance doing all they could to drive them out.

But on that holy night, Wilhelm simply wanted to celebrate the day with his friends and forget about the war. It had been one day short of a year since he had last seen Hannah, and the thought would not leave his mind, no matter how hard Höring and Jonas tried to rekindle his mood. He wanted the war to end, now more than ever. Three hundred and sixty-five days was three hundred and sixty-five days too many. He was tempted to walk east and continue until he arrived in Berlin, some roughly thousand kilometers away. But perhaps Aaron would share a bit of the generous Christmas spirit and fly him there. The distance would take less than three hours. In three measly hours, Wilhelm could be in Berlin and in another twenty-five minutes, be at his front door. What a Christmas that would be!

"Wilhelm, the war will be over soon. We're just trying to get a better armistice from Great Britain," Jonas reassured.

"Yes, we're trying to fuck them like they fucked us," Höring said.

It was a noble attempt to brighten his mood. But no matter how many Christmas lights hung around Paris, his mood stayed dark and desolate.

"I hope you are right," Wilhelm said, then downed the rest of his beer.

Christmas Eve was also the first day of Hanukkah, and at that moment, the Goldschmidts were probably lighting the first candle of the Menorah. The homesickness did not subside even after Wilhelm returned to his busy days.

"Good thing you're not going up with me. You've got enough weight on your mind to crash us," Aaron remarked.

It was now Wilhelm who was silent during their pre-flight checks. His mind was in Berlin and on Hannah.

It was 29 December, and Germany was about to launch the largest bombing raid of the war on London.

"I miss Hannah. I miss my home," Wilhelm said.

"I hear you," Aaron said.

"All set," Wilhelm said.

"Shall I go end the war?" Aaron asked, flashing a half-hearted smile.

"Is Berlin on the way to London?" Wilhelm asked.

"I suppose we could sabotage the heading indicator," Aaron said.

As the pilots around them climbed up the ladder into their planes, Aaron paused.

"We're firebombing," Aaron said. He was unsure if he should or could tell Wilhelm, but he wanted him to know what that meant. It meant hell itself would fall on London.

"Next time we are granted leave, I'll fly you to Berlin. Introduce me to this Hannah. You talk so much about her I feel like I know her. I also think I may love her. I will have to steal her from you," Aaron joked. He extended his hand and Wilhelm shook it.

"See you later," Wilhelm said.

Aaron nodded, climbed the ladder, and took his seat. He closed the glass canopy and gave Wilhelm a final wave. The planes roared as they lifted into the air and crossed the Channel like a swarm of bees.

It was the last time Wilhelm ever saw Aaron.

"His tail was completely shot off. Went into a mad spin of black smoke before he crashed into the Channel. I looked for a parachute but didn't see any," a returning pilot said.

Wilhelm had grown close to Höring and Jonas, but Aaron was at a maturity level Wilhelm tried to reach—a man who wanted to live his life and fulfill his life with purpose. His father had told him to not get close to anyone, but it contradicted what being human meant. But Wilhelm had to admit, it would have been easier. He liked to think Aaron had survived the landing and swam to shore. He wished the pilot who had told him could have left out some of the details that deflated that hope. But Aaron's words came back to him...

"There are worse ways to go."

Kanada

In Greek mythology, Sisyphus had been condemned to an eternity of rolling a boulder uphill only to watch it roll back down, and he would have to push it back up again—over and over again. Nothing summed up Hannah's days in the field better. And with each passing day, her strength diminished exponentially. Of the original twenty-five workers, only eight remained.

The Rottenführer stared for nearly an hour. Hannah did her best to summon what hidden strength may have been dwelling inside her. But the spring was dry and had nothing to offer her. During the two-mile hike back to the camp, Hannah's body threatened to collapse. She would have been powerless to stop it. At times, her legs did give out, but Trugnowski's giant hand caught her by the elbow and kept her on her toes. During some of the return marches, his hand would never leave her. He was still almost mute but, for some unspoken reason, he helped her. But no matter how much Trugnowski covered for her, her lack of productivity had been noticed. As the group walked toward the gate, the Rottenführer put his leather glove-covered hand across Hannah, stopping her.

"Not you," the Rottenführer said, pushing Hannah toward another group of thirty.

There were both men and women, familiar faces and unknown, in the group, and they were either silent or speaking incessantly in a language Hannah did not understand.

"You will be taken to the showers," a guard said.

Hannah and those who understood German were beyond excited at the prospect of a shower. Hannah had not had one since she had first arrived—a day and month she could not remember. Her legs found a temporary strength at the prospect of hot water pelting them. Her skin was coated in dirt and desperately needed a good washing. It was doubtful she would be given shampoo or even soap, but just to watch the grime flow down the drain would be enough to lift her spirits.

Armed guards were on both sides, and they kept the group moving past the barracks and through the fence. Hannah and the prisoners were led to a building Hannah had never seen. It was nearly black with a brick chimney double the height of the building. The rumors in the camp whispered new arrivals were sent in the same direction—new arrivals who were never seen again. But there were hundreds of people who arrived at a time. Women with long hair and dressed in their own clothes. Hannah knew all too well how drastically different a woman looked after her head was shaven. But that rationale only explained the women. It did nothing to address the children. Children in slacks and dresses were still children, even in striped pajamas. There were hundreds of children who had arrived at Auschwitz—Hannah had seen them on her arrival—and their screams as they were pried from their mother's arms were unforgettable. She never saw the children again. Perhaps, they were boarded onto another train. Or, perhaps, something much worse had happened to them.

The temporary strength in her legs vanished. With each step, her heart beat faster until it nearly beat out of her chest. The chills on her arms and neck were like blades of grass on a windy day. Her hands were sweaty. Every ounce of her body told her to take flight. She needed to escape. But she was caught in the middle of an unsuspecting herd—like a water buffalo unaware the lion was close.

"Remove your clothes and place them on the hangers. Remember where you put them," a guard instructed.

Those who understood German undressed, and the non-German speaking prisoners followed shortly after. Maybe Hannah's nerves were poorly founded. She followed in removing her clothes and placed them on a hanger. But until the water from a showerhead poured out, the uneasiness would not leave. Why would they tell them to remember where they put their clothes? It was a rational thought. But a cold realization dawned on her. The Nazis were preventing panic. They had done the same with the luggage tags on the trains. That had been a ploy of deception. But the prisoners pushed her forward. She was naked in front of men, but that was the last thing on her mind. She stepped through an open door and into another room.

The walls were concrete and stained with smoke. A series of lights cast a yellow hue upon the walls. The room was empty but had a macabre invisible feeling that hung like a fog. There were no showerheads, but the ceiling had removable circular coverings, and the prisoners looked up toward them and waited for the water to fall. Even if they were going to be pelted with a fire hose, water was water.

But as the others waited for the water to fall, Hannah was fixated on the walls and the fingernail scratches on them. She breathed rapidly, but there was no air to fill her lungs. The door slammed shut, creating a terrifying echo and causing shivers to erupt on her arms. The hatch-like door locked, and the room groaned like a ghost. The other prisoners sensed the impending danger and rushed to the door, pushed against the walls, and tried to reach the removable ceiling covers. The room filled with a snake-like hiss that amplified off the walls. Hannah and the prisoners were rats who had been forced into its burrow, and the snake had coiled itself around them. There would be no escape.

The prisoners dashed away from the two canisters of Zyklon B, an early pesticide until its lethal effects had been tested on Russian prisoners of war. Hannah was the furthest away from the ceiling openings. People coughed and screamed. Hannah fell to her knees and covered her mouth with her hands. An invisible plastic bag pressed over her face. Her frantic inhales brought no salvation. As her body fought, her mind left the cold room. She was back at her parents' home with Wilhelm for Hanukkah. Her mother and father smiled at her as she lit the last candle of the Menorah. But the hissing noise stopped. It may have been minutes or only seconds, it was impossible to tell. The lock on the door cranked, and the door swung open. The guard yelled for them to leave. Hannah and the prisoners rushed through the door like a wave. They hurried to grab their clothes but, in their hysteria, no one could remember exactly where they had put them. Instead, they reached for the closest pair of clothes in an attempt to leave as quickly as possible.

Hannah grabbed a pair of pajamas, half-expecting the owner to yank them from her hand. But no one cared. She pulled the pajamas on and then her shirt. In the shuffle, the pajamas were now too short, barely covering her ankles, but the wooden clogs she ended up with fit perfectly.

The prisoners were ushered back outside. Men were atop the building that was Crematorium 1. Something had gone wrong with the canisters. The words "mechanical failure" were spoken amongst other words that, even though Hannah had spoken German her entire life, she had not heard until her late teenage years and words Heinrich routinely spoke after losing a round of cards.

"Do we bring them to the wall?" a guard asked.

The leader mulled the suggestion over. "No. Save the bullets. When it is fixed, we will bring them back."

Hannah had averted death, but only temporarily. She needed to find herself in a position of value again, or she would be killed. She did her best to hide it from Eleanor and assured her nothing had happened. But that night, not even complete exhaustion could bring her to sleep. She could have been dead. She should have been dead. As relieved as she was that she had escaped death, there was the awful reality that hundreds, if not thousands, hadn't been blessed with a similar fortune. Had God intervened? But how hubristic to believe that. But it had to be more than luck and a mechanical failure. But whatever it had been, she was not foolish enough to think it would happen again. She wouldn't last one more day in the field nor would the Rottenführer be pleased to see her. He had sent her to die, and if he saw her, he might rectify the fortunate mistake. Her moment came the following morning during appell.

"I need someone to aid in the cleaning of the toilets," Standartenführer Usinger said.

"I will do it," Hannah volunteered.

Hannah had never been one to speak in front of large numbers of people, but nothing short of her life depended on being reassigned.

"Very well," Standartenführer Usinger said. His lips puckered as if he were biting down on a lemon. Only a Jew would be so eager to clean shit.

Trugnowski nodded to Hannah and marched to the farm for more manual work. His once muscular frame was gone. His horse-like strength had faded.

The guards did not want to stand in such filth and breathe in such foulness, so Eleanor and Hannah had the bathroom to themselves. They were each equipped with a short spade, and they shoveled the feces from the hole and placed it into a bucket that was to be emptied elsewhere.

"Breathe through your mouth," Eleanor advised.

But the smell, although bad, was no different than any other smell at the camp. Hannah had not had a shower in only God knew how long. The pajamas she wore were covered in dirt and sweat, and now that it was January, the wind and cold went right through them and into her very bones. When the winds were exceptionally nasty, they threatened to freeze her bones to ice. The brutal wind was blocked and the inside was marginally warmer. But warmer was warmer, no matter how marginal.

"Will you teach me English?" Hannah asked.

"Yes," Eleanor replied in English.

Hannah had not abandoned hope of being able to leave the camp someday, but she knew there would be no place in Germany for her. She had thought about Paris or London, but New York City seemed to be the safest place for her. As far as she knew, the Americans were not at war, and the country was a land of opportunity and embraced those who were different.

The English language was not as poetic as French and entirely confusing. But Eleanor was a patient teacher, and it gave her something to do. She loved teaching, and Hannah could see that, and at times, it was frustrating how patient she was. She was entirely in her element when teaching. Hannah now understood when Wilhelm described the way she looked when she took photos or painted.

They started small with greetings. But as soon as she thought she understood the rules, the pronunciation, and the spelling, there was always an exception. Words like "read" and "read" that were spelled the same but pronounced entirely differently were beyond infuriating. There were dozens of them, and contractions were even worse. To help with her spelling, Eleanor had Hannah write words and sentences in the dirt, and it was a good thing it was not paper, for she made her fair share of mistakes. But the key to learning anything new is devoting time, and time was something she had plenty of.

For the first few months, it had been the nights that had been comforting and the days, hellish. But her days, although doing a job that months ago would have made her vomit, were filled with deep conversations and learning. Hannah was a student with a private teacher, and her lessons extended beyond English. It was so much more. There was no letter grade, certificates or diploma but the gift of a kindred spirit to share an immense crucible with.

Aiding in the reversal of day and night was the spread of Typhus fever. The barracks had become an infected and dangerous place. Each cough was a potential death sentence, and Hannah slept with her arm draped over her face. Even if she could not see them, the barracks was covered in a plague of poltergeists, looking for people to terrorize. During its worst night, the fever claimed twelve.

Each day brought new prisoners. They were separated left and right. Left meant life and right meant death. But the hundreds of new arrivals also brought with them thousands of possessions—possessions that were not returned to even those who were spared their lives. Each day, Hannah saw the new arrivals, and she and Eleanor had been around long enough to know who among them would be dead within the hour. Young children, mothers, and the elderly were a demographic the Nazis had no use for. The Jewish possessions and plunder were moved to a building known as Kanada.

The nights were freezing, and when a woman died, she was looted for bread and her pajamas, taken. The corpse drew out what little body heat one had, so the body was rolled onto the floor. In the mornings, it was a horror to see three or four women stiff as boards on the floor and as cold as the winter outside.

During a bitterly cold morning, on their way to the bathrooms, Hannah and Eleanor were stopped by one of the low-ranking guards.

"You are needed elsewhere," the guard said.

Hannah had heard similar words before—words that had brought her to the gas chambers. She wanted to run, but Eleanor looked at Hannah and squeezed her hand.

"It's okay, Hannah," she said.

But so many had thought the same. Hannah knew what waited for them. She would rather be shot than willingly walk back into that horrific chamber. She tried to pull her hand away, but Eleanor secured it.

"Trust me, Hannah," she said.

Hannah nodded, her eyes taking in Eleanor's certainty. Her faith was rewarded. The guard led them to Kanada. Eleanor smiled at Hannah, squeezing her hand once more.

"Sturmbannführer Waltz, I have two workers for you," the guard said.

Sturmbannführer Waltz was dressed in black and would have been handsome had it not been for the maniacal way his eyes caught the light. He was a man who prided himself on his appearance. His boots were polished, his face, cleanly-shaven, and his clothes, pressed. Yet, no matter how well his clothes were pressed and his face shaven, it did nothing to draw attention away from the scar that covered nearly half of his left-side. He inclined his head, and the guard left.

"What you are about to see cannot be shared with anyone. Now that you will see this, there is no leaving. The only way out is through the chimney," Waltz said, pointing to the smoke coming out of the gas chamber that was Crematorium 1.

Waltz opened the door of the wooden building. The women inside scurried about, sorting through mountains of shoes, coats, pants, and thousands of suitcases that stretched the length of the room and almost reached the massive ceiling.

"You will search through this. You will find women's coats. And you will find men's coats. You will find me fifty coats every day, or you will be punished. Do you understand?" Waltz instructed.

"Yes, we understand, Sir," Eleanor said.

Waltz was taken slightly aback at her German. He pointed to Hannah, "women's jackets" and then to Eleanor, "men's jackets."

The room was a moratorium of life—families forced to fill a lifetime of possessions into small suitcases. Massive piles of eyeglasses, rings, and watches as tall as Hannah were near the front. It was a great plunder of the treasure of the Knights Templar lore.

"You will be searched upon the ending of each shift. Pray we do not find anything on you," Waltz warned. He stared at them both, fully aware of how uncomfortable his disfigured face made them and left.

The place was nicknamed Kanada by some of the prisoners, as they believed Canada to be a country of wealth. The sight was enough to make Hannah's eyes water. When she first sorted through the cascading heaps of clothes, it was like sorting through trash, but after finding her first coat, the horror of it all avalanched upon her. Each shirt, coat, dress, pants, and pair of shoes belonged to someone. She was grave robbing, even if she had not dug up the grave.

"Look for food," Eleanor said. She spoke in English as to not be overheard by unwanted German ears or snitches in their midst.

Hannah's vocabulary had improved greatly, and some words stuck better than others. But "food" was a word that nearly caused her to drool like a dog waiting for a treat. No English word sounded more heavenly than food.

A frail woman, slightly older than Eleanor, came over to Hannah and Eleanor and pointed to a spot on the floor. "You speak English?" Hannah asked. The woman shrugged and both nodded and shook her head. She had simply ascertained food would be on their mind.

A pile of canned foods was hidden under a few coats and suitcases. Hannah took the knife the woman offered and stabbed it into a can of pineapple, sawing at it to open it enough for the juicy fruit inside to pour out. Before it was fully opened, Eleanor pushed the can to Hannah's lips for her to drink the watery syrup. Hannah took a gulp before giving the can to Eleanor and letting her have a drink. They dug their dirty fingers into the half-opened can and pulled out pieces of the circular slices. It revitalized their malnourished bodies the moment they bit down. It was the first genuine smile the two had in months, and after a diet of bread, imitation coffee or tea, the occasional slice of sausage and bowl of watery soup, the pineapple was so sweet that it tasted like pure sugarcane. It was tempting to eat the entire stockpile.

"We need to bring Trugnowski something," Hannah said.

"Nothing that will cause a search. We need to be careful," Eleanor cautioned.

Hannah nodded, and she and Eleanor sorted through the clothing. They intended on doing this job permanently for, with each new train arrival, there would be more and more food making its way into Kanada. They opened suitcases and piled their findings on the floor. Both Hannah and Eleanor were nervous to steal food, but when the other women grabbed food to bring back, they too looked for food that could be hidden. Six potatoes, still relatively fresh apart from a few spots of mold and grown sprouts, filled a new arrival's satchel she had brought along for the train ride.

It was less invasive and far easier sorting through food than a person's jacket. Hannah used the knife to cut the potato in half the long way, slicing off the mold and sprouts, and shoved the potato into her wooden clog, resting it against the side of her foot. Eleanor took the other half and did the same. As she finished adjusting her wooden clog, the door opened, and Sturmbannführer Waltz stepped in. He had a habit of walking with his hands behind his back and resting on his elbows to ensure none of the Jewish "filth" touched him.

"How many coats for you?" Waltz asked, standing over the two piles of coats, neatly folded.

"Sixty-two," Hannah answered. She had counted them five times. She knew if she was a single coat off, she would most likely be punished.

"And you?" Waltz asked.

"Sixty," Eleanor said.

"Above average," Waltz remarked, surveying the room, trying to find something displeasing. "Your shift is over."

Hannah, Eleanor, and the four other women stepped through the door. Two guards came forward and patted the women down. It was a more thorough search than any had hoped. Hannah had counted on her grimy pajamas, body odor, and the fact they were "diseased" with Judaism would lead to a simple eye search for protruding pockets. Hannah tried to calm her breathing, for she considered Waltz a dog who could and would sniff out fear. The guard roughly smacked her arms and legs before nodding at the Sturmbannführer. Waltz stared at the women before giving a nod of his own for them to leave. But walking naturally with a half of a potato in your shoe was difficult and required more of a shuffle than a walk.

When they moved through the food line and joined Trugnowski, he had already finished his bread and piece of sausage.

"I may be dead in the morning. I will not die with uneaten bread," Trugnowski said.

"Take out your bowl," Eleanor whispered in English.

Trugnowski had been forced to listen to Hannah's dinner lessons and had picked up some English due to sheer annoyance. He held out his bowl. Hannah kept a lookout for approaching guards while Eleanor slid the potato half from her clog and slipped it into Trugnowski's empty bowl. It seemed disgusting to eat an uncooked potato stored in a sweaty, dirty clog, but Trugnowski almost drooled enough to fill his bowl.

"How?" he asked.

"We worked in Kanada today," Hannah explained.

"Thank you," Trugnowski said.

189

"We will try to bring more if we are able," Eleanor added.

"Do not get caught because of me," Trugnowski said.

But Trugnowski needed it. Of those who had worked the field with Trugnowski and Hannah that first day, only the two of them were alive. He had a stubbornness about him that seemed would not allow him to die.

The gong struck, and the prisoners rose to their feet and rushed back to the bathrooms and then to their barracks.

"I'll bring you back a rock tomorrow," Trugnowski said, cracking a smile—his first since Hannah had known him.

Trugnowski left, and Hannah and Eleanor followed the mass of women.

"I have not seen Kitty," Hannah mentioned.

"Nor have I," Eleanor said.

They searched for her in the line for the bathrooms, but when they returned to the barracks, Kitty was already in bed, sweating profusely, yet shivering.

"Kitty, are you alright?" Eleanor asked.

"Don't touch her," Hannah said.

Eleanor paused with her hand hovering mere inches above Kitty's forehead.

"She is sick. The same as the others," Hannah said.

Typhus continued to run rampant in the camp, aided by the fact that nearly everyone had lice. Kitty's arms were covered in red blotches. She mumbled in her sleep, and her forehead was covered with sweat. Hannah and Eleanor slept nearly face-to-face. They wanted to keep as much distance between themselves and Kitty. But with so many people packed in like sardines in a can, it was impossible. There was no worse feeling than leaving a dying friend. But there was truly nothing they could do for Kitty. When the morning gong woke them, Kitty was not in bed. Her body was on the floor, nude, her pajamas and headscarf taken. Hannah and Eleanor paid their respects silently from afar—at least her suffering had ended.

They returned to Kanada each day, sneaking precious amounts of food into their mouths and hiding food in their clogs to keep giving Trugnowski lifesaving portions. After a few months, Kanada was no longer a building but an area. The Jewish possessions stretched the entire length and reached the top of the fence line that separated Kanada from the gas chambers. But it did not block the disturbingly clear view of children and mothers standing, waiting for the chamber. The mothers looked about nervously as their children played. Hannah wanted to yell out to them that they were waiting for their deaths, but if she had, she too would find herself back in the chamber.

Gas chamber usage increased greatly after the head of the SS, Heinrich Himmler, had seen them in action. The extermination of the Jewish race was the Final Solution to the problem and threat the Jews posed. Some mothers held newborn babies in their arms as they entered the gas chamber—a sight that was a sledgehammer to the heart. Trugnowski had been reassigned to work in the chambers where he lifted the corpses onto a cart and burned them. Their ashes were spread into the pond behind the crematorium. On windy days, the ashes fell like snow. Hannah would rather clean a million toilets than load one dead person, but Trugnowski did not have that choice.

The smiling children she saw moments ago were now cold corpses. Their deaths were neither instantaneous nor quiet. Their screams carried out of the building and over the fence line. The spring weather was warm with a bright sky, and it seemed impossible that something so macabre could occur under such a peaceful sky. But the screams were so loud that the Nazis worried the new arrivals would hear them and pandemonium would ensue. To counter this, the motor of a lorry, parked beside the building, was switched on to drown out the noise. During the times the motor ran, disturbingly more frequent, it was impossible to talk. But during the quiet moments, Hannah and Eleanor carried on conversations in both German and English.

They had also found a gap in the bottom of the fence, which they increased by digging away the dirt. They stashed food there and Trugnowski, on the other side of the fence, was able to grab the food and eat it throughout his shift. Sometimes, he would leave a rock for Hannah and Eleanor and each time they smiled.

Hannah and Eleanor worked in tandem, searching for men's jackets, and after ten were found, they switched to women's or vice versa. They kept their numbers within five of each other, knowing any greater discrepancy could lead one of them to the chambers. They ate four times during their shift, and when it was winter, they wore coats as they searched but always made sure to take them off by the time Waltz came by.

At first, Hannah lost track of the days, but now, she lost track of what month it was. Was it snow that fell or ashes? On another indistinguishable day, the motor of the lorry had run steadily, but it finally shut off.

"How come you never had children?" Hannah asked.

It had rained most of the day, and a permanent gloom had been hanging in the gray sky for days.

"We tried but were unable," Eleanor said.

The wound was still fresh and always would be. She would always want to be a mother.

"I'm sorry," Hannah apologized.

"Far less cruel than the fates that await those over the fence," Eleanor said.

The motor of the lorry rumbled again. More unfortunate souls were dying. When the motor shut off some fifteen minutes later, Eleanor resumed the conversation.

"And you and Wilhelm? Will you have children?" Eleanor asked.

"I hope so," Hannah answered.

Though she had not given much thought on it since arriving at Auschwitz, she had wanted children prior, and if she was able to leave someday, she would still want them. The conversation went quiet as they resumed searching and sorting men's and women's jackets and coats. They had finally reached some of the stockpiles buried beneath and behind hundreds of others. Between a blue suitcase and wedged between a dress and boots was another coat. It was nearly inside out, and the black fur-collared dress coat was caked in boot marks and cobwebs. Hannah brushed aside the boots gently, knowing the integrity of the pile could be compromised at any moment and bury her in an avalanche of suitcases, clothes, and shoes.

As the coat pulled free, the initials E and J with an overlapping G in gold thread became visible. Hannah's airways closed. She held the jacket close to her. The gold thread only verified a truth she had already known but did not want to accept. It was her mother's favorite coat. One she, no doubt, would have worn for relocation. The unknown had allowed her to think her parents had made it to England or New York City. The unknown had the ability to be either cruel or kind.

"Hannah?" Eleanor asked. She paused and stepped closer to her.

"It's my mother's coat," Hannah mumbled.

The words stabbed her like a knife through her still heart. Thoughts had always been almost harmless in comparison to words.

"I'm so sorry, Hannah," Eleanor said, rubbing Hannah's back.

"I hope they were sent right to the chambers. That they didn't have to wilt away to bone. I hope they didn't have to go through this," Hannah said. She slid down the pile and to the floor. Her mother's jacket was pressed against her face, soaking in her tears.

Eleanor knelt beside Hannah and squeezed her hand and wiped Hannah's tears. "You need to keep being strong, Hannah. There will be a time for grief—a time where you can let it wash over you and ponder why this happened. But that's for a later time. You need to concentrate on surviving," Eleanor said.

"We're never leaving here, Eleanor. The only way out is through the chimney. Remember? We've seen too much," Hannah said.

The outer layer of the coat had taken on the smell of mildew, dust, and the stench of Auschwitz—burned corpses. But the inside of the sleeves had retained the smell of her mother's perfume and of her home. She took whiffs of it like a drug, but the high it brought diminished with each sniff. Everything they gathered was sent back to Germany for use by its citizens. Hannah kept her mother's coat buried. She pushed on the piles to cause them to cascade. She would not let her mother's hand-designed and handmade coat be worn by the wife of some Nazi elitist.

"Don't lose hope, Hannah. It's the only thing we have," Eleanor said.

But hope had been lost. Her parents were dead. Wilhelm very well could be too. She wanted a life beyond Auschwitz, but she had always envisioned her parents being in that life. But it did not matter. Sturmbannführer Waltz would not let them leave. She would die here like so many others. She could not fathom an estimate toward the number of people she bore witness to going into the gas chambers. Those who had given up fighting for life, but wanted to die on their terms, stormed the electric fences to either be electrocuted or shot by the guards. Hannah was silent the rest of the shift, even with Eleanor's attempts to talk in both German and English.

During the line for food, Hannah skipped the soup. Her appetite somehow was gone. The watery soup would have done little to stifle it anyway. Trugnowski and Eleanor were in line together, and Eleanor no doubt told him what had happened. When Trugnowski sat beside her, she tossed her piece of bread to him.

"You are not eating?" he asked.

Hannah only shook her head.

The November winds were mercilessly cold and ripped through her tissue paper-like pajamas. She shivered, causing goosebumps to erupt on her flesh. Eleanor and Trugnowski spoke, but Hannah was too fixated on the guards in the watchtower to hear. It was an unequivocally better way to die than the gas chamber, starving to death, freezing to death, working to death or from a slow-forming disease. She was in tears as she trudged forward. She hyperventilated as she drew closer to either being shot or hit with thousands of volts of electricity. She had moved past every other prisoner. A few more steps and either a bullet or electrocution would come. A measly two more steps and her pain and suffering would end. But two hands wrapped around her and squeezed her like a vise.

"You are not a quitter," Trugnowski said, forcing Hannah away from the fence.

"Just let me go. Please," Hannah pleaded.

Trugnowski spun her around. The rain still fell, going on for nearly twenty-four hours straight, and the ground was a muddy slop. "You have lost your family. I have lost my family too. Your parents did not have the opportunity to fight, nor my wife and children. But we do. Each day we live, each day we do not give into those fucks and die, annoys them. They want us to lie down like a turtle on its back. But I am no fucking turtle. Neither are you," Trugnowski said.

Hannah's tears mixed with the falling rain, but Trugnowski knew they were there. He pressed her head against his chest and hugged her. Even when the first warning rang out, Trugnowski did not let her go. He was prepared to stay with her for as long as she needed. Hannah broke away and took Eleanor's offered hand and joined her back in the barracks.

All that night, Hannah awoke to sobs as the realization she was not in a nightmare dawned on her. Her mother in her favorite jacket kept coming to her and then her father beside her. Children were biased and considered their own parents to be the greatest in the world, but to Hannah, it was true. They were more than parents. They were her best friends, her role models, her closest confidants. They were the kindest people who kept to themselves but always greeted people with a warm welcome. Hannah could not stand to be awake. It hurt too much. During the deep abyss of sleep, her mind was idle and all her thoughts, washed clean. Each time she awoke, Eleanor was there to try and comfort her. Sometimes, it was a whisper telling Hannah to hold onto fond memories and keep them alive and other times, it was simply lying in silence with her.

Hannah's mood and morale did not improve over the next week or even the next month. She could not understand why Trugnowski continued to resist death. It was so welcoming. Why live in such conditions? Was it truly worth living another month? Hannah did not want to be there another winter. It truly was an absolute frozen hell. She used to find the cold air filling her lungs rejuvenating—a reminder she was alive. But now, it only reminded her that death crept and lurked behind every corner, pointing its finger at her. Forget the Nazis and their gas chambers—they were only death's instruments and did its bidding. Starvation, freezing, and sickness were the hounds of the beast.

But Auschwitz took away her sense of individualism. She was now a number. Hannah Elsa Goldschmidt was dead. 19653 was left in her place—a walking skeleton with protruding eyes, wearing baggy pajamas that made her look like a ghost. But as she reflected, she realized she truly was a ghost. She was caught between worlds—not belonging to this life anymore but, for some reason, unchosen to join the next. She had no possessions and nothing to separate her from any of the other haunted souls who wandered the courtyard.

Hannah had always held faith that this life was not it. There had to be more. But now that she knew for certain her parents were dead, she wanted to believe in heaven exponentially more. Yet, she truly feared she would never see them again. She started to join the groups that still actively prayed while the guards were not watching. She wanted to hear it. She wanted to hear from someone else that there was a kingdom in heaven and her parents were waiting for her.

The rain continued to fall, thunder struck, and when the skies cleared and the sun shined, it only made the view of the damned on their march to the chambers that much clearer.

"I can't watch this anymore," Eleanor said.

Every day, she was forced to watch children wait for their deaths—children who had yet to experience life. She had taught so many children and she, better than most, appreciated the wonder of a child.

"Don't look," Hannah said.

It was an immediate reaction of her, but she understood for some people, there was a magnetism that would not allow them to look away.

"I can't dig through piles of children's shoes and coats anymore," Eleanor said.

She had finally broken. She had been Hannah's rock since the train. If she broke now, there was nothing stopping Hannah from crashing over the waterfall. Of the near two thousand conversations the two had had, Eleanor's beliefs had only been brought up once—on the train ride where she had told Hannah she had been anointed an honorary Jew.

"What do you believe in?" Hannah asked.

It was certainly a private question, but Eleanor was her surrogate sister.

"Nothing," Eleanor answered.

The words were a truth she had accepted since she was a young teen. She wanted to believe, but the skeptic in her stopped her.

"There is a heaven, Eleanor. A place where we reunite with all we have lost. Whether it is above the stars or in your heart or your mind, it does not matter," Hannah said.

It must have had made it so much worse to be branded a Jew but not be granted the strong faith in God. Hannah had asked her often about her husband, Liam. Eleanor knew he would have signed up for the war the moment she stopped answering the telephone.

"I am glad he doesn't know where I am. There is nothing it could do but bring him pain," Eleanor said.

"Do you regret it? Saving those children?" Hannah asked.

"Not for a second. Those children are somewhere smiling, laughing, learning, living."

Eleanor had certainly lived longer than a child's age, but at thirty-four, she had hardly lived a full life.

The conversation ended abruptly because Sturmbannführer Waltz approached. Hannah, Eleanor, and the eight other women, a number needed to keep pace with the new inventory, stood dismissively. Hannah hated it. She was a beaten dog scared of her master.

"You are not maintaining the quota," Waltz said.

Yet, Hannah and Eleanor had. The only problem was the quota was almost always one more than the day before. If they found two hundred coats, he would require two hundred and one the following day. It was just another way the Nazis tried to make the Jews feel useless. But Hannah and Eleanor were wise to the Nazi game. There were days when they found a hundred coats, but the day before had been significantly less. To counter such a flux in numbers, they hid the coats, and the next day, they started with double-digit coats without any time expiring. It allowed more time to search for food. They dug five additional holes and filled them with food. During lucky searches, they found apples and oranges in the packs, purses, and bags of the fresh arrivals. But no matter what the food was, it saved Trugnowski's life.

"You add thousands of objects a week. Yet, we are still only ten. We need more, one to sort through for dresses and skirts, another for men's pants and trousers, and…" Eleanor began explaining, but Waltz cut her off.

"How many workers do you require?" Waltz asked.

"Twelve," Eleanor answered.

"Try again."

"Children."

"We have no use for children at this camp."

"They require less food than adults, and they have much more energy. We could double our numbers. They can easily reach the back piles and sort through them," Eleanor reasoned.

"We have no use for children at this camp," Waltz repeated.

Eleanor had tried the argument several times, and most of it was valid. But Waltz and the Nazis had no use for crying children or decrepit elderly. Each day, a period of which dozens upon dozens of children were killed, Eleanor too died bit by bit.

"You will get three adults. I expect the numbers to be reached or you'll be wafting through the chimney," Waltz said and then marched toward the door.

"Sturmbannführer," Hannah shouted. She had to nearly jog to keep up with his gazelle-like march. He paused. "Can you tell me how the war is going?" Hannah asked. She had not gotten a spec of information in months.

"Germany prevails much to your displeasure," Waltz answered.

"My husband fights for Germany," Hannah said.

"Jews are not allowed to serve in the military. We have no need for rats," Waltz said.

"He is not a Jew."

"You lie."

"What use of a lie would I have?"

"It is illegal for a non-Jew to marry one."

"We were married before the laws were passed."

She refused to give specifics in fear of Wilhelm getting killed. The Nuremberg Laws were passed in 1935, and it was obvious Waltz studied her to see if her age made sense. But what was there to study? Her hair was shaved, her skin sickly and pale and covered in dirt and draped in pajamas over a frail skeleton. It was hard deciphering one woman from the next.

Waltz nodded and continued on. Though Waltz was cold and had no problem watching innocent people step into the chambers, he was not the cruelest officer in the camp. He generally let Hannah and Eleanor work without interruption as long as they met their quota. But as the number of people working in Kanada grew so did the number of guards, for Waltz must have thought there was more of a likelihood to steal. But Trugnowski's life depended on it, and both Hannah and Eleanor were willing to accept the punishment if caught.

After finishing the work day and getting their supper, they walked away from the food line to eat.

"Stand watch," Hannah said.

Trugnowski towered over her and blocked her from view. She stood beside his bowl and lifted her pant leg out of her clog. Rice fell into the bowl. She and Eleanor had torn a small hole in the lining of their pocket and stuffed it with rice. The rice traveled down their leg and collected in the pants' leg tucked into the clog. He would have to wait until the next day when his hot coffee would be poured into his bowl to soften it up.

"Where will you go when you are free?" Trugnowski asked.

Hannah and Eleanor split one piece of bread and gave Trugnowski the other. They had made sure to eat near the end of their shift. They were by no means full or even satisfied, but Trugnowski needed it more.

"England," Eleanor said.

"Your husband ... is he a good man?" Trugnowski asked.

"A sweet man with a charming smile that sends chills down my arms," Eleanor gushed.

It was awful to think Wilhelm and Liam fought on opposite sides and could have fought against one another.

"I will get the fuck out of Europe. Australia. Swim with crocodiles," Trugnowski said.

The gong struck, and another day at Auschwitz ended. But those moments eating dinner were the best part of Hannah's day. Hannah had always been a firm believer in surrounding herself with strong and positive people, and she was grateful she had found Eleanor and Trugnowski. Eleanor had such a calm, soothing presence, and nothing baffled her or dampened her spirits. Trugnowski had an intimidating presence, but it was his resiliency she envied greatly.

Three days later, Hannah and Eleanor had quite the array of food for Trugnowski, including rice, bits of broken carrots, peas, and cut potatoes.

"Put your bowl on the ground," Hannah said.

"Save it," he said.

"You need to eat," Hannah said.

Trugnowski looked from Hannah to Eleanor.

"I will have no need for it," he said.

"What is happening?" Eleanor asked.

"There were a hundred young men unloaded today. Stronger than me. Younger than me," Trugnowski explained.

"Impossible. You are made of stone," Hannah said.

"I heard one of the guards. They do not know I speak German. I will not make it," Trugnowski said.

"Then we make a run for it. Together. We sneak out tonight and take our chances," Hannah said.

Trugnowski lifted his pant leg and removed his wooden clogs. His feet were swollen and a disturbing blend of purple, blue, and black.

"I cannot run," he said.

"You have to try," Hannah insisted.

"Even if I make it, they will punish those who remain," he said.

Those who had successfully left the camp did so knowing ten people were starved to death because of it.

"People will die anyway. Go," Hannah said.

"They will kill you and Eleanor. I cannot do that. I will not do that," Trugnowski maintained.

"We will go with you. We will help you walk until we find a train or a bus or something," Hannah said.

"You will only get killed. Hannah, thank you, but I have only come to say goodbye," Trugnowski said.

"You said you wouldn't stop fighting!" Hannah yelled.

"I will march with my head high, not bent," he said.

"Please. Don't. I can't lose you too," Hannah begged.

He lifted her chin and forced her to meet his eyes. "I would have died a long time ago if not for you."

"I would have died the first day in the field. You helped me. Why?" Hannah asked.

She had never asked. It was a dog-eat-dog world inside the camp where the moment someone perished, they were searched for food and their pajamas, taken. And at that time, Hannah had absolutely zero to offer him.

"You have quiet strength. Like my wife," Trugnowski said.

"We will think of something," Eleanor reassured.

"I have accepted this. You are a fine woman, Eleanor. Take care of each other," Trugnowski said. The gong was about to strike, and the masses would break for bathroom and barracks. "Keep fighting. When you can't fight anymore, fight again," Trugnowski said. He kissed Eleanor's forehead and squeezed her hand. She, like Hannah, had tears flowing from her eyes. Their dirty faces were washed clean where the tears fell.

"Goodbye, Hannah," Trugnowski said.

Hannah planned on taking his words "keep fighting" literally and was not going to stop in her attempt for him to embrace his own mantra. The gong rang out, and the masses scurried. She clung to the tips of his fingers, and he gave them a squeeze before breaking the grip. Taller than most, he was visible the entire way. He limped as he followed the other men, but the Rottenführer stopped him. Two guards had their guns raised. The man's lips moved, but the words he formed were indecipherable. Trugnowski nodded and followed the officer, the two guards aiming their guns at his back. Before they arrived at it, their destination was known to Hannah and Eleanor.

In between buildings ten and eleven was a connecting wall. In front of the connecting wall was another removable wall, constructed from logs and covered with black-painted cork. It was where prisoners were shot, and the black cork was there to protect the wall behind it. The gas chambers were a well-tuned death machine but were not cost-effective to kill one person or even a dozen. In those cases, they were either hanged or shot.

Hannah dashed after Trugnowski. With each step, her feet were greeted by a baseball-bat-like hit from the ground. Eleanor hurried to keep up, calling Hannah's name, but to Hannah, it was distant and faded. Hannah's other senses had been numbed to increase her vision. Her vision was crisp and clear and locked on Trugnowski. Hannah flirted with time. She may not make it back before the gong struck the final time. But she didn't care.

"Turn around," the Rottenführer commanded.

Trugnowski was at the wall. The hundreds of bullet holes in the cork were testament to what he would soon face. Hannah's body froze, rooted to the spot, in a further attempt for her vision to sharpen even more. She could no longer even feel the ground beneath her feet. Eleanor was beside her, squeezing her hand.

"Turn around," the Rottenführer repeated, his voice more forceful.

But Trugnowski would not turn to face the wall. He would stare into the eyes of the Rottenführer. Trugnowski took a deep breath and stood tall—his head held high as he looked up at the night sky.

"Fine," the Rottenführer said.

He fired off a shot that struck Trugnowski in the stomach. He was forced back into the wall. He used his hands to cover his wound. A second shot hit his chest, and a third proved to be fatal. He slid down the black wall, leaving a streak of crimson. His head slouched to the right, his eyes still open. Hannah's face was too filthy for her tears to travel down parts of her face. Her vision, which had been eagle-like in its sharpness, was now cloudy.

"We have to get back, Hannah," Eleanor said, sniffing back her runny nose caused from crying.

Now that Hannah's vision was compromised, her other senses came back to her. The permanent smell of roasting corpses, the howling wind, and a return of strength to her legs were among them, but none more than a sense of time. It had frozen when Trugnowski stood against the wall and, now, moved twice as fast to make up for it. They sprinted as the invisible clock struck down. They were mice amidst hawks they could not see. The gong rang as they stepped into the barracks. They searched for a vacant spot and had to lie sideways to fit.

"His pain is over," Eleanor consoled.

"And ours only grows."

"He wants us to fight. We would dishonor him if we did not."

201

The only two constant things in their life at Auschwitz had been each other and Trugnowski. Every other friend or acquaintance was gone, whether it was by gas chamber, starvation or disease. Breakfast the next morning was heartbreaking. Hannah kept waiting for Trugnowski's tall frame to march toward them. During their shift in Kanada, even the dug holes beneath the fence were cause for grief. Hannah and Eleanor were silent during their shift, and even Eleanor and her undefeated spirit and resolute flame flickered.

"I want double of yesterday's numbers. By this time tomorrow, this place will be triple in size," Sturmbannführer Waltz instructed.

Apart from the obvious that thousands of possessions would flood into Auschwitz and the thousands of possessions were brought by hundreds of new arrivals, there was a subliminal truth lurking in Waltz's words—the long-tenured prisoners no longer had a place at Auschwitz.

"Sturmbannführer Waltz, may I speak with you?" Eleanor asked.

"Make it quick," Waltz said.

Eleanor struggled to keep up with Waltz's march. Their conversation was either too far away or spoken too quietly for Hannah to hear. She continued to toss women's coats into one pile and men's into another. The other women working did not speak German nor English, and even if they had, it was unlikely Hannah would have spoken to them. She could not stand to get to know one more person only to see them die.

"What did you have to talk to him about?" Hannah asked.

Eleanor's conversation with Waltz lasted all of five minutes, a seemingly short conversation, but the longest between a Jew and a Nazi Hannah had witnessed.

"I wanted to know how many were arriving and offered ideas on how they could save time on our end," Eleanor said.

Hannah got the strange feeling Eleanor was not being entirely honest, but it most certainly was not a malicious lie. Hannah suspected Waltz had confirmed that tomorrow they would enter the gas chamber and not Kanada. Eleanor's worried or nervous look only amplified Hannah's own worry and nerves. Eleanor was silent as she worked, and Hannah was too troubled to mention it. They snacked on food more that day than any other.

"Eat more," Eleanor said.

Two guards watched over them while Waltz left for one of his meetings. But both were generally lazy and not very observant. It was easy to sneak a mouthful of food three or four times a shift, but Eleanor kept handing Hannah more food.

"What is going on?" Hannah asked.

She was caught in a conundrum. The truth was painful and scary, but so was the unknown.

"Do not react to what I am saying," Eleanor said in English. Hannah could only nod. "They are going to be sending hundreds of us to the chambers to make room for the new arrivals. But they are sending some to another camp. Waltz has agreed to it," Eleanor said.

"So we can die someplace else?" Hannah asked.

"We have to get off the train before it stops."

"How? The doors are locked. The only window, barred. Some of the cars do not even have that."

"Find one problem, find a solution. Small victories, Hannah."

Appell that night was a miniature eternity when the Rottenführer finally approached them. His meeting had been with the higher-ranking officers as well as the commander of the camp, Rudolf Höss.

"The Reich will be sending some of you, along with a few of the officers, to Belzec. There is more work needed there. You will assist the officers as needed on their journey. When your number is called, step forward," the Rottenführer announced.

The air was thick with hope. Everyone prayed silently for their number to be called. No one knew how many numbers would be called, but after each number was read, the hope faded. They were literally lottery-type odds of having your number called. Each time a number was read, someone was ecstatic, and each time, there was a person a digit or two away who was devastated.

"…19653…" the Rottenführer read.

The number was tattooed on Hannah's flesh and mind, but she stared at her forearm nonetheless. Hannah wanted to turn her head to look at Eleanor but had learned to stifle that desire. But Eleanor, no doubt, wore a smile.

The Rottenführer lowered his clipboard. He had no more numbers to read off. "Follow Sturmbannführer Waltz to the train," the Rottenführer commanded.

Hannah not only had her number memorized but Eleanor's too. It had not been read. Hannah turned her head, ignoring the dangerous ramifications of breaking appell policy.

Eleanor's eyes were glazed with tears.

"Eleanor?" Hannah asked.

"Go, Hannah," Eleanor said.

Those who had had their numbers read hurried after Waltz. The train would not wait for them.

"Why?" Hannah asked. It was the only word that she could form.

"I could only get you. Go, Hannah. I'll be fine," Eleanor said.

Hannah risked missing the train, and the jealous spiteful eyes of those around her were anything but subtle.

"Live, Hannah," Eleanor said in English.

Hannah's body was going to tear itself apart. Her heart wanted to stay. Auschwitz had been a visceral hell—the likes of which Hannah could never have expected. She had had her reservations of what the destination of the train was—so many had believed the great lie of a Jewish resettlement. But Hannah had only survived because of her deep-rooted friendship with Trugnowski and Eleanor. Hannah knew what staying meant. It meant, the next day, Eleanor would be sent to the gas chambers, and for that reason, her body tried to pull her away. Her soul was caught somewhere between the struggle. It tried to mediate and consider both options. Could she live with such a selfish action as abandoning a true friend? A part of her wished the choice would be removed from her hands—that Waltz either dragged her to the train or shot her where she stood. She considered what the new camp would be like. The devil she knew was better than the one she didn't. And there would be no Eleanor there—just a dark unknown she would have to face alone. But her thoughts went to Wilhelm. Perhaps, there was a future for the two of them. Fifty years from now, she would look back at this moment as the opportunity where she reclaimed her life. With that, her heart let go of the rope and walked over and joined her body and mind.

"I'll never forget you," Hannah said.

Eleanor smiled. Somehow, she had stayed positive, stayed kind, stayed human in a place designed to strip all remnants of humanity. She had saved Hannah's life. She hadn't stopped a bullet from striking her or rescued her from a burning building, but she had saved the small fragment of life Hannah clung to—the ember that barely flickered in the torrential downpour. She had breathed life into it.

Hannah stared into Eleanor's kind blue eyes before she finally turned and hurried after Sturmbannführer Waltz. She tried to keep her eyes forward, but with each step she took, the desire to see Eleanor one final time grew. She turned. Like with Trugnowski, her other senses dulled to allow her vision to sharpen so she could see Eleanor's face one last time. The sign reading "Arbeit Macht Freit" loomed over her head. She joined the other fifteen toward the train tracks. In English, the sign read "Work Shall Set You Free"—another lie of the Reich.

The train waited for them like a black stallion of iron and metal. It was much sleeker and meaner than the cattle cars Hannah had ridden into Auschwitz on. But it did have one cattle car. The Nazis were certain not to let such foul creatures as Jews ride along with them. Hannah stepped aboard the cattle car. The door slammed shut and then locked. As the train shrieked and powered ahead, Hannah pressed her nose against the cattle car and looked through a small crack for her last image of the place she had spent the last number of unknown months—a place that, in a weird morbid way, had been her home. Auschwitz was the devil's vacation home—a home away from hell. She cried for what felt like hours until she could not cry anymore.

She thought of her mother's coat she had left behind. It was all that remained of her existence and, soon, even that would be gone. When she closed her eyes, the train's shrieking morphed into the cries of those who had died inside the gas chambers, demanding justice and remembrance.

She had no idea how long they had traveled. Hannah stood beside the barred window, glancing outside. The bars of it were on the inside and were burnt orange with rust. The cold air that blew into her lungs powered her once more. It was life blowing in between the horizontal bars. With each breath she took, she became drunk on the notion of escaping. She would not die like a sheep sent to its slaughter. Trugnowski had willed her to fight, and Eleanor had allowed her to do that by getting her a spot on the train. It would be a dishonor to allow herself to be taken prisoner at another camp.

"Find one problem, solve one problem," Eleanor had said.

Hannah pulled on the bars, bits of rust came floating down as she did. She removed her headscarf and wrapped it around the bar and tugged on it. The other women aboard knew what she was trying to do, and they had the same feelings of hopeful emancipation as Hannah. One pointed to the wet floor and motioned wringing out the scarf. Hannah nodded and dipped the headscarf into the urine-and-feces-filled bucket and wrapped it around the bars and pulled. More rust came floating like snow as the bar moved but a quarter of an inch. She removed the scarf and, together, she and the other women pushed up on the bar to try and move it back into place. They repeated the process over five hundred times before they exhausted their final strength. But finally, the bottom bar snapped off at the connecting points to the window.

The train traveled too fast to jump, but Hannah waited for any signs of deceleration. But the others were not as patient, and instead, dove headfirst out of the train, not caring where the train was or how fast it was traveling. They had chosen death their way. But Hannah was no longer looking to decide her death. She looked to embrace her moment to reclaim her life. Only three had yet to jump, Hannah included, but at the first sign of the train slowing down, the two women squeezed through one after another in quick succession.

Hannah was alone, and timing would be imperative. If she jumped too soon, she could be killed or injured, and if she jumped too late, she could be captured. But if any guard had been looking out of the window, they may have been able to see the women leaping from the train.

The train shrieked and decelerated. Hannah's insides lurched forward, and she nearly lost her balance as the train rounded a bend. Outside the window, there was nothing but blackness and silhouettes of trees. She took a deep breath and flung herself through the window.

The Battle of Stalingrad

Any hopes of the war ending within the first year vanquished when Germany launched Operation Barbarossa—the planned invasion of the Soviet Union. While many of the soldiers cheered upon hearing the news of the betrayal of the non-aggression pact, Wilhelm knew his path would take him east and keep him from returning home to Hannah. Jonas tried defending the action by saying it was all part of Lebensraum or "living space"—the belief that the land occupied in the western parts of the Soviet Union was needed for the advancement and growth of the German race.

Wilhelm wanted the war to be over. Germany had had a score to settle with France and Britain, but Russia had been knocked out of the fight early during the Great War and had signed a non-aggression pact at the outset of this war. Why seek a war with them?

Wilhelm traveled from the coastline of Northwest France through Southern Germany and across Austria, Hungary, and into the Ukraine. The Germans raced toward the Dnieper River that divided the Ukrainian country in two. The fighting had been much like it had been in France, and Germany covered large amounts of land quickly. The fields were on fire and crops burned to ash. The buildings were destroyed too, leaving nothing but rubble where they once stood.

"Who did this?" Jonas asked.

Wilhelm, Jonas, and Höring were a part of the tip of the spear—no other Axis forces had rolled through.

"They did. So we cannot use any of it," Höring said.

Hundreds of acres of crops burned to ash—crops thousands depended on for survival. The Soviets had embraced a military tactic called Scorched Earth. But even though the fields were burned and the wooden buildings had crumbled to giant bonfires, there were still people left behind who were now homeless—women and children who had nothing to do but stand and watch in fear as the German army, with its beast tanks, roared and marched past.

It was late June 1941, and Wilhelm had hoped to spend his summer at Lena's cottage in Northern Germany, not on a battlefield in the Western Ukraine. Although there were casualties, the battle on the eastern front had yet to show the strength of numbers the Soviets possessed. Day after day, the German army rolled further into the Soviet Union. Perhaps, the war would not be as extended as initially feared.

"A greater German Reich, boys," Jonas said. He had preached in annoying detail how much the German people had benefited from the war. Germany was now in control of all Western Europe, save for Spain and Portugal. "Franco is a supporter of ours," Jonas said when asked why there was no planned invasion of Spain.

General Francisco Franco Bahamonde was the military dictator of Spain. If he did choose to enter the war, it would be to join the Axis powers. Almost all of Northern Africa was under German rule. The Desert Fox, a moniker given to German General Erwin Rommel, had led victory after victory. But each country conquered meant they were now subject to the Nazi's racial laws. It was unlikely Wilhelm and Hannah would be able to live in any of them, except the Lebensraum.

Each night, Wilhelm stared up at the stars and watched everything around him fade away. He took a deep breath and, for a moment, believed Hannah was beside him, staring up at the same awe-inspiring view. But there was always distant artillery and gunfire to snap the mirage and bring him back to Ukraine and the war.

By late August 1941, Wilhelm and the Germans had made it to the Dnieper River and the city of Kiev situated on both sides of it. It was the largest battle Wilhelm had been a part of. Shells and artillery exploded everywhere. Tanks launched a storm of shells that rained down like hail, and blasts ripped through the sky like meteors. The Germans had brought the 1st and 2nd Panzer Armies and the 2nd, 6th, and 17th Infantry Armies. It seemed a million men were fighting for the Soviet Union with a thousand tanks. But the Germans had the air superiority outright.

By 1 September, the Northern German forces had pushed the Soviets south. Wilhelm and the Sixth Army were to push into the city of Kiev. Kiev was the heart, brain, and throat of Ukraine, but to get to those vital organs, Germany had to go through its fists and fangs first.

Wilhelm's nerves scurried through his veins like a scared animal looking for an escape. He hated the anticipation of the first bullet. It always scared the hell out of him and momentarily paralyzed him. But it was not a single bullet ripping through the air but a million. German soldiers were struck down. Bits of flesh and blood blasted into the air. Mortar rounds exploded. The Germans returned fire. Wilhelm had been separated from Höring and Jonas as they sprinted for cover behind a building. Clouds of concrete dust covered them as buildings were blasted apart by artillery. Any soldier daring enough to peak their head around the corner was met with a bullet. Wilhelm unloaded his Gewehr 41 at brave Soviets charging forward.

"Move!" an officer yelled.

Wilhelm and the others sprinted from behind their cover and dashed forward. Pieces of rock and dirt flew as shots fired by snipers on rooftops narrowly missed them. Two men fell dead beside Wilhelm before the shooter on the roof was struck with a bullet. His body slid off and splattered on the ground. German planes flew overhead, riddling the ground with bullets. German Wehrmacht soldiers used flamethrowers to engulf both buildings and soldiers in flame. Wilhelm stood with his back pressed against one of the buildings. The stone vibrated from the tremendous explosions. At least a dozen soldiers did the same, waiting for a moment to advance further.

The roof and top floors were decimated when a German plane, smoking and leaving a trail of black, crashed into it. The impact knocked Wilhelm and the other Germans to the ground. The pebbles and rocks cut into his hands as he pressed himself to his knees. The man next to him rose to his feet, but a massive chunk of the roof and wall crushed him and splattered blood onto Wilhelm's face and chest.

"It's coming down!" a soldier yelled. He pulled Wilhelm to his feet and dashed out of the cover the building had provided. A bullet dinged and knocked the soldier's helmet off, and before he could reclaim it or even react, a second bullet ripped in and pierced through his forehead. He dropped face-first, and Wilhelm tripped over his body. It was a moment of luck because bullets whistled past where he had stood. He ran on hands and feet as the building collapsed.

Panzer tanks barreled through the rubble, and the machine gunners laid waste to any Soviet soldiers within sight. Wilhelm's nerves caused his hands to shake, and he took deep breaths to try to counter it. Even if the enemy was less than two meters away, his hands shook too much to guarantee his aim would be accurate enough to take him down.

The fighting was fierce, but Germany continued its dominance and created a wall that encircled the 37th, 5th, 21st, 40th, 38th, and 26th armies of the Soviet Union and divided and conquered them. After nearly a month of fighting, the city of Kiev was taken by the Germans, and a week later, the remaining Soviet armies surrendered. Over 600,000 Soviet soldiers marched out of the city in surrender.

"Well, Wilhelm. What is your verdict? Does burned fields and concrete rubble beat Rome in historical beauty?" Höring asked as the captured soldiers left the battlefield.

"We still could be on our way," Wilhelm said.

"War will be over soon," Jonas stated a bit too confidently.

It was easy to think the Soviets were like ants fleeing an anthill. Did the Soviet Union have enough men to replace the over half-million who were now prisoners of the German army? The Soviet Union had been dealt a serious blow, and it was easy to fall for such optimism. But each time Wilhelm had fallen for it, his hopes were crushed.

The Sixth Army continued east and, a month later, fought the Soviets in the Battle of Kharkov and again in the spring of 1942. But like the British, the Soviets had a resolve of steel. The nights and days following battles were filled with reflective silence. Bodies had to be collected, and every able man was required to do so.

Wilhelm retreated to his journal and wrote about the sights and sounds of hell—things that never needed to be said aloud.

"There's no method or reasoning behind it," Höring said when Wilhelm closed his journal. He had gotten better at understanding when Wilhelm was writing to let him finish before he spoke.

"Behind what?" Wilhelm asked.

"Who lives ... who dies ... it's just dumb luck," Höring said.

During by-gone days, a soldier could alter his odds and even the war by improving his swordsmanship. But in this hell, everyone was meat for the grinder. It was putting your life in the hands of fate. Fate was like the old emperors of Rome—either pointing their thumb up or down to decide the fate of the gladiators in the arena.

"Just keep doing what you are doing," Wilhelm said.

"That's just it. I don't know what it is I'm doing. Have I done something every single night before battle? Do I have some mannerism or a lucky omen?" Höring asked.

"You are overthinking it now," Wilhelm said.

"Goddamn right I am," Höring said, the fear causing his voice to crack. His fingers shook as he lit another cigarette. He took three therapeutic puffs from it. It calmed his nerves. "Hannah have any friends?"

Wilhelm smiled. Höring too. It was the thousandth time Höring had asked.

"What about your French girlfriend?" Wilhelm asked.

"She is in France. I need a German wife and, preferably, a mistress in every country we conquer," Höring joked.

Heinrich's face flashed in Wilhelm's mind.

"One of my best friends from back home was always lucky with women. Heinrich Hess is his name. I would not doubt if he has a girlfriend in every country," Wilhelm said.

"He in the same sinking boat as us?" Höring asked.

"Yes, but I don't know where he is now. I have not seen him in two years."

"You will have to introduce me to him when we are done here. I could use some lessons."

Wilhelm smiled. He opened his journal and slid the pencil into the spine.

"What's with the flower?" Höring asked when he saw the page.

On the page was a drawn rose. It was not as good as one of Hannah's drawings, but Wilhelm had picked up techniques during Sunday morning drawing sessions.

"It is a blue rose. It is Hannah's favorite flower," Wilhelm said.

"I'll keep an eye out for them. Stalin probably had them all burned though," Höring said, taking a final drag before flicking the cigarette and rising to his feet. "A bit quiet. How will I ever sleep without the constant bombardment?" Höring asked. He smiled, patted Wilhelm on the back, and left.

Each night, Wilhelm pleaded to the unknown to either let him dream of Hannah or dream the war to be nothing but a nightmare. He wanted nothing more than to wake up beside Hannah. It did not even matter where. It could be in their bed at their apartment. It could be at Lena's cabin or on one of Lena's couches in her house, at Josef and Emma's or his father's.

Summer had been Wilhelm's favorite season but, yet again, he could not enjoy it. June, July, and most of August came and went, and the invisible Caesar graced Wilhelm, Jonas, and Höring with a thumbs up. But the stagnant thumb twitched. The soldiers of the Sixth Army scrambled into formation.

"What's going on?" Wilhelm asked.

"General der Panzertruppe Paulus is about to make an announcement," Jonas said.

Wilhelm followed the soldiers rushing by and then stood in silence as they waited. Had the Soviet Union capitulated? Or, at the very least, sought a seize fire? Paulus stepped forward. He was a tall man of six foot four inches with a slender frame. He was in his early fifties and had resumed command of the Sixth Army earlier that year of 1942. He held much respect from his troops and had enough medals on his uniform to cause it to hang lower on that side.

"We have been bestowed a great honor," Paulus started, "a great honor that will require sacrifice and perseverance. Our Führer has entrusted us, the Sixth Army and the 4th Panzer Army, for this mission. Joining us are the 3rd and 4th Romanian Armies, the 8th Italian Army, and the 2nd Army of Hungary. But make no mistake, this mission, this grievous task, is our responsibility. We are to attack the city of Stalingrad. Our Führer will accept nothing but absolute victory! We will fight down to the last man! There will be no retreat, no surrender! A thousand-year Reich!"

"A thousand-year Reich!" the entire army yelled.

"Fuck," Wilhelm muttered as the soldiers moved out.

"It will not be any different than any other battle," Jonas said.

"Wilhelm's right," Höring said.

Jonas paused and waited for one of the two to elaborate further. Höring nodded for Wilhelm to explain.

"It is Stalin's namesake city. They will not retreat like they have so far. They will defend it fiercely," Wilhelm explained.

"Russians are inferior to Germans," Jonas said, shaking off the fear that had temporarily taken hold of him.

"So are monkeys. But I'd be afraid of them too if they were holding a gun," Höring said.

Höring compared attacking Stalingrad as knocking on Stalin's own front door and throwing a pile of cow shit at his face when he opened it.

Wilhelm found little rest that night, and as they moved east, the nervousness in his stomach felt like a caged creature desperate to break free. He was not the only one, for all over the camp, men squatted and released an onslaught of diarrhea or vomit onto the ground, bringing new meaning to Scorched Earth. It took over a week until they were close to the Volga River, the longest river in Europe and where the great city of Stalingrad sat. The Luftwaffe's bombers soared toward the great Soviet city to its supply lines across the river and dropped hell that engulfed the earth in flames and, from the distance, seemed to rise into space.

The next morning, with the rising sun, the Luftwaffe unleashed a number of bombs impossible to count. Höring said it had looked like Armageddon crashing through the atmosphere and plummeting toward Earth. In a matter of seconds, the industrial city had been knocked back to the Stone Age. The Luftwaffe had done its job. It was now the duty of the foot soldiers to take the city.

"Good luck, Wilhelm," Höring said.

"You too," Wilhelm said, giving his friend a hug.

Jonas was hunched over and vomiting.

"Bet you wish you had a banana for the monkeys now, don't you?" Höring teased.

Jonas held up a middle finger as he heaved onto the ground.

Every soldier ensured their firearms were clean and in good standing. Nobody wanted to charge an enemy with a questionable firearm. As the Germans advanced, tank and soldier, the wind died. Buildings were half destroyed and the city's civilians, caked in concrete dust, wandered about like zombies. Soviet tanks bulldozed over the rubble, their barrels sending boulder-sized shells at the Germans. Soviet troops came from every corner and, in an instant, chaos and pandemonium broke out. Soldiers fired from the windows and fell to the ground when shot. It was a fight for every street and every building. Soldiers were thrown out of the top floor. Portions of buildings collapsed and fell all around.

Wilhelm and the soldiers near him fired a frenzy at the charging Soviets, but they were like bees swarming to defend its hive. A German stepped forward and ignited his flamethrower. There was no more terrifying sound. It was a dragon that opened its mouth, roared, and belched fire. The Soviets were consumed by fire, and no matter how much they squirmed or screamed, the flames did not die. Some shot themselves to end the pain, and others thrashed about until death took them. The fire took no chances at being duped and kept burning until the bodies were charred black.

"Keep moving!" the soldier with the flamethrower yelled. But by turning, he had exposed the tank, and a bullet punctured through, and the tank exploded. Even from twenty feet away, the heat burned Wilhelm's eyes, and he dropped his weapon to rub them. The tanks were merciless and ran over the injured. Mortar rounds exploded everywhere, and grenades were thrown back and forth.

It was too painful for Wilhelm to open his eyes. He patted the rubble for his gun, grabbed it, and tried using his forearm to rub his eyes and end the pain. When his eyes finally did open, they were filled with moisture, and his excellent vision was now that of someone who needed three-inch thick eyeglasses. Bits of rock landed on his boots where bullets narrowly missed him. Nearly blind, he had no idea how much of a sitting duck he was. Somebody grabbed him and threw him to the ground.

"Jesus Christ! What the fuck is the matter with you!" the voice yelled.

"My eyes…" Wilhelm mumbled. His vision was clear enough to see a red cross on the uniform of the man who knelt beside him.

"What happened?" the medic asked.

It was a different voice than the man's who had just yelled at him.

"Flames. I can't see well," Wilhelm said.

If the sights were half as cruel as the sounds, he was thankful he couldn't.

"Fall back! It will fade! Rejoin when your vision…" the medic's words were cut short as a bullet hit his neck.

Blood poured from the wound onto Wilhelm's face. He struggled to his feet, now faced with the dual task of trying to wipe blood from his face and rub his eyes while trying to see where he ran to and locate the enemy.

When he reached the German line, it was filled with hundreds of injured, and each begged and screamed for help. His vision improved minute by minute. Soldiers around him pressed down on bullet wounds, applied tourniquets, and treated burns. How some were still alive was impossible to understand. Men who were burned all over their bodies, missing arms and legs, some nothing more than a torso, reached or screamed for help.

When his vision fully returned, Wilhelm searched for Jonas and Höring briefly before having to move back into the city. It was, on a much smaller scale, the feeling of jumping into cold water. It was best to jump in than dip your toes. But this water had sharks lurking beneath the surface, and there was blood in the water. The Germans pushed further and further into the city, but at the cost of thousands of lives. Wilhelm fired from behind a pile of concrete rubble, covering for two other Germans as they charged forward. He waited for them to provide cover before he climbed over and sprinted forward.

"Shit!" one of the two yelled. Six Soviets sprinted out of the building to the Germans' right. They wielded spades, chair legs, and axes. Their ammunition had run out, and they fought with whatever Stalingrad had to offer. Wilhelm was tackled to the ground. A Soviet pressed a chair leg against his throat. Wilhelm grabbed a piece of concrete debris and smashed it across the Soviet's head. He drove it down again and again. Bits of blood and brain covered the concrete and Wilhelm's face. He removed his Sauer 38h pistol and fired two rounds into each of the two remaining Soviet attackers and pulled another German to his feet, but the moment he was standing, he was shot in the throat.

He collapsed on top of Wilhelm. A grenade bounced and rolled toward him. He mustered his strength and turned the dead German over and dove head-first over the pile of debris. The grenade exploded and showered him with rocks. He lost his rifle, and he had only a few shots left in his Sauer 38h pistol. He fired at any Soviet close by, but he was the only German in the vicinity. In a city of millions, he was alone.

He searched the dozens of bodies nearby for a weapon and grabbed a pistol from a dead German. A shot rang out louder than any other and, less than a second later, a sharp pain ripped through his chest, the force of which sent him onto a pile of rubble. He pressed his hand against his chest, and the white concrete dust covering his hand now turned crimson.

Fleeing

When Hannah landed on the rock-hard ground, her elbows and knees taking most of the impact, it hit back. The train carried on, but the screeching and flashes of bright oranges and yellows was a grave warning. The train was coming to a stop. Every fiber appeared to have quit on Hannah. The cold ground that surely had bruised seventy percent of her body now, somehow, soothed her. It was rest. Her bruised, swollen feet pulsated, and she would have as much success attempting to stand as pushing the train. But the train gave one last shriek, one last warning. Hannah's brain processed the danger and sent a surge of power to her body. The train let out a high-pitched whistle and a cloud of smoke. When the doors of the cattle car were opened and there were no Jews, the Nazis would search every barn, house, cellar, and closet to find them.

Hannah forced herself to her feet with a groan. It had been months, maybe even years, since she had run. Her clogs slid back and forth, nearly causing her to face plant. She took them off and tossed them aside. The branches and leaves she ran on could cause her no further pain, but her feet threatened anarchy as she scurried toward the cover of the forest. Shouts followed by whistles and boots hitting the ground released an adrenaline response in Hannah. Fate had taken a kind turn. Many of the officers had German Shepherds—but none of the officers aboard the train. Had they, there would have been a zero-percent chance of escape. She raced between the trees in a serpentine pattern, chancing glances behind her to see how close the Nazis were. Each snapping twig betrayed her location.

Screams of terror informed Hannah the fortune of some of the other women had run out. Gunshots echoed, almost causing Hannah to scream. Whether the shots were executions from point-blank range or the shots of a hunter shooting a fleeing prey was impossible to decipher.

The cover the woods had offered ended. Hannah came to a clearing with only a lone farmhouse with a rusted black truck parked near it with its lights on and engine running. The barn door was open, and the silhouettes of two men inside were cast from the truck's headlights. Hannah hurried to the truck. The manure in the truck bed would have been smelt by most at five meters away, but the smell of ripe shit went unnoticed to a woman who had become familiar with the smell of death. She climbed onto the bed and shoveled the manure on top of her to conceal herself. She positioned her head between the two horizontal slabs of wood that made up the sides of the bed.

Two voices, speaking a language unrecognizable to her, grew louder as they approached the truck. One voice faded away, no doubt as he moved to the house. The truck door slammed and, seconds later, the truck bounced as it sputtered forward. Hannah brushed the manure away from her face and gasped. The rushing air filled her lungs. The road led to an unknown destination, and her view was too limited and the sky too dark to make any guesses as to where she was.

The truck slowed when the man came to an intersection and waited at a stop sign. Hannah lifted her head from the manure. A string of cars came to a halt. Flashlight beams scanned the nearby fields. The Nazis had begun their search. Barks rang out near the front of the line of automobiles. They belonged to only one breed of dog—German Shepherd. The truck could have gone straight or right or even back the way it had come. But the flashing coming from the back left was another warning. Hannah brushed the manure back over her face and did her best to make sure she was completely covered in it. She had to take delicate sips of air or risk inhaling the manure. Claustrophobia set in instantly.

The truck crept forward as the search continued.

"We are searching for escaped prisoners," a voice said.

Even muffled by the manure, the ominous voice was familiar. It belonged to Sturmbannführer Waltz.

"I … not speak… ugh … German no well," the man in the truck said.

"What are you carrying?" Waltz asked.

He did not care in the slightest if the man understood or not. But Waltz's question was answered as soon as he approached the back of the truck. A strong whiff of shit hit his nostrils, and he stepped back offended.

"Where are you going?" Waltz asked.

Hannah had no more sips of air and had to fight the urge to rise up from the manure and gasp for breath. The idea of dying by suffocating on shit was worse than being shot. But one thing was for certain—she would never step aboard that train again. She would rather die in a flatbed of manure than be a cow sent to slaughter. The man in the truck spoke again in his own language to reiterate his inability to speak or understand German while the manure was stabbed by the tip of a rifle, inches from Hannah.

"It is just a pile of shit," the soldier said, nearly gagging.

The number of cars stopped increased with every passing second, and the headlights from the automobile behind threatened to illuminate Hannah like a stage light.

"Move along," Waltz said.

The man must not have understood what he had been told because a hand hit the top of his truck that almost caused Hannah to jump.

"Move!" Waltz yelled.

The man drove forward, and after the truck struggled audibly to achieve higher speed, it accelerated enough to create a comfortable distance between it, the driver, and Hannah from the Nazi search party. Hannah pushed her hands free from the manure like a corpse breaking through its grave. She shoveled the manure off her face and sucked in air with huge exaggerated gasps.

As her breathing steadied, she tried to wager a guess about where she was. The train had moved east—perhaps Poland or Czechoslovakia? All that mattered was that the driver didn't speak German and he drove away from Waltz and the Nazi search party. For the first time, since arriving at Auschwitz, the stars were an endless highway of possibilities, an unexplored pathway leading to an infinite number of destinations. And for the first time, she was able to grasp all she had lost. She had grieved at Auschwitz, but survival took precedence. But now, as she lay in the bed of the truck with nothing but stars and solitude, her thoughts turned somber.

She thought about Eleanor and the fate awaiting her. What had she done to warrant such a selfless act of compassion and heroism? She thought of Trugnowski and the way he had stood strong and tall until the very end. She thought of her mother and father. The date of losing a loved one can never be forgotten—something remembered down to the minute. But Hannah did not know the minute, the hour, the day, the month or even the year—a tombstone etched with a question mark. As the road sped by beneath her in a black blur, so many she loved were rooted now in the past. But Wilhelm had made the stars a constant reminder of him, and it was impossible for Hannah to gaze upon them without thinking of him. He was the one thing that pulled her forward. As she contemplated on everything and everyone she had lost, defeat was never so enticing. But her soul demanded her to continue on.

The truck slowed as it approached another farmhouse. It sounded like the final cough of a sick man before the engine was killed. The truck door croaked as it opened, and the door slammed. She expected the farmer to walk around the truck and stare down at her, but the door to the house opened and closed with a creek and a thud. She lifted herself from the bed of the truck and toppled over the side. The cold air nipped at her, and her stained pajamas did little to protect her from its bite. She checked the truck for the keys and was not surprised to not find them there. Her body was as brittle as glass. It was going to shatter at any moment. Her feet had quit on her and refused to lift off from the ground. In her frail state, even the relatively calm winds nearly blew her over. Her mouth did not have a spec of saliva, and swallowing was painful.

She hobbled toward the large barn, the color of which was the same faded red as the cattle car that had brought her to Auschwitz. She tried pulling open its heavy doors, but the wind was a cruel jokester and slammed them shut. On her second attempt, she was able to squeeze through the opening. The cows inside mooed. Was it normal for a cow to moo in the middle of the night or would the farmer come out to investigate? Near the doors was a water pump. Hannah put her face in front of it and pumped. She took in as much of it as she could, but most of it ran down her chin and doused her pajamas. Water had been such a luxury at the camp, and to be in a situation now where she could drink herself to death with it was unfathomable. After nearly drinking her weight's worth, she limped away from the pump. Even inside the barn, the chill found its way to her, and her drenched pajamas caused her to shiver. Her feet throbbed. She lifted her left foot—thorns punctured the bottom. She grimaced as she pulled them out.

Every stall in the barn was occupied by a cow, except for one. Hannah opened it and stepped inside. It had equal amounts of mud and hay. Her body tremored from the cold. She gathered all the hay in the stall and used it to insulate herself and tucked her hands into her armpits and buried her face in the hay. She drifted off, whether from tiredness or passing out, to a deep sleep filled with a series of dreams that flowed from one to the next but had nothing in common. Eleanor and Trugnowski were both in them as well as her parents. The last dream was of Wilhelm, but it was entirely confusing. His German morphed into a language she could not understand. She snapped awake and gasped.

The farmer stood outside the stall, speaking the same word she had not understood Wilhelm speak in her dream. His wide, round frame covered nearly all the stall, and his glasses were so filthy that it was possible he had not seen Hannah. But he shouted again.

"I am sorry," Hannah said, grabbing hold of the wooden horizontal beam and struggling to her feet.

The farmer's angry tone instantly changed when he saw her striped pajamas. Hannah, although eyes open, was anything but coherent. She was beyond exhausted, beyond starved, beyond weak. Her hands and feet were numb, and the numbing crawled further up her arms and legs. She hovered between this world and the next. She was powerless to do anything when the farmer opened the stall and scooped her up in his arms. She had expected to be dropped onto the cold, hard ground, but the farmer carried her to the house and inside. She drifted in and out of consciousness, the colors of the room faded, and images blurred together. She felt nothing—not the cold wind attacking her as the farmer carried her inside, not even the farmer holding her. There was both an expanse of black and then white—a symbol of a temporary state of unconsciousness and death.

Over the course of the next week, she seldom awoke—only long enough to take in the walls, faded egg-white in color, and the maple wood flooring. She was in a bed, freezing under the covers but dripping with sweat—somehow burning to death while simultaneously freezing. Her insatiable tiredness was finally appeased. She opened her eyes, and her vision corrected itself. The room was rustic, and the home's owners were surely nemophilists. Now that her sleepiness had faded, a worry and curiosity as to exactly where she was and with whom had taken over. She flipped the damp, sweat-logged covers off and stepped onto the floor. It cracked and groaned with each footstep.

She stepped out of the bedroom and found a staircase a few feet from the room. She descended the stairs, carefully holding onto the banister for support. With each step, the smell of frying eggs and sizzling ham became so defined that she could taste it. Its aroma was glorious. Her stomach gave a strong push forward in an attempt to burst out of her. A tall, slender, red-haired woman standing over the stove turned to look at her. She hurried toward Hannah and gently rubbed Hannah's face. The man on the kitchen chair turned his body, his large belly getting caught on the table. It must have been the man from the truck, but it had been so dark and Hannah so nearing unconsciousness that she could only assume. The farmer and his wife spoke to one another. The topic was no doubt Hannah.

"I do not speak your language," Hannah said.

They didn't speak German but, at least, it would let them know she did not speak their language.

The woman took Hannah's hands and offered her a smile and escorted her back upstairs—an encouraging direction than the alternative of the front door and the terrors outside. The house was modest and a combination of smells of fire from the living area fireplace and cedar from the dressers and desks in each of the rooms. It was the sort of home that most likely had been in the farmer's family for generations and had changed minimally since it was built—probably two hundred years ago.

The farmer's wife led Hannah back into a bedroom and pulled clothes from the second drawer of the cedar dresser. She kept them folded in her hands and led Hannah into the bathroom. She placed the clothes on the bathroom counter and grabbed a towel from the cabinet beside it. She turned to the bathtub and pulled the shower curtain out of the way and started the shower. The woman offered another smile and left.

It was still a mystery who they were and what their motive was. But the idea of a hot shower was too much, and Hannah lifted the striped pajamas over her head and pulled the headscarf off and took a frightened step backward when she caught her reflection in the mirror. Who was the person staring back at her? Her hair, now longer than a shave, was still inches shorter than the last time she had seen her reflection. Her body was grotesquely thin and every bone, fully visible. Her face, once full of life and color, now seemed to be months into decay. Her eyes, once as bright as red giant stars, were now faded, dulled, white dwarves approaching their end. She stepped into the tub. The clear water that ran down her head and body turned black at her feet. She shampooed her hair twice and lathered her body with soap three times. She then took the razor from the ledge and shaved her armpits and legs.

The water massaged her throbbing feet, tensed shoulders, and achy back. She sat, her arms draped over her knees, and let the water cascade onto her. Apart from her shower with Wilhelm on their final night together, it was the greatest shower of her life. As she dried herself off and wiped the mirror clean from the condensation, for the first time in months, she felt like a human being. The shower did not bring back length to her hair or add weight to her skeletal frame, but she was clean—clean for the first time in months, maybe, even years. And that was a start. She took one final look at her filthy pajamas on the bathroom floor. She had expected to die in them. They were her coffin, a coffin she wore every day. It did not matter if the clothes on the sink did not fit. They were different, and what a marvelous thing that was!

Hannah dressed and opened the door and walked down the steps. She had appeased her tiredness and her need for cleanliness. Next on her list was food.

The farmer and his wife rose from the kitchen table, but Hannah was fixated on the two eggs, a piece of bread coated with a thick layer of butter, and home fries on the plate and a glass of milk beside it. She wanted to make no assumptions the plate was for her and waited until the woman gestured to the seat. She crammed bits of egg and toast into her mouth and took gulps of milk between bites.

The farmer and his wife waited as Hannah devoured the plate in less than two minutes. The farmer then left the table and returned moments later, fighting to unfold a map of Europe, using the salt and pepper shaker on opposites ends to secure it. He placed his stubby finger near the border of Poland and the Czech portion of Czechoslovakia. His finger covered nearly a dozen cities, but Hannah was somewhere near Ostrava. Hannah pointed her own finger on Oświęcim, the site of Auschwitz.

"Nazis. Which countries are they in?" Hannah asked, even though it would not be understood.

"Nazis?" the farmer's wife asked.

Hannah nodded. She pointed to Germany. "Nazis," she said.

She moved her finger to Poland and again repeated the word Nazis.

The farmer's wife caught on and pointed to country after country—Albania, Czechoslovakia, Austria, France, Montenegro, Luxembourg, Macedonia, Croatia, Belgium, Denmark, Greece, Hungary, Italy, Norway, the Netherlands, Yugoslavia, Finland, Lithuania, Poland, San Marino, Serbia, Ukraine, and the Soviet Union. The invisible noose around Hannah's neck tightened with each tap of the woman's long finger. There was no safe haven in Europe.

The farmer's wife barely left the kitchen that day, and Hannah did not leave the table. She ate and ate, and an hour later, she ate more. She stayed a week, each day her strength returning tenfold. She would ask no more from the kind farmer and his wife. The penalty for harboring a Jew was death, and Hannah did not want that on her conscience. She was no longer in Poland, but Auschwitz was only a short train ride away. Her gut told her complacency was death. She had to keep moving.

"Thank you," Hannah said.

The farmer's wife placed her hands on Hannah's and held up a single finger and went to the counter. She grabbed a satchel and placed inside it a dozen hard-boiled eggs, three potatoes, two loaves of bread, a triangle of brie cheese, and a jug of milk.

The farmer had one last gift too. He removed a gold pocket watch, a compass below the clock, from his shirt pocket.

"No. I cannot," Hannah said, holding her hand up to refuse.

The farmer shook his head, placed the watch in her hand, and gently pushed her hand away.

It had been in their best interest to report her to the Nazis or, at the very least, banish her from their home. But instead, they chose compassion. Hannah would have died out in the cold forest. The food, bed, clothes, and shower had not only saved her life but also kept her flickering ember spirit burning.

Hannah placed the satchel over her shoulder and gave one last appreciative glance at the two Samaritans. It was early, and the sun had yet to fully rise. She opened the gold pocket watch and made sure her heading was south. She had no place in mind but made sure to stick to walking through the wooded areas and avoid the main roads. Her stamina and strength were still far from recuperated, and she stopped frequently to rest.

The silence of nature only brought back haunting memories of shrieking and whistling trains. On most occasions, she was able to shake it off. But what she had thought was in her head was reality when she stepped through the end of the tree line. A train station was ahead. The sight of the train paralyzed her. Hannah had never loved nor hated trains before. She had found them to be less thrilling than planes or even cars, but now they were a symbol of the horror she had been through. Her entire body wanted her to run in the opposite direction, but the train was her best option for covering ground and fast.

"Find one problem, solve one problem."

Eleanor's words came to her like a pep talk.

The search radius for her was small, yet she was still in it. She needed to create a greater distance between her and Auschwitz. Although she had showered, her hair was slightly longer, and even in different clothes, it was not enough to fool Waltz. He was as predatorial as a dog and equally cunning. She lurched toward the train, pausing when her eyes found something potentially dangerous. She tried to stifle the nerves and lightheaded feeling that had taken over her. She stood amongst a hundred people, waiting for the train to arrive. Hannah approached the ticket window, and the woman inside leaned forward.

"Excuse me. Do you speak German?" Hannah asked.

"Little," the woman answered.

"Where is the next train going?"

"Vienna. Would you like to purchase a ticket?"

"No, thank you."

But Hannah had every intention of being on the train, she just had no money to purchase a ticket. She would have to sneak on.

The train approached from the close distance, shrieking as it decelerated to a stop. An irrational fear took hold that as soon as the doors would open, Waltz and an SS platoon would step off. But was it so irrational? A person looking to escape would surely go to a train station.

The train's doors opened, and the passengers inside the train forced their way past those trying to get on. During the commotion of boarding and exiting, Hannah hopped down onto the tracks and climbed onto the train's caboose. After all the passengers had boarded and the doors had closed, the train powered forward rhythmically.

The wind and temperature were unforgiving, but the gray midi dress and matching jacket she wore were much better suited for it than the striped pajamas. She lifted her feet onto the caboose and used her satchel as a pillow and ensured her chest and legs were covered by the metal railing. The rejuvenation she had after a week of straight eating and sleeping was taken over by sheer exhaustion once again. Sleeping was easier than the sporadic depressing thoughts that went through her head. She had no dreams, nor could she remember at exactly what point she had fallen asleep. She had become well acquainted with a shrieking train and the squealing as it slowed. But her sense of smell took control over her, and with her bag so close to her nose, she could smell nothing but the homemade bread. She tore off a piece and appeased both her sense of smell and stomach, and she brought her attention back to the screeching train.

She had arrived in Vienna. She hopped off the train before it stopped completely and dashed off the tracks. Hannah followed the mad dash of people heading toward the heart of the Austrian city. It was hard not to be mesmerized by the city's grand opulent standing with its buildings piercing the sky like the tips of a jewel-covered spear. Austria was the home of Hannah's favorite painting and had always brought a calming wave and now, only envisioning it, was no different.

Hannah stayed in the city for two weeks, sleeping in one of the city's parks or in alleys. She scouted the outdoor cafés, and when the patrons would leave, she would grab their leftover food from the plates before the waiter or waitress could clear them. But her time in Vienna had to be limited. Not only was the city and the country of Austria under Nazi occupation, it was also pro-Nazi.

Hannah had to get to France and from France to England. It did not matter France was under German control. France and, especially, Paris were not pro-Nazi, and its citizens were less likely to turn her in.

Hannah's time hanging around the outdoor cafés paid off with more than just leftover food. She discovered that an Austrian-flown airplane made frequent trips from Vienna to Strasbourg, France. It would be extremely gutsy to attempt to sneak aboard, but the prospect of being able to travel whether by foot, car or rail to France seemed unlikely. It was to her advantage that the flight took off during the nighttime hours. It made it much easier to sneak onto the airstrip, but there were still searchlights that scanned the strip, looking for any trespassers.

Her time with Sturmbannführer Waltz and Jakob Hauser, his rank no longer known, had taught her cunning. She scouted at night, listening to names, ranks, and conversations. On her third night, she made her move. She dashed across the small runway and hid behind a Nazi officer's black automobile, so polished that it was mirror-like in its reflection. When the loading of the cargo paused, she took her chance and sprinted up the ramp and hid behind one of the crates. She sipped in breaths and exhaled slowly.

The two guards finished loading the crates of cargo, one talking about a big-breasted Austrian he had seen the night before, and the other was far too busy imaging the woman to check the plane.

"Find one problem, solve one problem."

The next problem was the tumultuous ball of nerves in Hannah's stomach. She had never flown before, a nerve-racking experience on its own, but she had illegally snuck on a plane used to benefit a regime that wanted her exterminated.

"You are the pilots of this plane?" a German voice asked from outside the plane.

The voice was muffled, and had it not been for the man having great diction and enunciation, his words would have been lost.

"Yes, Sir," another voice replied.

Austria was a pre-dominantly German-speaking country, and it provided a huge advantage to be able to understand what the Nazis were saying. Warnings and information could be attained. Apart from Eleanor and Trugnowski, it had been her ability to speak and understand German that had aided in her survival. Those who could not understand it were at a serious disadvantage.

"Where do you fly to?" the first voice asked.

Without even seeing the man, Hannah knew he was an officer. They carried themselves in a different way—well-mannered and supremely confident.

"Strasburg, France," the second voice answered.

"Not anymore. You will fly Brigadeführer Huber to Berlin," the first voice instructed.

"Yes, Sir," the second voice said.

Hannah's eyes bulged open so wide that the whites of her eyes were probably visible in the black space. Though the plane was hardly for personnel transport, especially top Nazis, it did have an additional seat—a seat now filled by a general of the SS. The plane's ramp rose and closed, trapping her inside. She had escaped the hawk, only to be brought right back to its mouth.

The plane powered forward, and its front lifted off the ground. The fear of what to expect from flying came all at once. She had had her trepidations about flying, but that was when she was flying into France, not the heart of the Nazi empire. Her ears popped as the plane lifted off, and she thought her stomach might fall out of her mouth. She was unsure whether or not she would have preferred being able to see out. She had often heard people talk about the bird-like views of the world, but she saw nothing but the dark cargo area where she had hidden.

As the fear of ascending into the air in a tube weighing hundreds of thousands of pounds dissipated, the awful feeling of knowing in a few short hours her time as a fugitive, perhaps even her life, was at an end set in. When the plane's back opened, there would be no hiding—no escaping. She would be questioned and the barcode tattoo on her left forearm, discovered. But Hannah would not board another train like a sheep again. She would not let them take her alive. There had been a time, after finding out her parents had perished, when she had wanted to die. But now she wanted nothing more than to live. Her life was only beginning. But if it were to end, she would make them waste the bullet.

She checked for anything that could be used as a weapon, but there was nothing. The only ideas she had—lifting a crate and bashing it over someone's head—failed as soon as she tried to lift it. Her second plan, opening the crates and hoping they were filled with weapons, also failed. The crates would only open with a crowbar. She literally had nothing to do but wait. In ways, the flight took a lifetime and in others, it lasted only a few precious seconds.

The plane descended, catching bits of turbulence as it did. Hannah's breathing grew louder and faster. She had one hope—that the back would not have to be opened. The shipment was to be flown to Strasburg, France. What need was there to open it? But the realist in her had stabbed the optimistic soft balloon that was hope. Nothing was done without the Nazis' knowledge. They would not let a cargo plane fly from Austria to France and not know what was inside of it. Of course, it had been checked in Vienna, but the Nazis proofread and dotted their Is and crossed their Ts with obsessive detail. There was no way the plane was not going to be searched.

The wheels of the plane bounced off the runway, and Hannah held onto the cargo netting to prevent herself from falling over. The plane skidded to a stop. The engines died, and there was nothing but silence. As she hid behind the farthest crate, an idea of genius or madness struck her. It would be hard, if not impossible, to explain herself if she was found cowering behind a crate. But if she made herself known, it would be much easier to do so. The wrong decision would cost her her life.

She pounded on the back of the plane and screamed. Once again, her mind and body were on different sides. Her mind commended such a different way of thinking, but her body felt betrayed, and all her strength vanished. For a moment, it appeared she would go unnoticed. But the ramp lowered. A black hat swallowed the runway lights, and the silver Totenkopf reflected them. Hannah did her best to neglect her body's severe warning and show fear. She had to disobey its innate fight or flight response.

"Finally," Hannah said in relief after the back of the flight was opened.

She stepped down the ramp. Five Nazis stood at the foot of it. Two looked to be common foot soldiers, and the other three were officers with various degrees of ribbon and medals adorned on their black leather uniforms.

"Who are you?" the highest-ranking Nazi asked.

Hannah studied his uniform. Lena's soliloquies about patches, ribbons, medals, and ranks had paid off.

"My name is Hannah, Hauptsturmführer," she said.

"Hannah who?" the Hauptsturmführer asked.

He wanted to remain in control of the conversation, but her knowledge of his rank had caught him off guard.

"Hannah Hauser," she said.

"Why are you on this plane—hiding?" the Hauptsturmführer asked.

"I wasn't hiding. My boyfriend works at the airstrip and, well, I'm rather ashamed of it now, I let him talk me into sneaking off for a few private moments. He said he will be right back. Like a fool I sit and wait, and the next thing I know, the ramp is closing and we are lifting off," Hannah said.

"Your papers," the Hauptsturmführer demanded, extending his hand.

"I do not have my papers. I was not planning on traveling. Where are we anyway? Are we in Berlin?" Hannah asked.

Even if the Nazi in Vienna had not told her, she would never forget the Berlin skyline. The city was her home.

"Your accent is not Austrian," the Hauptsturmführer said.

"No, it is not. It is German. I lived in Berlin until I moved to Vienna for schooling," Hannah said.

"What seems to be the problem, Hauptsturmführer?" another voice asked, approaching them.

The men jumped into a salute. The man, decorated with a dozen more insignia and medals than any of them, stood before them.

"Brigadeführer Huber, this woman was aboard your plane in the cargo area," the Hauptsturmführer said.

"Continue," Brigadeführer Huber said.

He had dark eyes and his hair, which matched his leather jacket, was combed over to the right. He looked over Hannah with a satisfied gleam in his eyes as he rubbed his thin mustache.

"She claims she and her boyfriend sought a private embrace. She was stuck on board when her boyfriend left," the Hauptsturmführer explained.

Brigadeführer Huber scrutinized Hannah's disheveled appearance and messy hair, which had grown long enough to not draw comments. She certainly did appear to have had a man's hand running through her hair and under her blouse.

"What is your boyfriend's name? Last name first, please," Brigadeführer Huber asked.

"Gruber, Tobias," Hannah answered.

Though the last name had been a shot in the dark, she did know that a Tobias had worked at the airstrip, along with Lukas, David, Simon, and Conrad.

"Schütze," Brigadeführer Huber called.

The two foot soldiers stepped forward and fell to his command.

"Bring the pilots here," Brigadeführer Huber commanded.

The two soldiers hurried to the front of the plane and, less than ten seconds later, the two pilots were brought to Brigadeführer Huber. It was not under gunpoint, but one wrong move or answer and it would be.

"May I remind you two that I am an extension of the Führer himself, and to lie to me is to lie to him. Lies will be treated as treason, and treason will be met with death. Is that clear?" Brigadeführer Huber threatened.

"Yes, Sir," the two answered.

"Miss, please tell me the pilots' names," Brigadeführer Huber said.

She had but seconds to answer. Realistically, she could not be expected to know every person who worked on the airstrip. There were at least fifteen on every shift and over six shifts. But Brigadeführer Huber would accept nothing less. But to guess incorrectly would be much more incriminating.

"I do not know. Women are not allowed on the airstrip," Hannah said.

"Yet, you claim to have been," the Hauptsturmführer said in suspicion.

"That will be enough, Hauptsturmführer," Brigadeführer Huber said.

The Hauptsturmführer slouched like a dog who had been scolded by its master.

"Do you know every single German soldier?" Hannah asked, straddling the line between confidence and rudeness.

"Careful now," Brigadeführer Huber cautioned, waving his finger at her in warning. He turned to the two Austrian pilots. "Is there a Tobias Gruper who was working on your shift?" he asked.

"Gruber," Hannah corrected.

She had lied about the name, but she also had a strong feeling Brigadeführer Huber was testing her to see if she could remember her lie.

"Tobias Gruber," Brigadeführer Huber said, nodding respectfully.

The two pilots looked at one another.

"There is a Tobias, but I do not know his last name, Sir," the taller of the two said.

"And you?" Brigadeführer Huber asked the second pilot.

"I know of Tobias but could not guess his last name, Sir," the second pilot agreed.

"Have you ever seen this woman before?" Brigadeführer Huber asked.

"No, Sir," both answered.

"You do not know the girlfriend of Tobias?"

"Let's hold off on using girlfriend. He has a lot to make up for if I ever get back," Hannah said.

The whole illusion would be over if Brigadeführer Huber asked to see her forearm. But her physiology was a picture-perfect Aryan super race, albeit still an incredibly thin one.

"What does Tobias look like?" Brigadeführer Huber asked.

Hannah had no idea. She had memorized names not faces, and in the dark, she would not have been able to tell a black man from a white man. But, sometimes, life throws moments of fortune and luck.

"He's a bit taller than me. Dark hair, almost black. A bit puffy around the mid-section," one of the pilots said.

The question had not been intended for him, but in the pilot's defense, the last line of questioning had been directed at the two of them.

Brigadeführer Huber scowled.

"You can call him fat. He is," Hannah said.

Brigadeführer Huber remained silent as he pondered over his choices. The runway was cold, and the winds had picked up. To continue his inquiry meant he would have to stay out in the cold. Even his usually comfortable leather jacket became more rigid and unforgiving in such conditions.

"Hauptsturmführer Ludwig," Brigadeführer Huber beckoned.

The Hauptsturmführer stepped forward, still dismissive.

"Yes, Brigadeführer," he responded.

"See to it that these pilots are refueled. They are to fly back to Vienna and return Tobias Gruber his beloved girlfriend," Brigadeführer Huber instructed.

"Yes, Brigadeführer," Hauptsturmführer Ludwig said.

"Safe travels, Miss," Brigadeführer Huber said.

"Thank you, Brigadeführer," Hannah said.

The Hauptsturmführer delegated the duty to the two SS-Schütze before following Brigadeführer Huber. It took much longer than Hannah had hoped to get permission to board the plane. Not only did it have to be refueled, but there was also a series of safety checks that bordered on the line of obsessive.

Hannah did not have to play dead to keep the bear from attacking her. She had to convince the bear she was one of them. The longer she was there, the more the bear sniffed and watched her. It was an act that fleeted with each passing second.

"All set, Miss," the shorter pilot said.

She nearly skipped to the front of the plane but passed it off as an uncoordinated step and walked with annoying indifference. The seat was small, even for her, and she had to keep her legs pressed tightly together or her knees would hit the two pilots' elbows. She kept an eye on the runway, half-expecting a swarm of soldiers to be sprinting down it while the two pilots flipped switches and called out procedures.

"We will have you back in Vienna in just a few hours," the co-pilot reassured.

The plane sped forward faster and faster.

"Where were you to land?" Hannah asked.

"Strasbourg, France," the co-pilot answered.

"To hell with Tobias. Take me to France," Hannah said.

The two pilots exchanged glances. They had been given an order from the Nazi command. They were much more worried about disobeying it than being late on the shipments. But the two were connected, and if the cargo did not arrive shortly, they would have to face the wrath of a different officer, and one perhaps of a higher rank.

"France it is," the pilot said.

The front end of the plane lifted off the ground, and Hannah's body twitched with nerves but, luckily, the pilots only considered it flight jitters. Yet, it had nothing to do with the flying. She found it to be exhilarating. It had everything to do with that she had escaped the hawk's nest and was once again leaving her home city.

Hannah could not help but smile in awe of the stars. She was closer to them now than she had ever been. The sky was a black canvas, and it seemed as if she had the ability to move the stars as she pleased with just a lazy flick of her finger. She loved the night and the glimpse of heaven it provided, but it was the sunrise that was truly awe-inspiring. The sky was a palette of pastels of oranges, reds, and yellows. The sun lifted spirits and brought the promise of better days. To Hannah, it meant one thing—hope.

Unexpected Friend

Blood ran down Wilhelm's arm and off his fingertips. His right arm trembled from the pain. He lifted his left to reclaim his helmet that had been knocked off. A second shot ripped into the concrete, creating a small puff of smoke. Bits of rock shrapnel ripped into Wilhelm's back. He was in the scope of a sniper.

He crawled into a crevasse between the two heaps of rubble filled with concrete and corpses. Russian voices came from both sides above. Wilhelm's rifle was out of the pit, and he only had a Luger P08 pistol he had taken from a fallen German—its eight shots not nearly enough for the number of voices. The voices grew louder. Wilhelm pulled one of the Soviet corpses onto him and sprawled his arms out and placed the Soviet face-down on the concrete rubble in an attempt to conceal himself. Men jumped into the pit, their boots grinding rock as they landed. They kicked German bodies and prodded them with the end of their rifles to check if any were still alive. A shot rang out, and a man yelled at the shooter. It was unwise to waste ammunition on the dead. The voices grew quieter as the men climbed out of the crevasse and dashed away. The immediate threat was gone. But somewhere in the upper floors of a building was a sure-handed sharpshooter.

Wilhelm's entire hand was covered in blood, and it was easy to see why the Soviets thought he was dead. He brought his finger to the source of his pain. "Fuck," he said, grimacing. The sun had set, but the city itself was cast in firelight and flames. He needed to get out of the street. But was he clear of the sniper's scope?

He grabbed a helmet and a rifle from one of the dead, first checking it for ammo— empty. He placed the helmet on the end of the rifle and raised it out of the cratered pit. When no shots were fired at it, he took his chance. He crawled toward the apartment building to his right and, after he was inside, pulled himself to his feet. He used the banister as support to climb up the stairs. Climbing up one flight was hard enough, but for that reason, the upper floors were the safest. His right arm hung limp, and he used his left to aid his weakening legs. He stumbled inside a room and collapsed against the wall. The room was vacant, and anything left behind had been destroyed. Wilhelm pulled his knapsack off his back and looked for something he could use to stop the bleeding. Although the wound was far from his heart, a great thing, the threat of bleeding out was real. He found a small packet of sulfa powder. He ripped open the packet using his teeth and sprinkled the white powder onto his chest. It would aid in preventing an infection.

Wilhelm kept his hand on his pistol, but as he sat there with the pain and fatigue sweeping over him, his blinks grew further apart until his eyes could not open. Stalingrad was the last place for one to fall asleep. It seemed impossible one could. The gunshots alone should have been loud enough to prevent it and, with the artillery and mortar rounds, it was enough to wake the dead. Yet, it was a scurrying mouse that woke Wilhelm, and it only took an instant for him to realize where he was. It was frightening he had been able to sleep in such an environment. How close had he been to being discovered or killed? Yet, if he was to die during this battle or outside it, dying in his sleep was the best way to go.

The mouse stood on its hind legs, sniffing the air before it dashed away. A blast of artillery fire erupted, and the dividing wall between apartments exploded. Wilhelm coughed from the smoke and concrete dust that filled his lungs. His cough echoed. But as the smoke and dust settled, Wilhelm realized it was not an echo. It was a different cough. There was a man in the other room. Wilhelm reached for his pistol and raised it. The man's uniform was covered in blood, white dust, and grime, but there was no mistaking the uniform of a Soviet soldier. The Soviet too raised his pistol.

They shouted at each other in German and Russian to put their gun down. They held their pistols outstretched for so long that Wilhelm felt like he was no longer holding a 1.92-pound gun but a 42-pound cannonball. He breathed heavily, knowing his life hung in the balance. Every single fiber of his being told him to fire but one—a small, faint voice that reminded Wilhelm the Soviet had yet to fire. Wilhelm's hand trembled, and he could no longer hold the gun up. His arm fell limp to his side.

The Soviet stared at him blankly. Though he did not lower his gun, he appeared less certain now. Wilhelm closed his eyes. His body twitched, waiting for the bullet. He let Hannah's face fill his mind. His breathing escalated while he waited and waited, but the shot did not come. He cautiously opened his eyes. The Soviet too had lowered his gun. The two sat and stared at each other through the rubble and dust. Moonlight trickled in, but it would be impossible to react quickly enough should one decide to fire. Water dripped from parts of the ceiling. The battle outside had quieted down slightly, but distant gunfire and artillery could still be heard.

The Soviet had not moved in minutes but raised his hand. Wilhelm reached for his pistol, but the Soviet pointed to the ceiling and spoke in his native Russian. Wilhelm tipped over his hands to show he did not understand a single word of it. The Soviet nodded and put the tips of his fingers together horizontally and brought them down. Wilhelm looked up at the ceiling. With the faint light, the cracks in the ceiling were visible, which combined with the water dripping from it, he was able to gather what the Soviet was trying to tell him.

"Can I come over there?" Wilhelm asked, pointing to himself and then to the other room.

He discretely holstered the pistol and rose to his feet with his hands clearly visible. The Soviet looked uneasy as Wilhelm approached. He had his hand on his gun but did not raise it. Wilhelm crawled over the destroyed wall and slid down the rubble. The movement had increased his pain, and he collapsed against the wall. The Soviet had a tall frame and sported a week-old beard, and even amongst all the dirt and dried blood, he was still handsome. The Soviet's black eyes went to his hands clutching his stomach.

"Are you hurt?" Wilhelm asked, pointing to the Soviet's stomach.

The Soviet removed his hand. A shard of glass, three-inches long, stuck out of his stomach. He nodded to Wilhelm. Wilhelm pulled the neck of his shirt down to show his own wound. It was clear to Wilhelm why the Soviet had not shot. He was in the same pain and predicament as Wilhelm. The Soviet reached into his knapsack. Wilhelm shot his hand toward his pistol. But the reaction was unneeded. The Soviet removed two small disposable syrettes. He poked one of the needles into his stomach and tossed the second one to Wilhelm. It was morphine to help numb the pain.

Wilhelm shook from the excruciating pain, and the area around the wound throbbed. He took the syrette and stabbed the needle into his skin, close to the wound. His chest had been chewed on by Cerebos, the hellhound of the underworld. But the beast fell to an unexpected slumber from the strum of a harp or, in this case, a needle. A feeling of relaxation spread over Wilhelm.

"What is your name? I am Wilhelm Schreiber," Wilhelm said.

"Alexander Kozlovsky," the Soviet said.

"Thank you for the morphine," Wilhelm said, holding up the syrette, hoping it would help translate.

Alexander nodded before his eyes fell to the shard of glass protruding from his stomach. Wilhelm used his arms to crawl toward Alexander to examine the wound.

"We have to pull it out," Wilhelm said. His motioning hands were impossible to lose in translation.

Alexander nodded and dug into his knapsack and removed a pack of gauze and put the strap of the knapsack in his mouth and bit down. Wilhelm grabbed the edge of the glass and carefully pulled it out. If he went too fast, he could cause further damage if the shard was caught on any tissue or muscle or, worse, slice a vein or artery. The further the glass was removed, the more blood spilled from Alexander. Wilhelm tossed the glass aside and pressed the gauze against the wound. The shard was roughly an inch wide, and nearly half of it was covered in blood. Wilhelm reached into his own knapsack and removed another packet of sulfa powder and ripped it open. He waited for Alexander to nod his approval. The Soviet did so with a deep breath. Wilhelm lifted the gauze, and the blood wasted no time in embracing the opportunity to drain out of his body. Wilhelm poured the powder onto the wound and pressed the gauze back onto it. Alexander nodded at Wilhelm's chest. He kept his left hand on his own wound and used his right hand to examine Wilhelm's. He searched for an exit wound but found none. Alexander used the last of the gauze and pressed it against Wilhelm's wound. The morphine had made Wilhelm more relaxed than he was before being drafted. It disconnected him from his body and the pain it felt.

Was Alexander in the same situation as Wilhelm—forced to fight a war he did not want? Yet, Alexander fought to defend his family and his home. Wilhelm knew he and the German army were the evil force in this battle.

The deep relaxation Wilhelm had fallen into increased exponentially until it was impossible for him to keep his eyes open. But the moment the harp of morphine stopped playing, the three-headed beast awoke and tore at his chest.

Alexander's head rested on his own shoulder, but he awoke when Wilhelm's foot scraped against the concrete pebbles. Alexander reached into his knapsack and removed a silver flask. He gave an innocent smile before taking a swig. His grimace told Wilhelm it was not water. Alexander spoke again, and he held the flask out for Wilhelm to take. Wilhelm took it and repeated Alexander's words in Russian. He had an idea of what was in the flask, but after taking a swig, he was absolutely sure. The liquid fire burned on its way down his throat, and his chest exploded with napalm. It was Russian vodka. How stereotypical the Russian would have vodka. Wilhelm was unable to break stereotype. He reached into his bag and removed a bar of German chocolate. He had been saving the bar for months. He wanted to wait until the day he found out he was going home. But there had been so many instances where he truly thought the war could be coming to a stand-still only to have it escalate elsewhere, and dying with an uneaten chocolate bar was sinful. So, Wilhelm opened the chocolate bar, broke it in half, and gave one half to Alexander.

"German chocolate," Wilhelm said.

"German chocolate," Alexander repeated.

He toasted his half to Wilhelm before taking a bite. It was the best bit of food either of them had had in months. The chocolate was creamy, rich, and smooth. It must have been the first time Alexander had had German chocolate, and it appeared to be a borderline sexual experience.

Wilhelm searched his knapsack for more food. He liked to save rations, as he never knew when they would come in handy, and now was that time. But it was his only chocolate bar. The rest was army rations of rye bread and legumes.

A slow, drawn-out creek filled the room and, less than a second later, the ceiling in the other room, the one Wilhelm had taken refuge in originally, collapsed. Alexander held an imaginary nail and hammer in his hand and struck the two together. Wilhelm took it to mean Alexander had built similar buildings before becoming a soldier. Wilhelm too tried charading his career by putting his hands on an invisible wheel and mimicking using a shifter. He removed four five-by-seven photographs and flipped through them and showed Alexander a picture of him and Hannah in front of the 1935 Mercedes-Benz 500K convertible. Alexander spoke, and Wilhelm could only assume he was asking who the woman was. Even if he had asked a car question, Wilhelm would rather talk about Hannah. It rejuvenated his motivation to get home.

"My wife, Hannah," Wilhelm said.

Alexander said only one word after he dug free a photo from his pocket. It was faded, torn, and dirty. The photo showed Alexander next to a woman with black hair and a baby in her arms. He spoke as he pointed to the people in the picture. Wilhelm could pick out the words Helen and Victor and was able to figure out the rest. He nodded with a smile to show he understood. From the same pocket, Alexander removed a small rectangular card. Though it looked different and was in a different language, Wilhelm knew what the card was. Wilhelm removed his own conscription card. Alexander nodded. Perhaps, it was another reason he had shown Wilhelm compassion and mercy.

Though Alexander hated to waste his vodka, he made sure to pour some over his wound in an attempt to help stop the infection from spreading. He grimaced before offering the flask. Wilhelm grabbed it, poured some over his bullet wound, and took a small sip. There was not much left, and he thought it would be rude if he finished it.

Both were far away from the blasted-apart opening, but it did not drown out the sound of relentless firing. Alexander spoke. Though Wilhelm could only guess what he had said, Alexander had said it with a poignant somberness. Wilhelm could only think of one sentence—hell has risen. It was no longer below him. It was not a punishment for the unrighteous. Somewhere atop one of the few still-standing buildings in Stalingrad, the devil was laughing at the carnage and chaos of the battle below. Alexander had not asked for the war. He had not deserved it—nor had Wilhelm, nor had the millions of men who had been put into the inferno. The painter Dante and his painting Inferno came to his mind. Dante spoke of hell being divided into levels—nine of them. But the Battle of Stalingrad had descended past what Dante imagined hell to be. It was all that and more. The ground was littered with the dead and dying. Soldiers covered with black dirt and white concrete dust crawled and limped, looking for help, leaving a trail of crimson blood in their wake.

Alexander turned to look at Wilhelm. The horrors of what he had seen reflected off his black eyes. But there was pleading in them as well. Alexander pointed to the picture as a whole and spoke one poignant word. Wilhelm understood. Alexander wanted to return to his wife and son. He wanted to leave the war behind. He simply wanted to go home.

"Home," Wilhelm said, pointing to the photo of Hannah.

Wilhelm had always considered Erich his best friend. But the two were different people. Erich had eagerly signed up and become a member of the SS. Heinrich had not been eager for war, just like Wilhelm, but he was a soul who could not remain complacent. He had a permanent feeling of being unsatisfied. It was not only in respect to the number of women he had dated. It was much more complex than that. He struggled to find where he belonged. Aaron had been much more sophisticated than any of Wilhelm's other friends. But he had even more grand plans than Heinrich. He really wanted to change the world. Höring and Jonas were polar opposites of each other, and it was Wilhelm who had brought the two together. He identified with them in certain things, Höring more so, and even though they were the same age, Höring was much "younger" than Wilhelm. But with Alexander, Wilhelm had found his exact match—a carbon copy of his very essence. Alexander did not want to change the world. He did not have ideas of glory, and he knew where he belonged. He belonged with his wife, Helen, and their son, Viktor. It was all he wanted. It was for that reason Wilhelm bonded with Alexander on a level he had never done with anyone apart from Hannah. It did not need conversation. They were two men, amongst millions, who had been tricked into entering Hades' underworld. They had dived into the pool of souls, and after entering Hades' domain, he never let you leave.

Wilhelm was jealous Alexander had been able to have a child with the love of his life. Helen had a son to love and raise. He had left Hannah alone.

Wilhelm's shoulder and chest throbbed, and his hand trembled. With Alexander's help, they had been able to reduce the amount of blood loss. But he still bled, and the wound needed to be cleaned and sealed. The same was true for Alexander. He bit his lip and groaned whenever he moved. Both were now unable to stand to piss in the corner. Instead, they simply rolled over to urinate. Both knew if they did not get medical aid, they would die. But the stairwell was covered with debris, and the other end of the building had received a bombardment of artillery. They were too far up to even consider jumping from the gaping hole in the wall. Even if the fall did not kill them, there was a likelihood their legs would break and an almost guarantee of an onslaught of gunfire.

A thought came or, rather, more of a story than a thought—stories of legendary warriors who cauterized their wounds. It was extremely painful and could lead to infection. But it would buy him and Alexander days, if not a week. But how could he communicate it to Alexander? He pulled out his knife and pressed the blade against his stomach and groaned and tapped the steel with his finger and acted like it was hot. Alexander nodded. Both looked through their packs for something to burn. Alexander removed his lighter, and together they were able to put enough paper in Alexander's tin cup to cover the entire blade of the knife in flame.

Wilhelm removed his last two syrettes of morphine. He poked one into Alexander's skin, allowing time for it to travel over his body and a feeling of euphoria to take over. Alexander took off his belt and folded it over. He would bite down on it to prevent himself from biting his tongue. Wilhelm used his canteen to collect the water dripping from the ceiling above them and doused the wound with water in a last attempt to clean it before he counted down with his fingers. Alexander took deep breaths and put the belt in his mouth and bit down, his fingers squeezing it. Wilhelm grabbed the knife. The silver steel had transformed into a fluorescent orange. Alexander took a final deep breath and closed his eyes. Wilhelm pressed the blade against Alexander's wound. The skin hissed like a snake as the skin seared together. Wilhelm pulled the knife away. Alexander spat the belt out and let out a word that Wilhelm could only guess was "fuck." Wilhelm allowed Alexander to steady his breathing and the initial trauma to fade and used the last syrette of morphine on himself.

The knife was back inside the tin cup. The flames danced up and reflected glimmers of silver off it. Alexander handed the belt to Wilhelm, and he wrapped it around his knuckles. Alexander nodded. The knife was now a glowing orange again. He poured the water down Wilhelm's chest to remove both the dried and fresh blood, and then he grabbed the knife from the tin cup.

Wilhelm brought the belt to his mouth and bit down. He had set the photo of Hannah against his knapsack, and he concentrated his gaze upon it. The excruciating pain the knife would bring was to buy more time—more time to return to Hannah.

The knife glowed as Alexander brought it toward him. The pain felt like the devil himself had placed a finger upon his flesh. It sizzled and seared. He bit through the leather and squeezed the belt with trembling hands. Even with the dose of morphine, it had been almost worse than being shot. At least the bullet had come by surprise. But to see the glow of the fiery blade slowly approach his flesh had made it worse. Wilhelm raised his canteen to his mouth, his hands shaking so greatly that the water inside splashed out.

Alexander tossed the knife on the ground and leaned back against the wall. His deep breaths grew softer until his head slouched. His chest heaved up and down but much more relaxed now that he had fallen comatose. Wilhelm's senses dulled. He could no longer smell smoke or the rotting corpses of the city. His hearing was next. Everything was distorted and slow. His vision was blurry, and the black dots in the corners grew until they covered his entire sight. When he woke, he had no idea how long he had passed out for. To him, it had been a blink, but it was no longer night, telling Wilhelm at least four hours must have gone by.

Alexander was awake too, and judging by his face, he had been waiting for Wilhelm to wake. He used his hand to mimic writing. Wilhelm nodded and removed his journal from his knapsack. He offered the journal and the pencil to Alexander. He took it and said what Wilhelm assumed was thank you. Alexander had poor penmanship, and the words were all connected in a singular line. At the end of the page of a long letter, he signed his name.

"Helen," Alexander said and returned the journal.

Wilhelm nodded. Even not being able to read a single word of the letter, he knew what it was. It was a goodbye. If Alexander died, if the Soviets lost the battle, he wanted to give his beloved Helen closure. Wilhelm wanted the same for Hannah. He wrote Hannah's name on the top of a new page. As the words flowed from pencil to page, tears filled the corners of his eyes. He wrote memories, promises, and wishes. Conveying his feelings for her on one page was an impossible task. But most of all, he wanted Hannah to know how much she had changed his life. Being able to be with her for as long as he had been made him feel much older than the twenty-three years he was. The years with Hannah had meant more to him than twenty or thirty years without her ever could.

"Look to the stars and you will find me there."

Wilhelm signed his name and stared at the letter. He tore the page from his journal and wrote his address far more legible than any word in the letter. It would go nowhere if no one could decipher where to send it. The Soviet and the German exchanged letters, locking eyes. They had made a solemn vow to seek out the other's spouse.

They ran short of food rations, and the water they drank from the dripping ceiling was far from sanitary. The cauterization of their wounds had worked, and they were no longer bleeding, but they had exponentially increased their chances of contracting an infection. The deck was stacked against them, and neither Stalingrad nor death fell for bluffs. They examined their wounds every hour for signs of infection. The gun and artillery fire were now nothing more than annoying houseflies. It was the buzzing of the Luftwaffe aircraft, like a swarm of hornets, that truly paralyzed them with fear. The bombs they dropped destroyed entire buildings. The swarming came. Wilhelm and Alexander braced themselves, sheer terror in their eyes. Bombs exploded close by. The floor and the entire building they had taken refuge in shook. The planes were close. Wilhelm and Alexander covered their heads and braced for the explosions.

The neighboring building exploded and sent a fresh wave of concrete dust that filled their lungs. The ceiling of their building broke, varying in size from pebbles to slabs, and crashed down through the floors below. The floor gave way at an angle. The structural integrity of the building was decimated.

Alexander and Wilhelm slid down into the apartment building a level and a room beneath the one they were in and crashed to the floor. The ceiling of the room was on fire, and they would have suffocated had it not been for the massive opening in the outside wall. They crawled like mice through a tight opening. The flames roared and engulfed the wall. They threw their knapsacks through the hole. Alexander crawled through and offered his hand to help Wilhelm. The flames roared with frustration for the two escaping its wrath. They hurried to their feet. The flames shot through the opening in the wall. The opposite wall was open near the top of the 2.4-meter tall room. Alexander tossed both of their knapsacks over and reached for the wall. His cauterized wound stretched as he pulled himself up. Again, he offered his hand and yanked Wilhelm up. The two fell over the other side and landed on a pile of concrete rubble.

They were anything but comfortable and worried the flames would spread, the ceiling would collapse or a bomb would drop right on the building. It was hard to believe the room had once been someone's home and, in a lot of instances, had become a grave. In the corner, weeks into decay, was a family of four. The apartment was filled with their possessions. With no place to go, they had elected to stay in their home. The smell was putrid, and Wilhelm and Alexander vomited. The refrigerator had been knocked down, and all the food inside had spoiled past the point of stomaching it. They found a mattress covered with blood and bullet holes and dragged it into the fridge. They were able to rest on the mattress with their heads safe from any falling debris. Three years ago, the rotting meat and moldy vegetables would have made Wilhelm puke, but they were nothing in comparison to the corpses in the corner.

The ceiling of the room, as well as the two floors above it, was gone. Rain fell and soaked their clothes. The water burned when it pelted their wounds, the color of which had been a bright pink but was now blotched with disgustingly yellowish-white pus. Its meaning was clear to both. Their wounds were infected, and if they remained untreated, they would die. They were left with nothing but silence and the awful smell of decay. How long he and Alexander had been in the apartments neither knew. But the food rations were long gone and the water too. Dysentery was sure to come from the grime-covered water they had resorted to drinking. Everything they had done only delayed death. But, now, time was up.

Both were deep in memories, but the silence was broken by gunfire from the floor below them. They shifted from the fridge and sat up in heightened alert. They looked at one another. The approaching soldiers meant fatal news for one of them. The muffled voices couldn't be distinguished as German or Soviet, but the gunshots that followed were a known language to every man. Even quieter than the voices, which had fallen silent, were the footsteps outside the door. Doors on the floor were kicked open. Wilhelm's pulse quickened. Alexander breathed heavy and quickly, but it offered no relief. They had but seconds until the door was kicked in.

Alexander spoke, but Wilhelm only understood the words "Soviet" and "me." Wilhelm repeated similar words. If they were Soviet, Alexander would try to stop them from shooting Wilhelm and Wilhelm, the same. "Helen," Alexander said. Both he and Wilhelm raised their hands in surrender. The door opened. The men wore gray uniforms, not military green. They were German.

"Don't shoot!" Wilhelm screamed.

But it was too late. A shot fired. The bullet pierced through and out Alexander's forehead. His head snapped back and fell limp against the fridge—his eyes still open. In a fraction of a second, a life had ended. A second ago, Alexander's hope of seeing his wife and infant child was alive, but in the next second, Helen had become a widow and Viktor, fatherless. Wilhelm could not take his eyes off him as the Germans cleared the room.

"Are you injured?" a medic asked.

Wilhelm had not cried a single time during his years fighting. He had lost friends and acquaintances, but none had brought him to tears. But with Alexander's death, he had lost a reflection of himself. The ability to be a human being in an arena of beasts designed to strip compassion, mercy, and empathy seemed an impossible feat. It could have been the Soviets to advance from the firefight below. It could have been Wilhelm dead against an overturned fridge. How many moments of seconds had influenced what had happened? How many missed and hit bullets had brought the series of events that had transpired to being?

Two men grabbed Wilhelm at the elbow and forced him to his feet. Others patted Alexander's body for supplies and ammunition—grave robbing. Wilhelm had done it, but to him, they had been nameless, almost faceless men. He cocked his head back to look at his fallen friend and comrade one last time. His tears fell freely. Alexander deserved better than to die in some dilapidated wasteland. He did not deserve to have his body rot against a pile of rubble. A lightheadedness descended upon Wilhelm, and the pain in his chest and shoulder returned. The sunlight blinded him as he was dragged out of the building.

"He needs medical attention," the medic said to the driver of a truck filled with wounded and perished soldiers.

Wilhelm was lifted onto the truck. Bodies were haphazardly tossed beside him. Arms and legs protruded off the edge. The truck left the damaged and destroyed building and Alexander behind. Wilhelm watched before the pain became too great and he fell to darkness.

Back into the Fray

Wilhelm's cauterization of his wound had saved his life. The doctors had told him as much. But his fear of getting an infection was well founded, and for the next three weeks, he drifted in and out of consciousness. Each time he awoke, there were different people on the bunks beside him. He was given things to drink, food to eat, pills to swallow, and ointments to rub on his wound. Each day, the pain in his chest and shoulder lessened. After a month, Wilhelm was cleared to return to combat. The devil atop the buildings snickered at his misfortune. There were no empty beds at the aid station. Hundreds had been cleared for combat, and the last thing any returning soldier wanted to see was the truckloads of injured or dead soldiers.

The initial blitzkrieg success that had been the staple of the German advance had, for the first time, failed them. The Soviets had chosen Stalingrad as the city they would defend to the last Russian. Stalin's words were not an empty threat. During the initial three months of the battle, the Germans had captured ninety percent of the city, but the Soviets stood fast and stout. They also proved to be much more cunning than General Paulus had expected. The heart of winter was upon them, and the freezing winds swept through the city like a fog. The Germans were not prepared for such weather. The battle had started in late August, and none of the Sixth Army nor the others who fought wore clothing to match temperatures that dropped well into the negatives, and with their supply lines cut off, there would be no winter gear coming.

Wilhelm loved winter walks but only when dressed for it. His ears and hands were frozen, yet not numb to the pain the cold brought. He kept his hands buried under his armpits and switched from left to right in pressing his ear against his shoulder. Wilhelm and four other men were shoulder-to-shoulder in a foxhole. Hardly comfortable, it at least blocked the wind.

"They will send reinforcements," a soldier said.

Whether it was to someone in particular or to himself was unclear.

"No one is coming. We're cut off," a soldier said, his mouth exhaling a cloud.

"What do you mean?" the soldier asked.

The desperation in his voice told Wilhelm his first comment had been a pep talk to himself.

"Our supply lines have been cut off. While we charged forward dick first, the Soviets went around the back and, now, they are fucking us in the ass," the soldier said.

"We need food, winter clothes," another said.

The pissed-off soldier pointed behind them. "There isn't anything coming from that way but death," he said before pausing, "We are in the cauldron now."

The phrase stuck, and the area they were encircled in became known simply as the cauldron, and it was not a great moniker for the Germans. The pot was cooking. Somewhere, hopefully, Höring was telling Jonas a massive "I fucking told you." Wilhelm had not seen either of them since August. The foxhole had become home. The four other men crammed inside all looked the same. Most of the time, their faces were buried in their jackets. Throughout random bits of conversation, Wilhelm only picked up last names. There was Schneider, Keller, Bergmann, and Sauer.

"We are in hell," Schneider said.

"Hell? I think hell is a bit warmer than this," Keller snapped back.

"Well, give me a ticket," Sauer said, his face buried in his jacket.

"Your soul is nothing to joke about," Schneider said.

Schneider was an awful guy to be in a foxhole with. Facing mortality every day was hard, but Schneider took every joke too seriously and threatened people with damnation.

"The devil can have my soul for a Goddamn jacket," Keller said, letting out an exhale that created a mushroom cloud.

"Keller, you will be sadly mistaken if he takes that offer," Schneider said.

"Yeah, well, I'll be mistaken and you'll still be freezing your ass off," Keller retorted.

"What about you, Schreiber?" Schneider asked.

He also had the annoying habit of making others choose sides.

"Yeah, I'd sell his soul for a jacket," Wilhelm joked.

The others laughed, but it quickly turned into coughs.

Wilhelm's face was past numb, and sitting on the cold, hard ground made his ass grow colder every second. His lips were so chapped that every time he smiled, luckily not often, they split open, and his runny nose had frozen around his nostrils.

"Screw this. Start a fire," Keller demanded.

"You are not putting a bullseye on my back, asshole," Bergmann said, lifting his head to look at Keller.

"The explosion will at least be warm, Bergmann," Keller said.

Such a cruelty to have the means to warm themselves with a fire but could not.

"I'm pissing icicles," Bergmann said from out of the foxhole with his back to them.

"Don't piss into the wind, asshole," Keller said.

"You still got that picture of your wife?" Bergmann asked.

"Why?" Keller asked.

"I need to get hard to piss," Bergmann said.

"I would sell my soul for that," Sauer teased.

"Eat shit, Sauer," Bergmann said as loud as he dared to.

The foxhole filled with laughter, but each time morale increased, the temperature dropped even further. Wilhelm and the Germans no longer fought just the Soviets. They fought winter, and winter was born to Russian parents. The Soviets were raised in it and, more importantly, were dressed for it. The number of soldiers who froze to death was startling. Every morning, fifty or more would be found to have perished overnight. Those living ransacked through the dead for food and clothing. Bodies were stripped naked, and after the ten thousand horses were killed for meat—a sound Wilhelm would never forget— the dead were eaten. No one could judge, for only with your life on the line do you know the depths you would go to save it. The highlight of one night had been Bergmann coming into possession of a blanket large enough to cover the foxhole.

Inside the foxhole, Wilhelm stared at the medal his father had given him—the blood pump of the world.

"What is that?" Sauer asked.

"It is my father's medal from Verdun," Wilhelm said.

"Why do you keep looking at it?" Bergmann asked.

"We are in Verdun," Wilhelm said.

The hole took a solemn turn.

"The meat grinder," Schneider stated.

"Frozen meat," Keller corrected.

All the horrific sights, sounds, and smells Wilhelm's father had seen he now had too.

"Where the hell is our resupply? We have no food! I can't even find any Goddamn snow that is not covered in blood or urine to melt down!" Keller yelled, kicking the frozen wall.

No one wanted to venture out from the small pockets of safety if not needed. Their time to fight again would come, and each day, the noose the Soviets had wrapped around their necks pulled tighter. Each week, the foxhole grew smaller. Sauer died in his sleep. Schneider came down with such a deep cough that he started puking blood. He was taken out of the fight but died days later. Bergmann was hit by a mortar round and bled out on a pile of concrete and wooden rubble. Keller died eight days later when he found himself in the scope of a sniper.

Each day, bits of humanity were stripped away in order to survive. Wilhelm no longer asked fellow Germans their names. There was a hundred-percent chance one or the other would be dead in the next few hours. One such unfortunate soldier had had to remove his jacket when it caught on fire. By the time he had wandered into the apartment building Wilhelm and twenty others were defending, there was nothing that could be done for him. But morbidly, the fire was welcomed, and they huddled around the eighteen-year-old as his body burned.

Wilhelm and the Germans waited in silence for the Red Army to advance down the destroyed and beaten road in front of the apartment building. When they finally came, they were riddled with lead. But without any time to react, the wall was blasted apart, and

Wilhelm was thrusted backward. Those closest to the wall were killed, and those who survived did so with varying degrees of shrapnel.

"Soviets!" one soldier yelled before he was shot down.

Wilhelm's rifle was too far away for him to reach. His only option was the flamethrower on the dead German's back. He grabbed it and squeezed the handle. The fury of hell came surging from it. It spread nearly twenty-five meters and scorched the seven Soviets with the flame. Their screams completely overpowered the sound of the roaring flame. Wilhelm had grown accustomed to the cries of war, but there was none more terrifying than a man on fire. Wilhelm had burned seven men to death. It was at that moment Wilhelm realized the devil's greatest trick of all. War turned soldiers, both Soviet and German, into his minions and demons who did his bidding.

After the bodies stopped squirming, Wilhelm dropped the flamethrower in horror at what he had done. He was the only one alive in the room or on the road. He dashed out of the apartment building and ran back to rejoin the German force. Inside the cauldron, it was clear Stalingrad had been won by the Soviets. It was known by all—from the soldiers to the officers—all the way up to General Paulus.

"He will not let us surrender," a soldier said, melting a bit of snow in his tin cup over a fire.

They were behind one of the few still-standing buildings and could enjoy a fire to warm them.

Everyone in the circle knew who "he" was—Hitler. He would not have his pride wounded from such a defeat. They all knew what it meant. They would have to fight until they were killed, starved or frozen. No one would leave the cauldron alive.

"A pilot has agreed to take letters back with him. If you boys have someone back home you want aware of your fate, I suggest you write a letter and give it to him," an officer announced.

Wilhelm still had the letter he and Alexander had swapped. It felt like it had been so long ago. So much had changed. Wilhelm had developed such a coldness to killing. He was an animal—a wolf who did not second-guess killing the sheep. Only the Soviets weren't sheep. They were wolves too. Each fight and each victory was earned through blood and sweat. He knew if he had met Alexander now, he would have shot him instantly. He could not even trick himself into thinking otherwise. He considered himself fortunate he had met him at a different time and when he was a different person. The thought of Alexander made Wilhelm cling to what little humanity he had left. The rest had been jettisoned off a steep cliff, and what did remain hung on by its fingernails, its grip faltering. Was he still the same man Hannah loved?

Perhaps, if Hannah was able to read his journal and all he had done and had been done to him, she could understand. But Wilhelm had lost his pencil, and by the time one was passed to him, the pilot had boarded his plane. They were brave to fly into the cauldron, and some never made it back out. They dropped off what supplies they could, and though it may not have seemed like much, the sight of canned herring was enough to make men cry for those who had feasted on rats and, in the extreme, other men. Word spread that General Paulus had given the pilot his wedding ring to return to his wife in Germany. If General Paulus did not plan on leaving the cauldron, no one should.

"You know what I am thinking of?" one soldier asked.

They were huddled together in the freezing blackness.

"A warm bed and a woman to warm you?" a fellow blonde soldier answered.

"I'm thinking of every plate of food I never finished. The bits of bread from my sandwiches. Never had a strong liking for bread. I'd pick the crust off. Now, I'd kill a thousand Russians for one piece of bread with butter spread on it," the soldier said.

Coughs echoed up and down the lines. Everyone had a cold, whether minor or severe.

"I would have rather died in North Africa—my feet in the Mediterranean, my back on the warm sand as the sun beat down upon my face," one said through a shiver.

"Not me. I never wanted to be a soldier. There was a brothel I frequented in Hamburg. There was this Negro woman with breasts out to here. I want her to smother me to death with those," one said, using his hands to demonstrate.

They tried to laugh, but only deep, painful coughs were swallowed up by the brutal wind.

"What about you?" the soldier directly across from Wilhelm asked.

"Warm in my bed with my wife by my side," Wilhelm said.

Wilhelm thought about Hannah all that night. He could only hope she was well and that fortune had taken a more desirable turn for her. He wanted to pull her picture from his pocket, but his fingers were too rigid. The snow had stopped falling, and the winds had died too. The entire air around them was frozen. Wilhelm and the Sixth Army were freezing to death, and there was nothing he could do.

Josephine Moreau

The plane landed safely in Strasbourg and the two pilots, after their cargo was unloaded, took Hannah to a local restaurant for breakfast. Neither appeared to be Nazis or even Nazi sympathizers, but she had an impression that they were keeping a close eye on her. Whether they were worried about failing Brigadeführer Huber's command or simply being gentlemen, she could not tell. Though she did not know their motive, she did know she was not getting back on the plane.

She ate her order of apple-cinnamon French toast and excused herself to use the restroom. She discretely, filled with shame, took the tip from a table as she passed by and entered the woman's bathroom. A woman was at the sink, washing her hands. Hannah entered a stall and waited for the woman to leave. When the woman left and the door behind her closed, Hannah stepped out and hurried to the window over two meters from the ground. Well out of her reach, she ran to the garbage can and turned it upside down. She took quick glances to the door, praying solitude would continue for moments longer. She climbed onto the garbage can and was able to reach the window sill. She slid it open and pulled herself up through the opening. She dropped onto the hard ground and rushed to join the huge crowds on the street. Even if she was in occupied France, it was unwise to speak German and expect to be given directions to the train station. As an alternative, she asked in English, and only after asking nearly ten people did she get an answer.

The two Austrian pilots surely had discovered she had escaped. The only question was would they alert the Nazis? If they feared repercussions from Brigadeführer Huber, they more than likely would.

The train station was less than ten blocks away, and Hannah had to balance a fine line of looking to be in a hurry and looking like she was running from something. When the train station came into view, Hannah had to stifle her relief. She had only arrived at the station. She still needed to acquire a ticket, board the train, and the train needed to leave. She walked to the window and bought a ticket for the next train to Paris using the stolen tip money.

"Twenty minutes," the older, gray-haired woman said.

Twenty minutes was a lifetime—far too long. It would not take a genius to figure out someone wanting to run away would look for a method to do exactly that. Hannah took her ticket and stood next to the tallest men she could find. She wanted to turn her head and look, but one glance was all that was needed to be spotted. She checked the pocket watch the farmer had given her. It had to have been broken, only three minutes had passed. And the next time she checked, only a minute.

After seventeen more anguishing minutes, equating to nearly fifty glances at her watch, the train finally pulled into the station. After the passengers stepped off the train, Hannah, fighting visions of a human cattle car, stepped on and occupied a window seat. She blocked her face with her hand and looked toward the aisle. Whenever she saw black leather boots walk past, she fought the urge to look up. When the last passengers were seated, the train jerked forward, and Hannah left the eastern French city of Strasbourg and the two pilots behind. The tracks passed south of the city of Verdun and the famed battlefield of the Great War.

Nearly thirty years earlier, the fields would have been littered with French and German men. Petyr Schreiber had fought on that very field and, according to Wilhelm, a part of him had died there. The fields looked too peaceful to be the resting place of hundreds of thousands of men. The rows and rows of white crosses of the memorial Douaumont Ossuary were perfectly in line and stretched past what the human eye could see. History had been ignored. Would anyone have wanted war after walking the hallowed grounds?

The forty-six-meter high bronze death bell was silent. The lantern of the dead, rotating red and white, only shined at night, but the white crosses sparkled in the sun. The sacrifice of so many was impossible to forget. But the deaths of thousands at Auschwitz were unknown to the world—no bells chimed for them, no lights shone. Thousands disappeared with nothing to remember them by but the mountains of possessions in Kanada.

Hannah's thoughts were depressing and reflective until the Eiffel Tower broke over the horizon. When the train shrieked to a stop, most passengers began retrieving their luggage. Hannah had none and was the first to step off the train. The next batch of passengers waited to step on, and Hannah disappeared into the crowd.

Hannah had used all her stolen money on the ticket to Paris and, not that she had wanted to, she could not make a habit of stealing. It was a sure way to get into trouble. There were few cars on the streets, but cafés were on every street corner, serving Parisians and German soldiers alike. The entire city was romanticized—from its historic beautiful buildings to its narrow streets of cobblestone.

Of all the cafés, there was one busier than all the rest, and all points led to it. The name of the café, "Givre Strudel," or "Frosted Strudel," was in white letters against a red canopy. It had both indoor and outdoor seating and no vacancy for either. The chairs were wicker and the tables, glass. The plates were filled with edible art, and judging by the food, the place specialized in pastries. Clouds of smoke wafted off the end of cigarettes from people enjoying an after-lunch smoke. Bust boys cleared and washed tables while waitresses flirted for better tips.

Hannah opened the door to the café, and the waitresses dropped their heads at the sight of another customer. A woman with olive skin and thick, flowing brunette hair spoke. She studied Hannah's confused expression.

"We have no seating available at the moment," the olive-skinned woman said in broken German.

"I would like to ask about a job," Hannah said in German.

She followed the woman as she cleared tables and loaded the dirty dishes into a plastic tub. The woman studied Hannah once more. Her eyes, blue and green in color, each fighting for dominance, pierced through Hannah. The woman nodded, indicating Hannah to follow her. Hannah did, and the woman made meandering past the customers and staff look like an elegant dance. She used the plastic tub to push open the kitchen swing door.

She dropped the tub down next to the sink, the dishes inside clambering against one another. The woman spoke in French again, and a man dried his hands on his apron and hurried through the swing door.

"You speak German. You are in Paris," the woman said.

"Do you speak English?" Hannah asked in English.

"I do. And I speak some Boches too," the woman answered.

"Boches?" Hannah asked.

"German," the woman said.

She paused ever so slightly and wore a look that told Hannah to get to the point.

"I would like a job," Hannah said.

"Yes. I understood you when you said it in German. You are from Germany?" the woman asked.

"I am," Hannah replied.

There was no point in denying it. Her accent would betray any lie she told.

"Why are you here?" the woman asked, mixing a bowl of white frosting with a spatula.

"I need a job. I have no money," Hannah explained.

"Not much of a dresser either, are you?" the woman said.

She cleaned the spatula on the edge of the mixing bowl and grabbed a whisk and whipped the frosting.

Hannah was still dressed in the clothes the woman from the farm had given her. The farmer's wife had a huge heart but little taste. The clothing was fine for the farms of Czechoslovakia, but it was not fine for one of the most fashion-conscious cities in the world.

"I have nothing," Hannah said.

The woman slid the bowl down the counter to the pastry chef and wiped her hands on a towel. Again, she studied Hannah.

"Michelle, I will be leaving for lunch. I will return shortly. With more help," the woman said.

"Okay, Josephine," Michelle said.

"Follow me," Josephine said to Hannah.

Josephine was the most popular person at the "Givre Strudel" and, perhaps, all of Paris. She could hardly make it past a table without the patrons starting a conversation or throwing their hands up, waving and flashing giant smiles. She was voluptuous but could hold a conversation with the brightest mind, and her wit was as sharp as a tack. Her kindness was not exclusive to the French but to the Germans as well, and it took twenty minutes to travel three tables.

"How is everything, gentlemen?" Josephine asked in German.

"Perfect as always, Josephine," the highest-ranking officer said in French.

The other German officers nodded politely between their puffs of cigarettes. Josephine returned the smile, and after twenty-five minutes, they had finally made it outside. Luckily for Hannah and Michelle, who was told Josephine would return shortly, Josephine only offered waves and smiles to the outdoor patrons.

"How long have you been in Paris?" Josephine asked.

"Just today," Hannah said.

"Fresh off the train. There are some things to remember. The city is a different place during the day than it is at night—beauty and the beast. There are rules. We have strict regulations on everything, but there are ways around that," Josephine explained.

"Where are we going?" Hannah asked.

She did not want to sound rude but wanted to be cautious, even skeptical, of everything.

"If you wish to work for me, you will dress like a woman and with clothes that fit. You look like you are wearing a potato sack."

Somehow Hannah did not take offense. The outfit certainly would not have been in her wardrobe.

"There are so few cars," Hannah remarked.

During the flight out of Vienna, the roads were filled with headlights, but in Paris, they were ghost-like.

"The Germans take the gasoline," Josephine explained.

They walked five blocks and crossed three intersections before Josephine ascended four steps to the entrance door of an apartment building. She inserted her key and opened the door. They stepped inside. Most of the doors on the floor were open and rooms, vacant.

"The building used to be full. Many left before the city was taken," Josephine said.

No doubt the Germans had broken into every apartment and had taken whatever they desired. Josephine's apartment was on the top floor, and Hannah was not surprised at how well kept the apartment was. Josephine was a sharply dressed woman who had an eye for fashion and decorating, and every hair on her head was where she wanted it to be. Hannah discretely looked over the apartment. A framed photo hung on the mantel—Josephine was surrounded by four men, one her age and three much younger. It was far too personal to mention and, instead, Hannah acted like she had not noticed it.

"You do not like the Germans?" Josephine asked.

"I like them fine," Hannah said.

Josephine grinned. "I saw your face at the Strudel. I've cast that look at a man or two before."

"No, I do not like them," Hannah said.

"That is your right. But when they are eating at my café, you will treat them no differently than you would a man from Paris. Understood?"

It came as a surprise she owned the café and an absolute shock she did not mind Germans.

"Why did you leave Germany?" Josephine asked.

"Paris was calling," Hannah answered.

It was a lie and one Josephine did not appreciate. She stared at Hannah with her dagger-like eyes and then resumed searching through her closet for clothes that would fit two criteria—one, clothes that would fit Hannah and, two, clothes she was willing to part with.

"Put these on," Josephine said.

She turned away from Hannah. But for Hannah, after Auschwitz, changing in front of a strange woman caused no discomfort.

"How does it look?" Hannah asked.

Josephine turned. Hannah was in a sky-blue summer dress and a pair of white heels.

"Dress is a bit baggy. I will put a belt around to tighten it to show your petite figure," Josephine said.

"I have a belt," Hannah said, reaching for the leather belt she had worn.

"No leather belts. It will warrant questions. All leather is to be used for boots for German soldiers. Do not wear it again," Josephine said.

Hannah nodded. She knew at that moment there would be as many rules to surviving in Paris as in Auschwitz.

Josephine wrapped a cloth belt around Hannah's waist and tightened it.

"For the finishing touches…" Josephine said, twisting open a tube of lipstick, nude in shade. It was not nearly as vibrant as Josephine's fierce red, and Hannah approved of that. Her goal was to blend in, not to be noticed by every man in Paris.

"Are you planning on staying in Paris?" Josephine asked.

"I would like to get to London," Hannah answered.

Josephine laughed.

"Is that funny?" Hannah asked.

"The Germans will not allow you to go to London," Josephine said.

She led Hannah out of the apartment and locked her door and wiggled the door handle to ensure it was locked.

"Do you speak any French?" Josephine asked.

"No," Hannah answered.

"That won't fly. I'll let you serve the Germans. Pick up what the other waitresses are saying. We close at seven. We will talk again after that."

Hannah was being thrown into a lake, and she would either sink or swim. But she had survived much worse than learning to speak French on the fly while serving the very soldiers who rounded up people like her.

Inside the café, it was nearly eighty degrees, and Hannah had to fight the urge to roll her sleeves up and risk her tattoo being seen. It would mean nothing to Josephine or any of the French, but high-ranking German officers were sure to know what it was. A vacant table was occupied by a group of German officers. Hannah prayed silently that none of them had been to the Hauser household.

"Welcome. Can I start you off with something to drink?" Hannah asked.

"Just water for the table, please," the oldest of the group said.

"Very well. Do you need more time to look over the menu?" she asked.

"Your German is quite good. Are you not from France?" the soldier asked.

He looked like the poster child of Hitler's Aryan race fantasy.

"I grew up in Germany. My parents moved here when I was fourteen," Hannah lied.

"Your first day?" he asked.

"It is. I am sorry, but did you want to order something to eat?" Hannah asked.

"My apologies. Of course, you are quite busy," the German said.

It was rude and, perhaps, the man was only being polite. But in her experience, anything more than two questions was an interrogation. She scribbled their orders down on her pad in English, and Josephine had to translate it to the chef. When one table had everything they needed, a hand shot up and another table was in need of more water or more napkins or wished to pay the bill.

"Until we meet again, Miss," the German said, holding his field cap out in front of him.

"Thank you for stopping in," Hannah said.

Somehow, she felt strangely guilty for her rudeness. The man had been overly polite with both his conversation and tip. It was a good reminder for her that not all German soldiers were evil. For every Waltz, Usinger, and every Rottenführer she had met, there were people like Wilhelm, Erich, and Heinrich. A hope rose in her. German soldiers entered the café every hour. The next could be Wilhelm. But each time, she was met with disappointment.

The day flew by with little time to even use the bathroom. Josephine had to remind hopeful customers it was past closing time. The other waitresses said their goodbyes, and Josephine locked the doors behind them.

"You did well today," Josephine said.

"I served forty-seven people. Twenty-three ordered the frosted strudel," Hannah said.

"You don't need to remember that sort of thing," Josephine said.

She nearly burst out laughing before her eyes narrowed and pierced Hannah with her razor-sharp stare.

"I am sorry," Hannah said.

The old habit of Auschwitz was hard to break. One miscount and Hannah would have been sent to the gas chambers. But she had always remembered a second number too—the number of men's coats Eleanor had found.

Josephine's eyes were a fearsome defense while Hannah's were a glaring weakness that revealed every feeling and thought.

"Are you alright?" Josephine asked.

"Yes," Hannah lied.

Josephine stared at Hannah. A lone tear hung on the corner of Hannah's eye. She hoped if she blinked quick enough, it would not fall. But it did. No more questions could follow, for there was a pounding on the glass door that nearly knocked off the "CLOSED" sign.

Hannah jumped. Josephine did not. She walked to the door and unlocked it. A man took in Josephine's appearance and charmed her in French. He stepped inside and had not expected to see anyone else. Josephine and the man spoke to each other again.

"I am sorry. I did not realize you still had a customer," the man said in English.

Josephine must have told him that Hannah could not speak French.

"She works for me. She started today. Hannah, would you please get a piece of strudel for Mr. Durand?" Josephine asked.

"Certainly," Hannah said.

The man smiled. He was as charismatic as Josephine. He was not one of the men in the photo on her mantel, one of whom Hannah assumed was her husband. Josephine did not have a ring on, but her hands spent a large majority of time in dough, frosting, and cake batter. But it was the sort of late-night meeting sure to cause gossip. The man looked slightly uncomfortable. He was handsome with black hair with a dusting of gray and had a thin mustache. If Josephine was single, Hannah held no fault in her taste.

Hannah went into the kitchen. Only words, not sentences, drifted through the swing door and into the kitchen. But all were in French, and Hannah did not understand a single one. When she opened the kitchen door, the conversation fell silent.

"*Merci*," Durand said, flashing a suave smile. It was the sort of smile that was equal to a dozen pick-up lines and had surely entranced many a woman when he was in his twenties. He used his fork to cut a slice of the frosted strudel and took a bite. His eyes rolled back as the flavor hit his taste buds. "Josephine tells me you do not speak French. Excuse my accent," Durand said in English.

"You will have to excuse mine," Hannah said.

"German?" Durand asked.

"Yes," Hannah answered.

He took a sip of the coffee Josephine had poured him and puckered his lips.

"I do what I can with what I get," Josephine said.

It was imitation coffee. Hannah had had a cup between tables, and if Durand thought this coffee was a poor imitation of real coffee, he should have had the "coffee" at Auschwitz. Durand finished his coffee and used his fork to scrape up the remaining bit of frosting from the plate. He stood and put his top hat back on. It sat on an angle. Durand flashed a smile as he pulled out money for his purchase.

260

"Josephine Moreau, a pleasure as always. I thank you. And to you, Miss, I apologize, but I have forgotten your name," Durand said.

"Hannah. Hannah Smith."

"A pleasure meeting you."

Durand inclined his head and walked to the door with a slight limp.

"Tomorrow at ten. Be back here," Josephine said to Hannah.

"Thank you," Hannah responded.

Hannah had solved the mystery of getting work. Now, she had to settle the problem of her gurgling stomach and finding a safe place to sleep. She opened the door and had stepped half-way out when Josephine spoke again.

"Where are you staying?" she asked.

"I don't know," Hannah said.

She had lied enough.

Josephine sighed. "Give me five minutes to finish up."

She sorted through the cash register, and knowing silence would be appreciated while she counted, Hannah remained quiet. She took to refilling the salt and pepper shakers, pushing in the white chairs and sweeping under the tables. Josephine announced she was ready and met Hannah at the door. She shut the lights off and locked the doors behind them. What Josephine had said about the city being different at night was evident almost immediately. The number of German soldiers standing guard was double. They looked like stone gargoyles in the darkness, and the whites of their eyes glowed in the dark.

"Do your parents know you have come to Paris or did they wake up to a letter saying you ran away?" Josephine asked.

"My parents were killed."

It would have put less negative attention on her if she had said they had passed away. But passed away was such a peaceful way to describe death—something that should be reserved for people who died in their sleep at an old age. Hannah would not lie about that. Her parents had been taken from their home and murdered.

"I am sorry," Josephine said. She was not a bashful woman, nor did she swallow her words often, but she recognized Hannah did not want to speak about it and let it slide— for the moment at least. "The city's allure during the night has been lost. My husband and

I used to sit on our roof and look at the lights. They were so mesmerizing and enticing," Josephine said.

She paused ever so slightly before she unlocked the front door of the apartment building. She locked it, even though she knew it would do little if the Germans wanted to enter. After stepping inside her apartment, she set her keys on a glass dish beside the door. "I will give you some blankets and a pillow. The couch is much more comfortable than it looks," Josephine said.

She had no idea the type of bed Hannah had slept in at Auschwitz, and having a fluffy pillow and a firm, comfortable couch made her giddy.

Hannah thanked her as Josephine put the needle onto a record player. Music played softly in the background. No matter how hard she tried not to look, Hannah continually found herself staring at the photograph on the mantel. Hannah had only been in the apartment twice, but there was nothing to indicate that the four men in the picture were still living there. Each conclusion she came to was more negative than the last. If they were her sons, it must have been a delightfully noisy household and, now, the silent apartment must have been strange and unwelcoming for Josephine—an absence she tried to replace with music. Josephine disappeared down the hallway, and Hannah crept to the photo to see if any of the three younger men bore a resemblance to Josephine.

"My husband, Mathis, and my sons, Noah, Adam, and Leo," Josephine said.

Hannah had not heard Josephine's footsteps. Whether it could be classified as snooping, Hannah was unsure.

"Sorry," Hannah said.

"I wouldn't have it up if I didn't want it seen," Josephine reassured.

"They are handsome. You all look very happy."

"We were." The past tense was not missed by Hannah. "Mathis was killed during the Fall of France, Adam during the Dunkirk evacuation. Noah and Leo are missing," she said.

"I am sorry," Hannah said again.

She truly was, yet how could Josephine serve the very officers who gave the commands that brought the death of her husband, one son, and possibly two more?

"So am I," Josephine said.

The loss of her parents would be an eternal struggle for Hannah, and even though she found no comfort in it, her parents would have chosen their deaths over Hannah's—

without question. And the way Josephine's usually piercing eyes wilted into pools of tears, it was clear she would have too. But unlike Hannah, Josephine's tears did not trickle down her cheek. Josephine walked into the kitchen and prepared a pot of tea. Hannah studied Josephine as she did. Eleanor had been a woman of a quiet, reserved strength. Josephine too was a strong woman, but it was much blunter. Like some kind of sorcerer, she was able to transform her emotions into an impenetrable and unreadable armor.

"Are you hungry?" Josephine asked.

Politeness dictated Hannah to refuse. But politeness was trumped by a gurgling stomach.

"Regrettably," Hannah said with a guilty smile.

"An honest answer at last."

"Josephine, I am sorry, but…" Hannah started to say, but she had no words to finish it. At least, that wasn't another lie.

"We all have our secrets, Hannah. I have mine. But you need to work on your lying, or you are going to get hurt."

It was true. She had tried lying to her parents about Wilhelm, and it ate her up to the point where she had to come clean.

Hannah had expected some intricate French delicacy and was delighted when Josephine set a peanut butter and jam sandwich on a plate beside her. After twelve hours of baking, sautéing, roasting, brewing, and frying, cooking was probably the last thing Josephine wanted to do. But even a sandwich deserved some showmanship. She made a crisp diagonal cut and garnished the sandwich with strawberries and blueberries.

"Thirsty?" Josephine asked.

"Do you have milk?" Hannah asked.

The milk the farmer and his wife had given her was both delicious and filling.

"No. It is rationed for children only," Josephine explained.

"Tea will be fine. Thank you."

"Sure."

Josephine poured the tea from the shrieking kettle pot into two teacups and spooned a cube of sugar into her lemon tea and, after Hannah nodded, added one to hers as well.

"When did France fall?" Hannah asked.

Josephine's eyes were neither piercing daggers nor pools of tears. They were perplexed and unable to read Hannah. The whole world knew the month and year.

"What happened to you, Hannah?" Josephine asked.

"Nothing. I am fine," Hannah said.

"*Connerie*," Josephine retorted.

"I don't know what that means."

"It means bullshit."

Hannah covered her face with her sandwich, but her eyes betrayed everything.

"June 1940. How long ago was that, Hannah?" Josephine asked.

Hannah could not even tell her the day's date.

"Maybe I should leave," Hannah said.

Josephine would not stand for another lie, and Hannah could not blame her for it. Yet, her secret needed to stay in the dark.

"If you wish it. Be careful. Curfew is over. If you are caught, they will ask for your papers. You do not have any. You are German, yet you fled your own country. I am asking why. The Germans will demand to know why," Josephine warned.

Hannah was frozen half-way between Josephine and the front door, unsure to stay or leave.

"Did you kill someone?" Josephine asked.

"No," Hannah said.

If Josephine could detect a lie, hopefully, she could sense the truth too.

"I am going to ask you a question, Hannah. I would appreciate the truth."

Hannah could only nod. She hated being questioned. She was back in the study in Lena's house or at her parents' bare and stripped home being unknowingly interrogated.

"I am letting you stay in my home. I am breaking the law in harboring you. I am willing to do this if you are a victim, but if there is any reason the Germans could be looking for you…" Josephine paused. "I am a mother who hopes to see her two sons alive again. Please do not do anything to stop that from happening."

"Please don't make me say it," Hannah pleaded.

"I am not them, Hannah. I will not force you to do anything," Josephine promised.

Hannah was paralyzed with indecisiveness. She had learned to trust herself and her instinct. Yet, now, she was unable to decide. She wanted to trust no one. It was the safest not only for her but Josephine too. She had trusted Eleanor and Trugnowski, but they were in the same situation as Hannah with nothing to gain from it. Josephine could turn Hannah into the Nazis. It was the smartest thing the woman could do.

"Are you a spy?" Josephine asked.

It was the last thing Hannah expected to be asked.

"No," Hannah said.

"Of all the cafés in Paris, you stop at mine. You are a German. There is no hiding that. You have a clouded past and an aura of mystique you will not shed no matter how many times I ask you…"

"Spy. Why would I spy on you?" Hannah asked. But now it appeared Josephine had something to hide, and she too was not confident enough in the other to say anything further. They were at a standstill. "I am not a spy. I promise you I mean you no harm," Hannah said.

Josephine studied Hannah's face. Hannah did her best to meet her eyes with her own.

"You will need something to wear to bed, I suppose?"

The next morning came in an instant. Leaving the couch seemed like an impossible feat. It had grown in its comfortability as the night had gone on. The blankets had trapped Hannah's body heat and kept her warm.

Josephine pulled open the blinds, and a bright light flooded the room. Hannah shielded her eyes from it, but Josephine yanked the covers off her, and all the heat that had been trapped inside scattered away.

"If you want to stay here, it will not be free. Make me breakfast," Josephine said.

"I thought you did not demand," Hannah said.

She smiled softly, suppressed a yawn, and walked into the kitchen.

"I had a full stomach during that conversation," Josephine said.

Hannah lit the stove's top burner and cracked open four eggs over the skillet.

"What is in London?" Josephine asked.

"Nothing," Hannah said truthfully.

"The war is there too. But they are not under occupation. The Germans tried but failed. They turned their attention elsewhere—the Soviet Union," Josephine said.

"I thought they were allies."

"So did Stalin."

The farmer's wife with a tap of her finger had told Hannah as much but not why.

"And America?" Hannah asked.

"They stayed out of the war until December '41. The Japanese bombed them," Josephine replied.

Hannah was ashamed for being excited about America entering the war in such circumstances, but hopes of America liberating Europe filled her heart and mind.

"The Allies fight in the Pacific and North Africa. No one is fighting Germany on the western front," Josephine added.

Hannah used the spatula to scrape the scrambled eggs onto two plates. After the small breakfast, Josephine picked out another set of clothes for Hannah to wear. Josephine applied lipstick, a deep merlot in color, and black eyeliner to accentuate her eyes. After, the two walked to the "Givre Strudel." It was easy to see the city had reclaimed its charm. The head baker, Louis, was already hard at work, making the pastries, and when the doors opened at seven, patrons rushed in.

"Oberführer Köning, gentlemen, were you waiting outside since dawn?" Josephine asked, addressing a group of German officers that had just entered.

The merlot lipstick caught the men's attention and did not let leave their mind.

"Madam, I may have to order you to open early," Oberführer Köning said with a smile.

He was a tall, thin man nearing his mid-sixties, and the way his eyes lit up as he looked at Josephine's busty figure told Hannah the wedding band on his finger was little more than a fashion accessory.

"Gentlemen, may I introduce my beautiful niece, Hannah?" Josephine said.

Hannah tried to smile but came off looking nauseous. "Hello. It is great to meet you," she said in German.

"A German niece. You never mentioned that before. A pleasure to meet you," Oberführer Köning said.

"Can I get you something to eat or drink?" Hannah asked.

"You have your aunt's hospitality," Oberführer Köning remarked.

"Let me wager a guess. Oberführer Köning will have the éclair. Standartenführer Ziegler never goes against his superior's command, yet his pastry choices differ, and he cannot follow him on this. He will have the Pain au chocolat," Josephine said.

The German officers were completely entranced by Josephine's charm.

"Untersturmführer Engel is hoping on advancing past Standartenführer Ziegler and, therefore, will also order the éclair. Hauptscharführer Voigt simply wants his croissant, and he wants it now," Josephine continued.

She finished with a curtsey, and the German officers applauded. Even Hannah was mesmerized by her. Josephine was a snake charmer and the leather-clad Nazis, her snakes. Hannah had always considered herself an introvert and shied away from being the center of attention. But Josephine turned heads when she entered a room and held the attention in her hands like a ball of clay and molded it into whatever she wanted.

"Your aunt is quite correct, Miss," Oberführer Köning commented.

Hannah smiled nervously before walking to the kitchen. She tore the order from the glue spine pad and hung it on the line of orders with a clothespin. When Hannah returned, Josephine still commanded the German officer's attention.

"Hannah, would you please bring these gentlemen some coffee? I am sure the onslaught of meetings will need to be combatted with a strong cup," Josephine said.

Hannah paused and waited for further direction. The word strong was not applicable for the coffee they had served Durand. She was also unsure if it was wise to speak English in the company of Germans. Her mouth opened slightly, but she decided against it and moved through the kitchen swing door.

"My innocent niece. I offered to have her in France every summer, but where does she want to go? England," Josephine said in French.

The German officers laughed, apparently fluent in French.

"She does speak German. There will be more need for that than French," Untersturmführer Engel said.

He smiled politely. It did not suit him. His teeth were stained yellow from decades of cigarettes and coffee.

"German is not going to woo us French girls, Untersturmführer Engel," Josephine said as she blew a kiss goodbye.

In the kitchen, Hannah looked around for legitimate coffee.

"Need something?" the chef asked.

He spoke in English but had a thick French accent. He was also too busy applying a perfect scoop of ice cream to a slice of apple pie to look at Hannah.

"Coffee for the Germans," Hannah said.

The chef turned to look. "Josephine tell you?" he asked.

Hannah nodded.

"Follow me."

He rang the bell to alert the other waitresses an order was ready and led Hannah through the kitchen. Waves of heat washed upon her, causing her eyes to burn. The other chefs and bakers appeared to be unaffected by it. The chef led Hannah into a small office where a single pot of coffee was brewing.

"I thought this was illegal," Hannah said.

"Germans like good coffee. The shit is for us French," the chef explained.

"*Merci*," Hannah said.

She had planned to call him by his name, but she did not know it.

"Frank," he said.

"*Merci*, Frank."

"You want to thank me, make the next brew from toilet water," he said with a smile.

"Don't tempt me," Hannah joked.

She grabbed the pot of coffee and moved back into the kitchen and through the swing door and to the table.

"Are you going to talk about upping our ratio of butter and cream in this meeting? Otherwise, I'm going to have to change the name to the Strudel and drop the Frosted," Josephine teased.

"I am afraid not today," Oberführer Köning answered.

"Tell me, Oberführer Köning, why are these meetings not in my café? Or is it a law they must take place in some abandoned warehouse and beneath ground?" Josephine asked.

Hannah filled their cups with true black coffee.

"Fill it to the top, girl," Hauptscharführer Voigt ordered.

Hannah suppressed the urge to dump the entire scolding hot pot onto his head.

"Well, I will have to make sure those of higher rank are satisfied before accommodating a grunt," Hannah said.

The entire café fell silent. Josephine cast a nervous eye toward Hannah. The entire table stared at her. Hauptscharführer Voigt steamed like a kettle of tea. His superiors, solemn-faced. Their eyes had the maniacal glare the most terrifying of Nazis had. But the glare changed into a gleam, and laughter erupted from the officers at Hauptscharführer Voigt's expense.

"She has your wit, Josephine," Oberführer Köning said.

Hannah finished pouring the coffee and headed back into the kitchen. She steadied her breathing and her shaking hands.

"Food for the German officers," Frank announced.

Hannah had picked up several words and Frank, knowing she was new to the French language, spoke much slower. She grabbed the tray of food and pushed through the swing door. Remembering things had always come naturally to Hannah, but her skills had become so much keener and developed during her time at Auschwitz. Forgetting something, anything, meant death.

"Well, gentlemen, I am afraid if I have failed to convince you to come out of your basements and use my café at your convenience, I must try to bribe my fellow countrymen. Until tomorrow, I bid you adieu," Josephine said.

She strutted away and waited on a recently occupied table. It did not take long for the German officers to scarf down their food. Hauptscharführer Voigt's stares were as powerful as the heat waves in the kitchen. It took a week for him to forget the remark. The officers came in each day without exception and without exception, their orders remained consistent. Josephine always struck up a conversation that lasted anywhere from a quick greet to thirty minutes.

Another day had flown by, and Hannah flipped the "OPEN" sign to "CLOSED." A pounding on the door came before the sign had even stopped swinging. She took a step back, and her stomach leaped into her mouth. A man, his face concealed by his top hat, stared through the glass door at Hannah.

Radley Durand

The man at the glass door of the "Givre Strudel" removed his hat and smiled apologetically for scaring Hannah.

"Josephine, Mr. Durand is here," Hannah yelled.

"Let him in," Josephine yelled back.

Hannah unlocked the door and pulled it open.

"Good evening, Hannah," he said.

"Hello, Mr. Durand."

"Please, please, I am no mister. My name is Radley."

Though he was undoubtedly French, the way he thoroughly studied her was Nazi-like. Hannah could only smile uncomfortably as a response to his examining gaze.

"Would you like something to eat?" Josephine asked.

"No, not tonight. Are we ready?" Durand asked.

"Yes, we are," Josephine said.

Hannah was unsure as to whom Josephine was referring to as "we." Durand and Josephine? Or, was she included in it?

"Hannah, Radley is going to escort us home. There has been some trouble on the streets the last few nights," Josephine said.

Radley was a man who appreciated the way a good suit made him feel, and he appeared to have a favorite. He wore the same one he had on when Hannah had first seen him. But his limp was much worse than Hannah had originally noticed. In all, Durand did not seem like the fighting type.

"After you," he said, swinging his arm open to let Hannah and Josephine pass.

The wind had picked up, but Hannah was dressed for it, unlike during those frigid nights at Auschwitz. Shadows moved, but they scurried way too much to be German soldiers.

"Who are they?" Hannah asked.

"Homeless," Josephine answered.

Yet, it only seemed to be the partial truth—a partial truth that was confirmed when they walked past the street on which they should have turned.

"Where are we going?" Hannah asked.

Both Durand and Josephine were as silent as the night.

"Please answer me, Josephine," Hannah said.

She spoke in French, so there was nothing lost in translation. But no answer came. Hannah considered all her options: she could continue to follow the woman who had befriended her and the suave stranger or she could take off running. But, if she did, she would be caught by the Germans and would most likely be sent back to a concentration camp.

Durand walked toward a dented metal door. He slid it open and stood aside. The streetlights around the corner cast no light on what was inside.

"If you please," he said.

"Josephine?" Hannah asked.

She pleaded with her eyes. Surely, if Josephine could read lies, she could read the sheer terror in them now.

"Do what he says, Hannah," Josephine said.

Hannah stepped inside the black warehouse. What little light there was vanished when the door slid and slammed shut. To Hannah, she was back in Auschwitz and stepping into the gas chamber. Lights powered on. Hannah shielded her eyes. The warehouse had not been in use since France had surrendered. But it wasn't the wooden pallets or machines that caught her attention. It was the dozen men who surrounded her. Josephine stood next to the door and Durand, in front of Hannah. She had nowhere to escape.

"Who are you?" Durand asked.

"Hannah Smith," she said.

"Are you a spy, Hannah Smith?" Durand asked.

He pulled a pistol from behind his waistline.

"Please, don't," Hannah pleaded.

The barrel of the gun was inches from her forehead and so close that she could smell the gunpowder.

"Answer the question," Durand commanded, his voice echoing across the desolate factory.

"Josephine, please, I told you," Hannah pleaded.

"Don't look at her. Answer the question," Durand said.

"No, I am not a spy. Why do you keep asking me?"

"Do you know how many cafés there are in Paris?"

"No."

What a bullshit question!

"Hundreds. Yet, you come to Josephine Moreau's 'Givre Strudel.'"

"What do you want?"

She had found her strength. She did not want to die—far from it. But she would embrace it in the way Trugnowski had. Durand would have to use that gun.

"Are you a German spy?" Durand asked.

"I have answered your question," Hannah said.

"Why did you flee Germany?"

Only the truth could help her now.

"I will not answer in front of all these people," Hannah said.

"You are not in a position to make demands," Durand said.

"Only you and Josephine. Otherwise, you can shoot me," Hannah said.

The power had shifted. Durand now looked to Josephine. But her piercing eyes peered at and through Hannah. "Everyone else, leave," Josephine commanded.

She walked toward Hannah and Durand. The other men hurried toward the three exits in an attempt to not have twelve mysterious men pile out of an abandoned warehouse at once.

"Hannah, I have been kind to you, have I not?" Josephine asked.

"You have," Hannah answered.

She would not argue that.

"It is time you tell me the truth. You say you are not a German spy, but you are filled with secrets. Why did you flee Germany?" Josephine asked.

Hannah paused. Could words give justice to what she had seen, smelt, and heard? And, if she could find the words, would she have the strength to speak them?

"What do you know of what is happening to the Jews?" Hannah asked.

"We have heard rumors they are being sent east to an all-Jewish city," Josephine replied.

She gave Durand another look. No doubt thinking Hannah was deliberately trying to change the topic.

"There is no city. Jews are being sent to camps and killed," Hannah said.

Durand lowered the gun slightly as he processed the significance of what he had heard.

"What are you saying, Hannah?" Josephine asked.

Hannah pulled her left sleeve up and rotated her wrist so that her palm faced up. The number 19653 in black ink was perfectly visible and made her vulnerable in the same way as the day it had been carved into her.

"What is this?" Durand asked.

He lowered the gun and gently grabbed her arm to examine it.

"When we arrive, we are tattooed with a registration number," Hannah explained.

"Arrive where?" Josephine asked.

"Auschwitz—the killing camp," Hannah said.

"Hannah, what are you talking about?" Josephine asked.

"They take all Jews, Gypsies, homosexuals, enemies of the state. The elderly and young children are killed as soon as they step off the trains. Those who can work are forced to do so. They starve us. They shave our heads and take all our possessions," Hannah said.

Originally hesitant, revealing the truth released an immense buildup of pain, hurt, and fear. Durand and Josephine looked at one another—neither knowing how to react. They had expected a lie but not what they had just heard. There was no faking that level of emotion. Because of that, the horror and shock of it all showed on their faces.

"You are Jewish?" Durand asked.

"My parents were killed there. I escaped. I snuck onto the back of a manure truck, and a farmer and his wife took care of me. I boarded a train to Vienna and hid inside a cargo plane flying to Strasbourg. I came to Paris with nothing but the clothes the farmer's wife had given me. I want to get to London and from there to New York," Hannah said.

She had put all her secrets on the table. She was at the mercy of Josephine Moreau and Radley Durand.

"They cannot commit mass murder," Durand said after moments of silence.

"You know nothing of what they are capable of—the propaganda they have been brainwashing the Germans with," Hannah said.

"Hannah, thank you for sharing this with us. I am sure that was not easy for you. I will repay your honesty with some candor of my own," Josephine said. She put her hand on the gun Durand still held by his side. He understood and concealed the gun back in his waistline. "Hannah, Radley and I are part of the Maquis—the French resistance," Josephine said.

"I thought France was defeated," Hannah said.

"France was defeated. The French still fight," Durand said with a hint of pride in his voice.

"The reason I asked if you were a spy is because it is my duty to gather information for the resistance," Josephine explained.

"The information Josephine gathers she gives to me and we plan action," Durand added.

"What do you mean?" Hannah asked.

"We find out where meetings are taking place, where shipments of supplies are coming in, which alleys the drunk Germans like to piss in," Durand explained.

Every short and long conversation Josephine had had with the German officers had been initiated for the purpose of gathering information, and anything useful was given to Durand and the Maquis.

"We could use you, Hannah. I do what I can, but I am French. You are German. You look like them. You talk like them. They will open up to you in a way they never will with me," Josephine said.

"I can barely stop myself from shaking when I serve them coffee. I am not good at lying," Hannah said.

"And I want to pour hot coffee on their head. You learn to deal with it," Josephine said.

"France has Jewish families too, Hannah. Just think about it. I will not let you get hurt. I swear it," Durand reassured.

It was hard for Hannah to take that as an unbreakable vow as, moments earlier, he was ready to shoot her.

"That's enough for one night, Durand," Josephine said.

She was aware of the toll the last twenty minutes had taken on Hannah.

"Yes, but, if you please, I would like one final moment with Hannah—in private," Durand said.

Josephine looked at Hannah and studied her face. Hannah gave an uncommitted nod.

"Make it quick," Josephine said.

She walked to the sliding door, opened it, and stepped outside but left it open.

"I apologize for frightening you. But we cannot be too careful. The Germans are like dogs. They are cunning and smart and sometimes lick their own ass," Durand said and smiled.

It was genuine and, somehow, the fear in Hannah lessened.

"Josephine is a strong woman. You will be safe with her," he said.

He pulled out a cigarette and lit it.

"Do you smoke?" he asked.

"No," Hannah answered.

"Good. Me neither."

He took a puff and nodded for Hannah to leave first.

"I have men on every block. You will get home without incident," Durand said.

His words proved to be true. The shadows in the alleyways scampered about like rats. Josephine was quiet on the walk back to her apartment and even after they were back inside.

"I am sorry, Hannah. I had to know what you were hiding," Josephine said.

"I understand," Hannah said.

Josephine hid a dangerous secret herself, and self-preservation was near the top of her list. She and Wilhelm had kept the fact she was Jewish from their closest friends. The fewer people that knew, the safer it was.

"Please don't hate Durand too much. It was my idea," Josephine said.

"When he first came to the café, I thought…" Hannah started, but Josephine interjected.

"We were intimate? Radley is a handsome man. But my heart still belongs to my husband and my boys. Radley, to his wife and children," Josephine said.

"Aren't you scared?" Hannah asked.

"No, Hannah. I have lost everything in my life," Josephine said.

For the first time, Josephine acknowledged her sons, Noah and Leo, were most likely dead. She had repaid Hannah's vulnerability with her own. Hannah compared her own life to Josephine's. She had lost her parents. She had lost Eleanor and Trugnowski. She had lost her friendship with Lena. Heinrich and Erich may be dead too. It was only Wilhelm who filled her veins with a tenacity to survive.

"And Radley? Has he not lost everything?" Hannah asked.

"His story is his to tell. I would not feel right in telling it," Josephine said.

"If I choose to not help?" Hannah asked.

"That means you are choosing, and that is exactly what we are fighting for."

The next morning came without further discussion, and Josephine acted in a way that made Hannah question if last night had even happened. Once they arrived at the "Givre Strudel," Josephine put on her charming façade.

"Gentlemen, may I take your coats?" she asked Oberführer Köning and the other officers.

"That won't be necessary, but thank you," Oberführer Köning said.

"Are we interested in trying something new today, gentlemen?" Josephine asked.

"You are persistent," Oberführer Köning said.

"Let me show you why you gentlemen dine at my café instead of the hundreds of others in Paris," Josephine said.

"Hannah," Oberführer Köning called.

Hannah was at a nearby table, and even it was an order, she wanted to finish waiting on the two elderly French women. When she finished jotting down their order, she walked over to Köning's table. If Josephine was able to subdue hate and rage—extremely volatile emotions—Hannah could stifle her fear.

"Yes, Oberführer Köning?" Hannah said in German.

"What do you recommend from your aunt's menu?" Oberführer Köning asked.

"Croissant avec pomme," Hannah answered in her best French.

"Shall we make this interesting, Josephine?" Oberführer Köning asked.

"I did not think you to be a gambling man, Oberführer Köning," Josephine said.

"I am always up for a good wager if the reward is worth the risk. We shall try the croissant avec pomme. If we are in agreement it is good, I shall give you the cream and butter you desire," Oberführer Köning said.

"And, if by some strange miracle, you do not?" Josephine asked.

Köning had all the power in choosing, and he could lie to get what he wanted.

Hannah scrunched her toes to hide her nerves.

"The meal is on you," Oberführer Köning said.

Hannah relaxed her toes and smiled.

"Five croissants avec pommes, Hannah," Josephine ordered.

Hannah disappeared into the kitchen and passed along the order slip. She went around the café and refilled the cups of coffee for its patrons. The kitchen was packed elbow-to-elbow with waitresses and cooks, and Hannah waited as Frank put the finishing touches on the croissant. The smell of melted butter and cinnamon apple filling her nostrils was enough to make her salivate.

"Smells delicious, Frank," Hannah said.

"Good. I made one for you too," Frank said.

"You are the best," Hannah said.

She grabbed the tray of food and carefully pushed open the swing door with her foot.

"I do not want to be accused of playing favorites, so I will let you decide which croissant is yours, but I will start with Oberführer Köning," Hannah said.

The German officers laughed, but Hauptscharführer Voight's was hardly genuine. Hannah was selling her status as Josephine's niece extremely well, and the fact was not missed by Josephine. Oberführer Köning grabbed the largest croissant, and they went in rank until Hauptscharführer Voigt was left with the runt of the litter.

"Somebody needs to suck hind tit, Voigt," Untersturmführer Engel said.

Oberführer Köning grabbed his fork and, like a surgeon, sliced the croissant to ensure his first bite would contain equal amounts of croissant, apple, and cream. He closed his eyes as he chewed. The other officers were less delicate with theirs and ate two bites to his one.

"The verdict?" Josephine asked.

"Butter and milk used in this?" Oberführer Köning asked.

"Of course," Josephine said.

"There is a shipment arriving tomorrow. I will see to it that you receive ten times your allotted ration," Oberführer Köning said.

"I underestimated you. I thought you would not pass up the chance for a free meal," Josephine said.

She wiped a bit of cream from his lip. Her touch caused his face to redden.

"An excellent choice, Hannah. Thank you," Oberführer Köning said.

Hannah and Josephine left the officers, granting them privacy to finish their meal and conversation. The rest of the day went by much like the last week had.

The "Givre Strudel" was loved by Parisians and had the German stamp of approval, and when wealthy citizens from Germany visited Paris, it was the "Givre Strudel" where they ate breakfast and lunch. When one table vacated, there were two or more parties trying to swoop in and claim it. Thanks to the heavy and fatty foods of the café, Hannah was returning to her normal, albeit petite frame. While she would wait for Frank to finish adding the final touches to his creations, he would tell Hannah about Stephanie, his four-year-old daughter. He would bring her home something every night. Josephine had to disappear into her office just before closing. If not, the customers would stay all night. If the patrons were able to vote for a new president, the name Josephine Moreau would flood the ballots.

The last customers left the café shortly after seven that night. Hannah shut the door and locked it, but unlocked it seconds later. Durand knocked only once and smiled when she opened the unlocked door. Nearly every night, she would lock the door, walk away, and then he would knock.

"Good evening, Hannah," Durand said.

"Josephine, Durand is here," Hannah called.

"A few minutes," Josephine shouted from her office.

"Hannah, I wanted to apologize again. Can I ask you about that tattoo on your arm?" Durand asked.

Her right hand instinctively went to the tattoo. It was like a scar—a scar she was very conscious of.

"You said you received that at Auschwitz in Southern Poland?" Durand asked.

"Yes, in Oświęcim," Hannah said.

"We receive some information from the English on certain occasions. I wanted to tell you I have passed this information on to my contact in the British Intelligence Agency," Durand said.

The idea of the British discovering such atrocities and putting an end to them was a warming feeling. She would love to see the British and American troops storming under the Arbeit Macht Freit sign hanging over the camp entrance and liberating the unfortunate souls.

"Thank you," Hannah said.

Durand offered Hannah a seat, and after she sat, he took the seat across from her. His left leg protruded from underneath the table and was completely outstretched.

"It wasn't easy for me to see France fall and fall so quickly. Six weeks, Hannah. I fought in the Great War. Months of fighting to capture one trench to the next. And the Germans took the whole country in six weeks. I wanted to enlist, but I took shrapnel to my left leg during the Great War," Durand said, nodding in the direction of the aforementioned leg.

In addition to the pain it caused, he had no dexterity and would not be able to do any of the running, crawling, and crouching the duties of a soldier required.

"I want to fight in whatever way I can. The Americans fight in the Pacific and the British in North Africa, but they will look to open a second front. It is our job to raise as much hell as we can until they do," Durand said.

The swing door was hit open, and Josephine came through, delicately balancing three cups of coffee in her hand. Durand grabbed two of them and placed one in front of Hannah.

"Some big news today—there is a shipment coming tomorrow," Josephine said.

"Good work, Josephine," Durand commented.

"Thank Hannah. She helped, even if it was by accident," Josephine said.

"The Maquis thanks you, Hannah," Durand said, raising his glass to her and taking a sip of his watered-down imitation coffee and puckering his lips. "I hope coffee is on it."

"What will you do? How will you find the shipment?" Hannah asked.

"We send men to scout the streets. There are only handfuls the Germans use. We will find it and give the people of France their food back," Durand said.

All three took sips from their cups. The silence was still uncomfortable.

"You are married with children?" Hannah asked.

"Yes, I am," Durand answered.

"Why do you risk your life and their lives? Believe me, Mr. Durand, the Nazis won't just kill you but your whole family," Hannah said.

She did not mean for it to sound so cold and cruel but only as a warning. It was how the Nazis made their subjects submit to their will.

"My son fought for France. He was one of the hundreds of thousands who were able to escape Dunkirk, thanks to the kindness of French and British alike. Fishermen braved the bombing and downfall of machine gunfire to do their part. Josephine transmitted secret messages that allowed for such a thing to happen. Thanks to their heroism, my son is alive, married, and expecting his first child," Durand said.

Hannah considered it. She was alive because Eleanor had sacrificed her life to let Hannah take her spot on the train. If she could help in any way to limit the power of such hate and discrimination, she felt obliged to do so.

"I will pass information that I get. But I will not push for it. I have no desire to return to Auschwitz," Hannah said.

Her fingers were wrapped around the hot cup of coffee, and she was both relieved and nervous about what she had said. Durand placed his hands gingerly on hers.

"That will never happen. You are staying with Josephine. She knows how to get hold of me," Durand said.

"How can I trust you? Why should I trust you?" Hannah asked.

He could not expect her to ignore the fact he had pointed a gun at her.

"It is something that I must earn," Durand said.

A moment of silence descended. All three took a sip of their coffee. After they finished their cups, Hannah took them into the kitchen and washed them as Durand and Josephine went over the details of the next day's attack on the shipment.

The entire next day, Hannah was filled with a nervous energy, which she did her best to conceal. She asked Josephine every twenty minutes if she had heard how it had gone. But Hannah did not need to ask Josephine. Oberführer Köning and the other German officers had been disrupted during their meal, and they had hurried out of the café. Hannah nearly broke out in a smile. It was a smile returned by Durand that night.

"Care to brew a proper pot?" Durand asked when Josephine opened the door. He held out a can of coffee with both hands. As Josephine brewed the pot, Hannah interrogated Durand about the heist. He answered each question truthfully and in great detail.

"Are they all dead?" Hannah asked.

"Some ran," Durand said.

She prayed Wilhelm was not among them. She had no idea where he was, and each German killed could be him. It was hopeless to try and describe him to Durand, and her photographs were in the Kanada building at Auschwitz or had been burned.

Josephine returned with the pot of coffee in one hand and three cups in the other. She added cream, sugar, and chocolate. It was the best coffee of Hannah's life.

Durand returned every night that week, and the three enjoyed coffee and conversation. Durand liked his coffee black, and Josephine liked hers with two spoonsful of sugar and a dash of cream. Coffee had become something of an addictive comfort, and Hannah grew to like hers with a spoonful of sugar and a fourth of a cup of cream until the black roasted coffee turned caramel in color. But, by far, her favorite was when Josephine added whipped cream and chocolate.

"I hear you like to paint, Hannah," Durand said during a late-night cup.

"I do. But I haven't done it in so long," Hannah replied.

"Durand is quite the artist himself," Josephine said.

"Are you?" Hannah asked.

"Many years ago, when I returned home from the war, it seemed to give me peace. Fields, forests, sunrises, and sunsets—that is the hopeless romantic Frenchman in me, I guess," Durand said.

Hannah knew exactly what he was talking about, for she felt the same way about painting, drawing, and photography. There was something intrinsically relaxing about nature. While cities like Paris, Berlin, and New York had become cities of steel, there were places that looked no different than they had thousands of years ago. Hannah loved the big city, but the majesty of a grassy field, the leaves on a tree blowing in a soft wind, and a nighttime canvas of stars were never lost on her.

"Wilhelm had bought me a camera. But I lost it at Auschwitz," Hannah said.

It was the first time she had mentioned Wilhelm to either of them and to anyone since Eleanor and Trugnowski.

"Who is Wilhelm?" Josephine asked.

"He is my husband. Wilhelm Schreiber," Hannah said.

"I was not aware you were married. Is he in Germany?" Durand asked.

"I don't know. He was drafted. He left Christmas day 1939. Things were getting perilous for us Jews, so I left to stay with his father. But I returned to find my parents, and I was caught and forced on a train," Hannah said.

"Did he know you were a Jew?" Josephine asked.

"Yes. He did not care. He loved me," Hannah said.

She had not intended to utter the word "loved." She had wanted to say "loves." But, subconsciously, she had used the past tense. It was another way her ordeal at Auschwitz had taken positive human emotions, like optimism and hope, from each person. Or, like Josephine, was she accepting a truth deep down she knew?

"He loves you still," Durand said.

Josephine could not offer such compassionate words, for she had been in the same situation as Hannah.

"I can't believe it's been almost three years since the day I saw him," Hannah said.

When Hannah had arrived in Paris and Josephine had told her it was April 1942, she could hardly believe it. It had seemed unbelievable she had survived for so long in a camp that had perfected the art of mass killing.

That night, Hannah did not sleep for more than half a dozen ten-minute naps. Her mind was on Wilhelm. She visualized every dance, every kiss, and every embrace the two had shared. She had thought about asking the German officers for information on Wilhelm, but even if they knew him, new questions would be asked and only endanger them both. It would not take long before Hannah Smith was exposed for being Hannah Goldschmidt—the runaway Jew.

Hannah celebrated Hanukkah in silence that year. Josephine did not care if she practiced it in her apartment, but Hannah was determined not to sacrifice Josephine's wellbeing for it. Her faith was resolute in her heart and mind where it would always be safe.

The "Givre Strudel" was only half-filled for the first time since Hannah had worked there. The German officers had flown back to Germany to celebrate the holiday. Durand had stopped by early that day. He said he would be returning to his home in Sevres—a city located thirty miles southwest of Paris.

"I would like to extend to you an invitation to spend the holidays with my family and me. Josephine is invited, of course," Durand said.

"Are you sure?" Hannah asked.

Durand smiled. "I believe so. Allow me to think on it once again," he said as he rubbed his chin, "Yes, I'm sure."

"Can I talk with Josephine first?" Hannah asked.

"Hannah, my dear, you are a woman. You do not need to ask me or anyone else for permission," Durand said.

Durand, like Wilhelm, viewed women as their equals, and being a gentleman had nothing to do with it. Hannah admittedly hadn't liked Durand early on, but that was understandable, given that he was about to shoot her for being a German spy. No, it had nothing to do with manners and holding open doors. It was his complete trust in Josephine and the partnership the two shared. He took in every bit of advice she had to offer and allowed her to call the shots. If she worried the information she had been given was too personal or too risky or obvious, she would tell Durand to not act on it and he would listen. The Germans constantly tested the French to see who had become obedient and who had not. Sometimes, the information obtained was too easy to be true, and it was. It was leaked so that the Germans knew who the rats were.

Hannah walked through the kitchen swing door. The kitchen, which was usually packed elbow-to-elbow, filled with sizzling and searing and waves of heat, was empty, silent, and cold. Josephine was in her office and on her fourth glass of wine.

"Are you alright?" Hannah asked.

The vibrant blue and green of Josephine's eyes had faded, and the whites had turned red from crying.

"I am fine," she said, sniffing back her runny nose.

"Radley has invited us to his home for the holidays," Hannah said.

"I know. You should go," Josephine said.

"You won't?" Hannah asked.

"No. I will spend Christmas in the same place I have for the last twenty-one years," Josephine said.

"I will stay with you. You shouldn't be alone," Hannah said.

"Go, Hannah. I am not alone," Josephine said, raising the bottle of wine on her desk.

Wine would always be synonymous with Hauser. What type of fine wine would be drunk at the table on Christmas?

"I know how hard it is around this time," Hannah said.

"It always feels like 'it is around this time,'" Josephine said.

It was true. There was not a day that passed when Hannah did not think about her parents and Wilhelm. Feelings of melancholy and nostalgia attacked without warning as if they were some kind of poisonous gas that had been inhaled. There was no antidote except letting it run its course.

"Since it happened, not a day has gone by when I have not thought about the twenty-ninth of October," Josephine said.

Although the date's significance was unknown to Hannah, she guessed it was the date of the death of either Mathis and Adam or that of Noah and Leo's disappearance. But it was none of those.

"The Stock Market Crash happened in America that day. Two weeks earlier, we had decided to leave Paris to live in Chicago. But the country started drowning in debt and starvation. The job Mathis had lined up was gone. So, we stayed. If we would have left for America, my husband would still be here and my three sweet boys," Josephine said, wiping her runny nose with a red handkerchief.

Life was a series of moments shaped by fate and chance.

"My boys loved Christmas, Hannah. When they snuck off to bed, Mathis and I would lay the presents under the tree. We would take the plate full of cookies for Father Christmas, pour a glass of Christmas wine, and sit on the couch. We would look at the tree lights and drink and eat," Josephine said. She wore the glistening tears in her eyes proudly. For the first time since Hannah had known her, Josephine Moreau's tears left her eyes, but only four of them—a tear for each of her beloved men. "The boys would rush to wake us in the morning and had such excited smiles on their faces. What kills me is imagining the horror on their faces when they realized they would die. That my promises—that I would always keep them safe—were empty," Josephine said.

She sniffed back her runny nose once more and rose to her feet.

"Merry Christmas, Hannah," Josephine said.

She kissed Hannah's forehead and hugged her. Her appealing perfume was completely overpowered by the smell of the Chardonnay.

"Merry Christmas, Josephine," Hannah said, her voice reflecting Josephine's sadness.

She wished there was something she could give her. Something she could say. But if she had something or had known what to say, she would have given it to herself years ago.

Josephine returned to her bottle, and Hannah walked through the empty kitchen to Durand.

"Josephine is staying," Hannah said.

They walked outside. Hannah locked the door behind her. Snow fell steadily through the frigid, windy air.

"I imagined she would. The holidays belong to God, but its nights belong to demons," Durand said.

Pain, hurt, anguish, and despair fed the demons, and Durand had unwillingly fed his for years.

"I expected you to drive a car," Hannah said.

Instead, he drove a dirty, beaten-down truck that Hannah had her doubts about it staying in one piece.

"Unfortunately, I do not have much use for a car on the farm," Durand said.

He started the truck, and it whimpered like an annoyed old dog that had been woken from a nap.

"Doesn't your son get annoyed that while you're in Paris, he's working the fields?" Hannah asked.

"I imagine he does," Durand said, smiling and laughing.

The truck sputtered out of the city, the Eiffel Tower receding in the rearview mirror until it disappeared. The snow fell faster, covering the roads with a white powder.

"So, you wish to get to London?" Durand asked.

"I do," Hannah said.

"There are ways. But it is extremely dangerous, and only the rich or important can leave."

Hannah had always planned on making it to London, but over the last few months, she had become aware of how unlikely it was. She was neither rich nor important.

"It is beautiful here," Hannah said.

Every tree branch and blade of grass was covered in snow, but the winds were a reminder of how dangerous a snowstorm could be. But it was also relaxing and, compounded with the heat inside the truck, Hannah fell asleep and stayed asleep longer than she had in weeks. Durand softly rubbed her shoulder to wake her.

They traveled on what must have been a gravel road, judging by its bumpiness. A short wooden fence stretched from the start of the road up to the farmhouse. The truck slid to a stop and groaned as the engine died. Six dogs sprinted toward them. Hannah's eyes lit up in fear. She had only been around the German Shepherds used by the Nazis, and her experiences with them had been terrifying. Durand's dogs were of the Beauceron breed and had a muscular black frame with brown tinting on their nose and legs and cropped ears. They barked and growled at the stranger next to their owner, and only after Durand rubbed their ears did they relax.

"Hannah, this is Unus, Duo, Tribus, Quattuor, Quinque, and Sex," Durand said, affectionately introducing Hannah to his dogs.

"One, two, three, four, five, and six in Latin?" Hannah asked.

"My daughter named them. Causes a bit of an awkward conversation when we have English-speaking guests and my wife calls for Sex," Durand said, smiling his jovial smile.

When the door opened and Durand stepped in, two young girls dashed at him with more force than the dogs had. Durand kissed their foreheads repeatedly, alternating between the two.

"Hannah, I would like to introduce you to my beautiful daughters, Abella and Elaina," Durand said.

Abella had dark hair like her father and was a few weeks shy of turning ten years old. Elaina was six years old, had dark blonde hair and, according to Durand, she looked exactly like her mother.

Hannah smiled. The two girls beamed at their father. The dogs stormed about and skidded along the wooden floor. Durand removed his jacket and hung it on the coat rack. He helped Hannah with hers, and she was pleasantly surprised to find she was not cold after parting with it. The house was heated by a roaring fire in the sitting room, and the oven had been put to heavy use, cooking turkey, potatoes, and an apple pie.

A woman with a welcoming smile stepped into the kitchen and rushed toward Hannah.

"You must be Hannah," the woman said.

Hannah extended her hand, but the woman grazed right past it and wrapped her in a hug, her long, flowing, ash brown hair covering Hannah's face. Her skin was tanned and her eyes, olive green in color.

"Hannah, this is my wife, Madeleina," Durand said proudly.

"It's so great to meet you, Hannah. I have heard so much about you," Madeleina said.

"Thank you for having me. I know Christmas is a time for family," Hannah said.

"Family and friends," Madeleina corrected.

"Where are Sevrin and Simone?" Durand asked, sneaking a carrot from the vegetable tray on the wooden counter.

"Finishing getting ready," Madeleina answered, slapping his hand away from the vegetables. She was well aware of all his tricks.

"It looks delicious, Mrs. Durand. I wish I was able to bring something," Hannah said.

"Nonsense. We asked only for your company. And, please, call me Madeleina."

The house had a soothing warmth to it, and comfort came to Hannah immediately. It was a rustic farm, and the house perfectly blended the appeal of antique nostalgia and modern designs. It was recognizable how laid-back Durand was at his home and with his family. They were an affirmation as to why he fought and why others should too.

A man Hannah's age came into the kitchen, holding the hand of a woman with pitch-black hair. The man had inherited his mother's feminine looks but had his father's body and black hair. The woman was the sort of French beauty Heinrich would have fallen for.

"Hannah, my son, Sevrin, and his wife, Simone. Is the baby sleeping?" Durand asked.

"Yes, I just fed him," Simone said, smiling politely and shaking Hannah's hand.

Sevrin did the same and escorted his wife to the kitchen table.

The dinner was wonderful—full of filling, delicious food, and hearty laughs and smiles. But Hannah could not share in them. Everything reminded her of her parents and of Wilhelm. When she closed her eyes and the laughter filled her ears, she was at her parents. Sevrin and Simone were the ghosts of Christmas present, showing her what she could have had had life not been so cruel. She was thankful the baby was asleep in the other room, for she did not think she could handle it. Shame spread over her for looking so depressed, but Durand's life had been blessed with moments of luck.

Even more special was the fact that everyone at the table, except Abella and Elaina, who were too young, appreciated how fortunate they were. Hannah had never taken that for granted, yet there was a certain level of appreciation for life that only death or a near-death experience could give—a certain enlightenment only achieved through a crucible of heartbreak. It was enough to make Hannah lose her appetite, but she had never left food on a plate since escaping Auschwitz, and she finished every last bite.

"I'm going to show Hannah the horses," Durand said.

Madeleina washed the dishes. Durand had planned on drying them, but he had studied Hannah throughout supper—there was something wrong.

"She needs it," Madeleina whispered and kissed his cheek.

"Girls, I need two heroes to help dry the dishes," Durand said.

Madeleina knew the hurt inside Hannah's blank stare, for Durand had worn it for years after the war had ended.

Durand whispered to his daughters and, although disappointed, they hurried to the sink to help their mother.

"Hannah, I would like to show you something," Durand said.

He grabbed both of their coats. Hannah rose from the table and lumbered toward him. He helped her with her coat while Madeleina hurried toward her.

"Here, dear, it is quite cold out," Madeleina said, putting an indigo wool beret on Hannah.

The air was frigid, and flakes of snow blew into her face when the door opened, but it was welcomed. The ghosts of Christmas had created a panic in her that made breathing difficult. The air rushed into her lungs as they trekked through the ankle-deep snow.

"Are you feeling alright?" Durand asked.

"I am fine," Hannah said.

Durand smiled sorrowfully. "That will not work in this household, Hannah. I said that for ten years, and my wife called *connerie* on me every single time."

"I shouldn't be here, Radley."

"Yes, you should."

"I'm not talking about here. I'm talking about being alive."

"I know."

They stopped next to the horse stable and rested against the fence. The snow fell in dancing swirls.

"The fields of France were littered with the number of men who should be here instead of me. White crosses stretching further than I could see," Durand said.

"Eleanor gave me a seat on the train that could have been hers. It should have been," Hannah said.

"She chose you, Hannah. Take solace in that. The men who died around me did not. They were only standing in the wrong spot."

"Are you going to tell me it goes away?" Hannah asked.

A flash of heat made her boil inside her coat, and her face reddened. She hated when people said that. It would never go away. How could it? How could you forget the memory of your parents being murdered or a woman who had become like a sister sacrificing her life for yours?

"No. It does not go away. But it gets easier," Durand said, "Not a day will pass that you do not reflect upon it. I was a different man when I returned home. I wasn't around for Madeleina or Sevrin. She raised him alone while I sought the unreachable bottom of the bottle. I wasn't a good man. I'll never forget the way Madeleina looked at me—like it was the first time. She didn't recognize the man she saw. I felt that way every time I looked into a mirror and wondered if I would recognize the man I was when I left for war in 1915. Or was he dead and too stupid to realize? One night, I stumbled in drunk and left the door open. Rain pelted inside, and I collapsed onto the floor—covered in my own vomit with angry tears falling from my eyes. Sevrin came from his bed crying. Loud enough for Madeleina to hear. She came into the kitchen to find me passed out with Sevrin sitting beside me—drenched from the rain and frozen to the bone. He came down with pneumonia. I tried to apologize over and over. But she reacted in a way much worse than anger. She no longer cared. I was a bullet, Hannah. As it ripped into her flesh, I caused her immense pain, but the further I tore into her, eventually, the wound became numb. She told me, 'You are alive. I do not know why you were spared when so many were not. But you need to decide if you want to live or exist.' You need to let it out, Hannah. It can't be caged forever. You give it too much strength."

She had no response, but it did not require one.

"Before I forget…" Durand said.

He reached into his coat pocket and pulled out a small, rectangular box wrapped with Christmas paper.

"You shouldn't have," Hannah said, sliding her finger into the paper and tearing it.

"Compliments of the Germans," Durand said, pocketing the torn paper.

Hannah had to hold the box out to catch the moonlight.

"A camera!" Hannah exclaimed.

Her eyes swiveled from the camera to Durand. Her mouth was wide enough for snowflakes to fall onto her tongue.

"Merry Christmas and Happy Hanukkah, Hannah."

"Thank you, Radley."

Her first camera had been such an integral part of her life. It had captured so many moments that she had shared with Wilhelm, her parents, and her best friends. She would never get those photographs or those moments back. But it was Durand's way of telling her to create new ones.

"Care to join me back inside?" Durand asked.

"In a moment. I would like to take a few photos before I do," Hannah said.

Durand nodded and trotted back to the house through the snow. Hannah readied the camera to snap a few photos of the starry sky and moon. When she took her first picture, it sent a wave of comfort through her that she had not felt in years. She loved taking photos. She loved capturing moments. She loved capturing life. As she looked through her lens at the stars, Wilhelm's voice came to her.

"Look to the stars."

She placed the camera strap around her neck and let the camera hang. She gazed up at the stars and raised her hand, fingers dancing with the air, to catch the falling snow. She danced slowly like she and Wilhelm had done. Only this time, she was alone. She could only hope he was alive and staring up at the same sky she was.

Red Army Victory

Mother Nature had sided with the Soviet Union, and its invisible bite was massive and sharp, It dropped the already freezing temperatures into the negative twenties. Many Germans froze to death quickly, and many stood from behind their cover and let the snipers take them.

"Not the worst way to go," one soldier said.

"Better than freezing to death or starving," another agreed.

Wilhelm had not been able to write in days. He no longer had any dexterity in his fingers to grip the pencil. The one cathartic exercise he had had been taken away from him.

Wilhelm and the Germans were on a rock at sea—the waves and water just short of washing over them. But the tide was coming. The rock would soon be underwater, and the sharks would feast on them.

"Wilhelm?" a voice said.

It was hard to decipher where the voice had come from. Nearly a hundred men moved past him like frozen zombies. But the man who had spoken crouched and sat beside him.

"Höring?" Wilhelm asked.

His face was bearded and dirty, but his shit grin belonged to the Höring Wilhelm knew. It was the first time he had seen him since they had first entered the fray months ago.

"You bastard!" Höring said, wrapping Wilhelm in a hug and eyeing him up for injuries.

"I thought you had died," Wilhelm said.

"I thought we both had. I saw you being carried out on a stretcher. I called your name, but I think you were out of it. I thought for certain you were going to die," Höring said.

"Shot in the chest by a sniper. You get through unscathed?" Wilhelm asked.

"Stabbed in the stomach with a rusty piece of steel," Höring said.

"And Jonas?" Wilhelm asked.

Höring's excitement vanished as he shook his head.

"How?" Wilhelm asked.

"He got hit in the knee and fell out onto the road. I tried to help him, but a Soviet tank ran him over. Those fucking bastards!" Höring said and kicked his foot against a slab of broken concrete.

What a God-awful way to go.

"Were you able to get a letter out?" Wilhelm asked.

"No. Did you get one to Hannah?" Höring asked.

Wilhelm shook his head.

"I'm sorry. But everything you would have said, she already knows," Höring said.

Even though it was still a frozen hell, sharing a foxhole with Höring lifted Wilhelm's spirits. They talked about the battle and the awful things they had done and seen. But, mostly, they talked about the fond memories of Paris and northwestern France during the pause in battle.

"Africa would have been better," Höring remarked.

"Dying in a desert doesn't sound any better," Wilhelm replied.

"At least I'd still have a *schwanz*. I think mine froze off," Höring joked.

Somehow, amidst all the death and desolation, they laughed.

The sound of artillery grew louder day by day, hour by hour, and the noose burned around the Germans' neck.

"Remember the cafes in Paris?" Höring asked.

"Jonas ate a dozen Éclairs," Wilhelm recalled.

"Puked it up," Höring added.

"And went back for more," they both said together.

They grinned and laughed.

"Sure wish we could go back there someday," Höring said.

"Me too," Wilhelm responded.

Höring stared out of the foxhole toward the dangerous looming distance.

"When I die, I hope my body burns. I don't want it out there—in some heap of corpses, stripped of my possessions and clothes," Höring said.

So many young men had accepted they would die—men yet to experience life.

More troops came through, but unlike walking like frozen corpses like they usually did, they sprinted.

"What the hell is going on?" Höring asked.

"General Paulus is going to surrender. There are murmurs coming from outside his camp," a soldier said before hurrying after his buddies.

"Where the fuck are you going?" another asked.

"Out of this fucking city!" the soldier yelled back.

"Wilhelm, I heard the men talking. We do not want to be Soviet POWs. They will work us until we die. Something about payback. We need to get out of here," Höring said.

Would Wilhelm's father think less of him for abandoning his post? Would he be disgraced? But the battle was lost. It had been for weeks. A competent ruler would have surrendered months ago. It was Hitler who disgraced his own soldiers by refusing to let Paulus surrender. But where did Höring or the other soldiers expect to go? They were completely surrounded. But a thought warmed his chest, flooding strength back into his frozen body—death was guaranteed. Did he truly want to die frozen in a pit? No. He would die trying to return home and to Hannah.

"Let's get the fuck out of here," Wilhelm said.

They grabbed their rifles and sprinted toward the back of the camp. Nighttime was their best chance at an escape. They were not alone. Over two hundred Germans tried to sneak through the thick Russian lines. While everyone pushed west, Wilhelm grabbed Höring's arm and ushered him toward a lone plane. One of the brave German pilots who chanced the onslaught of anti-aircraft ammunition was still in the cauldron. The pilot sat in the cockpit, completely unaware of the gunfire, artillery, and mortars. But, as Wilhelm and

Höring drew closer, it was clear as to why he was so peaceful. He was dead. A frozen mass of ice.

"What are we doing, Wilhelm? He's dead! We have to get out of here!" Höring said.

"We are going to fly out of here," Wilhelm said.

"You can fly?" Höring asked, his voice a mixture of surprise, relief, and doubt.

"Aaron showed me."

"Have you logged any hours?"

"No. But we are not going to be able to sneak through those lines. Listen to that! They are getting mowed down! Our only chance is over them."

Höring looked at the plane and then toward the source of the terrifying gunfire. At that very second, men were dying. The plane was their best chance—their only chance.

"There are worse ways to go," Höring said.

"There are worse ways to go," Wilhelm repeated.

The pilot was on the chubby side and, now, all two-hundred pounds of his five-foot-ten frame was dead weight. Wilhelm and Höring struggled to lift him out of the cockpit. The discarding of the pilot's body was anything but honorable, and it hit the ground like a block of ice. Sporadic gunfire was exchanged somewhere in the west as the fleeing Germans were met by the Soviets. It grew louder. The noose that was the cauldron tightened one final time. Those inside it inhaled their final breath.

Wilhelm and Höring climbed into the Junkers Ju 52 airplane. It was much larger than the Arado Ar 96 that Aaron had flown.

"Are you flying out of here?" a German soldier asked, stopping in his tracks while his eyes searched for Soviets.

The plane could fit eighteen soldiers, but there were supplies in the back.

"Hurry on," Wilhelm said.

The soldier looked at Wilhelm and Höring as if he had been accepted by Jesus. He hurried on. A group of six saw the plane and scrambled on without invitation.

"What are we waiting for?" one asked.

"The cargo wasn't dropped. Meaning, something wasn't working," Wilhelm said.

The seven in the back became twelve.

"Get the supplies off," Höring ordered.

They were supplies they absolutely would have and had killed for. But now, to fit more men, they needed to get them off the plane. But they were twenty, and if there were any more, they risked being too heavy to take off.

"We have to go, Wilhelm," Höring said.

Wilhelm nodded. Leaving meant forsaking the men sprinting toward the plane. But it was either saving himself, Höring, and the twenty odd men or subjecting himself to the same fate. Wilhelm pushed the throttle forward, and the plane came to life with a mechanical buzz. He tried visualizing every flipping switch and every gauge check Aaron had done. He pulled on the yoke, and the front end of the plane lifted off the ground but bounced back down again.

"Come on, come on!" Höring yelled, his leg shaking up and down.

The front end lifted off once more, and the plane rose off the ground and climbed higher and higher into the sky. Those aboard screamed with excitement as they rose above the boiling cauldron. The tanks and soldiers below sent small orange and green flashes of firelight.

The flight certainly wasn't smooth, and there were a dozen gauges that Wilhelm had no idea what they were for. He checked those he knew—his airspeed, artificial horizon, altimeter, heading indicator and, lastly, his fuel gauge. It was less than half, but it would be enough to get them out of the cauldron, out of Stalingrad, and out of enemy occupation. Perhaps enough fuel to get to Poland. From there, Germany was only a train ride away and then the nightmare would end. He would go to Berlin and find Hannah, and they would leave. He did not know for where. Hannah had always loved New York, but Wilhelm was a German soldier and hardly expected to be given sanctity. But there would be time to decide where to go. He only cared about finding her and nothing about the destination.

The sky lit up and exploded as the Soviets on the ground fired anti-aircraft guns. The plane shook violently when a shell exploded mere feet away from the plane. The sky flashed like a strobe light, exploding thunder that ruptured eardrums. The back end of the plane was struck. The outside air shot into the plane with a high-pitched whistle. The artillery ripped through the steel hull and through an unlucky passenger.

"Pull up!" Höring yelled.

Wilhelm pulled on the yoke, the veins in his forearms pulsed, and his hands shook as he tried to will the plane to climb higher toward safety. It shuddered from the pressure, but the plane obliged to his command. The shells exploded harmlessly below. Höring and Wilhelm smiled.

"We made it," Höring said.

But no sooner had the words left his mouth, the 88-mm caliber shells ripped into the plane's right wing. It broke off and sped toward the earth like a meteor. The warning alarms went haywire. The plane was punctured with holes like Morse code. The passengers were sucked out of the spiraling plane. The gauges spun freely. The propellers broke off. The ground came closer and closer. Wilhelm could do nothing but brace for impact. The plane smashed into the ground. The front end fell forward, Wilhelm's body whiplashed, and his neck was forced out of place. Patches of fire ignited all over.

Wilhelm looked himself over. His head pounded like a drum. He had to turn his whole torso, his neck was too stiff, in order to see what condition the other men aboard were in. Nobody moved—some had been torn and blasted into pieces.

"Wilhelm," Höring called.

"I think everyone's dead," Wilhelm said.

He struggled to remove his seatbelt. It had done its job, but it had gotten so tight that it left bruises.

"We have to get out of here. The Soviets will be here soon," Wilhelm said.

"Wilhelm," Höring called again.

Wilhelm succeeded in removing the safety belt and tossed it to the side.

Höring turned his body. A two-inch-wide piece of metal had ripped through his stomach, and when Wilhelm looked, he noticed it had punctured through his back and ripped through the seat. The moment it would be removed, Höring would only have seconds before he bled out.

"Am I going to die?" Höring asked, his hand shaking violently and his head jerking back and forth.

Wilhelm wanted to lie. He had seen it done by medics nearly two hundred times. How else do you calm a dying man? But Wilhelm couldn't. Whatever lie his mouth would tell, his eyes would betray. Something warm ran down his face and dripped onto his hands. He thought it was tears, but it was red in color. As he put his hand to his head, a sharp pain erupted through his body. He had a gash across his head, and more blood gushed out when he pressed it.

"I didn't want it … to end like this … I wanted to go home, Wilhelm … I wanted to go home … now I can't … what comes next? Where do I go now?" Höring asked.

The unknown terrified him. Would these be the last few seconds that he existed?

"There is something after. You will go there. First, you will sleep. Your body will heal. Your scars will fade. Your loved ones who are already there will be notified, and they will prepare for your arrival. There will be beer and food and even those cinnamon rolls from that café in Paris. All your friends and family will be there waiting for you. Who is there that you were closest to?" Wilhelm asked.

"My grandfather," Höring said.

He spat blood from his mouth. The fear of what was awaiting him forced tears. His body was failing. His hands shook uncontrollably, and the color faded from his face, his skin turning ghost-white.

Wilhelm grabbed his hand. "Your grandfather will meet you at the Gates. He will make sure you are comfortable, and he will answer all the questions I cannot. You will walk into that room, and everyone you know will be there. They will raise their glasses to you. There will be no more pain. No more sadness. Every day will be the best day of your life," Wilhelm said.

Höring gasped for breath, and even though the wind attacked his lungs, he could no longer breathe it in. His lungs had given up, and his heart soon would follow. Höring's eyes filled with fear. Wilhelm could only stroke Höring's face as tears and blood trickled down his own. The life in Höring's eyes was gone, but his body twitched spontaneously for another few seconds.

"Fuck," Wilhelm muttered through sobs.

He collapsed back into his seat. Even his salty tears caused a burning pain. His face was smeared with tears and blood as well as with grime and oil. He climbed out of the plane and fell to the frozen ground. Men sprinted at him with their guns drawn. Any hopes he had that they were German evaporated when they shouted at him in Russian. Wilhelm raised his hands above his throbbing head. Just holding his hands in the air was a struggle. He was like Atlas, carrying the weight of the world on his shoulders. They kept shouting, and one of the ten men aiming his gun at him would most likely get an itchy trigger finger.

Wilhelm only hoped what he had told Höring was true. His mother would meet him. Wilhelm nearly smiled at the thought. It wouldn't be so bad. He would spend each day with his mother and his grandparents. Höring and Jonas would be there, maybe even Heinrich and Erich. He would wait for his father and years down the line, he would greet Hannah. His mother would be able to ease all his worrying with one stroke of his hair and one hug. No, it would not be that bad at all.

The barrel of a rifle was pressed into the gash in his head, and the searing pain seemed to rupture his skull into powdered fragments. Wilhelm had trouble hearing anything the Soviets were saying. Yet, strangely, the sounds of hell in the form of gun and artillery fire, even so far away inside the cauldron of Stalingrad, were perfectly clear. Another rifle poked his back and prodded him to move. Wilhelm kept his hands behind his head, and when the Soviet wanted Wilhelm to move right or left, he slapped the rifle against either side. The taps were anything but gentle, and bruises formed around his ribs like a bad rash.

As he marched on, more and more Germans joined his line. The heat of the fire from the plane had warmed his body, but after marching for a mile, his body returned to the homeostasis level of freezing it had been at since winter had set in. His feet sank into the snow, and his boots and socks were soaked. German prisoners in the line fell, and if they could not rise to their feet, they were stabbed with bayonets. Those whose hands fell were shot. But it was not only Wilhelm and a few dozen Germans who were being forced to march. The entire German army had surrendered the city.

General Paulus had ignored Hitler's suggestion (order) of suicide before surrender. Wilhelm had never spoken with General Paulus, but Wilhelm's respect increased for him, for the general would rather surrender than allow any more sons of Germany to sacrifice their lives for a lost cause. The date was 2 February 1943 and, after months of catastrophic fighting, the great Battle of Stalingrad was finally over. But a fear spread amongst the Germans that they would all be executed. It was a fear well-founded. They had killed thousands and thousands of Soviets, and there was surely a desire for revenge. The Germans had had the same feeling. The battle had become personal. It was impossible for it not to have.

The Soviets looked upon the Germans being ushered out east of the city with complete disdain. Wilhelm recognized the emotions on their faces, visible through the grime and blood. They were the same emotions Wilhelm had experienced. He had expected the Soviets to be some mythical, demonic force, and the same was true of the Soviets' mentality toward the Germans—monsters of Moscow, beasts of Berlin. But both sides looked disappointed to find the enemy to be just men. But in their eyes was also hate. The average Soviet was expected to live a meager twenty-four hours after he entered the fray with a final death tally that would never be known.

Wilhelm and the over ninety thousand Germans began the long march from the devil's playground and deeper into Russia.

The Offer

The spring of 1944 came with much longing. Winter had always been Hannah's favorite season, but the last few had soured her taste. The cold, dark days were an invisible weight that fell upon her shoulders and threatened to collapse her. Spring meant clear skies and longer days of sunlight. Even if it rained, she found the sound relaxing. But it also made her think of everyone she had lost and all those inside the concentration camps left to meet a terrible fate. Even the heavens cried over their fates. Rainy days also meant quieter times at the "Givre Strudel."

Hannah had become nearly fluent in French and, despite her accent, she blended in as a French woman. She had taken nearly a thousand photos with the camera Radley had gotten her. Hundreds were of the city and dozens were of Josephine and Radley. Despite both loving the spotlight, neither were entirely keen on having their picture taken. Hannah had visited Radley's farm half a dozen times and received lessons on the French language from his daughters. The resistance continued to grow in number, and the information Josephine passed on continued to be valuable and led to many raids on resupply caravans. Hannah passed on what information she could but was still unwilling to join the true fight. She had only one goal—to blend in and not draw attention to herself.

The rain had been falling for what seemed like a week straight, and the German officers had not been to the café. Josephine had grown incredibly irritated and felt helpless. Radley was much calmer. Each night, he would stop by at the café for information. "Then, we shall simply talk," he would say with a smile when there was no information. But, one night, he had a new level of excitement about him that Hannah had rarely seen apart from when he pulled down the long gravel road to his home. He nearly danced toward the radio and turned the dials. Songs and speeches came in and out of signal as he fine-tuned the dial.

"What is this?" Hannah asked.

"Radio Londres," Durand answered.

"This is London! The French speaking to the French!" the voice on the radio announced.

"They give orders to the resistance," Durand said.

It hardly seemed like orders more than it did incoherent ramblings. The channel was pro-French and, from the safety of London, degraded Germany. But it was surely being listened to by the Germans.

"Isn't that dangerous?" Hannah asked.

"Coded messages. Only a select few know how to translate—those who speak to the offices in England," Durand answered.

Josephine placed a plate next to Hannah and Durand. Both had an apple strudel with a perfect spoonful of frosting and cream on top of it.

"I'm expected to give the leftovers to German soldiers. So eat," Josephine said.

Hannah had been able to try everything Josephine was able to cook up, and each surpassed the last. She was truly talented at not only making mouthwatering food but also turning it into art. The dishes looked so perfect that it seemed a crime to run a fork through them—the type of art the Nazis prided themselves on destroying. Hannah would much rather give the dish and its creator a mouthful-of-food smile and a thumbs up than see a smug Nazi eat it with ambivalence. But Durand had no problems and did not even think of the amount of time Josephine had spent in making the edible art. It was unintentional—not everyone had an eye for such things. Hannah particularly loved the fresh vegetables that were given as a side in some dishes. Josephine had always believed in a wide array of colors for vegetables.

"Magnificent," Durand commented after defeating the strudel in less than two minutes. Hannah had yet to take her third bite. She preferred to savor such things. Durand, on the other hand, was already scraping his fork against the plate to pick up every speck of strudel and frosting he could.

"The Desert Fox has come," Durand said when the radio program ended.

"What is that?" Hannah asked.

The whole program had been like a silly nursery rhyme. But the words "desert fox" had never been spoken.

"Erwin Rommel—Germany's greatest general. He was seen moving northwest from Paris," Durand explained.

Erwin Rommel was respected for his military prowess by both the Americans and British.

"That means they must think there is an invasion coming," Josephine added. Durand nodded. He had been talking about a proposed invasion from the Allies since Hannah had met him. "When did he arrive?" Josephine asked.

"Uncertain. Late February or early March. He is scouting the beaches of Normandy," Durand said.

"They will be sending soldiers and supplies. We need to figure out where they are coming from and stop them from reaching Rommel," Josephine said.

"Yes, we do," Durand agreed.

An awkward silence fell. Josephine and Durand stared at Hannah with an intensity impossible to ignore.

"What is it?" she asked.

"Take a walk with me, Hannah?" Durand asked.

Months ago, she would have pleaded to Josephine for her not have to. But things were different now. She trusted him. But the nervous energy he exuded was uncomfortable.

"Radley, what is it?" Josephine asked.

"Join us. I do not want to risk this being overheard," Durand said.

Josephine sighed with annoyance. They had held a thousand secret meetings after hours in her café, and if it was bugged, they would have been arrested or, most likely, killed by now. But, nonetheless, the fresh air might do her well. The rain had finally stopped, and there was not a better time to see Paris than at night. The water from the rooftops fell rhythmically. After Hannah and Durand stepped outside, Josephine flipped the lights off and locked the door. Durand carried on in annoying silence as he led them toward the Eiffel Tower blocks away.

"Will you be speaking before we reach the Atlantic?" Josephine asked.

Hannah had thought the same thing but did not want to come off as rude. But it was the sort of bluntness Josephine possessed that Hannah envied. She was a woman who valued her time. Hannah had always wished for this trait. Sometimes, she believed it was the difference between a victim and a victor. But, even if she did possess it, she would not have said such a thing to Radley. Both he and Josephine had done so much for her, and the least she could do was to let him walk in silence and gather his thoughts.

"I spoke with my contact in London, Hannah. I told him of your desire to receive refuge there," Durand said.

A smile spread over Hannah's face. She had grown to call Paris a home of sorts, yet it was a home with no locked doors, so to speak. She could never feel safe with Nazis roaming the streets.

"What did he say?" Hannah asked.

"He has agreed to help you," Durand said.

Hannah impulsively hugged him, but as she pulled away, she could tell from his face there was much more to it than a free trip to London.

"They want her help," Josephine said, her voice full of disappointment.

"They do," Durand said.

"How could you do this, Durand? You know she wants no part of this. She has been through enough," Josephine said.

"I did not say that she would. I would not do that. But I would leave the decision to Hannah. It is her life, her opportunity, her choice," Durand said.

"What do they want?" Hannah asked.

"The German officer that comes into the café is reportedly involved with the defenses orchestrated by Rommel…" Durand said.

"Oberführer Köning?" Hannah asked.

"Yes. He is a man who likes to put pencil to paper. He keeps a journal, a calendar, on him at all times," Durand continued.

Hannah had seen it sticking out of his jacket pocket every time he had eaten at the "Givre Strudel." But that was his winter coat. He would not be wearing the long, black leather trench coat with May approaching.

"The war is a game of codes, Durand. Surely, an Oberführer does not reach that rank by being so blatantly stupid as to write things in a notebook?" Josephine snapped.

"It is in code. We, however, believe we can decipher it," Durand said.

"What are you hoping to find?" Hannah asked.

"What rail stations the soldiers and supplies will be arriving in Normandy," Durand answered.

"Why not just destroy them all?" Hannah asked.

"Some are vital for Paris' survival," Durand said.

"If one is destroyed, they will simply use a different one," Josephine said, struggling to stay calm.

"We wait until the train is on the tracks. We destroy the tracks ahead of the train and behind it," Durand said.

"He will notice the notebook is gone when he leaves," Hannah said.

It would be impossible not to.

"We are doing all we can to focus the attention elsewhere to draw the Germans away," Durand said.

"Is Normandy where it is going to happen?" Josephine asked.

"We do not know," Durand said.

Rumors of several possible landing spots had circulated, but it was far too dangerous to send out a for-sure location, and if there had been, Durand would not have known about it.

"They will arrest her if they catch her. She will be interrogated. They will see her tattoo, and she will be killed," Josephine tried reasoning with him.

"I am not telling her what to do, Josephine," Durand said politely.

Hannah's tattoo had become difficult to hide. It would look suspicious if she wore long sleeves during the spring. She had made a habit of keeping a towel draped over it or keeping it covered by the food tray.

"Why me?" Hannah asked.

It seemed like a job Josephine could have done though she seemed adamant about wanting no part in it, and Hannah could not blame her. Oberführer Köning did not strike one as a cruel man, but he certainly was not an idiot.

"You have gotten closer to him and the other officers than any French man or woman could. It is because you are German, Hannah. They let their guard down around you more than they can with Josephine," Durand explained.

It was true. Josephine had gotten as close as she was able to with her wit, and her sexual charisma had teased Köning, but unless she was willing to sleep with him, it could do no more. Even then, afterward, the power her body held over him would be over. But he gained a feeling of comfort speaking in his native tongue, and Hannah had learned the art of lying. She constantly made remarks that pleased the Oberführer—talks that included how lazy the French were and how barbaric the eastern people of Europe were. Each comment that elevated the German race had made her his preferred waitress—even ahead of Josephine.

"Can I think about it?" Hannah asked.

"Of course, Hannah," Durand said.

There was no pressure in his voice, and she knew he had only told her to give her an option. She respected him for not forcing her one way or another but valuing her own opinion.

"Hannah, we have to get going or I will be late," Josephine said.

"Josephine, there are other ways to get information," Durand said.

"Like stealing a notebook from a high-ranking Nazi officer?" Josephine jeered.

She had not agreed with Durand on telling Hannah the offer. She knew how much Hannah wanted to get to London and knew she was considering it. But, in her mind, it was a suicide mission destined to fail. She stormed away from Durand, and Hannah covered the distance between the two.

"I have to go. I will think about it," Hannah said.

"You best hurry," Durand said, nodding toward Josephine who had created thirty feet of distance between Hannah and her.

Hannah rushed after Josephine, but the walk to her apartment was filled with silence. The silence continued inside as Josephine changed into a maroon, low-cut dress that highlighted her voluptuousness.

"Are you sure you want to do this?" Hannah asked.

"There are other ways to help the resistance that don't require stealing or shooting," Josephine said.

"Be careful."

"Just be sure you are awake when I get back."

Hannah nodded, and Josephine gave one last look in the mirror before leaving. The apartment took on an uncomfortable silence. Hannah turned the record player on for background noise before grabbing her sketch pad and drawing a rose. It lacked the fierce blue of the one Wilhelm had given her, but it was the best she could do with what she had.

She found herself looking at the clock as it crept painstakingly slow toward 9 p.m. She rose from the small kitchen table, went into Josephine's room, and grabbed a matte black dress from the closet. Josephine had been kind enough to adjust many of her own dresses for Hannah to wear. Not only was she curvier and more endowed than Hannah but also taller. She put on a pair of long black gloves that went up to her elbow and covered her tattoo. She looked herself over in the mirror. The person reflected back was so drastically different than the one in the farmer's bathroom. She had come so far since that day. She was a survivor in all definitions of the word. But "survivor" was only a temporary status while in a Nazi-controlled country.

Hannah knew where Josephine was—"Les Sauvages" dance club in downtown Paris. It was where many a German soldier and officer went to pick up French women. The streets and sidewalks of Paris all led to the club like ants leading to the same ant hill.

When Hannah arrived at the club, German soldiers were kissing French woman outside the entrance, and more passionate and inappropriate acts were being performed in the alleyways. As Hannah opened the door, the powerful music of trombones, saxophones, and a piano caused her eardrums to vibrate. The club was packed with dancing people. The mahogany bar was filled with patrons extending their empty glasses and pints to be filled by the overwhelmed bartenders. The room was thick and muggy, and everyone was glistening with sweat. Conversations were being held in both French and German and the universal language of laughter. Cigarette smoke wafted to the ceiling. It was an intoxicating atmosphere that made it impossible to not want to dance. The place was filled well beyond its recommended limit, and the prospect of finding Josephine seemed dubious at best.

Men, both French and German, offered to buy Hannah a drink, but she waved her hand in refusal. It was way too loud to be heard over the band. Only after a couple left the dance floor did Hannah spot Josephine. She was dancing with a German officer in a way that mothers would shield their children's eyes from. Josephine was well aware of how weak her body could make men. She was also quite the dancer. Had Hannah not been surrounded by predators, she would have danced too. As the song finished, applause broke out for both the band and dancers. Josephine followed the German officer to the bar, but her smile vanished when she saw Hannah.

"What are you doing here?" Josephine whispered.

"You were late. I was worried," Hannah said.

"This must be your niece Hannah?" the German officer asked.

"Yes. Hannah, this is Sturmbannführer Ernst Heiden," Josephine introduced.

The man turned, and the light hit his face. Hannah had seen him before—several times at Lena's house. He was one of the many officers Jakob entertained.

"Have we met before?" Sturmbannführer Heiden asked.

He stared long and hard at Hannah's face, and although he still had a smile on his own, it was a façade. Beneath that friendly mask was a cold calculating machine searching the archives of his memory, trying to find her.

"No, I do not believe so. Perhaps at Josephine's café?" Hannah asked.

Josephine's face showed no signs of worry, but her fingers had tensed. It was fortunate it was impossible not to sweat inside the club, for Hannah's perspiring forehead would have given her secret away.

"No, I do not think so. You are Lena Hauser's friend, aren't you?" Sturmbannführer Heiden asked.

"I think you have me confused for someone else," Hannah said.

Sturmbannführer Heiden did not break his gaze, and if she flinched, the game would be over and he would have won. She stared back into his dead gray eyes while he tried to stare beyond her brilliant blue. Josephine strutted away from both Hannah and Sturmbannführer Heiden, and for a moment, Hannah thought Josephine had abandoned her—but for only a moment. Josephine often said that once a man has sex on his mind, he will abandon all reasoning and think of only fulfilling his lust. Sturmbannführer Heiden looked to his side. Josephine was no longer there. His face showed he had realized he had spent an inordinate amount of time staring at her attractive and far younger niece.

"Excuse me," he said and began searching for the top of her head near the bar.

Hannah knew exactly where she was but, to add to the illusion, she let him wander as she crept beside Josephine.

"Are you stupid?" Josephine asked, not looking at Hannah and trying to make sure no one else saw her.

"I am sorry," Hannah said.

"You could have been caught, Hannah. You should leave," Josephine said.

She was right. Josephine had told her to stay home, but she was over an hour late, and Hannah would not sit passively by, wondering if her friend was in need of help.

"I had to know you were okay," Hannah said.

"I found you," Sturmbannführer Heiden said from behind them.

The invisible hair on Hannah's arms stood up like a deer in headlights. Hannah and Josephine turned. Sturmbannführer Heiden smiled at them. Both were elated that he had smiled but neither showed it. Hannah had a look of indifference on her face, and Josephine scowled at him in a way that made him question whether he had truly seen war.

"You left," Sturmbannführer Heiden said.

"I did. I don't play the opening act. I'm the headliner," Josephine said.

"I simply thought I recognized your niece. I have had too much to drink and the lighting is poor, I could not tell. I am sorry," Sturmbannführer Heiden said. He apologized to Hannah, and she looked at him with even greater indifference.

"Are you going to buy me a drink or do I need to find a French man who can properly treat a woman?" Josephine mocked.

"Best not ask a French man to fight for his woman or the fight would be over very quickly," Sturmbannführer Heiden quipped.

Hannah knew Josephine wanted to lash out and strangle him.

"Soixante Quinze for both myself and my niece. I hope you brought a ladder because you have to climb yourself out of quite a hole," Josephine said.

The drink looked like bubbling liquid gold. It was a mix of champagne, gin, lemon juice, and sugar and was garnished with a lemon wedge. Josephine finished hers in one long, continuous gulp, whereas Hannah sipped away at hers.

"Dance with me," Sturmbannführer Heiden said, but his request hovered on the line of a command.

"I will meet you there. I have gossip to spread with my niece," Josephine said.

Sturmbannführer Heiden nodded and stumbled toward the dance floor. Josephine turned her back to him and removed a small vial of liquid. In length, it was roughly the size of her pinky nail but less than a quarter of an inch wide.

"Take this. In twenty minutes, buy us another round and pour this into his glass," Josephine instructed.

"What is it?" Hannah asked.

The need to whisper ended when the band began playing again. They could barely hear without shouting into each other's ears.

"Let's just say, he'll wake up and won't remember he even met me," Josephine said.

Hannah did her best to give enough of a standoffish look to scare off any brave men from approaching her. The band was exceptional, but it was ironic that a band of Negros was deemed worthy to play music for the Third Reich. Like so many other ethnicities, Negros were viewed as inferior. The clock on the wall was too far away for Hannah to see so, instead, she simply counted each song that played. After four songs, she ordered another round of Soixante Quinzes. The bartender lined them up, and Hannah took out the required francs to pay the bartender. She discretely removed the topper from the vial and poured it into the glass on the far right. After the contents stopped bubbling, she nodded toward Josephine who came with Sturmbannführer Heiden following closely behind her.

"Another round," Hannah said, holding out a drink for both. This time, Josephine sipped hers, and Sturmbannführer Heiden drank it in two giant gulps, but a fifth of it ran down his chin.

"Shall we step outside?" he asked. He had intended to whisper, but he was drunk, and whispering was not something a drunk person was capable of doing.

"Please. Do you expect to take me in an alleyway?" Josephine asked. It was entirely his plan, and his face showed it. "We will go to my place," Josephine said.

Sturmbannführer Heiden rubbed his hands across her back, his lust fully consuming him. The beast in him had seen the full moon.

"I will meet you there," Josephine said to Hannah.

Hannah looked at the way Sturmbannführer Heiden's hands were exploring Josephine's back. It was possible he would stick to his original idea and have his way with her in the alley. But Josephine nodded her assurance, and Hannah accepted it and headed toward the exit. The fresh air was incredible in comparison to the stagnant, muggy cigarette stench of "Les Sauvages." The sheer number of men and women embracing one another in the alleys was disturbing. Drunk German soldiers stepped outside for fresh air to vomit onto the streets or urinate along the walls. Their stares were stronger than the cool night chill. Hannah was a gazelle standing in tall grass surrounded by lions. Yet, she was no gazelle, and if any German was foolish enough, they would soon find that out. They cried out pathetic attempts to try and seduce her, none of which were gentlemanly. Hannah ignored them but kept glancing over her shoulder to ensure they were not stalking her like lions through the tall grass. She reached Josephine's apartment building and hurried to unlock the door. A feeling of relief surged through her when she stepped inside and locked the door.

Hannah poured a glass of water and disappeared into Josephine's bedroom. Josephine had told her to stay in there as she would not bring another man in her bedroom. Instead, they would use the couch—the same couch Hannah slept on every night. There were three beds available for use between the two empty bedrooms, but she could not blame Josephine for wanting them to stay empty. She had been beyond hospitable, and Hannah had zero complaints with the arrangement. She sat on the edge of the bed, but as a deep exhaustion set in, she curled up near the foot of the bed and struggled to fight off the desire to sleep. The front door of Josephine's apartment was thick and heavy and did not open quietly. Hannah sat up and tried to listen to the whispers coming from the living room. Any hopes the voices had of being quiet were betrayed by their drunken stumbling. They collided with chairs and nightstands. Hannah crept close to the door to try and better hear what was being said. After what felt like the entire night, the door opened, and Josephine nodded for Hannah to step out. What she had thought had been the entire night had only been twenty minutes. Sturmbannführer Heiden had passed out on the couch with his pants undone. His neck was covered in lipstick stains, and Josephine's dress was undone.

"He passed out before…" Josephine said.

Hannah had not asked, but she had wondered whether they had had sex. Josephine sat at her kitchen table and lit a cigarette in a black cigarette holder and took five quick puffs.

It was the first man she had kissed since her husband had died. Even if she had done it for the resistance, it had not made it any easier. She never smoked inside her apartment, and the fact that she was told Hannah it was eating her inside out.

"Did he talk?" Hannah asked.

"Yes. I kept telling him we needed to see the countryside tomorrow. He told me he was scheduled to guard the tracks for a supply train coming in tomorrow morning at ten," Josephine said.

"That's wonderful. The supplies are no doubt for defending against the invasion," Hannah said.

"They are. But it is not the supply train we need," Josephine said.

The information they needed was in Oberführer Köning's notebook. The entire night was Josephine's attempt to remove the burden of choice from Hannah. It was far too dangerous in Josephine's opinion. Yet, she was doing things just as dangerous if not more so, but Josephine was a French patriot, a widow, a bereaved mother, and a woman scorned. She would die for Mathis, Adam, Noah, and Leo. And she would die for France.

"I know this could not have been easy," Hannah said.

"We must all do our part," Josephine said, taking a hefty puff from the cigarette in her trembling hand. It was clear to Hannah that Josephine would have to make peace with it alone.

"What do we do with him?" Hannah asked.

One quick knock on the door made it look like they had been silently waiting for their cue. Josephine hurried to the door and looked through the peephole before opening it. Durand stepped in with three other men. Hannah had seen them before. They were often the same men who escorted her and Josephine home. The tallest of them was Franco. His eyes were hidden by his gray ivy hat. The second and third were twins and had recently turned seventeen. The only thing that helped distinguish Glen and Greg was a small black mole on Glen's chin.

"You are going to have him killed?" Hannah asked.

Dozens of witnesses had seen how much Heiden and Josephine had danced and drunk together. They had even been spotted leaving together. When Heiden would be reported missing, Josephine would be the number one suspect.

"Unfortunately, no," Durand said.

"They will bring him back to one of the clubs. It is not uncommon for people to pass out in the alleys," Josephine explained.

"I want to go," Hannah said.

She clearly had not learned her lesson the first time about near misses. But it was as safe with Durand and his men as it was in the apartment. It also seemed impossible for her to rid herself of the feeling of uselessness for having spent most of the night hiding in Josephine's bedroom.

"You are either very brave or very stupid. Durand, you keep her safe. I am going to bed," Josephine said, handing Durand her tube of lipstick. She was preoccupied with her own thoughts and wanted some time alone. She disappeared down the hallway.

Greg and Glen lifted Heiden from the couch and struggled under his weight. "It may be quicker if we drop him out of the window," Durand suggested, winking at Hannah. It was a risky mission, for a firefight would ensue if they were seen by other German soldiers. The danger clouded the muggy spring air. Hannah stepped down from the apartment's stoop. Every shadow or figure moving in the dark caused her heart to beat faster and her breath to shorten.

"Relax, Hannah, they are with us," Durand said.

The entire walk had been scouted, and if they happened to be approaching German soldiers, one of Durand's men came and silently pointed for them to turn either left or right. A woman approached them, moving with earnest haste. "You're late," she said. The woman brushed away her shiny, pumpkin-colored hair from her blue eyes. She was beautiful, and her busty figure was brazenly displayed. Durand handed the woman the tube of lipstick Josephine had given him.

"Who is this?" the woman asked as she puckered her lips and applied the lipstick.

"Hannah. She is part of the team. Hannah, this is Clauvette," Durand said.

The woman had no time for introductions, so Hannah only inclined her head toward her.

"My team has the soldiers inside dancing. But they will be back out shortly," Clauvette said.

Glen and Greg dropped Heiden into the alleyway. Clauvette bent down and kissed his neck and lips. She unbuttoned her shirt and allowed her breasts to spill out. "If you have to be in the play, you may as well be the star," Clauvette said as she took Heiden's hand

and put it up her skirt. Hannah was taken aback at Clauvette's indiscretion. "Do you boys want to stay for the show?" Clauvette asked, turning to look at them.

"I think so," Franco said.

"It will end with us getting shot," Clauvette said.

"Hannah does have a camera," Durand joked. Hannah lightly hit his arm. Franco and the twins thought it had been a genuine suggestion and tried to hide their disappointment after realizing it had been a joke. "Okay, come on, boys. Time to go," Durand said, waving his hand like an air traffic controller. They sulked but hurried away, Hannah and Durand behind them.

"So, the plan is he wakes up next to Clauvette and doesn't second-guess anything?" Hannah asked.

"When Clauvette is done with him, he won't be able to think of another woman for a month," Durand said. Hannah could not question that. It appeared he would be dreaming of her based on what she had done while he was unconscious. "She is a prostitute," Durand added. There was no judgment in his voice, but he could tell Hannah had been wondering how someone could be so comfortable with their body and sexuality. "She is well skilled at getting information. While she brings the German to her bed, his belongings are searched," Durand continued.

"Everyone does their part," Hannah said.

"Not all. There are some who prefer the Nazis. They continue to rat us out," Durand said.

Even if one was not willing to openly rebel against the Germans, how could any French-loving or liberty-loving person, for that matter, prefer Nazi rule over what had once been a free society?

"No news on the invasion?" Hannah asked.

"None," Durand answered.

"I have been thinking of the offer a lot," Hannah said. Durand chose to remain quiet. He would not force Hannah in any way, nor would he let anything he had to say impact her decision. "I still don't know. It terrifies me," Hannah said.

"It is a decision not to be made lightly," Durand said.

Hannah fell quiet again. The decision, although always her own, must be made by her and her alone. She respected Durand for not trying to lean her one way or the other. Yet, she also respected Josephine for trying to keep her from doing it. It meant she had her best interest at heart. The two had become surrogate parents of sorts. But they could never replace her true parents and neither tried. Josephine was more of an aunt and, often, Hannah was on the receiving end of Josephine's irritation.

"Tonight was not easy on Josephine," Hannah said.

"I can imagine not. It was not asked of her. She volunteered," Durand said.

"Did you know her husband?" Hannah asked.

"No. But he must have been quite the man to win over a woman like her," Durand said.

"I feel so terrible for her," Hannah said. Durand laughed. It was hardly the reaction she had been expecting and horribly inappropriate. "Why are you laughing?" she asked.

"Hannah, you really are too kind," Durand said.

"What do you mean?" she asked.

"Your heart breaks for Josephine. Yet, you have lost equally. That is what we are fighting for. For every horrible thing the Nazis do, there is someone doing an equally great selfless act," Durand explained.

A list of names and faces came to Hannah—Lena Hauser, Eleanor Cole, Rafel Trugnowski, the farmer and his wife, Josephine Moreau, and Radley Durand.

Durand bid Hannah goodnight, and when she entered the apartment, she quietly opened Josephine's bedroom door to ensure Josephine was sleeping and not crying. But it appeared she had done her share of crying before sleep had granted its mercy. Sometimes, sleep did not offer an escape. Dreams were torturous. They allowed one to see, to feel, and to hear those who were no longer alive. With such a huge decision to make, it was likely Hannah would not have to worry about dreams.

The Decision

Hannah tried to find comfort, switching from sleeping on her back to her stomach and on her side. She awoke, unsure whether she had slept for hours or minutes. But it didn't matter. She had received all the rest she would require. She checked the pocket watch the farmer had given her. It was only quarter to five. It was Sunday, and the café was closed. Josephine had had much to drink at "Les Sauvages" and even more after Heiden had passed out. An empty bottle of wine was on the table along with the photograph of her, her husband, and her three boys. Hannah cleared the table and gently put the photograph back on the mantel. Josephine's tears had smeared the glass frame. Hannah wiped it clean with her sleeve.

She quietly dressed and left the apartment. Hannah strolled across the city, the sun barely peeking over the horizon. The nocturnal had gone to bed a few short hours ago, and only the most ambitious moved about the streets. Hannah dashed toward the warehouse Durand had taken her to when he had suspected her to be a spy.

"What are you doing here?" Franco asked.

"Franco, I need to borrow a car," Hannah said.

"For what?" Franco asked.

"I need to see Radley," Hannah answered.

All of Durand's men had been told Hannah and Josephine were extensions of himself. If they should require anything, it was to be done. Franco worked the nights, and his shift was almost over. Gas was at a premium, and he would have preferred if Hannah would have come eleven minutes later. The problem would have been someone else's. Even still, he led Hannah to a faded and rusted black truck.

"You know how to drive?" he asked.

"Yes," Hannah said, taking the keys from his hands.

"Do you know how to get there?" Franco asked.

Hannah was generally bad with directions but had been to Durand's enough to have memorized the way. She never remembered things by street names but, instead, looked at the landscape around her, the buildings, the homes, and the trees. When the truck coughed to life, Hannah doubted if it would even take her to the end of the road.

"She'll make it. Don't worry," Franco reassured her. He had worn the same worried look on his face the first dozen times he had driven the car too.

"I hope so, or I will be calling you," Hannah said with a smile.

"Drive safe," Franco said, waving a salute as Hannah pulled away.

The truck found its legs and steadied its breathing. Hannah had missed driving. It was not the same without Wilhelm, but the solitude brought upon by the open road allowed for some of the best contemplation. It was peaceful, and it was the first time Hannah had truly been alone since Wilhelm had left. Sure, there had been moments of isolation when in the bathroom, but during the last few years, she had been without it. She had felt lonely almost always, even amidst the company of others. Yet, now, truly alone, she felt oddly less so. The drive granted her nearly an hour—an hour in which she went over the decision she must make. She had expected to go back and forth on her decision the entire way. She hated making decisions. Yet, there had been one thing that she had never had to second-guess or question—Wilhelm.

Durand was out in his field, a garden hoe in his hands, while his horse enjoyed a moment's pause. Durand stood tall as the truck approached. He looked uneasy at first until he recognized the truck. He dropped the hoe and limped toward the truck when Hannah stepped out. He looked so different in his dirt and sweat-stained white t-shirt, denim pants, and suspenders than he did in his suit and top hat.

"Hannah, is everything alright?" Durand asked, checking her for injuries like a paranoid parent.

"Can I ride your horse?" Hannah asked.

The horse in the field looked bored, and there were four more in the stable, eating an early breakfast of hay.

"Sure," Durand said, holding the middle part of the word longer than normal.

He had no problem with Hannah going horseback riding, yet he hoped she had come for something more important. They walked toward the horse, and Durand grabbed its reins and led it to the stable. Hannah was silent as Durand prepared two horses for riding. He helped Hannah get up onto the saddle and sit. He was much more adept and was able to pull himself up without much difficulty despite his bad leg. He had ridden on horseback during the Great War and had learned how to mount and dismount quickly. Yet, with his bad leg, he was rarely able to ride for long periods of time. The horses trotted along, enjoying the warmth of the rising sun. The blue sky was full of white, wispy clouds with a flashing layer of blinding hues of orange and yellow over the horizon. They stared in silence for several moments before Hannah spoke.

"I thought about my choice," she said.

She had almost gotten lost in the sunrise. A trance had set upon her, which was almost impossible to break.

"What have you decided?" Durand asked.

"I want to do my part. I want to get to London."

Josephine and Durand had made her feel welcome, but she could never truly feel safe in a city or country under Nazi rule.

Durand's face was a mix of contradictory emotions—both worried and proud. "I will make the arrangements," he said.

"Thank you for not trying to dissuade me one way or the other," Hannah said.

"I told you I would work to gain your trust. I can't do that by telling you what you should do. I trust you will make the right decision for you," Durand said.

Hannah was invited in for breakfast and spent the day helping Durand with farm work. It was familiar in so many ways and, yet, strangely new. Water breaks were something she had not been blessed with at Auschwitz, nor did she feel like a gazelle whose weakness was being observed by a lion. At that exact moment, there were thousands of people working past the point of exhaustion and starvation. Hannah would not allow herself to live in fear. She would not allow herself to live half a life. She would not sit idly by while others tried to stop the evil tyranny. Evil prevails when good men and women do nothing. As Hannah watched the sunset from atop the wooden fence, Durand surprised her by bringing two blank old canvases and a paint set for the two of them to paint.

"It has been quite some time," Durand said, trying to find his first stroke of the brush.

"Just start," Hannah said.

Uncertain of where to start, Durand had been hovering his brush over the canvas. Hannah had instantly put her brush to hers. It was an hour of silence, and even though the colors of the sky were the same on both canvases, how they perceived the sunset was profoundly different.

"No wonder why the Nazis destroy art," Durand said as he examined his own piece.

"It is fine. You are quite good," Hannah said, doing her best to encourage him, for he truly was.

"You have improved at lying, Hannah, but I call *connerie*," Durand said with a smile.

Hannah signed her first name and gave the painting to him.

"A gift," Hannah said.

"To be revered on rainy days," he said.

Durand drove Hannah back to Paris, and it did not take long for her to drift off. The lack of sleep the night before and the hard day's work in the field had worn her out in a way she had not felt since she had left Auschwitz. When Josephine opened her apartment door and saw Durand and Hannah, she knew Hannah had made her choice. Hannah anticipated a lecture, but Josephine was silent as she walked to her cupboard and removed three wine glasses from the shelf. She popped the cork out of a bottle of Sauvignon Blanc and poured a glass for each of them.

"If we do this, I want passage for Hannah within twelve hours. Oberführer Köning is not a mindless monkey like some of these Nazis. He is smart. I will not let Hannah be subjected to interrogation. They will discover she is a Jew. We do this in one week," Josephine said.

Both Durand and Hannah motioned to interrupt, but it was Durand whose voice carried the loudest.

"Josephine, the invasion is coming soon. We cannot wait a week. It may be too late," Durand said.

"We do this smart, Durand," Josephine said, "Hannah has been living undercover as my niece for two years. If one day she doesn't show up, it will raise suspicion. Tomorrow, I will tell the Germans my niece is returning home. We tell them she is leaving on Friday— that she is working the morning shift and catching the one-o'-clock train to Munich."

Neither Durand nor Hannah could find fault in her logic. The most important part of a lie was in the details—details truthful to some degree.

"The notebook will obviously be in German. You will not have enough time to read it all. You must look for dates and locations. There are three railroads the Germans use for resupply. We have given them each a number," Durand explained. He unfolded a map from his breast pocket. In red pen were hand-drawn railroad ways. "Gare de l'Est, Gare du Nord, Gare de Bercy," Durand said, pointing to each on the map.

"They will no doubt have given each a code name," Josephine said.

The Germans had used the Enigma coding machine almost exclusively since the war had started. It looked much like a typewriter, and when one letter or key was pressed, a second keyboard letter would light up. Three rotors were used for adjusting and acted like the hands of a clock—Hour. Minute. Second. The front of the machine had a plugboard that paired two letters together using a connecting wire, much like an operating switchboard. There were exactly a mind-boggling 158,962,555,217,826,360,000 possible combinations.

"He will have the month's numbers on him," Durand said.

"Month's numbers?" Hannah asked.

"Each month, the Germans send out the settings for the machine. It is how they are able to adjust the settings to make sense of what was sent," Durand explained.

Instructions showed how to adjust the rotors and plugboard to a starting position. The code was typed, and the cryptic message appeared one illuminated letter at a time.

"If Hannah steals his sheet, he will know," Josephine said.

"Agreed. Hannah takes nothing with her," Durand said.

"I can write it down. But, instead of numbers, I will write down orders of food. I will use the menu," Hannah said.

They went over the details over a dozen times. Josephine would not settle for surprises. She had always thought Durand had not given as much respect to the Germans as he should have and, therefore, underestimated them. The next morning, Josephine told the German officers Hannah would be leaving that Friday. Hannah told them her boyfriend, Wilhelm, was returning home from duty. Josephine had sold it perfectly. Tears filled her eyes when she said she would miss her. They went over and over the plan that night and, again, the following night to the point where Durand had to step in and call it quits. Josephine wanted every detail planned out. She wanted an escape route and plan in place for every possibility.

On Thursday night, Josephine was in an awful mood. Durand had been on the receiving end of a dozen scowls and three verbal bashings. He went outside for his end-of-the-night cigarette and hoped Josephine would cool down. But it seemed unlikely. The dishes Hannah had washed from their supper and Josephine had dried were nearly broken when she slammed them into the cupboard.

"You are mad at me," Hannah said, keeping her eyes on the plate she was scrubbing.

Josephine stopped drying the dishes and took a deep breath. "No, I am worried," she said.

"You did well with the Germans. The way your eyes teared up..." Hannah said.

"What did I tell you about lying? Put some truth in it," Josephine cut in.

Hannah wrapped her arms around Josephine, soap spuds falling off her hands.

"Thank you," Hannah said.

"You brought life back to this place," Josephine said.

"Come with me."

"Your future is elsewhere. Mine is here. Paris is my home—my family's home."

Durand opened the door and peeked in to test whether a plate would be thrown at his face. When he saw Hannah and Josephine hugging, he decided it was safe for him to step inside. Franco was behind him, no doubt because Durand had said there was extra strawberry pie.

"Franco, please take a photo," Hannah asked.

She grabbed her camera from the nightstand next to the couch and handed it to Franco. She kept her hand around Josephine's waist to prevent her from sneaking out of frame. Durand stood on Hannah's other side, and Franco snapped the photograph.

"I promised Franco pie," Durand said.

Josephine grabbed a plate she had dried less than thirty seconds earlier and carefully lifted a piece of strawberry pie with a fork and set in on the small plate. Franco thanked her after stuffing a large piece into his mouth.

Hannah looked at the clock. It was nearly ten. "You should be going. Madeleina will be worried," she said to Durand.

"No worries. I told her I would be staying here tonight. I will make sure I am here if needed," Durand said.

Hannah smiled. It would comfort her even that night when she tried to fall asleep. She often had visions of the door being broken down and SS officers sprinting in to snatch her.

"I hope you like the chair," Josephine said.

"It looks quite lovely, but I was under the illusion that hospitality dictates I sleep in your bed and you sleep in the chair," Durand said, casting a subtle wink in Hannah's direction.

"Give me your fork, Franco," Josephine said, extending an open hand.

"What for?" Franco asked.

He still had roughly one-and-a-half forkfuls left, and the idea of abandoning his eating utensil so close to finishing caused a feeling of melancholy to sweep over him.

"I am going to stab him with it," Josephine said.

Franco's true allegiance would have to become clear … and it did. He scooped up the last bites and handed over the fork.

"Traitor," Durand said.

Franco shrugged as he rose from his seat and walked toward the door, his shoulders dipping and swaying.

"You will do fine, Hannah," Franco said.

"Thanks, Franco," she said before he left the apartment.

Josephine walked down the hallway and grabbed another pillow and blanket for Durand.

"Do you need anything else?" Josephine asked.

"No, I am fine. Thank you," Durand said.

"Good night," Josephine said.

"Good night," both Hannah and Durand answered.

Hannah went into the bathroom to change into her pajamas and brush her teeth. When she stepped back out, the hallway and living room were pitch black apart from the small bit of moonlight shining through the closed blinds. Durand tried to get comfortable, shifting his body and trying to cover his feet with his blanket. Hannah was as quiet as she could be but bumped into nearly everything in the dark. She finally found the couch and laid down.

"I'm scared," Hannah said, her words cutting through the muggy silence.

Her thoughts were on what tomorrow would bring.

"Good. It means you have something left to fight for," Durand said.

He often said there are two types of people—people who had something to fight for and people who had nothing left to lose. Durand had something left to fight for. Josephine had nothing left to lose. Which group did she belong to? Had she lost everything? Or, did she too have something left to fight for? But she quickly realized she did have something left to fight for—her life and a fresh start.

"I won't let them take me alive," Hannah said.

"It won't come to that," Durand assured her.

Hannah was old enough, mature enough, to know that though he meant his words, there was nothing he could do to ensure they would come to fruition. She did not expect to sleep much that night but, oddly, she did. It seemed her mind had grown too exhausted to filter through the millions of thoughts—both consequential and insignificant. She wondered how long she would have slept if Durand had not roughly woken her.

"Sorry. I have been calling your name for damn near a minute," Durand said.

Apparently, Durand had started with a soft shake and a whisper, but only after shaking her and nearly screaming did she wake. The answer to how long? All day. Josephine was dressed and sitting at her kitchen table. Two plates full of eggs and hash browns were placed in front of the empty seats. Hannah was too nervous to eat and slid her plate over to Durand. As he finished his second helping, Josephine picked out a dress for Hannah. A small suitcase sat at the foot of the neatly made bed.

"What is this?" Hannah asked.

"It's some things I threw together. I will have you looking like a true Parisian when you go to London," Josephine said.

"I will send word. I will see you again," Hannah said.

"I hope so," Josephine said, stroking Hannah's blonde hair.

Durand stood short of the door frame and did not take another step forward, for it would be widely inappropriate to step inside another woman's bedroom.

"It's time," he announced.

Hannah took a final look at the place that had been short of home for two years. She would miss it all—the smell of candles and perfume she had once considered too strong but, now, nothing but soothing, a deep breath upon entering the apartment sent a feeling of relaxation through her, much like a deep breath of winter air, the kitchen table where they shared suppers, glasses of wine, and late-night snacks, the couch, and the space that had been her room. Durand put a soothing hand on her shoulder and carried her suitcase in the other. Hannah was grateful the morning sun was strong and the temperature nearly seventy degrees already. There was no value one could put on a sunny day to help lift one's mood. Durand nodded with encouragement before turning left. Hannah and Josephine continued across the intersection toward the "Givre Strudel."

It was stifling inside. Josephine had gradually increased the heat inside and passed it off as a broken heater. It was all in hopes of getting Oberführer Köning to allow them to hang up his leather trench coat. Hannah served four tables within the first two hours. She continually glanced at the door, waiting for the Nazi to enter. An hour passed from his normal arrival time. She continued to swap concerned looks with Josephine. But finally, the Nazi officer entered the café. Of course, he was not alone. As usual, he was not alone. Untersturmführer Engel, Standartenführer Ziegler, and Hauptscharführer Voigt accompanied him, and each of them showed different levels of annoyance at the heat inside the café. Hauptscharführer Voigt looked as if he was ready to withdraw his pistol and shoot someone.

"I see the heater is still broken. How wonderful!" Oberführer Köning remarked, his sarcasm as thick as the air.

"My apologies, Oberführer. You know us French. We like to be fashionably late," Josephine said.

"I would like to have a word with the repairman when he does arrive. It is not gentlemanly to keep a woman waiting," Untersturmführer Engel said.

"And today is young Hannah's last day in Paris," Oberführer Köning said.

Hannah walked toward him, taking a deep breath and wearing an artificial smile as she did. She had a part to play—a part that would send her to London.

"I was hoping you would forget. At least on my aunt's behalf. She has been a wreck all morning," Hannah said.

"Oh, Josephine, you cannot blame a German for wanting to return to their motherland. It calls to us all," Oberführer Köning said.

"May I take your coats?" Hannah asked.

Each waited for Oberführer Köning to choose and would follow his decision, but each silently prayed he would decide to take the jacket off. It was nearly ninety degrees, and the heat increased from all the bodies packed into the café like sardines.

"I suppose," Oberführer Köning said.

Hannah did her best to show no excitement as she collected the leather jackets.

"Hang them on the coat racks," Josephine said.

Hannah nodded and turned left toward the men's and women's bathrooms. Separating the two was a coat rack filled with spring jackets. Hannah marveled at the lengths some women went to to remain fashionable. Even if it was fifteen to twenty degrees cooler outside, it was still far too warm to be wearing a spring jacket for the sake of fashion. But, then again, Köning was wearing a long black trench coat. He was the worst offender. Hannah hung up the jackets and walked back to the table. If she took longer than necessary, it would draw attention to her.

"Can I offer you something to drink? Perhaps, an iced coffee?" Hannah asked.

"Definitely something cold. I will take the iced coffee," Oberführer Köning said.

The other three once again followed the highest-ranking officer in ordering the same thing.

"I hope you don't mind, Josephine, but we will be having some guests. New soldiers have just returned from combat. Those with honors have been invited here on our behest," Untersturmführer Engel said.

He raised his hand to the air, looked toward the door, and waved for whoever was outside to enter. The door opened, and soldiers dressed in black stepped in—two dozen in all. They were SS, but to Hannah, they were Dobermans. Their black leather boots went up to their knees, and they wore the swastika band on their left arm. At their sides was the Luger P08 pistol, and in their arms, they held the Gewehr 43 rifle.

"Is my food so awful that they must wear helmets and carry rifles into my café?" Josephine asked.

She had kept her cool considerably well. Luckily, the sweat that dripped down Hannah's forehead could be attributed to the heat and not the sudden wave of fear and nerves that had flooded over her. The German officers only smirked at Josephine's comment. Every open seat in the café was occupied by the SS, and those that had been filled by French patrons were strongly encouraged to be emptied with an unbroken German glare.

"Hannah, would you please fill up some pitchers of water for the soldiers?" Josephine asked.

"Of course. I'll be back with those iced coffees as well," Hannah replied.

"Your French has improved greatly. Do you still remember how to speak German? Or have you forgotten?" Hauptscharführer Voigt asked.

"I forget nothing," Hannah said in flawless German.

How she hoped he had understood the subtext of her words. She would never forget anything the Nazis had done. If it had not been Josephine's café, she would have been tempted to lock the doors and let the Germans die of heat exhaustion. Hannah walked through the swing door of the kitchen and filled the silver pitcher with ice and water. Josephine came through the swing door seconds later and grabbed Hannah's arm at the elbow and pulled her inside her office.

"It's off," Josephine said.

"No," Hannah argued.

"Hannah, there are close to thirty soldiers in there. More men than Durand can supply right now. If something goes wrong … if you are caught, it is over. You will be killed or sent back to that God-awful place," Josephine said.

"I can do this," Hannah assured.

"I know you want to get to London, Hannah…" Josephine began.

She had not finished speaking, but Hannah cut her off.

"It is bigger than me, Josephine. We are doing this so the Nazis cannot stop the Allied invasion. We are doing this for your family, for my family, Durand's family, and for every other family who has been torn apart by them," Hannah said.

Josephine stared at Hannah in silence. Hannah had arrived in Paris a beaten, frightened girl. But, now, a strong resilient woman stared at her, and she liked to think she had some small part in that.

"Bring out the coffee. I will take the pitchers. While I engage the Germans, you take the journal and go into the toilet. You have one minute. Chances are one of these bastards will have to take a piss, and I don't want him rounding the corner as you're putting the journal back," Josephine said.

Hannah and Josephine stepped out of her office and grabbed the four pitchers of water Michelle had filled for them. Regina was busy making the four iced coffees for the German officers. They were oblivious to how dangerous the atmosphere had become. Josephine had not involved any of them in her activities in the French resistance.

"Gentlemen, your iced coffees are being prepared right now. It will take just a few more minutes," Josephine said.

She and Hannah moved past their table. They set the pitchers of water on the tables, and Hannah returned to grab the ice coffees while Josephine started her act. Hannah was tempted to spit into the iced coffees but withheld the urge. What they were going to do would be far worse. She grabbed the four tall iced coffees and pushed open the kitchen swing door with her foot.

"In no particular order, Hauptscharführer Voigt," Hannah said.

It had been a long-running gag to serve the lowest-ranking officer his food and drinks last. But, because of that, Voigt always had a scowl on his face.

"Are you ready to order?" Hannah asked.

She had her tattoo covered by a white towel she used to wipe condensation off the tables. Hannah jotted down their orders before disappearing through the kitchen swing door. It was another minor annoyance to have the Germans look over the menu only to order the same thing they had ordered almost every day. She handed the order to Frank, and as Regina moved toward the swing door, Hannah crept right along behind her. As Regina went forward to the tables, Hannah diverted right toward the bathrooms. Hannah looked behind her to check if anyone was coming around the corner. The front glass door was within sight, and many German soldiers were outside, waiting for a table. Hannah's fingers shook slightly as she crept toward the coat rack. Oberführer Köning's jacket was at the end. She had purposefully placed it there so she could hide behind the coatrack and find it easily without having to sort through the multitude of coats.

She grabbed the journal and turned toward the bathroom. She turned the lock and opened the journal. The black book had a connecting black ribbon used as a bookmark. There were letters that had been written but were yet to be sent out. She flipped through the pages with frantic frenzy. The imaginary clock in her head counted down ten seconds at a time. A page was folded up into eighths near the front of the journal. Hannah unfolded it. On the left-hand side was a column that read DATES. The other columns stated which three of the five rotors were to be used, the exact starting point, and the letter pairing for the plugboard. In her hands were the Enigma code settings.

The date was 21 April, and Hannah only needed to copy the numbers for the remaining days of the month. The Maquis knew German troops and supplies were moving in before May, but they didn't know exactly when or where. The first letters and numbers she wrote were sloppy because of her trembling hand. She gave it a violent shake, and her penmanship became much bolder than it had been before. Every letter was a bullet—a bullet that would not strike its target in seconds but days. She flipped through the pages, looking for any mention of troop movement. But everything was in the same fine German writing and nothing stood out. She knew the codes would not appear to be words at all—rather, just an onslaught of letters in a discombobulated order. She found it between two unfinished letters—one addressed to Oberführer Köning's wife, Elsa, and one to his son, Conrad. She did her best to write the coded letters as fast as she could, but it proved challenging. It was not like reading words and being able to glance and translate. She had to see each letter of the word for it would make all the difference in whether or not the French resistance would be able to translate it.

She finished and pocketed her order book into her apron and closed the journal, making sure the black ribbon was on the same page it had been. She opened the door with her left hand, the book in her right and concealed behind her back. She poked her head out and narrowly missed being seen by a German soldier who had stepped into the men's room. She had dodged a near miss, but the Germans outside the front door stared at her through the glass. It was impossible to know whether they could see through the glass or only saw their own reflections from the high sun. The longer she waited, her chances of being caught increased. Hannah stepped out, placed the journal back into Köning's jacket pocket, and rounded the corner. She collided with someone hard enough to be knocked to the ground. The order pad fell out.

"My apologies, young Hannah," Hauptscharführer Voigt said, standing over her.

His apology lacked any sincerity whatsoever. He bent down and picked up the order form and looked at the ridiculous amount of lettering on it. She had jotted down the Enigma code settings on the front page and the coded messages near the middle.

"So many orders today?" Voigt asked.

"It is a running tab of what has been ordered for all of our customers," Hannah said, trying to keep a calm façade.

"Why do you do such a thing?" he asked as he continued to read.

Hannah knew the Hauptscharführer had not seen Oberführer Köning's journal, for the letters in there were extremely private. But it did not mean he had not received the same Enigma code dates as Oberführer Köning. But what need would there be for every one of the officers to have the codes if they worked exclusively under Oberführer Köning's command? Having so many copies was an unnecessary risk of them being stolen by the Allies.

"Why do you have numbers and not meals?" Hauptscharführer Voigt asked.

"Because I did not feel like writing out apple strudel nine times," Hannah answered.

"You seem to be in a hurry," Hauptscharführer Voigt said.

"Yes, as a matter of fact, Hauptscharführer Voigt, I am. Oberführer Köning's éclair is most likely done, and it is best served warm. But, in this heat, it is nearly impossible to deliver it without the frosting melting off and ruining the dish. But if you wish to continue to interrogate me on how my aunt runs her business and knows what to stock so she doesn't have to tell a customer she ran out of something, then please continue. Otherwise, your superior requires his breakfast," Hannah said.

Hauptscharführer Voigt scowled a moment longer before handing over the pad and stepping toward the bathroom. It made Hannah smile when he found out the door was locked. She took long strides toward the kitchen swing doors. Durand stepped into the diner. Hannah wanted to stop to look at him, but if she did, it would draw unwanted attention to both herself and Durand.

"If you can find a seat, it is yours," Josephine said from the German officers' table.

"Thank you, madam," Durand said, inclining his head.

Hannah stepped out of the swing doors with a platter full of food the German officers habitually ordered.

"What will you do back in Germany?" Oberführer Köning asked Hannah after finishing his first bite.

"I do not know. Maybe, take the first month of summer and just enjoy it with my boyfriend," Hannah answered.

"Send him our regards for fighting so fiercely on behalf of the Reich," Standartenführer Ziegler said.

Hannah was sure every German soldier who had been fighting either in the east against the Soviets or in Italy and North Africa against the British and Americans would be delighted to know high-ranking SS officers were enjoying pastries every morning in Paris.

"I will. I hope to bring him back here. But I will be asking if the heater has been fixed before I do," Hannah joked.

The German officers laughed before shifting their undivided attention to their breakfast. Hauptscharführer Voigt sat and found the spoonful of butter that usually topped his croissant had melted into a puddle that surrounded his croissant like a moat surrounds a castle.

Hannah stepped toward Durand, sitting alone in a corner of the café. His leg stuck out straight, and he wore a look that told Hannah he had had the same thought about locking the doors and letting them all die of heat exhaustion.

"Can I get you anything else?" Hannah asked.

"No. Just the coffee. I'm afraid the company has left a rather sour taste in my mouth. I am having to suppress the urge to vomit," Durand said.

The German soldiers around him couldn't possibly understand the French he had spoken so quickly. Hannah sniggered and tore the order and coded message from her pad. She signed it at the bottom and set it on the table. Durand let it sit there as he tried to finish his cup of coffee, but it was too weak and watered down. He rose from his chair, pushed it in, and tossed enough francs to cover his bill and leave Hannah an overly generous tip. He seized the order form, pocketed it, and limped toward the door.

Hannah stopped by the German officers one last time.

"Gentlemen, it is time for me to say adieu and auf wiedersehen," Hannah said.

"It has been a pleasure getting to know you, Miss Hannah. I wish you safe travels," Oberführer Köning said.

The other officers nodded politely except for Hauptscharführer Voigt, who only curled his lip upward in the slightest amount. Hannah smiled and followed Josephine to her office for their final goodbye.

"I will never be able to repay you," Hannah said.

Josephine only pulled Hannah into a hug and brushed Hannah's hair away from her face to behind her ear.

"Take care, Hannah," Josephine whispered.

She wanted to tell Josephine so much more than what she had. But Josephine was not one for such emotional talk. Hannah hurried toward the back exit, Josephine's smile giving her the will to leave. Durand was waiting outside. He gave her an encouraging smile and squeezed her hand. The truck Hannah had used to visit Durand was parked two blocks ahead. Durand placed her suitcase in the back of the flatbed, and the two hopped in.

The truck sputtered out a puff of black smoke from its exhaust before it jerked forward. They drove to the warehouse where the German Enigma machine had been brought to see whether the information Hannah had gathered was worthy of sanctuary in London. It had not been Durand's decision, and he had fought to have Hannah on the boat while they looked, but the higher powers of the resistance and the British Intelligence deemed otherwise.

"I do not like leaving Josephine behind," Hannah said.

"She will play her part well," Durand reassured.

A man stood with his back against the warehouse, smoking a cigarette. His leg was raised, and his foot rested against the sheet metal door. He took a final puff before he tossed his cigarette and slid the door open. Dozens of people were inside. Some Hannah had seen before and others, she had not. Plenty were far above Durand in rank. Every person was indirectly or directly staring at the Enigma machine on the wooden table. A resistance fighter, a woman of Hannah's age, was seated at a chair in front of it and ready to set the starting position.

Durand removed the messages from his pocket and handed it to a man in his late sixties. He was balding on top and was short. To ask who he was would draw red flags so, instead, Hannah remained quiet. She would do nothing to risk her spot on a ship to London. The balding man handed the sheet of paper to the young woman sitting in front of the Enigma machine. She lifted open the top, adjusted the rotors first, and swapped out the middle one with rotary number four. The plugboard took the longest. The wires had formed some sort of knot that would make any seaman proud.

"I am ready," the young woman said.

Durand sat beside her, a pencil and a blank sheet of paper in front of him.

"Ready," Durand said.

The woman typed U on the front keyboard, and N lit up on the second. The woman typing called out each letter, and Durand repeated it to confirm. Hannah looked over Durand's shoulder. Words came to life from cryptic code, words including "train," "Normandy," and "resupplies" but, more importantly, there were exact times, dates, and locations. Those who were quicker at putting the letters together into words erupted into smiles. Durand looked over the message before handing it to, who must have been, the highest-ranking man in the room.

"Secure supply lines to Normandy. Five thousand troops to arrive in Paris on 26 April at 1 p.m.," the man began to read.

The report detailed which railways, which German officers, and which supplies would be coming in. With this information, the French could destroy the railroads, call in Allied bombing raids and, plain and simply stated, wreak havoc on the Germans. People erupted into cheers and hugs. Durand rose from his chair and spread his arms. He wore a proud smile as he hugged Hannah. Months ago, Hannah had thought she was going to be shot inside that warehouse for engaging in espionage against the French and Allies. Now, she had provided vital information for them.

"How will we know when the invasion is coming?" Hannah asked.

"When the English tell us Joseph has a mustache, we will know," Durand answered.

It was another cryptic radio message that would sound like nonsense to any German listening, but it would be the sound of liberty approaching for every French.

"Miss," the high-ranking, balding Frenchman said, interrupting Hannah and Durand's embrace.

Hannah turned toward him, and the man stared her down. He dug into his pocket and removed a series of documents, passports, and tickets—all held together with a rubber band. He handed it to her, and Hannah removed the rubber band and looked through the stack. There was a passport granting her admittance into England. The name on it was Hannah Smith. Also, in the stack was a ticket for passage aboard a ship departing from Saint-Valery-en-Caux.

"Your papers. Your request to enter England has been approved by the British Intelligence Agency, Ms. Smith. They thank you, the French thank you, and I thank you," the man said, bowing his head.

Hannah was silent as she stared at the papers. It was a strange thing to have her future condensed down into a passport and a ticket.

"Ship leaves in three hours. We should go," Durand said.

Hannah nodded. She wanted to say goodbye to Josephine one last time and wished she would have come with her. But the ghosts of her family were in Paris—they were both her anchor and her chains. Stealing from the Nazis had been one of the most terrifying experiences of Hannah's life and, yet, she could hardly recall a time when she felt more alive. She had made a significant difference in the war.

"Hannah," Durand said, putting his hand on her shoulder.

Hannah had yet to move. She had nodded she was ready to leave, yet her feet remained glued to the floor as if she had stepped on wet concrete and let it dry. Hannah nodded again and lumbered toward the door.

"Are you alright?" Durand asked.

"I am leaving people I trust behind for another unknown," Hannah said.

"London is far safer than Josephine or I can make Paris," Durand said, squeezing her shoulder to offer encouragement.

He started the truck and pulled forward. They drove in silence, a hundred emotions crossing her mind. She was not as elated as she had thought she would be. Instead, a feeling of loss spread over her again. Would she find someone who would look after her with as much devotion as Josephine and Durand had? But she continued to remind herself they were alive. She was not losing them in the way she had lost Trugnowski and Eleanor. She tried to find how she would say goodbye to Durand and had expected more time. The nearly two-and-a-half-hour drive seemed to have taken fifteen minutes. The truck was more than happy to shut off and sighed when the engine was killed. It looked as though over a hundred boats and ships were in the port.

"Radley, I don't have the words," Hannah said.

Durand placed a hand on top of Hannah's and shook his head. "It's auf wiedersehen, not goodbye."

They stepped out of the truck, and Durand lifted her luggage from the flatbed. Nazi guards blocked the entrance to the port.

"How do we get past them?" Hannah asked.

"Your papers will grant you admittance. This is as far as I go," Durand answered.

Hannah lifted onto the tips of her toes and kissed his cheek. "You are a good man, Radley Durand," she said.

"Perhaps, I could get that in writing so my wife has proof," Durand joked, flashing his intoxicating smile—how Hannah would miss it!

She took her suitcase from him and gave him one last look before faltering toward the Nazi guards. She extended her passport and ticket. The guards looked her over. The last time she had had her identification looked over, she had been thrown aboard a train to Auschwitz. She turned her head to see whether Durand was still there. Perhaps, there would be time to dash back to the truck if the papers were determined to be falsified. The guard searched for signs of tampering and forgery on a passport tampered and forged by the British Intelligence Agency but found none.

Durand was still there, looking on with a strength that wafted toward Hannah with the sea breeze. The Nazi guard stared hard at Hannah before nodding. The other guard lifted the boom barrier and allowed Hannah to step through.

"Hannah!" a voice rang out.

Hannah turned. Josephine dashed toward her with remarkable agility, considering the length of her heels.

"I had to see you off," Josephine said.

She took Hannah's hands in her own and squeezed them.

"I will see you again," Hannah said.

Although she wanted it to be a statement, it hovered on the line of being a question.

"You will," Josephine said, stroking Hannah's hair.

"Thank you. For everything. I wouldn't have made it without you," Hannah said.

"*Connerie.* Now go," Josephine said, wiping Hannah's tear away with a rub of her thumb.

The Nazi guard pushed Josephine out of the way. Hannah crossed the gate barrier, and as she did, Durand wrapped his arm around Josephine.

"This way, Hannah," a nearly eighty-year-old man said.

The man had hair as white as clouds and was extremely frail-looking. His ship looked worse and was only twice as large as the truck Durand had driven her in.

Hannah stepped aboard. The old man was joined by two others—one who was a quarter his age and another, no more than twelve years old. As they removed the ropes securing the boat to the dock, Hannah looked on as Josephine and Durand waved goodbye. The boat pulled away from the wooden dock, and Hannah blew them a kiss goodbye. The details of their faces were no longer visible. She could only make out Durand's near-black hair and thin mustache and Josephine's thick, flowing brunette hair and fierce maroon lipstick. As the distance furthered, she could only make out his suit and her burgundy spring dress. When she could no longer see the dock or the coast, she turned away.

The English Channel was remarkably calmer than normal, and the sun was high. Hannah was thankful for that. She did not want to be aboard a boat of that size should the waters turn choppy and the skies, gloomy. Hannah was uneasy and untrusting, but the fact that the three men aboard the ship comprised a three-generation family lessened it. But she could pay little attention to any of the three men. Her thoughts had taken over, and she had no ability to maintain small talk. They were like the reel of a movie, which needed to run the length of the film before it would stop. Her entire life had been lived in Europe and, now, she was leaving the heart of it behind. She could only hope that, someday, she could return.

Prisoner of War

The vicious Soviet winter finally lifted. The frosted ground thawed. Wilhelm had no idea where he was, nor did he know how much time had passed since he had tried to fly out of Stalingrad. He had marched nearly all day, every day, and every day, the number of Germans diminished. Some never woke for the next day's march, and those who fell too far behind were shot.

The days were filled with a stronger sun than any day in Stalingrad since the battle had started. But the end of the weeks or month-long march was at hand. A large fenced-in area with towers on each of the four corners loomed ahead. Soviet soldiers jeered at the German prisoners. But there were far too many Germans, nearly 91,000, to accommodate in one camp.

Wilhelm's life depended on being herded into the camp. His feet were covered with blisters and, no matter how numb his frozen feet were, he could feel each blister shoot pain up his leg with each step. He would not make another long march. If he was forced to keep moving, his legs would quit on him. But fate took a kind turn.

A push on his back ushered him inside the camp. A long line formed. Soviet soldiers demanded the Germans to announce their name and rank before entering.

"Schreiber, Wilhelm. Obersoldat," Wilhelm said.

The Soviet wrote down the information, and Wilhelm followed the rush of Germans to the center of the camp. A colonel dressed in a gray suit covered in military medals and decorations stood in front. The whispers of the Germans died down. The Soviet soldiers turned to attention. The highly decorated Soviet spoke and then paused to allow the German translator to catch up.

"My name is Colonel Vladislav," he said, "I am the high-ranking officer at this prisoner-of-war camp. You are just that—prisoners. You have lost your battle. I will not stand for uprising at my camp. You refuse to do the work that is handed to you, you will be shot. You will not be asked twice. Before anyone mentions the Geneva Convention, I will remind you of how we Soviets were treated at your camps."

The Geneva Convention was terms of how prisoners of war were to be treated. It guaranteed certain rights, including a set number of calories, which stated they should be entitled to the same as the capturer's enlisted men and determined by rank. The Soviets had not signed it and were not subject to any of its laws.

How could they blame Wilhelm for how the Soviets were treated at German camps? Or, most likely, ninety percent of the men there?

"You owe a debt to the Soviet Union—a debt that shall be paid through hard work or through death," Colonel Vladislav said and then turned away.

A bell rang, and the tenured prisoners rushed toward the food line like dogs hanging around the table at Thanksgiving.

Wilhelm hurried to join the line. It may be likely those last would get little to none. The food was scooped out with a ladle and placed inside a tin bowl. It looked like a thick, soggy slop.

"What is this?" Wilhelm asked.

"Kasha," the German ahead of him answered.

It was a Russian word, and Wilhelm had no idea what it meant. But if he had to guess, it translated to "shit."

"Um, it's buckwheat porridge. Boiled. Sometimes we get meat. Today, we don't," the German added.

Wilhelm placed a spoonful in his mouth. It lacked taste and was like chewing drenched cardboard. But each spoonful appeased his appetite.

"How long have you been here?" Wilhelm asked.

"I don't know," the soldier replied.

The soldier's dirty blonde hair, if subjected to a good shower and scrub, would probably have been similar in color as Hannah's. His face was sunken in, he had a thin frame, and his long nose was like the Jewish propaganda posters in Berlin.

"We tried surrendering to the Americans. But they wouldn't let us," the soldier said.

Höring had been wise to state they should not be captured by the Soviets.

"Where were you fighting?" Wilhelm asked.

"Southern Italy. Bailing out the damn noodles. You?"

The Italians had sometimes been referred to as noodles or pasta by some of the Germans. It was definitely not a term of endearment, which one would think was odd, seeing as they were allies. But the Germans, more specifically German young men, had to constantly aid the Italians as they lost battles and land.

"Stalingrad," Wilhelm said.

The soldier's face turned grim. "You fought at Stalingrad?" he asked.

Wilhelm nodded.

"We heard it was the second Verdun," the soldier said.

Stalingrad—a single word that brought a torrential onslaught of faces, names, sights, sounds, and smells. Wilhelm would forever have a permanent chill in his bones from the winter spent there.

"Tell me how to survive in this place," Wilhelm said.

The soldier's words were shockingly boring. However, he told Wilhelm to expect a change now that spring was on its way.

"Try to pick up as much Russian as you can. The guards seem to speak a dozen different languages. But the higher-up ones speak Russian. If you can speak it, you make yourself more valuable," the blonde-haired soldier said.

Several languages were spoken in the Soviet Union—Russian, Belarusian, Ukrainian, Lithuanian, Latvian, and Finnic to name a few—and was one of several reasons the Soviet Union had allowed itself to take heavy blows to the head before it raised its hands and struck back. Orders had been given in multiple languages and much was lost in translation. It also did not help that Stalin had purged (executed) many of the Soviet Union's top generals out of fear of betrayal and uprising.

The soldier showed Wilhelm to one of the housing buildings. Bunks lined up along the wall and were four-rows high. Wilhelm was not alone in climbing onto an empty bunk. It was too small and only had one blanket and a pillow that was little more than an inch and a half thick, but it was the best sleeping arrangement Wilhelm had had since he was in the infirmary.

It took thirty seconds for Wilhelm to fall into a deeper sleep than he had in months. There was no steady artillery fire or explosions that woke him. Not even the loud snoring coming from beside, above, and below him could wake him. In his dreams, he found Hannah, and when he did wake to the sound of a ringing bell, reality had never been as cruel.

Wilhelm followed the blonde-haired German to morning breakfast. Wilhelm was not shocked, though entirely disappointed, to see kasha was also the breakfast of choice.

"So, do you speak Russian then?" Wilhelm asked.

"Bits. Not enough to be dangerous. We have to learn like dogs," the blonde German said.

Beaten dogs most likely.

Wilhelm raised a sloppy spoonful of kasha to his mouth. Breakfast was expected to be eaten quickly so the work could start.

"Have any skills?" the blonde soldier asked.

It was a question that affected Wilhelm in a way he had not expected. It almost made him cry. It had been so long since he had done anything for fun. He hadn't touched a guitar since he had left for war. He hadn't been around fast modern cars, only panzer tanks. He hadn't done anything in so long that he could hardly remember what he had been good at. His hobbies came back to him, and their absence was never more profound.

"I helped on airplanes back in France," Wilhelm said.

"Listen, I know nothing about that stuff. But I don't want field duty. If I can talk them into letting us go to the factory, can you teach me?" the blonde soldier asked.

"Sure," Wilhelm said.

The hundreds of Germans were separated into different lines based solely on physical appearance. Those who were tall with broad shoulders were put into lines of hard manual labor. Those who looked to be intelligent (generally based on who wore glasses) were put into lines involving more complex tasks.

Wilhelm looked around to see to which line he would be pre-selected to join. He was tall, and though he had lost much weight during the last month of Stalingrad, he was in much better shape than some of the prisoners. The blonde soldier squeezed his way toward one of the Soviets. Wilhelm shadowed him. The blonde soldier spoke with much struggle and was only able to say a few words, one of which Wilhelm knew to be airplane based on the way the blonde soldier used his hand to mimic a takeoff. He even made the sound of the engine. The Soviet pointed at Wilhelm and spoke.

"Nod," the blonde soldier whispered.

Wilhelm nodded, and the Soviet nodded to the right. Wilhelm and the blonde soldier joined the line of roughly eighty prisoners. As they marched to the fence entrance, a dozen guards with PPD-34 submachine guns at the ready stalked beside them.

"That was Russian?" Wilhelm asked.

"More sign language," the blonde soldier said.

He grinned, but as they approached the machine gun-carrying guards, his grin vanished.

"Don't get any ideas. I've seen a dozen men shot down. They barely broke a stride too," the blonde soldier whispered.

"Where are we?" Wilhelm asked.

What would he do if he escaped? Where would he go? He didn't even know where he was.

"I don't know. They didn't exactly hand out maps," the blonde soldier said.

A half-dozen military trucks with canopies covering the cargo portion of the truck were parked outside the fence line. The Germans loaded into them. The armed guards stood vigilant, looking like guard dogs, hoping for somebody to run.

"These are American. Saw the same ones in Southern Italy," the blonde soldier said.

Wilhelm stepped into the back of the truck and took a seat along the left-side bench. The truck had two benches, and they were filled beyond what was comfortable. The back door lifted and slammed shut, and the truck charged ahead.

"Where are you from?" the blonde soldier asked.

"Schönfeld. And you?" Wilhelm asked.

"Würzburg."

Every turn caused Wilhelm's body to move with it. Even with the ride being incredibly bumpy and uncomfortable, it was strangely relaxing. Wilhelm had always loved driving. Even if he wasn't behind the wheel, there was something relaxing about a drive.

The truck pulled to a stop, and the back door dropped. Two Soviets stood with their machine guns pointed at the Germans to prevent them from charging out.

The factory was a tall building that was larger than any football stadium Wilhelm had seen. It was covered in sheet metal, and some sections looked as though a strong wind would send the covering soaring through the sky. The Germans were led inside and, somehow, it looked even bigger than it had from the outside.

At the far end were complete bomber aircrafts. The middle was filled with planes being assembled and before that were assembly lines producing engines, propellers, throttles, yokes, and other parts. Soviet guards were spaced every fifteen feet, creating a fence of flesh.

In addition to the Soviet guards were Soviets who managed each area. Again, the Germans were selected at random to work different portions of the assembly line.

Wilhelm and the blonde soldier followed a Soviet worker who looked far too old to still be working. He had a gimp to his step and a walking stick to correct it. His name was Sanjik Mikhailov, but he had a nickname that Wilhelm and the blonde soldier had given him— "Old Uncle Joe." The American president, Franklin Roosevelt, had called the Soviet leader, Josef Stalin, Uncle Joe, and since the man looked like a much older Josef Stalin, thick mustache included, the nickname fit. Old Uncle Joe was also far easier to remember and pronounce than Sanjik Mikhailov.

The man's voice was strong, raspy, and he would trail off the ends of his words. His Russian was entirely different than any other Wilhelm had heard. He understood the language barrier and showed how each part was to be assembled into the plane. Instead of speaking, he simply used his walking stick to poke them.

"This pilot you helped, he didn't crash on takeoff, did he?" the blonde soldier asked.

It was a joke, and his smile showed it, but Wilhelm found no hilarity in it.

"He left for a bombing raid over London and never returned," Wilhelm said.

"Oh, I am sorry. I was trying to be funny. I should have asked first," the blonde soldier said.

Wilhelm only shrugged. The man had meant no offense. It was impossible to find anyone who had not lost a friend.

"He was a genius. He had a life of plans," Wilhelm said.

He had always envied and respected Aaron for that. Wilhelm was spontaneous and a procrastinator. He thought only of the present, mostly because the present had been so damn perfect. The present now made him long for the great memories of his past or the unknown events of his future.

"And you? What plans did you have?" the blonde soldier asked.

He was poked for talking.

"To marry the love of my life," Wilhelm said.

"Did you?"

"I did."

"Lucky bastard."

Wilhelm was poked, and it was not because he had screwed up but because he had stopped working. His mind transported him from the present to the past. But Wilhelm fared much better than the blonde soldier. Wilhelm had worked on German planes and, though the Soviet bomber was different, he had a good idea of what the plane should look like when assembled and what each part did and how to ensure it was in proper working order. He gave the blonde soldier information on each part they placed inside the plane. Some required the use of a hoist and others, a precise touch.

Old Uncle Joe looked at his pocket watch every twenty seconds and groaned. He poked Wilhelm and the blonde soldier in the ribs and pointed to different parts of the engine with his walking stick.

After they assembled the first engine on their own, Old Uncle Joe inspected it. He let out grunts when something was displeasing and sighs when something was satisfactory. Whether it was done in an attempt to bridge the language barrier or it was an idiosyncrasy he had always had, Wilhelm could not tell. But Old Uncle Joe was much kinder than some of the other workers or guards. He even offered Wilhelm and the blonde soldier a drink from his flask. The moment Wilhelm swallowed the drink, he recognized it was the famed and lethal Russian vodka. Wilhelm repeated the words Alexander had said when he passed the flask. Old Uncle Joe nodded and repeated the same.

The factory was anything but quiet, yet it was in comparison to the heavy artillery and gunfire exploding day and night at Stalingrad.

Wilhelm had had many morbid thoughts during the battle, and they were hard to break. During breaks in battle, meal times or rest, Wilhelm would often look around at the hundred or so soldiers close by him and wonder who amongst them would live to see another sunrise, eat another meal or even take another breath. He stopped asking for names, even stopped seeking conversation. He only sought comfort in his journal. But that was no way to live. His father had been that way. Was the way he too acted some genetic trait or the way every battle-experienced soldier felt? As he and the unnamed soldier worked on a new plane, Wilhelm took the first step in reversing his outlook.

"My name is Wilhelm," he said.

He had fought next to men who had died. Brothers in arms yet strangers. No more.

"Torben," the blonde soldier said.

The next several months were filled with the same activities, and each day, Wilhelm picked up bits of Russian. Like any new language, he learned how to curse first, as they were Old Uncle Joe's favorite words. Wilhelm knew roughly thirty words, and eight of them were a derivative of the word "fuck." But after the first two months, he was able to communicate everything he needed to in order to get his work done.

"Good morning," Wilhelm said after arriving on another day.

Old Uncle Joe was smoking a cigar that was down to a nub, but he was a stringy old bastard and was frivolous with everything.

"Morning," Old Uncle Joe replied.

He had a habit of not adding good to his mornings and, instead, he preferred to simply state it was morning.

"We need to talk," Old Uncle Joe said.

He was usually grumpy and had a permanent scowl on his face. Yet, his lips, which were usually closed and straight, were curled in a way that looked like a horizontal "S."

Wilhelm and Torben followed him to a corner out of earshot between two guards.

"What is my name?" Old Uncle Joe asked.

"Sanjik Mikhailov," Torben answered.

The pronunciation was dreadful.

"So, you do know it? I hear you have a different name for me," Old Uncle Joe said.

343

Wilhelm and Torben looked at each other. They had never used the name while he was around, but they had been more careless with it over the last few weeks.

"What is the name, Wilhelm? Go on, tell me," Old Uncle Joe said.

"Old Uncle Joe," Wilhelm mumbled.

Torben had pleaded to Wilhelm with his eyes to remain silent in hopes of continuing the façade of innocence. Old Uncle Joe's face scowled, and his eyes squinted. But then they opened, and his mouth formed a smile. Bits of dust seemed to fall to the ground as his mouth formed into something it had not in the several months Wilhelm and Torben had known him.

He shook his walking stick at the two before he nodded for them to get back to work. Old Uncle Joe was tough and demanded work, yet he treated Wilhelm and Torben with a level of respect absent in most Soviets. But there was always a poke to be had. Torben swore the man simply liked to poke things.

"How did you get involved in this?" Wilhelm asked while working next to Old Uncle Joe.

His Russian was far from perfect, and perhaps the order of his words was wrong, but it was close enough for Old Uncle Joe to understand.

"Mother Russia asked me and, once more, I need to suckle at her breast," Old Uncle Joe said.

"That must be one saggy tit if he is nursing on it," Torben whispered in German, searching through the wrenches for the 178 millimeter.

War had affected everyone, not just the soldiers who had to fight and die. Women were moved into fields of employment predominately occupied by men, and the elderly, who had earned relaxation, were required to help. Stalin did not believe in handouts, and every Soviet was expected to serve a purpose, and if they did not, they were killed.

"Do you have … woman … ugh?" Wilhelm asked in broken Russian.

Sometimes words were hard to find.

"Wife," Old Uncle Joe said.

Wilhelm had heard the word before on several occasions and the fact he had forgotten was frustrating.

"Wife," Wilhelm repeated aloud and silently a dozen times. It better stick, he thought.

Torben looked uneasy at how personal Wilhelm tried to get.

"She passed," Old Uncle Joe said.

"Because of the war?" Wilhelm asked.

Old Uncle Joe shook his head and pulled his cigar from his mouth. "No. She missed the war. I am thankful for that."

Wilhelm could understand. He missed his mother every day yet, strangely, he was thankful she did not have to live through another war. She was a kind person who was almost too compassionate. When she would hear bad news or someone she loved was feeling low, she would become prone to what Wilhelm called symptoms of sympathy. She would get stomach aches and become restless. She could not sleep at night and would often cry.

"I understand," Wilhelm said.

He had paused too long to not receive a poke, and this time, it dug into his kidneys. Another whistle signaled the end of the workday. Wilhelm and Torben nodded goodbye to Old Uncle Joe and joined the lines to exit the factory and be brought back to the camp. The hot August air was thick with humidity, and the men reeked of sweat. Wilhelm did not know how close he was to Stalingrad, but it was hard to fathom the brutal cold could turn into something so hot. The gates of hell had opened, and the thick veil of steam and heat wafted upon them.

Wilhelm and Torben sat at the back of the truck, removing their white t-shirts and rolling their pants up to their knees. The canopy covering had been removed, but any prisoner contemplating freedom would have to risk being shot by the soldiers in the surrounding jeeps or run over.

The breeze from the speed of the truck was the best part of Wilhelm's day. It was the only time the weather was comfortable. Wilhelm loved the heat but that was when he spent much of the summer at Lena's cottage and nearly all day in the lake behind it. Yet, every soldier who had been at Stalingrad knew how torturous the winter had been. The bright skies and burning sun provided warmth, relief and, most importantly, hope.

The soldiers sat with their arms raised to let their armpits air out. Sundays were their days to shower, but it was only Tuesday, and everyone smelt awful already. Some men, unfortunately, had a stronger disposition to sweat. Some were as oily as a fish, and Wilhelm sympathized with them over how uncomfortable they must have been.

"Keep driving until you reach the Pacific," one soldier said.

Nearly everyone was in agreement.

"Keep driving until you drive into the Pacific," another said.

Now, they were all in agreement.

Wilhelm's back had gone from a lobster-red sunburn to a nice tan, and he only got darker or peeled from that point after. But just as some were more prone to sweating, some were more prone to burning. The gingers in the group had learned they could not take their shirts off, for the sun had a hatred for their freckled skin.

One poor bastard had burned to a purple, and his skin was full of water blisters. He was in the infirmary for weeks. He now kept his long sleeve shirt on even in nearly ninety-degree weather. Torben fell somewhere in the middle. He neither really burned nor did he tan. His skin seemed to redden and turn tan overnight, but by the afternoon, he would return to his natural pale color.

The truck pulled to a stop, and the Germans groaned as, once again, they became aware of how hot and muggy it truly was. They were ushered through the fences and back behind them. The meal lines formed and Wilhelm and Torben waited in line, the sun beating down upon their neck and shoulders. The main summer meal had been Okroshka, a cold soup of raw vegetables, boiled potatoes, and meat. Meat was not always a given, as the Soviets ensured they themselves had plenty of food first. But when it was available, it was usually beef.

After receiving their bowlful, they moved toward one of the tables under the roofed areas. No meat floated in the soup, and it was mostly potatoes, but Wilhelm had been lucky for he had two cuts of a carrot in his. As they looked past the camp and through the fence, there was nothing else in sight. They were well past the middle of nowhere with nothing but grass fields and a blue horizon.

The heat continued, and the sun did not set until nearly nine by which time Wilhelm and Torben were back in their bunks. The room was much larger than the truck but did not have the benefit of open air to help the smell. Some men had doused their white t-shirts in water and worn them on their heads like turbans to mitigate the heat.

During the day, Wilhelm was too busy to think of his situation. But at night, it flooded in. His greatest release of stress and emotion had been writing in his journal. The end of a long page was like the drag of a cigarette. But Wilhelm had no journal now, and the withdrawal kept him up. The release in the form of pencil to page was gone. The horrible thoughts in his head had no place to go. They were poison. Some nights, he only slept three hours. In a camp filled with snoring men, if you were not quick to fall asleep, the unsynchronized bass snores and soprano sleep whistles were as good at keeping someone up as pouring cold water on them.

In late June, the Soviets had left the doors of the quarters open to allow more airflow, but one night, a German prisoner had taken off. He had not made it to the fence before he was gunned down, yet his actions had cost the others. The door would remain shut no matter how stifling it was. It was always a few that ruined it for all.

By the time Wilhelm had fallen asleep, the bell rang as a wake-up call. A small hint of excitement spread during breakfast, and as Wilhelm and the others hopped onto the trucks, some even smiled. It was like waiting for a rollercoaster to begin. The moment the trucks pulled forward, the breeze washed over their faces. When Wilhelm closed his eyes, he imagined being on one of his drives with Hannah.

When they entered the factory, it appeared Old Uncle Joe hated the extreme heat more than any. His scowl melted, and his forehead dripped sweat.

"Fucking hot in here too," Old Uncle Joe said.

He removed a flask and took a swig before offering it to Wilhelm and Torben.

"Sips, not gulps, you greedy assholes," Old Uncle Joe said.

Wilhelm took a sip while Torben flirted between a sip and a gulp, figuring it was worth the risk. Old Uncle Joe snatched the flask from Torben and pocketed it.

That morning, Wilhelm and Torben were poked more times than they were in the last two months combined. They did not work fast enough for him, and Torben was ready to break the stick. It was impossible for Old Uncle Joe to poke the overwhelming thick heat, so he had to settle for the two Germans.

When the break whistle blew, Torben left to go to the bathroom. Old Uncle Joe sat with a glazed look in his eyes. The cigar in his mouth wafted out smoke, but it appeared he had forgotten it was even there.

"Something wrong, Joe?" Wilhelm asked.

It snapped Old Uncle Joe out of his trance, and he took a deep inhale of his cigar. The end of it lit up with red and orange as the embers reignited.

"I got married this day, forty-nine years ago," Old Uncle Joe said.

Wilhelm did not know the date, but it had to be early August.

"Think of the good times," Wilhelm said, trying to console him.

"Makes me miss my children," Old Uncle Joe said.

"I didn't know," Wilhelm said.

"Of course, you didn't. I never told you. I lost two sons in the Great War. My daughter died during childbirth a few years after the war ended. My wife and I raised her child. He died fighting you lot," Old Uncle Joe said.

Did his grandson look like Joe? Wilhelm was too afraid to ask. What if he had killed him? What if the faces of the men he had killed that flashed in his head every night fit the description of Joe's grandson? A braver man would have wanted to know.

The mystery behind Old Uncle Joe's scowl had been solved. Being a man who had been cursed in losing so many loved ones, no one could blame him.

"Why do you not hate me?" Wilhelm asked.

Old Uncle Joe took a soothing puff from his cigar and sighed. "Because you are somebody's grandson. Somebody's boy. And if mine were in your position, I would hope they would be treated well."

"You served, didn't you? During the First War?" Wilhelm asked.

Old Uncle Joe nodded. "I did. I was a pilot. I fought in the Battle of Tannenberg. You Germans beat us to bits of shit and piss. I had fought in battles before. But what I saw while up in the air was something entirely different. I saw hundreds of men mowed down. The fields full of gas and smoke. A fucking mess."

Old Uncle Joe pulled the cigar from his mouth, his hand quivering, and blew a fat cloud of smoke.

"If I hold you responsible for following your orders that means I can be condemned for mine. And if that's true, we're all going to hell," Old Uncle Joe said.

He took quick puffs from his cigar, looking like a baby sucking a pacifier, and it was equally soothing.

"Break is almost over. Go get yourself a drink," Old Uncle Joe said.

His shaking hands did not go unnoticed. Wilhelm's father's had done the same thing all of Wilhelm's life. The distant stare in Old Uncle Joe's eyes was a look every veteran of combat wore from time to time. He was back in that airplane flying over the fields of what was once East Prussia and now Poland, reliving the atrocities war forced young men to commit.

Old Uncle Joe spent the rest of the day slouched in his seat, taking swigs from his flask and puffs from his cigar. He seemed to blink once every hour.

Wilhelm was torn. A part of him wished he could see what Old Uncle Joe did while another part of him was thankful he could not, for the demons that descended upon him in the dark were all he could bear. To add any more risked him being dragged to hell by them.

Warfare had changed drastically from the Great War to the fighting erupting over Europe and the Pacific twenty odd years later. The trench and chemical warfare that had been staples in the Great War were gone. But there had been an even larger gap from fighting in the late 1800's until the Great War during 1914–1918. It was hard to believe that in the American Civil War, during the years 1861–1865, swords and muskets had still been used. Two men alone with mounted MG42 machine guns would have been able to wipe out entire cavalry charges.

There were a handful of moments that shaped—that defined—a person's life. But some moments shaped and defined the lives of others—sometimes, a dozen, others, a hundred, and sometimes, millions. 28 June 1914 before 11 a.m. was one such moment. In Sarajevo, a nineteen-year-old by the name of Gavrilo Princip drew his pistol and, from a distance of 1.5 meters, gunned down the Archduke of Austria, Franz Ferdinand, and his wife, Duchess Sophie Chotek. And from that event, the Great War broke out. The Treaty of Versailles, to end the Great War, only brought a stalemate, and in 1939, the Second World War started, which brought about its own series of events that brought Wilhelm to a factory somewhere in the Soviet Union. Could so many events be explained by anything but fate?

"Feels weird not being poked," Torben said.

For the first time, they had gone the entire second half of the day without being poked. It was not for perfect work either. They had actually screwed up once and their daily total was two less than the day before. But Old Uncle Joe's trance did not end that day.

The next month, Old Uncle Joe fell deeper into the mess of his mind. He must have done a fair share of drinking before he arrived, for he slurred his words even more than normal. It was now October, and the cool autumn was welcomed, especially by those who burned in the sun. They had lost ninety-three men to the heat, and had it not been for Old Uncle Joe sneaking Wilhelm and Torben sips from his water canteen, they may have fallen too.

It was a proud moment when Wilhelm and Torben saw the bombers completed. They had built them, and as they drove out of the opened hanger, it was not hard to feel like they had accomplished something. It was the type of pride a hard day's work brought—much the same feeling Wilhelm had when he had sold his first car. But as the engines roared to life, Wilhelm was reminded of the mission of the bombers. These were not planes for supply drops, travel or to see heavenly views. They were to drop hell on the cities below—German cities where his loved ones were.

It was November when Old Uncle Joe finally resumed his poking. He made up for the last few months by poking Wilhelm and Torben what felt like every thirty seconds.

"Pace yourself. You'll cramp up," Torben said to Old Uncle Joe after being poked all morning.

Both he and Wilhelm were fluent in Russian by now, and it was mostly because of Old Uncle Joe and the stories of nothing he told. While most prisoners worked in silence and the guards around them too, Old Uncle Joe did not mind a conversation as long as the work was done.

"You should have seen the women in Italy, Wilhelm. Tanned skin. Those accents. And the pasta…" Torben recounted.

They had two entirely different experiences. Yet, Wilhelm could appreciate that once the artillery fire and gunshots started flying through the air, battle was battle.

Torben had claimed to sample nearly every type of pasta during his weeks of inactivity. While he ate filling, delicious pastas with tomato-based or milk-based sauces, Wilhelm ate horse, nothing or something he would never tell a soul. There were also no beautiful women in Stalingrad because there were no women—not that it would have mattered. Even if he had not seen Hannah in nearly four years, she was still his wife, and he would remain faithful.

Torben had visited the Colosseum, St. Peter's Basilica, and the Trevi Fountain. Everything Wilhelm, Höring, and Jonas had discussed doing, down to the pastas and gelato, Torben had done.

Torben had skinny-dipped in the Mediterranean with an Italian woman and, after, they had made love on the sand. They had spent two weeks together. He had written her address on a cocktail napkin from a small restaurant, but it had been taken during his capture.

"So you don't remember it?" Wilhelm asked.

"Please. Think I would forget a woman like Francesca? That address is tattooed on my brain. When this thing is over, I'm going to marry her. All of this ... this shit I've had to do will have been worth it. I can forget about it all. Bring Hannah. We're getting married right on the Mediterranean. You will love it. Then you can go see all the sights," Torben said.

Every day, Wilhelm and Torben would ask Old Uncle Joe for updates on the war. It was not that either was eager for Germany to lose, they were just eager for the war to be over. They would have to stay in the camp until the fighting was over. Otherwise, every released man would be put back into rotation. But Old Uncle Joe had little news, and when he did, it was safe to say the news itself was no news at all, as it was a month or two old.

Wilhelm and Torben finished another engine and used the hoist to lower it into the bomber. The break bell rang out through the factory loud enough to be heard over the equipment. Yet, this one wasn't a break bell. It was a warning bell. Enemy (German) planes had been spotted, and Wilhelm and every other single person in the factory knew the building was the sort of target pilots drooled over. They crouched and waited for what may or may not come. Old Uncle Joe sat in his chair with his walking stick resting on his lap.

"Joe, what are you doing?" Torben whispered.

"If I am to die, I shall die comfortable," Old Uncle Joe said.

Wilhelm could not find fault in the logic. If a bomb broke through the ceiling and crashed on the floor, the explosion would be vast enough to destroy everything inside. There would be no escaping it.

The warning bell would ring if enemy planes were within thirty kilometers and, sometimes, could last two or three hours. It was an awful feeling much like a tornado drill. Yet, tornados, even if they did touch down, did not have set targets or course adjustments. The bombers delivered catastrophes that were a natural disaster in scale but with the hunting prowess of lions, and the factory was one massive, weak, defenseless lamb.

The bombers sounded like swarms of bees but amplified and gave warning, but, luckily, no sound came. The bell rang once more, and the Soviets shouted to get back to work. Even the Germans who had not been able to pick up much Russian knew what those words meant.

"Bit of a different feeling than being the one who drops them, huh, Joe?" Torben asked.

"I was throwing grenades from my plane. Not dropping God's fury," Old Uncle Joe slurred.

Torben smirked before disappearing around the other side of the plane.

"Joe, I have wanted to ask you something," Wilhelm said.

His voice was quiet. He had not fully committed to speaking.

"Going to need to speak up," Old Uncle Joe said.

"I have wanted to ask you something," Wilhelm said a little louder.

"Then ask. I'll keep my stick at the ready," Old Uncle Joe said.

"Do you know an Alexander Kozlovsky?" Wilhelm asked.

Old Uncle Joe sat in silence, trying to find an Alexander Kozlovsky in his memories.

"I don't believe so. That's not a German name."

"No. He was Russian," Wilhelm said.

"Who was he to you?"

"We were in the same building at Stalingrad. He saved my life—more than once."

"Did you kill him?"

"No. But I didn't save him either."

When he was taken prisoner, the letter Alexander had given him was taken and burned. Unlike Torben, the address on the letter was not tattooed on his brain. He only knew Helen Kozlovsky lived in the Soviet Union, an expanse of over seven million square miles.

Old Uncle Joe took a deep puff of smoke that told Wilhelm he was preparing to speak for longer than normal and wanted to make up for the missed puffs with one long, drawn-out drag.

"You know when I was flying over the battlefield, I was reminded of Matthew 13:49–50. 'This is how it will be at the end of the age. The angels will come and separate the wicked from the righteous and throw them in the blazing furnace where there will be weeping and gnashing of teeth.' I realized I was looking down at hell itself—a view that makes angels cry. I can only hope that when I die, the view is equally profound," Old Uncle Joe said.

"I hope it is," Wilhelm said.

Old Uncle Joe poked Wilhelm, but it was much softer—more of an assuring poke—than any of the other hundreds he had received. Wilhelm and Torben never said it out loud, but they both knew they had been extremely fortunate to have been assigned to work for

Old Uncle Joe. The Soviets hated the Germans and with good reason. Germany had betrayed Russia and attacked after a non-aggression pact had been signed. From what Wilhelm had been told, a large number of surrendering Soviet soldiers had been executed. And the war's fiercest fighting—fighting from block to block, building to building in the namesake city of the Soviet Union's leader—had cost a million Soviet men their lives. There was no shortage of reasons for the Soviets to loathe the Germans.

The hopes of the war ending by Christmas were spoiled. The war raged on. The camp grounds were covered in five inches of snow, and the sky had frozen. Wilhelm took the opportunity before curfew to stare up at it. He tried to let the camp buildings, the fences, and the watchtowers fade away so he could focus on nothing but the luminescent flashes of white and blue stars. And when everything beside him faded away, he was beside Hannah once again.

D-Day

The shores of Portsmouth were foggy and dreary. Even if Hannah knew to expect such weather, it was contradictory to the mood she should have been in. Somehow, she thought it should have been full of a bright, high sun, like somewhere on the coast of the Mediterranean. As she walked away from the docks, the clouds flashed with electricity, and a downpour fell like water bullets. A man holding a black umbrella and dressed in a long tan trench coat stood on the other side of the street. His head was dipped, and the brow of his face was covered by a fedora of the same color as his jacket. He looked up.

Hannah covered her eyes to prevent the torrential rain from falling into them.

"Ms. Smith?" the man asked.

"Yes," Hannah answered tentatively.

The man extended the umbrella to cover Hannah. "My name is Otto Wesley. I am Radley Durand's British contact." He had a smile on his face, but a charming smile often hid the fangs of a snake.

"He never gave me your name," Hannah said.

She had yet to step under the umbrella because it would bring her close enough to him for him to grab her. From the distance she stood, she could run if need be. Josephine had warned her of double agents.

He reached into his breast pocket, and Hannah instinctively took a step back. He brought his hands up quickly, realizing she had taken it for him reaching for a gun.

"Sorry. I am just going to remove my identification. Is that alright, Miss?" Otto asked.

Hannah nodded. But she turned her feet ever so slightly, in case she had to break out in a run. Otto reached into his breast pocket once again and removed a wallet. He opened it and showed Hannah the photograph and his name and rank beside it. But it meant little to Hannah. She herself had owned a forged passport and carried falsified papers on her as they spoke.

"I have a car across the street. I will take you to London," Otto said.

Hannah had still yet to step under the umbrella and toiled over whether or not she should trust him.

"Durand said you would not be eager to trust. I understand. Would you like to get a cup of tea first?" Otto asked. Hannah nodded but still did not step under the umbrella. "Here, you take it, Miss. I am fine," Otto said, handing the umbrella over as if it were a gun.

Hannah took it, and Otto led her across the street to a small corner café. It lacked the panache of the "Givre Strudel," and it looked like it was over a hundred years old and like the last place one would want to order a cup of tea. That was alright with Hannah. She ordered a pale ale. It was different tasting than the German beers she had had. The ale was decent, but German beer was far superior. Halfway through the pint, her nerves lessened and the chills the rain had given subsided. If she finished the pint, she would be a block past drunk and defenseless to stop anything. Otto had ordered a cup of lemon tea and stirred it an annoying amount of time before taking a sip.

"Why are you not fighting?" Hannah asked.

He was in his forties by appearance, yet he still looked fit enough to fight. It was a personal question and a rude one at that. She did not trust Otto, but if it turned out he was who he said he was, she did not want to start off on a bad foot with the agency that had gotten her into London.

"I'm sorry. That was very rude," Hannah said.

"It is quite alright. I believe we can do as much good collecting intelligence. There are fine young men fighting and dying. If we can gather information that helps save their lives, I believe it to be worth it," Otto said.

Hannah was ashamed of the question and wanted to hide her face in her pint of beer but refrained.

Otto sensed Hannah had finished her drink. He enjoyed another sip of his tea that flirted with becoming a gulp before it burned his throat.

"Shall we carry on then?" Otto asked.

Hannah had yet to make a decision on his trustworthiness or his honesty but decided it did not matter. If he was going to drive her someplace to kill her, he would do so. She would keep her promise to herself that she would rather be killed than board another train.

"Yes," Hannah said.

Otto smiled and escorted Hannah outside. The rain had somehow increased, and it looked as though the entire English Channel had risen and fallen on Southern England and would allow the Germans to blitzkrieg into London with their tanks.

"Weather takes some getting used to. But it has been one of our greatest allies since this war began," Otto said.

They dashed across the street toward his black car that was entirely conspicuous and screamed government. Otto spent the drive talking about how the stormy seas had repelled the German invasion. But as Hannah looked out of the window, the Germans may not have invaded, but their torrential onslaught of bombing had certainly wreaked destruction. It was amazing how a single building remained untouched when the buildings around it were nothing but rubble. It was a part of the indelible spirit Hannah had heard on the radio at night, sitting with Josephine and Radley. She had to give his resolve her approval and respect him for knowing it could have been much worse.

The drive was north of two hours, and the rain followed them every minute of it. Otto pulled the car over. Hannah stepped and looked for a building that exuded the type of opulence the Reich Chancellery had. Yet, the buildings on the block were dingy and beaten down. Had the bombing done this or had the buildings always looked that way?

Hannah and Otto crossed the street, and he waved his gratitude at the car that stopped to let them cross. The address on the building read "54 Broadway" and a brass plaque read "Minimax Fire Extinguisher Company." The lackluster exterior was an exact match of the interior. The building had nine floors, and a woman was seated behind a receptionist desk on the first level. She was in her late sixties and looked as though she had slept a total of sixty some minutes combined since the war had started five years ago. The two greeted one another with pleasantries.

"I will let him know you are on your way up," the woman said.

"Thank you, Jane," Otto said.

"What is this place? Why have you brought me to a fire extinguisher company?" Hannah asked.

Otto was silent as he ascended the steps, and Hannah was forced to follow in matched silence. They reached the top floor. It was filled with wooden partitions separating desks. Otto led Hannah toward an office. Unlike the cubicles, the office had a door to allow privacy and discretion. Otto knocked on the open door.

"Sir, Hannah Smith is here," Otto announced.

"Send her in," a man said from inside.

Otto nodded, and Hannah stepped into the office. Otto reached for the door and closed it as he stepped out. Hannah wished Otto hadn't—not because she trusted or liked Otto, it was too early for an opinion, but because he had been the most familiar thing in a building of oddities and secrets. The man behind the desk was in a suit, and judging by the amount of sweat on his forehead, he was miserable in it. Hannah could not blame him. The entire building burned in an invisible flame, and Hannah considered spraying the whole floor with a fire extinguisher they claimed to sell.

"Ms. Smith, a pleasure to meet you. I am Stewart Menzies," the man introduced himself, rising from his desk and offering his hand.

Hannah shook it and took the leather armchair Menzies offered her. He sat back down and brought his fingers together and raised them to rest below his nose. A golden file with a button and string closure was on his desk.

"Do you know who I am, Miss?" Menzies asked.

Hannah shook her head.

"I am Chief of Military Intelligence, Section 6."

He reached for the file at his desk and twirled the string free and flipped it open. Hannah's own picture stared up at her from the top left.

"What is this?" she asked.

"Your file," he said. He removed a stack of photographs of Hannah outside Josephine's apartment, outside the "Givre Strudel," and at "Les Sauvages." "We don't grant access into England without doing our due diligence," Menzies said.

With so many photos sprawled on his desk, each one made Hannah feel more violated than the last. Her love of photography was in question. She had used it as an innocent art form, but whoever had taken these had been a voyeur lurking in the distance like some kind of pervert.

"What does it have in there?" Hannah asked.

"We know that you are not Hannah Smith ... that you are actually Hannah Goldschmidt, born to Josef and Emma Goldschmidt. I know that you are Jewish. I know that you spent a significant portion of time at Auschwitz concentration camp in Southern Poland," Menzies said.

The entire speech caused a range of emotions to storm through Hannah's blood that made the storming outside look like the tears of a toddler. When he said her parents' names, her heart stopped. "Significant portion of time" seemed like the most insensitive way to describe her experience at Auschwitz. The man had read life-altering and heart-breaking events as if they were simple dates and facts.

"Your testimony to Radley Durand is one of the reasons we became aware of Auschwitz," Menzies said.

"Good. Have you shut it down?" Hannah asked.

"No. It is still in occupied territory. We believe there are in excess of forty thousand camps."

Her heart fell from her chest and settled in the pit of her stomach. Forty thousand? Auschwitz was an unspeakable horror. It had to be a singularity—a rarity. To think the acts of that awful place had been mimicked and duplicated over forty thousand times was devastating. Was she the last living Jew in Europe? How could anyone else be alive?

"I am going to ask you a few questions, dear, and I must tell you that for some of these questions, I already know the answers. I have told you bits of what I know about you so that you are aware we cannot be lied to or made a fool of. You may get lucky but, understand, if we find out you are lying, your sanctuary here will be at an end. Do you understand?" Menzies asked.

Even if his tone had meant to be gentle, it came off like sandpaper.

"I do," Hannah said.

"Who taught you English?"

Hannah's heart resting at the bottom of her stomach was kicked by an invisible foot as Eleanor's kind face flashed before her.

"A woman at Auschwitz."

"A fellow prisoner?"

"Yes."

"Do you remember her name?"

"Of course I remember her name. I shall remember her until the day I die. She saved my life. Eleanor Cole. She was from York and worked as a school teacher in Germany. She snuck thirty-two Jewish children from the school before the Nazis could take them. They branded her an honorary Jew for it," Hannah said, struggling to control her emotions.

"Branded? You mean, tattooed?" Menzies asked.

Hannah turned her left arm over and set it on Menzies' desk. The black numbers 19653 with the black triangle underneath was as pronounced as the day she had gotten it.

"Why did you want to come to London?" Menzies asked.

"I wanted to get out of Nazi-occupied territory," Hannah answered.

"You want to stay here?"

"I don't know. I don't know where I belong."

It was the most truthful answer she could give. Deep inside the parts of her mind that harbored her most vulnerable thoughts was the prospect that she would never find a place that was home.

"You did well under pressure with the mission assigned to you. Would you consider doing more?" Menzies asked.

"More?" Hannah asked, taken aback by the question.

"Become an agent for the British Intelligence Agency," Menzies explained.

"I just escaped, and you would ask that I go back? I have been branded a Jew. It is not safe for me," Hannah said.

"The world is at war. No one is safe."

"I understand that there are jobs to be done. I am willing to help. But I will not go back there while the Nazis are in control."

"Very well."

"Was the information I gathered useful?"

"We shall know in the coming days. I will keep you posted."

"Thank you."

"You acquired the information. It is the least we can do."

"No, thank you for granting me entrance."

"War is hell and hell is war. You have had your fair share of both."

She certainly had. But the city of London had also taken its fair share of blows.

"You are a woman who has had to keep many secrets in order to survive. The area I ask you to help with will require the same. Any information you overhear is top secret. To tell it to anyone is treason and punishable by death, do you understand?" Menzies asked.

Hannah nodded.

"I am afraid I will need a verbal response," Menzies said.

Hannah realized her entire conversation had been recorded by a microphone hidden somewhere in his office. She guessed either under the lamp or in one of the six ballpoint pens stored in the pen holder on the left-hand side of his desk. "I understand," Hannah said. She should have figured the conversation would have been recorded, yet she still felt violated, much the same way she had when she saw the photographs of her taken without her knowledge.

"Excellent. As our French agents may have told you, there will be an invasion to open a western front. The Soviets in the east have stopped Germany and are pushing them back," Menzies said.

"What do you need from me?" Hannah asked.

"We cannot spare anyone. While our young men fight, our women are producing in the factories so they have guns to fire, helmets to wear, and planes, tanks, and trucks to transport them," Menzies said.

Hannah knew nothing of factory work, but if it would grant her amnesty, she would learn.

"Yet, there is also a need for nurses to treat the wounded. It is not an easy job, but I think you'll find it gratifying," Menzies said.

Had they seen in her file that her mother had been a nurse? Hannah had given up hope of becoming one long ago.

"I will do everything I can," Hannah said.

"Our hospitals get flooded with injured every night after the bombing ceases. The Canadian, American, and British soldiers who will invade will require nurses. Will you help where needed?" Menzies asked.

"Yes," Hannah said.

"Good. From this moment on, you are Hannah Smith. Raised in Ludwigsfede, Germany until you were nine when you moved to London. It will cover up the reason for your accent, as there is no denying you do have an accent," Menzies said.

Hannah nodded.

"I am going to introduce you to Kay Summersby. She is currently working for the American General Eisenhower as his personal assistant. But she spent a great deal of nights driving ambulances through London, escorting the injured to hospitals. She will be a valuable resource to you," Menzies added.

He pressed a button on his phone and, seconds later, the door opened with Otto standing at the door frame.

"Yes, Sir?" he asked.

"See to it that Ms. Smith is given a proper meal and night's rest. Be sure to give her a rundown on procedure before you drop her off at her hotel," Menzies instructed.

"Yes, Sir," Otto said.

Menzies stood from his chair and extended his hand. Hannah rose and shook it. "We shall be seeing you again, Miss," Menzies said.

Hannah smiled and followed Otto out of the office and toward the stairwell.

Otto took her to a nearby restaurant. Hannah did not even have to look over the menu. Her dinner was chosen for her because there had been extreme rationing in England. She was served a baked potato with less than ten shreds of cheese and a sliver of butter. After dinner, Otto took her to a hotel not far from the MI6 headquarters.

"Are you coming up?" Hannah asked after she was checked in.

"It would be improper. But I would like to go over a few things if you please," Otto said.

He offered the lobby sofa for Hannah to sit on. The lobby was much more opulent than the outside had looked. It was filled with gold and scarlet and the wallpaper, a crisscrossing of the two. Golden chandeliers hung from the ceiling and cast a bedazzled glow across the gold-tiled floor. The couch itself was crimson and placed beside the dormant fireplace. Otto removed a series of pamphlets from his breast pocket and set them on the coffee table in front of them, pushing aside the newspapers in the way.

"You have your passport and papers, correct?' he asked.

Hannah nodded and lifted them out of the purse Josephine had given her.

"Excellent. This is your ration book," Otto said, holding up a tan booklet, roughly the size of a journal.

It had the words "Ration Book" engraved in black, block letters and the date 1944–45 on the right-hand side with an octagonal stamp near the bottom center that validated the booklet.

"There are coupons in here and instructions on how to get your allotted food. Hope you're not a big bacon enthusiast," Otto said.

Hannah took the book and flipped through it. There was rationing on about everything and the allotted amounts per week. Sugar, loose tea, meat, cheese, preserves, butter, margarine, lard, and sweets were just a few of them. But there were stipulations based on health conditions as well. People with diabetes were able to surrender their sugar coupons for more of something else. But the rations were not limited to food. Clothing, soap, fuel, and paper were also limited. Like any government writing, it made her question if she would ever be able to figure it out before starving to death.

"Best to just get in line and watch the person ahead of you. Easiest way to learn I believe," Otto advised.

Had Menzies had her mind bugged too?

But Otto lost her attention. She stared at the sign above the fireplace: "BLACKOUT MEANS BLACK."

"What is that?" Hannah asked, pointing to it.

"That is my last bit of instruction. It is the most important also. There are to be no lights on after dark. None. Any bit of light can give the German bombers a target. If you hear sirens, move down the stairwell and come back into the lobby, understood?" Otto asked.

The hotel building appeared to be the only thing left to bomb on the street. The nerves in her body pleaded her to run to the door.

"Don't fret. Tomorrow, I will show you London and then we shall meet Miss Summersby," Otto said.

He rose to his feet. He held his fedora in front of him and waited until he was given the okay to leave before putting it on. Hannah nodded for him to do so, but her eyes were fixed on the ominous sign.

"Goodnight, Ms. Smith," Otto said. He inclined his head, placed his fedora back on, and walked to the door but stopped and turned. "One last thing. Your room key."

He held out a lone key with a gold keychain with the numbers 414 inscribed on it. Hannah took the key and walked to the stairwell and climbed up the flights of steps to the fourth floor. She turned right and came to room 414. She inserted her key and opened the door. The room itself was pleasant enough with a small bathroom, a nightstand with a lamp, and a bed with a soft pink blanket covering it. It would be the first time Hannah would sleep in a bed in longer than she could remember. She set her purse on the nightstand and went into the bathroom to wash her face. She had meant to change into her pajamas, but as she laid down on the bed, her body experienced a comfort that it had been without for a long time. She went from drowsy to a deep sleep, skipping the usual stages in between.

In her dreams, she was back at Auschwitz, yet was granted permission to make a phone call. Sturmbannführer Waltz escorted her into his private quarters and commanded her to pick up the phone. She brought it to her ear, but there was no one there. She put the black phone, a white circle with a swastika on it, back on the receiver. The phone rang again and again but morphed into a different sound—a sound much more terrifying. Hannah shuddered awake, but the sound did not go away. She sat up in bed and crept to the window. Realization spread across her face and gave way to a deep-seeded fear. The warped sound was an air raid siren. The fallen of England screamed for the living to seek shelter.

Hannah jumped back from the window and scrambled to the lamp she had forgotten to turn off. It was still dusk when she had first laid down. Her fingers fumbled with the switch, and the room went black. She dashed to the door and opened it. Other guests of the hotel moved about the hallway. Some were frantic while others remained calm. Those who were calm must have been in the city long enough to know what they were doing, and she decided to follow them down the stairwell. She trembled, knowing, at any second, a bomb could fall through and explode the building into a heap of rubble. But the people moved aggravatingly slow. Slow had been the antithesis of everything that had kept her alive.

The lobby was full of every guest and staff member the hotel had. The lights were out, and the front glass doors had been covered with a black covering. A single light came from the open basement door, and people were shepherded down the steps like sheep. Oddly, there were no children amongst the fifty or so people crammed into the small basement filled with extra towels, cleaning supplies, and blankets. The sirens continued to cry out, sounding like the city of London itself was wailing. The warning lasted forty-three minutes if the pocket watch the farmer had given her was still on time. The sirens changed and gave the "all clear" to return to their rooms.

Hannah and the hotel guests and staff had been lucky. But the next morning, when Otto picked her up and they drove through London, it was obvious others had not been. Otto explained that most children had been moved to the countryside, away from the high number of bombing raids. Otto's son and daughter lived with his wife and her parents in Kiddington, roughly eighty miles from London. It had been a part of Operation Pied Piper that started back in 1939 and saw over 3.5 million people, mostly children, being relocated out of the densely populated metropolitans of London, Manchester, and Birmingham. Many of the relocations were outside England itself, including Canada and the United States.

Otto was a wealth of information and had a greater detailed knowledge of how the war had gone than Durand or Josephine could offer. It was not that they were unwilling to offer information, it was simply they did not know. The Germans controlled the newspapers and radio, and any news they received was most likely outdated by a week at best. Hannah had learned from Otto that over 91,000 Germans had surrendered at Stalingrad. Was Wilhelm among the living captives or the fallen of nearly 400,000?

Hannah began the day expecting to meet Kay Summersby, but she did not. Nor did she meet her the next day or any day that week. It was not until 13 May when Hannah had been brought back into the MI6 building that she met Kay Summersby. She was seated in the waiting area in a military uniform, her dark brown hair flowing in thick waves toward the back of her head. She had thin, high-arching eyebrows, and her nose tipped upward. She was in her mid-thirties and had a fierceness more resembling Josephine than the quiet resolve of Eleanor.

"Miss Summersby, may I introduce Hannah Smith?" Otto said.

Kay stood and made sure her uniform was in order before offering her hand to Hannah.

"Nice to meet you, Miss Smith," Kay said.

"A pleasure," Hannah replied.

"I will take it from here, Mr. Wesley," Kay said.

"Very well. I shall you see later, Miss Smith, Miss Summersby," Otto said, bowing his head to both women before walking to the staircase.

"Let us go for a walk," Kay said.

Hannah followed Kay out of the office building and onto the sidewalk. They walked in silence, crossing street after street. People, both civilian and government, were trying to clean up the rubble of the previous night's bombing.

"I used to drive an ambulance a couple of years ago. I spent my nights driving the injured to the hospitals. Do you know how many people I saved?" she asked.

"No," Hannah answered though she knew it was rhetorical.

"Nor do I. I just know there were a lot more who I didn't," Kay said.

Hannah appreciated that Kay took another turn, for she did not want to see who or what the people searching would find once the debris were moved.

"Are you married, Hannah?" Kay asked.

"No," Hannah lied.

To tell the truth meant she had lied previously. She would be deported back to France at best or held as a German spy if the English found out she was married to a German soldier. It did not matter that Wilhelm was not a Nazi. Most cities and people thought Germans and Nazis were one and the same. She would have faced the same stereotype if it had not been for the tattoo on her left hand branding her a Jew.

"And you?" Hannah asked Kay.

"Married. Divorced. Engaged. Single."

"I am sorry."

"So am I about half of it," Kay said, a subtle grin spreading on her face.

She told Hannah her engagement had ended with the death of her fiancé in North Africa. He had been sweeping for mines when one exploded.

"I work for the U.S. General Eisenhower as his personal assistant. I don't know what preconceived notions about secretaries you have, but there is important work that needs to be done. There is no room for spelling errors on reports or being late. You will hear information that could send the entire world into a frenzy. It is your duty to hear such information and process it silently and without emotion. You cannot let emotion show on your face when you move from room to room," Kay explained.

"I understand," Hannah said.

"Excellent. I am told you will also help out the nurses and doctors. Will you be able to handle death all around you?"

It went without saying, Kay did not know about the horrors Hannah and the Jewish people had been subjected to at Auschwitz and the thousands of other concentration camps. Hannah had seen hundreds of people brought to the gas chambers daily. She awoke every morning to find at least three or four women dead on the floor. She could handle it, but that did not mean it was easy. It was a part of being a compassionate human being and having empathy. The sort of cold indifference to death was something exuded by the Nazis. Hannah was proud to say that it did affect her.

"I am ready to do my part," Hannah said.

The rest of the day, Kay showed Hannah exactly what it was she did—from typing reports on a typewriter to transferring calls for the General to simply serving him a cup of coffee when he looked stressed.

"You need to be able to read them. These men are making decisions that will cost young men their lives. It isn't easy. You or I can't pretend to know what that feels like, so don't," Kay said.

Hannah had not met General Eisenhower, but if the weight of his decisions stressed him, he was a far better man than any of the Nazi officers she had met.

The day with Kay ended shortly after six, and Hannah was told she would be picked up on the fifteenth to aid in a meeting. Hannah waved goodbye and stepped back into the MI6 headquarters. Did anyone ever wander in looking to buy fire extinguishers? But something told her there was someone in the staff who knew everything about them to further sell the lie.

Otto had been talking to Jane the receptionist, but both fell silent when Hannah stepped in.

"Good evening, Miss Smith, the chief would like to speak with you," Otto said.

Hannah nodded, and even with Otto's smile, she knew it was a ploy to trick her into a sense of comfort. Hannah ascended the staircase until she reached the top floor. Most of the staff inside were packing up to leave or had left apart from a man in the corner, toiling over paperwork under the heat and light of a desk lamp.

"Good evening. You wanted to see me, Sir?" Hannah asked, knocking on the side of the door frame.

"Yes, Hannah, please sit down," Menzies said, offering her the chair in front of his desk.

Hannah stepped inside and sat.

"Can I get you some tea?" he asked.

"No, thank you," Hannah refused politely.

Had she not seen the way Jane and Otto had reacted to seeing her, perhaps she would have gone for a cup. But now, she was nervous and knew something had happened and it was not good.

"Very well. Hannah, I have some good news that I'm afraid will be overshadowed by some truly awful news. The codes you stole led to a large supply train of troops, munitions, and artillery that was stalled outside Paris and raided by French resistant fighters," Menzies said.

It wasn't good news, it was great news. But Hannah couldn't even react to it. She curled her thumbs under her pointer fingers and squeezed and grinded the inside of her cheek with her teeth.

"And the awful news?" Hannah asked.

Menzies appeared to have wanted to drag out the silence longer.

"But the German officer you stole it from placed his blame on you. Josephine Moreau lied for you and took the blame, and I am afraid she was killed."

During her first time in Menzies' office, Hannah's heart had fallen to the pit of her stomach. She had thought it could not fall any further. But the pit of her stomach had only been a precipice to a much further fall—one that was unending. Her heart had severed all tethering that held it in place and, now, it fell and fell and fell.

"I am afraid there is more tragic news to be said. Some of the information stolen was planted by the Nazis. French resistance moved to a location said to have had V2 rockets, but they walked into an ambush and were killed. Radley Durand was among them," Menzies said.

Perhaps, Hannah was wrong in being proud of her empathy. Her life would have been so much easier had she not cared and had she not loved. The list of the fallen continued to grow, and each time, Hannah felt personally responsible. She had stolen the information against Josephine's warning, and it had gotten her killed. Had she listened to her, Josephine would be alive—Radley too. Madeleina and his children came to her mind and the awful news they had or would receive.

"I am truly sorry, Hannah," Menzies said.

Sorry would not erase the guilt and devastation. The word had little impact, especially from a man who had never met them. How too short a word love was. Four letters could not encapsulate the emotions she felt toward Josephine and Radley, her surrogate parents who had looked after her in Paris. Every memory she had with the two replayed cruelly in her mind—every smile, every laugh, every deep conversation. She had made a note to ask Menzies for information on Eleanor's husband, Liam, but what was the point? Surely, there was only more heartbreaking news to be shared.

"Take as much time as you need. If you require anything, please do not hesitate," Menzies said.

She rose from her chair, her legs wobbly. Menzies could tell she was anything but alright, but grief was something each person must deal with and in their own way. Otto wore a solemn face and wanted to say something as he drove her to the hotel. But Hannah was grateful he had not. It was easy to distance oneself when hearing of the deaths of people. Though it was still sad, they were just a statistic. Did two people truly make that big of a difference amongst a population of billions? But when the person was given a name, a history, characteristics, and idiosyncrasies that made that person different from any other person on the face of the earth, it made it unbearable.

The bombing sirens did not go off that night. Would she have even gotten out of bed for them? Hannah had wanted to return to Paris for visits if the war had ended with a Nazi Germany defeat. But now, there was nothing there for her. She did her best to pretend she did not know their fates. She wished Menzies hadn't told her. She could go on with the illusion that both were fine and would live long lives into their nineties. But she had seen too much death to fall to such naivety. She would always assume the worse. The part of Hannah that held onto the belief that Wilhelm was still alive began to second-guess itself. Was she just being naive?

The next day, Hannah called Otto to tell him she was not feeling well and slept the entire day away. A deep sleep was the only place where the pain could not attack her. It was her safe zone. The following day, she was again tempted to stay in bed and sleep to escape her reality but knew, if she did, it would become an addiction—a drug to escape reality.

It was 15 May 1944. Kay would be picking her up for some sort of meeting at St. Paul's school. She needed help seeing that all guests were greeted with a drink, meal, and all necessary documents. Hannah forced herself to shower and prepare for the day. As she unzipped her suitcase, the nostalgic smells of Josephine's apartment wafted toward her and formed invisible fists that sucker punched her. Hannah had made a permanent habit of hiding her tattoo, but she decided she would no longer. She would not pretend it had not happened, that she was not Jewish, and would not treat it as if she had done something wrong.

She lumbered downstairs and waited until Kay's black government-issued car pulled up alongside the hotel.

"I hear you received some terrible news. I am sorry," Kay said.

Hannah only formed a heartbroken smile.

It was the only reference Kay made of it. She was a conscientious observer and could tell Hannah did not want to speak of it.

Hannah had thought a meeting between such influential military leaders would have been held somewhere larger than a school, but she did not know of St. Paul's at all. As Kay drove up the road, a boom barrier blocked their admittance and armed guards held up a warning hand that would surely have been followed by the raising of their rifles had they not slowed down. Hannah paid little attention to them. Instead, she was flabbergasted by the ridiculous size of the building. It looked more like a gothic castle than a school. It had an antique quality to it Wilhelm would have loved. The building was built in 1509, and even four hundred years later, it stood strong. How could the Nazis not bomb such a massive target? Or did they have some remnants of humanity and would not bomb a school?

Kay was given clearance. The boom barrier lifted, and she drove forward.

"Most will not be arriving for another two hours, but we need to get everything ready," Kay said.

Kay introduced Hannah to at least a dozen women, but she had done so too fast for Hannah to pick up all their names. She had heard Jessica, Annabelle, Agatha, and Carol but could not put the name to the face. Kay led Hannah through the school and into the room where the meeting would be held. A large, rectangular table had been set up, and a large map of Europe hung open on a wheeled cart.

"Lay out the water glasses and teacups to the left-hand side of each seat," Kay instructed.

She put down name holders designating where each guest would be sitting. Hannah only saw a few of them before she left to get the glasses. General Montgomery, Prime Minister Winston Churchill, King George VI, and General Eisenhower were among them. Hannah did as Kay instructed and, when she finished, asked if there was more she could do to help.

"Place these at each seat. These are top-secret documents. Do not look at them," Kay said.

Hannah nodded and took the tall stack of folders that looked identical to the file Menzies had had on her. The words "TOP SECRET" were stamped in red on the front cover and invited wandering eyes. But Hannah did not want to look, for Kay had said the plans put in place would lead to the death of hundreds, if not thousands, of men. Even if she had wanted to, the folders were sealed, and once they were opened, there would be no hiding it.

"They are starting to arrive. Pour the water. I shall prepare the tea," Kay said.

Hannah filled the glasses, but when she got to Prime Minister Churchill's glass, Kay stopped her. Hannah nearly spilled the water from the tin pitcher onto the top-secret document, the table, and the floor.

"The Prime Minister prefers his water to have a bit of a kick," Kay said, holding up a bottle of Johnnie Walker Red Label whiskey. She poured enough till the bottom of the glass was covered in the amber liquid and nodded for Hannah to pour the water in.

"Good day to you, Miss Summersby," a voice said with great diction.

The man stepped inside the room. He was balding with buzz-cut white hair and adorned in an army green uniform with colored insignia on his chest and stars on both of his shoulders. He was in his fifties but looked slightly older.

"Good day to you, General," Kay greeted.

"Good day to you, Miss," the General said to Hannah.

"A pleasure to meet you, General," Hannah said.

Kay had not intended for Hannah to be in the room when the leaders came in, but it would be rude to sneak out now.

"You Americans are always too early to such things," an older man commented, slurring his words.

Hannah recognized his face immediately. He had been called the English bulldog when Hannah was in Germany. He had a permanent scowl but, after taking a sip of his water, became jollier.

"Prime Minister," the General greeted.

"General Eisenhower," Churchill said, nodding his head politely.

Neither man had taken their seats as other senior personnel entered the room. There was too much small talk for Hannah to gather who each man was and nobody, except Prime Minister Churchill and General Eisenhower, was by their seats. Another man entered in a military uniform and a beret atop his head. He had a strong chin, a thin mustache, and stood only five-and-a-half-feet tall.

"Monty knows the definition of a fashionably late entrance!" Churchill remarked.

Like General Eisenhower, the man moved to his seat. The name Bernard Montgomery was typed on his white placeholder. General Eisenhower wore a look of disapproval. The half-dozen conversations fell silent when the last member of the meeting stepped into the room. Everyone stood and turned to face the man stepping in. He was dressed in a well-tailored suit and was handsome with hair parted to the right and a cleanly shaven face, but he looked uncomfortable having the eyes of the room upon him. As the men took their seats, the last man to enter took the only remaining spot. The man was King George VI.

Kay nodded to Hannah, and the two hurried to the door as the conversation went from social to business. The meeting lasted for hours, and Hannah only stepped in when someone buzzed for assistance. Most often, it was to refill water or serve coffee or tea. Hannah did her best to drown out what was being said. Hannah, Kay, and the other women served them their lunch, and when the meeting ended, Hannah and the other twelve women went in to clear the used glasses, teacups, plates, and silverware from the table. Kay took a moment to speak with General Eisenhower, and Hannah was sure to maintain enough distance as to not accidentally eavesdrop or be accused of it.

"Do you need help with anything else?" Hannah asked after Kay ended her conversation with General Eisenhower.

The glasses and teacups had been brought into the school's cafeteria and had been washed, dried, and put away.

"Yes. We are going to Portsmouth," Kay said.

Kay explained in greater detail in the car as she drove Hannah back to her hotel, yet there was much that was left out. She had been given "filtered" information, as the who, what, when, and why had been left out. She only knew she would be moving back south to Portsmouth. Not that the London weather had been as nice as she had hoped, for it had rained all but one day since she had arrived, it was Portsmouth that had been filled with the chilly, crisp Channel air and stormy waves. But many of Hannah's questions were answered when she arrived shortly before ten the following morning. Thousands and thousands of soldiers, vehicles, and ships filled the city and its shores. Something massive was going to happen in the next few weeks that could decide the war. It was the invasion Josephine and Radley had hoped for.

General Eisenhower had temporarily moved into the Southwick House, not far from Portsmouth, to be closer to the troops. Kay had become his close confidant and, sometimes, Hannah would not see her for hours. To Hannah, the Southwick House itself resembled the American White House with its white columns and colonial design. The most distinct feature of the house though was the map of Southern England and Northwest France. It stretched the entire wall and was nearly fifteen-feet tall. Red lines signaled troop movement. It was information the Nazis would kill and pay any price to have.

It was now June, and the entire city was buzzing with anticipation. Hannah had spent the first three hours of her day, starting at five, learning and remembering how to stitch and treat the bleeding of a wound. She became well acquainted with administrating morphine, cleaning wounds, and dressing them. The career her mother had had before a law took it from her and prevented Hannah from doing she now learned. There was no better way for Hannah to honor her.

On 4 June, Hannah was woken at a few minutes past two in the morning by her ringing phone. Kay had called and told her the Allied commanders would be having a meeting at four and she required help preparing. Hannah had grown accustomed to getting little sleep, but even she had trouble leaving the comfort of her bed. It called to her to return as if it had put her under some trance. Hannah ran her fingers under the cold water and rubbed her eyes and splashed cold water on the back of her neck. It ran down her back, and shivers erupted, breaking the trance. She had been staying within walking distance of the Southwick House and did not want to trouble anyone at such an hour to drive her roughly three-quarters of a mile. The sea breeze awoke her and even gave her a chill that remedied any sleepiness she had. She prepared both tea and coffee and made herself a cup to ensure the trance of tiredness had no way of returning.

General Eisenhower, Air Chief Marshal Sir Arthur Tedder, General Montgomery, Air Chief Marshal Sir Trafford Leigh-Mallory, Admiral Sir Bertram Ramsay, Lieutenant-General Frederick Morgan, among others, arrived at the house intermittently over the course of ten to fifteen minutes. Hannah made sure each gentleman did not require anything before she left the room. On her way out, Captain James Stagg was discussing the next day's weather.

There was so much to be done that Hannah missed lunch and only caught supper at quarter to seven. The army rations were hardly fine cuisine but much better than the civilian rations. Hannah was not allowed to leave the area around Portsmouth. No one or nothing could—not a letter, postcard, phone call or telegraph. The poor men who had hung up the map in the house had been forced to stay. Though they were prisoners, they were allowed to move about the camp and do odd jobs. They were given army rations, but each man was married. They had left for work in the morning and never returned home. Their wives were worried sick, and when they would be allowed to return home, they would have a lot of explaining to do. But secrecy was of vital importance—a secrecy almost ruined by a crossword puzzle with the word "Neptune." It was the code for the naval assault crossing, and the army had scrambled to find out who the spy was amongst them. Her German accent would put Hannah on top of the list. But luckily, it had been an unfortunate coincidence committed by a Surrey school headmaster months earlier.

A few days earlier, on 1 June, Hannah had taken extreme pride in hearing a poem broadcasted over the BBC.

"Les sanglots lourds / Des violons de l'automne," it had said.

"When a sighing begins / In the violins / Of the autumn-song."

Kay had told Hannah it was a call for the French Resistance to carry out further railroad sabotage and meant the invasion would take place within two weeks. A nervous energy had set about the camp, and a permanent case of jitters had taken a parasitic hold on Hannah. Even on the days she did not drink coffee, it was one too many.

She did not return to her room until quarter after eleven but, surprisingly, wasn't tired. But she needed more rest and simply laid in bed and stared at her ceiling until the trance of tiredness seized her again. It did but, again, it was short lived. It was like she was in a car and constantly missing the turn to the house of sleep. Her phone rang shortly after two— Hannah was needed again at the Southwick House. The trance of tiredness pinned her to the bed with its invisible hands. Hannah yawned, her blinking threatening to turn into sleep. She lifted herself from the bed and stumbled toward the bathroom to complete the same process as the days before.

Kay seemed to have been working for nearly forty-eight hours with only a moment of sleep. Once again, General Eisenhower and the others filed into the room, and Hannah ensured each of them had a cup of tea or coffee. Captain Stagg started his weather report before Hannah and the other aids left the room. The meeting was much shorter than the previous one. D-Day would definitely be the next day. The entire war was building to this one event, and the entire outcome of it could very well depend on whether the invasion was successful or not.

Throughout the day, the soldiers found out their orders. The tension, anticipation, and worry were as palpable as the sea breeze. Hannah saw General Eisenhower several times over the course of the day, and he wore the hopes and fears of every soldier on his face. Not even his piercing blue eyes could hide the emotional toll the decision had on him. Yet, he exuded a calming strength in how he stood tall with his shoulders pressed backward and his chest out.

At quarter after eight, Hannah gathered in the main room of the Southwick House, standing a foot away from the radio. The second half of the poem would soon be broadcasted by the BBC, as another coded message signaling the invasion would start within forty-eight hours.

"Blessent mon Coeur/D'une langeur monotone," the radio said.

"My heart is drowned / In the slow sound / Languorous and long."

Hannah smiled. At that moment, in Paris and cities throughout France, hundreds of French men and women were cheering. They were ready to cause hell. The American and British airborne troops would leave around eleven, and Hannah wanted to pay her respects to the men who would go first. Some had shaved their heads into Mohawks and pumped themselves up. Others looked as though they would be sick. They would parachute behind enemy lines before the main invasion would begin. No sleep would come to her, and she didn't even bother getting into the metaphorical car to try and find the house. Instead, she wandered about the camp and stared up at the night sky.

As dawn broke, Hannah bore witness to the hundreds of ships carrying thousands of soldiers in a combination that equaled the largest armada in the history of warfare preparing to leave. A high-pitched shriek came from the camp's speakers. It was enough to cause men already on high alert to jump. Allied Commander Eisenhower's voice came through, and the soldiers fell silent.

"Soldiers, sailors, and airmen of the Allied Expeditionary Force," his voice said.

There was no movement, no other sound. All eyes and ears were fixed on the General's voice. The nervous waves rising and falling in their stomachs were worse than the Channel's.

"You are about to embark upon the great crusade toward which we have striven these many months. The eyes of the world are upon you. The hopes and prayers of liberty-loving people everywhere march with you. In company with our brave allies and brothers-in-arms on other fronts, you will bring about the destruction of the German war machine, the elimination of Nazi tyranny over the oppressed peoples of Europe, and security for ourselves in a free world. Your task will not be an easy one. Your enemy is well trained, well equipped, and battle-hardened. He will fight savagely."

The hair on Hannah's arms stood up. Chills spread across her body, and she was not alone. If only the damned people of the concentration camps could hear the General's speech. If hope was a small seed, Eisenhower's words were water, sunlight, and shelter from the storms.

"The tide has turned! The freemen of the world are marching together to victory!" General Eisenhower continued. There were cries and screams of approval. "I have full confidence in your courage, devotion to duty, and skill in battle. We will accept nothing less than full victory! Good luck! And let us all beseech the blessing of Almighty God upon this great and noble undertaking."

The speaker fell silent. It was the greatest speech Hannah had heard in her life. She had heard Hitler's addresses her entire teenage years, and she could not argue or deny he was a great orator. He instilled passion with his words. But Eisenhower had delivered a speech she would remember for as long as she lived. The camp was silent, but his words had lit a fire in his men. Hell, it had lit a fire in Hannah.

The American, British, and Canadian soldiers loaded onto the ships. The seas were covered in ships, and the sky, a canopy of planes. The ships powered over the choppy channel. It was a truly awesome sight and display of might. The waves were violent, and it seemed the Channel was pleading the men to turn back as if it knew the carnage that would befall them should they continue. The entire camp was filled with nerves, and they did not leave with the Armada. Quite to the contrary, the nerves increased. Everyone was too nervous to speak.

The minutes took hours, and the hours took days. General Eisenhower and the high-ranking officers received updates, but Hannah steered clear of the house if she was not needed. If the invasion failed, the injured would be returned to Portsmouth. If it was successful, and only after the beachheads were secure, Hannah would return to France to tend to the injured.

She stared across the Channel. If she stared hard enough, long enough, would she be able to see the horrors transpiring on the beachheads? Had the Nazis defeated the Allies and, at that second, the hawks were on their way to England?

Hannah returned to the house to serve lunch, and after an hour, she returned to take the plates. Hardly anything had been touched. Food had become a luxury in most places in Europe, yet she could not blame the Allied commanders for not eating. Hannah was far too nervous for her stomach to worry about hunger. She sat outside the house with her hands on her knees. When the door opened, she rose to her feet. She would not be sitting when a high-ranking officer walked past.

"Come inside, Hannah," Kay said, stepping out of the house.

Hannah followed in after her, and Kay paused in between the entryway.

"The invasion was a success. Our troops are in France," Kay said.

A smile spread across Hannah's face. It was not returned. Kay had a somber look about her, the antonym of how she should have looked.

"What is it?" Hannah asked.

"There are many injured and dead. We need nurses to go to Normandy and help treat them," Kay said.

There were thousands of Americans, Canadians, and British troops in Normandy, yet she could not feel safe. But she also recognized the unfathomable sacrifice the troops had made. She owed a debt to Josephine and Radley—a debt that would only be repaid when "Vive Le France" was shouted by the people of a free nation once again. She also owed a debt to the British for allowing her sanctuary when they understandably could have denied her based on her heritage. Yet, another debt was still to be owed—one that had yet to be acquired. She planned on moving to the United States to become a citizen of the freest nation in the world.

"I will go," Hannah said.

She would do her part.

"Thank you, Hannah. Be safe," Kay said.

Hannah nodded and hurried to the building she had been staying in to change into her nurses' uniform. It was a faded, grayish blue with a red cross on the left breast. She hurried to the ships leaving in less than twenty minutes. The other nurses were all ready to go and understood the severity of what they were about to do. Most nurses would go in a few days, but a small few joined the doctors and medics.

The order was given, and the nurses rushed onto one of the five ships. Thoughts of what the other coast would bring filled her mind. They made her worried, and the rough seas made her nauseous. One alone was enough to make her seasick, but the two combined made her throw up twice on the journey over. She could not imagine what the soldiers aboard the ships had been feeling. She spent the ride trying to keep her thoughts on all she had learned. There would be men needing morphine and others who would need their wounds cleaned. There would be men with missing limbs, blasted in half, and bleeding to death who would be calling for help. It was an impossible thing to plan for.

"Listen up, ladies. There are five beachheads that need attendance. This ship is unloading at Omaha Beach. Save who you can. Pray for those you cannot," a voice announced over the intercom.

Hannah had seen the red lines on the map at the Southwick House, each pointing to a spot on the Normandy coastline—Utah, Omaha, Gold, Juno, Sword. The amphibious ship barreled onto the shore and stopped. Hannah squeezed into the line of nurses sprinting onto the sands.

"Oh, my God," a nurse whispered to herself, paralyzed by the sight.

There were no words for such savagery. The beachhead was riddled with steel hedgehogs and craters. Hundreds upon hundreds of bodies littered the sands. Some were in pieces along the beach and others bobbed along the shore. The waves washed blood water onto the sandy beaches. Cries came from those still alive. They held up their blood-covered hands, trying to signal for help. It was almost impossible to move without accidentally stepping on a body or body part.

"Be careful of mines!" a nurse called out.

The entire shoreline was riddled with them, and each step Hannah took could send her fifteen feet into the air and landing in three or four pieces.

"Help me! My legs!" a soldier cried.

The man was covered in blood and sand, and his legs were buried under a fallen soldier. Hannah used all her might to push the soldier off. The body rolled off, and his dead, open eyes stared into hers. But when Hannah looked down at the wailing solider, there were no legs. There was nothing but bloody stumps with bits of clothing and tendons dangling from above the knee. It was remarkable the man was still alive. But he had only moments.

"You're going to be okay," Hannah said.

She struck him with morphine and rose to her feet, but the soldier wrapped his hand around her ankle.

"Don't leave me," he pleaded.

His face went from pale to white.

"I'll be right back, I promise. You're going to be fine, handsome," Hannah said.

His grip was faltering, and as she lifted her foot, his hand slipped off. She rushed to another soldier nearby. He had a bullet hole in his stomach and clutched at it with his hands, blood pouring between the cracks of his fingers.

"Over here!" Hannah yelled to a group of soldiers carrying stretchers.

A hundred white stretchers were carried across the beach. Two soldiers came and carefully lifted the wounded soldier onto the gurney. Hannah poured sulfa powder onto the soldier's abdomen and placed his hands atop it.

"Press down," Hannah instructed.

The two soldiers carried the wounded soldier away, and Hannah went back to the man who had pleaded her to stay. His eyes were open, and his chest was still. The yelling for help grew quieter with each passing moment. It was a terrible game where the time on the clock decreased not by seconds but by minutes at a time. Hannah was forced to simply ascertain a soldier's chances with a look. Precious seconds "wasted" on a soldier who would not make it meant that another who would have had a chance had been neglected too long. Hannah ran to a soldier who was screaming and writhing in pain. If he had enough vigor for that, he still had some strength.

"Where are you hurt?" Hannah asked.

The soldier turned and glared at her.

"You're a fucking Kraut!" he yelled.

"I am here to help you. Where are you hurt?" Hannah asked again.

"Get the fuck off me, Nazi!" he screamed.

Hannah was knocked onto her back.

The soldier reached for his pistol. But an army doctor knocked it from his hands before he could fire a shot.

"She is with us, soldier. How can we help you? If you don't tell us, we can't help you," the doctor said.

Hannah knelt beside him. The tide washed up around her. Her mind flashed to think of what would have happened had the doctor not knocked the pistol away. She would have been dying and bleeding on the sands.

"My fucking leg!" the soldier yelled.

The doctor moved his hands gently around the leg. A geyser of blood shot up into his face and Hannah's. The soldier yelled and pounded the beach with his fist, sending bits of sand flying into the air. Hannah wiped the blood from her eyes. But for Hannah, whose face was being sprayed by a constant seas mist, the blood was warm and disturbingly comforting.

"Morphine," the doctor said.

Hannah struck the morphine into the soldier's other leg, and the doctor splashed the wound with the water brought in with the tide. The dirt and sand washed away, but the blood poured out.

"Another morphine," the doctor said.

Hannah listened and struck the man again. His eyes rolled back and he passed out.

"We need to take the leg," the doctor said. The tide washed over the leg again, and bits of the man's bone became visible. "I need you to get a stretcher. This man will bleed out in less than five minutes if we don't hurry," the doctor instructed.

Hannah rose to her feet and sprinted past the reaching hands of those in need. To her, she was sprinting through a cemetery and those already dead and buried were pushing their hands through and reaching for her. Only they weren't dead, but Hannah could not afford to stop and look back at all those she would leave behind. The impromptu infirmary was occupied well beyond what could fit under the tent. A cart was overfilled with amputated feet, legs, hands, and arms.

"There is a man who needs an amputation," Hannah said to anyone who would listen.

Two men grabbed a blood-stained gurney and hurried to follow Hannah. They helped load the soldier onto the gurney and carried him to the infirmary.

After an hour, the cries fell silent. The washing waves were the only sound. Hannah sat barely out of reach of the tide. She had thrown up only once—the cause of which had nothing to do with the sights and sounds. They certainly were disturbing, but Auschwitz had prepared her for it. It was the heartbreak for the dead and dying on the beaches of Normandy.

The waves lamented the fallen. The poor souls who littered the sands had entered the jaws of death itself—a meat grinder, as Wilhelm's father Petyr had called the Battle of Verdun. Bodies had been annihilated, and the bits of guts and flesh were picked at and eaten by gulls. Soldiers mourning the loss of friends fired shots into the air to scare them away. The bodies were placed onto the back of a truck as respectfully as possible, but the cleanup of the bodies would take days if not weeks. But Omaha beach was not an anomaly. The beaches of Gold, Sword, Utah, and Juno were littered with hundreds of more brave, young men. The final tally was a number too awful to consider.

General Eisenhower had spoken of the elimination of Nazi tyranny over the oppressed peoples of Europe. It was for people like herself, for Josephine, for Radley and his family, and for the thousands inside the Nazi concentration camps. The fallen had given their lives not just for their families and friends back in the United States but also for unknown strangers throughout Europe and for generations of people yet to come.

The ultimate sacrifice was to give one's life. Hannah would have done it for her parents, for Wilhelm, for Eleanor and Trugnowski, and Josephine and Radley. But she knew them.

She loved them. These young men had given their lives for strangers. It was something Hannah couldn't understand. She could only hope every person around the world and for decades to come could understand what had happened.

Priests moved about the beach, blessing the bodies of the fallen. The trucks carrying the bodies brought them to their temporary grave. It was only three-and-a-half-feet deep, and the bodies were lined shoulder to shoulder. Bulldozers pushed heaps of dirt on top of them. One of their two dog tags had been taken so the graves could be marked to indicate who was buried beneath. The amount of aluminum hanging from crudely made crosses made them look like stars shining in the night sky. When the winds off the Channel hit them, they chimed with melancholy. The sun had set, and the waves that had once been a peaceful lament were now eerie. The moon was full and the stars, bright. Not even night could hide the macabre beach.

Hannah gazed at the stars. Wherever Wilhelm was, she prayed he would not have to go through such a hellish ordeal as the men who had stormed the beaches of Normandy that fateful day in June.

New Deal

The moon was full and bright and the stars around it, equally so. But the curfew was set and Wilhelm, instead of staring at the best sky since arriving at the prisoner-of-war camp, could only stare at the cobweb-infested wooden ceiling of the barracks. But Torben had shared news minutes before lights out that had diverted Wilhelm's gaze from the white-speckled black canvas to Torben's face.

The United States, Great Britain, and Canada had invaded France days earlier. Germany was now waging a war on two fronts. A major news story like that demanded details— details unfortunately not available. Prodding for information was a good way to get into trouble, and for that reason, Wilhelm steered clear. But Torben wanted to know. He wanted to know when the war would be over and when he could marry Francesca and return home to his mother.

"Tell us, Joe," Torben pleaded.

It was the next morning, and they had just arrived at the factory. Both had agreed Old Uncle Joe was their best play for information but also agreed to slowly press for it, not greet him with an interrogation.

"Do I look like I work in Soviet intelligence? Keep working," Old Uncle Joe said.

"I tell you what. When we're free, Wilhelm and I are going to take you to Germany for a proper drink. Something that goes down smooth and doesn't cause your throat to bleed," Torben said.

"I have had that drink. But I have been from my mother's breast for some time," Old Uncle Joe said, countering Torben's weak jab with a vicious hook.

He smiled, and Wilhelm and Torben could not help but laugh. Old Uncle Joe gave Torben a poke with his walking stick. The work had become much less stressful since the Soviets had pushed the Germans back into Ukraine and the bombing sirens no longer rang. Wilhelm and Torben did not deserve the poking anymore for screwing up, yet they still expected it. Old Uncle Joe shared what details he could when he could. He was prone to falling asleep on his stool, and Wilhelm or Torben would give him a soft tap with their boot to wake him. But Torben had gone too long between pokes.

"Your arm too tired, Joe?" Torben asked.

Wilhelm was on the other side of the bomber and enjoyed the hiatus from being poked.

"Joe?" Torben asked.

Wilhelm waited for an answer.

"What's going on?" Wilhelm asked.

"Get over here," Torben said.

Wilhelm hurried to the other end of the plane, nearly kicking over a box of tools as he did. Old Uncle Joe dropped his cane and collapsed into his chair. He sweated profusely and gasped for breath.

"What is it?" Wilhelm asked.

"My ... chest," Old Uncle Joe gasped.

"Get help!" Wilhelm yelled to Torben.

Torben nodded and sprinted toward a Soviet soldier. Sprinting drew the attention of every guard, and they raised their guns. Torben stopped dead in his tracks.

"Need help!" Torben yelled, pointing to Old Uncle Joe.

"Hang in there. Help is coming," Wilhelm said.

Old Uncle Joe's breathing was raspy and his face, ghostly pale. His sweaty palms grabbed Wilhelm's hand. He took one final inhale, and his chest did not move again. The guards dashed over with their guns raised. Wilhelm threw his hands up and stepped away.

"What did you do to him?" a Soviet officer asked.

His eyes were the same color as his uniform—a faded green. His hat had a red stripe across it with a gold hammer and sickle at the front. He was one of the supervisors of the labor areas, and he almost always had a cigarette in his mouth. His name was Captain Sokolov.

"Nothing. I think he had a heart attack," Wilhelm said.

Captain Sokolov nodded. "Your name?" he commanded.

He held out his hand, and one of his junior officers handed over a clipboard with the names of all the Germans working at the factory. He took a puff of his cigarette. The end threatened to fall off.

"Schreiber, Wilhelm."

Captain Sokolov took another deep puff that finished off the cigarette and then tossed it on the floor. The junior officer put his foot on the cigarette and squashed it like a bug, extinguishing the red embers. Captain Sokolov licked his finger and flipped the pages over the clipboard until he came across Wilhelm's name.

"Wilhelm Schreiber. Obersoldat? A private?" Captain Sokolov asked to clarify between German and Soviet ranks.

"Yes, Sir," Wilhelm said.

"With your detailed medical examination, I thought you to be a medic. Do you have any training in such things?" Captain Sokolov mocked.

It was obvious what Captain Sokolov was doing, but Wilhelm was powerless to stop it. He could only answer respectfully.

"No, Sir."

"You will never advise me again, is that clear?" Captain Sokolov asked.

"Yes, Sir."

"And you, blonde German shit, what is your name?"

"Kuhn, Torben. Obersoldat."

Captain Sokolov held the clipboard out for someone else to take it, and one of his junior officers did. Sokolov removed another cigarette and lit it.

"You rush at a guard again, and you will be hanged. Do you understand me, Obersoldat?" Captain Sokolov asked.

"Yes, Sir," Torben said.

"Excellent. Now I have found the Germans to be much like dogs. Beasts. If trained properly, you can teach them to shit outside," Captain Sokolov jeered.

He spoke elegantly, but deliberately fast in his native Russian. He wanted his orders to be missed so that the Germans could be punished. The officers around him laughed. Both Wilhelm and Torben could understand Old Uncle Joe, but he had always spoken lazily slow and repeated himself if needed.

"You have shit inside my house. It is exactly 15.56 kilometers from the front entrance of this factory to the gates of the camp. You will run back for the next seven days. If you are not back before dark, you will be brought outside and shot like any other misbehaving dog. You will be followed, so any thoughts of running to your freedom I suggest you swallow," Captain Sokolov said.

He smiled and blew a cloud of smoke from a fresh cigarette into their faces. He turned to leave while his men lifted Old Uncle Joe's lifeless body. There was only an hour left of the shift, but the loss of Joe made it feel so much longer. There were no pokes and no conversations. The Soviets had sent over another guard. He was an active soldier, and his only words were "faster, faster." As the prisoners shuffled out at the end of the shift, Wilhelm and Torben looked on as the trucks drove off. It was not yet the heart of summer, but it was hot. The best part of the day, driving in the open top truck, had been taken from them.

"Move," a Soviet said from behind the wheel of a jeep. The guard next to him snickered. Wilhelm and Torben jogged over grassy fields somewhere in Western Russia, the guards aiming guns and smiles their directions.

"Think we can take the jeep?" Torben asked in German.

"Can you stop bullets?" Wilhelm asked.

Wilhelm could not blame him for asking. If they could get past the two guards, they would have a vehicle to try and escape. But they were also somewhere in Russia with an unknown number of kilometers before they could be free of the Soviet Union's massive hammer and sickle. The Soviet guards did not let Wilhelm or Torben know what time it was or how long they had been running. They were truly running blind with an unknown predator stalking them from behind and running them down. Wilhelm's feet pounded. His boots were not ideal for long-distance running. His throat was a desert, and his tongue was a dried sponge. His sides felt as if spears had been stabbed into them, and his body threatened to collapse. Torben had an equally tough time of it, and with each passing moment, Wilhelm considered Torben's question more and more.

If they didn't make it in time, they would be shot. Their fate could have been decided already. They could be dead men running to their own grave. Why shouldn't they risk their lives for a chance at freedom? But Wilhelm had spent too long contemplating his decision. The gates of the camp loomed ahead. Captain Sokolov approached them, the smoke of his cigarette evaporating into the early night sky.

"I am shocked that you both made private first class," Captain Sokolov said.

Torben and Wilhelm bent over and gasped for breath. Their white t-shirts were drenched in sweat. The aches and pains Wilhelm had experienced while running only increased exponentially now that his body was still.

"Bring them inside," Captain Sokolov ordered.

Captain Sokolov would hang them inside the camp to send a message. The sky was at battle between day and night, but Captain Sokolov did not care it was still partially light out—only that it was partially dark. Wilhelm had seen a dozen men being hanged, their corpses swaying and left for days at a time as a reminder. When a German was too weak to perform the tasks given to them, the Soviets had no use for them. Wilhelm and Torben had no choice but to move inside the prison camp and wait for their fate. Wilhelm tried to plead with Torben with his eyes. He wanted to tell him he was wrong. They should have tried to overtake the jeep. But he would not be caught showing anything that could be conveyed as weakness. Wilhelm had seen too many men die to whimper over it.

Sokolov stepped in front of the two. "Congratulations, dogs. You have made it."

Their plates of food were tossed at their feet. As they bent down to pick them up, they were kicked to the ground. Their faces landed into their plates of kasha. The Soviets laughed, and a mix of rage and embarrassment fought for dominance in Wilhelm. But his rage was much stronger and almost defeated his sense of reason. It called for Wilhelm to snap out and retaliate.

Torben bit his lip and dug his nails into the dirt. Wilhelm reached his hand into his bowl, but Captain Sokolov kicked his hand away.

"You are dogs. Dogs eat with their mouths, not their paws," Captain Sokolov sniggered.

To not eat was a dead man's wish. They were not keen on the idea of eating like a dog in front of the entire camp of hundreds, but survival demanded being pushed past comfort zones and civility itself. So, Wilhelm brought his mouth down and slurped up the porridge.

"Good boy," Captain Sokolov said, roughly petting Wilhelm's head before lighting another cigarette.

The Germans around Wilhelm and Torben made no mention of what had happened, for they each had experienced something similar. They had not found it funny in the slightest because, like Wilhelm and Torben, they too wanted to survive.

"Fucking asshole," Torben said. He cleaned off the bit of kasha off his face as he and Wilhelm limped to the barracks. Both were far too exhausted to enjoy the half hour or so before lights out. "I hope he doesn't make us lick our own asses," Torben said.

Wilhelm fell asleep instantaneously when his head hit his pillow. He had not thought about Old Uncle Joe at all until the next morning when he awoke. With the new day came a strong dose of guilt. He and Torben knew things had changed for them and changed for the worse. Old Uncle Joe was a good and kind man. Their new guard was unsatisfied with anything they did, and even if by some miracle they had assembled a thousand bombers before lunch, he would find fault in it. They were also under the scrutinizing eye of Captain Sokolov. He grinned at them, knowing how hard their run would be under such a strong sun and weak legs. The run that day was twice as hard and the day after, three times harder. Wilhelm's feet were covered in blisters and bruises of purple and blue, and his unkempt toenails cracked and broke.

Captain Sokolov smiled each night as it got closer to the deadline. Apart from always having a cigarette hanging from his lips, nothing brought Sokolov greater joy than watching Wilhelm and Torben eat and drink like dogs. Wilhelm and Torben had made it each of the seven days, and even though both could barely walk, they were sure to stand tall around Captain Sokolov and the guards—not out of pride but knowing if Captain Sokolov saw how sore they were, he would sentence them to another run.

Every morning, Wilhelm's legs were like uncooked spaghetti noodles—hard and brittle—and would snap if he tried to stand on them. But every night, through the course of a long day, his legs would cook and become flimsy and threaten to give out. The soreness and pain in his legs didn't go away even when lying down. But worse than his legs were his tormenting thoughts.

"We should have gone for the jeep," Wilhelm said.

He stared up at the ceiling, his mind too busy to silence the snoring around him or dull his thoughts. Stalingrad was hell and nothing short of it. But he was a man during it. Sokolov dehumanized him, humiliated him, and dominated him in a way no self-respecting man should tolerate. But what choice did he have?

What if fate had presented an opportunity to escape and Wilhelm had been too afraid to seize it? But worse than that, he had dissuaded Torben from attempting it. He knew Torben had heard him, and it was a testament to how close they had become that he did not answer. It was so much more than going for the jeep. It was going after freedom—after life itself. And if freedom and life were elusive, well, at least, they would have met death on their feet and shaken its hand like men rather than cowering in the fetal position Sokolov forced them in.

Land of Liberty

The sacrifice of the fallen was stained on the sands of Normandy. The bodies had been cleared, yet the aura of loss and martyrdom was something the tide could not wash away. The air was thicker than it had been, and it was impossible to breathe in the salty air and not be overcome with emotion.

Hannah had been told the causalities of each of the beachheads, an estimated number north of ten thousand—estimated—an acceptable range higher or lower than the true number. The word made her angry and heartbroken. The true number needed to be known so each man who had died could be remembered. There should be no estimates, guesses or approximations. The sights and sounds affected each of the nurses' differently. Some fell ill while others cried in each other's arms. Hannah stood alone and grieved in reflective silence. Kay had said General Eisenhower's son had graduated from West Point the same day men of equal age crossed the Channel and stormed the beaches. Hannah could only imagine the conflicting guilt the General felt. General Eisenhower stood on the shore, the waves washing short of him, and stared in somber silence toward the Channel. He squatted down, grabbed a handful of sand, and let it fall between his fingers.

"These men are making decisions that will cost young men their lives. It isn't easy. You or I can't pretend to know what that feels like, so don't," Kay had said.

Near the camp, men sorted through the dog tags of the fallen, and others typed last names, first names, and ranks. A man typing finished another page and set it on a stack of papers nearly two inches thick.

"What will they do with them?" Hannah asked.

"They'll notify the family," a nurse said.

Families that had no idea their son, their brother, their husband or their father had died. They could be laughing and smiling at that exact moment with no way of knowing their lives had changed forever. But it would be closure families of the concentration camps would not get. There would be no answers to what happened.

The boat ride back to Portsmouth was quiet apart from the ship ripping through the waves. Hannah was once again leaving France and the European mainland behind. And again, her heart was heavy, contemplating the unfathomable loss of human life. Kay had stayed with General Eisenhower, as she should have. She was a close confidant, and whether the relationship was something more Hannah did not know nor did she care to. The city which had been home to thousands of Allied troops for the last several weeks was now a ghost town of haunting memories. The paths that had once been beaten with pounding boots were now silent. The laughter coming from the camps was gone. Only the wind swept through them with shrilling melancholy.

Hannah walked past the Southwick House and kept heading north. She had no ride to London, yet she did not want to try and fall asleep. She had helped as much as her heart would allow her to. She walked through the slow falling rain for an hour until she came to a bus stop. The bus route had not been operational at night ever since the outbreak of the war. Headlights were a good target. But it did have a payphone. She lifted the phone off the receiver and spun the number dial and called the one man she knew who could get her out of Europe.

"Minimax Fire Extinguisher Company. How can I help you?" a familiar voice answered the call.

It was Jane.

"Direct me to the man upstairs," Hannah said.

"May I ask who is calling?"

It was close to three in the morning, and Jane had either stayed extremely late or started her day extremely early.

"Hannah Smith."

A long pause made Hannah question if Jane had hung up.

"Hannah?" Menzies asked.

There was interference in the audio quality.

"Chief Menzies, I want to go to America," Hannah said.

Another short pause.

"Where are you?"

"About four miles north of Southwick. By the bus station."

"Stay there. I will send an agent."

"Thank you."

She placed the phone back onto the receiver and took a seat on the bench. Sprinkling rain quickly turned into a torrential downpour. It seemed the entire world was crying over what had happened, not just in Normandy but throughout Europe and the Pacific. Hannah had no idea how long she sat there with the rain soaking her clothing and flesh. Even if the rain chilled her to her very bones, it soothed her. It was music as it ricocheted off buildings and hit the streets and sidewalks. Her thoughts drifted to Wilhelm. Normandy was an awful event but, like Auschwitz, it was not a singularity. To think Wilhelm had not seen horrors like the Americans, British, and Canadians had was foolish and disrespectful. She sat in the darkness until a pair of headlights came toward her. The black car looked almost invisible in the darkness before it pulled to a stop.

Otto exited the car and jogged toward her. "Hannah," he called. He helped her to the car and turned the heat up. Reaching into the back seat, he grabbed a green and white plaid blanket. Hannah wrapped it around her body. "Why are you not in Portsmouth?" Otto asked.

"I was. I saw the beaches," Hannah said.

The way she had said it and the look in her eyes told Otto it was too awful to speak of. He had been quite the gentlemen to Hannah and respected her desire for silence. She only stared blankly out of the window as the road sped by. She only knew they had reached the Minimax Fire Extinguisher Company building when the road stopped moving.

"Do you want to change first? I am sure we can scrounge up some clothes," Otto asked.

"No, I am fine," Hannah said. She had been through much worse than being soaking wet.

"Very well," Otto said. He allowed Hannah to ascend the steps herself. She left pools of water with each step she climbed. The office was empty, and the only light on in the floor was the one coming from Menzies' office. Hannah stepped into his office.

"You look a fright," Menzies said, looking at the blanket draped over her shoulders and wrapped around her. He rose from his desk. "Let me get you something," he said.

"I am fine," Hannah said.

"What happened, Ms. Smith?" Menzies asked.

"I was in Portsmouth like you asked. I helped the wounded during the invasion."

"Yes, Kay Summersby gave a great review on your behalf. It seems you served the Allies quite well."

"Will you help me get to America?"

Menzies was silent, and Hannah expected a disappointing answer. He would make her serve yet again—perhaps, infiltrate the high German society or serve in North Africa.

"Yes, I will. Your part in the war is over, my dear. You have sacrificed much and have done what you can. I thank you and the mothers of the boys you helped treat thank you," Menzies said.

"The dead won't hear you," Hannah said.

Menzies gave her a grim look with eyes filled with apology.

"There are no ships leaving from London to New York, I am afraid," Menzies informed.

Remarkably, Hannah did not feel dejected. She had grown to consider New York to be as unreachable and mythical in status as Atlantis.

"You will need to travel to Glasgow. I shall arrange it. You will travel aboard the Queen Mary. She is the fastest ship in her majesty's fleet. It currently serves as troop transport," Menzies said.

"Excellent. When can I leave?" Hannah asked.

"There is a train that leaves at six, some two and a half hours from now. I shall make the proper arrangements. You are welcome to stay until then. Are you sure I cannot get you something to drink?"

"Just water, please."

"Very well."

He disappeared for roughly twenty minutes, ensuring Hannah had a spot on not only the train but the Queen Mary as well. When he returned, he had a small tin cup of water and a dry blanket made of wool. Hannah thanked him as he handed her the water. Menzies removed the wet blanket from her shoulders and covered her with the dry one. It was considerably warmer than the drenched flannel one she had been draped in.

"You did well, Agent," Menzies said and smiled softly.

"Promise me you will shut the camps down?" Hannah said.

"We will do all that we can," Menzies said.

It would be too late for thousands. At that second, many of the prisoners in the camps were dying in their bunks. More would die when the sun would rise and the trains would arrive.

Exhaustion finally set in, but Hannah would not risk oversleeping and missing her train. The train ride to Glasgow, Scotland would be roughly four to six hours, and she would have nothing to do but sleep. Her small suitcase of clothing Josephine had given her was returned to her, and she went into the women's lavatory and changed out of her blood-stained and rain-soaked grayish blue nurse's uniform into an emerald, sleeveless, knee-high summer dress. Hannah watched the clock, and at 5 a.m. sharp, she said her goodbyes. It was not a fraction as difficult as it had been saying goodbye to Josephine and Radley or Eleanor and Trugnowski. She did not know either Otto or Menzies as well and knew they had gotten use out of her. They never would have extended a helping hand had Hannah not extended one first.

Otto drove her to the train station and offered to wait until she was on the train, but Hannah politely refused.

"Go get yourself some breakfast," she said.

Otto smiled, handed her another stack of tickets and identification papers and got back into his car and drove away. The train was already there, and Hannah and the other passengers waited for permission to board. The train was much more inviting than the cattle car to Auschwitz had been, yet the same fear of the train remained. The shout came to board. Hannah took a deep breath and willed herself to step aboard. She feared she would step onto the train and to an empty room, a floor covered with human waste, a bucket, and a thick fog of heat. But the train was far from that. The seats were soft gray cushions with overhead storage, and clean glass windows to see the English countryside. She took a seat by the window and secured her suitcase between her feet.

It was another twenty minutes or so until the train sputtered forward. A loud shriek echoed outside. Hannah watched as the city of London disappeared beside and behind the train. Her eyes closed and, soon, she was fast asleep with the side of her head resting against the glass window. She had finally arrived at that metaphorical house after weeks of driving by it and missing the turns. If she woke the entire train ride to Scotland, it was only to shift in her seat to find the most optimal comfort she could. But even in her deep sleep, her body could feel the train slowing down, and she awoke without much struggle. The train was empty apart from fathers and mothers visiting children who had been sent far north, away from the Nazi nighttime bombing blitz. Hannah followed the dozen passengers ahead of her and stepped out to a torrential downpour. Lightning flashed, and the clouds rumbled like a growling dog, and every once in a while, it barked.

"Miss Smith?" a woman asked.

"Yes," Hannah said hesitantly.

"I have been expecting you. Chief Menzies called. I am Agent Sorcha," the woman said in a thick Scottish accent. She was dressed similar to Otto, and she had short, curly, dirty blonde hair. Her lips were chapped, and her fingers looked to be as long as rulers. Hannah was reminded of the famed pilot Amelia Earhart. She held the umbrella in her hand further out to shield Hannah from the rain. "I will take you to the Queen Mary. It isn't a far drive," she said.

Hannah had to laugh internally over how the car Sorcha drove and the car Otto drove were identical. She could only hope that when they were undercover, they were a bit less conspicuous. Sorcha was right. The drive lasted ten minutes. They made it to the waters of Firth of Clyde of Glasgow in northwest United Kingdom.

The Queen Mary itself looked almost indistinguishable from the Titanic. Hannah had heard much of the famed shipwreck both in school and from Wilhelm. The only difference that could be seen from land was that the Queen Mary had three funnels, not four, and the ship had been painted navy gray.

"That's the Queen Mary?" Hannah asked.

"Ey, the Grey Ghost we call her. Fastest ship in the war. Hitler has a bounty of two hundred fifty thousand and the Iron Cross for any U-Boat captain that can sink her," Sorcha said proudly.

The ship had looked small, but with each dozen feet they moved closer, the size of the ship increased proportionately. The ship itself was over a thousand-feet long and over a hundred-and-eighty-feet high. It had been a luxury liner before the war had broken out and, during the war, had become one of England's most reliant ships. It was Prime Minister Churchill's preferred ship to cross the Atlantic on.

"Safe travels to you," Sorcha said.

"Thank you," Hannah said.

Sorcha did not delay and returned to her car. An English soldier stood at the rail. Hannah walked across the ramp connecting the dock and the ship and handed the tall, lengthy soldier her ticket.

"Welcome aboard the Queen Mary, Miss," he greeted, stepping aside and making room for her to enter.

The ship had dropped off roughly a thousand Americans who would join the fight in the European theatre and, now, would be bringing a German immigrant back on its return journey. Hannah suspected other members of government were on the ship and knew both Americans and Brits crossed "the pond" to deliver information too valuable to risk being intercepted. But even with the other people aboard and the countless crew, Hannah once again was alone. Yet, this time, it appeared to be so much different.

The Queen Mary sped away from the coast of Scotland and toward Ireland, leaving a sea of waves in its wake. Hannah had not been home in over four years. She had traveled all over Europe yet, now, she was leaving the continent behind. She sailed across the world alone to an unknown place. When she was a child, she had imagined visiting New York with her mother and father. When she met Wilhelm, it was him by her side in those dreams. But the reality was much lonelier.

Even though it was past noon, Hannah traveled below the sea deck to find her staying room. The lavish liner had its furniture removed and replaced with triple-tiered bunks of wood for troops to sleep on. The ship's tapestries, paintings, china, and crystal had been removed. The fine woodwork in the staterooms and dining rooms had been covered in leather. Hannah had a modest room with a bunk, much like the three-tiered bunks with a small circular window to look out. She pulled the black curtain over the window.

The ship approached dangerous waters, and if a torpedo blasted into it, there would not be much chance of surviving. If anyone did, it would be through sheer luck, much like the way anyone had survived the storming of the beaches. If the ship was struck while she slept, there would not be a better way to go.

Hannah took a look at the pocket watch the farmer had given her and set it on the counter beside her. The air outside the ship had been cool, and it was hard to believe it was summer. Yet, the Northern Atlantic had its own climate. The chill that came off the water penetrated through the ship's hull like no torpedo could. Hannah lifted the navy-colored blanket and white sheet and crawled into bed and tossed them back over herself. She had always needed to fall asleep on her back, yet that was before she had slept on wooden beams they called bunks in Auschwitz. Even the more comfortable places she had stayed had not given her the instant relaxation and comfort your own bed could give. It all had given Hannah the ability to sleep anywhere at any given moment. She slept so deeply that no dreams came to her.

When she woke, the room was covered in darkness. She reached for the pocket watch and grabbed it and went to the window. She pulled open the black curtain, and the glow from the night sky cast enough light for her to see it was after 11:30 p.m. But now that she was up, she was no longer tired and knew if she laid in bed, she would simply stare at the ceiling. Even that was tempting because of how warm the bed had become. But she had already flipped her covers over, and any heat trapped inside had disappeared. She put her shoes back on and left her room. The halls were barren, and as she made her way up to the sea deck, there were only a few crew members around. Hannah had never seen the stars so perfectly clear with no city lights to ruin the view. The black expanse went on forever, and it was truly amazing how many stars were in the sky. It was incredibly peaceful. Even the water was calm, and it was impossible to tell the difference between where the ocean ended and where the sky began.

When Hannah looked over the railing, and the sights of the ship were out of her peripheral, she floated through space itself. It was hard to believe the world was at war for out here, there was nothing. That was terrifying, yet freeing in a way few ever experienced. She was a pilgrim waiting to discover the new world. Hannah stayed on the deck until two in the morning until she went back to her room and fell asleep. She awoke early the next morning and bothered every crew member she could find to see what she could to do help. She was not eager to be a useless appendage, nor was she keen on being in someone's debt. But there was not much she could do apart from cleaning, as the other positions required months of military training. Her help had been politely refused nearly a half-dozen times, and if she asked any more, she would have been considered a nuisance—something she too did not want. She went the entire next day without speaking a word to anyone. The government officials were locked in their rooms, and the crew members were far too busy. The Queen Mary was now well over half-way across the Atlantic.

Hannah found a deck of playing cards and killed several hours playing solitaire or shuffling the cards. She had not held a deck of cards since Lena's house so long ago. As she shuffled, the games they had played and the memories they made came back to her at once. At dusk on the fourth day, Hannah was told the ship would reach New York City by midnight. She waited until eleven before putting the cards into her suitcase and hurrying up to the deck so she could see the city as they approached. But it was nothing but blackness in the horizon for the next half hour until the bright lights of the New York skyline rose like ignited steel giants. The Statue of Liberty was bathed in spotlight, inviting the troubled, lost souls of the world.

"Give me your tired, your poor, your huddled masses yearning to breathe free," it said.

The Statue of Liberty stood proudly at what her country stood for.

Hannah's eyes glistened with tears of joy. She had finally arrived in New York. There had been so many near misses, so many moments that could have gone the other way. Something else besides the chilly sea breeze washed over her. It was a feeling of security for the first time—not just since the war had broken out but since she could remember. Hitler had risen to power when she was thirteen. Her childhood years were filled with too much innocence for her to remember anything bad. Wilhelm had once read her a quote about the ancient Greek city of Sparta: "Sparta has no walls because you, her warriors, are her walls." The same was true of the United States. There were no walls, no fences, no motes. Yet, the brave fighting men had seen to it that there was an invisible barrier. To try and cross it, one would be met with a tenacious defense of freedom.

The Statue of Liberty reminded her of one of the old Spartan sculptures of a warrior holding his shield and spear. The Statue of Liberty had no shield, no spear. Instead, its weapons were a torch, a beacon of light for damned souls caught in darkness, and a tablet with the date July 4, 1776—the date when the colonists under British tyranny cried out in a singular voice for freedom, demanded rights, and yearned for the pursuit of happiness. The statue itself was on Liberty Island, but it was Ellis Island all immigrants went through. The island was synonymous with sanctuary. Every feeling Hannah hoped and expected she would feel when she reached America she felt. Her tears showed worry, fear, and anxiety, but her smile showed relief, excitement, and hope. It was such an emotional overload that she stopped breathing momentarily.

"Welcome to America," a crew member said.

The ship would not stop at Ellis Island. Instead, Hannah would have to step off with the Queen Mary's crew and find another boat to take her to the famed island. Much like Sorcha had been waiting for her in Glasgow, there was an American agent waiting for her when she stepped off the Gray Ghost. The very air smelt like hot dogs, beer, and exhaust. It was the smell of freedom.

The agent wore a short-sleeve white dress shirt with a skinny black tie, and black browline glasses covered his face. He took quick uncommitted puffs of his cigarette. In his left hand, he had a two-by-three-inch photograph, and as the people aboard the ship moved past, he took quick glances from the photograph to the crowd. "Hannah Smith?" the man asked, spotting Hannah. He looked from her to the photograph in his hand.

"Yes," Hannah said.

The man did not hide that he worked for the government, and that made Hannah less worried than she had been in France or England.

"I am Agent Dunn of the Federal Bureau of Investigation. My boss, Director Hoover, has been contacted by Director Magruder of the Office of Strategic Services. Chief Menzies of England has asked that the United States of America offers you asylum. We must first ask you some questions. Follow me please," Agent Dunn said.

The agent led her to a small dock, roughly a quarter of a mile from where Hannah had stepped off the Queen Mary. The boat waiting for them was smaller than one of the lifeboats aboard the Queen Mary, and it swayed when they stepped on. Another agent operated the engine, and when Hannah and Agent Dunn secured themselves onto the boat, the agent brought the boat humming forward.

"Agent Connors," Agent Dunn introduced, nodding ever so slightly to the other agent.

Hannah could barely hear him over the chainsaw humming of the boat. Bits of the sea sprayed her face, but she did not mind. The boat skipped along the waves like a smooth stone. The main building on the island came into view. It was a red brick in the style of Renaissance Revival. The American flag was limp from the non-existent wind. The boat ride took mere minutes, and Hannah was thankful for that, as neither of the two men said anything. Agent Connors navigated the boat and killed the engine once they reached the island. Agent Dunn stepped off first.

"Take your bag with you," he instructed Hannah.

Hannah grabbed the suitcase and followed the agent into the building. The Statue of Liberty looked like a titan from such a close distance, and it stood tall with its back to her to ensure nothing came from Europe to harm her. She made a note to herself that one of the first things she would buy would be a miniature version of the statue—something she could put on the windowsill of wherever she ended up.

The immigrant building was not particularly busy at such a late hour. A family from the Middle East, Muslim by the looks of the woman's dress, paced around nervously. They had a large family of seven, and Hannah could appreciate the nervousness in their eyes. They were wondering the same thing Hannah was—was there truly a safe place for them? Seated at a table far from Hannah was a family who looked to be from Ireland although Hannah felt shameful for classifying them based on the fact the father had fire-red hair and the family had an affinity for plaid. But when the man spoke, there was no mistaking his prominent accent.

"We're going to need you to shower and be looked at to make sure you aren't carrying a disease," Agent Dunn said.

Shower—the lie the Nazis had told to keep the unsuspected prisoners calm. He led Hannah through the massive entrance hall and down a separate hallway. Hannah paused.

"There's a towel and soap in there. Should be everything you need," Agent Dunn said.

She stepped inside, and Agent Dunn waited outside to give her privacy. She removed her shoes and stepped onto the floor. It was ice cold and sent a frozen stab up her legs.

She slowly took her clothes off, and the room seemed more like early January than early June. It was relatively dark and only increased her unsettling feeling. She set her clothes on the bench and stepped into a shower stall. She turned the dial and shivered when the cold water hit her back. She adjusted the dial, and the water turned so hot that steam rose out of the shower. The chill she had gotten from sitting out in the rain only truly subsided when she was sleeping aboard the Queen Mary, but as the hot water ran down her body, it finally left her for good. A small squeeze jug of shampoo and a bar of soap with the paper covering intact were on the soap holder attached to the shower wall. Hannah scrubbed her head and squirted a small bit of shampoo into her hand and lathered her hair.

Thousands had arrived at Auschwitz and had been told a shower was through a door. The train ride took days and people were covered in sweat, human waste, and an invisible yet palpable body odor. A shower was heaven. Yet, what awaited was not hot water, shampoo, and soap. It was death. The fact was not missed by Hannah. Agent Dunn had said she would be taking a shower. Though he would never know how much, the fact Hannah entered the room to find a shower gave her a sense of security she would never forget.

Hannah grabbed a folded white towel on a rack near the sink. The water slid off her goosebump-covered body. She dried herself off and hurried to dress, stepping on her damp towel to keep her feet warm before the cold floor ruthlessly attacked them. The room had a permanent chill, half of which could be attributed to the dull gray coloring and half to poor lighting. Hannah used the bits of the towel that were dry to finish drying her hair the best she could by grabbing bits of it and wringing it out. She pushed open the door. Agent Dunn waited at a respectable distance. He was joined by not Agent Connors but a much older, white-haired man.

"Hannah, this is Dr. Cameron," Agent Dunn said.

"Hello, Hannah. I'm just going to give you a quick check under the hood. Is that alright?" Dr. Cameron asked. He had a gentle voice, but even if he had asked permission, Agent Dunn wouldn't.

"Certainly," Hannah said.

Dr. Cameron checked her hair, face, neck, and hands, something unofficially known as the "six-second physical." "She's running like new," Dr. Cameron said with a smile.

"Thanks, doc," Agent Dunn said.

"Any time," Dr. Cameron said, pointing a finger at Agent Dunn and then leaving to check on the Irish and Muslim families still pacing.

"This way, please," Agent Dunn said.

It was hard to fathom the number of people who had traveled through the building, people in the same situation as Hannah, escaping persecution and tyranny. Hannah had expected to be brought into an office, but Agent Dunn sat at a table. It was here people waited to be accepted or rejected.

"I need to ask you some questions, Ms. Smith," Agent Dunn said.

"Can I go by my married name? Schreiber?" Hannah asked.

"Passport says Smith. It's an American name. Your accent will draw enough attention. You don't want a Kraut name," Agent Dunn said and nodded to the open chair. Hannah took the seat. He slid her suitcase over, and as she lifted it to put it on the other side of her, she could tell the contents inside had been shifted around.

"Find anything you like?" she asked.

Agent Dunn's face blushed ever so slightly. "It's a precaution. You're from Germany. The United States of America is at war with Germany," he explained.

Hannah had made a mistake. She did not think they would have allowed her onto the Queen Mary only to reject her when she arrived. Where was she to go? Once again, Hannah was being interrogated as a German spy. Only the warehouse had been substituted for what looked like a giant cafeteria.

"I am a Jew first. The Germans are killing us," Hannah said.

"What are your goals in living here?" Agent Dunn asked.

"I want to be safe."

Agent Dunn nodded. He stared unabashedly at her. No doubt he knew everything she had been through the last five years. He tapped his pen on the stack of papers on the table in front of him as if confused while taking an exam.

"What are your thoughts on Hitler?" he asked.

"He is a dictator hell-bent on ruling the world and exterminating an entire group of people," Hannah said.

"Good. We think he's an asshole," Agent Dunn said. He smiled and shuffled the stack of papers neatly together. "You will report to me for the first six months you are here. No, this isn't standard, but you're not a standard immigrant either."

"Report?" Hannah asked.

"Check in once every two weeks and tell me what you are doing—if you've found a place to live and a place to work," Agent Dunn clarified.

"I am to stay in New York?"

"Yes. For the first six months. After that, you can go wherever you want. Can I have your passport please?"

Hannah reached into her pocket and removed the stack of papers and found the thick, navy-colored passport and handed it to Agent Dunn. He searched his pocket and removed a stamp and flipped open the passport. He pressed the stamp down and slid the passport back over.

"Welcome to the United States of America," he said.

The word "accepted" was in thick red letters, the shade of which perfectly matched the red J that had been stamped on her German one. The red that prevented her from having any future now guaranteed one. Agent Dunn rose from the table, and Hannah followed him. For a small moment, she allowed herself to think of the millions of people who could trace their heritage to the building she stood in. Hannah was lucky the leadership of the United States hadn't forgotten their ancestors had come from overseas and allowed her in.

Agent Dunn was quiet on the return trip to the city and only handed Hannah a business card that had his name, office address, and telephone number on it. "On the back of that card, you'll find another address of a temporary place for you to stay. Don't be afraid to call. Good luck, Ms. Smith," Agent Dunn said.

"Thank you," Hannah said.

She had no idea what she would do, but it didn't matter. She had made it to America, and she was far out of the reach of Hitler and the Nazis.

V-E Day in the Red Square

Somehow, Wilhelm had been in the prisoner-of-war camp for over a year and a half. And, as if it were a direct order from Satan himself, Captain Sokolov ensured every day was a fresh hell for Wilhelm and Torben. Familiar faces perished over the eighteen months, but new Germans took their place.

After the Allied invasion in Normandy, the German army could not stop the Allies from establishing a foothold in France. The Soviets capitalized on their unexpected blow at Stalingrad and delivered a flurry of punches as they pressed from the east. Captain Sokolov could not help but boast with each report that came in stating that the Germans had retreated further west. Wilhelm wanted to call him a coward for being at the camp while thousands of others fought and died, but two things stopped him from doing that. He did not want to be hanged on the gallows at a prisoner-of-war camp somewhere in Russia and, secondly, he felt like a coward himself. He had been captured and held prisoner for a large portion of the war.

Wilhelm and Torben, along with the rest of the camp, stood and waited for Captain Sokolov to give his new orders for the day. After smoking what seemed like the longest cigarette in the history of tobacco, he spoke. "We are to leave this camp. We will begin our march. Those who cannot keep up will be shot." It was hardly informative—just another method to annoy. Leaving the camp seemed exciting. Wilhelm had seen nothing but it, the factory, and the green fields in between. But where were they going? Was there truly a destination or were they on a death march?

Wilhelm wanted to go back to his bunk and gather what few possessions he had, but the Soviet guards blocked him and the other Germans. They would only be allowed to take what they wore on their backs. Luckily, the thick heat of July and August were gone, and October brought a cool breeze. The Germans were forced to march eight hours a day and end the day's march by putting up a perimeter fence of barbed wire. They were served minimal food and water and, by the time the additional chores and eating were finished, Wilhelm and the other Germans were allotted less than five hours of sleep before they were forced to wake up and deconstruct the fence they had assembled the night before. Wilhelm had never seen Captain Sokolov happier than when he watched the exhausted and famished Germans struggle to march.

"They are going to march us until we all die," Torben said.

They had already lost a dozen men, and they had marched for five days with seemingly no destination in sight. Wilhelm had no retort and no energy to exhaust on speaking. He couldn't remember the last time there was spit in his mouth, and the last time he urinated, he could tell by the color, a dark yellow, he was extremely dehydrated. Captain Sokolov had made a habit of emptying his canteen of water every night onto the ground, knowing every German there would kill for it. It was most fortunate that Sunday was rest day. There were still odd jobs to be completed, but none required a fraction of the amount of energy required for eight hours of marching.

"Schreiber. Kuhn. Dig the latrine," Captain Sokolov ordered.

Wilhelm and Torben had become so familiar with each other that they could speak "fuck you" with their eyes, and their eyes were quite the talkers. They used two spades, no longer than eighteen inches, that required both to kneel to reach the ground. The hole was barely six inches deep when a stream of urine filled the hole and splattered them. It cascaded down both their arms. They fell over backward, the remaining urine spraying off their boots. Captain Sokolov smiled, a cigarette dangling from his lips. He had his right hand wrapped around his dick and shook off what piss he had left.

"I thought if it was wet, it would make it easier to dig," Captain Sokolov sneered.

Wilhelm had visions of clobbering Sokolov in the head with the spade, but if he had any hopes of ever seeing Hannah again or anything at all, he needed to refrain. He bit down on the inside of his lip hard enough to taste blood. He didn't need to see Torben's eyes to know he had the same reaction. Captain Sokolov stood over them with his dick in his hand, daring one of them to react. Wilhelm could tell by Torben's face he was contemplating to drive the spade across Sokolov's pathetic *schwanz* and cleave it off. When neither did, Sokolov shook himself off, zipped his pants, and left.

"If a bomb could drop right down his fucking throat…" Torben began.

"It would have to go up his ass first," Wilhelm interrupted.

Both grabbed handfuls of dirt and wiped their arms and then continued to dig deeper. Soldiers were in line before they even finished. It came as no surprise Wilhelm and Torben had latrine duty every day, and each day, Captain Sokolov pulled the same disgusting gag. He was like a child who had fallen in love with a joke and told it over and over, except the joke had never been funny. Each night, Torben and Wilhelm exchanged inhumane ways of killing Sokolov—none of which would have done well to dissuade the Allies they were not Nazis. The longer it went on, the more inhumane the deaths became. Torben was especially creatively cruel. Wilhelm's favorite included paying for the airfare to fly Sokolov to Australia and have him feasted upon by a pack of dingos and applying a generous amount of honey onto Sokolov's pants and tying him to a tree and letting a grizzly bear seek out the sweet, golden, thick liquid.

Every German smelt like death and would need at least half a dozen showers before the smell would go away. Women would gag if they got within a block of them and would probably cry and spew vomit if they got within earshot. Wilhelm imagined every flower in the "Rote Blumen" wilting the moment he stepped through the doors. But he and Torben smelt worse than any of the others. It was because the royal prick Sokolov pissed on them every night. Some nights, it was more than a splatter. He urinated on them directly. Their shirts were far from the pure white they once were. They were covered with grease, dirt, blood, sweat and, now, thanks to Captain Asshole, they were stained with his dehydrated, disgusting, dark yellow piss.

That night, they used the small, almost useless, spades when another guard moved toward them. Wilhelm and Torben braced to get urinated on. Captain Sokolov had finished what seemed like the thousandth time, and Wilhelm couldn't possibly believe even the

Soviets still found it funny. If there was any positive to be had, it was the fact that, apart from a cup of coffee in the morning and night and the occasional swig from his flask, Captain Sokolov hardly drank. If he had seen to drink as much water as was available to him, Wilhelm and Torben might have drowned in urine.

"Here," the guard said, holding a water canteen by the side of his leg. Wilhelm took the canteen. The contents of it must have been urine. It had been a gag no German had fallen for in weeks, and there were usually signs of suppressed giggling or smirking. But the soldier appeared without any. Wilhelm sniffed it. Nothing triggered any warning signs. He brought it to his mouth and took a sip. The water was lukewarm, but it was enough to satisfy his dry mouth. He passed the canteen to Torben, and he took a drink that between the two of them left the guard with hardly anything left. He took the canteen and walked away. Neither had ever seen the guard before. He would have surely faced reprimand if Captain Sokolov had seen it. He had committed a random act of kindness.

In one moment, Wilhelm had learned one of the most valuable lessons of the war. Wilhelm did not want the Germans as a whole to be reduced to the Nazi ideology and to five prominent figures of Hitler, Goebbels, Eichmann, Heydrich, and Göring, and Wilhelm could not reduce the Soviets to Captain Sokolov or even Stalin himself who had committed multiple purges of his military and whose labor camps led to the deaths of hundreds of thousands if not millions. Alexander, Old Uncle Joe, and the unknown guard had shown kindness, whether absolute or fleeting.

After nearly two months and forty-seven dead, they arrived at the destination. The great Russian city of Moscow was less than nine kilometers away. Their new camp would not lead to any factory jobs. Instead, they would farm the land to help feed a starving nation. The hours were much longer than the factory ones had been—sun up to sun down.

Wilhelm considered himself blessed when the first snow fell and blanketed the fields. There were still tasks needed to be done—feeding the cows, pigs, and goats—but the sun rose later and fell earlier than the spring and summer months. Besides seeing Hannah dance under the falling snow, he had never cared for winter, but it had become his favorite season. He and Torben would milk the cows and drink some of the milk before bringing it to the farmer. They were lucky the guard who watched them found the barn too foul and would elect to stand outside. It may not seem like much, but to get extra calories whenever possible sometimes made the difference between life and death.

The holiday season came and went without Wilhelm even knowing it. Winter increased colds and flu, but the holidays brought an epidemic of homesickness. It was not until early February when Wilhelm found out what the date was. Wilhelm and the other Germans were brought out of the barracks and forced to stand and wait for Captain Sokolov. It was frigid, and they were hardly dressed for it. They had been given the most crudely sewn sweaters to wear, and each had a variance of holes. Torben called some of them Swiss cheese sweaters.

The same rules applied as in Stalingrad. Any soldier who died was fair game to be stripped of anything valuable. Neither Wilhelm nor Torben were proud of it but some nights, they kept each other awake. When it appeared all had fallen asleep, they crept about the bunks, checking to see if any had died. It was how they both received their second sweaters, another pair of socks, and a pack of smokes. The socks were almost more important than the sweater. It was impossible to keep feet dry, and wet feet led to fungus and disease—something called trench foot. They kept a dry pair in their pockets, and when the pair they wore became soaked, they switched, wrung out the wet pair, and placed them in their pockets, hoping the friction against their legs and body heat would eventually dry them.

"Going to just let us fucking freeze out here," Torben whispered.

They had been standing outside in the freezing cold for over twenty minutes. Wilhelm had considered himself lucky. He was in the middle and sandwiched between two men. It was the body heat he was after, and every soldier was closer to the man beside them than they might care for.

Captain Sokolov walked forward with a thick jacket covering his body, a fur Ushanka hat on his head, and the love of his life between his lips. Torben had devised a plan of ransom that involved not stealing but "kidnapping" Sokolov's cigarette supplies. He was willing to believe in exchange for the cigarettes, he would grant him and Wilhelm their release.

"How long is that cigarette?" one man remarked.

It defied logic. But the red ember at the end of his cigarette died off as it fell to the ground and was squished by a fellow officer. That lazy asshole couldn't even step out his own light. Sokolov stepped forward and took a deep breath. His tar-covered black lungs had probably taken in less than five percent of the oxygen.

"The Soviet Union continues to drive back the German army. While tucking their tails between their legs, they left behind something horrible. In Southern Poland, a camp of Jewish prisoners was liberated. These were death camps where Jews were sent to be gassed to death. I am told there may not be a single European Jew alive today. I want you to reflect on what you fought for and what your people did," Captain Sokolov said.

As he walked away, lighting another cigarette, and disappeared, a hundred conversations broke out.

"What is this bullshit he's talking about?" Torben asked but knew Wilhelm couldn't possibly have the answer.

"I don't know," Wilhelm said.

Hopefully, it was another ploy of Captain Sokolov—a way to kill any morale or pride left. But he had spoken grimly, and his usual sly smile was absent. Had Germany committed such an atrocity?

"They can't do that," Torben said.

But they had instituted innumerable policies as a part of the Nuremberg Laws. Wilhelm knew first-hand the law's impact on Jewish people and Hannah's deep fear of "relocation." He had seen the shops vandalized on, what history called, the Night of Broken Glass. Hitler had never lied once about what his intentions were for the Jewish people. He may not have openly said he would gas them and wipe them from the Earth, but he did say they were to blame for a great deal and had no place in Germany or Europe.

"Hannah is Jewish," Wilhelm said.

Torben had been the one wanting assurance, but he sensed it was his turn to do the same for Wilhelm. Wilhelm had told Torben about Hannah, not her Jewish heritage but everything else ten thousand times. It was likely every German in the camp had heard of Hannah, but he kept her secret his secret. He waited to see how Torben would react.

"This can't be true, Wilhelm. They can't get away with killing thousands of people," Torben reasoned.

He completely breezed over acknowledging the importance of what Wilhelm had said. Wilhelm was unclear if Torben had never cared or if he felt too betrayed to care. But he was horrified at what they had been told, and even if the doubt of his words showed in his eyes, Wilhelm appreciated the gesture. But there was nothing Torben could say to make him feel better. He spent the better part of the night staring blankly at the ceiling inside the barracks. Only one question went through his mind—a question more complex and thought-provoking than how the universe was created—what was Hannah's fate? And from that stemmed infinite questions. What had happened to her? Where was she? Who was she with? Was she safe? But all the questions brought him back to the question that had started it all—what had been Hannah's fate? If she was alive, his desire to live would stay resolute. But if she was dead, he wanted to know. He wanted to know if he could give up and die—end the slave labor, the marches, being urinated on, end the constant state of hunger, thirst, and sheer exhaustion he was in. Torben tried without success to keep Wilhelm's spirits up. But Wilhelm was a ghost who was neither connected to the present world nor the life that came after. Wilhelm did not even care when Captain Sokolov pulled his classic prank the next night, and for the first time, Captain Sokolov got no joy from doing it. Like some bullies, if there was no response, the game was no longer fun.

As the early months of 1945 passed, it had become clear Germany would lose the war. The great Battle of the Bulge launched by the Germans in the forested Ardennes had been their last major offensive. The Americans and British had defeated them after Germany had gained the upper hand. The melting snows and warmer temperatures meant more hours were required on the farms. The Germans hated the brutally cold winters, but spring brought its own issues. The daily work had increased three hours, but to Wilhelm, it eliminated tormenting thoughts for another three hours of his day.

Torben and Wilhelm shared a unique bond. Wilhelm had been the optimist from his time of arriving at the camp until February of 1945 when he found out about the concentration camp. Afterward, Torben took over the reins and became the positive beacon. He talked of Francesca and his parents and detailed down to the meal of what his first day back in Würzburg would be like. His persistence paid off. The tide switched back in Wilhelm's favor. He allowed himself to think about the future and took Torben's offer of attending his wedding and being a groomsman. Instead of thinking of themselves as prisoners, they thought of themselves as work colleagues who lived together. They planned a trip to Rome. Torben knew all the secret, less-crowded but better-tasting restaurants. They planned trips to Paris, Egypt, New York—anywhere but Russia.

After supper one night, Captain Sokolov ordered the Germans to stand and wait for an announcement. He stood in silence as he finished his cigarette. Even if the weighted stares of three hundred German prisoners were noticed, he did not show it. He finished his puff and let out a cloud of smoke.

"Prisoners, it is my duty to inform you that your Führer, Adolf Hitler, is dead—dead at his own hands. He put a pistol to his head as he cowered in his bunker. The Soviet Union in their might have invaded the city of Berlin, and the Americans are closing in. This war will be over in days. I consider it my duty to keep you informed of your country's actions. You have my word that when I receive news the war has ended, you will be made aware. That is all," Captain Sokolov announced.

No German cried out with joy, but if they felt anything similar to Wilhelm, they were screaming internally with relief. Torben put a hand on Wilhelm's shoulder to signal he too felt the same unspeakable relief. The end of the war meant the Soviet Union would have no reason to keep soldiers. Wilhelm could not find fault in their reasoning for keeping them while the fighting continued. But every soldier had family throughout Germany. They knew what damage bombing could do, and even if civilians were not the target, it was impossible for there not to be casualties. If the Soviets were in Berlin, they would not bomb the city with their own troops in it.

The following morning and the one after, the German prisoners expected Sokolov to inform them the war was over. But it wasn't until 7 May that Hitler's successor, Karl Dönitz, surrendered. But Stalin wanted the Germans to surrender in their own capital city of Berlin, and Soviet Marshal Georgy Zhukov oversaw as Field-Marshal Keitel signed a ratified surrender. The European theatre of war drew its curtains to a close. Wilhelm's time as a soldier and prisoner was over.

"Form lines. Those who step out of line will be shot. Those who ask questions will be shot twice," Captain Sokolov commanded.

It appeared Captain Sokolov was upset his reign was at an end and hoped he would be able to shoot one more German. Wilhelm and Torben did nothing to give Sokolov an excuse and literally slouched to appear shorter.

As they marched, it was clear it was not just the prisoners in Wilhelm's camp but also dozens of other camps near Moscow. They were herded like sheep toward the Red Square. The famed Saint Basil's Cathedral looked like ice-cream cones on the beautiful spring day. Lenin's mausoleum was one of the most revered buildings in all of the Soviet Union. The red, castle-like building was the State Historical Museum. It was a city like so many in Europe, rich with history, but Wilhelm would not stay to explore it.

Thousands of people cheered on the streets. Soviet flags waved proudly, and posters of Stalin were held high. But the deafening cheers turned to boos when the Germans marched through the square. Wilhelm had heard booing at sporting events, but it was nothing compared to the hate that radiated from the crowd. These were people who had lost nearly everything and everyone. Millions of Soviets had died in the fighting, and there was not one person in the crowd who had not lost a loved one. It was an awful feeling, seeing the glaring faces of someone who hated you unequivocally without ever having met you. The hate ascended to the high command. Josef Stalin looked down from Lenin's mausoleum.

"They have so much hatred," Torben said.

"Can you blame them?" Wilhelm asked.

Torben shook his head. No one could.

"It is a small price to pay for going home in one piece," Wilhelm said.

Torben agreed wholeheartedly. It was nothing short of a miracle that he, Wilhelm, and the thousands of German soldiers had not been killed. It was even rarer for neither to have had lost a limb. Wilhelm had been injured several times, yet he was beyond grateful he had both his hands, both legs, and he could walk, run, jump, write, play music, dance, and so much more. He would be able to go home in one piece—physically at least. The horrors of war were something that never truly went away. They would be like achy bones that were worse on cold mornings. There would be nothing to alleviate them. But returning to a normal life and to Hannah would be the best remedy.

When the Soviet national anthem played, both the Soviet soldiers and the civilians turned their attention to the red flag with a yellow sickle and hammer and chanted the words. The Germans stopped their marching. The Soviets would have taken great offense if they had not. Wilhelm was confident he could speak for the thousands of other Germans in saying they did not want to do anything to anger the Soviets further. If someone would have sneezed in the middle of the national anthem, they would have been strung up by their neck and hanged.

After the Soviet parade of victory and the march of German defeat, Wilhelm and the Germans marched back to their camp. After getting a bowl of soup that was mostly water with a few bits of vegetables, Captain Sokolov demanded the Germans stand at attention once more. It was the moment Wilhelm and the others had been waiting for—the moment Wilhelm had waited for since his fingers slipped from Hannah's on Christmas 1939. That was nearly six years ago—65 months, 1,964 days, 47,136 hours, 2,829,466 minutes. But no matter how precise the time was, it all added up to an eternity and a lifetime ago.

"The war is over, and there is no longer a need for this camp," Captain Sokolov said.

It was too much for some to contain. Smiles spread. Tears fell. Hopefully, Captain Sokolov had not seen the smiles or the number of casualties of the war would increase. A feeling of euphoria spread over Wilhelm. A weightlessness took hold—the sort of invisible feeling he experienced when he kissed Hannah.

There was not a single German who would not have preferred to have been captured by the English or Americans. Not only did they not have the same sort of animosity and thirst for revenge as the Soviets but, more importantly, they had signed the Geneva Convention. But it was over. None of that mattered now. Wilhelm had wasted five years of his life—the best years of his life. But Wilhelm was still only twenty-five years old. When he left, and when he found Hannah ... *when* he found Hannah ... she had to be alive. The gray, gloomy clouds that covered his thoughts parted, and the rain stopped. The bright sun was about to burst through the thin-veiled clouds and cast an expansive light upon the world for the first time in over five years.

When he found Hannah, they would have a few years of catching up to do before starting their family. They would spend their Saturday and Sunday mornings with Hannah painting or drawing while Wilhelm would play the guitar. He would have to learn it again, and he hoped his fingers would start playing the chords they used to. They would travel anywhere and everywhere. He didn't care if they didn't have money for it. They would each carry a pack filled with food and supplies and travel the countryside. He would take her to Austria and to the lake that had been the muse for her favorite painting. He would take her to Paris so they could dine on pastries during the morning, view the art museums during the day, and dance the nights away. He would take her to New York, perhaps on their anniversary on 30 June. He would take her to see one of the American movies at the cinema. They would order popcorn and Coca-Colas. But why stop at New York? There was so much to see in America. They could go to Chicago and see the home of the famed mafia leader Al Capone. They could head north to Milwaukee for a taste of home in the form of a dark German beer and bratwurst. From there, they would travel west to the city of stars and see the famous Humphrey Bogart and Katharine Hepburn.

There would be so much catching up to do with Heinrich and Erich and his father too. Even with the two being able to go a week speaking six words, converting that to years meant they had acquired enough words for a conversation. He would invite Torben too. He had become as close a friend as Heinrich or Erich and, in ways, more. There was no brotherhood like the one of soldiers. Men who fought together had a commonality no amount of time could create with someone else and, concurrently, no amount of time could take away.

It was an impressive feat that Wilhelm, mere moments ago, had no plans that extended beyond a day, but now had the next five years of his life mapped out in seconds. Wilhelm even gained a level of acceptance for the way Sokolov had been. May he have a joyous life in the Soviet Union and may Wilhelm never have to see him again. He had no plans on sleeping the night in the camp. He would leave as soon as the gates opened.

"We're going home," Torben said, smiling wider and brighter than at any point Wilhelm had known him.

"We're going home," Wilhelm repeated.

He and Torben hugged. Soldiers all around them celebrated, prayed, hugged, and almost danced. But a gunshot stopped all of it.

"I am not done speaking!" Captain Sokolov yelled.

Smoke wafted out of his pistol that pointed down at his side. Wilhelm considered it a poor shot on Sokolov's part, as it seemed unlikely he would pass up the opportunity to shoot a German. Torben and Wilhelm exchanged looks. The war was over. He couldn't kill anymore. But that didn't mean anyone was willing to test that theory, and the Germans fell silent immediately and faced Sokolov.

"Though the war is over, its effects are not. Hundreds of cities have been destroyed. Thousands are homeless, and millions are starving. There is much work to be done. Each of you is responsible for this. You are required to help rebuild what you have destroyed," Captain Sokolov said.

Wilhelm was back in that plane, trying to escape over the Battle of Stalingrad. He had soared higher and higher only to be shot down. The same had happened again. He just wasn't seated in the cockpit. He crashed and burned without ever leaving the ground.

The Germans had somewhat been able to hide their joyous stupor, but disappointment was much harder to mask. Whether it was shoulders slouching or mouths falling open to audible gasps or downright sobs, each was devastated. Wilhelm had helped build the Reich Chancellery building, and it had taken months to finish one building. He had seen Stalingrad. The entire city was a wasteland of stone and steel. It would take years, not months, to repair the one city. The Soviet Union was a massive area that stretched from Eastern Europe to the Pacific. To repair every last city would take decades.

Wilhelm looked over to Torben. A tear trickled down his dirt-covered face. He knew too. He knew he would never get to marry Francesca on the shores of the Mediterranean. He would never eat his mother's cooking again. All the trips he and Wilhelm had planned would never happen.

Wilhelm had always doubted if he would make it home. He had tried to remain optimistic he would see Hannah again. But now, he fully realized he would never be allowed to leave. He would never return to Germany. He would never return to Hannah.

New York

Hannah had fallen in love with the city of New York. It was easy to blend in with a city of millions of people from different countries, races, and creed. There was a place for everyone in New York and in America, Hannah included, and she had no problem finding work.

She found a job at a manufacturing plant in New Jersey. Agent Dunn had acquired a small apartment in Midtown for her. It was three blocks from Times Square. Even though she was in a city of millions, her apartment was considerably lonely. To counter that, she would walk around Times Square. When she had traveled all of lower Manhattan, she went further until she had traveled all five boroughs.

As the months of summer of 1944 drifted away and autumn swept through the streets of New York, Hannah enjoyed walking through Central Park. It slightly reminded her of the Tiergarten in Germany and the walks she and Wilhelm took. The resemblance was never stronger than during autumn when the crimson and gold leaves fell, covering the walking paths.

When news broke the Americans had defeated the Germans in the Battle of the Bulge on 25 January 1945, she allowed herself to get excited over the possibility of the war ending.

As the winter ended and the flowers bloomed in spring, reports came in that Germany, although standing, was poised for a knockout blow. When she found out Hitler had died on 30 April, she didn't feel the peace she had hoped. He had cheated the true justice he had coming to him. She wanted him to face the wrath of the Allies and see him hanged. She was not raised to desire such a thing, and it was not a Jewish belief nor of any civilized religion. God would unleash his own judgment against him and the other Nazi High Command. Yet, a part of her found it hard to believe he had taken his own life. He had preached of a thousand-year Reich and, though it was impossible for him to see it to the end of that reign, she could not imagine him giving it up so easily.

It was Tuesday, 8 May, when news broke that the war in Europe was over. When Hannah crossed the Hudson River, excited New Yorkers shouted it from block to block. As she made her way toward Times Square, it appeared all of New York City was packed into it. People screamed in jubilation, drank in celebration or gave thanks in prayer. The ships in the surrounding harbors let their sirens wail, and the streets were covered in a snowfall of paper flakes. Hannah had never seen so many people in the same high spirits as that day, nor had she seen such a collection of different people all get along. Bottles of alcohol were passed around. People kissed, and Hannah herself was kissed on the cheek, forehead, and lips by at least a dozen soldiers. She could only laugh and smile.

The party that ensued went on well past dawn, and Hannah did not make it back to her apartment until 5:20 that morning. It was not something she liked to do, as it required her to sleep most of the day away to recover. It was also the first time she had gotten drunk since before Wilhelm had left, though there had been many close calls at Josephine's kitchen table. The alcohol seemed so much worse and so much more potent than it had six years earlier. She had always awoken with a slight pounding headache from nights of drinking with what she considered slight waves in her stomach. But what greeted her when she woke up at half past noon was a sledgehammer banging against her skull. Her stomach sent waves high enough to capsize ships, and her dizziness made her second-guess if her eyesight had suddenly gone horribly awry. The hangover did not go away that day. It was an annoying houseguest that invited itself in and sat on the couch.

Hannah checked in with Agent Dunn a few weeks later and disclosed she wanted to go to school for nursing. He took it upon himself to make a few phone calls, and a week later, Hannah found out she had been accepted to New York University. She had experience in treating combat soldiers, and those who had made it home and required further medical attention were transferred to one of New York's many hospitals. Most had been from the European theatre of war, and Hannah volunteered to help. The experience of D-Day was worth more than four years of classes. You could not read in a book the horrors sight, scent, sounds, and touch could bring. After proving her worth, she quit her factory job and accepted a part-time position for the month of June.

Hannah asked Agent Dunn when it would be safe to travel back to Berlin, but he warned her the city was in ruins, and it would take months for it to be cleaned up. The war in Japan neared its end, and America contemplated any means necessary to end it.

On 6 August, Hannah was checking the morphine drips when the new American president Harry S. Truman's voice came through the radio.

"Sixteen hours ago, an American airplane dropped one bomb on Hiroshima, an important Japanese Army base. That bomb had more power than 20,000 tons of T.N.T," Truman said.

The room was almost always quiet, but at that moment, it was as quiet as space with only the faint drip of the morphine somehow amplified in the silence.

"We are now prepared to obliterate more rapidly and completely every productive enterprise the Japanese have above the ground in any city. We shall destroy their docks, their factories, and their communications. Let there be no mistake, we shall completely destroy Japan's power to make war," Truman continued.

"It's the atomic bomb," a soldier said.

Hannah was at the foot of his bed, checking his chart.

"What is that?" she asked.

"The end of the world," the soldier said and then turned his head from her.

When Hannah read the New York Times the next morning, the soldier's words proved true. She shuddered after finding out the Nazis had been after that very technology. Though she preferred the Americans winning the race, it was a technology not worthy of any man or group of men. It was a power only God should have. 60,000-80,000 people were estimated to have been killed instantly while thousands more had died of wounds and, later, radiation. Yet, for some unknown reason, Japan refused to surrender. Truman's warning was not an idle threat.

Three days later, on 9 August 1945, the second atomic bomb was dropped on the city of Nagasaki, and on 15 August, Japan made it known their intention to surrender. On 2 September, aboard the USS Missouri, the namesake ship of President Truman's home state, the Japanese signed their surrender in Tokyo Bay. The greatest event in the history of mankind was over.

Hannah called Agent Dunn every week, asking when she could return to Germany, and every week, his answer was the same. He had transferred her to Agent Clarkson within the Office of Strategic Services (the precursor to the Central Intelligence Agency). Hannah had never met Agent Clarkson. He was stationed in Washington, but he had voiced his concern about a strong worry that the Nazi Party was not extinct but dormant. They believed they had a large trove of chemical weapons that could be unleashed in the city. Though he did say the choice was Hannah's, he strongly suggested she stay in New York until the situation improved. Hannah's heart told her to go. There were so many people she wanted to see again—Wilhelm most of all. But she needed to be smart. She had not seen Wilhelm in nearly six years. The two could wait a little while longer. But so often, throughout the war, her optimism had been poorly founded. What if they couldn't wait a little longer?

The horrors of the Holocaust had been printed on the front page of the newspapers in advance of the Nuremberg Trials, a prosecution of prominent members of the Nazi Party that extended to not only military leaders but political and economic leaders as well in November of 1945. The country of Germany was no longer a singular unified nation but divided into four sectors as well as the city of Berlin. The northwest was under British rule, the southwest under French, the southeast under American, and the northeast under Soviet. The Germany Hannah had grown up in had changed drastically when she was a young girl, and it had now transformed again. The Allies, the Soviets most of all, had punished the German people for the crimes of such a small few. She could only hope the true people responsible, those who had not committed suicide, were brought to justice.

She looked through each morning's paper for updates on the lengthy trial. But like her return to Germany, it took much longer than she had wanted. Finally, in 1946, the trial ended with the death sentencing executions of ten prominent members, which was carried out on 16 October 1946. Herman Göring, commander of the Luftwaffe and member of Hitler's inner circle, had been sentenced, but he committed suicide in his prison cell. Most had requested death by a firing squad, a military execution, but the motion had been denied.

Instead, they were hanged. Their crimes were not military but crimes against humanity itself. Hangings took from fourteen minutes to twenty-eight minutes before death finally came—something that only reiterated her belief in God. She called both Agent Dunn and Agent Clarkson to the point of annoyance. She asked if there was anything either of them could do to track down Wilhelm. When both said it was beyond what they could do, Hannah let her heart win and, on 23 November 1947, boarded a plane to fly back across the Atlantic to Germany.

As the plane descended, the ruined heap Berlin had become took shape. Though the city had been under the rule of monsters and demons, it was her home. There were so many places she had gone and seen that were now heaps of rubble. Her first stop was the apartment she and Wilhelm had shared. But the building had been destroyed. She had a small hope that she would walk up the steps, knock on the door, and be greeted by Wilhelm. But if he was not going to be there, she would prefer the apartment to be rubble than walk into an empty apartment or an apartment occupied by someone else. It would either be an eerie graveyard covered in a foggy mist or it would have felt like their apartment was cheating on her by allowing new people to live in it and Hannah walking in during the act.

The next place she would go to would cause absolute devastation. She remembered the way perfectly. No amount of time could take that away from her. She came to her parents' shop and her home above. The windows had been boarded up. The walk to it had been like the receding waters before a tsunami. Instead of turning away and heading for safety, Hannah followed the receding water and, now, the tsunami of emotion and pain washed over her. She put her hand on the doorknob and turned it and, like a conductor, it sent an electrical shock of memories through her.

The door swung open, and Hannah was met with the stench of mildew. Cobwebs covered every corner, and the floor was covered in dust and debris. The once vibrant gold paint had now lost its luster. The shop was nothing like she had remembered or wanted to remember. Every tux her father had sold, every coat her mother had sewn had been in that room. The black dividing curtain still hung, and Hannah pushed it aside and ascended the steps. Each step she took caused her heart to beat faster. It knew the pain it would be forced to feel and did everything it could to stop her. As she reached the top, every last thing her family had owned was gone—the couches and beds, the nightstands and kitchen table, the photographs on the wall, and the dishes in the cupboards—all of it was gone. All the zest and love the home once had was gone too. Even the smell of her home was gone. But she could feel her parents there more than she had over the last few years. Even still, she wished she had never come. Visual memories were the most dominant memories a person had and, in some way, she had destroyed them. If her home had been a person, she would now see flashes of their corpse and not their life.

"I miss you. I love you more than I can put into words. I think of you all the time." Her voice choked with emotion.

Somehow, saying it aloud helped, yet made it so much more poignant. Her vision blurred from the thick, salty tears, and her chest heaved. She had to hold onto the banister to stop herself from falling down the steps. She wanted to sprint but, instead, could only lumber through the deep snow and blowing winds. But, with each step, her heart steadied its beating.

The Americans had set up a center to help German families discover what had happened to their beloved sons, brothers, and husbands. Though it was seldom they were able to help and, most times, they could only offer encouragement, Hannah persevered and stood in line for over an hour.

"Name you're looking for?" the American soldier asked in German.

"I am looking for Schreiber, Wilhelm, please," Hannah said in English.

She hoped English would give her words more meaning and make the American soldier understand Wilhelm was not just a name but so much more.

"One second, please," the soldier said, disappearing into a group of a dozen other soldiers looking through names in the files.

The place was set up under a large, army green canopy, and most of the files had been taken off German dog tags from soldiers killed during battles with America. They had taken the dog tag information and created an alphabetical list of names.

The soldier returned less than three minutes later and shook his head. "I am sorry, Ma'am. We have nothing on him. Do you know where he was fighting?"

Hannah could only shake her head. She knew nothing he had been through or had done since he left that fateful Christmas day eight years earlier.

"Could you look up two other names for me, please?" Hannah asked.

The soldier looked at the long line but nodded.

"Heinrich Hess and Erich Brinkerhoff," Hannah said.

The soldier went back and looked through the massive stacks of paper. Each name on that list would cause heartbreak for whoever asked for it. The soldier returned with a clipboard in his hand.

"Heinrich Hess was taken as a prisoner in 1944 in Normandy, France. He was sent to the States and held there," the soldier said.

Heinrich had been on the same beaches hours before Hannah had been. He had seen the horrors of the beachheads. But her good friend was alive.

"And Erich Brinkerhoff?" she asked.

"Unteroffizier Brinkerhoff was killed during the Battle of the Bulge. Sometime late 1944 or early 1945," the soldier informed.

From the way the soldier had said it, it was clear he did not care. Erich was a member of the SS, and they were unanimously hated by the Allies. But Erich had sought the position as a way to gain favor with Lena's father. He was a good man with a kind heart and an intoxicating laugh—intoxicating. That's exactly what had happened to him. He had been poisoned with ideals.

Hannah thanked the soldier and stepped aside to allow the next person in line to step forward.

Hannah had not spoken to Lena since she had saved her life, but the friendship the two had shared was something Hannah wanted to revive. Perhaps, Lena now saw the error in her opinions. But more importantly, Lena had lost the love of her life, and Hannah wanted to be there for her. So, she hailed a cab and spent the entire car ride to the Hauser residence wondering how Lena would react to seeing her. But as they drew closer, a question came to her that caused her stomach to flip. What if Jakob Hauser was alive? No sooner had the worry set in, the guilt for hoping Lena's father had died in the war had taken over. But she certainly did not want to walk inside and be the last Jew to die by Nazi hands.

The taxi pulled alongside the house. It was barely recognizable. The Nazi flag that had once waved proudly in front of it was gone, as was the flagpole itself. The house was unkempt, and the large lawn that once was covered in thick, luscious green grass was now dirt with craters from small explosions. Ida Hauser would never have allowed the house, or the landscape, to fall from such grace. She suspected that if Jakob Hauser had survived the war, he would have been imprisoned for his crimes, but the fear was still there. Hannah knocked three times and waited. When the door opened, Hannah was brought back to all the times Ida Hauser, wearing a white apron, had greeted her and Wilhelm. But it was not Ida Hauser, nor was it Lena, who greeted her.

"Can I help you?" a man asked.

"I am looking for the Hausers. Do they not live here anymore?" Hannah asked.

"Who are you?" the man asked, only opening the door wide enough for his head to poke through.

He looked to be in his fifties—unshaven, hair disheveled, and without a shower for days. Hannah was uncertain if she had ever seen him before. So much time had passed and the man was so unkempt that it was hard to tell what he would have looked like with a shower, clean shave, and a fresh haircut.

"My name is Hannah. I am a friend of Lena. I was hoping to see her."

"Come inside," the man said, opening the door wider.

But the man was a stranger in a house she once knew and, in some ways, he was even more of a threat to Hannah than if Jakob Hauser had answered the door. The devil you knew was better than the devil you did not.

"Who are you?" Hannah asked.

"I am Herman Janke. Ida's brother," the man said.

The man could have been lying, but Hannah stepped in and stayed close to the door. She was able to see into the living room where she, Wilhelm, Erich, Lena, Heinrich, and one of his many dates had sat in front of roaring fires during the cold winter months. It was hard to believe it had been almost a decade since she had stepped foot inside. Herman Janke had kept up the interior of the house as well as he had himself. Ida had always worked tirelessly to make sure the house was the cause of envy for all of Jakob's friends and those who were simply invited to exploit a potential gain. But the wooden floor that had always looked polished and mirror-like in its reflectiveness was now covered in a layer of dust, and the chimney would have embarrassed Ida. The inside was nothing but black soot, some of which had blown onto the floor when Herman had left the front door open too long on gusty days.

The Hauser house had always smelt like a pie was in the oven because, often, there was. The living room had smelt like smoke from the fireplace, not subtle but not overwhelming either. Some of the rooms smelt of lemon and citrus and the card room, like cigarettes. But now, the house had lost its smell. No pies had been baked, and the chimney smoke was overpowering. But she did not have to go into the card room to know the thick fog of smoke was still there.

"Did something happen?" Hannah asked.

Herman had been watching Hannah's eyes as they took in the house and the change in her demeanor. It was enough for him to answer.

"Jakob and my sister committed suicide days before the Soviets entered the city. They did not want to face the repercussions for what Jakob was involved with," Herman said.

Hannah knew "involved with" meant the genocide of Jews, Gypsies, homosexuals, and other "undesirables."

"I am sorry to hear. Your sister was always kind to me," Hannah said. But she was less sorry than what she had said. In truth, Jakob Hauser had gotten the fate he deserved if he was involved with orchestrating the deaths of millions. Though Ida certainly wasn't involved, she stood behind her husband.

"The whole thing is a fucking mess. Sorry for my language," Herman said.

Hannah found people who swore to be more honest. It meant they did not filter what they said and were generally more impulsive. Her parents had always told her to think before she spoke, but as she grew older, she realized that, sometimes, that wasn't always good. If you had to "choose your words," you weren't being honest.

"What about Lena?" Hannah asked.

"Her parents had encouraged her to end her life too. Her husband had been killed. But she had just had a baby boy. She would face whatever came. The Soviets stormed in with their tanks and troops and considered everything in Berlin to be their property. She didn't tell me, but I know they had a go at her—on more than one occasion. They shaved her head and put a swastika on her forehead with bright red lipstick. She wasn't allowed to wash it off. She held on for as long as she was able. I was too late. She ended it—for herself and her son."

Lena had not deserved the fate she had received. Hannah often wondered how grand and great life had been for Lena during the early part of the decade. She pictured endless parties and gatherings. Her family was rich and prominent. She loved Erich, and he loved her. It would have been easy for Hannah to have been jealous, and when she thought long on it, she had been. Hannah had faced horrors she would never forgive or forget, and so had Lena.

Lena had had to make the horrible choice of killing her child before taking her own life. Hannah could hardly fathom contemplating that let alone carrying it out. The time between killing her baby boy and killing herself was most likely a few seconds, but what anguishing bereavement she must have experienced, and for Lena, it certainly had lasted much longer than seconds.

Lena was far from being the only German woman to be raped by the Allies. Estimates—that God-awful, heartless word—conservatively figured around 100,000 women in Berlin alone. It was a horror Hannah had been spared from. Whether for love or lust, sex was a choice. It was a deeply intimate vulnerability, and she could not imagine the horror of having a strange man force himself upon her. Lena had saved Hannah's life and had been her best friend but, like so many others, she was now gone.

"Where is she buried?" Hannah asked.

"Out back," Herman answered.

He led her through the back of the house and to the patio door. As they passed through the living room, she looked up to the room where they had played cards on so many nights. For a quick moment, she thought she could hear laughter coming from it but knew the memory had become tangible in a way more like a dream than a memory. Herman opened the door, and Hannah stepped out into the snow-covered yard. But there was no tombstone, no monument.

"Where?" Hannah asked.

"I left it unmarked. I want them to stay at peace," Herman said.

It was an appalling thought that someone would dig up a dead woman. But Lena and her family were prominent Nazis, and there had been such a strong, but deserved, hatred for them since news of the Holocaust had broken. Herman, no doubt, had feared what would have been done to her body had he gone for a more traditional ceremony. Instead of being gathered by those who loved her, Lena had been buried by her uncle in secret.

"You were close?" Herman asked.

Hannah nodded. There was far too much to go into, and Hannah did not think she could say it without choking up. Somewhere inches in front of her and feet below was a woman Hannah had known and loved. It was the closest to closure Hannah was able to receive for those who she had lost. She had only seen Trugnowski shot down in front of the infamous black wall at Auschwitz. Eleanor, Josephine, and Radley had all been killed without Hannah seeing, and she only knew of her mother's passing from finding her coat at Kanada and had to assume her father had met the same fate.

She thanked Lena's uncle, and after a long caesura, she left. Berlin had beaten her heart with a club and left it in an alleyway to bleed out. But Hannah had experienced such a feeling before. She loved that city and the people who made it so special. But, now, they were all gone.

As she boarded a bus and headed south to Schönfeld, she found herself looking at the heaps of concrete and steel rubble. The buildings would be rebuilt, and one would never be able to tell the carnage once there. But to Hannah, Berlin was not a city of steel and concrete skyscrapers, building complexes, and homes. To Hannah, the city of Berlin had been like a rare China dish—a rare China dish the Nazis had taken and smashed into bits of porcelain. The dish could be put back together, but the cracks could never go away or be hidden. It would never be pristine again. The city no longer had the feeling of home she thought it would have when she returned. But her parents were the ones who had made it home. Even though she recognized there was not much of Germany that had been left untouched by war, she held out hope that Wilhelm's father was alive and well.

As the train took Hannah across the city ravaged by war and collapsed from conquest, she thought of how life seemed to be a revolving circle. Less than thirty years earlier, Europe was in the same state. However, Berlin was in a far worse shape than it had been at the end of the first war. Children stacked piles of bricks for fun, mothers showed both American and Soviet soldiers photographs of their sons, and women offered themselves to soldiers for packs of cigarettes and food rations. The opulent age of Berlin had died. But the damage was not exclusive to Berlin. The areas between cities were covered with craters, where heaps of earth had been blasted upward. Schönfeld had been one of the most beautifully simplistic cities Hannah had been to, but the cost of war had reached it too.

Hannah walked through the city and tried to remember where the "Rote Blumen" was. Her sense of direction was based on buildings and store signs, but so many of the buildings had been destroyed and store signs taken down due to closings. But walking gave her peace, and after meandering for an hour, mostly because of a decrease in courage, she found herself standing in front of the "Rote Blumen." It too had fallen prey to a devastated economy. Nobody had money to spend on flowers, given it was hard enough to acquire enough food to support a family.

425

The city moved with people but in such a different way. Before, it had been filled with busy people shuffling across streets filled with purpose and destination. Now, people wandered aimlessly like zombies. She left the closed, dark store and tried to ignore the pessimistic feeling growing in her stomach as she walked to Petyr's home. The house had not changed, and it was unclear if he had been extremely fortunate or if he had seen to repair any damages. Wilhelm had told her, and she knew from her time with him, Petyr was a meticulous man with several obsessive-compulsive disorders. He would not be able to allow damages to remain untreated.

She rang the doorbell and waited. Each second she waited only increased her worry and it was possible if she waited any further, she would puke. But the door opened.

"Hannah!" Petyr said as his eyes widened and mouth gaped open.

But after a moment of paralysis brought on by shock, he smiled. He seemed to have aged twenty years since the last time she had seen him. He coughed into his sleeve before opening the door fully and allowing Hannah to come inside.

"I am so glad you are okay," Hannah said, wrapping him in a hug.

"I was so worried about you. You left, and I didn't hear from you. I called your apartment every day. I even went to look," Petyr said.

It took nearly an hour to tell Petyr all she had been subjected to. The pain her words caused showed on Petyr's lined face. But she had not come for sympathy. She had come to find out about Wilhelm's fate.

"Petyr, have you heard from Wilhelm?" Hannah asked.

Her stomach was a rocky sea, and nerves flooded her bloodstream. The answer to all the questions and doubts over the last eight years would be answered over the course of the next few seconds.

"I haven't heard anything. One way or another. The last I heard he was on the eastern front," Petyr said.

Casualties were high on both the western and eastern fronts, but the eastern front had been the home of the war's bloodiest battle and highest casualties—the Battle of Stalingrad. It was not talked about in America the way it should have been. It was the true turning point in the war.

"I should have gone with you back to Berlin, Hannah. I am so sorry," Petyr said, his eyes pools of sorrow.

"You did not do this," Hannah said, taking his massive hands in hers.

"No, but Germans did," Petyr said.

"I am a German, Petyr. This was committed by some Germans, not all of Germany."

Perhaps, it was something Hannah would not have differentiated had she stayed in Germany. But every city, apart from Vienna, had had a strong hatred toward her because she was German. But she had known Germans who had been the antithesis of everything the Nazis stood for.

Petyr coughed again. It was much more violent than a common cough and seemed to originate somewhere deep inside his chest.

"Are you alright?" Hannah asked.

"Fine. Just a resilient cough," Petyr said. He rose from his couch and ensured his shirt was still tucked in and straight. "I have something to show you," he said.

Hannah followed him to Wilhelm's old bedroom. The door was shut. How long had it been since he had gone in? Petyr had always been an "out of sight, out of mind" type, and the events of the last several years made Hannah respect that way of coping.

He opened the door and for only a moment, after Hannah had taken a deep inhale, she thought Wilhelm was there. The smell gave her a temporary high as it brought an onslaught of memories and a sudden feeling of comfort. The room had looked exactly the same as the day she had left, and the manila folder was still against the lamp on the nightstand beside the bed.

"You forgot it when you left," Petyr said.

The sight of the manila envelope started an internal fight in Hannah. She couldn't decide if it had been a blessing or a curse. She knew what was inside the manila envelope would rip open unhealed scabs, and she would bleed all over again and, perhaps, fatally so.

"I'll give you some time," Petyr said.

He was not good with showing overwhelming amounts of emotion and was worse at being around it. As he descended the steps, Hannah could tell how far he was based on the volume of his cough.

She crept to the bed and sat, staring at the manila envelope, trying to prepare herself for what she would find. She slowly extended her hand for it and lifted the two metal clasps on the back. She reached inside, and her fingers pulled the glossy photographs out. She only saw the photograph for a moment before her eyes filled with tears. Her father and mother, wearing the coat Hannah had found in Kanada, smiled at Hannah from the photograph. Their love for each other and Hannah transcended the photograph and had become something palpable. Even the smell of the room had ripped the scabs open. It still smelt like Wilhelm. It had been the first thing to vanish from her memory. But it came swooping back to her in an instant. The next photograph was taken at Lena's cabin and showed Lena and Erich holding each other in the lake, the water below their hips. Heinrich pushed Wilhelm, and the woman next to Heinrich looked uncomfortable. Hannah had forgotten her name, and even that made her sad. But so much had happened and so much time passed that she could not recall even the letter the girl's name started with. The next photo was of her and Wilhelm dancing. Lena had taken it without their knowing until the flash went off. But it was one of Hannah's favorite photographs of the two of them. She loved the way the snow looked under the streetlight and the way she looked up into Wilhelm's eyes and the way his met hers.

There were a dozen photographs in all, and each was an unforgettable memory that brought back not only sights but also smells, tastes, and sounds. She could taste the wine from the photographs at Lena's home, hear their laughter as they frolicked in the lake at Lena's cabin, feel the coldness of winter in the photographs of her and Wilhelm standing under the streetlight with the snow dancing toward the ground, and she could smell the smoke wafting off the Hanukkah Menorah and the smell of the apple pie on the kitchen counter.

She slid her hand back into the manila folder, and at first, it found nothing but the sides. But then, it found something else. Hannah carefully grabbed it with her thumb and pointer finger. She knew what it was before she even saw it. She had spun it in her hand almost every night. It had brought her comfort and peace. The dried blue rose did not look any different than it had when she had last held it.

Hannah decorated the room with the photographs and placed the blue rose below the lamp and left the room and went to the kitchen. Petyr was boiling two potatoes and had a few vegetables cut up on the cutting board. He had grown his own vegetables, placing them in front of his windows so they could catch sunlight. The step-out porch outside his bedroom on the second floor had also been a garden, and it was too high for starving thieves to steal from it.

Both were quiet during dinner, and they rarely looked up from their plates.

"I am sorry about your shop," Hannah said.

The words broke the silence.

"There are worse things," Petyr said.

Even if that were true, Wilhelm had always said the flower shop had given his father the most joy. It reminded him of his late wife and being in the shop and working with flowers appeased his pain. Petyr was much more talkative than he had been any other time. He was hardly a people person and had kept mostly to himself over the years. They spent the meal talking about Hannah's degree in nursing and her life in New York City. Petyr only listened, only making a sound if he had to cough.

"Is it alright if I stay here?" Hannah asked as she washed the dishes and Petyr dried them.

"Certainly," Petyr said.

The following morning, Hannah went to the nearest Soviet headquarters and waited in line. Germans asked the Soviets for information about their missing men. Hannah had brought one of the photographs of Wilhelm, even though the likelihood of finding a Soviet who recognized him was slim. It would have to be by dog tags found or through prisoner-of-war reports. But the Soviets did not report their captured prisoners, nor did they take the time to catalog their dead enemy. Each person in line was shunned away, Hannah included. Hannah had briefly seen both the Soviet zone of occupation and the American, British, and French sections of Berlin. Even if all sections of the city were heaps of rubble, the Soviets had not made the same effort in helping out the people of Germany or rebuilding their destructed cities as their Allied counterparts.

Hannah returned to Petyr's, disappointed. Petyr had warned her as much. But Hannah started her mornings by trying again every day that week. Afterward, she helped clean, volunteered at the city's hospital, and returned to Petyr's for a game of chess. Petyr then tended to his plants while Hannah painted. She often closed her eyes to let flashes of the faces of Eleanor, Trugnowski, Radley, and Josephine fill them. She had not painted in so long and felt like she was dishonoring the fallen with her work. But each day, she improved, and the portraits gained greater detail. She asked and showed Wilhelm's picture to every young German man she saw, thinking perhaps somebody had served with him.

After two weeks at Petyr's, she successfully convinced him to reopen the "Rote Blumen." Even if they did not sell anything, Hannah knew Petyr had missed it. He showed her how to plant, water, and organize bouquets with themes that evoked loss, celebrations, and different seasons.

During that time, the British and American zones had become one and, soon, the French zone would join and would eventually form West Germany. It was clear the Americans and Soviets had radically different views on how to rebuild Germany. The Americans wanted to help rebuild their portion into a free market democracy. The Soviets, who had lost not only millions of lives but an unknowable amount of money, demanded the Germans produce for them.

Hannah's train rides into Berlin twice a week had shown her how different West Berlin was from East Berlin, and the gap grew with each trip. West Berlin was being rebuilt and the streets repaved while East Berlin had changed little since 1945.

Hannah did what she could in the hospital, but without medicines and supplies, there was almost nothing she could do. Each night, she looked through her photographs and spun the blue rose in her hand. The question of whether or not the manila envelope had been a blessing or a curse was more lopsided than Hannah could have imagined. She never thought leaving it behind had been one of the most fortunate moments of her life. Had she remembered to pack it into her luggage, it would have been taken by the Nazis when she had arrived at Auschwitz. Hannah found comfort in Wilhelm's old room, and when she cuddled with his pillow and closed her eyes, she could trick herself into thinking he was beside her. But for some reason, that night, she could not sleep a wink. She was attuned to every sound, and no matter how quiet Petyr tried to be, the opening of drawers and cabinets were amplified.

Hannah rose from her bed and went downstairs. Petyr was at the stove, preparing a cup of lemon tea.

"I'm sorry, did I wake you?" Petyr asked as he turned to pour the tea into a teacup.

"No. I could not sleep," Hannah said.

Petyr handed her the cup and reached for another one. He filled his and brought it to his lips without first blowing on it to cool it off. Hannah assumed he had taken to tea to help with his insatiable cough. The two sat in silence. Petyr's large hands completely covered his cup, his fingers tapping the glass. Hannah stirred her tea, and there appeared to be no end in sight as to when she would consider it properly stirred.

"What are you doing, Hannah?" Petyr asked.

"I guess I was deep in thought," Hannah said, setting the spoon down.

"No, I mean, what are you doing here?"

"I want to help out until Wilhelm comes home."

"Hannah, the war has been over for almost three years."

Hannah knew where his conversation was going, and she looked around the room for anything that could make him change the topic. She did not want to hear any of it.

"Hannah," Petyr said, gently placing his hand atop her much more petite one.

"They haven't declared him dead. I will not give up," Hannah said.

"War does not give gentle deaths. There are no family members gathered around to say goodbye. There is no documentation. The battlefields are riddled with thousands of dead. The armies need to be able to advance, so the bodies are tossed into a hole and covered," Petyr said.

Hannah did not want to picture Wilhelm being one of hundreds bulldozed into a hole. She had seen the horror of that at Auschwitz and Normandy. Petyr did not want to say more, but he was not getting through to Hannah.

"Hannah, Wilhelm is gone," Petyr said. His hands felt a rush of power before the strength left them, the tea in his cup washing from edge to edge.

"I can't believe that. I won't believe that," Hannah said, avoiding looking Petyr in the eye.

"Sometimes closure isn't something that can be achieved through knowing."

," Hannah said, shaking her head, refusing to believe.

"He loved you, Hannah. If he were alive, he would have come here."

"What if he did return to Berlin and I wasn't there and he is searching for me?" Hannah asked.

Petyr admired her resolve but did not encourage it. His trembling hand squeezed hers with surprising steadiness. "You have suffered enough, Hannah. Live your life. Go back to New York while you still can."

Hannah did her best to stop the tear in her eye from falling. But when Petyr had been unable to keep his hidden, her tears cascaded down her cheeks. Hannah could not remember how long the two of them had been sitting there, but when she finished her last sip of tea, it had gone cold.

Hannah gathered her things and kept the envelope next to her coat so there was no way she could forget it again. But there was something she had to do before leaving. She returned to the "Rote Blumen" and began the long, arduous process of dyeing a white rose blue. She cut the rose stem and set it in water and prepared the dye bath. She let the rose sit in the dye and returned to Petyr's. She wanted the same vibrant blue Wilhelm's rose had, and it would have to sit in the dye for much longer than the standard four hours. After dinner, she returned to begin the drying process. She let the rose hang upside down in the back of the shop and away from sunlight. She stayed another two weeks, and each morning, she continued to try and track down any information on Wilhelm's fate. But there was no information to be had, and with each failed attempt, she knew her time in Germany was coming to a close. When the drying process was complete, Hannah took the rose and slipped it inside Wilhelm's comic—the exact one he had been looking at when they had first seen each other a lifetime ago.

Hannah took a piece of thick white paper and Petyr's black ink ballpoint pen and wrote Wilhelm's name. The paper had already been stamped with the day's date—21 December 1947—using the stamp Petyr used on all orders at the "Rote Blumen." The ink from the pen spread smoothly. She poured every memory the two of them had into the letter, but it lacked a set direction. But such is the way of writing when it is filled with passion. But as Hannah reached halfway down the back of the page, she knew she had to say goodbye. Hannah signed her name. The tears that had been hanging precariously at the bottom of her chin fell, and the ink blurred. She folded the paper into thirds and slid it into the comic book along with the blue rose.

She gave the shop one final look and thanked God that she and her mother had wandered into it all those years ago. There were a handful of moments that shaped—that defined—a person's life. They had deliberated on if they wanted to enter but had some time to waste until the train to Berlin would leave.

Hannah returned to Petyr's, and even if he had encouraged her to leave and live her life, he looked shaken up at losing her. He recognized the pain that came from losing your soulmate and at too young an age. He had experienced it himself, and even if they were different genders, had nearly a fourteen-inch height difference, amongst hundreds of other physical differences, he saw himself in Hannah's blue eyes.

"Goodbye, Hannah," Petyr said, trying his best to smile, but the sadness showed in his eyes.

"Goodbye," Hannah said. She wrapped her arms around him, resting her face against his chest.

He placed his large left hand on the back of her head. "Take care of yourself."

"And you," Hannah said. She had her worries of how his cough showed no signs of ever going away, but Petyr kept assuring her it was something he had been dealing with off and on. Some days, it was worse than others.

Hannah had only her suitcase and her purse and made sure the manila envelope filled with the photographs and the blue rose was inside. She would not risk losing them again. Petyr walked her to the train station and waved her off, and she returned to Berlin. Hannah had told herself on the walk over she would not look, but seeing Petyr waving goodbye brought her back to when Wilhelm had left for war. She could not have imagined how drastically their lives would change. It was the last time she would ever see Wilhelm. She thought about that moment when she stood in their apartment as he and Heinrich walked outside to the cold, blowing snow. She had run after him and now, almost eight years later, she seemed to have known even then it would be the last. She was unwilling to let him go, but he was unable to stay.

She was seated on the train as the last few passengers took their seats. There was nothing she could do to stop herself from looking out the window. But as Petyr fell out of sight as the train sped by, Hannah was grateful she had taken the moment to look at him one last time.

The sights of ruined cities did little to improve her mood. It was not just her life that had changed over the last ten years but all of Europe. But now, she had only photos and memories of Wilhelm. She had already forgotten the smell of his pillow and knew that, over time, she would forget more. It was that that caused her additional pain. With each passing year, she would forget more and more about him. All his idiosyncrasies that made him who he was would be lost.

Hannah barely remembered getting off the train in Berlin and moving through the busy airport. But she found herself at her seat beside the plane's window, and the roar of the engines, signaling take off, was but moments away. As the plane lifted off the ground and soared high above Germany, she was not only saying goodbye to Wilhelm but to Germany and to Europe itself forever.

Freedom

There are many emotions that drive a person—emotions that elicit change, emotions that demand actions, emotions that can defeat a person's will. But Wilhelm had found there was no stronger emotion than hope. It was the promise of better. And by God, there had to be.

After the war had ended and the Germans had found out they would not be returning home, many men had lost hope. They accepted their fate, and hundreds of men died two or three months after the ending of the war.

During summer, Wilhelm worked the fields from sun up to sun down. During winter, he was often placed inside a cell large enough only for his bunk to fit in and a bucket to use for the bathroom. Solitude drove most men crazy. Minutes felt like days, and the walls did little to silence the screaming and crying coming from the other cells. But Wilhelm envisioned himself living a different life. He planned out his entire day in his fictitious life—everything from his scheduled alarm clock wake up time of 5:30 a.m. to shaving and showering. He would make Hannah breakfast before he went to work as a shift manager at a car manufacturing plant and discover hand-written notes from Hannah in his lunch. Each night, the two would go for walks and dance in their living room. Every three days in the make-believe world equaled one day in the real world. It was an exercise many would consider abnormal, but who was to say what was normal when presented with such a dire situation? Hope was something Wilhelm had not yet abandoned because hope had a name and a face. Hannah's voice, even if imaginary, kept his mind strong.

He looked forward to the end of each workday so he could disappear into his imaginary world. He thought so often of his other life that his dreams soon brought the world to life in a way his imagination could not. In his dreams, he could smell the banana bread in the oven or the popcorn on the stove. He could taste the wine and feel the snowflakes fall on his head. But, most importantly, he could feel Hannah's body against his. Her soft lips pressed against his chapped lips.

Torben could not understand how Wilhelm was so resilient, and Wilhelm could sense he had lost his will to care. Francesca, most likely, had moved on. But, most of all, Torben could not delve into his imagination the way Wilhelm could. He had nothing but the harsh, soul-breaking reality. Wilhelm did his best to lift his spirits during their workday but, no matter how hard he tried, he was unsuccessful.

It was 1950, and Wilhelm had turned thirty years old. But he was far younger than he was in his alternate-reality where he was forty-five. In that life, he had four children. His oldest was a daughter named Evelyn, two sons, Jonathan and George, and their youngest was Dolly (Dolores).

In July 1950, a horrible outbreak of typhus ran rampant through the camp. Wilhelm awoke each morning and checked his body for purple rashes and his forehead for any signs of fever. Ninety-seven people died that month alone from the disease. On 2 August, Wilhelm stepped out of his cell and waited for Torben to step out, but he never did. His body was carried out by two Soviet guards. Whether the fever had taken him or Torben forced Death's hand was something Wilhelm would never know. Torben was Wilhelm's last friend, and after his loss, it took Wilhelm weeks to disappear into the sanctity of the life he had crafted in his mind.

The weeks became months, and the months became years. But the hope Wilhelm held onto finally proved its worth. A commotion broke out in the camp. The prisoners whispered about and peaked toward the entrance.

"What's going on?" Wilhelm asked.

"They are letting us go home," a soldier said.

But he, like Wilhelm, had not allowed the news to be met without skepticism. The Soviets had held them so long, why would they release them now in 1955?

The Soviet officers approached them, and the forty-seven German prisoners stood at attention. They looked like skeletons covered in a thin layer of skin. No trace of fat or muscle could be found anywhere on their bodies, and their frames could not even support their backs, causing their shoulders to droop forward. But hate was a powerful emotion, and it rose in Wilhelm's chest.

Captain Sokolov finished what must have been his hundred thousandth career cigarette. Torben had wanted to see the man die but, again, life was far too cruel to allow such a minor victory. The Captain's visits were limited, and he was no longer a captain after achieving at least two promotions, but Wilhelm did not care to remember him as anything else.

"I am here to inform you that terms have been agreed upon between the Soviet Union and West Germany. You are no longer prisoners of the Soviet Union. You are free to leave," Captain Sokolov announced.

The Germans, although confused at Sokolov's mention of a West Germany, were too struck by his words of "no longer prisoners." They looked at one another, each wondering if the first man to move to the entrance would be shot. But Wilhelm had found a peace mostly derived from his alternate life. The feelings, the sights, the sounds he experienced in that life were things he would never feel, see or hear in his life as a prisoner. He had been too scared to try and claim his freedom years ago when he and Torben were forced to run from the factory to the camp. Perhaps, he and Torben would have been in Germany that second instead of Wilhelm still at the camp and Torben, dead. He moved past the other Germans and toward the fence entrance. Captain Sokolov inclined his head slightly as Wilhelm passed. Wilhelm looked up at the watchtower, but the normal guard on duty was gone. The fence was pulled open, and Wilhelm stepped out. It did not take long for the other Germans to follow him. Wilhelm was free.

A man greeted them outside the gates and introduced himself as a representative of West Germany. His name was Adolf Jung, and he looked to be in his early forties. He said he worked for Chancellor Konrad Adenauer. But neither the man nor his position meant anything to Wilhelm.

As Wilhelm sat on the transport truck, he thought of how many times he had sat on a similar truck and wished it was taking him home and not to a factory to work. He and Torben had talked about it often. The last five years had been the toughest without him. Over the course of the long ride to Germany, every friend he had made during the war and the fact none of them survived came to his mind. He thought of Höring and Jonas. He and Höring had almost escaped the Battle of Stalingrad. How different would the last twelve years have been had they succeeded?

When the trucks stopped, food rations and water were handed out. Every German drank theirs without a moment's pause. They were each given another refill, but Wilhelm saved his, knowing that most likely they would not get a third. Food had been so scarce and rationed over the years that even when the men told them to eat it all, Wilhelm and the others hesitated.

When they reached Berlin, there was a small gathering of mothers, wives, family, and friends waiting to greet them. Mothers wept into their son's chests, and children who had been one or two now greeted their fathers as teens. Wilhelm searched the crowd for Hannah. Every time his eyes fell upon a woman with blonde hair, his heartbeat increased, and his hope rose, but none of the women were his Hannah. Would she even recognize him anymore? Would he even recognize himself? He had not seen his reflection in a mirror in years, but his weight was down eighty pounds, he had a beard, and he was fifteen years older.

The city Wilhelm had fallen in love with was barely recognizable. The surviving buildings looked like skeletal fingers pushing up through the freshly dug earth of its own grave. He rushed past the spectators, trying to get to his apartment as soon as humanly possible. He passed the area where the New Reich Chancellery had once been. But it was gone. The building that had been the pride of the Nazis and cost millions of dollars to build had not even lasted twenty years. Wilhelm expected the city to be the same as when he had left. He had to keep reminding himself he had been gone fifteen years and nothing was immune to the changes of time. But it was his destroyed apartment building that caused his spirits to nosedive and skip along the hard ground. The rubble had been cleaned, and there was nothing to show he and Hannah had once shared a home on that very spot. The terrible fist of worry punched Wilhelm's stomach and clawed its way toward his heart. He had feared for Hannah ever since he had found out about the abominable Holocaust camps. Even more terrifying was the fact he was fifteen years behind the events.

He jogged as long as he could on his way to the Goldschmidts' home. But after two blocks, his weak body could no longer run, and his legs shook from malnourishment. He rounded the final corner and hoped to see the sign "Tailor, Tux, and Touch Up." But there was no sign. The windows Wilhelm had helped Josef put up were gone. Instead, the entire building was bricked. Wilhelm knocked on the door, and an older, chubby, gray-haired man answered.

"Can I help you?" he asked.

"I'm sorry. I'm looking for the people who used to live here. The Goldschmidts," Wilhelm said.

"I'm sorry. I don't know anything about them," the man said, already closing the door.

Wilhelm received another sucker punch, this time to his kidneys. Berlin had never felt too large for him before. It had been a land of unlimited possibilities with a horizon he would have never reached in the best of ways. But now, the city was a haystack and Hannah, the needle. The only information he had was Hannah was Jewish and the Jews had been rounded up and put into camps. He needed to know if Hannah had been one of them. But getting the Soviets to help him out seemed doubtful. He wanted to go to the Americans, but Captain Sokolov had said it had been the Soviets who had liberated the camp, but that was only one camp of thousands. A man named Konrad Adenauer had given him his freedom, perhaps he could give him his life back too.

Wilhelm crossed into the western portion of the city, and it was like he had walked across a sunset separating darkness and light. The western portion of the city had been rejuvenated and was well underway toward the process of healing while the east seemed to be caught in permanent gray skies and an eternal bleakness.

Wilhelm asked anyone he could where he could speak to either the German or American in charge and was pointed into the direction of Clayallee near the upscale suburban part of West Berlin called Zehlendorf. The guards stopped him and searched him before they allowed him inside. The building had a dozen offices, and Wilhelm went to the closest one with a worker who was not busy helping others. The man looked to be over a decade younger than Wilhelm, and Wilhelm tried to stifle the jealously bubbling in his stomach over his youth. The man was fortunate he had been too young to fight. Hitler had called upon the Hitler Youth to fight near the end of the war, and soldiers as young as fourteen were thrown into the fray. But this man must have been ten or eleven during that time. After missing the war, he had gone to school and received a great job right out of it.

"Hello, can I help you?" the man asked.

The nameplate at his desk read "Karl Heikmann," and his desk was stacked with manila folders and a picture frame facing Karl.

"Yes, I need help locating my wife," Wilhelm said.

"Please sit down," Karl said, offering the seat in front of the desk.

Wilhelm was far too worried to think about sitting, but his frail body could not support itself any longer, and he nearly fell into the chair. Karl looked at Wilhelm and could tell he had just returned home from a Soviet Camp. He was unshowered, unshaved, his hair longer than normal, and the clothes given to him upon his release looked like baggy bedsheets. Wilhelm also knew he undoubtedly smelt awful, and it was hard to tell if Karl was feeling sympathetic to his beaten-down appearance or suppressing a gag.

"Can I get you something to eat or drink?" Karl asked, but he decided he would call his secretary regardless of what Wilhelm answered.

"I'm fine," Wilhelm said.

Karl was already off the phone, and a woman popped in seconds later. It was impossible to tell if she had sprinted from across the building or was right outside the door.

"Yes, Mr. Heikmann?" the woman asked.

She had long blonde hair that hung over her left shoulder, and she appeared to be nearly the same age as Karl.

"Yes, Mrs. Heikmann, can you please bring my lunch in?" he asked.

"Certainly," Mrs. Heikmann said. She left, and Karl smiled like a child on Christmas morning.

"She is my wife. Try to keep it professional in the workplace and call her Mrs. Heikmann. Honestly, I just like reminding myself we're married," Karl said. He realized his comment was to a man searching for his missing wife, and his face blushed and his eyes bulged in horror.

Mrs. Heikmann returned with a paper bag and set it on the desk and disappeared without another word.

"I am so sorry. That was cruel of me. Please, tell me how I can help," Karl said, passing his lunch to Wilhelm.

"My wife, Hannah Schreiber. Her maiden name was Goldschmidt. She is Jewish. I have been in a prisoner-of-war camp somewhere in Russia since 1943," Wilhelm said.

As Karl wrote the name down, the awfulness of the end of the sentence connected. He paused briefly before he finished writing and pushed the lunch forward further.

"Please eat it. I'm fine. I had a large breakfast," Karl said.

Wilhelm was starved, so he opened the bag and removed the sandwich and potato salad inside. He emptied the paper bag, and a fork fell onto the desk. Wilhelm had never cared for mustard or mayonnaise, but that was before he had been starved for nearly fifteen years and ate only half a dozen types of food. Even thinking about kasha made him sick.

Karl asked a hundred questions, and Wilhelm was grateful for each of them. If he had asked only a few, it would have made him think Karl was going to do little to help. He asked everything from her address, previous address, next of kin, friends, and family in other countries. He asked Wilhelm for his place of residence, but Wilhelm struggled to find an answer.

"There are programs to help rehabilitate you—a hand to help you back onto your feet," Karl said.

But Wilhelm gave Karl his father's address and telephone number, and his eyes lit up. Perhaps, Hannah was there right now. The thought warmed his chest, and he could feel strength flowing back into his bloodstream. He was an absolute fool to not have checked there after visiting their old apartment and her parents' house. As Wilhelm rose to his feet, the realization also dawned he had no money for a train or bus ticket to Schönfeld.

"Is there something else I can do for you?" Karl asked.

Wilhelm had now eaten Karl's lunch and taken his money for the bus fare. Karl assured him it was not a problem, and Wilhelm could tell he was trying to rectify his poor choice of words earlier.

Wilhelm had missed the train by less than three minutes and was forced to wait another two and a half hours before the next one. He spent the remaining bit of money Karl had given him to buy a sausage and a Coca-Cola, just one example of American marketing all over West Berlin. The ice-cold soda was the most delicious thing he had drunk in over twelve years. His beverages at the camp had consisted of water or watered-down coffee or tea.

Waiting for the train was agonizing and, several times, Wilhelm contemplated walking. But reasoning would overcome the desire, and he would sit back down and glance at the clock behind him, roughly every forty seconds. It did not make waiting any easier when at 3:20, the designated boarding time, the train had yet to arrive.

Finally, at 3:45, Wilhelm and the train moved south toward his hometown. But the Schönfeld that had raised him was no longer. There were buildings he did not recognize and empty lots that had once been home to some of his favorite places. The candy shop he frequented with his mother was gone, as was his school.

He breathed a sigh of relief finding his father's home still standing. He turned the doorknob, but the door was locked. Wilhelm knocked and waited, but there was no movement inside. He looked for the spare key hidden in the dirt of a potted fern. Wilhelm scraped a layer of dirt away and pulled the stained silver key from the pot. He unlocked the door and stepped inside. The lights were off, and the house had more dust and spider webs than Wilhelm had ever remembered seeing. But cleaning the house was a chore Wilhelm had always done. But apart from the cobwebs and dust, the house had not changed. What a comfort it was that while everything in his life had changed, his childhood home stayed the same.

Wilhelm crept to his bedroom and opened the door. Possessions he had left in 1938 were still there in 1955—magazines that had not been touched in nearly twenty years and clothes he had not worn since he had moved to Berlin. He looked at every photograph on the wall, and with each glance and stare, his morale climbed out of the pit it had been stuck in for so long. He stared longest at the photograph of his mother. He would never forget her face, but seeing her smiling for the first time in years made him tear up.

He waited for an hour before he decided to visit his father at the "Rote Blumen." He was eager to see him and the look on his father's face when he saw he was still alive. But first, he needed to shower and shave for his appearance would not go undiscussed.

Wilhelm went into the bathroom and opened the drawer to the left-hand side of the sink and removed his father's clippers. He sheered his hair like a sheep, and the sink filled up with his long, wavy hair from his head and beard. He cut it the best he could, keeping it shorter on the sides and a bit longer on top. He looked for his father's razor and some shaving balm and shaved. He went to turn on the water, but not a drop came out from the sink. He stepped to the bathtub but, again, no water poured out. The city still looked to be healing and, perhaps, it was normal for the water and power to go out every so often. He grabbed a towel from the cupboard and wiped his face. His face had not been cleanly shaven since he had left for war, and it burned. His touch with a razor was not what it used to be. Small red pools of blood formed around his face. He felt ten years younger but didn't mind, as those years had been stolen from him anyway.

He went back into his bedroom and sifted through his shirts. He changed out of his baggy clothes and into a pair of slacks and a black shirt that, much to his disappointment but not shock, were just as baggy. He went to his father's room and sprayed some of his cologne on to mask his awful smell. Even without the shower, he felt more like a man and a human being than he had in longer than he cared to remember. He had not only looked like a savage, but he had also committed savage acts in the name of war. There would be no shower that could wash them away.

As he walked along the sidewalk, he blended in, and no one gave him a second look. It was all he wanted. It was a drastically different experience for returning German soldiers than it had been for American or Soviet soldiers. There had been an indelible pride for those who had fought for freedom around the world. The Germans received no fanfare, and those who had committed awful acts for the Nazi Party hoped they would return with no one the wiser.

Wilhelm arrived at the "Rote Blumen," but it was locked. Wilhelm stopped an elderly lady walking by.

"Excuse me, Miss, do you know what happened to the flower shop?" Wilhelm asked.

The elderly woman seemed the best able to answer his question amongst the people walking past. Wilhelm had a strong suspicion he knew her, but if he did, she had worn a younger face free of wrinkles.

"It closed two years back," the woman said.

"Do you know where the man who owned it moved to?" Wilhelm asked.

The woman's face changed. "Oh, I am sorry, dear. Mr. Schreiber passed away."

Wilhelm's head spun, and he put his hand on the wall behind him to secure himself.

"You are Petyr's boy, aren't you?" the woman asked.

Wilhelm could only nod. He had always believed there would be a time when he and his father would grow close—a time when their friendship would take off, a time when Petyr would no longer have to be a patriarch. He had seen glimpses of it after he had moved out. And now that he was a veteran of combat too, he wanted to speak to his father about the common horror they had experienced and their tour in hell.

"I am sorry," she said.

Wilhelm nodded, and the woman hesitated, unsure if she should stay to console him or give him space. She elected for the latter, squeezed his arm and left.

Wilhelm wandered aimlessly for hours. The comfort his childhood home had brought him earlier was now gone. It was a house full of memories, the good trumped by the bad, but the good were great. The house was now a mausoleum. Wilhelm had spent almost twenty years of his life in the city, yet it was a friend he no longer kept in touch with or had anything in common with.

He slept on a city bench that night, and before the sun rose, he forced himself to return to his father's home. He stopped at the utility department to have his water and power turned back on. He contacted Karl to see if he had made any progress. Wilhelm had no intention of waiting for answers and wanted to ensure Karl was properly motivated. But Karl had no answers to give.

When he forced himself to return home, he flipped the light switch on to test if it was working. When the bulb lit up, he went to the bathroom and showered for half an hour. The water circling down the drain was tinted brown. He scrubbed the bar of soap across his body a dozen times, and each time, he discovered places resilient to cleaning. He found that it gave him something to do—a task that kept his mind preoccupied. When he shut the shower off and dressed, he went to cleaning the next thing.

He started by wiping the cobwebs from the house and then washing the floors. After a week of calling Karl and cleaning the house until the floors could be eaten off of, he received a call to come to West Berlin. He boarded the train, and the vibration in his stomach from the fear of what he would be told did not go away when the train stopped. He approached Karl's desk, his back sweating, his hands shaking.

"Please, sit down," Karl said. Wilhelm took the seat and covered his mouth with his hand in an attempt to hide how nervous he was. "I have found Hannah's name on a list. Hannah Goldschmidt. But I'm afraid it's awful news, Wilhelm," Karl said.

Wilhelm's hand trembled. His stomach dropped. Fifteen years of worrying and wondering would be answered in the next few seconds.

"Hannah was sent to Auschwitz concentration camp between 1940 and 1941," Karl said.

Wilhelm's heart imploded.

Karl had been too young to have worked in the department after the war had ended in 1945 when thousands upon thousands of people had to be told a beloved friend or family member had perished in the war. It was something no compassionate human being could feel comfortable doing.

"Are you sure?" Wilhelm asked, his voice cutting out on him.

"It's her name. Her parents are on the list too—Josef and Emma. But beyond that, we'll never get more evidence. The Nazis destroyed much before their retreat," Karl said.

Wilhelm rose from the chair and wanted to say something as he left, but there was a golf-ball size lump in his throat that would not let him. He wiped his eyes and left the building. He wanted to disappear into the alternate reality he had created back in Russia. He tried to sink deep into his consciousness to try and walk up the concrete pathway leading to the eggshell bricked house he and Hannah had owned. But he could not. There was no house at the end of that driveway anymore. He wandered the streets of both reality and fiction.

Everything that was and everything that kept him alive was gone. There were so many moments when he thought his time was up—so many near misses where a bullet whizzed by his head or an explosion went off far enough away to keep him from harm. He had survived a shot through his chest and the infection that followed. He had survived Typhus fever, starvation, freezing, and Captain Sokolov's sadism. He had considered that maybe God had a vested interest in his survival and that his good graces were what had kept him alive. But it was the devil playing a trick on Wilhelm to keep him alive long enough to see there was nothing worth living for anymore.

But Wilhelm had known Hannah's fate when Sokolov broke the news of the concentration camps. Even if he had held onto hope, deep down, he knew. Hannah had asked him not to go—pleaded with him not to. But Christmas day 1939 had sealed their fate. Hannah had been dead for fourteen years. Wilhelm could only hope she was at peace and that one day, he may see her again.

Days Gone By

Time is a funny thing. Wilhelm's mother had passed away when he was only nine years old. Yet, at such a young age, a year felt like a decade, and by the time he was eighteen, her death, although something he would never get over, had felt like a lifetime ago. But time is on a hill, and it moves past in a way that years are more like months and months like weeks.

Wilhelm found little comfort in anything except the quest to reach the end of a bottle and the "Rote Blumen." He had opened the shop back up as a way to fill his nights. His daily nightmares subsided to once or twice a week and often were about Hannah living in Auschwitz, the horror of which was plastered on every newspaper, magazine, and news station, and his war-time friends being shot, stabbed, burned or frozen to death.

After three months of complete isolation, he went back to Karl to ask about his friends, Erich and Heinrich. But there was only more pain to be had. Erich had died in battle and Heinrich was last known to be a prisoner-of-war, but after a decade after the war had ended, he had not returned home. The Germans had been released by the Americans and British in 1945. It all added up to another heartbreaking truth—Heinrich was dead too.

The Americans and Soviets could not find any common ground, and tensions boiled to the point of eruption. They came to a head in 1961, when the Soviets built a wall through the city of Berlin to separate the American West and the Soviet East. Wilhelm took frequent trips to the city, and as the bricks were put into place to keep the East Berliners from fleeing to the West, it was impossible not to think the Third World War was only a few months away. Schönfeld was in East Germany, and although there was a strong number of East Germans retreating west, Wilhelm stayed. The flower shop and his home were the only constant things in his life, and he kept mostly to his hometown. There was a strong fear that the world was moving toward nuclear Armageddon. Neither side backed down after Soviet missiles were discovered in Cuba, just ninety miles from American shores. But that war would not require the sacrifice of young men. With one switch of a button, hundreds of thousands would die instantly—a terrifying thought—but for those who had fought in Europe or the Pacific, it was far less cruel than Normandy, Stalingrad or Iwo Jima.

Wilhelm's world consisted of the "Rote Blumen," the bar, the market, and his job at an automobile manufacturing plant—the only thing of his alternate reality to come true.

It stayed that way until 26 June 1963, when the charismatic and charming American president came to Berlin to speak. President Kennedy stood near Rudolph-Wilde-Platz with tens of thousands cheering for him. Wilhelm was on the other side of the wall along with another ten thousand trying to hear the president speak. Wilhelm was blown away by his speaking ability. He held the tens of thousands of spectators in his hand. Hitler had held a similar power of speech. But the two men had polar opposite ideals, where one saw power as the end goal and the other as a necessity to do good. How different would his life, the lives of millions, had been had John Fitzgerald Kennedy been the Führer of Germany and not Adolf Hitler? But five months later, the savior of peace and the leader of the free world was shot and killed.

Wilhelm spent his days assembling cars and his nights at the flower shop. Women came in and out of his life, but none lasted even as long as the flowers he sold. His longest relationship was with the "Zerbrochene Flasche," a local bar, which he frequented every Friday and Saturday night.

It was 1989. Wilhelm sat and watched the television as the Berlin Wall, which had divided a city, a nation, and the world, was torn down. His jet-black hair was now gray and thinning, and his face showed the stress of life. His nose was red from years of alcohol abuse and his ears had drooped. The next night, the news coverage was filled with drama surrounding the Wall. Many from Schönfeld had taken train, bus or automobile to Berlin to see it firsthand. But Wilhelm was not among them. He sat in silence and solitude in the "Zerbrochene Flasche." His only companion was his pint of beer.

The doors of the bar opened. A man, appearing to be in his mid-thirties, with a dark gray dress shirt and a black suit coat over the top entered the bar.

"Good evening," the man said in German. The man's accent was unmistakably American, an odd thing, considering he was in East Germany.

He took a seat beside Wilhelm and scratched his shaggy, slicked back, wavy black hair. Alfred, the bartender, stood in front of the man silently.

"Good evening," Wilhelm greeted.

"Beer, please," the man said.

He rubbed his mustache and nodded politely at Wilhelm. He smelled of leather and newspaper.

"American?" Wilhelm asked.

"Yes. Is my accent that bad?" the man asked.

"Noticeable. Are you fluent?"

"I took German in college. My father learned it when he was stationed over here."

Wilhelm took silent note that even though the man's father spoke German, he had learned it at college.

"That's nice," Wilhelm said.

He had always found strangers to be interesting. Every person had a thousand stories to tell. But over the last twenty years, he had rarely run into any. It had been the same cast of characters everywhere he went and the same dreadful conversations.

"Not really. He spoke English, German, and some French, but his preferred tongue was silence. And he was fluent," the man said.

"What brings you to Germany?" Wilhelm asked.

"That," the man said, pointing to the television.

On it, hundreds of people cheered as sections of the graffiti-covered wall came down.

"Shouldn't you be there?" Wilhelm asked.

"I was. My newspaper failed to get me a room at any hotel in West Berlin."

The bartender set down a glass of dark beer, and by the way the man looked at it, it was clear he was not a fan of it.

"Put it on my tab," Wilhelm said.

"Thank you, but that's not necessary. I get to spend fifty dollars a day on food and beverages, and so far, I've only had a sausage with *sauerkraut*. Let me get these," the man said.

He unfolded the paper Deutsche Mark from his pocket and set it on the table.

"Thank you…" Wilhelm said, holding onto the word, hoping the man would pick up on the blunt hint.

"Russell. Russell Kelly," the man said.

Hint received.

"Wilhelm Schreiber," Wilhelm said, offering his hand.

Russell shook it. "What do we drink to?" he asked, lifting his beer from the bar.

"To your father," Wilhelm said.

"To my father," Russell repeated.

Both men took a sip and reacted differently. It was hardly Russell's first beer, yet American beer was water compared to German. Wilhelm also had been drinking it far longer. The beer had as much effect as milk would have.

"What about you, Wilhelm? Married? Kids? All that good stuff?" Russell asked.

He took another sip of his beer and was able to enjoy it much more than the first sip, as he knew what to expect.

"No. Never happened for me," Wilhelm said.

"Can I ask you a question, Wilhelm?" Russell asked.

Wilhelm nodded between sips of his amber-colored beer.

"Did you fight in the war?"

Wilhelm sipped his drink without acknowledging Russell.

"Forgive me. It's a personal question. I know your story is much different than my father's. No parades for you. But the same pain, I'm sure," Russell said.

"I can't speak for your father," Wilhelm said.

"Well, I can't either. Nor can he. He … ugh … put a gun to his forehead a few years back," Russell said.

"I'm sorry," Wilhelm said.

"We were never close really. I thought by learning German, maybe we could have secret conversations that no one else could understand, but he only ignored me in two languages. I asked him about the war a lot, but he never said a word. After he passed, my wife and I cleaned out his dresser and found his medals and some old photographs and letters."

"Medals," Wilhelm said.

He shook his head and leaned back in his chair, his fingers rubbing the condensation on his glass.

"You have to justify the death somehow," Russell said.

He could only hope his sarcasm was picked up through his American accent.

"My father fought in the first war at Verdun. They gave him a medal too," Wilhelm said.

"Oh, God," Russell muttered.

He knew the battle and how destructive it was.

"I was never close to my father either. My mother, before she died, always told me to be patient—that I could not understand what he had been through. I wanted to understand," Wilhelm said.

"Did you ever?" Russell asked.

"Yes. To understand hell, you have to enter its gates."

"And where was that?" Russell asked, taking another sip that almost qualified as a gulp.

"At Stalingrad," Wilhelm said.

"You fought at the Battle of Stalingrad? That was the bloodiest battle of the entire war," Russell said, his face grim. He could only imagine the horror.

"I was in the Sixth Army," Wilhelm said.

"Wehrmacht, right?" Russell asked.

Wilhelm could tell Russell had studied the war, most likely in an attempt to understand his father much the same way Wilhelm had desired to know more about the Great War to understand his. It was a motive Wilhelm respected greatly.

"Yes. I was not a Nazi. But most people don't separate German from Nazi. One and the same," Wilhelm said.

"I lost two uncles. One at D-Day and another at the Battle of the Bulge. You're right. We don't differentiate," Russell said.

"I did not know about the camps, nor did thousands of other young men."

"Have you seen them? What's left of them that is?"

He waved the bartender over for another round. Russell had not intended to like the beer as much as he did but when in Rome or, in this case, Germany, one drinks beer. The flavor had come on strong, but with each sip, it settled better on his palate.

"No. I could never," Wilhelm said.

"My mom is Jewish. My grandparents were at Bergen-Belsen. They lived. I went with her about ten years ago," Russell said.

"My wife was killed at Auschwitz," Wilhelm said.

"Your wife was Jewish?" Russell asked.

The fact he was surprised spoke volumes about the hurtful stigma the war had on all Germans and the philosophy that they all hated Jews.

"Hannah Goldschmidt—the love of my life. When I left for war, she was captured—around 1941. I did not get released from Russia until 1955."

"1955? The war had been over for ten years," Russell said, hardly believing what he had just heard.

He knew Wilhelm was well aware of the amount of time and, once again, Russell understood his limitations as an interviewer. He was much better with a pen and paper in his hand.

"I'm sorry," Russell said.

Wilhelm waved it off. He was half-way through the fresh pint of beer that had been set before him. He grabbed a handful of the bar peanuts in the wooden bowl and tossed them into his mouth.

"Never remarried?" Russell asked.

"No. There were women, but none compared to my Hannah. When you meet the love of your life, you don't move on from that," Wilhelm said.

It was easy to tell his words were resolute.

"To the women we love," Russell said, raising his glass to Wilhelm.

Wilhelm raised his and took a sip.

"I don't want you thinking I'm some blind American who is ignorant to our own awful history. We went to war with ourselves to defend the abdominal practice of slavery. We killed nearly ninety percent of Native Americans when we came over from Europe. For

Christ's sake, the Ku Klux Klan is still active," Russell said, doing his best to console Wilhelm.

"Hate is something that is taught. The Nazis taught well," Wilhelm said.

"Brainwashed," Russell corrected.

They talked longer than either had expected and drank more than Russell had intended to. They each revealed intimate details that could only be revealed so quickly when alcohol was a factor. It lowered their guard and dulled the pain of old memories. It wasn't until closing time that Russell and Wilhelm left the "Zerbrochene Flasche."

Russell had caught only four hours of sleep that night when his alarm shrieked at him. He wanted to throw it against the wall but knew if he did, he would miss his flight. He sat up, and his head pounded as if hundreds of miniature men were hammering on it with chisels and hammers like some unexplored cave. He caught a Bloody Mary at the airport and left the garnishes on the side. Keeping the tomato juice and vodka down would challenge his stomach enough. As soon as he boarded the plane, he flipped the visor over his window and closed his eyes. Russell returned to Schönfeld on three other occasions, both professional and private, and each time, he was sure to catch half a dozen beers with Wilhelm.

As his seventies approached, Wilhelm retired from his factory job. He had lost the desire to keep the flower shop open and agreed to sell it. But he did not want to know if the building would be kept as it was, renovated or torn down. He packed everything up and had no idea how much his father had hoarded over the years. The basement was seldom used, and Wilhelm had never considered looking through the dozens of wooden crates and cardboard boxes. He only went down to the basement to go to the electrical panel if a breaker had blown. But what he thought would take twenty minutes turned out to last four hours.

He found an entire box of receipts and order placements, some written by his mother. She had flawless penmanship, almost calligraphic in its design. His own writing, like himself, was a mixture of his mother's elegant, crisp writing and his father's chicken scratch. Another crate was filled with thank-you cards and photographs from all the weddings and funerals the "Rote Blumen" had provided flowers for. Another box was filled with more private artifacts—photos of his parents he had never seen before and comic books that had been taken away from him because he had been reading them under the counter and not working. He recognized each of them and paged through them. The red cover of his favorite comic seemed to call out to him, and Wilhelm reached for it. The pages split open and a letter fluttered to the ground. Wilhelm grabbed it and unfolded the tri-folded piece of paper and read it.

"Oh, God," Wilhelm muttered, realizing what he had found.

He thought he had cried too much for there to be anything left in the reservoir. Seeing Hannah's handwriting renewed every memory and, like a tsunami, they crashed over him. It was proof Hannah Goldschmidt had not been a part of his imagination—something that he had thought up during the darkest days in Russia. Hannah was a woman he had loved, and she had loved him.

The letter made his body tremble and his stomach plummet. He nearly cried out when he saw the date on the top right-hand corner—21 December 1947, six years after Wilhelm had been told Hannah Goldschmidt had died at Auschwitz concentration camp in Poland. He was in a nightmare. He had to be. How cruel a dream it was.

He had often found her in his dreams though, over the years, they had become as rare as a lunar eclipse. But never had he been subjected to such a thing. If he was dreaming, it was the most awful realistic one he had ever had. The putrid mildew in the basement had no problem attacking his lungs. The letter in his hands was smooth but still threatened to give his dry fingers a paper cut. Her handwriting was exactly as he remembered it. Even the damn stamp was the same. The seven never stamped cleanly, and it was the reason he had replaced it. But when he unfolded the bottom of the letter, something fell out—a dried blue rose. It was from Hannah. It had to be. No one else could understand what the rose signified. Hannah was alive in 1947. If she was alive then, she could be alive now in 1995.

Russell Kelly

The cubicles of the Boston Globe were a steady sound of keyboards being struck, phones ringing, and copy machines printing. Russell Kelly was not a man who worked best with a clean desk. He needed clutter and background noise to work properly. He had a steady flow of late 1960's rock playing softly from his radio. But there were certain songs that should never be listened to on low volumes, and in those instances, he turned the music up louder until a punch from the other side of his cubicle told him it was too loud.

He stared at his blank computer screen. The cursor's flashing tried to draw Russell's attention back to it. His pointer fingers lightly tapped the "f" and "j" keys like the revving of a sports car at a red light. Finally, his mind flashed green, and his fingers started tapping the keys like a woodpecker. But he got a flat tire in the form of a ringing phone. He tried to ignore it, but a few more rings and he would get a dreaded voicemail. He hated taking calls but deplored listening to voicemails.

"Shit," Russell muttered. He pulled his hands off the keyboard and reached for the phone. "Russell Kelly, Boston Globe."

"Russell, this is Wilhelm Schreiber calling from Schönfeld, Germany."

Phone calls were a necessary evil of his job. But he was genuinely delighted to hear Wilhelm's voice.

"Wilhelm, I can honestly say I was not expecting your call. How are you?" Russell asked in German.

He found talking with Wilhelm to be almost therapeutic like confiding in a priest.

"She's alive, Russell," Wilhelm said.

"Who's alive?"

"Hannah. She's alive."

Russell sat up. He had heard a hundred stories of Hannah and knew her death had been the defining moment in Wilhelm's life—an event he never truly got over.

"What are you talking about, Wilhelm?"

"You have to help me find her," Wilhelm said, the years of desperate longing hanging on every pleaded word.

Russell stared at the unfinished work beside his desk and the flashing cursor. The words he had written were uninspiring to him—words he was forced to write. He knew he should finish it. It was what a sensible, responsible adult would do. But no matter the distance between Boston and Schönfeld, Wilhelm's pleading was unmistakable.

"I'm catching the next flight," Russell said, making sure there was no hesitation in his voice.

When he had returned home from his first trip to Germany, he had told his wife, Lauren, all about Wilhelm. She understood there were some people you connected to. Though she did not like the last-minute trip, she gave him her blessing. The flight seemed longer than normal, and the jet lag was worse than ever. It was the unique experience of time traveling either into the past or into the future but at the cost of being thrown into a blender. He traveled through Schönfeld and to Wilhelm's house. The door opened before he could even knock.

"Thank you for coming," Wilhelm said.

"What do you have?" Russell asked, setting his dress coat and briefcase down beside the kitchen table.

Wilhelm opened a bottle of Weizenbier (wheat beer) for Russell and then laid the evidence on the table. Russell removed a notepad, a blue ink pen, and a tape recorder. He had also brought his laptop but found writing with a good ballpoint pen to be one of the greatest feelings and a better way to retain information.

The table looked like a murder mystery or a missing person case. But that was exactly what it was—a missing person case that had gone cold fifty-four years earlier. Wilhelm showed Russell the letter and pointed to the date repeatedly as Russell read it.

"Now, I wouldn't be honest if I didn't say maybe the wrong date was stamped," Russell said.

"Please look into this," Wilhelm pleaded.

"If I was going to turn you down, I would have done it over the phone."

Russell listened as Wilhelm went over every detail he knew and took strong guesses at those he did not. Russell had heard much of it before but never took notes nor tape-recorded the conversation. Russell poured over the notes until after midnight, Germany time. He had now officially been up forty of forty-eight hours with only intermittent sleep on the plane ride over. Wilhelm fell asleep in his recliner, and after a heroic effort, Russell fell asleep at the table. He stayed another day and copied the photograph of Hannah Wilhelm had. She was nineteen in it, and Wilhelm had told him it was taken some time in 1938 or 1939. It was a torn and faded black and white photograph. Wilhelm had memorized every line and every curve, but it was hard for Russell to distinguish what Hannah had actually looked like.

"I have made a copy of this, Wilhelm, but the picture itself isn't ideal, the copy even less. If you're willing, I can take this photograph back with me. We have people that specialize in photo enhancement," Russell said.

Wilhelm was uneasy with the idea. The photograph had been a rosary for him over the past fifty-five years and the only evidence he had of her existence.

"I understand. What are your thoughts on coming to Boston? You hold onto the photograph," Russell suggested.

"I don't know. How would I be accepted?" Wilhelm asked.

"Like an elderly man. I wouldn't lead with the fact that you are a German World War Two vet though," Russell said with a smile.

Russell had added perks of seeing New York City and Boston, but Wilhelm only cared about the integrity of the photo. It was the only photo of Hannah he had. He would not risk it. Wilhelm followed Russell, a veteran traveler, through the airport and onto the plane.

Wilhelm had never flown on such a large airplane nor had he flown such a distance. It was hard to believe something so large could fly over an ocean so expansive. As he flew over Western Europe, plane rides with Aaron came to his mind but turned into his attempted escape with Höring over Stalingrad.

When they landed, JFK international airport seemed to have decreased the entire world to less than five thousand acres. Every country seemed to be represented. Russell was at home in the airport. He knew which lines to enter and how to speed past people without being rude. With his guidance, they went from the terminal to outside in less than twenty-five minutes. A long line of taxis dropped people off at the door.

"What hotel will I be staying at?" Wilhelm asked.

"Hotel? No. You're my guest. We've got plenty of room. Fair warning, we have two dogs, and both are big time droolers," Russell said.

Wilhelm asked if they could take a few short hours to see the city. He was mesmerized by the Statue of Liberty as they flew in and even more so on the ferry ride to it.

"I guess I kind of take it for granted," Russell said as they looked up at the Statue of Liberty.

He had flown out of JFK airport nearly two dozen times. He had seen the Statue of Liberty from the ground, sea, and air just as many. But Wilhelm would never understand how it or what it stood for could be taken for granted. It meant freedom for all who came. The United States of America was the beacon for those seeking liberty, and it always answered the call.

Wilhelm and Russell returned to the airport parking garage, and Russell unlocked his silver 1994 Lexus Es. The drive was four hours without traffic which, luckily, they missed a large majority of. Boston was a city of great colonial history, and Wilhelm knew of the most important events and people during America's thirst for independence. Wilhelm had always believed the American Revolution to be a war men would be honored to fight in, and it also happened to take place before there were machine guns that could mow down hundreds of men in seconds.

Russell lived in a luxurious apartment with his wife Lauren. She had hair the color of caramel, eyes like milk chocolate, and fair skin. Russell affectionately referred to her as his ice cream sundae. The two Dobermans Russell had spoken of barked and bared their teeth when they saw Wilhelm.

"Mars. Jupiter. Quiet down," Russell scolded, dropping the luggage by the door.

"It is great to finally meet you, Wilhelm," Lauren said, wrapping Wilhelm in a hug.

"Thank you. It is nice to meet you," Wilhelm said in broken English of a dozen pieces.

Jupiter and Mars sniffed Wilhelm and had yet to decide if he was to be welcomed or chased out.

"I may have had better luck if they were German Shepherds," Wilhelm joked and smiled weakly.

"They're all talk, Wilhelm. An hour from now, they'll be curled up by your feet," Russell said.

He poured three glasses of wine. Lauren could only offer a smile, for she spoke little German. She was a doctor, and the apartment had an organized, clean feel to it, much like the examination rooms at her work. Wilhelm had gotten the impression from the way Russell had talked about himself and Lauren that they both were deeply enveloped in their careers and neither had wanted to risk complacency and have children.

Lauren had done her best to learn a few bits of German so she could be a proper hostess. She showed Wilhelm the spare bedroom he would be staying in, where the towels were in the bathroom, and granted him access to anything he wanted to eat or drink in the kitchen. Jupiter and Mars followed them into every room. They would not trust the stranger with one of their humans.

Russell had drunk one too many glasses of wine, and the next morning, on his way to work, the miners in his head returned to hammer and chisel. He normally drank a cup of coffee with cream, but he found his headache to grow with each sip and switched to water instead when he arrived at his cubicle. He took off his dress coat and rolled up his sleeves and went to the water cooler. He waited until the editor of the paper, Matt Storin, arrived. Storin had been a graduate of Notre Dame, and Russell knew it was the way to start a conversation. Russell finished his cup of water and tossed it in a garbage can and hurried to Storin's office. He knocked on the door frame.

"Got a second?" Russell asked.

"Russell, good morning. Sure, I have a moment," Storin said, stopping unpacking his briefcase.

"Holtz going to win more than ten this year?" Russell asked.

"Great thing about being a Notre Dame fan is God is always on our side."

Russell sat and decided on how to choose his words.

"What's up?" Storin asked.

"I wanted to ask about a piece," Russell said.

"Alright," Storin said, leaning back in his chair and entwining his fingers.

"Back in 1989, I was sent to Berlin to cover the Wall. I had stayed in a city in East Germany called Schönfeld. I met an older gentleman there—Wilhelm Schreiber. He was a veteran of World War Two. He fought on the eastern front at Stalingrad. He was released as a prisoner of war in 1955, more than twelve years after he was captured. He was married before he left—a marriage that took place in secret because his wife Hannah Goldschmidt was Jewish. She was sent to Auschwitz between 1940 and 1941 and presumably killed. But, a few weeks ago, Wilhelm found a letter from Hannah dated 1947."

"What are you asking to write?" Storin asked.

Russell was slightly alarmed that Storin was not affected by anything of what he had said. But like a baseball hitter in a slump, he could only keep swinging.

"I want to find out what happened to Hannah. I think it would make a great story. Two lovers reunited over fifty years later," Russell said.

"Russell, this is Boston. One of the most Catholic cities in the country. We don't like Nazis. Nor do Americans. Nazis have been raised to mythology, said in the same breath as Satan and the black plague," Storin said.

"He wasn't a Nazi. He was in the Wehrmacht. He married a Jewish woman. Does that sound like something a devout Nazi would do?" Russell asked.

"It's not going to read well. Our own veterans are in their seventies now, Russell. We're losing guys every year. But there are still plenty of families who remember the war and what it cost them," Storin reasoned.

"This is a human story, Matt. This isn't an American story or a German story. It's a story about the human condition. It's a story about love. The war tore thousands of families apart. What he went through and what he lost ..." Russell argued.

Storin was still unsure and tapped his pointer fingers against one another.

"I know this man. The war never ended for him," Russell said.

"I'm sorry, Russell. This isn't something our readers want to see in our paper. Whether or not he was a Nazi, it won't matter in the public opinion. It will only read 'Former Nazi Looks For Old Girlfriend.' I can't do it. I'm sorry," Storin said, maintaining his stance.

Russell had struck out and wanted to storm the mound.

"Matt, come on," Russell begged.

"He was a German living in Germany during a reign of terror," Storin said.

"Would you punish an innocent kid from Alabama because the KKK lynched somebody? Would you punish a parishioner because the Catholic Church murdered thousands over the course of history?" Russell tried arguing further.

"Careful, Russell," Storin said, giving Russell a warning look over his glasses.

"We need to break down these myths, Matt. We can't stereotype or classify this way anymore. We're all so much more than that." Storin started unpacking his briefcase again. "I am going to pursue this thing," Russell said.

"That's fine. You have the Globe's resources, but it won't make print," Storin said.

Russell nodded and wished silently Notre Dame lost every game the next year. He had hoped if he had printed the story, it would go national, and if Hannah were alive, she would be able to read the paper. He would have the paper's extensive resources at his disposal but, apart from a few personal favors, it was all on him.

He brought the picture to a friend and co-worker of his named Robby who enhanced the photograph. When Russell returned the photograph, he also gave Wilhelm a printed copy of the refurbished image. It looked identical as it had when Hannah had given Wilhelm the photo decades ago.

Wilhelm stayed a week, but progress was slow, and he returned to Germany without much hope. Russell called him at least twice a month to give him updates, but both he and Lauren would travel for work, and there were some months where no calls were made. But in July of 1996, Russell got his first big break. Hannah had been mentioned in a single passage in a Nazi officer's journal. The name Hannah Smith had fit her description and age. Russell had been searching under Goldschmidt and Schreiber but now added Smith. The name appeared in several declassified documents of the British Intelligence Agency.

Russell and Lauren spent an hour every night sharing a glass of wine and pouring over thousands of photographs of the war, hoping to spot Hannah. Her picture was taped to the top left of the monitor, and they constantly looked from the taped photo to the pictures on the screen for any similarities. Their goal was to look at a hundred a night, and sometimes, they went above that and other times, below.

Russell was prone to moments of pounding his fist against the desk when nights came without success. One night, to make matters worse, his aim was off. He smashed his fist against the keyboard and sent the number keys flying from it. Jupiter and Mars came to him and licked his hand, and Lauren rubbed his shaggy hair away from his face.

"You're too hard on yourself," Lauren said.

"He's almost eighty, Lauren," Russell said.

"You're doing everything you can."

"Sometimes, I wonder if I had been able to do something like this for my dad if he would still be here."

"Your dad loved you. Your mom tells you that all the time."

"Well, he never showed it. Wilhelm's a good man. I don't want that war to claim another casualty."

"Then we'll start looking at a hundred and ten," Lauren said with an encouraging smile.

"Thanks, sundae," Russel said and returned the smile.

She squeezed his hand. It was coated with dog saliva. "Oh, great," she muttered, wiping it on his shirt.

Adding a further ten photos a night seemed like little, but over the course of a month, it was three hundred more photos, and because of that, they discovered Hannah had worked as a nurse and aide during the D-Day invasions. But the invasion was top secret, and no unauthorized photographs were allowed to be taken. But there were a few authorized photos of General Eisenhower saying goodbye to the paratrooping soldiers in which a young blonde girl could be seen.

Russell and Lauren had bought Wilhelm a computer, as mailing new developments took far too long. They had flown to Germany, and Lauren had shown Wilhelm how the computer worked. When they left four days later, he had been able to open his email and type, though it took him nearly ten minutes to write a single paragraph. To him, the keyboard had no pattern, and the letters shifted worse than the enigma code had. But when he opened his email and saw the photograph, the struggle had been worth it. The woman in the picture was Hannah. There was no uncertainty. The photograph was proof Hannah had experienced millions of memories since the date she had supposedly died.

In November of 1997, Russell uncovered that Hannah had checked into Ellis Island in New York in 1944. She had lived in New York City and attended New York University for nursing. She had received her degree in 1948. Russell and Lauren flew Wilhelm to New York and brought him to the immigration building on Ellis Island and showed him where she had signed. The signature matched perfectly with the letter she had left him apart from Goldschmidt being replaced with Smith. But a graphologist confirmed Wilhelm's certainty. The two signatures came from the same person. But the case again ran cold, and 1997 ended without further news.

The spring months of 1998 came without much word, and Wilhelm felt every bit of his seventy-eight years of life. Perhaps, it was for the best he did not see her. At least, in this way, she could remember him for the way he looked in his youth and not the wrinkled, white-haired, and slightly overweight man he now was. It wasn't a peace that had come over him as much as it was an acceptance. He would never see or find out what had happened to Hannah—not in this life. But the fact Hannah had lived years longer than 1941 was far more important to him.

It was yet another Thursday for Wilhelm, and his lunch consisted of a bun covered in liver sausage and the other end with peanut butter and jam. But unlike the hundreds of other Thursdays, his telephone rang.

"Hello?" Wilhelm answered.

"I found her."

The Blue Rose

It had to have been a dream—the same dream Wilhelm had for the last fifty-nine years. He had thought about, prayed, hoped, dreamed, and wished of returning to Hannah ever since he had left for war. There had been other women after his return in 1955—women who wanted his whole heart and had given him theirs, but Wilhelm could not. Hannah owned such a large portion of it, and what was left had been pieced and stitched back together but never whole. The women had either left or Wilhelm had ended it before they got too hurt. But he had stopped dating after turning fifty, and the last thirty years had been lonely.

The flight to New York was filled with nerves. Russell had only told him he had found Hannah and nothing more. Lauren had a glass of wine waiting for Wilhelm and Russell when they walked in. She made small talk while Russell disappeared into his study to retrieve his findings. Wilhelm was greeted by the dogs like a grandfather by his grandchildren. Lauren tried to put an end to their jumping and licking, but Wilhelm did not mind. A moment later, Russell stepped out of the room with a manila folder in his hand and took a seat at the kitchen table.

"Before we discuss Hannah, I thought you would like to know I found information about your friend Heinrich Hess," Russell said.

"Heinrich?" Wilhelm asked in disbelief. His face spread into a smile, as old memories rose from the depths to the surface. But then, he remembered Heinrich had never returned home, and his smile vanished.

"Heinrich was taken prisoner by the Americans outside Normandy in 1944. He was sent to Wisconsin and was a prisoner of war there until the war ended in 1945. He married an American woman by the name of Patricia Ainsworth in 1946. They lived in Wisconsin and had five children. He passed away in 1992 from lung cancer at the age of seventy-two," Russell read from his notes.

Though he was still dead, the news changed everything. Heinrich had lived a good life, still ten years shy of what Wilhelm considered a long life, but much longer than Wilhelm had thought he had lived. He could not help but smile. Heinrich had found a woman to stifle his uncommitted spirit.

"Thank you for telling me that," Wilhelm said. He could have been jealous, and in ways, he was, but he was not spiteful. He was beyond grateful his good friend Heinrich had lived a great life filled with love.

Russell, Lauren, and Wilhelm all stared at the manila envelope that looked an awful lot like a big gray elephant in the room.

"Wilhelm, I know after these past few years, you have developed certain presumptions or thoughts on what Hannah's life has been. I want you to tell me if you want me to read this," Russell said.

It was a symbol of the level of friendship Russell and Wilhelm had developed. Even if Russell had not been given the green light to write the story, he had spent nearly three years of his life researching and looking through thousands of photographs, documents, and newspaper clippings to figure out what had happened to Hannah. Yet, he knew, sometimes, the truth was more painful.

Wilhelm had pondered over the question ever since Russell had called and told him he had found her. He had tossed and turned in his bed and sat at his kitchen table in the middle of the night, trying to come up with an answer and, truthfully, he did not know. What good could come of it? It would not change the past. But he had to know if Hannah had lived a good life.

"Read it to me," Wilhelm said. His tone was soft and uncommitted, but he repeated himself with a confident and strong voice.

"Okay," Russell said, sliding a pair of reading glasses onto his face.

He opened the folder and pulled out a small stack of papers from the envelope.

"Wait," Wilhelm said. Russell's mouth had opened but no words escaped. He looked up and pulled his glasses off. "Do you have an address?" Wilhelm asked.

Russell nodded. To Wilhelm, it was unnerving how much information could be uncovered about someone. Strangers could learn intimate details only a few friends ever knew. It made him shudder to think what the Nazis could have done with such easy access to information.

"She lives in Lake Forest, Illinois," Russell said.

Lauren rose from her seat and disappeared into her own study and came back with three plane tickets—Logan International Airport to O' Hare International Airport.

"These are not refundable," Wilhelm said, looking at the tickets and hovering over the line of saying yes and saying no.

"This is our gift, Wilhelm. Whatever you decide to do, we will support it," Lauren said.

The tickets were not for until two days later, which gave Wilhelm plenty of time to mull over it. When he thought he had his mind made up on going, the unknown ushered in a plethora of questions. What if she was married? And what if her husband answered the door? Did she have children? Her life over the last fifty odd years had surely changed her. There are a handful of moments that shape—that define—a person's life, and she had undoubtedly experienced plenty. Every answer was in the manila folder. But, perhaps, he was too old-fashioned to want to learn about someone's life by simply reading about it. He wanted to have conversations and earn the trust that brought disclosure of personal thoughts. But Wilhelm had decided his answer. Hannah had been subjected to truly awful things and, no matter how much time had passed, he felt partially responsible for it. He needed to apologize to Hannah. He needed to see that those atrocities had not dictated her life the way they had for him.

Russell and Lauren rearranged their schedules so they could join him. It never had to be spoken, though Lauren was much more open to discussing it, but Russell and Wilhelm had developed something of a surrogate father/son relationship. Russell had never been able to gain an understanding with his father the way he had hoped. But he recognized the same demons that had dwelled inside of his father also dwelled inside Wilhelm. It was the primary reason Lauren had no problem with Russell devoting so much time to helping Wilhelm out. But oddly, some of their best nights together were at their computer screen, sharing a bottle of wine. It was time together every night, something that didn't always happen. Most nights, they were enveloped in their individual studies, working.

Wilhelm recognized the sort of union he and Hannah had was exactly what Lauren and Russell had—if they could only fully embrace it and minimize life's distractions. Lauren had come from a loving, supporting family. She and Russell considered each other equals. They supported and motivated one another to be greater than they were the day before.

Lauren sensed the nerves running through Wilhelm, but years in the medical field told her there was little one could do to help them. Honesty was the biggest priority, and one could not substitute truth with comfort. Wilhelm's nerves only worsened when they landed in Chicago and waited for the rental car. It was a gorgeous December day, and Lake Michigan was a frozen sapphire with steam rising from it. The skyscrapers of the city stood tall. Russell drove the rental car north toward one of the city's affluent suburbs. The homes were much larger than anything Wilhelm had ever stayed in, with only the Hauser's house being an exception. The roads and driveways were well plowed and shoveled, and the lawns were coated with half a foot of snow. If Hannah lived here, it meant she lived a comfortable life.

Wilhelm was in the very city Hannah lived. It was the closest he had been to her since they had kissed goodbye that fateful Christmas morning. He twirled the blue rose in his hand. Its color had faded, and its petals looked as though they could fall off at any moment. Both the blue rose and Wilhelm belonged to Hannah and, soon, both would be back in her possession.

Final Dance

The horrors of war never truly faded, but Hannah had learned to silence her demons. Her life in America had been everything she had hoped it to be. Her home contained a lifetime of memories and knick-knacks from her apartment in New York City, her first home in Milwaukee and, now, her home of thirty-nine years in Lake Forest. Photographs were everywhere, and some would say there were too many. Hannah had made the most of her life, but she never sat idly by when it came to elections. Democracy was something taken for granted by many but only because, even though colonists had lived under the unfair rule of a British King, Americans had never lived under the rule of a dictator.

She was active in Holocaust testimonies and worked to help Jewish survivors adjust to a life away from their homes and tried, through legal processes, to help return Jewish possessions to the families they were stolen from. In America, she had worked for Civil Rights and marched alongside Dr. Martin Luther King Jr and thousands during his march on Washington and his famed "I have a dream" speech. She had voted for General Eisenhower for president in 1950. There was no better man for the job, as the new war seemed imminent, than the Supreme Allied Commander of the Second World War. It was the first time she had voted in a presidential election, and only possible after she became an American citizen. She had volunteered to support the young John F. Kennedy in 1960 and had even traveled to Berlin to hear him speak to her former countrymen. But a bullet ended the charismatic president's life, and turmoil ensued. She had supported LBJ during the '64 landslide and President Kennedy's younger brother Bobby in '68 before a bullet ended his campaign and his life. She had strongly opposed the Vietnam War and joined the anti-war rally. However, she understood the sacrifice the young men made. She never spoke against the soldiers—only the war.

Her bedroom drawers were full of political pins and fliers and over five thousand photographs. She almost always had a camera on her. In her bedroom, she had drawings and paintings of every person who had helped her survive. But as time went by and her memories diminished, she could no longer remember the small details that made individuals stand out. She still had the painting of the sunset of purples and oranges done by Radley at his farmhouse. It hung in her hallway. She loved her two-story home, but it was empty now that her children were gone and her husband had passed away almost ten years ago. Truthfully, she had always preferred Milwaukee more than Lake Forest. It had a strong German aura that reminded her of her childhood home and the best years of her life with Wilhelm and their friends.

She kept every photograph of Wilhelm hidden in drawers, away from her husband's eyes and her children's. There were too many questions the photographs would attract, the answers to which would cause too much pain. They were like ships carrying treasure that had sunk in an ocean of memories—memories that she wanted to keep for herself. Children wanted to believe their parents were soulmates—the one in a million type. But the truth was though her husband had been kind to her, it had taken many years for their friendship to advance to anything further. Even after they had married, it took a decade for her to truly love him. Being a foreigner was a scary time during the 1950's and 1960's. The Red Scare made all foreigners out to be Soviet spies. Her husband, Clayton Lauer, had given her a sense of security she could not have achieved on her own. But now that her children had moved out and her husband had passed, Wilhelm's photos and the blue rose he had given her adorned her nightstand beside her bed.

The setting sun poured into the kitchen as Hannah dried the last of her dinner dishes. She was now seventy-seven years old, and the tattoo on her left forearm had faded and smeared. The black ink looked more forest green in color now. Her arm had age spots and had gotten saggy in her old age. She did not consider herself a vain person, but looking in the mirror had become a depressing necessity.

A dark red colored car drove past, and Hannah took special notice of it. She knew each of her neighbors' cars, and the neighborhood itself was in the middle of a series of left and right turns that were far away from any highway or busy city streets. Whoever drove past had intended to be driving on that road. A car door shut, and Hannah could tell it was her driveway the car had pulled into. She tossed the towel onto the kitchen counter and peaked through her living room blinds. The car pulled away and drove the same way it had come from. Perhaps, the driver was truly lost. But a soft knock permeated through the door and penetrated the house. Hannah opened it. An elderly man smiled at her.

"Hannah?" the man asked.

"Yes?" Hannah answered, studying the man's face. It was oddly familiar to her but in the most peculiar way, like she had known him from a dream or another life.

"Hannah Goldschmidt?" the man asked.

Hannah was taken aback and partially alarmed. She had never gone by Goldschmidt in America. Her name had been Hannah Smith until she had married Clayton Lauer in 1957 and taken his surname. She studied the man's face, but it was his eyes Hannah found. When he stared into her brilliant blue eyes, hers met his. And, in an instant, she knew exactly who the man was.

"Wilhelm," Hannah muttered.

In her shock was absolute certainty. Her hand went to her mouth to cover it, and she didn't blink for nearly a minute. Wilhelm smiled, tears forming in the corners of his eyes. He had always feared she would forget about him entirely.

"Yes, Hannah," Wilhelm said, holding out the blue rose in his hand.

She rushed forward and hugged him.

"How?" Hannah asked, her voice was barely audible.

"There is so much that happened, Hannah. To me. But to you too. I am so sorry for what happened to you and your parents," Wilhelm said.

Hannah could barely comprehend what he had said, for she had been rethinking the last five decades of her life.

"Part of me always thought you were alive, Wilhelm. I waited for you," Hannah said, taking the blue rose from him—it was the very same she had dyed and dried in 1947. "I lived with your father in 1947, helping in his shop. But he told me I needed to move on. I wrote you a letter."

"I was in a Soviet prisoner-of-war camp until 1955, Hannah. My father passed away before I returned home, and everything was in boxes and in storage, and the shop was closed when I returned home. Your name was on the list of victims at Auschwitz," Wilhelm said.

There had been so many events and significant people that had allowed Hannah to live such a long and fruitful life. Each name deserved a proper story, and to limit the length simply for convenience was a disgrace to their memory. Hannah invited Wilhelm inside and disappeared into the kitchen to prepare a cup of coffee. Wilhelm hovered in the living room, gazing at the dozens of photographs adorned on the wall—photographs of children she had and her wedding. Hannah had moved on in a way Wilhelm had never been able to.

Hannah, with two cups of coffee in her hands, looked on in silence. Wilhelm was hypnotized by the wedding photo. She had always been beautiful—young but beautiful—but in her wedding photo, when she was in her mid-thirties, she had truly transformed into a gorgeous woman. None of the other faces in the photograph were known to him, and Wilhelm's eyes kept returning to Hannah in that striking dress. A series of emotions washed over him—some soft like a calm tide and others, a rogue wave.

"He passed away a few years ago," Hannah said, interrupting the silence and breaking Wilhelm's trance.

"I'm sorry to hear," Wilhelm said.

"Stay here. I want to show you something."

Hannah struggled up the steps to her bedroom. Wilhelm continued to look at the photographs. Each one caused him heartache. They were memories the two of them should have shared—children they should have raised and vacations they should have taken. He could only hope the man in the photo had treated Hannah like the queen she was. Hannah came back down with a handful of framed photographs.

"I was staying with your father before I was taken to Auschwitz. I had forgotten a manila folder on your nightstand. All of these photographs and the blue rose you gave me were in it. Had I remembered it, it would have been destroyed or lost at Auschwitz," Hannah said.

Wilhelm took the first photograph in his hand. His younger self stared into the eyes of a young Hannah and was immortalized on the glossy five-by-seven-inch photograph. Their arms were wrapped around each other. Heinrich and a girl he had forgotten were beside them, and Lena stood in front of Erich. Even with the picture being black and white, Wilhelm was transported back to Lena's cabin. The sunshine beat on the back of his neck, burning his skin. The breeze wafting off the water made Hannah's hair dance. Their laughter echoed in his ears. The next photograph was of Wilhelm, Erich, and Heinrich preparing dinner on a Friday night.

"I saw Heinrich after the war. In 1950, he visited New York City, and I met him and his wife there. Patricia. It was so great to see him. They lived just over two hours away when I lived in Milwaukee," Hannah said, the memory bringing a smile to her face.

Heinrich had been fortunate to be sent to the western front. Fate had taken a cruel turn when it had sent Wilhelm to the east. Yet, fate had forced both him and Hannah to make cruel turn after turn to the point where they could no longer remember how to get out of the macabre maze.

The last framed photo was of Wilhelm and Hannah dancing in the snowfall in Berlin. The white border of the photograph was signed Berlin 1939. It was the last photograph taken of the two. The snow fell under the city light. Hannah and Wilhelm held each other close. The blue rose he had given her so long ago was inside the picture frame.

"You kept it," Wilhelm said with teary eyes.

Hannah nodded. She too had tears in her eyes. Wilhelm tried his best to keep his from falling. He had not come here to make her cry. There was so much to talk about—the forgettable and the unforgettable. But how do you pick up where you left off when it was nearly sixty years ago? They had been together for only less than two years. Hannah had been married to her husband twenty times longer.

They sat at her kitchen table, sharing glasses of wine, fits of laughter, and moments of tears. She told him about the farmer and his wife, Eleanor, Trugnowski, Radley, and Josephine, and he told her about Höring, Jonas, Aaron, Torben, Old Uncle Joe, and Alexander Kozlovsky. As she recalled her own heroes and listened to Wilhelm's, the difference between Catholicism and Judaism filled her mind. In Catholicism, the savior had come. He was Jesus Christ. But in Judaism, the savior had yet to come. But Hannah no longer found that to be true. The savior was neither a man nor a woman. The savior was a group of people. The savior was Eleanor Cole, Rafel Trugnowski, Josephine Moreau, Radley Durand, the Czech farmer, and his wife. And the savior was Wilhelm. Wilhelm had experienced the same—Hannah, too, had been his savior. The two had kept each other alive with memories of the past and hopes of the future, which overpowered the direness of the present during their crucibles. But their fates would never be one again.

Wilhelm rose to his feet and hugged Hannah goodbye. He walked out the front door. Hannah stood in her doorway. Flashes of watching him leave on that fateful Christmas morning came back to her. She had let Wilhelm go then. She had ignored her intuition and the terrible ominous feeling that had swept over her as he had left. She would not repeat that mistake again.

"Wilhelm!" Hannah yelled.

Wilhelm turned to look at her. Russell and Lauren were in the dark red rental car parked in the driveway. Their hands were entwined, and both were overcome with emotion. Russell had not expected his life to change when he had walked into that bar in Schönfeld, Germany in 1989, but it had. Both he and Lauren had a strong understanding that their careers came before their relationship. But Wilhelm and Hannah's story had redefined their priorities.

"I don't want you to think I got over you," Hannah said, gently taking Wilhelm's hands in hers.

"You don't have to explain, Hannah. You should have," Wilhelm said.

"I never got over you. I knew I needed to, but I just couldn't. I stared at our photo every day. I felt guilty that I loved your ghost more than my living husband. You were the man I wanted to spend my life with."

It was a truth she could never tell her children—the truth that Wilhelm Schreiber had been the love of her life. The more time had gone on, the more she had realized it. It was no fault of Clayton. It is a rare thing, perhaps the rarest of things, to find someone to connect with, share with, confide in, and have the level of intimacy and desire Hannah and Wilhelm had had with and for one another. Wilhelm's lip quivered, and the tears he had done so well to keep from falling slowly slid down his wrinkled cheeks. All the struggle finding Hannah had been worth it for that one sentence. Every minute of fighting in the fields, in the streets, inside the apartment buildings, every frozen night, and oven-hot day, every year in that Soviet camp was worth it.

The radio played loudly from the rental car. The song had been one Hannah and Wilhelm had danced to on countless occasions, and it was the final card Russell and Lauren had to play. They exited the car, smiled, and walked down the street to give Wilhelm and Hannah privacy. The headlights of the vehicle were like a spotlight at a theatre and cast them in a blue lighting. The stars shined overhead, and the snow fell.

"May I have this dance?" Hannah asked.

"Always," Wilhelm answered, taking her hand.

They danced slowly to the music, staring into each other's eyes. It was a mysterious thing that the crow's feet around their eyes vanished. The longer they stared, the more they found their wrinkles smoothening out and the skin tightening and regaining its healthy glow. Both their white hair returned to its true color—Wilhelm's to jet black and Hannah's to nearly white blonde. Their bodies shed the excess weight they had gained over the years, and age itself reversed like the hands of a clock. Hannah and Wilhelm were young again. Wilhelm held her close, the blue rose gently pressed between their hands. Perhaps, it was a mirage of what could have been or maybe a higher spirit had taken pity and granted them a Cinderella-type experience with an unknown curfew.

There are a handful of moments that shape—that define—a person's life, and Wilhelm could remember them all, but in that moment, he let go of every one of them, except Hannah. In those four minutes the song lasted, all was right in the world for the first time since 1939. Wilhelm and Hannah were dancing once again.

About the Author

 *Forever Fleeting* is the debut novel by Bret Kissinger. He has taken his passion of writing and history and combined them into a truly compelling novel set during the Second World War. He was born and resides in Wisconsin.

Other Works by the Author

Gone the Way of the Dodo Bird

The Final Edit

Scan the QR Code to join our mailing list:

Made in the USA
Middletown, DE
10 March 2025

72485841R00280